W9-BBK-713

ICE AND FIRE

"Now. Catherine. Strike now, or yield."

She thrust the knife forward, but at the last moment looked into eyes that reflected the storm. This strange, brooding man had become part of her. Frighteningly, he needed her now, though she had denied him in rage and pride as he had her.

As the knife clattered to the deck, a fleck of crimson over the Irishman's heart smeared against her breast as he swept her into his arms and crushed his mouth down upon her cold lips, kissing her as if the tempest raging about them were centered in his soul. Passion rose in fiery waves, pouring over the edge of the world, a descent into the inferno, bodies locked in a fusion of molten desire . . .

Avon Books are available at special quantity discounts for bulk purchases for sales promotions, premiums, fund raising or educational use. Special books, or book excerpts, can also be created to fit specific needs.

For details write or telephone the office of the Director of Special Markets, Avon Books, Dept. FP, 1790 Broadway, New York, New York 10019, 212-399-1357.

Christine Monson

Stormfire

AVON
PUBLISHERS OF BARD, CAMELOT, DISCUS AND FLARE BOOKS

STORMFIRE is an original publication of Avon Books.
This work has never before appeared in book form. This
work is a novel. Any similarity to actual persons or events
is purely coincidental.

AVON BOOKS
A division of
The Hearst Corporation
1790 Broadway
New York, New York 10019

Copyright © 1984 by Christine Monson
Published by arrangement with the author
Library of Congress Catalog Card Number: 84-90894
ISBN: 0-380-87668-X

All rights reserved, which includes the right to
reproduce this book or portions thereof in any form
whatsoever except as provided by the U. S. Copyright Law.
For information address the Denise Marcil Literary
Agency, 316 West 82nd Street, New York, New York 10024

First Avon Printing, June, 1984

AVON TRADEMARK REG. U. S. PAT. OFF. AND IN
OTHER COUNTRIES, MARCA REGISTRADA, HECHO EN
U. S. A.

Printed in the U. S. A.

WFH 10 9 8 7 6 5 4 3 2 1

To my beloved wingmate, Jon, and fledgling, Jenni.

Special thanks to Claudia Wall, Sergei Timacheff, and Anne Lorcy.

CHAPTER 1

Steel Pinfeathers

Tap, tap, tap. Alice shifted her unaccustomed weapon and her considerable weight at the same time. Tap, tap, tap, the nursemaid's broad foot briskly connected with the floor. She glowered at the angelically serene young creature who had her head stuffed under satin *point d'esprit* pillows. No angel, little Catherine!

Catherine was a minx. Small-boned, with a coltish grace and an unruly riot of black hair so fine it seemed to snap blue, Catherine usually resembled a disreputable urchin because of her indifference to dress. Her remarkable eyes, almond-shaped, heavily lashed, were an iridescent blue as restless in shade as opals. They had never been the eyes of a child, unless the child were fey Oberon's own.

Alice had hoped this past year in Bath would see Catherine develop into a fashionable young lady, but when Catherine arrived home for the Christmas holidays, she seemed little different from the hoyden who had mingled unselfconsciously with children of servants. It had not been unusual at Windemere to see fledgling cooks and dukes haul on the same rope in Tug o' War while a muddied Catherine yelled encouragement and dragged with the best of them. Alice's face turned wistful.

Catherine, daughter of John Enderly, viscount of Windemere, and countess in her own right, had been sent to The Gentlewoman's Academy in Bath after her mother's death five years past. Letters about Catherine from that establishment were disapproving. In the opinion of the

1

school directors, the countess had had her way too much and, thanks to her diplomat father, seen too much of the world for a girl not yet seventeen. The creature could be sly in four languages, but could not be caught being insolent in any of them. Her schoolmates invariably followed her lead, whether in reading discourses on female equality by that Italian woman, Gaetana Agnesi, or sneaking out in male attire to unsuitable entertainments. The viscount had merely been amused, but Alice, aware of the difficulties of Catherine's adjustment to the school, pitied her.

Catherine's posterior languorously shifted position, and her old nursemaid's sympathy evaporated as she scowled at that offending bit of anatomy. Alice might be unlettered, but she knew what spelled "come hither." She should have foreseen trouble a week ago on Christmas Eve when she told Catherine of the Parisian wardrobe the viscount had purchased for her. She might have known Catherine would deduce the new wardrobe carried a whiff of suitors along with innocent lavender. A witchy look had flickered through Catherine's extraordinary eyes, and to Alice's dismay, she chose to wear the most daring of the new dresses to greet guests for Christmas dinner. The crimson sari silk with iridescent flaming colors had enveloped her young body like sorcery, and Alice was now certain the trouble it brewed that night had boiled over. Just thinking of it made her temper seethe. Her foot, ceasing its impatient taps on the floor, came down with a peremptory crack.

The pillows exploded and Catherine shot up from the debris of silk. She blinked groggily, startled to see Alice in her mobcap standing guard over the bed with a rapier clenched in one fist. "What on earth . . . Alice, what are you doing? Have you lost your mind?"

The older woman harrumphed, "Buck naked, I see. Where's your nightdress?"

Catherine's eyes cleared, then took on a cat's studied indifference. "In the chiffonier," she answered coolly. Alice was a love, but also a tyrant. Besides, she had an idea where this discussion was about to lead. "Since when do you concern yourself with what I wear to bed?"

2

"Since that cheeky buck with a gleam in his eye and a French accent comes saunterin' out of yer bedroom at an owl's hour and shoves this sword into my hand. He says, says he, 'Don't let any more like me come through here.' And off he goes whistlin' like a banty rooster that's been at the whole henhouse." Alice's large hands welded to her hips and her eyes glittered. "Now, you tell me, missy, what went on in here last night!"

Catherine eyed her for a long moment, wondering if she should admit how far awry her week-long attempt to appear more intriguing than a marriageable, manageable heap of bank notes had gone. The cockerel in question was Colonel Raoul Louis d'Amauri, formerly baron d'Amauri, of the Grand Armée. The handsome Frenchman was the most appealing of the bachelor houseguests, possibly because his teasing brown eyes instantly saw through her masquerade. Despite his blue and scarlet dress uniform, he looked little older than herself.

Far less appealing was el conde Ramon Diego de Valera of Seville, whose black eyes gleamed with an insinuating intimacy that sat ill on a cold, hollow-cheeked face. He had pursued her like a vulture and had intimated her father favored his suit. She made it clear she found him revolting, yet she was on edge. The Treaty of Ildefonso the previous year had settled Spain's differences with France and united the rival sea powers into a formidable juggernaut. Could it be that her father was negotiating with Valera for a way to maintain England's naval superiority? Was she somehow the price for his services?

When she put the matter to her father, he flatly dismissed it. "I've no intention of marrying you to the count. You have possibilities, Catherine, we've yet to develop." As it turned out, the Spanish count had his own nasty ideas for her development.

Fortunately, her frequent company with Amauri held Valera sullenly at bay for a time, and her interest in the Frenchman gradually became more than merely polite as his charm drew her out. With chestnut hair and cinnamon eyes, he radiated a sunny vitality that engaged everyone, but his jaw and mouth had an unmistakable resolution that belied his guileless eyes. He had maneuvered her into

3

her first kiss, experienced on his part and intriguing on hers. How to prevent him from completing her seduction had become more of a contest than she had expected.

Just then, she decided how to handle Alice. Completely unabashed, Catherine swung slim legs out of bed and walked over to the dresser. Idly, she picked up a diamond-initialed hairbrush and began to give her hair long strokes. "Do you really mean to say, Alice, you slept through everything? Remarkable. Of course, Napoleon's army cannon-ading your bed couldn't awaken you, so how could a small skirmish between France and Spain over tiny England have any effect?"

Totally confused now, the maid frowned, then suddenly waggled the rapier at the dark smears on the coverlet. "Blood! Ye've gone and done it! Yer mother and grand-mother would be ashamed of ye!"

"Why? Neither of them was totally faithful to one man. As you've often told me, most of the trinkets I've been wearing were gifts to Grandmaman, and she did more than dimple for them." When her hair bloomed outward like a dark flower, Catherine dropped the brush on the dresser. I look pale and tired, she thought as she stared at the mirror. I have circles under my eyes, a headache, and the disposition of an adder. Yet that swashbuckling French-man insists I have the power to drive men mad. In spite of herself, she began to smirk into the mirror.

At that, Alice went into a fury. "Don't ye dare stand there lookin' like a cat in a creampot! How do ye know that belly won't blow up come spring?"

"Where's my peignoir, Alice? I want a bath. Mignon has seen to the hot water, I hope."

Snatching up a peignoir and slippers, Alice scurried fu-riously behind her mistress as Catherine headed for the bath. "Think ye're so smart after havin' done it once, no-body can tell ye anythin'. Let me tell you, there's no guar-antee ye ain't pregnant, missy!"

"Oh, yes there is," Catherine said as she tested the wait-ing bath water with her toe. "And I said France *and* Spain, Alice. I believe I mentioned last evening that two gentle-men were seriously inclined to bed me, did I not?"

Alice's jaw dropped. "Ye greedy little hussy! I ought to

take this slipper to yer backside . . ." She advanced with a glint in her eye.

Her prey slipped down into the gilt mosaicked bath and flicked a bubble at her. "Calm down, Alice. You'll have an apoplexy. As you're so fond of saying, 'There's no point bolting the barn door after the horse has run away.' Don't you think you should have given me solid advice last night instead of chortling over my sorry plight? While it is true that two *uninvited* men were in my bedroom and they both had my virtue against the wall, it's also true the blood on the bed isn't mine. I was pawed, not raped."

Alice sagged onto a stool. "Why, for heaven's sake, didn't ye call me?"

"The Spaniard threatened to murder you."

"Ah, ye poor lamb! That serious, was he?"

"That serious," Catherine replied dryly. "The Frenchman rescued me just in the nick of time." So close a nick, she thought privately, he must have been ready to bounce into my bedroom himself.

"For heaven's sake," said Alice again, "I thought they was just moonin' about."

"So did Father. He thinks I should be calm about such things."

"Well, what do ye mean to do?"

"Take his advice, naturally. Don't I always?"

A week later, John, the butler, handed Catherine into the coach schoolbound for Bath, then secured the few pieces of luggage. She had decided not to take the new wardrobe back to the academy, and Alice, chastened, had not insisted. Dressed in a high-ruffed white silk blouse, forest green velvet jumper with frogged jacket, silver gray bonnet, and loden cloak, Catherine was the picture of a well-bred student.

She waved to Alice and the tiny cluster of servants who gathered to see her off, then tucked her hands back into a silver fox muff as the carriage rolled away. Quickly, the graceful Palladian mansion receded into the trees of its surrounding parkland. Leaving the side curtains open, Catherine defied the chill to view the scenery, which was among the most beautiful in England. The lakes were ice-bound, their shorelines blending into rolling forests whose weblike networks of branches cut sere, abstract friezes against the gray sky. Though the lake country was shrouded in lonely silence, she loved its still seclusion.

Today she saw none of it, her mind preoccupied with the dismal prospect of returning to Bath. I owe it to Father, she reflected with dejection. He has never asked anything of me but this one obedience about school. Besides, revolt promised nothing but added monotony. Foolish as the school was, it was preferable to a convent or, worse yet, marriage; one more year and that grim prospect must be faced. Many girls of the senior form had already announced betrothals.

Catherine's mother's marriage had been arranged. The daughter of one of the richest men in France, Elise Enderly, as comtesse de Vigny, had brought to her marriage a considerable dowry, assurance of a great fortune upon the old comte's death, and rights of succession in the event of the deaths of two brothers. Unfortunately, when Catherine was six the upheaval of the French Revolution had swallowed the entire family and its estates. Her dowry already spent on renovations to Windemere, Elise was reduced to the position of a bad bargain.

All in all, Catherine had not suffered from the marriage. Elise was a vivacious woman, more like a sister than a mother, and if John Enderly was dismayed at being saddled with a penniless wife, he never showed it. An indulgent father, he encouraged Catherine's quick mind and, in turn, she idolized him. Although he was not physically demonstrative, she often thought he yearned to be a more sympathetic parent than his nature allowed. After her mother's sudden death, she was dismayed to be banished to school when they needed each other most.

Her first months at the academy had been plagued by nightmares. She became slovenly, a habit she still had to fight. She felt abandoned, unloved, and guilty of some obscure, terrible crime. At last, the sheer boredom of the school had calmed her, and outwardly she had adapted. She gave up begging to stay home because it so upset Enderly that he lashed out in tight-lipped anger. He reminded her of the months after her mother's accident, when she had been disoriented with hysteria, and had had to be restrained and confined. She would *not* return to Windemere with its upsetting memories. His rejection at such a sensitive time had stunned Catherine into submission.

As far as marriage for love went, she had no illusion that her father would grant her an indulgence he refused himself, and even less illusion about single women without family protection and financial support. She had not a penny of her own.

Love. Alice had said once that Elise Enderly had loved and been loved as few women ever were. There had been another, somewhere, sometime, whose memory had brought her mother sadness and delight. Elise had never spoken of him but his existence had shadowed John Enderly and instigated occasional bitter quarrels. Catherine knew it was useless to question Alice. The two had long ago decided to let Elise's secret die with her.

"It's all right, Alice," Catherine remembered answering softly. "I won't be like Maman. She lived and died loving the wrong man. I shall take care to avoid that."

Yet when Raoul had left Windemere, she had missed him badly. She had spent the rest of the uneventful balance of her visit arguing with herself that infatuation was not love.

Catherine caught up the cloak collar against her windward cheek and sighed ironically. Why even think about it? An immediate, efficient marriage loomed ahead like a well-oiled guillotine.

As the late-afternoon sun slipped toward the horizon, trees stretched fragmented shadows across the snow. Reluctantly, she closed the side curtains against the increasingly bitter chill, thinking Carson, the new driver, must be cold. She burrowed farther into the corner to brace against the sway of the coach and drifted into sleep.

Sometime later, Catherine awoke, vaguely aware something had disturbed her. Surely she could not have slept all the way to the inn. She blinked sleepily in the darkness of the coach and shifted position slightly, feeling cramped but not really uncomfortable. The coach's pace seemed faster and the wheels passed over ruts and rocks with jarring jolts. Perhaps that was it. A second later she was wide awake. *Too many horses.* The steady drum of the coach's team had been matched by other hoofbeats, which moved at the same relentless pace. Had her father summoned an escort because of some threat, perhaps from Valera?

With a fingertip, she drew back the side curtain. A horseman flanked the carriage. Her throat tightened as stealthy investigation revealed two riders on the opposite side. Even by the wavering light of the coach lamps, their faces could be seen clearly enough. These were not her father's men! Were they the Spaniard's hirelings? Carson had made no protest when they joined the coach, so he either knew them or had been coerced to continue driving without interruption.

Catherine felt in her pocket for the small knife she had decided to carry to discourage future Valeras and made up her mind. Bracing against the lurch of the coach, she cautiously stood and tried the latch of the roof hatch. The door's sudden heaviness warned that luggage was strapped across it. Bracing the weight against a shoulder, Catherine lowered the door as far as possible, then strained a hand through the opening and sawed clumsily at the luggage lashings. She was almost hurtled off-balance by the carriage's pitch, but finally the strap parted.

With the door still on her shoulder, she lowered it by fractions while she supported the descending luggage with the other hand. She lowered the small trunk to the floor and straightened. As she rubbed her back with one hand and clung to the strap with the other, she reflected that if her prospective bridegrooms were too grotesque, she might become a professional contortionist. She discarded her bonnet, then stood on the cushioned seat and cautiously raised her head through the opening. A rampart of luggage surrounded the hatch. Quickly, a valise followed the trunk into the coach, which left just enough room for her body atop the roof.

Catherine wedged elbows on either side of the hatch and pushed off the seat below. For one horrible moment she hung in space, legs scissoring, then heaved upward. Staying low, with a grimace at the pressure on her midriff, she

8

wriggled upward until her hip rested across the hatch rim. Clutching the remaining luggage straps with both hands, she panted, thankful for the darkness and muffling carriage racket.

Once Catherine had adjusted to the cramped space and closed the hatch, a new problem presented itself: the cold was penetrating, and even though the luggage broke the wind's whistling blast, she would soon become too numbed to escape. Between chattering teeth, she silently cursed her thin gloves and stockings.

She shivered violently, wondering when the coach would reach its mysterious destination. The blowing snow could not obliterate the sea tang in the air, so they were not headed in the direction of Bath; more likely, this was the Liverpool road. Thanks to encircling drafts and the snow gathering in her cloak folds, her nose began to run. With a spark of malicious glee, she wiped it with one next-to-useless glove and pictured Valera's face when he was delivered a red-nosed, blue-faced lump. Oh, that his ardor might become as frozen as her feet!

Just when she began to contemplate a perilous leap from the coach roof and flight through the woods, the coach slowed and entered the outskirts of a town. Distant harbor noises sounded above the vehicle's rattling progress over the cobbles: squeaking wood and slapping halyards; an occasional hollow shout over water; faint laughter from waterfront inns. This might be Chester or another of the modest ports that lined the channel to Liverpool. Someone must want to get her to sea quickly. She would be missed at school by tomorrow evening; certainly too late to prevent embarkation from England, but soon enough for the authorities to pick up the track if the coach had been spotted on the road. Even in Spain, Valera would not be safe . . . unless he dumped her overboard before the authorities reached him.

Gradually, the coach was surrounded by raucous sounds of harbor inns. Her ears pricked. Where there were inns, there were people: ruffians aplenty, too, but once she began to yell, few would be reckless enough to contribute to the abduction of a viscount's daughter. The coach was bumping slowly now . . . slow enough . . . *too* slow. It was stopping!

Even as one of the riders dismounted and approached the carriage door, Catherine gave a final decisive slash at a nearly severed lashing and the trunk crashed to the ground. In a flash, she shot over the opposite side of the coach. Ignoring long skirts that revealed a welter of petticoat and pantalette as she slid, she hung briefly onto a dangling leather strap to break the drop. She landed with outspread hands on the cobbles, and like a sprinter, aimed toward a lane of chandler's shops and taverns. Her feet slipped and she fell. Swearing at numb limbs that felt as if they were pricked by shards of hot ice, she stubbornly scrambled up and began to run through the heavily falling snow. The street was empty except for a dark figure rendered shapeless by whipping snow as it wove through light pools from the windows at the far end.

Oh, God, where were the people? There had been so many voices before; now there was only the sound of pursuit. Yelling at the top of her lungs, she headed for the nearest door. The shape up the street stopped and peered curiously at the scrambling young woman and the three dark, muffled men who ran after her. Using all her weight, Catherine slammed against a heavy tavern door and shoved it open. Men were everywhere: at the bar, tables, stairs. The room, full of yellowish smoke, stank of unwashed flesh and crude, greasy lanterns. The few women, astride laps, shrieked with laughter as they swilled rum, their chins and breasts shiny with spilt liquor.

Hanging on to the door, Catherine shouted, "Help me! I'm being kidnapped!"

Several people turned and stared, but the faces registered nothing. Frantic now, she screeched, "Listen to me! You must stop them. I'm—" A firm hand clapped over her mouth as the other twisted her around against a hard body so that her back was to the crowd.

"A new bride," a stranger's voice finished for her.

She felt, rather than knew, her back had the entire room's attention now. Staring upward, she caught a flash of bright blue eyes nearly as angry as her own and shiny blond hair before the man's mouth came down on hers to effectively stifle her. She wrenched; his arms tightened. She tried to stamp his toes, but he simply lifted her off her feet. Clamping his hand again over her mouth before she could emit more than an outraged yelp, he amiably commented to the crowd, "Would that the convent had bred into her another kind of spirit . . . Ow!" A furious foot connected with his shin.

The crowd was laughing now, and, burning with frustration, Catherine opened her mouth to yell again. Instantly, the lean blonde crushed her face against his chest to muffle her squalls. Doing a little dance to elude her drumming feet, he gave their audience an embarrassed grin. "My wife and I apologize for the disturbance. If you'll excuse me, it's . . . ah, been a rather long engagement."

A particularly outraged squawk was heard from the region of his chest and the crowd roared. Hoots and catcalls filled the place. A tall sailor stood abruptly, swaying slightly, then swept the bottles from a long plank table to the floor. Howls arose as drink spattered laps and clothes. Leaning over the table he bellowed, "Bring her over, Johnny Gentleman, and we'll show ye how it's done."

Catherine froze and the kidnapper stiffened. The tallest of the muffled figures behind them in the doorway moved forward. She could not see his face, but concluded it must be grimly impressive, for the crowd lapsed into surly silence. The second figure advanced, and leaving them to guard his retreat, the blonde backed quickly out the door into the street, where he abruptly heaved his prey over a shoulder, then headed toward the coach with her hair, loosened by rough handling, swinging about his knees.

Finding her arms free, Catherine clenched her hands together in a gathered fist and slammed it into the small of his back with all her might. The resounding *whoof* and stagger were satisfying but she was not dropped. As she raised her fists again for a second whack, the kidnapper snarled over his shoulder, "Try that winsome trick again and you'll find yourself served to that scurvy crew in there."

The fists hovered. "Do you think your master would like that?" He missed a step and Catherine knew she had scored.

"I have no master, so don't try me, Countess!"

At his use of title, she gave as sarcastic a snort as the stifling position would allow. "Well, it's a relief to know you've got the correct victim. I should hate to think you've made a mistake!"

Behind them, the cloaked accomplices were backing out of the tavern with drawn swords. Apparently, the dogs were beginning to howl again. Although her stomach felt as if it were being ground into her backbone, Catherine tried to assume a businesslike tone. "I'll double whatever you've been offered for this affair. You needn't tell your—oof—henchmen." She wanted to kick him again, for she sensed he was amused. "I'm certainly not familiar with thieves' cant, but whatever the phraseology, money's money, and you'd be a fool not to accept it. Your—ugh—blackguard employer will probably shoot you rather than pay you. I'll meet your terms when and where you name, but if you don't agree quickly, the offer will be made to your cronies." She eyed the distance between themselves and the two following behind.

Three more men, waving fists and mouthing threats and obscenities, emerged from the tavern; others joined them. Ironically, they had only seen her vaguely for a few moments, and bundled into a shapeless cloak at that, so no personal lust was involved, only the ravening of the pack to tear apart something they thought helpless.

From now on I'll never be without a knife, Catherine vowed, if there is a "now on." Unfortunately, the weapon had already been jostled into the snow.

"Well?" she prodded urgently. "What's your answer? Do you want triple your fee or next to nothing?"

"What's happening back at the Hound's Head?" he puffed, as if he had not heard.

Noting that a wooden sign bearing a painted canine silhouette creaked in the wind above the inn, she counted heads. "Six men with dirks and sabers are following us. Your friends are at our heels. If you're going to give me an answer, you'd better do it now!"

The kidnapper gave no reply, but tugged at the catch of his cloak, then quickly slid his captive over the front of his shoulder and, despite a flurry of kicking and clawing, wrapped her in the garment: head, shoulders, arms, and all. Lifting his burden again, this time in his arms, he began to run heavily through the snow.

He'll never make it, Catherine thought frantically. He'll slip and we'll all be caught! A vision of being stretched out on the greasy inn table while her erstwhile kidnappers lay in the trampled, reddened snow of the street was intensified by muffled cries and running feet. The fair-haired man did not seem to be headed for the abandoned coach; instead, he bobbed and weaved as if darting through alleys. Once, he slipped and fell roughly against a brick wall, but caught himself with a shoulder. He scrambled for balance, then was off again and running this way and that, until she lost all sense of direction. Suddenly, boards sounded hollowly under his feet and her weight sagged against his chest as if he were running uphill. She was scraped and bumped, both boot and crown, by the narrow sides of a low doorway, then dumped in a pile of cloth.

As soon as his hands left her, Catherine tested the tightness of her wrapping. Unfortunately, the blonde had no intention of allowing further options of escape. He whipped a length of rope around her ankles, then looped and strung it up her body and secured her arms. She swore, then thought better of it in case he might be encouraged to use a gag, a tactic which would invite imminent asphyxiation. A reassuring pat descended in the vicinity of her shoulder. "Now, be a good girl; otherwise our captain may be inclined to see how well you swim. I promise he'll pitch the evidence before being caught with it." After that cheery bit of advice, he left. Muffled voices were audible on deck.

Almost soothed into a semblance of calm by a rocking motion, she had already guessed they were aboard a boat. The hollow noise earlier must have been a gangplank. Orders sang out and ropes whistled through rigging. The vessel was pushed away from the wharf and wavelets rapped against the hull.

Her heart sank like a stone. Valera's got me now, trussed like a Christmas goose. Then her eyes narrowed. Given half a chance, I'll spit him on his own skewer, the oily rat, along with that villainous choirboy he uses for his dirty schemes!

The waves slapped harder as the vessel gained way toward the harbor mouth and began to pick up the first scuffs of wind from the sea. The receding town lights dulled in the growing snowstorm, whose flakes whirled and corkscrewed down to lie like soapsuds on the cresting, running tide, then melt into glossy black water. Unknown to Catherine, the villainous choirboy was on deck, leaning against the rail and thinking how much the night sea looked like her hair.

With his gloved hands tucked under his armpits, Liam Culhane brooded. He had sunk a long way to kidnapping helpless women. Well, not so helpless. He twisted to ease his backache. The countess fetched a mean clout. He could not get over her seeming lack of fear while being carted along like a market-bound piglet, and that with a pack of howling ruffians on their heels. He would have been killed on the spot, but her lot would have been worse. Perhaps she hadn't the sense to know it, although she seemed to know well enough where to aim when averse to being kissed.

Enderly's only child. What did Sean want with her? Ugly possibilities nagged at him. There was no knowing what was in Sean's mind, especially that part blackened by hate. Though his eyes could be sulphurous with the memory of it, in all the years of his growing to manhood Sean had never spoken of Kenlo and the massacre that had brought him to live at Shelan to be reared as Brendan Culhane's son and Liam's brother.

That day was branded into Liam's brain. He, his father, and Flannery had just disembarked from a curragh on the beach below Shelan when suddenly, across the sun-glared rock, had charged a wild, small figure in a dirty, hacked-off cassock. A rapier brandished high, blade glinting, it charged with a howl. "For Megan and Ireland!" Five steps later it was on its face in the grit, senseless. Brendan turned the body over, then swore softly when he saw the boy's face and a blood-soaked, makeshift bandage on his thigh. The dragon-engraved hilt of the sword lay across the open, unconscious fingers.

"Saints preserve us, that's Owen Roe's sword," rumbled

14

Flannery, a redhead so tall he blocked most of the sun from boy and man as he towered over them.

Brendan brushed dirt from the boy's bruised cheek, minutely examining his features like a scholar discovering some extraordinary but possibly dangerous treasure. Liam did not need to ask who the stranger was. He had been only two years old when his mother, Megan Culhane, had abandoned him and his father. A painted miniature of her in his room told him bluntly enough he was looking at his brother. The urchin had Megan's fine, straight nose. The eyes, like hers, were green; they had blazed from a long way down the beach, and Brendan had half drawn his sword even though the ludicrous apparition was obviously a child. Megan's sooty lashes swept across the boy's dark face.

From the look on Brendan's face as he smoothed the boy's hair, Liam instantly knew a truth he would have given his life not to have known: a truth Brendan would have given his own life to prevent him from seeing. Hot pain rose in him. His father thought him a scholarly dreamer, best suited to the priesthood. And Culhane did not need a priest for a son. This black-haired urchin's reckless charge had won him the protection, and love, of one of the most influential men in Ulster.

In time Liam had learned to accept what he could not change. The two boys were bound together by loneliness, and Sean tolerated Liam's company if he did not seek it. Beyond that, Sean was close to no one. While Liam readily made casual friends with the children on the estate, Sean was cold, curt, and unpopular. Still, as the boys of the household grew older, it was to Sean that they turned as leader. And at Sean that the girls began to look.

Even his position with Brendan was distant despite the lord's loving guile. While Sean accorded Brendan respect he gave no other and was at all times correct, affection was never evident in his behavior.

His relationship with Flannery, from whom he learned to fence, ride, and shoot, was coldly professional. As Flannery said, "He's training to be a killer and I'm the best killer he knows."

* * *

Now, ten years later, Brendan was dead, and Liam the bearer of his title; but Liam felt like an aide among generals. Flannery still gave him orders. He glanced toward the stern. At the wheel of the fishing yawl, with his great, cratered moon of a face and fiery beard reflected in the glow of the binnacle lantern, the giant looked the same as he always had except for a few streaks of gray.

Liam shivered slightly and thought about the girl. He decided to let her up on deck for a while. Fresh air might clear the chit's head. Fancy her talking as if she knew Sean—although it was possible. Sean never discussed either his plans or women with anyone.

When he tugged the cloak from the captive's face, she lay so pale and still he thought she had suffocated. Fearing he might have done murder, he jerked away the rest of the cloth. Her eyes flew open, and with amazing energy she tried to wriggle away. He hastened to soothe her. "I'm not going to hurt you . . . Oof!" A knee caught his thigh a nasty smack. Exasperated, he sprawled atop the heaving woolly sausage and pinned it. "For God's sake, miss, I thought you'd stifled! I was trying to free you."

The prisoner eyed him balefully. "I was asleep. If I were going to stifle, I should have done it long ago. In fact, I should be quite black. Perhaps you should have chosen a profession less demanding of your intelligence. And it's Countess to you, not miss!" She alternated so smoothly between blistering anger and cool impertinence that he could merely sit astride her and stare. Her dark brows nearly met. "Get off, you dolt! Unless you prefer to crush your victims rather than stifle them!"

Liam shifted to his knees and shoved his nose down to hers. "I suggest you don't insist upon the use of your titles where you're bound, *miss!* And you're lucky I extend you the courtesy of *that* term! If you can keep a civil tongue in your head, you may walk the deck."

"Not the plank?" the captive retorted tartly. "How gallant." At his frown, Catherine lapsed into sardonic silence as he undid the ropes. With a sigh, she sat up and slowly stretched cramped limbs. Liam was surprised at the girl's unconscious grace. Both Sean and Brendan had that same proud carriage of head, which might have been stiff with-

16

out the ease that accompanied it. She was well proportioned as far as he could tell under the cloak, although too thin and still a bit gangling. The small face with its high cheekbones and magnificent eyes had promise of beauty, and the mouth was decidedly appealing; he remembered the way it had felt in the tavern. Oddly, he thought he might have seen her before.

Catherine felt him watching as, skirts swinging, she paced up and down in the limited space. He was young. Certainly he was still capable of being easily embarrassed: that made him susceptible, but to what? His appreciative look lacked the intent appraisal of the Spaniard, even of Raoul d'Amauri; besides, she had learned to beware of leading a man on, even innocently. He was educated, at least to a point, with acceptable grammar and a touch of a brogue. Irish. The Irish were rumored to be idealistic about mothers, sisters, and virgins. Her image as a helpless waif was already dented, judging by the kidnapper's wince of pain as he ducked through the hatchway and escorted her onto the deck; however, sisters often inflicted such damage on siblings, and having had a retinue of surrogate brothers through childhood, she felt on fairly firm ground when it came to their management.

Once on the slippery deck, Catherine took in a lungful of air. Snow drifted into the bulwarks and whirled slowly about the single massive figure at the wheel. He had donned oilskins and hat and looked eerily like the legendary Flying Dutchman, but he was probably Irish too, with that flaming hair. She could not imagine why the Spaniard had employed Irishmen for his dirty work, unless they were allied in common hatred of the English.

Vigorously rubbing her hands, Catherine wished for her muff. The wind hit her directly in the face as she tugged up the hood and faced the rail. Because of the low fog, no stars were visible, so direction was a mystery. If the Irishmen were headed out to sea, they must expect to be met by another vessel; Valera could easily be moored up one of the coastal creeks, waiting to take his pleasure at leisure, then dump her body in a back marsh.

Desperation prodded her to action. Knowing the blonde was immediately behind her, Catherine deliberately slipped

17

on the wet planking. She managed to twist slightly so that when he caught her she could easily turn into his chest. All happened exactly as planned, under Flannery's sardonic eye.

Liam felt the girl tremble under the cloak. Poor little devil, he thought; she's frightened out of her wits. She must be holding together by sheer bravado. "Are you all right?" he murmured into hair that smelled perfumed in the sifting snow where the hood had fallen away.

A small hand rested against his chest. "Yes . . . yes, I think so. It was clumsy of me. I . . . wasn't thinking." His captive looked up at him gratefully, her eyes great shadowed pools. In them he saw desperation and a determination not to let it show, but beyond that, a mysterious beauty that caught at his heart. In the pit of his stomach, Liam had a growing dread of the fate that awaited the girl in Ireland.

She clung to him for the barest fraction of a moment, then released him and turned away. They both leaned against the rail and she resettled the hood of the cloak. Liam was a little disappointed; he had been watching the lift of the wind in her hair. Still not looking at him, she murmured, "You don't seem like a criminal."

Liam shifted his back to Flannery and answered with a tinge of discomfort, "I'm not, ordinarily."

Catherine noted his move to conceal their conversation. Flattening a palm, she turned it upward to catch the idly drifting snowflakes. "Do you know what your . . . employer plans to do with me?"

"No," Liam answered honestly. He did not know, but he had a fair idea.

"Not the confiding sort, is he?"

"He's not."

"And you're not a man who'd press the point."

He began to get angry again. "Why should I?"

"If I told you he intends to rape and possibly murder me, would that make a difference?"

"I don't know that and neither do you." Underneath his level rebuttal he was stunned by her blunt appraisal.

Catherine's hands tightened on the rail as she turned on him. "I do know! You'll be as guilty as the monster you

18

serve. You can stop it now. You won't accept money to cheat him, so you must have some sense of decency. If you help him, it will be the end of you."

Liam was glumly inclined to agree. He was accustomed to following where Sean led, and although he shrank from some of those paths, he respected his brother's judgment. Still, revenge was at the heart of the festering hatred Sean bore for their mother's murderers, and in that hatred, Liam did not know whether his brother was entirely lucid. What if Sean did kill the girl? Could he be a party to murder?

Reading indecision in his eyes, Catherine laid down her last card. "If you help me escape, my father will reward you with anything you ask, help you make a new start anywhere you like. You could make a respectable name for yourself . . ."

Liam's voice turned hard. "So . . . the English lady would graciously give me what's mine already, what you and your countrymen would have stolen long ago if you could beat down the final resistance of men like my 'employer'! Do you think you can wheedle concessions from people you've trodden underfoot? Come down from your pedestal, *my lady,* and have a good look at the source of your own wealth, a pittance of which you deign to share with me if I lick your feet as a proper Irishman should. Your father wrung his money and rank from dead bodies he strewed all over my homeland. Their lives paid for the clothes on your back! And by all that's holy, if my 'employer,' as you call him, doesn't throttle you, I may be tempted to do it myself, in memoriam!" With that, he swung his prisoner away from the rail and pushed her back toward the tiny cabin.

Catherine stiffened, hovering between cold rage and colder certainty that she was in the company of a fanatical madman. For a wild, fleeting moment, she thought of jumping over the side, but certain death had little appeal. Just before being thrust into the cabin, she spotted the third accomplice. He squatted near the stern where he relashed a small dinghy. The dinghy! The big craft would be impossible to manage, but the dinghy!

The blonde pushed her ahead of him into the cabin, then

stooped to clear his height through the doorway. Catherine spun abruptly, slammed the heels of her hands upward against his chin, and cracked his head against the lintel. When he reeled and caught automatically at his ringing head, she dove into his midsection, snatched his pistol, cocked and leveled it without a tremor. "Back out, Sir Patriot, with your hands clasped at the back of your neck. And don't suppose I'm a poor shot. You're a sizable partridge at this range and you've told me exactly where you stand, so move!"

Cheeks blazing and head throbbing, Liam moved. He would never hear the last of this, but injured pride did not provoke him to try anything stupid. The cold glitter of those sapphire eyes, so warm and beseeching a moment ago, assured him the girl was in no mood for rash behavior. He could almost feel Flannery shaking his head in disdain as he backed gingerly across the threshold.

The countess motioned him to a point several feet from Flannery and waggled the gun briefly at the big man's belly. "Drop your weapon, sir; call your companion and shed your jacket and boots. This man is dead if you delay."

Flannery calmly unhitched his belt and shrugged out of his jacket as he called briefly, "Come forward, Reagan. We're in the lady's company now." He indicated his inability to let go of the wheel long enough to remove his boots.

"Lash it. And you, Fair Hair, off with your top clothes."

Liam frowned. "Do you mean for us to freeze to death?"

"Letting you turn to ice would be an admirable way to preserve ammunition." She eyed the third man moving forward. "But I leave such tactics to you Irish . . . unless you continue to spew lies about my father. Hurry up!"

Liam sullenly tugged at his jacket as the third man joined him and was motioned to discard his clothes and weapons with the others. Catherine felt a growing uneasiness. They were too calm, too acquiescent. Seasoned villains could not be impressed so easily, unless . . . a fourth man was aboard. She leveled the pistol with both hands at the big man's belly. "Call the other one."

Flannery's bushy eyebrows went up slightly. "What other one? Ye're lookin' at the lot of us, little lady."

"Tell him to sing out, or you'll be lying amidst your din-

20

ner on the decking. I want that dinghy launched posthaste; these men can manage that very well without you. I shall count to three. One . . . two . . ."

Flannery interrupted, still with the same slightly amused look. "All right, Jimmy boy, the jig's up. Introduce yourself."

Abruptly, a crushing weight dropped onto Catherine's shoulders from behind and flattened her to the deck. The pistol was plucked quickly from her fingers as a tenor voice whistled reedily in her ear, "How d'ye do, ma'am. Sorry to drop in on ye like this." Red suns seemed to explode in her skull and her ears pounded as Catherine watched the redhead's big boots dance crazily toward her across the planking. He's going to kick me in the head, she thought dully. She tried to push the boots away but her fingers would not obey. The deck faded into blackness.

Flannery stood looking down at the unconscious girl and prodded Jimmy's leg with his foot. "Up with ye, lad, or ye'll crush the life out of her. She don't have the backbone of a cavalry nag."

Freckled, carrot-haired Jim Cochrane grinned as he hauled his two hundred lanky pounds off the captive who lay with black hair spilled across the wet deck. "She's got sufficient to put a fatal leak in a man's gut." He slipped a sly look at Flannery's belly. "Thought fancy doxies only knew how to crook their dainty fingers through teacup handles . . . and rings in men's noses." Now, he openly grinned at Liam.

Liam scowled, but Flannery chuckled. "Aye, the little chicky has steel pinfeathers. Must have got 'em from her da. They'll be plucked soon enough." He resumed his stance at the wheel. "Take the girl below, Liam. Tie her and don't dawdle. I want ye to spell me at the wheel."

Liam scooped up the limp prisoner and desposited her below, glancing resentfully at the still face as he tied efficient knots. How could any female be vulnerable one minute and mean as a mink the next? The witch probably deserved anything she got.

As Liam returned and took the helm, Flannery dragged a cigar out of his pocket. Poking it into the lantern, he puffed until it caught. "Tell you something, laddy.

We're not ten miles off Antrim. If she'd made it ashore to tattle to the authorities, the English would be on us like bloodhounds. On the other hand, maybe she'd have only shot one of us. I don't like bein' a leak-mouth, Liam, but Sean has to know ye were foxed. We can't afford soft spots."

Liam's blue eyes flared. "I didn't want this job. And you cannot claim we're doing it for the sake of home and country. We're doing it for Sean's sick hate. If he wants to break Enderly, why not aim for the man himself? That girl is barely seventeen. I daresay she knows nothing about her father's activities."

Flannery leaned on the binnacle and tapped his cigar so that the end glowed briefly like a hot, red eye. "Little Miss Enderly did quite a job in a space of ten minutes, didn't she?"

"For God's sake, she didn't put these words into my mouth. I thought of all this before we ever set sail from Donegal."

"Did ye now? Well, think again. Irish women and children have been made into proper hash by the English, though ye've never seen much of that. From now on I'll see ye do, should the stinkin' occasion arise. Ye've not seen pregnant women raped and bayoneted and babes bashed against the walls. Seen girls—and lads not five years old—abused and strangled." He bit off a piece of his cigar and spat it viciously downwind. "Then ye'll see the Enderly girl's no different from them, that she gets no pity. She's the enemy. Do ye think yer mother died of polite conversation with the English?"

Liam's lips tightened. "Megan was a spy."

"Aye, so ye heard that, did ye? Well, so she was, and a good one, too. But the other forty people in that village weren't spies; they were poor, dumb fisherfolk and they got the same as her." He chewed the cigar, twirling it thoughtfully. "Ye niver forgave her for leavin' ye. That's more like it, an't it, boy?"

"She was nothing to me. I hardly remember her." Liam's profile was stony as he checked the compass needle.

"No, I suppose it's what ye don't remember that

gripes at ye." Flannery yawned again. "It's been a long night and this cold's bitin' me bones. Hold her steady, 'til ye sight South Rock Beacon, then pick up five points north and rouse out Jimmy." He stubbed out his cigar. "I'm goin' below to sleep. Think on what I said. She's the enemy. The day ye forget it again will be a sorry one for us all."

Stiff and cold, Catherine awoke at dawn. Prison gray light wavered over the roughhewn bulkheads. Wrapped in blankets, the big redhead snored loudly in his hammock. Liam, an inert bundle, lay in a pile of sails at his feet. Her stomach growled when she shifted to renew circulation. As she burrowed awkwardly into her covering, Jimmy came below to rouse Flannery. Without giving her a glance, they left Liam sleeping. After some time, she drowsed.

The regular pattern of men changing watch and taking turns at the sails continued for the rest of the trip. Late in the day she was fed hardtack and coffee by the grinning Jimmy, who loosened the fetters but left her feet hobbled. Sometime after that, she slept again.

The next day seemed like one fitful nap, again broken by a single feeding. Catherine was awakened after nightfall when someone wrapped her tightly in the cloak again, head and all. She was lifted and carried, then lowered into other arms in what must have been the pitching dinghy. An icy feeling in the pit of her stomach warned they had reached their destination. Surf sounded and the dinghy lifted and rolled forward as the oars maneuvered, controlling the vessel's path up onto a pebbled shore with a grating shudder. The men in the bow went over the side and dragged the boat up onto the beach.

She was lifted again and passed over the bow. Then it seemed they walked and climbed forever, shifting her from man to man every so often. Periodically hearing dripping water, she imagined a cave or dungeon and bit the cloak to still her chattering teeth. Heels sounded on stone, then a finished floor. She was swung from a shoulder and dumped. Scared as she was, she felt a wave of rage at her captors' roughness. Well, let Valera enjoy her—if he could! She was dirty, smelly, mad as a hornet, and stiff as a board.

She heard Flannery's voice in a strange language, then Liam's; finally, a last one, deep and unfamiliar, in a tone of dismissal. The door closed and silence fell.

CHAPTER 2

Angel on Fire

Catherine rolled as the cloak was snapped away with an abrupt tug and dropped near her feet. For a moment, she lay rigid with apprehension, then cautiously opened her eyes to stare at a polished pair of boots carelessly crossed just beyond her nose. Her eyes followed the boots up long legs encased in black breeches to a white-shirted chest. While his head and shoulders were nearly obscured in shadow, the man seated before her was too tall to be Valera. Quickly she scanned the dim corners of the room searching for the Spaniard, then realized no one else was there. Nonplussed, she wondered what was going on. Who *had* kidnapped her, and why? Her attention darted back to the stranger. He leaned forward slightly and a dark face took form from the shadows, a form as beautiful as Original Sin must have seemed to Eve, with all its lure and its pain. As eyes the smoky green of storm seas caught hers and held, a phrase from Milton's *Paradise Lost* whispered through her mind:

His form had yet not lost
All his original brightness, nor appeared
Less than Archangel ruined . . .

He might be Lucifer, she thought. How sad he is.

Sean was equally unprepared for her. As the dark torrent of hair fell away from her pale face, her breathless, controlled fear was as tangible in the firelit room as a

25

small fist in his belly. God, she was young. He had pictured some blond, simpering bitch, unconsciously attributing to John Enderly's daughter characteristics he detested in Englishwomen. He had never imagined a dark forest creature, this childish Ondine. She has eyes out of legend, he thought. But legends sharply reminded him of Megan and the tales she had told him in childhood; the fleeting impulse to free the English girl left him.

Seeming to be unafraid now, the girl watched him as if he were some mythic beast caught in her virginal snare. Still, she paled and drew back when he rose and went to her with his knife unsheathed. He cut her bonds with two quick moves, then walked to the fireplace and poked the fire until it blazed. He turned and hunkered down to watch her chafe her wrists; they were purpled beneath the light froth of lace, but she made no murmur, and began systematically to rub her ankles. The silence was almost companionable.

In the heightened firelight he saw part of the reason her eyes were so compelling. Veiled by heavy lashes, they were slightly oblique, crested by brows like a lark's wings. Above high, slanting cheekbones, her features were finely chiseled, but placed upon a too-thin face; she looked a year or so younger than she was. The mouth was finely drawn, with a tender, full underlip. Dishevelment added to her appearance of vulnerability, but now that he saw his prisoner more clearly, he also noted the proud, almost arrogant set of head and the determined jaw.

Aware of his intent assessment, Catherine also saw it had subtly taken a hostile turn. She withdrew her attention from her ankles and met his gaze. She had seen the same hawk-hard cast of features among Moors of southern Spain, and his closely cropped black hair suggested Jacobin sympathies. "You've gone to a great deal of trouble to bring me here. May I ask why?" Her voice was soft, almost husky, but as clipped as a Prussian officer's. Sean might have smiled at her coolness if the situation had left any room for amusement.

"Your father owes me a debt."

She glanced at the handsomely appointed study, the huge painting of leopards *couchants* over the desk, the gleaming Celtic artifacts mounted on one wall. "Wouldn't it have been more civilized to send a solicitor?"

"Possibly. If the debt were merely monetary."

His indulgent tone annoyed her. "You must hate him very much to risk *other* men's lives to steal his only child."

"Few men have cause to hate him more, but I'm only one among his critics," he replied dryly. "And little risk was involved. Stealing you was simple enough."

"And not having been present, you're very sure of that?"

"If you managed, in some small way, to inconvenience my men and escaped with a few bruises, don't press your luck. You've arrived intact by my order. Personally, I'd like nothing better than an excuse to throttle you."

Her jaw lifted. "Do you intend to murder me?"

Culhane's eyebrows quirked. "Not at the moment." He rose and crossed to her. Her slim white throat was arched, her head with its thick, tangled hair thrown back as she looked up at him, her eyes unflinching. Still, he heard a slight gasp as he pulled her up on deadened legs. She made no effort to pull away, probably realizing she would fall if she tried to resist him. Backing, he forced her to take a few steps. Along with the waver of cramped limbs, he felt her tension, although her eyes showed nothing but defiant contempt. "If you're looking into my soul, I can tell you now it's black as the Pit," he drawled.

"If bullying defenseless women is the least of your sins, I must agree with you."

"It's amazed I am at how quickly you've blossomed from child to woman." His lilt had become mocking. "Moments ago, I could swear you were barely out of leaders."

"A short time in your company has sufficed to age me."

"Well . . . " He looked down at her faltering steps. "If you hope to totter home one day, you'd better mind your manners."

Her eyes blazed. "What will you do if I don't? *Threaten me to death?*" She tried to twist out of his grasp but he jerked her up so that her toes barely reached to the floor.

"It's time you understand your status here. So long as I intend to keep you, you're mine to do with as I like. You're in Ireland, girl, to see how the Irish live, and how they die, if I'm inclined to stretch your education that far. Here, my word is law, whereas you rate less than the least Irish pig."

Blinded with fury, she spat. The spittle struck him on the cheek and his green eyes went murderous. One hand left its bruising grip on her arm, and he backhanded her across the face. Catherine thought her neck would snap. Light exploded in her head as warmth flowed into her nose and mouth. The fire in the hearth dimmed.

He roughly picked her up and strode through the door into a dark foyer. Only the pounding pain in her head and neck told her she had not fainted. He carried her up a long flight of stairs, then along a hallway. Pausing almost in midstride, he shouldered open a door, went into a room, and unceremoniously dropped her in a straight-backed chair. When she immediately tried to get up, he firmly shoved her back, dunked a towel in a basin of water on the adjacent commode, and, tugging her head back by the hair, plopped the cold towel sopping wet across her face. She let out a squeal of shock and outrage as icy water ran down her chin and throat and worked its chilly way between her breasts. When she grabbed at the towel, he jerked her hands away. "Hold still! Your nose is bleeding a river. And keep your head back!"

Though furious, she realized the practicality of his order and obeyed, until he clamped her nostrils together. With frantic distress noises at being suffocated, she clawed at the towel over her mouth. He muttered an oath and, lifting the towel, swabbed at her cut lip with a corner of the cloth while she gulped for air. Gradually, the bleeding stopped as he roughly cleaned her face. She looked more peaked than ever when he finished, but her eyes were still mutinous. Tensely, she watched as he wrung out the towel in the basin, his strong hands easily twisting the heavy cloth. With a slight shiver, she remembered his remark about throttling her.

He quickly folded the towel, then dropped it on the marble-topped commode. Wearing a determined look that boded ill, he crossed the bold Moorish rug to a magnificently carved bed hung in oyster velvet. Sitting on the end of it, he leaned back on his elbows, spread his legs, and said, "Come here."

28

Her mouth went dry, but she did not budge.

"Do you require another box to clear your ears, girl?"

Catherine debated a retort, but bit her lip and went to stand just out of reach. To give him an excuse to batter her again was pointless. She could do little to stop him from doing as he pleased, but sooner or later he would drop his guard.

He thrust out a boot. "Take them off." She stared at him, a comical mixture of relief and outrage warring for a moment on her face. Then, with a look of complete disdain, she turned her back on him, hiked her skirts slightly, and with the boot between her skirted knees began to tug, only to straighten with a snort when he planted his other foot on her bottom and braced himself. "You'll do well to keep your head up or you'll start your nose bleeding again."

Catherine dropped the first boot with a deliberate crash and began working on the other one, thinking with what wicked joy she would crown him once she got her hands on the candlestick by the basin. As the other boot hit the floor, she squirreled out from between his knees, expecting him to lunge for her, but he simply lay back on the bed and locked his hands behind his head. With one good kick I could ruin the smug bastard, she thought grimly as she turned to face him.

Sean had just begun to think she might be tractable after all when he caught the gleam in her eye. "Try it." His voice was quiet but his eyes glinted like shards of green glass.

"Ladies who present no surprises are rather tedious, don't you think?" she replied wickedly.

"You've unladylike notions; but then, you couldn't look less like a lady now, and I've rarely met one capable of surprising me. There's clean water in the pitcher. Wash your face. You may hang your jacket on the chair."

Catherine turned on her heel and stalked to the chair, hung her jacket as directed, then carried the basin of darkish pink water to the commode. She emptied it with a heavy splash and refilled it. Stealing a glance in the mirror as she poured, she saw her features already swelling in a pale moon ringed in dirt and bruises. Her nose, neck, and jaw ached; her cut underlip was still bleeding. It's no thanks to that lout my nose isn't broken, she thought angrily, wincing as she soaked her face. His voice came over her shoulder, "You may as well take off the dress. Your dirty neck is showing and you might not have another bath for some time."

She kept the padded cloth clamped to her nose and retorted nasally, "You said I rated no better than an Irish pig; you can hardly object to my looking the part."

She missed his faint smile. "If you think a swinish appearance will discourage my men, you'd better know they're not in the least particular, but I am. Take off the dress. I'll have it off soon enough, in any case."

Damp hair sticking to her face, she grabbed the candlestick with both hands and whirled. "If you touch me, I'll kill you!" Her voice was low, but utterly determined.

Sean Culhane slipped off the bed in one fluid movement, and belatedly, Catherine realized she had not reckoned with his reflexes. She took a wary defensive stance, arms straining at the weight of the candlestick. Ignoring her, he unbuttoned his shirt, pulled it off, folded it neatly, and laid it on a carved chest. Wide shoulders and a black-furred chest tapered to a flat belly and slim hips. Clad only in snug breeches, he turned to stand with hip outthrust, hands hanging loosely. "That thing won't stop me," he said almost wearily. Before the words were out of his mouth, he was nearly on her. She swung the candlestick in a wide, lethal arc that he dodged with a swift, twisting side step. He closed on her, caught her wrists on the back swing, and crushed the tendons until, with a cry, she was forced to drop the heavy weapon. Then he thrust her back and around, twisting her arms painfully against her back. Just as quickly, he released her arms; but as she tore free, his fingers hooked in the dress and, with a jerk, ripped it down her back. He was already stripping her as she spun, clawing and stumbling over skirts which had fallen in a tangle about her feet. Wild-eyed, spitting hate, she caught his cheek and raked his chest while he half dragged her, half carried her to the bed. One chemise strap was ripped and hanging, the other slipping down her arm. Her hair swirled like a silken maelstrom as he picked her up and hurled her onto the bed.

Then, as he stood over her, his cheek clawed and his chest striped scarlet, his looming figure abruptly merged into a nightmarish haze of blood in her mind. It blocked out reality, tore her away to some other place, another horror from a source deeper than the threat of imminent rape.

When Sean stripped off his breeches, he knew she had seen a man before. Her eyes were wide, but not with startled innocence. He might have guessed a bitch of Enderly's would be no virgin. She edged away from him like a cornered animal, her eyes great desperate pools fixed on his bloody chest. Creamy skin gleamed in the shadows of the bed as the torn petticoat slipped up, revealing long, slender legs; but it was not desire that drove him now.

He climbed atop her, caught her hands and pinned them above her head, then threw a leg over her lower body. When she felt the pressure of his sex against her bare thigh, she suddenly went berserk and fought him in dumb, choking terror. Clamping her wrists with one hand, he methodically ripped the camisole and petticoat from her straining body, then lay full length upon her, forcing her to submit to his nakedness until she lay exhausted, heart thudding against his ribs. Sensing the trigger to her fear, he deliberately smeared her breasts with his blood so that her body was slippery under him. Eyes dilated until they were almost black, she lapsed into paralytic terror, lips moving in a pleading whisper, "No, no . . . no," as a litany, as if to herself. Sean's eyes, boring into hers, looked into a midnight void. Relentlessly, he pursued her into the void.

Rising to a kneeling position, then grasping her under the knees, he backed off the bed, pulling her with him until he stood on the floor with her defenselessly open to him, knees on either side of his thighs and feet dangling. He dragged her thighs wide. As if giving a death blow to an enemy, Sean rammed himself into her body with all the hatred pent in him, felt fragile membrane tear and heard her scream in agony. He thrust harshly, savaging her, fingers biting into her flesh when she twisted as if to escape a knife stabbing into her vitals. His hatred burst into her in a flood.

When he had done, Culhane stood like a spent animal, motionless but for the rise and fall of his chest. Catherine lay impaled, slack, her face averted and shadowed by her hair. He withdrew, then released her to lie sprawled and broken, like the women the soldiers had left in the ruins of Kenlo.

He collected the shreds of her undergarments and wiped them with the mingling of her blood and his seed. He crossed to the desk, wadded the garment, then began to wrap it in paper.

Catherine staréd dully as if in a trance, but when realization of his intention finally pierced her mind, she shrieked and flung herself across the room, nearly tripping as pain wrenched at her abdomen. Desperately, she snatched at the package. "No! You won't shame my father so! Give it to me!"

Sean eluded her as he would have a gesticulating drunkard. "Shame him? He has enough blood on his hands to taint the North Sea. Not an Irishman born won't raise a cheer as your unworthy father kicks into hell, a precipitous journey he'll be taking sooner than he knows."

"You're a liar! He's one of the most respected statesmen in England! He's never hurt anyone!" Stumbling, she made another futile grab. "You're not fit to lick his boots, you filthy cur! You're striking at his back because you haven't the courage to face him!"

Leaning over the desk with a contemptuous sneer on his dark face, Culhane interrupted her tirade. "He's respectable, twit, not respected! Oh, he's spotless enough to the eye. He does his murdering with a stroke of a pen. I'll wager he's never even quirted a horse. How do you suppose he's managed to rise two steps in the peerage? Well, I'll be telling you. He's an efficient butcher, as well as an accomplished thief and traitor. And as for my craven reluctance to carve him up in gentlemanly fashion, face-to-face, it's too good for him. By the time I've done with the bastard, he'll think hell's a holiday!"

"You miserable, lying . . . !" She hooked for his eyes and diverted his attention as her other hand snaked toward the packet and successfully flicked it out of his grasp. She backed with it toward the fireplace.

Culhane pulled a pistol from a desk drawer, cocked and leveled it. "Drop the bundle, girl. Your father's pride isn't

32

worth dying for." When she did not move, he murmured softly, "So, you'd not die for yourself, but you'd toss off in a trice for Papa. You've a slapsided notion of the way the world wags, girl, if you'll trade your life for a bit of dirty linen. For clean, now, that's another thing altogether, as you'll soon discover."

Eyes blazing in contempt, Catherine whirled and accurately chucked the bundle into the fire. As the packet began to flame, she tensely held her breath, waiting for the pistol explosion that would send her into oblivion.

Blackness clouded in Sean, the packet conjuring up the image of Megan's oil-soaked, blazing corpse. Imperceptibly, his finger tightened on the trigger. The girl was John Enderly's blood, she was Enderly; but a part of his mind, too familiar with the dreadful ritual of death, warred with his impulse to murder. He knew how small she would be in death. The bullet would explode that straight, proud little back to crumple her on the rug like a mangled kitten.

Catherine, hearing his strides eat the distance between them, lunged to block his way to the fire. Culhane knocked her aside. She fell to the carpet, then flew at his back and tore at his hair as he knelt to dig gingerly in the hot coals. Flicking the packet out of its glowing bed, he growled and shoved her off, then turned the gun on her as she came at him again. As the cold muzzle touched between her breasts, she froze in a crouch, panting with fury, midnight hair smoking about her face and shoulders, eyes opal-eerie. Without warning, Sean's loins blazed into a desire so intense he caught his breath. With a lust he had never before known, he wanted to take her. To feel her wind about his body, to arouse response in her as fierce as her suddenly savage beauty. Fiery serpents of light darted across their taut bodies as the chill tip of the gun trailed slowly upward between the soft breasts until he rested it in the hollow of her throat. He felt sweat trickle down his kneeling body, down the crevices where his thighs met his groin. Fighting for control, he gritted hoarsely, "Get back." As Catherine obeyed him warily, his voice was ragged with effort to hold himself in check. "I suggest you dress . . . *now.*" He indicated the direction of her clothing with the pistol. Without taking her eyes off him, she got up and found her clothes.

His pulse slowed as she quickly covered her nakedness, but where the torn dress did not meet under the jacket, the cleft of her breasts was an enticing shadow. No longer training the gun on her, but still watchful, he tucked the packet under his arm and moved toward the head of the bed, where he gave the bell rope a tug. Shortly, as he shrugged into a robe, a rap sounded on the door.

"Come in, Peg."

The woman, with graying blond hair loosely tucked under a nightcap and a plump body contained with equal carelessness in a voluminous robe of indeterminate color, seemed undisturbed to see a wild-haired young woman in torn clothing with eyes like bruises in her master's bedroom. Silently, she waited.

"Take her downstairs and show her where she's to sleep," Culhane ordered. "She'll begin her duties tomorrow. The slower she learns, the less she eats. If she makes any trouble, deal with her as I would. Good night."

The woman nodded at Catherine, indicating she should precede her. As the door closed, Catherine saw her rapist staring broodingly into the fire.

Before they started down the stair, the woman advised briskly, "In case ye've any notions about makin' a run for it, this place is well guarded and ye're as far from help as the moon. I've got arms like a hairy pugilist and a noggin to match, as well as five stone on ye. So move along. We'll both need our sleep for tomorrow."

Catherine, grateful for the protecting darkness, was too depressed to speak. Feeling torn and degraded, she clung to the banister as they descended.

Finally, in the bowels of the house, when she verged on collapse, the woman nudged her to stop. Choosing a key from a ring looped over her arm, the Irishwoman unlocked the heavy door and, lifting the candle high, motioned Catherine to enter. "'Tisn't much," she advised in her broad brogue, "but ye'll be glad enough for it at day's end." The flickering candle revealed stone walls and a high window too narrow for even a child to squeeze through, but perversely generous enough to emit an icy draft. The bed, a straw-stuffed pallet on a wooden cot, had only a single, tattered quilt. At home, Chippendale himself had decorated her bedchamber, petit salon, and bath.

The woman was already headed for the door. "I'll bring ye somethin' suitable to wear in the mornin'."

"Thank you, Margaret. I am to call you Margaret?"

The woman paused. "There's no need to thank me. I'm a plain woman and plain Peg will do." She closed the door behind her and locked it.

Catherine let herself sag. She lay huddled on the prickly pallet and sobbed until she went dry. Too exhausted even to pull up the cover, she dropped into a deathlike sleep.

An hour later, a scream rent the silence. Instantly awake, Sean unsheathed a dagger concealed amid the bed hangings beside his head. A sobbing cry welled up from the depths of the house. He slid out of bed, found his breeches, and pulled them on. Barefoot and Indian quiet, he padded into the hallway, then swiftly down the stairs. At the bottom he heard the tormented cry again, a crooning, keening, mourning sound eerie as a banshee's wail. His breath caught. It was the girl. Somehow he knew it was the girl. Thinking she might have attempted suicide, he tore down flights of stairs to the levels below the main floor. A candle glowed at the opened door of the cell where Peg stood in her rumpled gown and no nightcap, staring into the room. Grabbing her shoulder, he furiously thrust her aside. "Damnation, Peg, I told you to be certain . . ."

Catherine lay on the bed, face turned to the wall and shielded by one arm. Peg grasped his arm warningly as he moved to brush past her. "She's still asleep."

He looked at her dubiously.

"Oh, aye. It was her right enough. Wailin' as if fiends were at her and mumblin' some heathen gibberish. But I doubt she knows a thing about it."

He crossed to the pallet. Catherine, seeming to sense his presence, moaned and flung an arm outward as if to ward him off. Her eyes were faint blue shadows under the lids. Wondering what horrors they were seeing, he watched them flicker. Her nose was swollen, blurring the definition of her features. The parted jacket nearly exposed her breasts, and, without thinking, he pulled the ragged coverlet over her.

Peg, watching him with a speculative expression, announced rather loudly, "I'm thinkin' she could do with an extra blanket."

He looked up, green eyes unreadable, then glanced at the window and shrugged. "As you like. She's unlikely to last a fortnight without it." Shoving the knife into his breeches band, he left the way he had come.

Catherine lay inert, trying to think what miserable part of herself she did not want to move first. "There's a horrible creature in my head with a hammer," she mumbled.

" 'Tis a leprechaun, no doubt," Peg said, briskly stripping the blanket down to the foot of the bed. Because the prisoner was numb with cold, the additional draft had little effect.

"Leprechaun?" Catherine muttered dully.

"Aye. Mischievous little men. Some folk call them elves. They cause all sorts of trouble unless ye put out milk for them."

"Milk?" Catherine's eyes flew open with hope.

"Aye. But ye'll not be seein' breakfast for hours," said Peg, slapping a small pile of linen on the bed. "Nearly half the mornin's gone and ye've plenty to do, so ye'd better be movin'."

Catherine squinted into the dark. "You're confused," she said flatly. "It's still night."

"Night, me mither's bun." Peg sniffed. "The birds is caterwaulin'. Out of bed, girl."

As Catherine struggled to her elbows, a sharp pain shot through her neck and down her spine. Stifling a groan, she cranked her complaining body out of bed. When she had reached a more or less stable standing position, Peg thrust a worn, colorless shirt at her from the linen pile on the bed. Catherine looked at it. "You're joking." When Peg did not even blink, she sighed. Every muscle shrieking, Catherine worked her way out of her jacket, then into the shirt. One of Peg's own, it dropped directly over her head to her waist, ignoring her shoulders on the way.

"A tad large," Peg noted. "Pull it up and draw the cord

at the neck. . . . . Tighter. I want no good Irishmen bein'
tempted to sin. That's it. Rip off a strip round the hem and
tie it about yer waist." Peg stood back and surveyed the effect. "Well . . . ye won't be dazzlin' the Prince of Wales,
but it looks better than it ought."

Catherine tried to pull on her jacket but the narrow
sleeves refused to pass over the shirt, so with a sigh, she
firmly ripped the sleeves off the once-fine garment and
made a passable vest. She had slept in her boots, so at least
she was forgiven the necessity of bending over to put them
on; she thought she might collapse if she did.

"Come along with ye." Peg led the way through a series
of corridors, up a narrow flight of steps, then pushed open a
door.

The whitewashed kitchen was enormous. Windows,
which lined the far wall, had heavy shutters with musket
slits; deep-set casement wells indicated stone foundation
walls three feet thick. The place could easily be turned into
a fortress. Massive hoods sheltered huge hearths on the
near wall. Down the center of the room was a long row of
oak tables where several women were either up to their elbows in bread dough or making up vats of porridge and
slicing bacon slabs for the fireplaces. As Catherine's nose
twitched, her stomach let out a sullen growl. Two boys in
their early teens were stacking wood at the near fireplace;
one gave her a shy, furtive smile. As she smiled back, his
companion gave him a warning thump on the shoulder.
"Back to your work, Danny!" He turned back to his chore.
The women were less shy. One by one, as they became
aware of her presence, they stared. A wave of hostility
drifted toward her. Straightening her aching back, she
eyed them as coolly as if Peg were escorting her on tour.

"Know anythin' about cookin'?" Peg asked.

"Not a thing," was the crisp reply. "And I've no intention of learning."

Peg gave her a look. "Ye'd be wise, girl, not to quibble
over trifles."

Catherine started to retort, then realized the woman
was right. She had best tread lightly until she explored her
situation. She shrugged. "Very well, but don't blame me if
I burn down the place."

Peg led her to a table where a young blonde with rosy cheeks and Peg's blue eyes kneaded dough. With a sidelong look at Catherine, the blonde kept kneading. "Now," Peg said, "watch Moora here and do as she does."

Catherine wondered if raw dough was edible. It *looked* edible. She watched Moora's hands work and wind. Catherine filled her hands with flour. Nobody had asked her if they were clean. They were not. Moora plopped a wad of the creamy stuff on a board in front of her. Catherine dug her fingers into it, then tried a few experimental pulls. It was sticky and rubbery, but amusing to manipulate. Better still, it was turning a light gray. She adored the idea of feeding dirty bread to the enemy, but she was famished and the mound of dough was the only food in reach. Casually, she reached into the flattish wooden bowl that held fresh dough. Moora said without looking up, "Don't eat that."

"I've only had a few mouthfuls of food in the last few days," Catherine argued. "I won't be much use if I faint."

Moora's jaw set. "It's a rule. If you eat anythin' besides the regular meals, it's stealin'. Maude, there, handles thievin'."

Catherine looked at Maude's burly physique and man-sized hands that wielded a side of bacon like a demitasse spoon. She kept on kneading.

After a bit, Moora rolled her own portion into a fat sausage shape, then coiled it into a long knot. Catherine started to duplicate the pattern. "No. Another handful of flour or so for yer dough, then flour yer hands again before ye roll it."

For the next few hours Catherine folded dough, longing to pillow her head in the soft mass to sleep forever. At last, a bell sounded by the hearth nearest the door and her stomach gave a gurgle of joy. Breakfast! Everyone began to scurry about, clear tables, and set them with porringers, mugs, and spoons. Moora, without a word to her unwanted apprentice, joined the others. Catherine watched for a moment, wondering if she was expected to assist, until Peg waggled an imperative finger and pointed to one of several silver trays loaded with covered dishes monogrammed with the initial *C*. The beast's own breakfast, no doubt.

"Take that and follow me," Peg said. Moora and four girls picked up the other trays.

"But, what about . . . ?"

"Your breakfast?" Moora ironically supplied for her.

"Later," Peg intoned. With a sigh, Catherine picked up the heavy tray. By the time they reached the end of the long corridor to the dining room, she thought her wrists would break.

The first face she recognized was Liam's at the table's far end. Toying abstractedly with a water glass, he glanced up as Peg led the servants into the room. His startled look told Catherine the bruises on her face must have ripened. With a flush, he focused on his empty plate. She hoped his conscience roasted him!

As she trailed Peg and Moora past the chairs toward him, she saw only strange men until Flannery's flaming beard came into view. Possibly accustomed to his master's brutality, he apeared less surprised than Liam. The trays went down on a massive mahogany sideboard. The room was Georgian with dark green walls, handsome white wainscoting, and a carpet with a scarlet field bordered in green and gold. A George Stubbs painting of riders and dappled white hounds hung in a gilt frame over the sideboard. Across the room, long windows admitted the hazy glow of early morning and framed a landscape bleak as a drained sea adrift with clinging scraps of mist. A few trees clustered near the house, but beyond those, nothing whatever relieved the wind-blasted furze and heather-blanketed rock. A peach-veined marble fireplace held a cheery crackling fire which dispelled the morning chill. Due to the laggard winter light, candles in brass wall brackets and on the table had been lit.

As the dishes were uncovered, Catherine developed the attention of a starved dog. Crisp bacon wafted a heavenly odor to her nostrils. Poached eggs with lovely yellow yolks peeped from their deep dish. Kippers, golden cottage potatoes. And luxury of luxuries, black Jamaican coffee.

"Now, ye're to serve each gentleman yer dish from the left," Peg told her after dismissing the rest of the servant girls except Moora. "If he wants a bit, you spoon him out a bit. If he keeps lookin' at ye, give him more. Don't trip over

39

yer skirts, and tomorrow, tie yer hair back. Begin with the big chair at either end, dependin' on whether Moora or meself an't already there. I know it an't usual, but that's the way we do it at Shelan."

Shelan. Up until now, no one had mentioned names of anything or anyone.

"When ye're done, come back to this spot. If anybody wants extra helpin's, he'll crook his finger; you go runnin' and see what he wants."

You mean they don't whistle and expect me to wag my tail? Catherine thought irritably. I was so looking forward to relieving myself on some Irish gentleman's foot.

Thankfully, Peg and Moora headed for the far chair, the one where *he* must rest his villainous posterior. Catherine avoided looking in that direction and turned her attention to the choirboy. She doled bacon onto Liam's plate with precise plops. His neck was rosy, his embarrassment tangible as he muttered, "Thank you."

Catherine bobbed abruptly and whined in perfect Cockney only he could hear, "Ow, don't think nothin' of it, ducks!" Ignoring his choke, she went on to the next man.

Then she heard the Green-Eyed Beast's hateful, melodic lilt in the same strange language from the previous night and stole a look at him under her lashes. Insufferably at ease, he was sitting back, long legs stretched out under the table, a bleached linen shirt open at his tanned throat, his eyes on Flannery. Critically assessing the clean-cut profile etched against the window's hard, gray light, she reluctantly had to admit he was a man any woman would look at. Like her father, he used no gestures as he spoke. She noted with satisfaction the scratches on his cheek.

Of the two men conversing with Green Eyes, one was in his fifties, with narrow, crinkling blue eyes and a thick shock of gray hair. He was the only man with a proper coat at the table, and the oldest. Green Eyes' attentiveness to his comments suggested respect. The other was a red-haired, blunt-featured youth completely out of place in a polished room. Except for a coarse mouth, he resembled Flannery, but lacked Flannery's air of ironic humor. He

40

seemed to be making some argument and growing irritated with the others' tolerant disagreement. The rest of the men listened as they finished their food.

"Fetch the plates," Peg quietly directed at last. "Make sure the silver's laid slantwise across the plate so it don't fall off. Rouge, the young redhead there, don't bother with proper manners, so watch his plate . . . and his hands, too. Pick up from the right and be quick. Moora's gone for cobbler we've still to serve."

Catherine gave a silent groan. Oh, her godforsaken stomach. But at least she did not have to go near Green Eyes as she cleared. Moora brought the cobbler and, with Peg, served the upper and middle part of the table. Catherine's mouth watered as cream-drenched apple cobbler was placed in front of the men. Green Eyes waved the last course aside, but wanted coffee. To her dismay, Peg motioned her to take it. "From the left, remember," she said, handing her a cup and saucer with the silver coffeepot.

Praying the cup would not rattle, Catherine crossed the room with the heavy pot. If he tried a familiar pat, she swore silently, no matter what they did to her, she would empty the entire steaming potful over his head. She set the cup and saucer down without a clink. Although he must have known who was serving him, he spared her not a glance. She poured. He ignored. She retreated with the pot, madder than if he had pinched her. So, she was just one more virgin he had brutally used and given the toe of his boot! By the time she returned the pot to the sideboard, she was as hot as the coffee. And nearly giddy with hunger. Mentally, she called him every foul name she had ever heard and a few she made up on the spot. Peg nudged her. "He wants cobbler now."

Oh, *now* he wants it, does he? Grabbing the cream pitcher and packing a saucer under her arm, she picked up the entire remainder of the cobbler and marched to his chair. Moora moved to cut her off, but Peg stopped her daughter with a knowing, silent shake of the head. Catherine plunked down the pitcher on the table, then withdrew the saucer with a flourish from under her armpit, placed it with a sharp rap on his service plate, and ladled out cobbler in fat dollops. Green Eyes leaned back in his chair and watched her. The others were fascinated as a great pile oozed over the saucer rim onto the plate. She poured cream in a shining stream on the miniature mountain until, to her regret, it ran out before leaking from the table onto his lap.

Quietly, as if addressing a peevish child, he said, "Because you lack regard for our food, you'll do without your share of it today. Go back to your place."

Liam winced.

Cheekbones white with rage, Catherine stalked back to the sideboard. I don't regret it. I don't regret a scrap of it, she told herself furiously.

Moora edged away. Peg said nothing, simply removed the offending mess from the table, then resumed her place. Most of the men excused themselves, looking Catherine over in wonder as they left the room. Flannery, Liam, and the gray-haired man lingered on with Green Eyes.

Great Caesar's Ghost, Catherine though irritably, they must be recounting the history of the Roman Empire! I must have something to eat! A wave of dizziness washed over her. In the next moment, she sagged to the floor.

The men stared at the small heap on the rug. The gray-haired man instantly pushed his chair back, but Sean waved him to remain where he was. "Don't disturb yourself, doctor," he said in clipped English. "When did you feed her last, Liam?"

"Jimmy gave her hardtack yesterday noon," came the flustered reply, "but she missed two meals yesterday and two the preceding day."

"Hm. I imagine she *is* a trifle hungry." Sean appraised the heap. "Pity. She's going to regret sleeping through tomorrow's meals as well."

A pitiful moan issued immediately from the heap as it began to rouse feebly to a half-sitting position. "Wh . . . what happened?"

"You appeared to faint," came the expressionless reply.

"Oh," Catherine said vaguely. She lifted a hand to her forehead and sneaked a peek at him under sooty lashes. Narrow green eyes slanted back at her through lashes as thick as her own.

42

He smiled grimly. "We're all gratified by your rapid recovery."

One sapphire glinted at him from behind her hand. "I feel better now."

"Oh, good. I was afraid you wouldn't be up to a third act."

In an instant, she whipped to her feet despite a slight unsteadiness. "If you mean to starve me, I see no reason to work." She glared at him defiantly. "And I won't until I'm given a decent meal."

Unimpressed, Sean sipped at his coffee. "As you like. Peg . . ." He jerked his head toward the kitchen corridor door. "Take her back to her room. She'll stay there until she agrees to complete her duties. The hours she spends taking her ease will be deducted from her free time in future."

Catherine said nothing, but if her eyes had been carving knives, Culhane would have been whittled to a chip. Peg and Moora flanked her as she marched out of the room, slim back as straight as a board. When the women's footsteps had died away, Doctor Flynn leaned forward on his elbows. "Sean, she has no weight to lose. If she holds out . . ."

"She won't."

"That girl is more stubborn than you realize," Liam cut in. "She might have gotten away from us in Runcorn if she hadn't chosen the worst dive on the docks for a haven. And on board—"

Now Flannery spoke. "She made sheep's eyes at Galahad here and relieved him of his pistol. She was all for commandeerin' the dinghy and takin' her chances in a snowstorm."

Sean scoffed, "The little witch would have had a short row frozen to the oars."

Flannery cocked an eyebrow. "Long enough to maybe raise Antrim."

"She won't last in that hole belowstairs with nothing to eat!" Liam protested again.

"Did her sheep's eyes melt more than your brain?" Sean cut back curtly. "You could have lost the lives of your crew, not to mention your own, the boat, and that black-

43

haired baggage who can hang the lot of us." He stood up and leaned over the table, fingers splayed on the linen. "Now, get this through your heads. She's *my* prisoner. If I've a whim to flay her on Dublin Commons, it's nothing to you."

An awkward silence fell. Liam sat rigid, his knuckles white on the chair arms. Sean kicked his chair back. "I suggest we get on with the day's business."

Flannery and Flynn rose, but Liam remained where he was. "I'd like a word with my brother in private," he said tersely. Flannery and Flynn exchanged glances and withdrew.

With a short sigh of exasperation, Sean dropped into his chair. "What is it?"

"Sean, I may be a figurehead here, but I demand respect."

Sean raised an eyebrow. "Demand it?"

"I accord you respect . . ."

"I earn it."

"And I don't? Is that why you undermine my position? Do you expect me to accept public criticism?"

"Did you merit the criticism?"

"Yes, I don't deny it."

"Then you must accept it. You accepted a commission you nearly aborted. Had you given me a like responsibility I failed to carry out, I would be subject to your reprimand. If this were a formal army, I would be liable to court-martial."

"This isn't wartime and it was your private scheme—"

"That you agreed to see through."

Liam looked away in frustration, then back. "Very well." His voice was toneless. "I see your point."

"Good. Now that we've reached this stage, I concede *your* point. I should have spoken to you privately. I lost my temper." He held out his hand. "We're into the shank of the morning, brother. Shall we get on with the day's work?"

Liam hesitated. "On one condition. Don't starve that girl."

Sean's green eyes narrowed. "I won't bargain, Liam." He paused. "When she understands for the first time in her pampered life what hunger means, I'll feed her. Not before." He pulled Liam easily to his feet and gave his shoulder a slap. "Don't fret, Galahad. I've no intention of making her any skinnier than she is. Last night was like bedding a bag of rabbit bones." He turned away before Liam could tell if he was lying.

CHAPTER 3

The Swinging Star

When Catherine, who had instantly fallen asleep in her cell, opened her eyes, twilight revealed a mug of water on the floor beside her bed. Resisting the urge to drain it, she drank just enough to quiet her hunger pangs, then again slept half the clock around until late morning of the next day. In a stupor, she groped for the mug and, despite her restraint, downed most of it before the stomachache dulled. She wondered how long she could hold out; if the Irishman was capable of kidnap and rape, he was capable of letting her starve. He'll hang, she swore vengefully, and I'll dance a jig about the gibbet to show him how to kick his heels. But oddly, as she drifted back to fevered sleep, her mind evaded the point when the noose choked the life from the magnificent, marred animal who had attacked her in a kind of torment equal to her own.

Her dreams swirled and twisted like vapors over a marsh. Somehow the old, recurrent nightmare of being a child again, of running through a forest from some terrible unseen beast, altered. The heat was as oppressive as that of a jungle and she was now a young woman, but still wearing a child's nightdress and crying for her mother. As always, Elise appeared, dressed for riding. She silently took her hand and led her from the forest into a misted meadow split by a crumbling stone wall. Usually the dream faded away at this point; but now, a black-hooded executioner waited by the wall, his bare chest covered with crimson slashes. Among the cuts gaped mortal wounds;

46

sick with fear, she tried to run away, but no matter where she stumbled, her mother blocked her escape. The executioner seized her, threw her down on the wall, then ripped away her nightshift. She screamed uselessly for Elise. Then it seemed her body was being torn apart, as if she were being stabbed by curving blades, and in her agony she saw eyes glitter green hellfire through the slits of the executioner's mask. Pleading, she caught at her mother's habit, but the habit was covered with blood, and Elise's beautiful face was cold. "Now, it is your turn. But you cannot die. You will never escape me. I will follow you always . . . always . . ."

Ice touched her cheeks and forehead while someone held her down. She tried to fight free. "No, no. Lie quietly. You're beginning to feel better, are you not?" The voice was soothing. She began to relax until the aroma of hot chicken broth teased her nostrils. Her eyes flew open to see the gray-haired man from the dining room wave a spoon in front of her nose.

His blue eyes crinkled. "Ah, I thought Peg's soup would bring results. Not too quickly now; it's hot."

Obediently, she sipped. After several mouthfuls she lifted her attention from the spoon to scrutinize him.

"I'm Doctor Flynn. We met at breakfast the other day."

Flynn was brisk, but she sensed he was kind. It seemed she had caught a chill and spent a rough day and night. She sipped as he offered the spoon again, then asked wryly, "Won't the master of Shelan disapprove of my dining before I've done a day's work?"

"I think not. Liam didn't condone your confinement without food."

"Liam?" Now it was her turn to be startled. "Liam is master here?"

He guessed the source of her error. "Lord Liam Culhane is the twelfth Culhane of Shelan. The man with whom you . . . disagreed is his younger brother, Sean." To forestall more questions, he settled the blankets higher about her shoulders. "You should sleep now."

"That's all I've been doing for . . . how many hours now?" Despite her light tone, shadows crept into her eyes.

"Breakfast was three days ago. It's Friday, near dusk."

Slipping his fingers about her wrist, he took her pulse. "Don't you want to sleep?"

"Not particularly." Her lashes shuttered. "Sometimes I have bad dreams; fortunately, I never remember them."

He looked at her a long moment, released her wrist, then slipped the pillow from behind her and tucked her in. She had hardly been aware she was wearing one of Peg's roomy nightgowns.

"I don't believe you'll be having any more bad dreams tonight. Just think of having a solid breakfast in the morning."

Briefly, Flynn reported Catherine's recovery to Sean Culhane. His elbows on the desk, Culhane flicked a quill in his fingers. "When will she be up and about?"

"Tomorrow morning if she doesn't overtax. Naturally, she has to eat to regain strength."

"Naturally." Culhane's tone was dry. "Then there'll be no complications?"

"She's resiliant and determined."

A wolfish smile mocked him. "You admire the little wench's nerve for bearding the ogre in his den, don't you?" The smile grew grim. "She's a spoiled brat who has never been thwarted in her life. Her diamond-studded hairbrushes would feed an Irish family for life. Her French grandmother was a royal whore; her mother, an empty-headed doll who wasted her portion of one of the greatest fortunes in France. And like the rest of her lot, Miss Enderly has been taught to sell her erstwhile virtue for a solid price."

"Isn't it possible that your hatred of Enderly has twisted your judgment?"

The younger man smiled mirthlessly. "I'm a veritable corkscrew, doctor."

Flynn knew that smile. With a sharp twinge of pity for the Enderly girl, he took his leave.

Catherine wolfed breakfast. At last she sat back with a small, gluttonous smile of satisfaction at Peg, who sat in the opposite windowsill, watching her. They were alone in the kitchen. She stretched, eyes narrowed against the

48

morning light. "You're a good cook, Peg! That was splendid."

"Oh, I do well enough," Peg replied, not mentioning her cookery was acknowledged the best in the country. "Of course, famine is a fine appetizer."

Catherine cocked her head, still squinting. "Did Liam Culhane order his brother to let me have all this?"

Peg snorted. "Liam orders Sean to do nothin'!"

"But he *is* lord here, isn't he?"

Peg gave her a sharp look. "Doctor Flynn told ye that, I'm supposin'. . . . Well, it's true enough in a sense, but every soul on the place takes orders from Sean. Liam's a fine lad, and he paints pretty pictures, but he can't manage a flock of sheep. I wouldn't be tellin' ye this, but ye'd better know it. The only way ye'll go home is if Sean Culhane gives the word."

"Hmmm. I suppose it's hopeless then." Catherine stretched in the warm sunlight and locked her hands behind her head. She heard another snort from the sill and opened one eye.

"Hmph. Ye don't fool me. I know that purr when I hear it; it always bides trouble for a man. If it's beguilin' Sean ye're thinkin' of, he's a hard, bitter man, not a lamb chop. He'd have been beat near to death with battin' eyelashes by now if he gave a tinker's damn about a woman in the world."

Catherine grinned impudently. "Thank you for the advice, but I'd rather persuade him with a bullwhip."

Peg sniffed. "Dare say ye would, but it wouldn't mend yer maidenhead . . . oh, I know. I saw the sheets." Catherine did not move but a flush tinged her cheeks. "I don't suppose ye'll like me sayin' this, but ye're a lot alike, you and him. Aye, it's true. Like now, with that slitty-eyed grin and yer stretchin', ye remind me of a pair of cats: him a tom and you a half-growed she. Ye move alike, and I'll wager ye've even the same spittin' tempers!"

Catherine's flush grew hotter, though her voice was even. "You imagine it all, Peg. We're different people who come from different worlds. I cannot wait to return to my own."

A thoughtful look came into Peg's blue eyes, then faded

as quickly as it came, and she slid her bulk out of the sill. "Well, for the moment ye'll have to manage in this one. Help me clear these dishes and I'll show ye what ye're to do."

The duties seemed endless. Catherine was to make morning porridge and help Moora with baking. She was not to assist with service at Culhane's table until future notice; neither was she to serve the tables for the hundred or so roughhewn men who took breakfast in shifts in the kitchen. While they ate, with a good many stares, belches, and rattles of cutlery, Catherine worked dough at the pastry table. When they left, she was allowed to eat. None of the women except Peg would sit near her; they made it clear being at the same table with an Englishwoman spoiled their appetites.

After breakfast, she and two other women scrubbed a mountain of dishes. Then she was assigned housework, always where someone could watch her. She was allowed to return to the kitchen for lunch after the men had finished, leaving yet another mountain of dishes. After that, back to housekeeping. She had always known the maintenance of a large household was endless; doing the work herself gave her a sour appreciation of its true magnitude.

Dinner was served, first to the Culhanes and a small group in the family dining room, then to the mass of the men in a hall that ran the length of the central house. Although she was never in either room at mealtime, she had to set and clear the tables. By the time the kitchen was put in order after dinner, she was numb with fatigue and only too glad to be escorted to her cell.

For three weeks Catherine saw virtually nothing of Sean Culhane and Flannery, and little more of Liam, who spent most of his time on horseback, roaming the moors with sketch pads. Doctor Flynn she saw not at all, except for a brief post-illness examination. She missed Flynn's kindness, for while she was careful to give no sign of it, she felt her ostracism sharply. To these people, she was a cipher that represented oppression. Peg had no time to talk, and Moora, suspicious of her every move, reported everything she did to Peg. The information probably passed to Sean Culhane.

At first she lived in dread that Culhane would summon her to his bed, but he had not. Like a spoiled child's new toy, she had been discarded after he had dirtied her. Or tired of her. That possibility perversely piqued her vanity. Perhaps once he had taken her virginity, her inexperience was unappealing. He probably had mistresses all over the countryside.

But pique was slight in comparison to relief at being left alone. Each night in her cell, she uttered a fervent prayer that Sean Culhane might go deaf, blind, and impotent. Her battered, grubby appearance, coupled with Moora's inevitable presence, had effectively discouraged advances from the many men constantly in and out of the house; but now that the bruises had faded and her nose was back to normal, they began to appraise her in spite of her shabby clothes. When, in her ignorance, she tried to wash her velveteen dress as she did herself—in cold, soapless water —the results were disastrous. The jacket hem was raveled, the flimsy kid boots split. Once careless about appearance, she became obsessed with maintaining a semblance of her former neatness.

Escape was her real obsession. How far the estate was from a town with a British garrison, she could not discover. Virtually no one spoke to her except Peg and Moora; Moora was wary and Peg dropped only what she wanted, giving Catherine the impression she was waiting for something. The servants' conversation usually ground to a halt in her presence.

The main house, while unguarded, rarely lacked servants near its entrance, and men she assumed to be estate tenants were always about its grounds. A stone Restoration mansion with a terraced entry, it faced a graceful, semicircular bricked court; a terrace with French doors ran the building's length on the sea side. Though the mansion's furniture and draperies were well worn, their quality was fine and the rooms held a king's ransom in artwork. Paintings by Verrocchio and Velasquez and a small Cellini bronze were among the masterpieces scattered about the

51

private family rooms, like the Goya and Rembrandt etchings in Sean Culhane's bedroom.

The ground floor windows offered only a discouraging vista of starkly beautiful, desolate moors, while the upper stories gave a magnificent, precipitous view of the Atlantic. Furze and sea grass edged a cliff where a smooth lawn dropped abruptly away to the sea. To the north of the house was a battered ruin. Only part of a massive tower remained, bluntly prodding above crumbling adjoining walls whose shattered ramparts backed the sea and north country; the inland walls were low lines of rubble. Apart from the scattered outbuildings, several cavelike stone buildings clustered in a gully and were nearly invisible from either land or sea.

She supposed the gully buildings to be servants' quarters until the morning she saw "tenants" she recognized from the kitchen drilling with makeshift muskets of rakes and broomstaves. As they marched back and forth in a ragged mass beside the stone barn, her first impulse was to laugh, particularly when she saw them all scatter like a handful of peas and fling themselves behind troughs and walls, then point their ludicrous weapons at one another while Sean Culhane and Flannery roared imprecations at them.

In less than a week, the antics of the Irish no longer amused her. Drill lines were measured, the men less clumsy at their exercises. She recalled that the American colonials had defeated British soldiers by hiding in forest and field and sniping from ambush. After muskets replaced the staffs, Catherine began to take Culhane's puny force seriously. While they were dismal shots and appeared to have only a few guns, their marksmanship, like their drills, would improve. Culhane's ruthless discipline resolved any doubts.

Once, while she was polishing furniture, she glanced out of a bedroom window to notice Culhane in heated argument with one of his lieutenants. The incensed subordinate pulled a knife and took a swipe at the tall Irishman. Culhane's foot hooked the man's ankle and its owner landed in an awkward sprawl. When he attempted to rise, he found his knife hand pinned under his opponent's booted foot. Catherine saw his mouth gape in a scream as the boot heel crushed his fingers. Sean Culhane kicked the knife away, then to Catherine's horror, coldly kicked his attacker in the side, deliberately breaking several ribs. With a short, sharp movement, he summoned two men to carry the man away. Clearly, Catherine realized, the Irishman would have no resistance to his authority for some time. She must get away from the monster, and quickly.

Occasionally, ships at sea were so tantalizingly near that Catherine could make out their ensigns on clear days. One afternoon she leaned from a window and flailed away with bed linen, ostensibly airing it, until Moora yanked it from her hands and sailed it to the damp ground. She had to scrub for hours to remove its grass stains and, as punishment, wash the ballroom windows and scour the marble entrance hall.

Under Moora's ever-present guard, Catherine was still scrubbing the foyer long after she ordinarily would have been confined to her cell for the night. Back aching, she paused to wipe hair out of her face; the rag strip, which secured it atop her head, had an annoying tendency to slip. As she reapplied the scrub brush, the front door opened, and one by one, seven pairs of muddy boots tracked across the clean floor. Her head snapped up and she glared in speechless fury. Sean Culhane gazed down at her with lazy amusement. Liam and the others, a bit embarrassed, stood just behind him while Rouge Flannery smirked, ogling her damp, clinging shirt. "Good evening, Miss Enderly," Culhane murmured with mocking politeness.

Catherine's eyes shot sparks. Mad as a singed cat, she rose slowly to her feet, fine brows nearly meeting in her smudged face. Suddenly she flashed them a breathtaking smile, then swept a deep curtsy that would have served at a court presentation. Hooking her fingers around the bucket handle on the down sweep, she straightened and let fly an arching torrent of dirty water across the lot of them. "Good evening to you, gentlemen," she purred sweetly.

Though the men at the rear caught only the spray, the front ranks took the brunt. Flannery sputtered, beating at his beard. Rouge snarled and moved forward to reach for her but was interrupted by a long arm that snapped out to bar his way. Not looking at Rouge, Culhane said easily, "You've been neglected, Miss Enderly, to the detriment of your sunny disposition."

She watched him warily. Although quick reflexes had saved him from the worst, Culhane's hair dripped in spikes about his face. Were his lips actually twitching in an effort to suppress a laugh? The others were angry enough.

"Perhaps the exclusive company of women has grown tedious for you," he suggested mildly. She tensed. "Moora" —he glanced at the horrified young woman standing stock-still against the wall—"see that Miss Enderly joins the officers for dinner tomorrow evening." He gave his white-faced captive a hint of a mocking bow. "Sleep well, my lady." Then he waved his men toward the dining hall. As the door closed behind them, she heard an almost boyish explosion of laughter that might have been appealing had it not chilled her.

Feeling Moora's eyes boring into the back of her head, she defiantly planted her hands on her hips and faced her. The Irish girl's look of incredulous astonishment would have done credit to an owl. "What are you staring at?" Catherine demanded.

"Ye've got a nerve!" Morra spluttered. "I wonder Culhane didn't beat ye within an inch of yer life! Ye're daft!" Her voice rose steadily, but with a note of admiration.

"Perhaps; perhaps not. I have a temper. And I don't like being bullied." Catherine picked up the bucket and headed for the kitchen.

As Catherine sloshed water from the kitchen pump into the bucket, Moora, hands behind her back, watched almost shyly. She fidgeted for a moment, then insisted, "But Sean Culhane is master here."

"He's not my master, nor will he ever be."

Moora's eyes rounded. "He'd not be likin' to hear that sort of talk."

Catherine dropped a gluey handful of soap in the water. "I daresay he won't, when you tell him." She sardonically eyed the reddening girl. "Still, a new note may relieve the

54

monotony of the daily recital. Pity. I should like to think it's boring him to death." She began to lug the bucket back upstairs.

As they climbed the stair, Catherine heard a faint giggle. "Bored he'll never be, not with a cheeky wench near drownin' him on his own doorstep. And him laughin' it off! He never laughs!" She giggled again. "Didn't they look a sorry pack of wet hounds? That Rouge, he's the cur in the pack. I don't mind stayin' up the night, just to watch him get his comeuppance." They reached the foyer door and briefly her hand touched Catherine's wrist. "Rouge won't forget, though. See you don't ever find yerself alone with him."

"Thank you, Moora. I'll remember that."

As the night wore on, Moora opened up like a flower in her desire to know about Catherine's life in England: the dresses, the parties, the jewels. Catherine tried to explain that the past five years had been as commonplace as the routine at Shelan, but Moora seemed so elated by even scraps of information, that Catherine recalled all she could, feeling a twinge as she watched the girl's wistful face. How barren life was for so many; yet even wealth and position had not made her own life happy, though Moora would never have believed it.

Unused to late hours, Moora gradually became drowsy, and when Catherine casually asked if elegant shops were available in the vicinity, she muttered sleepily, "Not for twenty miles, more's the pity. Donegal Town's the nearest."

As Moora slumped lower into her chair, Catherine edged toward the library door. When her young guard's breathing became regular, Catherine slipped into the library and shut the door. Knowing she could not have long before the dining hall emptied, she immediately tried the slant-top mahogany map desk; it was locked. Culhane's desk was also secure, but she expertly ran her fingers under the ridge between the drawer sections. As she hoped, a wad of sealing wax on the far left pressed a key to the wood. She rather suspected Liam, not Sean Culhane, would use such an old ploy. The key fitted the middle drawer lock, which in turn released the side drawer catches. Flipping through the papers to find the key to the map desk, she found a couple of hand-drawn maps on letter paper; one was unfamiliar, but with a shock, she realized the other, jotted with a number 14 and a question mark, depicted the Windemere estate. Holden Woods, a three-fingered shape, about two miles north of the house, was heavily circled. The small forest was one of the finest walnut stands in England and provided a tidy portion of Windemere's incomes. Year-round selective timber operations would make it an unlikely hiding place for even a small concentration of strangers, and surely better ambush points were closer to the house. Then why . . . ? Suddenly she had a sick feeling that Culhane meant to destroy the timber as part of his plot for revenge. He might already have done it.

Slipping the papers back in place, she quickly searched the side drawers. The key she found in the top one fit the other desk. The map case opened without a click, but her ears, attuned for any betraying sound, heard the knob slowly turn on the library door. Snatching up an agate inkwell, she darted behind the door and flattened against the wall. As the door inched open, the widening hinge crack revealed a female figure. Moora's.

"Catherine?" she whispered. "Where are you?"

Holding her breath, Catherine hoisted the inkwell. Moora moved farther into the room. As her body cleared the door, Catherine knocked it shut with her hip and regretfully brought the inkwell down on the back of the girl's head. Moora dropped like a rock. Catherine slipped down beside her to anxiously test her pulse. It was steady, if a bit fast. Quickly, she yanked down the damask curtain catches, knotted them about Moora's wrists and ankles, then stuffed the girl's mouth with her own mobcap.

Breathing quickly, Catherine returned to the desk and went through the maps, at least half of which were nautical charts. Finally she found one that showed Donegal Town deep in the belly of a bay in Ireland's northwestern corner; its size suggested a garrison. At a twenty-mile radius from the town, Shelan could only be one of two places on the coast, but to head north or south was the question. She decided to ride south for five miles; if she did not reach the bay, she would have to head north to find it and trace its curve to Donegal Town.

She heard a muffled groan from Moora as she selected a bronze dagger with a peculiar undulating blade from the Celtic collection and thrust it into her waistband. As an afterthought, she pulled down a lethal-looking throwing ax.

As she crossed the room with the ax still in her hand, Catherine saw Moora's blue eyes widen in terror. Although any delay was risky, she stopped to touch the girl's shoulder. "I didn't want to hurt you, Moora, but Culhane means to give me to his men. I know you could have called them before coming to look for me. Thank you." Then she was gone.

The cold night air was intoxicating after weeks of confinement. None of the usual threatening rainclouds hung over the moon-painted moor. Reaching the paddock without interception, she cracked the stable door a fraction of an inch. A single lantern in the rear revealed the place was deserted. She slipped in and closed the door, took a bridle from the wall, and went from stall to stall looking for the thoroughbred gelding she had seen Liam use on his painting excursions. She found the gelding, then saw something better. In the last stall, a big black pawed restlessly. As she went closer, a grin spread from ear to ear. If her stallion, Numidian, had a brother, this was the horse. Arab blood showed in every line of his huge body, but his size indicated a Morgan sire. If so, he would have stamina. She began to croon to him in tones that would have had Numidian sitting in her lap. Though his eyes showed oyster white crescents and he wickered nervously as she approached, he stood quietly, glossy skin twitching as she moved into his stall.

"There," she soothed. "There, darling . . . I won't hurt you. You lovely, big fellow, you beauty. Oh, darling, I wish I had a carrot," she whispered as he nuzzled her fingers with soft lips. "If you get me away from here, I'll fill you to bursting with carrots. Anything. Come away with me." Gently, she stroked him all over, hands slipping down fine, oval-boned legs. She quickly saddled him, then grabbed an extra horse blanket to wrap about herself and led him to the stable door. She peeked out. The house lights reached toward her like fingers, but seeing no one, she walked the black out into the moonlight. He stood, a massive, inky shape. With a deep breath, she put a foot in the stirrup. If he revolted now . . . She mounted and found the other stirrup. He whiffed softly through his nostrils. She walked him slowly in a short circle, touched heel to his flank, and gave him his lead. He broke into a smooth canter; then they lightly cleared the paddock wall and were off to the southeast like the wind.

Catherine was drunk with joyful release as the chill wind swept away the fog of hostility that had surrounded her, and the black settled into a long, easy stride that ate the miles. With a sense of omnipotence, she ripped away the strip securing her hair and flung it into the darkness. Her loosened hair whipped about her head like a heavy flag, stung her cheeks, brought tears to her eyes and laughter to her lips. She felt like a Valkyrie, riding the clouds, scattering the stars.

Then, for the first time, a troubling thought struck her. Once she reached Donegal Town the British army would be about Sean Culhane's neck like a python, but what of the others trapped in the coils? The rebels at Shelan, particularly the mercenaries paid to train the amateurs, were a nest of adders that should be scattered at whatever cost. But the women and children? And Doctor Flynn? They would all be imprisoned or worse. And what, after all, of Sean Culhane? He might be tortured for information about his activities and other potential rebels. Hanging he certainly deserved, but to be broken and maimed? She tried to fight her softness, remembering she had been foolishly lulled into sympathy the very night he had raped her. What had been an ecstatic ride to freedom now held grim promise at its conclusion.

Sensing her change of mood, the black slacked his pace. The moonlit landscape that had seemed so bright was now cold and barren as it undulated like a vast sea of stone. The hills rose and fell in slow waves, one like the other, monotonous and still, and the stars in the purple night glittered shrilly. Then a single star swung in a pendulum arc low on the horizon and the rhythm jangled into erratic, deafening discord. Heeling the horse in the flank, Catherine sent him thundering due east. She leaned over his neck as his long stride opened out. "They're coming! Run, beauty! Oh, please run!" Then a star swung directly ahead. Catherine wheeled in a rip of pebbles and turf, only to see yet another star waltzing in the northern hills. Hoping to outmaneuver them, she decided to try to slip past their rear guard in the dark. Better to dismount and lose them in the coastal rocks than to remain an obvious target in clear moonlight. She thudded away from the lights, but before she had gone a mile, the slim hope that they had been too far away to see her clearly faded as the lights swooped toward her in a rapidly closing V. All she could do now was run as long as the black held out.

"There she is!" Liam shouted at his brother, who galloped a big roan at Liam's side ahead of a handful of horsemen. "If we don't head her off, the outriders will drive her over the rocks!"

"Not on Mephisto, they won't. The wench may go over his head, but that horse isn't fool enough to jump to perdition."

Exasperated by Sean's seeming lack of concern, Liam started to retort, but his brother, apparently deciding his precious stallion might be in danger after all, pulled away and spurred until his companion riders were hard put to keep up.

Sean himself did not know whether the girl's danger or Mephisto's urged him on. Mephisto knew the cliffs well, but goaded to his utmost speed at night, he might not be able to stop in time. He had a momentary vision of girl and horse cartwheeling to the rocks below. Mephisto, he would be sorry to lose, but the girl confused him. Everything she represented repelled and disgusted him, yet he wanted her. Every night these last two weeks he had sailed to the village across the bay and assuaged his desire in the pale body of Fiona Cassidy as he tried to blot the English girl from his mind; he thought he had succeeded, yet tonight she had scowled up at him with blue eyes smoldering from the smudged little face and he had wanted to snatch away the fastening of her hair and crush that mutinous mouth under his in front of all his men. Better if she was out of his life now.

He was close enough to see sparks spit from the black's hooves and dimly hear the sea crashing on the cliff rocks. Suddenly, inevitably, Mephisto neighed wildly and twisted back on his haunches. Rearing horse and rider silhouetted against the moon before the girl screamed and fell.

Catherine scrambled to her feet as the riders closed in. They halted, some twenty of them, just fifty feet away. As the spent, sweaty black nuzzled her shoulder, she soothed him, stroking his white-flecked neck and side. The men were too far away to see the tears brim in her eyes. Then she gave him a gentle push and murmured softly, "You must go, beauty. I don't want you hurt."

A whistle sounded from a tall, shadowed rider. "Mephisto." The horse obediently trotted to his master. Growing a shade paler as she recognized the voice, Catherine drew the ax from her belt and waited, hair whipping in the sea wind. The tall rider gave a nod to one of the others, who rode forward a few paces.

Liam's voice carried over the dull sound of the surf. "Miss Enderly, give yourself up. If you peacefully surrender your weapons, I give you my word of honor no one will hurt you."

His answer was a cool, derisive laugh. "You have no honor, none of you. And you've murdered peace. Now you'll have to murder me, because I'll never willingly return to Shelan." Her voice lowered. "Shall we get this over with?"

The mercenaries were openly amused. One let out a cat-call; another, leaning mockingly from his saddle, gave an ululating Irish war cry.

"Never let it be said an Irishman kept a lady waiting," the tall horseman said, and dismounted. As he stepped forward, the moon gave his eyes the translucence of pale glass. "Well, Miss Enderly," Sean Culhane said amiably, "here we are again, toe to toe. Do you recall the conversation during our last tiff, when you attempted to make a point with a candlestick?"

Catherine said nothing, merely watched him warily as he slowly advanced.

"I see you do. Now, if you don't throw that thing, I'll take it away from you. If you throw it and miss, you're going to think the culmination of our last argument was idyllic. If you don't miss, my men are going to throw you off that cliff after giving vent to their irritation at losing the source of their income. So don't be nervous, and take your best shot, Miss Enderly; you sure as hell won't get another."

Despite his efforts to rattle her, Catherine still waited. And despite his easy words, Sean's midsection prickled as the distance between them closed and he realized she meant to let him get close enough to try to bury the ax in his gut. At a twitch of her elbow, he dropped and rolled, hearing an evil whistle where his belly had been. Uttering a yelp, a rider scuttled aside. His companions' amusement vanished. As Sean came quickly to a crouch, his opponent stared at him with the cold intensity of a cornered lynx, the bronze dagger in her fist. His heart began to resume its normal pace. The girl had managed the ax with startling expertise, but he was relieved to see she was unaccustomed to a knife. She held the blade haft up instead of horizontally, blade out. He slowly rose, and drew his own knife, and let it change from hand to hand to glint moonlight along its blade. Mercilessly he began to tease her, closing all the while, feinting easily, his blade a distracting blur. Watching closely, she quickly shifted her hold on her knife and imitated his movements, stalking him as stealthily as a small Indian.

Culhane's grin flashed briefly white in the dark. "Not bad for a beginner, but you've much to learn . . ." Inches from her, his blade suddenly cut upward in an arc from the shadow of his body. Startled, she backed, nearly dropping her guard.

"Lesson one. Killing at a distance is one thing. Disembowelment at close quarters is less aesthetic. Have you ever seen a pig butchered, Miss Enderly? Not pretty, is it? Death on a knife is nowhere as refined as that, I assure you." His knife flicked, flirted with her body, forced her back. "The final moments are messy, usually because one

61

slash isn't sufficient unless the fighter is experienced. Would you like to die in stages, girl . . . or all at once?" His knife snaked out and caught her blade guard in a deft twist, wrenching it from her fingers. Throwing an arm up to ward him off, she stumbled back the last remaining inches to the cliff rim. Her feet slipped sickeningly from under her; then she rifled down into nothingness. Abruptly Culhane's powerful grip caught her wrist, dragged her upward. She tried to wrench free, and he swore as he caught her roughly under the armpits and jerked her to him. For a terrible moment they struggled on the crumbling edge of the rock face until the Irishman found his footing and fought them both to safety.

As if unaware of her near fall, Catherine pummeled his chest and kicked wildly at his shins and groin. With a growl, he reached for her scruff; she snapped at him with her teeth. He got a handful of hair, jerked her around so he could hold her by the arms, then pushed her to the edge of the precipice. "Look down, damn you! That dagger you dropped down there is irreplaceable. I ought to throw you after it!" Breath coming in sobs of frustration, she writhed, still fighting him. He shook her, deliberately letting her hang outward.

"For God's sake, Sean," Liam cried. "Stop it!"

Sean ignored him. "Look down, you little idiot! That's death, real and final. Look down!"

Unable to help herself, she looked. A dizzy void yawned at her feet, the jagged rocks a hundred feet below reaching upward like deadly fangs, the glassy waves deceptively soft as they hurled moonlight-dappled walls of water against the sheer rock face. "When you invited my men to hack you to death, you didn't really know what death was, did you? Did you!"

Strangely silent, she hung from his hands. He gritted his teeth. She expected him to drop her, the ninny. He dragged her from the rim until the plummeting view was behind them. Passively, she allowed him to snap her about, then stood like a sleepwalker, staring at his chest. Thinking she was still in the thrall of the height, he tightened his grip on her arms to shake her when he realized she was rigid, her eyes glazed blanks. "Catherine," he said

62

carefully. Her eyes flickered, then slowly registered. He knew she was aware of him when they flooded with despair.

"Bring me the roan's bridle." When one of the outriders handed it over, Sean pulled Catherine's wrists forward and lashed them in front of her. She made no resistance as he led her to the black; but when, instead of putting her in the saddle, he tied her to Mephisto's tail, she struggled like a wild animal, then stood with feet braced, eyes ablaze with humiliation and hate.

"Sean, this is intolerable," Liam protested angrily. "I gave Miss Enderly my word—"

"Which she didn't accept." Sean handed the reins of the mount he had ridden to one of the men and swung into Mephisto's saddle. "Flannery, head for the smithy and heat up the forge. The rest of you get back to your posts. Liam, I suggest you go with them. Your temper could use a cooling out. I'll escort the lady home."

Liam gave his brother a look of fury, sawed his horse around, and dug in his spurs.

Culhane nudged Mephisto into a steady walk. Catherine balked, then was jerked forward into an unwilling trot. The Irishman did not look back. She quickly found she could only walk for a few paces, but then had to take several running steps to keep up as they followed a path worn in the furze along the cliff. Before they had gone far, the sun bloomed like a burning rose over the moors. Wretched as she was, Catherine was relieved to be alive to see the glowing dawn. White gulls wheeled and screamed along the sheer cliffs, then spiraled downward into the sea to emerge with fish.

Free. They're free! Catherine thought desolately. Suddenly blinded by tears, she stumbled and fell, scraping her knees on sharp pebbles. But her captor kept moving. Dragged by the straps at her wrists, she scrambled up with tear-streaked cheeks and began to swear steadily at him under her breath. Feeling better, she began to swear at him out loud, warily, then at the top of her lungs. She finally got the hiccups and had to stop.

Without looking back, Sean said dryly, "Good. Your limited vocabulary was growing tedious. If you're going to swear, do it properly. You haven't the feel of it a'tall, a'tall. Listen . . ." The air resounded with profanity, musical and grand.

Catherine's cheeks flamed scarlet. If her vocabulary was limited, Sean Culhane's definitely was not. The oaths had roll and thunder. When he finished, he had not repeated himself once. Of course, the lilt added a certain élan.

She frowned at Mephisto's tail in consideration, then repeated his last phrase. She had no idea what it meant, but she liked the rhythm of it. A low chuckle came back to her over the Irishman's shoulder. "Better. But don't mince up to it. Belly up."

She took a deep breath and let fly a volley at his head.

"Again better. Now let one flow gently, follow with power, lull, then build to a peak, and so forth. That's why a good string of oaths sounds like music."

Catherine could not believe she was having this conversation. Apparently the brute had a perverse sense of humor. Still, swearing relieved her anguish. She had thought to die, yet here she was tied to a horse's tail, admiring the scenery and trading profanity with a villain who had abducted her, raped her, then dangled her off a cliff. I must be hysterical, she thought. Aloud she began noisily to sing "The Tart of Whitemarsh," then wound up with an unrequested encore of choice selections from her newly learned repertoire.

Culhane clapped obligingly and she dropped a mocking curtsy to Mephisto's rump. An amused drawl floated back. "That Whitemarsh drab should have been walled up with the pharaohs, but I've heard worse renditions in music halls. No doubt you learned it discreetly at Ye Dreary Gentlewoman's Academy."

"As a matter of fact, I didn't," she retorted. "I was sitting in a schoolmate's brother's clothes in the fifth row of a Drury Lane theater"—she squinted at the bright light glancing off the sea—"but I concede the academy was exceedingly dreary."

"Then why go? I find it difficult to imagine anyone convincing a female as mule-brained as you to do anything you didn't think of yourself."

"Other people don't always employ your blunt methods of persuasion."

"You believe your father's techniques to be less crude?" His tone was light enough, but she felt a prick of unease.

"He's as different from you as heaven from hell," she replied curtly.

Culhane gave a short, ominous laugh. "Somewhere, heaven and hell meet: at that point even you, Miss Enderly, might have trouble telling the difference."

"The same thing is said about love and hate, but there, sir, you'd be at a loss. I cannot imagine your loving anyone, being gentle, even kind. You're a piece of stone, unfeeling—"

"Particularly about sentimental rot."

"You speak of rot!" Her temper heated. "You're a swamp of hatred . . . you . . ." She stopped, realizing she was going too far. Picking a quarrel with a lunatic on an isolated clifftop was the height of stupidity.

"You were saying? That is, before you considered your death might add a fillip to my stench?" His voice was taut, dangerous.

"I want to live, yes. But not without freedom. Not starved and beaten and threatened with death at every turn. Not surrounded by those who hate me. I'll fight to escape to my last breath. Your treating me like a slave doesn't make me one." She was tired now, the surge of energy that had carried her from Shelan seeped away. Her feet were sore; her wrists chafed. The brief, enforced trots were becoming uncertain and more frequent.

"Miss Enderly, you've only had a taste of the Irish condition. For seven hundred years British ambitions have brought war to this land, and with it disease, famine, and death. What you've endured has been nothing. If you think a slap in the face, a lean mattress, a limited wardrobe, a few floors to scrub, and a single man between your legs is a miserable life, you've not begun to learn misery. The Irish will never tolerate the English heel on their necks. Shall we see how well you stand an Irish heel on yours?" Culhane gave Mephisto a kick and the horse moved into a trot.

By the time they reached Shelan, Catherine staggered and stumbled from side to side, nearly hanging by her wrists. Her lungs felt incinerated, her eyes stung with perspiration, and her hair clung to her head in damp tangles. When Mephisto came to a halt in front of the house, she sank gasping onto the cobbles. In a stupor, she heard voices and sensed people looking down at her, then dully heard Culhane. "Flannery, is the forge ready?"

"Aye." Flannery's voice lacked its usual bluff humor.

"Good. I'll join you directly. Jimmy, take Mephisto. Feed him oats and rub him down well. The wench ran him to a rag."

"Aye, sor." Jimmy, too, was humorless.

Catherine heard Mephisto being led away.

"Peg, you and Rafferty stow the girl in her cell. Feed her. Then scrub out her mouth with soap. She has the ear of a parrot for foul language."

Catherine glared up, incoherent with rage and exhaustion, then struggled to her knees, sputtering, "But you . . . you . . . ohhh, I hate you . . . you . . . !"

"Still limited, I see." Culhane's lips twisted in a smile that did not reach his eyes. "Get her out of here. And after you wash her mouth out, wash her all over. The baggage is meeting the men tonight." He turned on his heel, leaving his prisoner stunned and numb with horror. Rafferty sawed through her wrist bonds, then he and Peg got her under the arms and pulled. When her legs collapsed, they draped her arms about their necks and towed her into the house.

Peg followed Culhane's orders to the letter. With Moora's surly help, Catherine was summarily undressed, even to her knife, and dropped into a tub of steaming water. She let out a howl. "You're boiling me! Oh, Peg, I'll be burnt!"

"Only for your sins, dearie. Open up!"

She pushed, clawed, and kicked until her assailants were as wet as herself, but Moora held on to her hair while Peg rubbed her clenched teeth thoroughly with a blob of strong soap.

"Ohohhh, pfooo! Stop! . . . Phooey!" Her spitting stopped when Moora rammed her head underwater with definite relish. Peg then poured a bucket of water over her head. The bath Catherine had been longing for was a complete

66

ordeal. She was not allowed to scrub herself; Peg and Moora did every inch of her, with scrub brushes, until she was raw. Having the snarls combed out of her wet hair was the most exquisite torment of all. By the time Moora finished, Catherine was certain she would be bald. When her hair was finally clean, coiled, and neatly pinned on top of her head, Peg said, "Open." Giving her a black look, Catherine clenched her teeth. "Go along with ye, girl, it's stew."

She opened instantly like a baby bird. As she chewed, a tentative smile tugged at her lips. "Exchellent stoo, Peg," she mumbled with her mouth full of a second spoonful.

"A' course it is. I was cookin' while ye were skedaddlin'. Hurry up, girl, we haven't got the mornin' . . . good, good. That's enough. Up ye go." Peg and Moora each got a hand under her armpits and hauled. Moora supported her as Peg wrapped her in a huge towel, wagging her head and rubbing her charge vigorously. "Here I've been tryin' to fatten ye up, and ye run it all off!" Leaving her wrapped in the towel, they helped her to her pallet, then covered her with quilts. She wanted to speak to Moora, but Peg dragged her daughter out the door. Catherine nestled down and was asleep before she finished burrowing.

She was awakened by a banging noise and the feel of a cold weight around her bare ankle. In fact, one leg was chilly up to the knee. Sleepily pushing herself to her elbows, she was surprised to see Flannery, his hair flame bright in the barren gray room, hammering at something on the floor at the foot of the pallet. "Whatever are you doing?" she mumbled. Flannery kept pounding without looking up. She flopped back down, too sleepy to stay upright; then dim realization dawned. She bolted up, clutching the quilts under her chin as he applied the final blows to a long pin fitted through the hasp of a leg-iron around her ankle. Attached to it was a short chain and a ten-pound ball of shot. "Oh, no . . . even he . . ." Her voice was a soft, strangled cry.

He finally looked up into eyes that were black and too bright. Her face was bloodless. "I'm sorry, girl, but there's more. Ye'll have to sit up." Catherine obeyed in a kind of stupor, holding the quilts tucked under her arms. When he brought the collar out, her eyes slowly filled with tears. She lowered her head as if baring her neck to an executioner's ax. As he fitted the iron band about her throat, Flannery saw the childlike tendrils at her nape, the narrowness of her shoulders, how small she was, how desperately young. He rammed the bolt home. He left her staring across the cell, head held unnaturally high as if it would topple off her neck if she moved it. She looked like an effigy on a tomb.

Sean looked up as Flannery filled the library door. "Well, is it done?"

"Aye. 'Tis done."

He quizzically eyed Flannery as the redhead lumbered toward the desk. "Your tone could sink the British fleet. Didn't the English's new jewelry suit her?"

"She didn't say. Personally, I'd say it didn't suit her."

Sean deliberately misunderstood. "Oh? Does that mean it didn't fit? Or that she kicked you?"

"Oh, that thrall collar's a perfect fit," Flannery replied flatly, "exactly right for a woman or child." His tone hardened. "We haven't had slaves in Ireland for four hundred years, and I haven't been fightin' beside Culhanes for nearly fifty to bring 'em back."

Culhane started to interrupt, but Flannery waved him to silence. "In all these years, I've never known ye to do a stupid thing, but if ye parade that girl in irons, ye'll regret it. Every time a man who was on the cliffs last night sees her weighed down with chains, his gorge is goin' to rise. They're not laughin' at her now, y'know." His big hands gripped the desk edge. "Ye had twenty mounted men armed with pistols and sabers to take a girl on foot cartin' a pair of antiques. I've not seen many men who could face cold steel that well."

"Think, man. She knew I wouldn't have her killed. She figured I'd send one or two men at her. If she could make a brief show and keep her skin in one piece, she'd have the lot of you on her side. Little Miss Nobility Braveheart. It worked beautifully. She even fooled you, and I would have wagered your rock of a heart couldn't be dented with a pickax."

Flannery shook his head. "She was ready to die and ye knew it. I think that's why ye went out to her yerself, to keep another man from hurtin' her."

Culhane came to his feet. "That's enough, Flannery."

"I'm thinkin' it is, but shacklin' that bit of a girl is too much. I'll keep takin' yer orders for Liam's sake, but don't ask me to lay a hand on her again."

Long after sunset, two handsome whores in brazenly low-cut dresses strolled into Catherine's cell; the taller girl was a sultry-eyed brunette with flaring cheekbones and a wide mouth, the other a flaxen blonde with magnificent breasts and a confident strut. With hands on her hips, the dark one, dressed in crimson, surveyed the prisoner's slight body curled up among the quilts. "Faith, she's not much to look at!"

The blonde nodded. "Give a man too much to eat, and he's more interested in meat on his plate than in his bed. But, Jaysus, this wouldn't even pick his teeth!"

Anger gave back Catherine's eyes some of their life as she flushed at their blunt appraisal.

The blonde blew a loose wisp of hair out of her face. "Ye must have put Culhane out more than a bit. He's a moody sort at best, but he an't ordinarily nasty."

Crimson shrugged dreamily. "I wouldn't mind if he was in a black temper all the time, so long as he kept me on me back!"

Catherine was incredulous. "You *enjoy* his attentions?"

The brunette closed her eyes and acquired a lewd grin. "Like a cat loves her cream."

"But, he's . . ."

"Violent?" the blonde finished for her. "Sometimes. Then he's like a storm breakin', but sometimes he's slow and easy. No angel can play a harp better than Culhane plays a woman."

Catherine's eyes skeptically flicked over the pair. "I gather you're not forced to . . . entertain his men?"

"A' course not," the blonde said, beginning to paw about for the prisoner's clothes. "Invited is what ye'd probably be callin' it, when ye was a lady."

"I *am* still a lady!" Catherine retorted furiously.

69

"Now don't be gettin' upset," clucked Crimson, pulling firmly at the quilts. "Irene don't mean it personal."

Catherine clutched her last protection with the tenacity of a worried crab. "Personal! Culhane is turning me into a . . . he's no better than a . . . oh! Give that back! Stop it!" She scratched and flailed, but the two got her into her skirt and blouse. After a brief inspection Irene shook her head. The pair exchanged glances, then yanked at Catherine's neckline. She gasped and grabbed, but the drawstring slid to an impenetrable knot just short of letting the garment slip from her shoulders.

Both women nodded simultaneously. "That's better. Nuns is apt to spoil the lads' appetites."

Catherine glared downward. "I won't do it!"

They ignored her. "Leave her hair up, don't ye think, Milly?"

"Aye, she'll do fine."

Milly picked up the iron ball; then each got an arm between them, and by lifting the kicking prisoner clear of the floor, the two had her through the corridors in a trice. They set her down in front of the doors of the common dining hall.

Catherine's knees went weak. She was to be raped again, not once, but many times by many men. The remembered pain of her only experience thudded in her mind like a hammer, and color drained from her cheeks. She took a shaking step backward.

Crimson firmly stopped her. "Buck up now, dearie."

Irene whispered a last reassurance. "And don't be worryin' yer head about the irons. Some men like 'em!" They opened the doors, then shoved her through. She stumbled as dead weight jerked at her ankle. In the midst of bewildering noise and smoky candles, she numbly straightened, heart pounding. Sudden silence surrounded her, then a wall of stares.

Liam, at the head of his table, turned with the others when the arresting silence drew his attention to the door. Sean, facing that direction from the seat on his brother's right, impassively watched his prisoner's halting entrance as Liam's jaw tightened. The girl's eyes reminded him of a trapped fawn. Her feet were bare and hair loosely piled

70

atop her head escaped in tendrils about her cheeks and
throat. Around her neck, like an obscenity, was a narrow
band of iron; a heavier band was locked about one ankle.
When Liam heard the scrape of the weight, something
burst in his mind. Without looking at his brother, he rose
and walked the length of the room to meet her. The girl
gazed at him in bewilderment; then, as he stopped to pick
up the ugly iron ball, her eyes filled with stunned gratitude. Close to her, Liam could see the velvet texture of her
skin, accentuated by the blouse's rough material; for an instant he wished she were a whore he could carry away to
the darkness. He blushed, ashamed of his thoughts. "I cannot ask your forgiveness for bringing you here; what I've
done is unforgivable. I'm sorry with all my heart . . . my
lady." He offered her his arm.

She hesitated, then placed her hand on it and murmured, "Thank you, Lord Culhane."

Across the room, Sean felt the warmth of the radiant
look Catherine gave his brother like a twist in his gut.
When Liam turned to escort her from the hall, Sean uncoiled to his feet. His voice rang out, "It would be rude,
brother, to steal the wench away before she has been introduced. Surely you don't mean to keep so fine a piece to
yourself."

Flushing with anger, Liam stopped in his tracks. Feeling Catherine's fingers tighten convulsively on his arm as
he altered course, he slowly walked her to the head of the
table. "We'll have to brazen it out now," he whispered. "If
we don't stay, you will appear to be going to my bed."

"But if they believe I'm your mistress, they might leave
me alone!"

"You may yet go home again, my lady. Now, these people can only guess about my brother's relationship with
you, but were I to compromise you publicly, your reputation would never be secure." He covered her hand on his
arm with his own. "Don't worry. I'll get you out of the
room as soon as possible."

Heads craned as the pair made their way through the
room. Most of the spectators were merely curious about the
irons, but true to Flannery's prophecy, some of the men

71

who had seen the captive's courage on the cliff were angry, and a wave of murmurs rose in her wake.

Sean watched the couple with a grim smile as he thought angrily, Damn it, how does the wench contrive to give irons the effect of a virgin's nightgown? Half the men would flatten out and let her trip her dainty feet across their backsides!

As Liam started to seat her at the table, Sean stood and raised his wineglass in a mocking toast. "Ladies and gentlemen, I give you Lady Catherine Denise Enderly, comtesse de Vigny. You may have heard of her father, General John Richmond Enderly. As adjutant to the governor general some years ago, he did much to relieve Ireland of her excess population. To your continued good health, my lady!" He drained the glass, flung it to the floor, and ground it under his heel. Aware of her barely controlled panic, he gazed mockingly at the crowd. "You should see yourselves gawk. Have none of you seen an English blueblood before? Well then, you'll have a closer look!" His arm swept down the table and Catherine jerked back, thinking he was about to tear at her clothes, but his hand locked around a pitcher of wine and thrust it at her. "Take up your duties, Countess. They want a look at you."

"Lady Enderly has no duties," Liam said firmly. "I've promised her my protection."

"You wasted your breath, brother."

Liam whitened. His hand twitched, then moved for his dagger. Unarmed, Sean tensed, ready to dash the pitcher in Liam's face and relieve him of his weapon. Feeling Liam's convulsive movement, Catherine tightened her grip. "No, please! You must not, my lord." Her voice lifted with defiance. "As your brother says, too much blood has been spilled in Ireland, though he slanders my father as the cause. He shall have no excuse to malign Enderly honor further."

Tucking the ball under an arm, she pulled the pitcher from Sean's grasp with surprising force and surveyed with saccharine mockery the seated men who had not risen in her presence. "Please don't disturb yourselves, gentlemen." Some of the younger ones had the grace to flush as she sauntered off. Liam dropped into his chair with a furious look at his brother, who returned it unwinkingly.

As Catherine filled the tankards of the silent, fidgeting men at the nearest table, Irene and Milly quickly took her lead and began to joke with their patrons. By the time Catherine had refilled the pitcher a few times from large casks of wine and ale set about the room, the racket had resumed its normal level, much of it caused by lively discussion of the open antagonism between the Culhanes.

At length, although the men were becoming drunk and boisterous and their women acquiescent, she dared not reenter the tinderbox atmosphere of the Culhane table. The men subdued their coarse language in her presence, but their women, who seemed resentful, became more offensive. At first the men were slightly embarrassed, but as drink and nearness of flesh inflamed them, their hands stealthily groped at her flanks as she pressed through the tangle.

Finally, when a hand drove between her thighs, she exploded. Swinging the pitcher in a wide swath, she bashed every head in reach and soaked several innocent bystanders. Abruptly, a hand locked through her iron collar, then jerked her against the bare, hairy chest of Rouge Flannery. His breath reeked of liquor. "So, it's the bad-tempered little wench!" She dropped the ball and pushed away from him, but he lifted until the ring, cutting into the back of her neck, nearly dragged her off her feet. "Oh, no, ye don't. We an't met proper yet!" He smiled mirthlessly, his gray eyes like stone chips, then jerked her head back with his free hand and smashed his mouth down on hers. She arched wildly, stifled and choked. His lips were loose and wet, his thick tongue forcing its way into her mouth. Finally he withdrew, painfully arching her head back as he did so. "That's it . . . keep fightin'. Keep wrigglin' . . ." He thrust his crotch against her and manipulated her hips with his hand. When she stiffened with revulsion, his voice turned venomous. "Think ye're too good to be fucked, eh? Culhane said we could have a look at ye, didn't he?"

He hooked his hand in her neckline. "I'm havin' mine now." He jerked down and she screamed.

An ominously quiet voice sounded behind him. "I said you could look, Rouge. Not touch . . . not ever touch." Long brown fingers appeared on Rouge's shoulder, jerked him bodily away from the girl, then held him for that fraction of a second the sodden giant had left before a hard-clenched fist stretched his length across a table, smashing crockery and glassware, sending women shrieking. "Remember," Sean Culhane warned coldly, towering with bloody knuckles over the dazed brute, "because if you ever forget, I'll hang you!" He caught up the ball by its chain, grasped Catherine's wrist, and dragged her out of the room after him, leaving her to manage the torn blouse with one hand. She had scant time to rejoice over her rescue for he headed straight to the stair.

Guessing his intention, Catherine tried to tear free. "No! Let me go!" He turned so suddenly in midstride that she ran into him. With a muffled curse, he bent and, upending her over his shoulder, carried her like a sack of feed. He kicked open the door to his room and unceremoniously dumped her on his bed.

Instantly, she rolled off. She landed on the carpet at his feet with a bare leg suspended upward by the chain her tormentor held, giving him a fetching view of her naked lower body. Despite her furious grab at her slipping blouse, he glimpsed soft, rose-tipped breasts. With increasing panic, Catherine saw his eyes go hot and clouded, and, cheeks flaming, she tried to cover herself, but her efforts brought the skirts nearly up to her waist. Swaying slightly, he began to reel her in, and she realized with horror he was drunk.

Culhane jerked open his clothing, then crouched and thrust a knee between her thighs. He dragged her wrists over her head, his voice roughened with desire. "You rode my nag until he nearly dropped. Now I'm going to ride you . . ." Gasping at his swift, spearing invasion as his body covered hers, Catherine involuntarily arched against him, a movement that only drew his sex deeper into hers and a choked sound from his lips. He began to thud his lean, powerful body into hers with harsh urgency, as if with his re-

74

lease he could exorcise her, but the yielding caress of her warm, tight gloving lured him deeper. She was wild under him, fighting him, but her breasts were soft under his chest and her hair was a silken fan. His desire built into an unbearable tension at the base of his groin, then burst with a flooding warmth.

Slowly his breathing evened and he eased onto his elbows, looking at her with a hint of puzzlement in his eyes.

Catherine, who had experienced nothing but fear and revulsion, found her own satisfaction in an outpouring of contempt. "You're nothing but a disgusting, drunken animal! Less!"

His eyes narrowed coldly. "Despise me all you like, but if you know what's good for you, keep your legs open and your mouth shut!"

Her eyes dilated into a slanting, wicked stare, she slashed at his face. She whitened when his fingers caught and dug cruelly into her wrists, but continued her attempt to throw him off.

"You stubborn little bitch! I'll break you if it's the last thing I ever do!" Jamming an arm across her throat, he yanked down the blouse, then tore at the band of her shirt. Grabbing a fistful of both garments, he dragged them off her thrashing body. Only added pressure on her windpipe quieted her. She lay pinned, breasts heaving in a struggle to breath. Suddenly his weight left her, but as she whipped to a defensive crouch, he slipped the chain through an iron clip bolted to the bed and snapped its padlock shut.

Glaring at the clip, Catherine hissed, "Flannery had a busy day! You even deny me the privacy of my own kennel!"

Culhane began to strip off his shirt. "I've neglected your education," he said coldly. "You're my *cumal*, female chattel no better than a slave." He dragged off his boots. "As for privacy, you lost that when you tried to escape."

"I'll never be your slave . . . *your* anything!" she spat.

Ignoring her, he poured himself a brandy from a desk decanter, then smiled sardonically as he lifted the glass to his lips.

To her discomfiture, he slowly discarded his breeches. Eyes shying from his crotch, she focused on his chest, where she noticed a scar along his left side. Observing the direction of her attention, he said, "Knife. The other was from a bayonet." Her gaze roved his chest until he grinned faintly. "Lower."

And there, next to where she did not want to look, was the faded scar. She grimaced. "A pity your assailant wasn't more to the point."

Culhane's grin grew wicked. "Had he been, you'd shortly be a frustrated young lady." He assessed her body. Defiantly, she eyed him back, but gradually she flushed under his maddeningly minute inspection.

Sean's gaze lingered on small, upthrust breasts, tiny waist and flat belly, along slim, long legs, then returned at last to the curly pelt between his captive's thighs. The girl was fetching enough to tempt a saint, he considered critically, but what was there about her that attracted him? Women were merely an accustomed diversion, but this one was a paradox: innocent, yet seductive; appealing, yet defiant.

Catherine's eyes widened nervously as he knelt over her, his hands on either side of her head. "You've spent your rotten lust. What more do you want?"

"Everything," he murmured. Then, his hands never touching her, his cropped black head lowered. His lips found the delicate curve of a collarbone and lightly moved along her neck to the hollow of her throat. His lips were warm, brushing her flesh as lightly as a butterfly's wings, and Catherine's hands strained against his shoulders, fighting the strange sensation that flushed her skin. She had already learned to her rue that he would and could do as he liked, but her helplessness was galling. His kisses explored the shadowed hollows under her pinioned arms and lingered along the swelling undercurves of her breasts, making her twist in unbearable anticipation. She gasped as his tongue flicked her nipples. Teasing them into hard little points, he lashed them into aching fullness, then took them into his mouth, suckled and nipped them softly. Heat pulsed into her groin. "Stop it," she whimpered. "Damn you, stop it . . . oh, stop."

When it suited him, Culhane left her breasts and teasingly licked her ribs, moved down to her belly, then nuzzled the flesh along the inside of her thighs. As she lay weak and innocent, without warning the soft roughness of his tongue slipped into her. She arched and cried out, tears of humiliation spangling her lashes. "Oh, God, no!" Sobbing, she wrenched at his hair as she tried desperately to evade tremors of pleasure that swiftly mounted in intensity. She moaned, hating the sound, believing she would die if his torturing caresses did not stop, yet not wanting them to stop. With a soft laugh, he lifted himself from her and tugged her hands away. Vaguely disappointed, she lay slack. Sprawled. And open. She shuddered weakly as he entered her. There was no pain now, only ease and the powerful rhythm of his body, until finally he buried himself in the heart of her and from a long way off she heard his muted groan. Then, after a moment, she felt empty and strangely melancholy. A cover lightly settled over her. Hazily she knew she did not want to stay in Sean Culhane's bed, but she was drifting into sleep even as he extinguished the candle.

The moon was high when the Irishman was startled awake by Catherine's cry. She was sleeping on her back with a hand outflung, the other curled beside her head. In sleep, she was childlike, vulnerable. Her lips were parted slightly, the tender underlip begging for kisses, but as he started to answer their invitation, her face contorted as if in agony, her hands closed into fists, and her body convulsed. "No, please." The cry ended in a whimper. *"Non, Maman . . . je ne peux pas. Je t'en pris . . ."* Perspiration broke out on her brow as she went rigid, then just as mysteriously relaxed. He thought she had fallen into deep sleep again, when she crooned sadly, *"Là . . . là. C'est tout. Ça va maintenant."* Brokenly, she began to sing a disjointed French lullaby.

Careful not to awaken her, Sean smoothed back Catherine's damp hair and wiped the perspiration from her face with a corner of the bedsheet. All the while, he considered her speculatively. So the gibberish Peg mentioned is French and I'm not the girl's only ogre, he mused. Perhaps the key to these nightmares is also the key to her resistance. And if you use the key? another part of him asked. What will she be then? Nothing, he answered coldly. She'll be nothing to me. But the strange lullaby haunted him into sleep.

CHAPTER 4

Silken Irons

Awakened the next morning by a sullen downpour, Culhane opened his bloodshot eyes. His head pounded as if Mephisto had kicked it. Irritable and fur-mouthed, he sourly eyed his split knuckles inches from his face. He flexed them; they were stiff and sore. Yawning, he started to stretch, then felt something warm against his back. Turning gingerly, he found Catherine snuggled against him, soft hair tickling his shoulder. With a sigh, she burrowed closer and he scowled. The little wench hadn't the sense of a lamb sidling up to a wolf. Suddenly, as if she were aware of danger, her eyes opened, startling him with their blue, starlike intensity. They widened when her proximity to his naked body seeped into her consciousness. "Don't worry," he assured her grimly. "You wouldn't make more than a mouthful. And nothing appeals to me less than food at the moment." Taking no chances, she wriggled away. The smoothness of her body against his triggered an even less welcome reaction in his groin. He sat up abruptly, then grunted as his hangover detonated. He shot her a scowl. "Damn it, cover yourself if you don't want to spend the day on your backside!" Hastily she snatched up the bedclothes. Taunted by her breasts still impudently prodding at the sheets, Sean swore and hauled himself out of bed.

A cool voice came from behind him. "If I cure that headache, will you leave me alone?"

"Bargains, baggage? I thought you understood we were

beyond that." Cheeky little witch, he thought sardonically. Hot as flame last night; an icicle in the morning. He knew she had not reached complete fulfillment the night before, but he doubted if she realized that.

Catherine watched the Irishman warily, disliking his calculating smile. Was he thinking how easily he could cheat on any agreement? He was nothing if not unpredictable.

By hard daylight, it was less difficult to understand how her body had turned traitor. Sean Culhane was physically magnificent and beautifully proportioned. As he paced, the symmetry of hard muscle moving under his smooth brown hide hinted at dangerous strength her frail power had not even tested. Certainly he was an expert lover; otherwise he could not have aroused an unwilling partner— literally, she thought disgustedly, without lifting a finger. She must find a way to hold him at bay!

"Would you be thinking of hemlock for the headache, minx?"

She started with a guilty flush, then retorted sarcastically, "My mother had effective remedies for drunkards. I'll give directions to Peg, so you should be utterly safe unless you've also given her a reason to poison you."

"Your viper tongue serves well enough. What a fang in your father's heel you must be!" From her gasp of pain and rage, he knew he had inadvertently scored a hit.

"Ohh, I'd like to remedy that headache of yours with a hangrope! Poison's too quick for you, too decent . . . too . . ."

"Quiet?" he suggested ominously, grabbing his head. "Call Peg before I sail you out of the window like the harpy you are!"

Catherine scrambled across the bed for the bell rope, inadvertently treating the Irishman to a view of thigh and hip. As she tugged the pull, he sighed and grabbed for his robe.

"Well, and how are we this fine mornin'," bubbled Peg minutes later.

"Bloodthirsty," snarled Culhane, jerking his head at Catherine.

She ignored him. "Come closer, Peg. I've a recipe for

you." When the woman curiously obeyed, Catherine began to whisper in her ear.

"What's she telling you?" demanded Sean suspiciously.

Peg looked over her shoulder. "If ye knew, ye'd never hold it down."

Culhane gave her a black look, but in all his life he had never looked as forbidding as the brew that arrived. The color of long-spoiled milk, its stench brought sweat to his forehead. "This has more the look of revenge than remedy."

"You don't have to drink it," Catherine said sweetly. "Splitting headaches cure themselves . . . eventually."

"Bitch," he said shortly, and raised the mug.

"Drink it all at once," she prompted. Faintly green, he upended the mug and gulped. Turning a deeper shade of green, the Irishman expelled his breath. He gave them an anguished look and bolted for the terrace. Throwing himself half over the stone balustrade, he retched violently. Sometime later he reappeared. Though pale and wet with sweat and rain, his face lacked its sickly tinge. "Mary and Saint Michael, what deadly brew was that?" Suddenly, he frowned suspiciously at Catherine, then furiously at Peg. "That devil's apprentice has been helping in the kitchen. God knows what rot she's been slipping in the food with both grimy fists."

Remembering the dirty bread, Catherine could not suppress a wicked smile.

He glared at her as he poured a glass of water. "Smirk, will you? I'll wager you've never had a well-administered thrashing in your life, have you, brat?"

Hastily rearranging her expression, she backed away across the bed. "You promised you wouldn't touch me if I cured your headache! Well, you haven't a single twinge now!"

Culhane gargled and spat into a basin, then gulped the rest of the water. His glare over the rim of the glass became evil. "Oh, don't I though? Women create more headaches than liquor any day, and you're the prize pain of the lot!"

Slapping the glass down, he advanced determinedly on the bed. Bombarding him with pillows and bedding, Catherine hissed in panic, "You promised! Cheater. Villain. Liar!"

Through the hail of linen, he ordered, "Out, Peg!"

"Stay!" the assailed one pleaded.

"Out!"

As Peg vanished, so did Catherine's ammunition. Culhane's long reach grabbed her by the scruff and dragged her flailing body across his lap as his hand firmly descended on her buttocks.

Tears of rage and pain sprang to her eyes. In all her short life, no one had ever beaten her. Relentlessly, his hand came down harder. "Liar!" she shrieked. Every time he smacked her bottom she screamed, "Liar!" until her voice was stifled and filled with sobs. Suddenly she was stretched on the bed, the sheets cool against her stinging backside. Through her tears she saw thick-lashed, storm green eyes close to hers.

"No," he said huskily, "no liar. I said I wouldn't touch you like *this.*" And his mouth covered hers softly, warmly seeking, rousing a shimmering heat in her. Her lips parted helplessly and his tongue slipped between them, probing, teasing, then hungrily, fiercely, until she moaned. Then mercifully, he was no longer kissing her, though his eyes were dark and his breath ragged. "No more bargains, imp." His lips brushed hers in a whisper. "Remember."

Then his weight was gone and Catherine felt the same strange sense of loss as the night before when he had withdrawn from her body. Covertly watching him from under wet lashes, she was astonished when he turned his back and quickly pulled on his breeches. How could the brute extinguish his ardor at will and turn prudish when she knew perfectly well he had not the modesty of a savage? She sat bolt upright and, after a wince at the resulting pain, wiped harshly at her damp cheeks. "Do you intend to molest me or not?"

His back still to her to shield the bulge at his crotch, Culhane dunked a brush in his shaving mug and grinned into the mirror. "Disappointed?"

Flushing, she snapped, "Hardly! I'd simply like to know whether I may dress without fear of having my only clothing shredded during one of your . . . fits."

"Any wretch would be driven to a fit of frenzy in the chill of your welcoming arms." He calmly began to lather his face. "Still, you'd do well to acquire a decent regard for my property, although if you begin a brawl each time I utilize the rest of it"—his eyes raked her deliberately—"you can blame no one but yourself when you end up without a scrap to your back, a state which will no doubt provide fascination for my men, and inconvenience to yourself. I'll not have Peg's meager coffer depleted to indulge your foolishness."

Catherine was momentarily dumbstruck, unable to find a sufficiently scathing remark to put the monster in his place. "What you call foolishness, I call honor; although you're too coarse to recognize it. If my arms ever open to you in welcome, it will be from the grave."

Culhane's reply was heavily tinged with sarcasm. "I wondered when you'd get around to speechmaking. You were meek enough the night I divested you of your possibly technical virginity, which would have gone at auction at any rate. Why no noble oratory then?"

Her assurance slipped a notch. "I . . . I don't remember that night. The actual—"

"Ha!" Culhane's tone was scathing, but he watched her keenly. "There's the flimsiest excuse in history! Half of creation's females missing a maidenhead have had convenient lapses of memory." Wiping his face, the Irishman turned and his tone became lightly threatening. "Were my efforts so tame that they left no impression on your mind?"

Catherine's fingers locked into the chain links, her eyes the dark pools of desperation he remembered from the night he had first taken her. "I . . . you . . . I don't remember! I don't know!" The last was a defensive cry.

Relentlessly he goaded, "Come, girl, you must remember. Was it rainbows and roses?"

Eyes widening, she began to tear hysterically at the collar. "Take it off! It's choking me! I don't remember anything!"

Culhane swiftly crossed the room, took her by the shoulders, and shook her roughly until he dislodged her hold on the irons. She sagged away from him, dazed. "All right, Catherine. We'll let it go . . . for now. Be still." Noticing she had already badly bruised her neck, he released her abruptly and unlocked the manacle from the bed clip. She watched, unable to suppress the hope in her eyes, but it quickly died as he made no further move to free her.

"Peg will give you new duties, less pleasant than your current ones, although many of them will be outside the house."

Catherine felt a faint surge of relief and bewilderment. Nothing could be more unpleasant than monotonous confinement, but to let her range abroad after an escape attempt? Another thought struck her. "I . . . have no shawl."

"Peg will take care of that. As far as your personal service to me"—he dropped the chain—"you'll present yourself at my door each night. If I see fit to answer your knock, you'll enter and be prepared to bed me. That means you'll be clean and in a civil temper. If I'm otherwise occupied, return to your own quarters."

Catherine listened with rekindling rage. "If you expect me to play whore to your *grand seigneur,* you're much mistaken! It will be a cold day in hell before I come to service you!"

Culhane's eyes narrowed. "Service me or service my men, but take your choice here and now. I've no taste for overused women."

She paled. "But last night you threatened to hang a man if he . . ."

"Trespassed on my preserve. Off it, you're fair game. I'll not lift a finger if Rouge Flannery spreads you at my table with your toes twirled about my wine goblet." He watched her slim shoulders sag, and read defeat in lusterless eyes. "What's your decision?"

"There's nothing to decide. Whore to one or many, it makes no real difference, does it?" Her voice grew bitter. "I choose you. Better to have the loathesome act done with as quickly as possible. Shall I be permitted to return to my cell after you've spent your filth in my body?"

Culhane whitened and, catching the chain, wrenched her face up to his. "Be careful, Countess. If you don't please me, the barracks is a short walk."

Her eyes were black with hate. "If I die, it's no walk at

all, neither to your lecherous bed nor their flea-ridden cots, so perhaps you do leave me a choice!"

His teeth bared an inch from hers as his fingers caught painfully in her hair. "Hear me, girl. Do anything so foolish as to die without my permission and I'll have your father's head within the day!"

Her resolution faltered. "If . . . if I please you, will you spare him?"

Loosening his grip on the chain, he shook his head. "You can but delay the time." Her eyes went dead. "The prospect may seem less bleak by and by." He disliked the turn of the conversation. Her compliance was too much like that of a sacrificial maiden bravely offering herself to a troll. Her body, yet unawakened, might too easily become frigid. Still, did it matter what she became once he had had his fill of her? Why not take a revenge that would prove endless? Why did he want only to kiss that vulnerable mouth and brush away her cobweb terrors?

Abruptly he scooped up his shirt and pulled it on. Not until he had dressed completely did he look at her again. The rain-hazed light bathed her nude body in a weird, cold glow that limned her features like those of a da Vinci Magdalene, both pure and profane. The mothwing lashes were shuttered, the iron collar harsh against the shadowed hollow of her throat. Her fingers, caught in the chain, gave it intermittent little tugs. Deriving scant victory from her hopelessness, Sean left her.

When Peg came into the bedroom, Catherine, clutching her torn clothing together, stood on the balcony. She neither turned nor spoke, but gazed fixedly downward at the terrace below.

" 'Twould be twice a messy end, lass. Sean can hardly have perfumed the flaggin' with his upheaval."

Catherine turned, her eyes dark with desperation. "He means to make me his whore!"

Peg's eyes softened. "Ah. The young ruffian's told you it's either him or the dogs, eh?" At Catherine's bleak nod, the Irishwoman patted her hand. "Most of his black rage is spent on himself. I truly don't think he would hurt ye."

"It's not *that* I most fear! I cannot bear him. I cannot bear his touch. But he swears to kill my father if I . . ."

"You don't want to die. Terrifyin' as he seems, he's not Rouge Flannery. He's young and strong and clean as a whistle, not to mention he looks more than passable. It could be worse, lass." Peg patted her shoulder. "If ye meet him halfway, who knows . . ."

"I'll not be his whore!"

"Then hold strong. Don't let him best ye. 'Twill take more than an ordinary woman's wiles to tame him, I'll warrant ye."

"You're surely not suggesting I learn to *love* that brute!"

Peg began bustling about the room picking up bedding. "That's strictly yer affair, lass. Likely he's too hard and too much a man for a soft, gentlebred thing to handle. Ye'd want a manageable sort that never throws up in the peonies, who never wants ye so bad he tears yer clothes off"— she looked pointedly at Catherine's torn blouse—"but says please afore he tops ye without darin' to lift more than the hem of yer nightgown." She began to make up the bed. "Love Sean Culhane?" Peg looked at Catherine appraisingly. "Ye couldn't, lass. Ye could never love him enough. Ye're too stubborn, too stiff-necked, maybe too cold." She whacked a pillow into place. "That man's heart has an achin' empty hole all the love ye're capable of couldn't heal. He's near wild with the pain of it, lashin' at anyone who comes too close. Even Brendan—"

"Brendan?" Catherine interrupted, eager to take up any topic in order to leave the uncomfortable subject.

"His father," Peg said briefly.

"What of his mother?" Catherine persisted.

"Dead when he was a boy. Megan O'Neill Culhane, she was. Proud as Lucifer of the O'Neill," the housekeeper added pointedly.

"What was she like? She must have been beautiful."

"Beauty is as beauty does." Peg bustled around the end of the bed. "Sit here, lass, and let me sew that up. No need givin' the lads a view."

Now genuinely curious, Catherine was not diverted. "You mean to say Megan Culhane was less than she ought to have been?"

Peg jabbed the needle into the cloth as if it were her former mistress. "She took Sean off up the coast while Brendan was in Dublin's Newgate Prison. And she never came back, even after he was home."

"Is that why Sean Culhane is so bitter? Because of his parents?"

"The rift hurt him enough; Liam, too. But Liam grew up with a home and inheritance while Sean wasn't acknowledged as Brendan's legal son until he showed up here when he was ten."

"But Megan was his wife! How could he let his son be viewed as a bastard?" Catherine blurted, shocked. "What a horrible man!"

"No, not horrible. Hurt. He loved the lad better than his life, better than Liam, and in that he was wrong. In his eyes, Megan stole the son he should have had by his side."

"I still don't understand why he waited to recognize his son unless . . . Sean Culhane is *not* his son."

"A good many folk hold that notion, but none can say a thing against Megan. She was wild, but an open affair she never had. If ye could have seen Brendan and Sean together, ye'd know it an't likely. They were a like height, black Irish with an easy way of movin'. Brendan didn't have Sean's sinful good looks, but I an't never seen another man who did. Sean gets his moods from his mother. And his eyes. Those green eyes are Megan's."

Peg bit off the thread at the knot, then drifted on. "Maybe the lad was still too much Megan's or perhaps 'twas his coldness, but in all those years, he was never more than polite to his da. Megan deliberately filled Sean's life, leavin' no room for anyone else. When she died, 'twas like she tore out his heart and took it to the grave."

"You still hate her, don't you?"

Peg's chin lifted and she stared into Catherine's eyes. "Aye, I hate her. She's like an evil dream that comes back night after night, bringin' no good and no peace. In life, she was no better." Peg looked abstractedly past Catherine's shoulder, as if someone were there, then shook herself and glanced out the window. High overhead, the sun edged from behind rain clouds. "For pity's sake, we've wasted the mornin' entirely! Come along, girl. There's work to do."

Shortly, the countess de Vigny was in the kitchen court-yard, up to her elbows in a steaming vat of water so hot it reddened her skin. Rebellious tendrils of hair were plastered to her perspiring face as she shifted heavy, wet clothing with a long paddle, then wielded a washboard in gray water scummy with oil from the woolens. The first hour was the worst; after that the body achieved a monotonous, indefinitely sustainable rhythm. The two sturdy, ruddy-faced laundresses said nothing to her or each other.

Now I'm to be a mindless, hopeless drudge, she thought. The other women, who sneered at her efforts to wring out bulky woolens, put her to filling lines with dripping, wind-whipped wash that buffeted her. Her bare feet, bruised by loose flagging pebbles and the dragging weight, grew mercifully numb. The morning drizzle eased long enough to make line drying barely possible, but Catherine was too tired to be thankful, and as the sun sank, she dropped her laundry basket with the others in a storage room. Her whole body protested when she straightened, yet she still had to perform another duty that weighted her soul far more than chains.

In a daze of exhaustion, Catherine bathed in a water bucket in her cell. Without bothering with supper, she slowly mounted the stairs to Sean Culhane's bedroom. On his way down to dinner, Liam met her there. His face filled with startled dismay as she dully stood aside. She was white about the cheeks and lips. Damp hair stuck to her face, and the mended, liquor-stained blouse clung to her barely dried skin. "Catherine . . . Lady Enderly, are you well?"

"Yes." Swaying with fatigue, she wished he would be on his way.

"I . . . I wanted to tell you how sorry . . . I lost you in the crowd last night."

"You needn't apologize." She took another step up the stairs.

He caught her arm. "Are you going to Sean?"

"Yes."

His lips curled bitterly. "I can imagine what sort of choice he gave you."

"You mustn't interfere. I believe your brother might harm even you if you attempt to thwart him."

His eyes narrowed. "Are you so sure I'd lose a fight with him?"

"Peg tells me you've been taught to create beauty. I'll not see you mangle that calling by quarreling with him on my account. I ask your promise to keep peace with him."

"But his behavior is despicable!"

"It's all I ask," she said firmly. "Please don't make my existence here more difficult."

"Very well, I promise. Until the day I can meet him on my own terms." Seeing her start to protest, he cut her off. "That's all I can promise." His voice had a hard, determined note that was new.

"Very well," she replied softly. "I must go now. Good night, Liam Culhane."

"Good night, my lady." Wretchedly, he watched her ascend the stair and disappear.

Catherine stood before Culhane's door for a long moment, her thoughts bleak. Then, berating herself for groveling, she knocked sharply. Moora opened the door and Catherine started in shock. Was Peg's own daughter Culhane's mistress as well? As the Irish girl stepped back, Catherine tensely surveyed the room. The only light besides the banked fire was Moora's candle. Culhane was nowhere to be seen.

"He said ye're to wait." Moora's voice was cold, impersonal.

"I don't understand. Is he still at dinner?"

Moora ignored the question. "Ye're to be locked. Come over to the bed." Slowly, Catherine obeyed, and Moora clipped the chain into the hasp, snapped a padlock on it, then headed for the door.

Catherine clutched the bedpost. "Moora, please! At least tell me whether he's coming tonight."

Moora smiled caustically. "Ye'll have to wait yer turn. He's ruttin' across the bay."

Catherine sank to the floor as the door locked, and she leaned against the side of the bed, where she stared dully at the intricate carpet pattern. Slowly the tears seeped from her eyes and slipped down her cheeks. The fire had gone nearly cold by the time she slept.

Near dawn, Culhane knelt beside Catherine. She was pale and cold to the touch; he silently cursed her for stubbornly refusing his bed. Careful not to awaken her, he scooped her up. Her head slipped back over his arm, exposing her throat where he saw the collar had chafed the delicate skin with angry welts. Hadn't the little idiot thought to pad it? Or was she too damned proud?

He lowered her slight weight onto the bed and checked her ankle; it was raw and likely to fester if not eased. The feet were bruised and icy as his hands enclosed them. Lightly, he chafed them, then undressed and covered her before shedding his own garments. He slipped in beside her and tucked her small body against his own to warm her.

Much later, he awoke to find his captive tangled under him like a kitten fallen asleep in the midst of its play, her courtesan's lashes and sultry mouth incongruous on her young face. Her hair tumbled from the frayed bit of rag that caught it from her face. Carefully, he loosened the knot and, as he let down her hair, slipped his fingers through its long, silky weight. He lightly stroked an experimental finger between her breasts and down her belly. Deeply asleep, she stirred slightly with a faint sigh. He parted her thighs, then entered her warmth to find her sleepily yielding. When her lips parted in a moan, he covered them with his own.

Dazedly aware of a pulsing pleasure welling and ebbing like foaming, heavy surf through her body, Catherine opened to its throbbing source. With a gasp, Sean plummeted into the heart of her, felt for one brief moment of sweet torture what it would be like if she wanted him, loved him.

Suddenly Catherine became aware of the long brown body, the smooth, powerful muscles that coiled and uncoiled in the flat, hard belly moving against hers, eyes that burned like jade fire in the darkness. She arched wildly against him, digging her nails into his back in an effort to destroy his compelling rhythm, but not before his explosion inside her turned molten, sending streams of sweet agony flooding toward her soul. Slowly, the intense pleasure seeped elusively away, leaving her a fragile, empty shell.

The man's gaze was as wondering as the girl's when her lashes fluttered open and their eyes met. As if she were some lovely, precious idol, he slowly traced the small Nefertiti face down to the tempting underlip, swollen from his kisses. "Catherine?" he whispered huskily. "Yield to me. Yield . . ." His lips lowered to seal her surrender. As if eluding a cobra's hypnotic sway, she turned her head away and his lips found only the delicate curve of her jaw, just beneath her ear.

Sean hid his disappointment in the curve of her neck. Nibbling the tender flesh, he searched out the hollows of her throat at his leisure and maddened her with the traitorous excitement of her body, still helplessly sprawled under his. Lazily, his mouth moved lower, teased aroused nipples into aching, swollen buds that strained to burst into bloom. She whimpered, lashing her head from side to side, sending the lustrous mass of her hair spilling across the pillows in rivulets. With a soft laugh, he rubbed his cropped head across her breasts and belly, forcing a groan of frustrated fury from her. Lifting his head, he grinned mischievously into angry sapphire eyes, caught a tendril of her hair, and twined it about an impudently thrusting nipple.

As she stared at him in a confusion of rage and longing, Sean sighed with a wistfulness more mocking than he felt. "Thou Diana, with eyes of starfire and hair like the midnight tempest, flung recumbent in the heavens amidst glittering, wheeling nebulae, you make the blood of man run hot in him like the tides, tempt him to reach for the moon, howling, with useless fingers of foam. Thou remote goddess of the heart, who doth dash him earthward at the very pinnacle of his longing. Thou daemon temptress."

With a sagging jaw, Catherine listened incredulously to the Irishman's uncharacteristic lyricism. Would the villain's surprises never cease? He had sneaked across her sleeping defenses like a spy and forsworn frontal attack.

And undoubtedly he had conquered another as easily mere hours ago, with his glib tongue and lecherous skill. She did not mince words. "Get off me, you rutting brute! Your howls are more the stuff of satiety than longing. And your fingers have been dabbling in another's porridge pot, not groping for the moon!"

Culhane looked slightly startled, but not in the least guilty. His eyes narrowed. "Methinks, Celestial Diana, you have the instincts of a fishwife. Pray tell, who has been whetting your tongue?"

Unwilling to give Moora away, Catherine countered warily, "Who has been whetting your appetites, milord? Methinks it was yet another fishwife. Verily, her stink is still about you."

Abruptly, he shifted his weight off her. "Now, girl, we'll have it straight," he said coldly, swinging his legs over the edge of the bed and jerking the bellpull. "I keep no shrews." Rubbing her posterior, she glared up at him from the rug. He leaned down and lifted her mutinous chin. "If I'm inclined to bed six women a night, you'll not make a peep even if you're on the bottom of the pile."

"You exaggerate your capabilities, Milord Cockerel! And in any case, it's hardly likely I should attempt to attract your perverted attentions!"

He lifted a quizzical eyebrow. "Perverted?"

"If you propose that rape is normal, then so is every flying pig under heaven!" Caught up in righteous fury, Catherine scrambled to her knees. "And this morning, you ignoble sneak, you crept up on me!"

"Strange, your reception seemed so eager."

"If you think that feeble effort fired my blood, you've much to learn!"

"And you, little innocent, have even more to learn, especially about my capabilities." He gave her an evil grin. "You'll find my tutelage less tedious than the academy's." He got off the bed. "But your shrewish tongue is beginning to bore me."

"Surely you don't begrudge me the last of my weapons?"

His green eyes raked her as he shrugged into his robe and she was once more uncomfortably aware of her nakedness. "Not the last weapon nor the most dangerous, *p'tite,* although you've not yet learned to use it. Put on your clothes."

When Peg arrived in answer to his summons, Culhane told her abruptly, "Our Miss Enderly has displayed a special talent for nosing out fish; therefore, she'll assist at the pond. When the catch is cleaned, she's to rejoin the laundrywomen until the next fleet is in."

Catherine slowly tied her sash with a sinking heart. Cleaning fish could only be more unpleasant than laundry, knowing Culhane. Grimly, she tightened the knot, wishing it were about the Irishman's throat.

"Are you due free time?" he asked her casually.

"Yes," she answered sullenly. Sunday would be her first day of leisure in well over a month; she had been keenly looking forward to it, if only to sleep.

"You wasted a working day on an escape attempt and you left the foyer unfinished, so you've that yet to do over completely, of course."

"Of course," she echoed nastily.

"And the ballroom windows." He looked thoughtful. "Then there's a matter of nagging. For an indefinite number of Sundays you'll clean stables, take over milking duties, and empty chamber pots in the morning tide with Moora as company. Somehow, I don't think she'll give you another chance to brain her."

"May I go now?" she asked with unexpected quietness. "Or is there more?"

Culhane scrutinized her. Gone was the mischief, the insouciant impudence. In their place was dread of the dulling defeat of long hours of slavish work. "Not quite," he returned with equal quietness. Scooping a linen shirt from the chest, he ripped it into strips, then hunkered down beside her and wrapped the strips around the iron to thickly pad her chafed ankle. He stood, and threading a strip between her throat and the collar, bound it as well while Catherine stood silently. When his eyes met hers, he found them wistfully startled, just as that night when she had first gazed up at him as if she were a nymph from some dark forest pool. The shadowed depths of those lovely, haunting eyes lured him, and only Peg's presence prevented his kissing the soft mouth only a breath from his

93

own. "I'll be away for several days," he murmured. "Will that please you?"

Catherine's eyes went dark, unfathomable as an inky sea under the heavy lashes. "I . . . don't . . ." Then it occurred to her. The fourteenth. Today was the twelfth of February. Her eyes flared as if lightning had struck across them, then she accused, "You're going to England, aren't you? To Holden Woods!"

"So you found that map too!" His voice turned flat and cold. "Not a bad bit of deduction, Countess."

"What do you mean to do?"

"I mean to burn it," he returned bluntly.

"That forest is maintained by harmless woodsmen and filled with wildlife," she said with a soft note of pleading that startled him. "Many may die if you set it ablaze. Don't massacre innocents in your war. They're all that makes peace gentle."

"Do you number yourself among the innocents in my Herodian path?" he asked roughly.

"I'm no longer innocent," she murmured bleakly, her words only for him. "You've stripped every dignity from me save one, which even now you crave, only to tread it into the dirt." Her chin lifted imperceptibly. "I ask no quarter. Will you burn the wood?"

Culhane's eyes held hers. "I will." She turned away from him and left the room. "Find her warm shoes, Peg," he said quietly.

"Well, with her small feet, 'twill be no easy task." Peg rubbed her nose. " 'Course, there's trunks in the attic . . ."

"Just shoes, Peg."

She played with her keys. "There's been somethin' I've been wantin' to ask."

"What is it?" Sean asked impatiently. His ship, the *Mary D.*, was moored offshore and he would have to leave within the hour to catch the flood.

"Do ye intend sendin' the girl back alive?"

"The devil!" He flung a clean shirt to the bed. "What makes you ask that?"

"After ye left yesterday mornin', I found her on the balcony, starin' down at the stone flaggin'."

94

His irritation instantly faded. "I'll have Moora stay with her."

"Ye can't have her watched every minute. That's part of the trouble. The girl hasn't a moment to call her own, nor a stitch of warm clothes. The work ye give her . . . some it's well enough, but she's not as strong as those women in the laundry. And cleanin' stalls is man's work."

"She ran away, Peg. She must learn never to run again."

"Ye'd not tolerate a cage; ye'd run till ye died. Break her spirit and ye'll lose her."

Culhane's voice was cutting. "She's nothing to me but a spoiled Englishwoman! She's next to worthless as a mistress."

"Aye, the black looks ye give the lass tell me that. I wouldn't wonder if she *is* cold. What did ye do to the poor girl that night they carted her in to ye like a lamb to slaughter, batter her maidenhead with a stave? The sheets was bloody as a choppin' block and she nearly fainted on the stair!"

Yanking on his breeches under his robe, Sean cut across her tirade. "Stay out of it, Peg. Is that clear?"

"Aye, clear enough. And as ye've also made it clear the lass is naught to ye, why not let her go, or give her to Liam? She'd bloom in the arms of a lovin' man. Why not admit ye haven't the knack of givin' a woman what she needs?"

"Damn it, Peg, that's enough!"

"Aye, that's enough, alright," said the housekeeper unperturbedly. "Ye'll kill her; sooner or later, it'll come to that." She calmly jangled her keys as she walked out the door.

Late that afternoon, Catherine was up to her wrists in flopping fish. Having fished for trout at Windemere, she lacked the usual female horror of anything not already buried under parsley on a plate. Cleaning fish, though smelly and unpleasant, was preferable to laundry. Some of the fish went fresh to the house, some was salted for winter, while the rest went to market in inland villages and towns.

95

Moora, disinclined to talk to Catherine, periodically retired to vomit over the cliff. She passionately despised fish of any kind, and Culhane, as usual, had hit on the perfect punishment for her negligence with his prisoner. The other women sullenly eyed the English girl but for the most part ignored her, though Maude's sidelong glances were particularly venomous.

As she trudged back to the house with the other workers, Catherine felt like a rabbit watched by ferrets: some of those ferrets, she suspected, occupied the towers cornering the mansion. The men who had surrounded her on the moors must have been patrols; they could not have all come from Shelan. Their efficiency suggested a signal system; certainly the towers were natural signal points. Either the lookouts had missed her in the moonlit stableyard by sheer chance or had mistaken her for a man; the latter possibility presented opportunities. But one thing was certain. If she was caught trying to escape again, Culhane would certainly send her to the barracks.

Her gloomy thoughts were unrelieved by supper, where she was served stewed fish. In her room awaited a hand loom and a pile of yarn; in sum, her requested shawl. And for all her scrubbing in the bath bucket, a finny odor clung to her hands. Culhane had certainly achieved his aim, Catherine though sourly. She would never make snide remarks about anyone compelled to fish for a living again. She toppled into bed and, thrusting her hands over the pallet edge as far away from her nose as she could get them, fell asleep.

The next day was spent in the laundry yard under a slow, gray drizzle. As usual in damp weather, the lines of wash were hung before the kitchen hearths where the sagging lines hampered the cooks and put everyone in a foul humor. Catherine was hanging a shirt when Maude accidently backed into dripping woolen underwear and dropped a tray of stuffed quail. As the birds hit the floor, she flew into a rage. "Ye did this, ye foul English slut! Satan's spawn! Come to finish where yer da left off, have ye? Whorin' with the masters while honest folk be doin' the work. I'll teach ye to bedevil yer betters!" She snatched a carving knife and lunged at the startled girl.

Deftly sidestepping under a line and grabbing a pot of hot stew, Catherine pitched it into the Irishwoman's face. Maude screamed and scraped at her eyes. By the time she cleared them, her prey, armed with a broom, was across the room. The scullery lad, Danny, had disappeared.

Maude laughed disjointedly, gravy still streaking her heavy face. "Aye, slut! Pick up a toy! That's all I had to defend me family. Let's be seein' how well ye do!" She charged, slashing viciously. Blocking the woman on the backstroke, Catherine quickly ducked under the blade and rammed the butt of the broom into her belly, just below the breastbone. Maude doubled in agony, breath exploding in a convulsive whoosh.

With Danny at her heels, Peg, brandishing a pistol, rushed into the room as Maude, groaning, sat heavily on the floor with her arms locked about her belly. "What the devil's goin' on here? Lord preserve us, girl, have ye kilt the woman?"

"No, but I should have." Catherine wiped hair out of her face. Eyes narrowed, she bluntly warned her attacker, "Hear me, madam. If you ever address me in so rude a fashion again, or wave anything more threatening than a parasol, I'll ram this staff through the roof of your unflattering mouth. Indicate that you hear me or I'll clear your ears in the same manner!" Maude moaned and rocked. Catherine slowly lowered the broom then stared grimly at Peg and the ruined wash behind her.

"What happened?" demanded Peg, equally grim.

Briefly, Catherine told her.

Peg reached behind her and pulled Danny forward. "Is that the truth, lad?"

"Aye, 'tis, ma'am," asserted the boy, trying to ignore the ominous looks of his countrymen.

God bless you, boy, thought Catherine fervently.

"Maude, get up and stop blitherin'! Ye got what ye deserved and be damned to ye for yer foul temper!" Peg turned on the rest. "Well, stop gapin' and be about yer work! Annie, Kathleen, gather up that dirtied linen and take it to the shed. Maude'll be havin' a turn at it bright

97

and early tomorrow." She waggled a finger at Catherine. "Come along, girl, ye've things to do."

Dejectedly certain the quarrel with Maude had cost her more work, Catherine wandered with lagging feet after Peg, who stopped at her cell door.

"Come in, lass. I'm goin' to give ye a lesson in weavin'. No need to look so glum. 'Tis easier than landin' Maude Corrigan on her backside." Peg picked up the loom, planted her wide bottom on Catherine's pallet, and swatted the place beside her. "Sit." Catherine reluctantly obeyed. "Now, a shawl goes quick. The wool's already carded and spun, so ye'll have no trouble." She smiled faintly. "If Sean had his way, ye'd have to shear the sheep, but he wasn't specific, so we'll slip by."

Catherine listened warily, knowing Peg would have put up a terrierlike resistance to any criticism of Culhane by another. Now she not only implied disapproval of his behavior but seemed prepared to bypass his orders and offer a suggestion of alliance. Catherine decided not to bite. "Peg, why did that woman attack me? I've done nothing to aggravate her."

Peg began to thread the loom. "Watch as I talk, lass. I've yet some dinner duties." Her fingers worked deftly as she spoke. "Maude's family was killed by colonial Protestants, Orangemen, last year in Armagh. To her, colonials is English. She had naught but a broom to fight them off. They bayoneted her, and when she came about, her four-year-old twin boys and twelve-year-old daughter were dead; boys had been bashed against the walls, the girl raped and strangled. The house was burnin' about her ears. She crawled out into the yard and found her husband dead in his own water trough. She an't been right since."

Catherine had gone pale. "Oh, Peg, the poor woman. If I had known . . ."

"What would ye have done? Given her a light tap? She'd have slit yer gizzard." Peg patted Catherine's hand. "Now watch . . ."

That night Catherine dreamed of being chained with dead children in a burning ruin. High above the flames pealed Sean Culhane's laughter and, strangely, her mother's.

Peg shook her awake in the late morning. Catherine blinked at the light, shielded her eyes, then panicked. "I overslept! I'm supposed to be in the laundry . . ."

Peg gave her shoulder a reassuring pat. "Not today, ye an't. This mornin' ye've an appointment with Flannery." At the girl's bleak look, she hastened to add gently, "No, lass, not for another iron frippery." She stood back to watch Catherine dress, admiring her slim grace. "When ye've done with him, ye'll work at yer shawl. Maude's takin' yer duties today."

Catherine lit up like a spring morning and Peg's mouth puckered at the corners. "Ye've a glory of a smile, girl. I'm glad ye haven't forgot how to use it." When her charge was done dressing, Peg led the way past the stableyard to the foundry, where Flannery, bare-chested in a leather apron, streamed with sweat as he pounded on a glowing horseshoe.

"Good mornin' to ye, Mr. Flannery," Peg said cheerfully. "I've brought the lass for her lesson."

Flannery nodded at Catherine, then glowered playfully at the housekeeper. "What's this *Mr.* Flannery, me girl? I was pinchin' yer bottom before Rafferty wed ye, devil take his oily tongue."

Peg patted Catherine's arm. "Don't mind him. The old goat's more bleat than butt these days." She headed back to the kitchen, her skirts lifted to avoid the stableyard mire.

Flannery stuck his head out of the door and yelled, "Ye'd better lift those fine legs and run, wench! I'm about to chase ye to Tipperary!"

"Pooh, ye old fart!" was the fading reply.

Catherine giggled, then hastily put a hand over her mouth to feign a cough.

Flannery turned with a smile. "Now, don't be doin' that, lass. Laughter's the sweetest song in the ears of God."

The remark was so unexpected she was unprepared to respond. Faintly embarrassed, she lowered her hands. "I fear I've laughed little of late."

"Aye, 'tis sorry I am about my part in yer troubles. I've never put me hand to anythin' that shamed the makin' til those irons. The leg-iron is comin' off for a bit." He picked up the hammer, knelt, and knocked the bolt loose. Ignoring her astonishment, he rose and tapped the collar padding with a forefinger. "Sean's?" She nodded and his eyebrows rose slightly. "That's a rare concession. I wouldn't depend on another."

Her smile reappeared faintly. "I gather Mr. Culhane is unaware my punishment has eased in his absence."

"Oh, he'll know soon enough. There'll be waggin' tongues aplenty to disabuse him on his return."

"Isn't your place ordinarily with him?"

Flannery returned her intent look without a blink. "Ordinarily. I had other things to do." He whisked off his apron, then pulled on a shirt from a nearby peg. "Like givin' ye a bit of schoolin' on how to deal with the likes of Maude Corrigan." He picked up a wide-bladed knife with a cupped rapier guard. "Mind, I'll not be givin' ye this, if for no other reason than stickin' it in Sean might prove too great a temptation. Which brings us to another point. Don't go callin' a man's hand unless ye've got a good idea of what he's got to show. In fifty years of soldierin', I've only seen two men who could match Sean with knife, rapier, or pistol; both were cold-blooded killers for hire. Culhane only hires out to his personal devil, but he's a true killer. Don't go rattlin' his civilized cage, lass; it an't never locked." With that bit of advice, the Irishman took her into the foundry's rear courtyard and began a blunt, brutal lesson in wielding a knife.

Liam was in the stableyard loading sketch pads into saddlebags when he noticed Catherine skirting the paddock wall after her lesson. "Good day, Lady Catherine!"

She waved gaily. "Good day to yourself, Liam Culhane! Are you going to paint along the cliffs this afternoon?"

"No, I was thinking of going down to the bay. I've been working on the terns that gather near Quoin Rock . . ." His voice dwindled as he was seized by an urge to sketch her. Flushed from the bout with Flannery, her skin had a rosy glow even to the swell of her breasts where the neckline had slipped low. Abruptly aware of where his eyes had fallen, he hastily looked up to find Catherine openly amused.

"La, sir," she teased, "have you never seen a fishermaid before?"

Liam flamed. He occasionally eased his celibacy in the surrounding villages, and the earthy memory of what lay beneath the garments of the local girls did his composure no good turn. "I . . . was startled to see you alone and unguarded. Have you just come from the foundry?"

Imagining his shock if he knew the real reason for her visit to his blacksmith, Catherine lifted her skirts and gave her foot a shake to rattle the chain. "Mr. Flannery had adjustments to make in my costume." The young lord studiously observed the additional view he had just been afforded, but to his disappointment, the skirt was lowered again. "Besides, escape seems impossible with this chain and so many armed men about," she ventured innocently.

"It would be impossible with no one about," he replied grimly. "The moors surrounding Shelan are a maze of bogs and winding drumlin mounds; if you didn't stumble into a quagmire, you'd be lost in no time. Besides, Sean has rearranged the pickets so no one can go a mile without being seen night or day. His signal system of lanterns and mirrors can relay messages as far as England in a matter of hours."

Seeing her smile fade, he hastened to change the subject. "Would you care to see some of my sketches?"

She tried to summon a show of interest. "I've often watched you ride out across the hills and wondered what impressions you gather." She came nearer while Liam dug in his bag. He pulled out a sketchbook and he slowly began to turn the leaves. She was silent so long he began to feel she disliked the sketches. He desperately wanted her to approve his work. Eager to impress her, he had snatched up the first book in the bag; now, too late, he thought of others she might prefer. Page after page of cloud studies slipped by, delicately spun and seemingly artless, yet still painfully difficult after years of practice. He had captured the moving sky in all its moods, in every season, in every light.

As they came to the last, she said thoughtfully, "Your sketches are wonderful! Have you ever shown them?"

Feeling a foolish grin start to slide across his lips, he firmly controlled it. "In Rome, where I studied, I was beginning to show in a few galleries. I had received a commission from Prince Borghese for his collection when I was forced to return home."

"What a pity! Did your father recall you?"

"Ah, not exactly . . ." said Liam. "It was over a young lady."

"Oh," Catherine said sympathetically, "twice a pity."

She cannot have been a pretty child, he thought, distracted by her unusual facial structure, which was particularly striking in outdoor light. Without their maturing balance, her features would have warred with one another, possibly even have been ugly. Her straight, fine nose stopped a hairsbreadth before becoming too long a line; the nostrils flared a shade wide. The delicate line of her jaw softened a hint of obstinacy, giving the whole an underlying strength which kept her from being merely pretty. Her eyes were unforgettable, inundating the viewer in fathomless mystery. Suddenly, her lips twitched as if restraining open mirth. "Your perusal is so keen, I begin to fear I've improperly cleaned my teeth, or perhaps"—she screwed a finger into her forehead—"developed a Cyclopean eye. Farewell, sir! I must hie back to my dank cavern, there to gnaw the bones of the unfortunate unwary. Have a pleasant day a-terning, Liam Culhane!"

As he regretfully watched her hurry along the path to the house, Liam remembered he had once pressed his lips and body intimately against hers for a brief moment foolishly wasted. He would not waste a second opportunity! His hopes soared. Had it been his imagination or had she actually looked up at him in admiration, as if seeing him in a new light? With a high heart, he loaded his horse and rode off at a gallop toward the bay that gleamed like a mirage beyond Malinbeg Head.

CHAPTER 5

Nemesis

Three nights later, at midnight, flames snaked slowly over wood stacks scattered through Holden Woods, hissing when encountering damp timber. By half past, a small band of Irishmen had mounted horses as reddening piles tossed sparks skyward while trails of flame spread through the underbrush. Like riders from hell, the Irish sat, glowing effigies about the pyre. At a signal from their leader, they wheeled and galloped southwest in a wide circle to evade the house, which blazed with its own frantic light during an Enderly ball.

News of the blaze was not long in reaching the master of Windemere. With his back to his butler, John, and a pair of sooty, bruised timbermen, Enderly, his expression hidden by a bizarre peacock mask, stood looking at a handful of shivering merrymakers laughing on the terrace outside his study. Over their heads, paper lanterns swung in the brisk northwesterly breeze. "Holden Woods has been torched, John. See to the damage quickly and report to me. There's no need to alarm the guests."

When he was alone, Enderly went to his desk and unlocked a drawer. Stuffed into it were the packaged remnants of a bloodstained undergarment. He reclosed the drawer with deadly resolution.

Culhane corrected course a half point and gave the wheel to Sammy, ignoring the other's glum face. The *Mary D.* was beginning to round the sweep of Antrim, her sails

103

swelled under the late-afternoon sun that splintered off the water. They had been lucky, he reflected as he wearily stretched and walked to the rail. The wind might have given them difficulty had it shifted earlier; if it held this gauge, the *Mary D.* would make Shelan by nine o'clock the following night. Bracing at the rail, he rubbed his neck. Restless, he had taken two turns at the helm. His body yearned for sleep, but his mind refused to permit rest.

Jimmy's late departure and separation from the rest of the band worried him more than he let the others see. Too, despite their care, a woodsman might have spotted a clue to their identities. He wiped spray from the rail and rubbed it across his face. Leaving the foresters alive had been a mistake, yet the girl had a point; he would be no less a butcher than Enderly if he had allowed them to roast. As for the wildlife, a veritable stampede had scattered through the surrounding meadows; deer were probably waltzing with Enderly's guests. At the thought, a mischievous grin made its rare way across his lips.

He had assumed his hatred of the English had erased his ethics, yet the girl, spawn of the man he hated most, had recalled a code of justice that did not simply reflect his own and his people's wrongs. Was it that she asked no mercy for herself? God knows he had shown her little, and the mercy that he had shown her was dragged unwillingly from those depths of humanity he had long thought dead. Was it her moments of strange, soft, faerie beauty that often caught him unaware? At times, in her fatigue, she was almost plain, but then those incredible eyes would lift to him in hot defiance or mute wonder, catching his heart and sending it thudding after his racing pulse. Eyes like this burning sea of light and as unfathomable as the cool, eddying depths of her homeland lakes. The quickening breeze ruffled his hair, tickling his lean face and temples. He wondered whether he welcomed the fresh winds because they put Windemere's smoke behind him or because they hastened him onward to the black-haired girl who would be waiting in his bed, moonlight in her eyes.

As the longboat keel grated on the pebbled beach at Shelan, Flannery was waiting, his red mane lifting in the night wind. Culhane left the men to pull the boat up the beach out of reach of the incoming tide and walked to the tall, monolithic figure standing silent and apart. "Any word from England?" he asked briefly.

The redhead tersely related the signalman's news. Jimmy was dead. He had been fingered as a pickpocket by a tart he had annoyed in a waterfront inn. He had tried to board the *Sylvie* with a marine patrol at his heels, and the watch had been forced to shoot him.

In a black mood, Culhane went to his chamber, then sent Moora to fetch the English girl. His eyes burned from lack of sleep, his brain from misgivings and regrets. Privately, he would miss Jimmy's freckled, clownish face and impish wit. As he paced before the fire, he railed against the enemy that had taken the man's life, all the while with a bitter knowledge death was ever at all their shoulders. He had need of the girl's warmth this night to ease the chill of his soul.

Catherine finished another row of her shawl, then set the loom aside with a real sense of peace and accomplishment, the first she had known since her abduction. She decided to dye the wool a heather shade to recall the delicate tint of that dawn when she had first seen the dipping, wheeling gulls off the cliffs; the color would always remind her of freedom. As she rose to turn down the bed, a light tap sounded at the door. Her peace fled. She froze, heart beginning to pound. The door opened and Moora poked in her head. "The master's home. Ye're to go to him at once."

"Thank you."

Leaving the door open, Moora returned to bed while Catherine numbly sank to her cot. Even if it meant being condemned to the barracks, she could not go to a murderer's bed, even for her father's sake. She rose from the cot and locked the door from the inside, then disrobed. Keeping the long shirt on to hold off the chill, she brushed her hair with short, tense strokes, using a brush Peg had given her. Despite the shirt, she shivered.

Sean Culhane's reaction was not long in coming. Catherine was lying awake in the darkness, the cold moonlight streaming from the high window slit in a narrow wedge across the cot, when she heard a booted foot crash against the door. "Catherine!" The angry cry held a note of desperation.

Clutching the covers, she bolted upright and raised her voice clearly, praying only the anger and not the tremble in it would carry through the door. "I prefer the pawing of your men to your bloody hands. Find another whore, murderer!"

Suddenly the door reverberated twice, then exploded inward as a man's body splintered its moorings. Catherine rolled out of bed in one swift, desperate movement and backed away from the tall figure. His shirt undone, he stood, long legs thrust apart, his panting breath the only sound in the silence after the door's shattering crash. No light shone in the corridor behind him and she thought his eyes must truly be a cat's for he seemed to see her all too clearly in the dim cell, her shirt showing like his, a ghostly blue white in the moonlight.

"Murderer, am I?" he snarled. "Many an Irishman would sleep safer tonight if that were so!" Kicking a stool out of his path, he advanced toward the retreating girl. "So you prefer the barracks? Perhaps you need a taste of them."

Catherine stumbled back and abruptly felt cold stone, rough against her palms. "Get away from me!" she challenged, almost choking with the effort to conceal her terror. In one harsh movement he tore open his breeches and thrust himself full length against her, pressing her struggling body to the wall. Ignoring clawing nails that raked his shoulders and back, he roughly pushed the shirt above her breasts and trapped them against the fur of his bare chest. The Irishman lifted her, then inexorably moved her downward onto his erection. He tore into her, ravaging the warmth he had sought earlier as a haven. Her gasping pain tormented him, made mockery of his bewildering, angry need.

His rough entry into Catherine's unprepared body hurt him as much as it did her, but once inside her he could not stop, although he had not wanted her frantic with pain and fear. Looking into her face, he dimly realized her teeth were clenched to keep from crying out, her eyes glazed with pain and hate. With a shudder, he blindly buried his face in the side of her neck as he emptied in a kind of agony inside her. Spent, he released her and staggered back, chest heaving.

Like a discarded puppet, she slipped to the floor, her shirt and hair falling to shield her abused body from his eyes as he fumbled at his clothing. Her head hung between her shoulders as if her neck were broken. "Catherine?" he muttered hoarsely, moving to touch her shoulder.

Before his fingers reached her, she lifted her tear-streaked face and looked at him with such loathing and contempt it stunned him. Her breasts heaving under the thin shirt, she fought for breath. When she finally spoke, her voice was ragged but hard as a diamond cutting glass. "If you ever . . . touch me again . . . I swear I'll kill you, somehow, someday . . . horribly."

His smile was twisted. "I wonder . . . your father, of course, is a consummate killer. You may have inherited his inclination, if not his skill. In his prime, he dispatched masses at a stroke. I'll be curious to see if you can manage a single murder."

She lunged at him, hitting at his face and head, raging as he thwarted her with a shielding forearm. He shoved her back against the wall so hard it knocked the breath from her lungs. "It won't be murder," she gasped fiercely. "I'll merely give the hangman a holiday!"

He looked at her quizzically. "Perhaps you'll be giving me one as well." He left the room, his tall frame filling the door as he passed through it into the corridor toward the Raffertys' room, leaving Catherine to wonder at his ironic parting words. But curiosity was faint in comparison to overwhelming despair. Long after an embarrassed Rafferty came to guard her door, she sat dully on the floor where she had slid after Culhane had gone.

Finally Rafferty became disturbed and went for Peg. She bustled in and, clucking angrily, bundled the unresisting girl into bed. "Now, lass, there's no need makin' matters worse by takin' a chill. Sean Culhane may not have the rattled wits of a bedbug in a whore's mattress, but I hope I'll not have to say the same of you." She patted Catherine's shoulder. "Now, go to sleep. If ye're goin' to fight that bucko, ye'll need yer rest . . . and a small dose of advice. Keep that chin up. You won a battle tonight, even if the other side doesn't know it yet."

Turning her head to the wall, Catherine said nothing.

Through his bushy eyebrows, Rafferty looked up grimly from his stool at his wife as she came out of the cell. "She don't seem to be listenin' to your advice, Pego."

Peg shrugged. "She's doubtless wonderin' how many victories she'll survive."

Rafferty grunted. "Hmph. Not many at this rate. What do ye think of yer precious pet now?"

Lowering her voice so the girl could not hear, Peg confided, "I think he's half in love with her."

"What!" roared Rafferty. "Ye call bustin' in an oak door and"—seeing his wife's warning frown, he abruptly lowered his voice to a hoarse whisper—"brutalizing the lass *love?* Jaysus, woman, God help her the day he proposes!"

Culhane turned an ill-humored eye on breakfast the next morning. To his right, Captain Walter Ennis of the *Mary D.* noticed his host's frown and nervously picked at his eggs, thankful his own part in the raid had gone without a hitch. Having to shoot one of your own people was always a nasty business, and morale was uneasy for a long time afterward. The group at breakfast included the officers of the *Mary D.* They were as cheery as if the porridge had been served up in a coffin; even Flannery had nothing to say.

Peg prowled at Sean's elbow. "Eat somethin'," she muttered. "Black coffee works on an empty stomach like the grippe." He slumped in the chair and ignored her. "Humph. Yer troubles be comin' in fits and starts. Try runnin' a house; mine go on forever."

"Like your tongue," returned her target blackly.

"Mind yer own!"

"Leave off, Peg! I'm in no mood for badgering."

"I dare say." Peg raised a sarcastic eyebrow. "A bit of sleep would have eased us all!" Huffily, she stalked off to the sideboard for more cream.

Flannery stared grimly into his tea. Having been summoned at dawn to rehang the shattered door, he knew exactly what Peg implied; fortunately, Liam, who had been ticking like a bomb since his brother's return, did not. Flannery looked down the table. Liam, like Sean, was drinking only coffee. His fair coloring and fine features, which accentuated the tension in his neck and jaw, vividly contrasted with his volatile brother's pantherish good looks and sullen stillness. Flannery knew how deceptive Sean's attitude could be, with what deadly swiftness he could unleash ominous power. But, watching the brothers together now, seeing Liam's hooded eyes and long, pale fingers wind through the fragile handle of his cup, Flannery was reminded of a serpent's gleaming coil. A poisonous snake could bring down anything under heaven. For the first time, he wondered if Liam was the more dangerous of the two.

"Captain Ennis," Sean's voice cut across the scraping tableware. "Remain after breakfast. I have new orders for you."

The startled captain cleared his throat. "Yes, sir."

Sean stared pointedly at the group as if they were dawdling. "Peg," he ordered abruptly, "serve the custard."

"Now?" she asked, frowning.

"Now."

Custard was served and wolfed. Chairs scraped back as all but Flannery, Liam, and the captain made their excuses and hastily departed.

"There's a bit of household accountin'. If ye're to be busy this mornin', I'll be needin' a say-so on certain matters now," Peg stated stubbornly after the room had emptied.

Sean smacked his cup into its saucer and impatiently folded his arms across his chest. "Spew. You've been leaking all morning."

Stoically, Peg began, "Moora's lookin' runty. She asks to be let off fish."

"No."

Without expression, the housekeeper went on, "An extra sixty bushels of feed are needed for the household stock."

"Why?"

"Rouge didn't repair all the mortar in the north silo be-

109

cause some leaks was buried under grain. A good bit of feed is rotten."

Sean swore. "Replace the wheat after Rouge shovels out the silo and repairs the mortar. The cost of the feed will be deducted from his pay. Flannery, inform your idiot son that any more mistakes like this will drop him from the roster."

"I'll tell him," said Flannery briefly.

"Next," snapped Sean.

"Doctor Flynn requests three medical books from Edinburgh."

"He gets them. Anything else?"

"Maude went after yer lass with a carvin' knife."

Liam, holding his cup with both hands, burst its frail handle. The bit of porcelain clinked into his empty plate.

Culhane's eyes bored into Peg's. "When, and for what cause?"

"The day ye left. No cause but the old one. Ye know Maude's daft."

Sean's mind raced with an anxiety only Peg guessed was there; he had seen no cuts or bandages on the girl. "Who stopped the old witch?"

"Hmph. There was nobody to stop her. She'd have cut the girl to ribbons if the lass hadn't laid the discouragin' point of a broomstick into her hulkin' middle."

"Christ, a broomstick!" he muttered.

"She could have planted a knife in Maude's belly instead; enough were handy."

"Then why in hell didn't she?" demanded the dark Irishman.

"Because she's no killer," put in Flannery.

Sean's green eyes narrowed. "And how would you know that, Master Blacksmith?"

"I just don't think she has the knack," the giant said simply.

"Ha!"

"You won't be satisfied until she's murdered by some hothead with a score to settle, will you, brother?" said Liam, coming out of his chair with a snarl. "You parade her like a trophy of war. You deliberately make her a target, raising up the sins of her father!" He kicked back his chair. "What if no defense had been at hand, not even that pathetic broom? Where would you bury your prisoner, Sean? Under rotted feed?" Almost choking with fury, he missed Flannery's sharp frown and Ennis's look of sly interest. "But she'll be already dead, won't she? Where's the fun in that?"

"Shut up!" roared Sean.

Liam walked coolly toward him. "Make me."

Flannery pushed his own chair back. "Don't be stupid, Liam. He can take you apart."

"Not without some effort."

"Well, I'll be damned," breathed Sean, "if older brother isn't the errant knight to the damsel's rescue. I trust you're prepared to keep your visor lowered in the lady's presence, Galahad; few women have a taste for missing teeth."

His brother whitened with rage and drew back his fist while Sean merely looked at him, smiling grimly. Liam wavered, belatedly remembering his promise to Catherine not to initiate violence. "Come for me," he invited hoarsely.

"The hell you say," scoffed Sean. "You began this farce."

"Damn you," whispered Liam. "Come for me, bastard!"

Sean tensed and for a moment the others thought Liam's time had come. Even Ennis knew his accusation was an unpleasant possibility, that Megan had had provocation for taking lovers. Brendan had enjoyed occasional mistresses over the years; the portrait of one brunette beauty had hung in his room until removed after his death.

"Gentlemen don't brawl with bastards," Sean finally returned with icy sarcasm. "Have you forgotten your inane aristocratic code? Painting with shattered hands is trying, bully boy. Put steel in your fist, or better yet, a pistol.

"Now, as for the rumors of my questionable lineage . . ." He bit out each word. "I've killed for less public mention. For all purposes you are my brother, but when you call me bastard, you call our mother whore. Repeat that insult and you'll have your fight."

Knowing he owed his brother an apology his injured pride would not permit, Liam said stiffly, "So long as I know what your honor requires," and walked quickly from the room.

Wisely deciding this was a poor moment to continue discussion of Maude, Peg shook her head and returned to the kitchen.

"Now, Captain Ennis," said Sean coolly, relaxing again into his chair as if nothing had happened, "I'd like you and the *Mary D.* to take over the *Sylvie*'s sea routes for the next several months."

"You mean, the *Mary D.* is to make the munitions runs out of Normandy, sir?"

"That's it."

"Who'll be taking over my routes?"

"I haven't decided," Sean lied calmly. "I'll give you the required charts, rendezvous points, and timetables in my study an hour before you set sail. There'll be one problem. As an English registry vessel, you have a legitimate cover, but that registry will be a liability if an English cruiser spots you off the French coast." He raised his empty cup in token salute. "To your new citizenship, Captain. You're now an American."

"What?" blurted the Dover man. An Irish emigré, he had no loyalty to England, but like many Europeans he considered Americans colonial primitives.

Culhane grinned ironically. "Mad George's ships are unlikely to detain an American vessel as a smuggler. Britain wants no arguments at her backside to distract the navy while Napoleon is filing his teeth."

"I don't sound like a colonial; my men don't . . ."

"How do you think Americans speak? Some of them sound as English as you and me." He flashed a white, wolfish smile.

" 'Twill be more dangerous than smuggling ordinary contraband," persisted the captain. "My crew should be paid more, and I should receive a percentage . . ."

Culhane waved a negligent hand. "We'll discuss that after you complete a run. The pay will match your performance. Now"—the hand waved toward the door—"if you'll excuse us, Captain, I have matters to discuss with Mr. Flannery."

Awkwardly, the worried captain took his leave.

112

"Will the registry stand scrutiny?" asked Flannery.

"Aye, and so will our Hamburg syndicate."

Although Flannery had done his own share of smuggling, he was unfamiliar with the current, complex business operations of the Culhanes, so Sean took the opportunity to explain. "Max Lehrmann controls the syndicate bank in Hamburg. His backers are, of course, Liam and myself, and he makes handsome percentages from *Sylvie*'s trade in French contraband. In turn, Lehrmann, who is Swiss, assures neutral registry, while the bank provides a foreign currency exchange house with unimpeachable security for dealing with individuals and governments."

Sean toyed with his fork as he continued. "We use both the *Sylvie* and the *Mary D.* for smuggling currency, art objects, spies, and, of course, running munitions. Lehrmann screams; he doesn't like risking trouble with his own government.

"Still, with a fair wind the *Mary D.* can outrun almost anything afloat. *Sylvie*'s the real sharper, but you know that. You captained her yourself."

" 'Twas years ago," Flannery sighed. "Aye, she's yar, sure enough. Never thought that black-patched fop in Marseilles could turn out a beauty like that. We kicked our heels at British gunports for nigh onto five years." He smiled in remembrance.

In the rare times the two men relaxed together, they invariably discussed the sea, their common love. Sean leaned back in his chair, stretched his legs, and grinned. "You wouldn't consider resuming her command, would you?"

"I'm too old for gallivantin' about on a seagoin' racehorse." Flannery patted his paunch. "Takes a man with no fat to run guns. Maybe I an't as resigned to end in a noose as I used to be."

"Rot," said Sean briefly. "The only thing you fear is leaving Liam in my clutches."

"Your doin' him in an't what worries me. Any other man who said what he did this mornin' would now be harpin' with the angels. 'Course I don't know," the giant added slyly. "Of late, ye've been actin' ornery as a penned stallion with his favorite mare bein' nosed by a rival stud.

113

Keepin' that little filly wouldn't be more than a matter of revenge now, would it?"

Sean scowled. "The wench is nothing to me but an irritation. I brought her here for a purpose, and by God, she'll fill it!"

"If she lives that long." Flannery scratched his chin thoughtfully. "Aye, I suppose it wouldn't do to grow fond of her. Pity. She might have grown into a spittin' beauty. Reminds me of a girl I saw once in Brendan's arms at a Dublin ball. One dance they had, then she was gone in the crowd. She was the loveliest creature in the world. Expect she's a grandmother now."

Culhane stared at him impatiently. "Are you growing senile, man, that you're beginning to live in the past?"

"We live in a world of ghosts, you no less than I. We're condemned to that end by a crippled, perhaps dyin' cause. That lass has the soul of life: eager, impatient, curious! She's not chained to the past. Ruinin' her future will gain us naught."

Patience worn to a nub, Culhane rose abruptly. "Spare me your fatherly advice if Rouge is an example of its worth." Flannery whitened and Sean instantly regretted the cruelty of his heedless words. "Flannery . . ."

"Don't bother," growled the redhead, heaving his bulk out of his chair. He stalked out of the room.

Still troubled by his sharpness with Flannery, Culhane drifted into the study. At length, he dropped into the morocco leather desk chair and, with a toneless whistle, stared off into space. Then, after unlocking a desk drawer, he drew out paper, dipped a quill into the inkwell, and began to write in a quick, firm hand.

By late afternoon four sets of orders were deposited in separate envelopes, their seals stamped with the gold Celtic ring on his right hand. The first envelope contained directions Ennis was to deliver to France. If Ennis became nervous enough to break the seal, he would find only a series of coded dates, times, and incomprehensible substitutions keyed to previously relayed information. The second envelope contained "official" sailing orders for presentation to customs officers, while the third contained his actual orders, ports of call, contacts, and signals. The last envelope was addressed to the captain of the British cutter *Stag*.

Culhane rose from his chair and stretched, then began to pace, lost in thought. Though he was on the verge of putting into motion the laborious plans of a lifetime, he felt nothing but immense weariness.

Fatigue invariably seemed to lead him to brooding about the English girl. Only a crazy person would have dared to disobey his orders and attack her. Although Maude was mad, he could not bring himself to commit her to an institution; the woman had suffered enough. Punishment was useless; her addled mind would never accept the sense of it. The simplest tack was to remove provocation from her path. Maude would continue with laundry in Catherine's place, while Catherine would work full time at the fishery and in the house.

A final problem remained: Liam. Because of the English girl, Liam was becoming a willful, audacious rebel. If the transformation had blessed his brother with stronger self-control, he would have almost welcomed her influence; as it was, Liam's ill-timed outbursts endangered them all.

A month at sea would clear Liam's brain. Let him act as first officer aboard the *Sylvie* on her merchant passage to America and he would come back a new man. He would have little choice. Go, and with good behavior the girl would pull lighter duty; stay, and her duty doubled.

Two weeks after the *Sylvie* sailed for America with Liam snapping orders at a numb crew, the coastal cutter *Stag* surprised a smuggling ship, the schooner *Adele*, while she was unloading contraband in a secluded creek four miles from Windemere. The crew disappeared into the thick marshy wood surrounding the captured vessel. The *Adele* and her valuable cargo of French wines were confiscated and her owners, League, Tunney and Briskell, Ltd., notified. Because of their heretofore unsullied reputations, the owners protested with gradual success that the captain, who conveniently committed suicide, had been introducing his own cargos without their knowledge and altering the accounts. While temporarily embarrassed, they took their considerable loss with stiff but resigned smiles, having long ago been prepared for such an event.

The greatest loser was the syndicate's greatest private investor and the *Adele*'s actual owner, John Enderly. The local magistrate called politely at Windemere because of the estate's proximity to the creek in question. He requested the viscount to keep surveillance for smugglers and Enderly civilly agreed; in turn, the magistrate tactfully did not ask to inspect his warehouses. When the affair was concluded, John Enderly had lost nearly two thousand pounds sterling. The burghers of the syndicate he had bought out sub rosa twenty years before had lost a much smaller percentage of their personal fortunes, amassed with the long-term backing of their secret mentor. They assumed the ship's discovery had been a fluke, and for a time altered the routes of the *Adele*'s sister ships. The effort was pointless, for even their temporary withdrawal from smuggling would not have discomforted the viscount's nemesis in Ireland; he was in no particular hurry, and his scattered fishing fleet kept a close eye on both syndicate shipping and the British coast guard.

Catherine stared stonily up at the canopy finial above her head. For over an hour she had idly watched the canopy shadows grow more distinct. As the morning sun's slow climb gradually illuminated the room, she tried to ignore the bronzed arm thrown casually over her body and the sleeper's face buried in the hollow of her bare shoulder. Her tactics had changed to passive resistance. She silently appeared at Culhane's door each night, undressed matter-of-factly, and submitted to his caresses without a shred of reaction. Only the hate in her eyes made her seem alive. Invariably, with an oath of frustration, he left her and sailed to the eager arms of the fisher girl across the bay. Her nerves were on edge, as they had been all during the two weeks of Liam's temporary exile, although her lot had eased in his absence. There had been no more days in the laundry, no chamber pots, and best of all, no hampering leg-iron; Sean Culhane had benevolently decided to let her run in event of assault.

Still, while Liam's protection had been insignificant, his

presence had lent the situation a trace of civilized restraint. Certainly the unconscious brute who lay beside her had none. Despite his frustrated irritation with her coldness, he continued to take her as he liked. Sometimes, when weary from long hours of work, he adjusted her casually to accommodate his long-limbed body and fell asleep immediately afterward, although not without pulling her close like a child's favored plaything. Sometimes he took her as if he wanted to break down her resistance with sheer brute force. And sometimes he was gentle, with a slow, sure skill that left her trembling and breathless. She fought her body's response by concentrating on his ruthlessness, his brutality, his rages, his infrequent, unexpected tenderness . . . and the struggle would begin again.

Sometimes she spied a flicker of despair in his eyes when he turned away. Occasionally, when her knock at night drew no answer, she knew he was across Donegal Bay, and her small sense of victory seemed perversely sour. The thought of him in another woman's arms often kept her awake with graphic imaginings long into the night.

Catherine irritably turned on her side and dislodged him, but he merely sighed sleepily and pulled her rigid backside into the warm curve of his body. Not daring to move again for fear of awakening him, she chafed. Jealous? How could she be jealous of a detestable brute whose every touch made her seethe with rebellion? She would rather be vain and petty than remotely attracted to a tyrant who insisted upon instant gratification of his every whim. Finally, as if disturbed by her restlessness, Culhane turned away, leaving her free to slip out of bed.

Oblivious to scattered wall mirrors that reflected her nude body at many angles, she padded aimlessly about the room. Ruefully, she ran a finger over the ridged leather bindings of books along the wall. Simple diversions like reading were now incredible luxuries.

Catherine wandered to the desk, stole a quick look at the sleeping man, then eased the center desk drawer open; it contained little of interest except a brass letter opener. Her pulse began to pound. Suddenly, horribly aware this was her chance to kill the Irishman, Catherine stared at it, transfixed. Even as she reached for the thing, the possibility of a trap clanged a warning; but if this opportunity slipped by, there might never be another. Culhane had to be stopped from destroying her father. She slipped the letter opener out of the drawer, then crept stealthily toward the bed.

The naked man lay on his back, the hard beauty of his face turned toward her, his dark lashes curved against his cheeks. Asleep, he appeared younger. The ruthless, mocking lines of his mouth relaxed, he looked capable of warmth and laughter, even love.

Her shaking fingers tightened on the haft. She was not positive of the exact location of the heart; when she felt tentatively for her own, its thudding seemed to echo in her entire breast. The vulnerable hollow at the base of his throat offered the surest target. Catherine raised the dagger, then hesitated, appalled by its spasmodic jerks. "God forgive me," she whispered, and stumbled away, sickened with self-disgust. She had nearly reached the desk when a sound from the bed made her freeze.

The victim's voice was dry. "Flannery was right; you haven't the grit for murder."

Catherine whirled. Culhane rested casually on one elbow, regarding her lazily. "You . . . you weren't asleep," she hissed. "I knew it was too easy."

He lifted an appraising eyebrow. "Is that why you thought better of skewering me with a dull gimrack? Or did your delicate stomach recoil?"

Eyes narrowing to sapphire slits, she flung the letter opener at him, but because of her rage and the weapon's dismal balance, it struck the wall beside the bed and clattered harmlessly to the floor. Culhane, who had not even bothered to duck, laughed shortly, and swinging his legs over the side of the bed as he sat up, kicked the weapon safely under the bed. "If you're intent on imitating the deadly mantis who kills her lovers, Countess, don't vacillate over your prey."

"I'll remember that advice! Unless you intend a terminal remedy for my queasy stomach!" she hissed defiantly, still too angry to be afraid. Tangled black hair hanging nearly to her waist and feet planted apart, she fairly vibrated with the itch to scratch his eyes out.

He lay back on his elbows and smiled faintly. "Plot as much as you like. I much prefer you as you are now, spitting like a wet cat, to the limp-kneed twit you provide so monotonously of late for my bed. Come here."

She stared at him in disbelief. "I just tried to kill you! You cannot possibly desire me now!"

He twitched back the sheet and his white teeth flashed mockingly in his dark face. "You see? Flagrant proof nothing is impossible under heaven. Come here, Catherine."

Teeth and fists clenched, she advanced with dragging slowness, the tiny fires in her eyes snapping. When she stopped stiffly beside the bed, Culhane folded his arms under his head, a smile still playing about his lips. "Lie down on me," he said quietly.

"What whorish service would you have now, master?" she snapped.

"It's simple enough. Lie down. Gently." His voice was patient, but warned a knee to his groin would hurt her longer than him.

Gritting her teeth, she lay upon him, her creamy skin silken against him, her hair falling like a canopy about their faces. Irritated but intrigued, she waited. Mentally, she fidgeted. In her fiery mood and with the insufferable brute beneath her, she felt like the aggressor, as if she were about to rape *him*. The fur of his chest tickled her breasts and she squirmed slightly, then noted sparks of light playing in his half-closed eyed, sparks that flared in quick response to her movement. Instantly she stilled. "Kiss me," he whispered, and as her lips reluctantly lowered to his, his mouth was hot, opening under hers, yielding, searing, then slanting across hers with a hunger that threatened to consume them both. She lifted her head, her eyes uncertain. "Now," he whispered huskily, "kneel astride my hips. You're going to do the honors."

"No!" she breathed, trying to push away.

"Do it, Catherine." His voice was ragged but inflexible. Having learned open disobedience was useless, Catherine straddled his slim hips uncertainly, then held her breath; she had never touched a male organ with her hand. She stared at the shaft that proudly rose from his body. A man's sex seemed like that of an exotic flower, beautiful, dreadful, potent. She put out her fingers. His manhood was warm, warmer than the rest of him, and he caught his breath as her fingers shyly enfolded him. She could feel his quickened heartbeat under the smooth velvet of his flesh. "Now, Catherine," he whispered, his lean body taut with urgency.

Half reluctant, half fascinated, she slowly brought him to the entrance he sought, then, biting her lip, hesitantly eased him just inside her body. Although his arms were still beneath his head, he tensed. "Am I hurting you?" she inquired uncertainly.

"No, not in the way you think." His eyes were hazy as a rain-swept sea. Slowly, he began to move, arching his body gently at first and letting his loins rise under her relaxing thighs until overwhelmingly he filled her. She shuddered and her head dropped back, arching the slender stem of her throat. "Like Mephisto," Sean whispered. "Ride my body like the stallion's back. Ride me, little one, as if you could go on forever . . ." His body arched in a driving, deepening rhythm, his arms and hands now pressed down against the sweat-dampened sheets.

Catherine's heavy hair fell in a swaying stream as her head lolled in a near delirium of sensation, yet a spark of resistance still burned; desperately, she concentrated on it, fanning it like a backfire set to control a raging holocaust. As Culhane found his own incendiary release, her nails jabbed painfully into her thighs.

His spent body polished with a fine film of sweat, Sean saw from under his lashes that the girl had cheated him again. Long, angry scratches marked her skin, and her eyes, while dazed, were once more defiant and filled with bitter triumph. At the moment he should have been closest to her, he had been alone. She moved away from him with distaste. As she retrieved her folded clothing from a chair and turned her back to dress, her disdainful look gave way to one of confusion.

At lunchtime that afternoon, after the fishery workers laid down their tools and headed for the house, Catherine climbed the rise to the pond to wash her hands. When she finished, the fishery was already deserted. Shaking her hands to scatter the droplets, she glanced at the stone blockhouse on the pond's far side. Idly wondering how fish were salted and dried, she lifted her skirts to avoid the muddy bank and wandered around the stony shore. Ducking inside the cool darkness of the blockhouse, she discovered the Irish had a unique way of storing fish: behind several rows of salt-encrusted fish were many more rows of muskets. Moving up and down the rows, she rapidly counted some fifty weapons; two damp oilskin-wrapped bundles against the wall contained more. She touched a bundle, then licked her fingers: salt. The muskets had come in by sea, possibly aboard the fishing boats which could pick them up anywhere along European coasts; France in particular would relish revolt at Britain's back door. The arms must be being hauled up the cliff at night, she realized, for she could not have missed seeing such activity by day. A case of lead ingots for shot rested against the rear wall, but it obviously represented only one shipment or part of one, surely not enough to supply Shelan's men. Perhaps the arms were in the blockhouse temporarily, to be stored in greater quantities and security elsewhere, perhaps even transported under loads of fish by wagon to neighboring markets.

Catherine felt cold. If Sean Culhane was shipping arms all over Ireland, national rebellion might be imminent. A disquieting coincidence strengthened that possibility. In the past two weeks, most of the male faces at Shelan had changed. Only about thirty men, who appeared to be hardened mercenaries, looked familiar. What if Culhane was training rebel guerrillas in rotating groups and sending them back home to wait a signal for national insurrection? How many such vipers' nests were secreted about the country?

CHAPTER 6

Pandora's Box

Sean sighed as Fiona worked fatigue from his neck and shoulders with her strong, well-shaped hands. His worn chair was comfortable, the fire low on the stone hearth of her Donegal Bay cottage, reminding him of long-ago peaceful evenings in Kenlo. A few miles above the bay, the Kenlo hut and its village companions had been settled like handfuls of debris pitched amid bleak coastal crevices and ravines where the sea droned and flickered with long, rushing strings of froth that raked toward shore.

By day, he and his mother had lived like peasants, but nightfall brought a metamorphosis as secretive as a butterfly's emergence from its gray, common husk. Dinner was a formal ceremony, which provided Sean's social training and gave substance to his heritage. Conversation usually concerned either Irish politics and ruling families, or world affairs that related to Ireland. By the light of a towering gold candelabrum, bronze-haired Megan taught her son how to be a king. When dinner was ended and its trappings—the candelabrum, the fine porcelain and silver—hidden away, the Irishwoman would take out her lute and seat herself before the fire. As she thoughtfully plucked the lute strings, making small adjustments in pitch, her son impatiently dropped cross-legged at her feet. When she glanced at him through her lashes, he caught a gleam of amusement and thought, as he often had, that she deliberately teased him. Still, her scel tales, the sagas of the boy

122

hero Cu Culainn, and the fantastic *Courtship of Étaine* were well worth the wait.

As she bent over the lute, the firelight gave the highlights of Megan O'Neill's auburn hair the intensity of stained glass. Her fine-bridged nose and smoothly carved features were the heritage of royal Gaelic lineage mingled with the Hispano-Moorish strain. Her smoldering green eyes suggested sensuality equal to her almost Satanic pride. Megan was carelessly aloof from the villagers, but when alone with her son, her pealing laughter was the release of utter freedom. She was purely woman then, as she would never be again if she ever assumed her rightful place in the world beyond the village, and with a sense of guilt, Sean had been secretly glad of their obscurity.

Megan's voice began low, then rose imperceptibly to a keening cry as she sang the first of the ancient Gaelic songs. Songs from the dust of shattered Rome. Of mistlocked secrets and the Old Ones. Of tribal savagery and clash of arms in forgotten wars. Of fire and death and mourning in pagan chants forbidden by the Church for centuries. Then sagas of heroes bold on sojourns to the world's end, and lays of *amour courtois,* richly tapestried with knights and ladies and fabulous beasts.

Try as he might, Sean could remember few of the ancient chants. Gaelic was his native tongue, but when Megan sang of Ireland's obscure origins, she seemed to have a pact with the past that excluded him, perhaps because she knew herself born to be an Irish queen, while he often felt like a prince of shadows. He did not know who he was.

Once, a village bully had foolishly called him a bastard. The insult had trembled between them until Sean rammed headfirst into the boy's stomach. The battle was a brief, violent encounter. Sean had the O'Neill nerve and the black side too; before he had been beaten senseless by the bully's cronies, he had bitten off the boy's ear. No one named him bastard again; they simply avoided him.

Finally one night, the last candle in Kenlo had gone out, the village stopped looking like a cheery spatter of lighted dollhouses, and the British-led Orangemen had come. Most were Irish Protestant Militia, members of the re-

123

cently formed Volunteers. Because most of the British occupation forces had been siphoned to America to suppress the revolution and abroad to face imminent war with France, Irish Protestants had seized the opportunity to force concessions from the lord lieutenant of Ireland. In spite of a recent wave of religious liberalism, the most radical Protestants intended to ensure by terrorism that their Catholic brethren should entertain no ideas of rebellion in the weakened circumstances of national security. Of the Kenlo raiders, only their chief lieutenant and a handful of noncommissioned "advisers" were British. Their commander, General John Enderly, adjutant to the viceroy, knew massacres were more apt to start trouble than to end it. Sean learned years later he had meant to stir up rebellion to line his own pockets with confiscated property. The raiders were to leave no survivors, no evidence of his machinations, but the night they had swarmed with their torches like deadly fireflies among the sleeping huts of Kenlo, they had left one alive. To carry the guilt of obeying Megan's order to run. To remember. To hate.

Feeling the reality of Fiona's fingers at his shoulders, Sean opened his eyes, deliberately cutting off the nightmare memories that always came with fatigue. And he was deathly tired. His workdays averaged sixteen hours, often with but a few hours' sleep. The company of his quarrelsome young mistress gave him little respite. In the two weeks since the letter opener incident, he and Catherine had bickered more than they had lain together. Frustrated by her resumption of stubborn apathy in his bed, Sean spent most of his nights in the village. Fiona gave him the peace Catherine's arms denied, and she was Irish: those two things were all he required at the moment—those and her earthy, uncomplicated eagerness for his body. As his head fell back, she kissed his lips, hair in a pale red-gold curtain about his face. Lazily he kissed her back, then roused as her breasts under her chemise brushed his shoulder. Her mouth moved on his, tongue probing until his blood simmered. Pulling her around onto his lap, he tugged at the chemise lacings.

* * *

Silence gathered about the limp, exhausted lovers as they lay side by side on the bed. Opening his eyes when Fiona's lips brushed his cheek, Sean grinned with drowsy satisfaction and she obligingly plumped the pillow behind his head, then snuggled back onto his shoulder. "You talk less and bed a man better than any female in Donegal," he observed sleepily. "That sterling virtue will take you far."

Cynical amber eyes flashed at him. "Oh, I wouldn't be knowin' about that, bucko. I've never even got as far as yer fine house at Shelan."

"It's nothing but a dusty museum," he replied calmly, knowing what she angled after.

"You're there, and too damned far away! Ye've come to me nearly every night of late, each time later and more bone weary than the last. One night ye'll say the devil with it and I'll be seein' no more of yer scowlin' mug. 'Tisn't fair to either of us."

"We've known each other a long time. Is that telling you nothing?"

"Aye, it's been a long time since ye was fourteen. A hot-blood virgin with the devil in his eyes and a form like pure sin." Her eyes softened with remembrance. "I was a dreamin' chit o' twelve who thought she'd met up with the Dark Prince. I gave in to the serpent, and lo, Paradise!"

"You're the closest I've had to a permanent woman," he murmured against her hair, "but we both know I'll never marry."

"Ye've always been hard, Sean," she whispered, "never needin' anybody."

Her face was hidden against his shoulder, but he could guess at the tears. He tightened his arm about her. "It's you who doesn't need me, Fiona. You'd be unhappy at Shelan."

"Like that girl?" She bit out the words.

"That girl?" he asked, not altering his voice.

"Did ye think ye could keep a woman long without some she-cat tellin' me the good news?" Fiona sniffed openly.

"What did this she-cat tell you?"

"That ye've an English prisoner who's a grand lady, and pretty, and sleeps in yer bed."

"While I sleep with you." Sean turned on his side and

125

kissed her into silence, then took her again. Long after she slept, he stared into the fire.

Before sunup, Fiona walked with him to the jetty that served Pier Harbor. The stars were melting in the blue-gray light and silvering waves curled peacefully, rushing over the rocks and receding monotonously. A shawl about her head and shoulders, she watched as Sean boarded his boat, quickly made ready, cast off the stern line, and ran up the sails; they slapped the swaying mast as the boat swung into the wind. When he rejoined her on the jetty, she reached up to turn his jacket collar higher against the chill. He caught her fingers gently. "Fiona, I won't be back."

Her amber eyes widened and turned fearfully up to his green ones, now dark as running storm seas. "I'll not plague ye about Shelan again," she pleaded in stunned panic. "I'll wait, as long as ye like . . ."

He shook his head. "You've waited long enough. You ought to have a man all your own, and children. You're too beautiful, too fine to be wasting your life watching for a night sail."

"But, it's me lot," she protested, tears filling her eyes. "There's naught for seafarers' women but waitin'! If not for ye, then another."

He lifted her strong face to his. "Then another, Fiona. Don't throw your love away on me."

Her amber eyes gilded. "I . . . I never said I loved ye," she blustered. "Never, ye cheeky rogue. Why, 'tis but a bit of a toss I expect . . ."

His lips brushed hers. "Good-by, sweet lass. It's glad I am you don't love me." He smoothed a tendril back from her face, then turned away.

Fiona stood, frozen in pain, as he cast off and tightened the sheets of the sloop-rigged yacht to catch the first puffs of offshore breeze. She was still standing there when, well out into the harbor, he turned to wave.

Sean was glad to be at sea, glad to have his mind occupied. The trim thirty-four-foot yacht demanded all his attention. A smaller version of the graceful *Sylvie,* her teak decks and brass running gear glistened with spray above

126

the spanking white of a sheared hull. Sails cupping the breeze, the yacht heeled over with wake dancing high. As she skimmed across the bay with the wind over her windward beam, depression settled over the Irishman. His last haven was gone and he had been right to leave it, yet the loneliness Fiona had eased for so many years seemed overwhelming.

Already, like ghostly butterflies, sails of fishing craft hovered over the bay, some well past the headland. Casting an eye to the wind, he tightened the foresail a notch. Against a sky rapidly paling to mauve, seabirds shrieked over the waves. As a sense of peace swept him, Sean realized part of the reason for his nightly sail was love of the quiet hours of evening and early dawn at sea. Fiona had been part of that love, part of his restless youth.

At the moment he changed tack to clear the point, the coast guard cutter *Stag*, 150 miles away, surprised the smuggling ship *Pandora* napping peacefully near the same English coastal creek where her unlucky sister ship had been seized. While *Pandora* had rocked at anchor during the night, one of Culhane's Windemere agents had silently swum up to her stern, tightly tangled a weighted leather pouch into the rudder chains, and departed. As dawn lightened the sky, marines sprouted from the marsh cattails on both sides of the *Pandora* and captured her, crew and all. When the British prize crew attempted to sail her away from her mooring, they found her rudder fouled; a check of the stern discovered the incriminating pouch, "obviously" thrown overboard when the crew was surprised. Like her legendary namesake, *Pandora*'s pouch released all manner of evil sprites in the form of secret running orders and contraband cargo lists forged with the signatures of League, Tunney and Briskell.

By the time Sean secured his yacht to cork buoys off Shelan and rowed the dinghy ashore, *Pandora*'s crew was being prodded ashore by bayonets wielded by marines who, in their leafy camouflage crowns, resembled a band of bacchanalian revelers.

That afternoon, Catherine, intent on avoiding the muddy shallows of the fishery pond, walked out on the narrow, decrepit dock to scrub her hands before lunch. When she turned, the way to shore was cut off by three women; the rest of the workers had disappeared. One of the women was Maude. Gripped by icy apprehension, Catherine stood, fingers dripping. Maude lumbered onto the creaking dock, her eyes pinpoints of mad, gray light, her tattered, colorless clothing giving her the appearance of some hulking derelict risen from the sea.

"What do you want?" Catherine asked quietly.

The pinpoints flickered. "Pray for your soul, slut."

The closer Maude came, the more Catherine knew any attempt to reason with her would be a waste of breath, yet she dared not retreat from the huge woman. Like drab vultures, the others waited on shore; one of them, she was startled to see, was Moora. Maude, sensing her dismay, struck with blinding speed, bringing her huge fists downward in scything arcs that would have broken her target's collarbones if Catherine had not recoiled just in time, nearly losing her footing on the irregular boards. Maude charged, but the heel of her victim's hand caught her in the throat, and with a croak of pain, she caught Catherine blindly about the ribs, dragging her into a deadly embrace. Catherine twisted a leg about the woman's bulky calves, then shoved with all the force she could muster, toppling them both into the pond. The shock of cold water closing over their heads loosened Maude's grip. Ramming her hands against the woman's jaw, Catherine broke free.

As her head cleared the surface, she dodged a flailing grasp, back watered, dodged the Irishwoman again, and tried to swim away. Then she spied Moora, who, not ten yards away, was awkwardly paddling a fat, narrow river skiff she had found tangled in the reeds. "Moora, help me!" Catherine swam for the boat, long skirts tangling about her legs, then, eyes widening, ducked just before the flat of Moora's paddle slammed down with a forceful crack on the water. Before the Irish girl could lift the unwieldy weapon, her victim reared up, grasped the blade, and sharply jerked it. With a shriek, Moora capsized. She went down like a stone as the boat bobbed away in the low chop of the struggle. The woman on shore began to scream and Maude flailed toward them with clumsy determination. Upending

128

like a water bird, Catherine dove downward. Although partly blinded by mud kicked up from the bottom, she caught sight of colorless hair wafting in the dank water. She grabbed and hauled, breaking the surface with her erstwhile attacker, and, towing her by her hair, headed for shore. Despite the Irish girl's struggles, Catherine dragged her to a safe spot in the shallows where she pounded her on the back. Moora gagged and retched.

"Maude! Maude's drownin'!" the third woman shrieked. Catherine staggered to her feet and looked in the direction the frantic woman was pointing. Maude's dirty kerchief showed above the water; her upturned face gaped like a wounded fish. Sighing, Catherine pulled off her hampering skirt and the one shoe she had not lost, then ran into the deeper water, wincing as her bare feet encountered sharp stones on the bottom. She closed the distance to the drowning woman with clean but tiring strokes. Circling just out of reach until the flailing Maude predictably sank, Catherine grabbed her hair. With the horrible glare of a Medusa, the woman reached up with sudden, insane strength, grasped Catherine's wrist with both hands, and pulled her close. Her hands shifted to Catherine's throat, then dragged her under.

Head pounding in a red mist, Catherine struck with all her force at the Irishwoman's belly and face, but her blows quickly weakened. When Maude finally became aware of her own danger and clawed for the surface, Catherine was already unconscious and sinking toward the muddy bottom.

"Mr. Flannery! Mr. Flannery!" The north tower lookout stumbled into the foundry and hung gasping from the doorjamb. His eyes widened in surprise as, instead of the jovial redhead, he found his commander-in-chief. Bare to the waist, torso smeared with black grease and sweat, Sean Culhane was paring one of his stallion's hind hooves in preparation for shoes cooling in the tank.

Culhane's green eyes slanted wickedly from the gloom at the messenger. "What the devil are you doing away from your post?"

Wiping his hands on his leather apron, Flannery came into the foundry from a back storeroom as the man stam-

129

mered, "The limey lass, sor. They're drowndin' her in the pond . . ." The words were hardly out when Culhane exploded by the man, slamming him against the jamb; Flannery was right behind him.

One of the laundrywomen waved frantically to a spot some fifty feet out in the water as Sean kicked out of his worn work boots on the pebbled shore. He raced through the shallows, then angled out in a flat dive. He tucked and sliced under, eyes straining for some sign of life. On shore, a gathering crowd curiously milled about the pacing Flannery. He caught his breath as Sean's dark head broke the surface of the pond alone. Sean dived, and dived again. Flannery shook his head. "It's been too long."

Sean's chest felt as if it were stabbed by hot pokers and his head pounded horribly, yet he drove deeper into the murky darkness. Suddenly his outstretched, straining fingers brushed cloth and he seized it like a madman, pulling until he felt it give. Clouds of mud roiled up from the bottom. More carefully, he tugged, then felt a body under his fingers. Hauling it upward against his chest, he fought for the surface. At last his head cleared the murk and he gasped with pain as his starved lungs filled with air. A small, silken head like a drowned kitten's fell across his shoulder.

With the last of his strength he got Catherine to shore and nearly collapsed atop her as they reached the shallows. Flannery roughly ordered the crowd back. Catherine was deathly pale, her lids and lips blueish. Her head lolled limply as Sean dragged her up the shore just far enough to roll her on her stomach and rhythmically empty her lungs. He began to pump water out of her, but finally there was no more—and no sign of life. The watchers became restless, even those gaping at the victim's scantily clad body. Noticing their avid eyes, Flannery abruptly ordered them away. He touched Culhane's shoulder. "It's no use. Ye've been at it long enough."

"Leave me alone, dammit." Desperately, the dark Irishman flipped Catherine over and brought the heel of his hand down hard between her breasts. Flannery, the laundrywoman, and the sodden Moora stared at him as if he had gone berserk. He hit her again and again, and Flannery had just taken a step toward him when Catherine coughed weakly. Water tinged with blood trickled from her mouth. Heart thudding in his chest, Sean pressed his mouth to hers and breathed. A ragged, bubbly breath mingled with his. When the long moth-wing lashes fluttered and he saw again the incredible blue of her eyes, he wanted to take her small face in his hands and make love to her mouth until she protested; only her dazed, shivering weakness stopped him.

"Flannery," he rasped hoarsely, "get a cloak or blanket—something." As Flannery headed off at a lumbering run toward the house, Culhane shifted to one knee. He steadied himself, waiting until his mind began to function again. "What happened here?" he demanded, lifting his head at last to stare unwinkingly at Moora and her stricken companion.

" 'Twas her, milord! The English bitch!" the laundrywoman hastily volunteered. "She pushed poor Maude from the pier, then came after us with a fish knife." The woman looked to Moora for support, but Moora stared through her.

"So English jumped all three of you with a scraper, did she? She's a real terrier, wouldn't you say?" he grated.

The woman cast a desperate glance at Moora, who turned her head away. The laundrywoman went as pale as the girl lying on the ground. Her hand to her mouth, she began to back away from the swiftly mounting fury in her master's eyes, then bolted for the cliff path. Moora sat unmoving, hair stuck to her face and clothing flapping heavily in the rising wind.

Culhane looked down at the slim girl they had nearly murdered. Her color had improved slightly, but she seemed disoriented and trembled with cold. Wishing Flannery would hurry with the cloak, he chafed her hands. Although he could have carried her to the house, he did not want to parade her unclad body past gawkers still hovering near shore. "Get out of here or I'll have the lot of you boiled in oil!" he roared. Instantly, they scattered. His attention ominously turned to Moora. "Well, Moora? Shall we have your bilge now?"

Moora met his eyes and told him the blunt, ugly truth.

" 'Twas all Maude and me. Annie just watched when Maude pushed her in," she said flatly. "I tried to brain her with the paddle, but fell in. I never learnt to swim. She pulled me out, then went back for Maude."

"I ought to hang the pair of you! What the devil got into you, Moora?"

"One fish too many," she muttered, absently watching Flannery approach at a trot with a cloak flung over one brawny shoulder.

Sean stared at her. "If you've been driven to murder, why not lie, too?" He angrily indicated the pale, shivering girl who moaned incoherently. *"She's* in no condition to protest. I might have believed you, if not Annie."

Moora's blue eyes held a strange look. "Milady wouldn't believe I wanted to kill her, and even after . . ." She paused. "She could have let us die."

"Don't dismiss the possibility of your demise too soon, girl," he snapped. "Even Peg wouldn't chide me now for letting you swing."

Coming up to them, Flannery handed Culhane the cloak, which the younger man wrapped about the nearly unconscious girl with swift care. Cradling her in his arms, Sean quickly carried her toward the house, her small feet dangling from the cloak's heavy folds, her dripping hair resoaking his shoulder and sending icy trickles down his ribs. As he took the stairs to his bedroom two steps at a time, he yelled orders at the startled servants. "Get a tub of steaming water upstairs with towels and liniment! Step lively!"

He had barely laid her in the big bed, stripped off her wet clothing and tucked the covers high about her ears, when the kitchen boys filed into the room with buckets of hot water. Flannery and Rafferty carted in a huge copper tub, Peg at their heels with the demanded liniment and towels. Her blue eyes crinkled with agitation as she plopped her load on the end of the bed. "What's this I hear about Moora?"

"Let's fret about one thing at a time." Sean patted her shoulder, then grimaced at the black mark left by his hand.

She shook him off, staring at Catherine's white face and tangled wet hair on the pillow. "What's Moora done?"

"Flannery will explain everything," he said gently, escorting her to the door. "Moora had a dunk in the pond and needs your looking after."

Peg twisted at the door. "But what about this poor lamb?"

He eased her out. "Don't concern yourself, Peg. I'll take care of her."

"You!" the anxious housekeeper sputtered. "You blitherin' blackamoor, what do you know about nursin'?"

"She's all right, Peg. Just chilled and a bit dazed." He pushed firmly, added, "I can manage," and closed the door.

When the tub was clouded with steam, Sean shooed the others out. Wiping his hands clean on a towel, he uncovered Catherine's arm, poured liniment into his palm, and began to rub her down, briskly starting with the fingertips and working upward. She stirred as he reached her shoulder. Covering her again, he slipped her other arm free of the covers and repeated the process. Catherine blinked as he started on her feet. "What . . . what are you doing?"

"Rubbing your toes." He began to stroke between them.

Having one's toes massaged was a strange but remarkably pleasurable sensation, she thought groggily. Her head raised a fraction. "Is Maude all right?"

"Yes."

She watched him work his way up her leg, easing the numbness with his strong hands as clinically as a doctor. Except a proper doctor, she considered, would not have spiky hair and lashes and be half-naked, wet, and sooty. "You're dripping on the bed," she protested feebly.

"So I am." His unexpected grin was a startling white in his smudged face. Her lips twitched as she unconsciously started to grin back, profoundly relieved to be alive. She sternly managed to work up a small frown instead when he flipped back the covers and vigorously massaged her torso. "Stop that," she protested.

Again his grin was like a boy's. "I've half a mind to tickle you back to life, you wriggling imp. Turn over," he ordered. With the wounded dignity of a sodden cat, she obeyed. His voice was brusque, but his hands were gentle,

133

and already the ache in her chest was fading. Despite her muffled squawk, he rubbed her chilly derriere. As he slowly worked over her back and shoulders, she slipped into a warm, euphoric stupor. All too quickly, she was jolted into wakefulness as she was turned over, lifted in powerful arms, and pressed against a cold, furry chest. Her eyes flew open as Culhane inexorably lowered her into the tub of hot water. "Oh! Don't!" she squealed. "It's too hot!"

Her tormentor was unperturbed. "Stop squalling. It's exactly what you need."

"*More* water?" Ignoring her, Culhane began to scrub her heat-flushed skin vigorously with a bar of scented soap. She scowled at him, spitting bubbles away from her face. "Just once, I'd like to bathe myself!"

He dropped the soap into the tub with a splash, and said casually, "Fall to."

Fiercely, her wrists rubbed the soapy water from her face. Then, ignoring him, Catherine began to apply the soap with leisurely dignity. Her head snapped around when his sodden breeches hit the floor, but she had little time to protest as he slipped into the tub. "There isn't room for two," she sputtered, trying to evade his long legs and exploring toes. With a grin, he held out his hand for the soap. Glaring at him, she deliberately dropped it, but was forced to repent the impulse as his fingers sought the slippery bar in the most unlikely places. She was flushed and furious as he victoriously fished it up. "One might easily believe your brains are between your legs. Don't you ever think of anything besides fornication?"

"Ah, 'tis a temptin' morsel you are, lass," he responded in a lilting drawl and with an exaggerated leer. "Just enough to whet a man's appetite and leave his belly lean. It's not greed but starvation that keeps me howling at your door." He wiped a handful of lather off his face and dabbed it on her offended nose. "Your hair is gluey, little one. Wash it."

She grabbed his head and ducked him, pushing herself up. "Your hair is soapy, sir. Rinse it!"

He came up sputtering and grabbed her in a bear hug before she could escape the tub. He pulled her down, shrieking. Grabbing the soap, he ducked her in turn and scrubbed

her head. "That's for children who play in the bath."
Ignoring her squeals, he ducked her again, then grabbed a
bucket of clean water from the floor beside the tub and
dumped it over both their heads. As water splashed everywhere, Catherine howled, struggling to her knees. Laughing, he rubbed his cropped head against her breasts and
belly and she began helplessly to giggle, digging for his
ribs and shrieking as he tickled her. Suddenly their slippery bodies sliding together made her eyes widen, and a
flaring desire to couple with him made her shudder. All
too sensitively aware of his small antagonist's change of
mood, Sean brought his mouth down hotly on hers, stifling
her breathless gasp of surprise. She struggled feebly, but
her hardening nipples rubbed wetly against his chest and
the hard heat of his loins thrust against hers as their bodies tangled.

Quickly, he caught her up in his arms and carried her to
the bed, then covered her slippery body with his own. Exhausted from her ordeal with Maude, Catherine pushed
weakly against his shoulders and twisted, but her writhing only made his breath come more raggedly in her ear
and his body slide more intimately against hers. He
slipped a wet finger between her thighs and she cried out
against his mouth as he brought her to exploding, arching
pleasure.

He kissed her throat, her breasts, her mouth, whispering love words, sex words, until her thighs parted of their
own accord to receive his first slow thrust. Each deep,
warm stroke of his manhood intensified a burning, pulsing
ache in her loins. She gave up fighting for feeling, for
yielding, for the sheer urgency of his life within her, the
source of life banishing death.

Sean took her languorous body with a tenderness he had
never before shown her or any other, wanting to lose his
soul utterly in her softness, to take her thorny, stubborn
spirit inside himself and ease the prick of her fears. When
at last the quickening rhythm of his desire carried her
with him to fulfillment, he found effortless peace. Afterward, he drew up the covers and brought her close to him.
"You haven't won yet," she whispered sleepily.

"Not yet, little one," he whispered back, and brushed her forehead with his lips as she burrowed closer.

Near midnight there was a hesitant rap at Sean Culhane's bedroom door. With drowsy reluctance, Culhane disengaged from Catherine's body and slipped out of bed. Opening the door a crack, he peered out, smoothed his hair, then opened the door completely. "What is it?"

Rafferty stared at his naked master and cleared his throat. "Ah, Peg thought ye might want a bite of supper, seein' as—" He touched his forelock to Catherine, who, like a small, ruffled owl, regarded him from the bed. "Evenin', miss . . . ye an't had dinner today."

Seemingly oblivious of the other man's embarrassment, Culhane nonchalantly turned to Catherine. "Are you hungry, English?"

Rubbing sleep from her eyes with a fist, she nodded. "Starved."

"Tell Peg she has two for dinner." He started to close the door, then added casually, "Clean this mess up, will you?"

Rafferty scowled as he tramped back downstairs. "Lord of the manor, bah!"

Catherine rolled up the sleeves of one of Culhane's shirts and grinned as she took a handful of material in at the waist of his breeches, which threatened to drop about her ankles. Recklessly, she pirouetted. "Rawther dashing, 'ay wot? Mawster Brummell would be green!" She gave them another hike and looked at him mischievously. "Your household may think you've developed a peculiar taste in bedmates."

He grinned as he tucked in his own shirt. "Your school days of passing as a boy are done, girl."

Frowning, she peered skeptically into the pier glass. "I cannot have changed so much in two months!"

"Take a roving bachelor's unprincipled word for it, lass. That little broadside could sink the King's Navy. As for those topsails, pack them into one of your Le Roy dresses and Napoleon himself would heave to."

Ignoring his roguish grin over her shoulder in the mirror, Catherine said abruptly, "You were well informed before you abducted me, weren't you? Even about the contents of my wardrobe." He turned and began to rifle through his chest. She advanced on him, still gripping her drawers. "Was Mignon, my new French maid, one of your spies?"

"Use this for a belt." He slapped a scarf into her hand. "Your birthday ball during the Christmas holidays was a great success; the London papers covered it with complete gush about your wardrobe."

As they walked downstairs, Catherine commented, "It's good of Peg to hold dinner. Her days are long and this one must have been particularly difficult."

"She's hoping to divert my inclination to hang Moora by her thumbs," Culhane laconically replied.

Catherine came to an instant halt. "Please don't hurt her! She has a wretched existence. The fish make her ill . . ."

"Why do you say her life is wretched? People elsewhere in Ireland are starving in droves. Moora will be as round as her mother by the time she's forty. And she has Sundays off. What do you have?"

She unconsciously laid a hand on his arm. "Don't you see? You and I have known all sorts of advantages. Moora cannot even read. She could be a lovely young woman, but instead she's worked like a farm beast from sunup to sundown. And the cruelest part of it is she's totally, miserably aware of her lot. She has every right to hate me!"

"But no right to murder." At her anguished look, he covered her hand with his. "Don't worry, I won't stretch her thumbs, even if she does bake croissants like rocks."

Not completely mollified, Catherine slowly accompanied him down the final flight. He had not said he would forbear from punishing Moora, and she was well aware that what Sean Culhane did not say could fill volumes.

Peg, waiting at the foot of the staircase, looked Catherine up and down and sniffed, "Barefoot." She glared at Culhane. "She'll catch her death! Supper's in the Rose Room." With that, Peg flounced upstairs.

As he seated her in the rose-silk-lined salon next to his study, Catherine could swear her escort looked a trifle sheepish. He surveyed the elaborately set, damask-covered table critically. "I wonder where Peg got the flowers?"

Sniffing the delicate perfume of the arrangement of winter roses between lighted tapers, Catherine smiled. "She has a plot in the kitchen garden. It seems incredible that Ireland has flowers even when the rest of Europe is buried in snow."

He slipped into his chair. "We owe our even climate to the Gulf Stream; it brings warm waters from the tropics as far away as South America."

Rafferty shambled in with a towel over his arm and a chilled bottle of champagne. As he dourly poured glasses for them in the approved fashion, Culhane commented dryly, "The larder must have been short of leftover stew tonight." Averting his eyes, Rafferty plugged the bottle into the ice bucket and shuffled out.

"What a lovely room," Catherine murmured, surveying the fine paintings and crystal chandelier. She sipped the champagne, her eyes twinkling mischievously over the rim of her glass. "So intimate. Do you entertain here often?"

"I don't usually bother with preliminaries," he said flatly.

She laughed without humor. "No, you don't. In that sense, our first meeting was unforgettable."

He started to reply when Peg bustled in with a tray of cold meats and cheeses. At a decorous distance from the food was folded a pair of men's woolen stockings. Her nose tickled by bubbles, Catherine blinked and sneezed over her champagne. Culhane laughed. "Be a good girl, English, and don Peg's offerings."

Peg snorted, but she did not budge until Catherine had pulled on the stockings and thanked her. " 'Tis glad I am to see some has manners about the place," she huffed, with a look at the unrepentant rogue grinning back at her. "Don't ye smirk at me. Rafferty's right, ye know," she gruffly admonished him as she headed for the door. "Ye've got all the charm of an Irish mule." His roar of laughter followed her out of the room.

Catherine stuck her nose up over the table as she finished adjusting the stockings. "She adores you."

He looked at her for a moment with his long-lashed

green eyes and sipped at his champagne. "Yes, I suppose she does."

Giving a last twist to the stockings, she eyed him thoughtfully. A good many women probably adored him; he made other men seem tame as sheep. The white shirt, loosely open to his slim waist, set off the dark good looks of his Moorish ancestry. Long fingers negligently about the glass of pale amber champagne as he relaxed in the opposite chair, ruffled black hair curling slightly about his face, he regarded her lazily. Suddenly realizing she was staring back with open assessment, Catherine flushed and sought refuge in her champagne.

"Don't drink that so quickly," Culhane warned. "It works havoc on an empty stomach."

"Thank you for the advice, but I was virtually weaned on champagne."

Serving her a portion of meat and cheese, he grimaced. "What a spoiled little hussy you must have been!"

"Completely," she mumbled unabashedly with a full mouth. She drained the champagne and held out her glass with an impudent smile, eyes iridescent in the candlelight.

Culhane refilled her glass. "Did your grandmother teach you to use your eyes like that?" he asked suddenly.

She stared at him in bewilderment. "*Use* them? How do you mean?"

He smiled slowly at her confusion. "You're singularly unaware of yourself. Haven't men ever flattered you?"

She picked at the meat, irritated. "Of course. But flattery is mere verbiage, and in my case, embellished with expectations of dowry."

"You think a man would want you only for your money?" he murmured, absently popping a grape into his mouth.

She took another sip of champagne to cool her cheeks. "No, not entirely. There's a title to consider, and of late . . . just before I left England . . ."

"Before you left?" Sean pursued intently.

"Men seemed to find me appealing for other, ah, more basic reasons," she finished lamely.

"I can imagine," Sean commented a trifle sourly. "And how did you react?"

"I . . ." Suddenly weary of his prying, she snapped, "That's really none of your affair. Besides, what difference does it make now why they wanted me? I should have lost my freedom in any circumstance. Marriage for a woman is a prison, the prisoner only more or less willing to endure her confinement. Whether a man wants to delve into her bank account or her bodice, it's all the same."

Sean's eyes fell to the cleft of her breasts as her gestures loosened her shirt from its makeshift belt. Unaware of his warming gaze, Catherine waved her glass and unexpectedly giggled. "I'm no longer a candidate for any man's marriage bed, thanks to you. Used goods is what I am." She grinned wickedly, leaning forward, not noticing his restlessness. "But a mistress can play her own game. Why shouldn't I be wanton, since I cannot be wed?"

She hopped out of her chair, snatched the bottle before he could stop her, and, oddly graceful despite her tipsiness and floppy stockings, postured lightly about the room. "To think, I'm free after all. I've just been too sour to realize it." She took a swig from the bottle and beamed at him. "All because of you, Eros Tyrannus." A thought struck her and she managed a more or less straight line to his lap. As she snuggled up to him confidingly, Culhane firmly removed the champagne bottle from her fingers. "What do you think I should do? Should I take a great many lovers or just one rich, dotty old man?" Not waiting for an answer, she pondered, frowning, "Young lovers must be like puppies: a great deal of trouble. One sweet old man would probably do nicely." She brightened. "Perhaps he'll only want to stroke me once in a while." She leaned back in his arms and peered at him from under long lashes. "Would you like to stroke me?"

"Very much."

She giggled, and growled throatily, "I'll wager you would. Peg says you're a real tomcat."

He grimaced, then tapped her on the nose. "You might fall in love, little cynic. Then what?"

Vigorously, she shook her head, sending her hair swinging. "Oh, no. Never. To be in love is to be a cat's-paw. You and I are too wise for that." Her owlish expression gave way to a frown, and she tugged at her shirtfront with puzzled irritation. "I'm hot. Why does cold champagne make one hot?"

"I don't know, little one."

She dabbled her fingers in his champagne glass and trailed them wetly down her body from throat to waist. "That's nice." She dabbled them again and ran them across his chest. "See, it's marvelously cool." Sean swiftly caught her fingers. "Don't you like it?" she asked in a small, dazed voice.

"It's time you were in bed."

"Oh!" She looked at him sagely. "You want to take my clothes off." Slipping out of his arms, she glided over to the fire, hips swaying provocatively albeit with a slight lurch. Abruptly, she sat on the floor and began pulling off the stockings.

"What are you doing?"

"Undressing. I've been quite obedient lately. Haven't you noticed?" She stood up and clumsily unknotted the scarf. A second later the breeches dropped to the floor.

"Kit, not here," he protested roughly.

"Why not?" she said fuzzily, working on the shirt buttons as she got to her feet. "It's a lovely room. Just like the inside of a rose. And we've a lovely soft couch." A finger waggled at the silk chaise lounge. "I once saw a lady—well, not precisely a lady—take off absolutely everything on a stage in front of a roomful of men. So, you've no need to worry about my undressing in here. Rooms like this are designed for seduction; Papa has them at home." She paused, thinking. "The actress disrobed so slowly I was bored, but the men seemed to prefer it." A silken shoulder slid free of the shirt and Sean's protest stuck in his throat. Then the other shoulder appeared and the creamy translucence of her skin made his loins ache as her small breasts curved above the garment. Noticing his eyes, she smiled and hummed softly to herself. By maddening degrees that played merry hell with his restraint, she let the shirt slide to the floor and stood there, a small, warm Aphrodite.

As if in a trance, she moved to the divan and lay upon it, languidly arching her body. "Come, dear jailer." She lifted her arms to him. But even as his lips found hers, tasting intoxicating wine and dazed desire, her arms slipped

141

limply from his neck as she dropped for the second time that day into oblivion.

Sighing, he lifted her in his arms. Her head slipped over his arm as he picked up the bottle of champagne, checked the foyer, then quickly ascended the stair, his mind and body a knot of frustration. After tucking his beatifically limp burden into bed, he pulled off his clothes and flung open the terrace doors. Standing stark naked outside on the cold flagging, he poured the still-chilly contents of the champagne bottle on the source of his tension.

Early the next morning a head-wagging Rafferty scooped clothing off the salon carpet, while upstairs a miserable Catherine had her head held over the terrace balustrade. Sometime later when, on Culhane's order, breakfast arrived upstairs, she groaned and bolted for the terrace again, wearing only a sheet. Peg shook her head. "Those flowers'll never show their poor heads next season!"

Stumbling back into the room, Catherine hiked the sheet up and kicked at it irritably as it vindictively tried to trip her. Keeping well away from the tray, she sidled crablike over to the bed, then crawled in with a pitiful moan.

"I'll have breakfast at my desk, Peg," Culhane said helpfully.

Plopping the tray down on the desk with a bang that made the bundle in the bed cringe, Peg scolded, " 'Tis ashamed ye should be, porin' all that liquor down the poor child; and after all she's been through!"

Her victim started to protest, when to his surprise, Catherine weakly defended him from the bed. "Please don't shout, Peg. It wasn't his fault. I . . ." Suddenly her eyes widened and she buried herself in the covers with a wail of horror.

Culhane threw back his head with an ungallant hoot. "So, you *do* remember, you sly little boozer!"

Holding her throbbing head, she reared upright, nearly gasping with pain and losing the dignity of her sheet. "You're mean! You're the meanest man in the world . . ."

"If you don't mind spending your charms on a meager

142

audience, I don't mind applauding your amateurish but energetic efforts."

"Oh!" she shrieked, and burst into tears.

Her distress was so obviously genuine that Sean went to her and gathered her into his arms. Sitting on the side of the bed, he nodded the bemused Peg out and tucked Catherine's head into his shoulder despite her tearful struggles. "There, there. Don't cry. You were quite good, really." Catherine groaned and weakly punched at his ribs. "Shhh," he soothed her quickly, "I'm teasing, minx. You had a bad time yesterday. Anyone would have wanted to get tight."

She peered through wet lashes up at him. "Have you ever nearly died?"

"Yes. It isn't much fun, is it?" She shook her head and turned her face back into his chest. "If it's any consolation, I've also been much drunker than you were, and for far less reason."

"But you weren't ass enough to strip," came the muffled, woeful reply.

His lips twitched. "Don't be too sure. Drunk enough, I'd peel for the queen."

She pulled back, intrigued. "You would, wouldn't you?" Quick suspicion danced in her blue eyes. "You haven't taken off your clothes for Princess Caroline, have you? She may not be queen yet, but she has a well-rouged reputation . . ."

Sean pinched her pale cheeks. "What do you know of rouge, brat?"

"Enough. I'm not a child," she retorted. "I wouldn't put it past you to bed a sow if you thought she'd squeal state secrets."

He chucked her under the chin. "Refrain from prying into my affairs and I'll refrain from telling the world you're a sot." He got up and began to rummage through his chest.

Catherine, watching him, suddenly asked, "Did I let you make love to me last night?"

He slowly shook his head. "Why?"

"I . . . I just wondered."

143

"Shall I correct that omission now?" he asked softly, a rare smile easing the lean hardness of his face.

"Oh!" Hastily she clapped a hand to her forehead as he took a step toward the bed. "I still have a headache."

His smile subtly resumed its familiar mocking lines. "For one so young, you're quick to find refuge in dog-eared bedroom diplomacy." She flushed and their easy intimacy was gone.

Culhane slammed the chest lid and said abruptly, "Little else in my wardrobe suits your needs. Peg will bring appropriate clothing if your nose and taste can bear the mustiness of outdated gowns. There may be even, God forbid, petticoats and pantalettes. But," he warned grimly, "if you put on a corset or panniers, I'll tear 'em off." He fished in his pocket and came up with a small, flat object.

She tensed as he came toward her and his fingers found her throat. She decided he was going to kiss her or strangle her, and she had no idea what had prompted him to do either. Looking with some amusement into her wide, uneasy eyes, he unlocked the thrall collar and removed it. Her eyes went cloudy. "Why?" she finally managed to ask softly. "Why now?"

"Partly good behavior," was the laconic reply; then he added more gently, "and partly because heavy jewelry doesn't suit you; but don't ever try to run away from me again." His last words were low, but she did not underestimate their warning.

"I'm sending you to work with Doctor Flynn at the infirmary, but don't get any ideas. If I weren't sure of security, I wouldn't assign you away from the house.

"You'll join me in the salon for dinner each evening, and hereafter, you'll share my bed. Peg has already brought up your things." He saw her brightening gaze dim, and his next words came leaden. "Don't look so forlorn. I'll make love to you again only at your desire."

She was confounded. "You won't touch me?"

He smiled faintly. "Inadvertently, perhaps. To avoid one another absolutely in even so large a bed is impractical."

She considered his proposal, eyes narrowing. Why would he suddenly relieve her of his attentions when she had been so obviously on the verge of capitulation?

Her behavior in the salon had been a shameless invitation. Why shouldn't she use his body as casually as he had hers? That was it! He refused to be her stud. His arrogance demanded more. He wanted to ensnare her mind, perhaps even her love. She was still wearing a slave collar, only now it was silken, invisible. Her eyes flared. "Do you think sheer lust will lead me into betrayal of my father, country, whatever honor I have left? Can't you just let me be!" She was frantic, almost hysterical, but he did nothing to calm her.

"Not yet," he said quietly. "Soon, perhaps. I hope so, for both our sakes."

There was a tap at the door and a flushed, dusty Peg led Danny and Rafferty in with an old trunk and several boxes covered in faded silks. Shooing the gaping porters out, she gave a nod to Sean. "Ye've a messenger waitin' downstairs."

His face a polite mask, Culhane turned to Catherine. "Rafferty will bring the dogcart to the front door at noon. You'll take lunch with Flynn. Rafferty will pick you up later. Tomorrow and thereafter, you'll drive yourself."

Catherine smiled bitterly. "How clever of you to choose such a quaint mode of transportation for me. I can see Fido kicking dust in the faces of your guards."

His lips quirked. "And a pregnant Fido at that. Don't look so horrified; she isn't due for a month." With that tidbit he strolled out of the room, leaving her to cope with alterations, camphor, pins, and Peg's nervous fingers.

The messenger had a sheet of decoded signals. Dismissing the man, Culhane scanned the note on the way to his study. It indicated Messrs. League, Tunney, and Briskell had fled to France after cleaning out their office safe of incriminating papers and a cache of their clients' funds. Like rats, they had kept an escape hole and gotten off with their lives, if not their wealth. The syndicate account at Lloyd's was in escrow while the organization's other investments were being investigated. Trial for captain and crew would be immediate and the lot of them were talking to save their skins. The local magistrate had paid John Enderly a second visit and made tactless reference to his warehouses, but had not produced a search warrant. Sean smiled grimly. The blow to Enderly's purse would amount to a fortune. Now, all the Irishman had to do was wait to see which way he would jump.

CHAPTER 7

The Atlas Myth

Catherine adjusted her heather shawl as the thatch-roofed stone infirmary appeared around a bend of the path. Doctor Flynn might live in solitude, but he had chosen his surroundings for natural luxury. Verdant heather stretched for miles and the view was breathtaking. In the fresh breeze, boats at anchor in the harbor danced at their moorings.

When the door flung open and Flynn briskly strode out, Catherine had a moment's misgiving. What if he should attribute this elevation in her position to Culhane's approval of his new concubine? But, as he helped her from the cart, the doctor's obvious delight to see her dispelled her uneasiness. He ushered her into a sitting room reserved for waiting patients. Empty at the moment, its worn furnishings had a coziness Shelan's rooms lacked. Flynn's head just cleared the lintel as they walked through the corridor that led to a small kitchen and apartments to the rear. In the center of a round oak table carefully laid with linen, pewter, and sturdy blue Delft plates was a small butter crock hastily stuffed with his handsomest flowers. Only dinnerware laid backward revealed a woman's hand was lacking in the preparations. Catherine felt oddly as if she wanted to cry.

After a succulent chowder followed by cream-drenched gooseberries, the doctor gave his new assistant a tour. The ward was a long, cot-lined, whitewashed room partitioned to separate the sexes. Several windows ensured a light, cheery interior on the bleakest days. The ward was spartan but immaculate; he informed her that a slow-witted lad from the nearby village of Ruiralagh came to clean and perform orderly duties. The dispensary was equally spotless.

Her first task at the infirmary was a simple one. Doctor Flynn's eyes not being what they used to be, she was to read aloud to him his new surgical texts from Edinburgh; Latin terms cropped up on every other line. Fortunately, she had been tutored in Latin and managed reasonably well. Quickly fascinated by the workings of the human body and techniques of repairing it, she began to ask intent questions that first amused Flynn, then pleased him.

Upon returning to Shelan, Catherine realized she would have to rush to make herself ready for dinner. Her wardrobe had been hung in an armoire brought down from the attic that afternoon, and a scented bar of soap was tucked in one of the drawers. She noticed her brush rested cosily beside Culhane's shaving things near the washbowl. With a slosh of water from the pitcher, she scrubbed hastily at her face, then spent more time on her hands, wishing for cream to ease their redness and broken nails. Sighing, she swabbed her dripping face with the towel and patted at damp tendrils of hair. After brushing her hair until it shone, she decisively placed the brush at the end of the commode far from Sean's gear. Pulling her hair to one side with a bit of ribbon, she gave it a few twirls with her fingers. With her head tilted to one side to study the effect, she wondered suddenly why she was going to so much trouble for a man she detested? She gave the curls a yank, but she was irritated to see their disarray had more appeal.

Still fiddling with her hair, Catherine ran down the steps, then slowed abruptly to nod decorously to Culhane's puzzled, staring officers who milled about the foyer. Every male head in the room turned to admire the flushed young countess's progress through the crowd and her charming, if somewhat hasty, exit.

She closed the salon door and sagged against it. Clearly, greater freedom went hand in hand with increased exposure as Culhane's mistress. She could imagine the bawdy remarks to be bandied about the officers' table tonight.

She stalked over to the marble fireplace, seized a poker, and stabbed viciously at the fire. Returning the poker to its stand, she sourly eyed the table laid with shimmering crystal and porcelain. The lack of windows in the room added to its aura of cozy intimacy, as did the faded, finely patterned silk wall covering. The furniture was Louis XV; the chair seats upholstered in pale-colored petit points of the changing seasons. Bits of gilt winked in the firelight. Idly, she drifted about, looking at the paintings and water-colors: among them were Liam's lovely, delicate sketches, a Botticelli pen drawing of a nymph, and a David of *Freedom at the Barricades*. The Botticelli, while worth a small fortune, might have been purchased by a past master of Shelan; but the David, despite a Jacobin theme popular among dissident Irish, was no more than a few years old and, like many other paintings in the house, represented a tidy investment. She could not understand Sean Culhane, with his obsession for pumping Shelan's resources into guns and rebellion, permitting such expenditures.

Culhane's deep, melodic lilt startled her. "Do you like Boucher?"

Her eyes slid over the chalk drawing to which he referred as she turned to face him. "No."

The Irishman shrugged out of his dripping cloak, his feral presence making the room's pastel colors seem tepid. "Indeed." One black brow quirked. "Why not?"

"I find his work insipid."

"Is that all?" He was a trifle mocking as he gave the bell rope a tug to summon Rafferty to take his wet cloak.

Her chin came up. "If you mean he reflected a venal society, yes, I've noticed that too."

"Bravo, Countess. Perhaps tutelage at Shelan has proved enlightening."

"I don't need to have my head pushed under the mire to realize it exists!" she retorted. "Have you brought me here tonight to quarrel?"

Rafferty knocked and Culhane shoved the cloak through the door. Scrubbing a hand across his wet hair, he came to stand beside her. "No, English," he said tiredly, "only to keep me company."

Looking at him sideways, Catherine noticed white marks

149

of tension and fatigue at his cheekbones, and the sag of his shoulders. She brought a chair and set it before the fire. "You're tired and chilled," she said firmly, answering his ironic look of surprise.

He dropped gratefully into the chair, and without even a grimace at the mud, she dragged off his boots. He grinned faintly. "Does this concern mean you've lost your itch to cut my throat?"

Without expression, she set his boots before the fire. "Peg told me you saved my life yesterday. No doubt the rescue suited your purposes." Crossing behind him to the table, she poured claret into a goblet. Her voice softened as she handed him the wine, although her hand abruptly withdrew as his fingers brushed hers. "Whatever your intent, I thank you for it." He gave a brief shrug and eyed her thoughtfully.

"You're looking at me strangely. What are you thinking?" she asked with a child's serious intensity.

Sean let his head fall back against his chair. "I'm thinking, little one, you're incredibly appealing in that old blue dress and I'd like to kiss you, to lie quietly before the fire with my head in your lap and trust that torrential rain outside to wash away all our inevitable tomorrows."

He sipped his claret in silence and continued to survey his prisoner as if he had no thought of her discomfiture. "Something's odd about that dress," he announced finally.

Startled, Catherine stepped backward as her critic rose from his chair. To her embarrassed annoyance, he began to undo the fichu of her dress. Although no longer fresh, the airy shawl concealed the daring exposure of her breasts, pressed high by a square-cut, tightly fitted bodice. "Please don't," she pleaded indignantly. "The fichu is entirely suitable. I thought the clothes were to be worn as I chose . . ." A distinct coolness settled about her shoulders as the light scarf slipped away. Seeing the warmth in his eyes as they roved over her throat and breasts, she felt a wave of apprehension.

"Surely you know fichus are no longer worn by sophisticated women," he teased.

"I have no wish to be sophisticated . . ."

"Only suitable." He grinned and she wanted to kick

him. As the slant of her eyes grew more wicked and her flush deepened, he drawled, "I don't recommend your starting a row. While I can think of nothing I'd like better than to tumble you on the rug, I think your resulting shrieks would soon be more those of pleasure than outrage. The men in the next room should find the vocal progression most titillating."

"Oh!" She stamped a foot and glared. "A buck rabbit in rut is more of a gentleman than you!" With her sudden motion, Sean caught his breath. "Stop staring at me!" Her voice and foot rose at the same time, and he quickly caught her wrist.

"Stop bobbling every time you move and perhaps I can." He dragged her to the table, pushed her down into her chair, and gave the bell a tug. "I should like to dine in peace, Countess. Shall we preserve the amenities, or have you forgotten them in your brief sojourn among the peasantry?"

"My manners are hardly in question," she hissed. "You're the one who suggested a roll on the rug!"

He laughed easily as he retrieved his wine from the mantel and sauntered back to the table. "Your neckline made the suggestion. Under the circumstance, I cannot be held responsible."

Her eyes narrowed. "I suppose in a like manner, you feel absolved for attacks on my father!"

Culhane's humor disappeared. "You're in no position to cast blame on anyone. You knew nothing and cared nothing for the condition of my people before you came here. It's remarkable that your oblivion extends to your father's activities as well. If you seek to hound me into rejecting your company, disabuse your mind. Tonight we'll dine together, converse politely together, and bed together. Adjust yourself."

"I wish I'd let you freeze," she grated.

"No you don't," he said calmly.

The door opened just then and Catherine, biting off her retort, looked up. "Moora!"

"Milady." Averting her eyes, Moora began to serve the plates.

Catherine tried to ease the girl's discomfiture. "I'm very glad you and Maude have recovered."

Astonishment banished Moora's shame. "Maude's well enough, I suppose. Better off than me, havin' her rest under the cold, wet sod." She caught her master's warning look too late, and stood tensely, twisting her hands in her apron.

"She's dead?" Catherine stammered, and turned to Culhane. "But . . . you said . . ." Her eyes dimmed. "Oh, God."

"That will do, Moora," Culhane curtly dismissed the pale servant girl.

"Why?" Catherine murmured. "Why didn't you tell me?"

"Because I knew you'd be upset."

"May I attend the services?"

"Maude was buried this evening."

"Is that why you were late . . . and so wet?"

"Yes." He did not add that the local priest had chosen to regard the circumstances of the madwoman's death as dubious and refused to perform the last rites, that only he and Flannery had been at the gravesite to inter the body.

"Buried in a dark hole in the rain," Catherine whispered numbly.

He leaned over and caught her face in his hands. "It could have been you. Be glad to be alive." She stared at him, saying nothing. His hands lowered. "Drink your wine. All of it, quickly." Like a child at an imaginary tea party, she obeyed. "Now start on the roast pork and don't stop until you've done." Even though his own food grew cold, Culhane refilled her glass and prodded her to eat and drink until a trace of color returned to her face. Deliberately, he talked monotonously of inconsequential nothings until her lids drooped, then gathered her up and carried her to bed.

That night fearful nightmares left Catherine shaken and drenched with perspiration. In semiconscious moments she clung to Culhane in terror. Unable to understand her incoherent cries, he could only hold her, whispering softly, and though exhausted himself, would soothe her into troubled sleep, only to find her thrashing a short time later.

Haggard, his eyes burning, Sean watched the sunrise and rubbed the dark stubble of his jaw as he stood at the windows. Catherine was sleeping fitfully. Crossing to the commode, he poured a bowlful of cold water, then shoved his head into it. Still dripping, he shaved quickly and dressed. He swung on a cloak against the damp and went out to saddle Mephisto.

As Catherine, pale and drawn, rolled over to greet Peg and a breakfast tray, Sean knocked on Doctor Flynn's door. By the time she had donned a rose woolen dress, wrapped the heather shawl mantilla-fashion about her head, and driven the dogcart to Flynn's door, he was saying good-by. "Is someone ill?" she asked.

Doctor Flynn took her hand. "No, but this young mule is bucking for trouble." He looked at Culhane. "You cannot train men from dawn to dark and spend every free moment over account books without breaking your health. Atlas was a myth."

Culhane shrugged. "Atlas was a fool; he served everyone's interests but his own."

Flynn scoffed. "And you don't?"

Culhane stonily returned his stare and, with a brief nod to Catherine, swung up into his saddle, then galloped the big black away toward Shelan. Flynn shook his head. "There goes a fool, indeed. He'll end in a noose if that wolf pack he leads doesn't turn on him first. He's too fine to treat his life so cheaply."

Frowning against the sun-pierced haze, Catherine looked up at him. "I'm forced to disagree, doctor. He's a ruthless, dangerous man. I doubt if anyone at Shelan will ever be a threat to him. He holds that wretched place in a grip of iron, pitiless and unfeeling."

A glint appeared in Flynn's eyes. "You've cause to complain of ill treatment, but I believe you judge him too harshly. It's Culhane prestige that holds Shelan together, not Sean. The Irish are a stiff lot in some ways. Sean is rumored a bastard, and they won't follow bastards, even legally accepted ones; that was proven by the O'Neills' clash over the Tyrone succession in Queen Elizabeth's day. If Liam went, the rest would scatter like winter leaves."

Her eyes narrowing, Catherine's fingers tightened on her shawl. Flynn had unwittingly supplied the key to Shelan's bloodless destruction.

The oblivious doctor stared at the horseman cresting the horizon. "If Sean Culhane seems to be made of iron, it's because he's had to be. You've seen the brutal life of the common people; yet it's far better at Shelan than in most parts of Ireland. Because of Sean, scores are fed, clothed, sheltered, and given a purpose beyond their usual futile existences. You say he's unfeeling, yet he came here today out of concern for you."

She stared at him in astonishment, then grimaced. "I must have kept him awake all night."

"I don't believe Sean thinks of himself often. He's autocratic, but he's the most selfless man I know."

"He regards me as property. He maintains me as such. The day he tires of me will mark the end of his concern."

"But surely you don't suppose he means to kill you?"

"I know too much," she said flatly. "At times, he seems to forget how much he hates me, but he always remembers."

He patted her hand. "You've had enough of fear and death of late. It's time you thought of life. A young woman in Ruiralagh is giving birth today. I want you to assist the delivery."

"But I know nothing about babies."

"If I doubted your abilities, I wouldn't ask you to come. Sean knows you're with me; he'll not look for you tonight."

Twenty-one hours later, Eileen Devlin gave birth to a healthy baby boy whose red, shriveled face wrinkled into a toothless wail moments after he emerged from his exhausted mother. The three who had waited so long for him were convinced he was the handsomest baby in creation.

From the study windows, Sean saw a small, warm-colored figure kneeling on the hillside against a sea of sweeping furze. He threw on his jacket, left the house, and quickly strode across the rising moor. Catherine did not hear him until he was nearly touching her. The shawl

154

draped over her head and shoulders and the serenity of her tired face as she turned to him resembled the ageless madonna in the Kenlo chapel. She had planted a handful of white, starlike wild flowers from Peg's garden in the fresh earth of Maude Corrigan's grave. He noticed her fingerprints in the raw, thin soil. Although their stems were a trifle limp, the flowers waved bravely in the breeze from the sea. "They're called stars-of-Bethlehem," she told him quietly. "If they survive, they'll cover the hillside one day."

He dropped to one knee and tamped earth around a forlorn bloom that was trying to blow over. "How's the baby?"

She smiled, a soft light in her eyes. "A beautiful boy. Doctor Flynn says it was a relatively easy birth for a first child. Only a common, everyday miracle."

Sean started to touch her cheek, then reluctantly withdrew his dirty fingers and rose to his feet, drawing her up with him. "Get some sleep. You need it."

She gazed up at him, the windblown shawl casting angular shadows across her fine-boned face. "And you? When will you rest?"

"Tonight." He smiled faintly. "If we can put off the customary quarrel."

Her lips twitched. "I believe my restraint is equal to your own."

That evening when Sean entered the salon, he whistled softly in pleased surprise. Her hair caught up in a loose, rippling cascade, Catherine waited by the fire in a watered silk gown of a pale green that accented the iridescence of her eyes. Tiny cream lilies were embroidered with gold threads on the lace-bordered bodice panel, and snug sleeves ended at the elbow in a froth of lace ruching. The lace was faded, the gold tarnished to bronze, and her hair too long to be coaxed into tightly coiled ringlets of a past era, but by the amber candleglow her aura was softer, more wistfully appealing than that of any powdered beauty. "Turn," he ordered softly. Gracefully, she obeyed. Blue-black hair that fell nearly to the small of her back seemed to tug her small head back slightly on her slender neck, giving her naturally ramrod-proud carriage a defiant look. Her waist seemed little more than a wisp, and her small, high breasts were creamy perfection. "Aye," he breathed, "it's a real blueblood you are, Countess. If your grandmother looked anything like you, old Louis must have galloped after her the length of Versailles, gout and all."

Smiling demurely, she gave him a deep curtsy.

"That dress calls for pearls," he observed. "Unfortunately, the family coffers have been bare of such trinkets for some time. Still . . ." He moved closer to her, dropping his jacket on a chair. "I prefer you without jewels." Smiling as her eyes widened, he hooked a finger under the ribbon at her throat. "Even this competes with your eyes, English."

Unlike the previous night, she stood without protest as his fingers undid the ribbon, brushing her neck as he withdrew it. His eyes held hers so long her confidence was undone. When he started to touch her cheek, she backed away, babbling hastily, "We're having quail tonight. I hope your fatigue endures such tedious fare; it's so difficult to extract meat from tiny game fowl."

"No less difficult than to extract a response from fairer game," he replied slowly.

Cursing her weakness for dressing to please him, she murmured, "Shall we sit down?" He politely stepped aside to let her pass and she did so swiftly, but somehow he arrived at the table in time to seat her with exaggerated courtesy. While they waited for Rafferty, the silence grew ponderous.

"I hope you slept well," Culhane said conversationally. If it were not for the faintly mocking gleam in his green eyes, she could almost believe he was solicitous.

"Very well, thank you. I was quite lazy; I didn't rise until late afternoon." Her dark blue eyes briefly lifted to his, then slid away again.

"My men must have found the sight of you coming down the stair a pleasant aperitif."

Angry spots of color appeared on her cheeks despite her firm resolution not to fight. "No one saw me. I came down early."

His lips curved lazily. "Were you so eager for my company?"

"Hardly eager," she snapped. "I resent being paraded as your mistress."

"If I wished to parade you, we would be dining less privately. Why so reluctant, Countess? You're not unappealing. And your grandmother was a courtesan, so why the prudery? You're a little stuffy for one so young."

She glared at him. "Compared to you, Attila was stuffy. And my grandmother was no courtesan, whatever your sordid information!"

"So much for your restraint," he commented dryly. "Wasn't she a mistress of Louis XIV?"

"For a matter of months, yes! Her husband's position and fortune were at stake."

"Oh? I heard she profited personally. A matter of a diamond and sapphire collar and some other trifling baubles."

Catherine flushed. "They were gifts. Why shouldn't she have taken them? Louis had what he wanted."

"A practical attitude, my lady. You may be more of a mistress at heart than you think. I wonder . . . what would you trade to protect a man you loved?"

"I've never been in love, and with any luck, I intend to elude that state."

"I think not, Countess. You remind me of a small porcupine: all barbs on the outside, but vulnerable on the inside."

"Then I must beware the hounds, sir," she returned tartly.

"Aye," he grinned slowly, "take care they don't turn you belly up."

Her hot retort interrupted by Rafferty and his tray, she glared at the uncomfortable man the entire time he served her. He hastily waited on Sean, then withdrew, and she stabbed viciously at a crisply browned bird, which instantly skidded across the plate and landed stickily on the fine Aubusson rug. Culhane burst into a rude hoot of laughter. She scowled at him so fiercely that his amusement mounted. Gradually, her own sense of humor tickled by his infectious laughter, Catherine began to giggle and finally joined his mirth completely.

Attacking dinner with hearty appetites, they both finally sat back surfeited. "I'm beginning to understand why the wilted ladies of Mother's generation fainted at every turn," Catherine sighed. "It's impossible to both breathe and eat in this dress."

Sean grinned wickedly. "Shall I ease your dilemma?"

"I think not, sir. Lacings are all that prevent my exploding." She rose, and carrying her brandy, went to sit on the rug before the fire, skirts blooming outward like a silken flower. Sean followed and seated himself beside her, an elbow resting on one upraised knee. He silently offered to replenish her glass. "No, thank you. I prefer to mount the stairs on my own tonight." Her smile turned thoughtful. "Doctor Flynn says you went to see him because of me. Why?"

His green eyes were unreadable. "We both needed sleep. Any other questions?"

"No," she replied softly, "no other questions." She studied his profile in the glow of the fire: the straight nose; the hard, sensual mouth; the lean, stubborn jaw; the proud carriage of the dark head; the hazy green of his eyes under their black lashes. "Doctor Flynn is right; you look exhausted. Isn't there anyone to whom you can delegate authority?"

His lips curled. "Like Liam? He's next to useless. Flannery? He's nearly sixty. Soft slippers before a hearth are all he wants, and he's earned them. These last nights I've begun to share his inclination." He stared into the fire several long moments.

Suddenly he uncurled and stretched his length on the rug, dropping his head into her lap. He sleepily looked up into her startled eyes. "Wake me when you tire of playing pillow. I need only a few minutes . . ." His words trailed away as his eyes closed. Seconds later, his head dropped toward her and his breathing evened.

Catherine sat motionless for a long while. Utterly relaxed, he looked boyish and she could at last visualize him as younger than Liam. He seemed defenseless. Very lightly, she began to stroke his temples and brow, smoothing back the black, ragged fringe of his hair. Then, almost without her realizing it, her fingertips wandered to his lips, traced them.

His hand came from nowhere and gently caught her roving fingers. Green eyes stared dazedly into hers. Twisting out of her lap, he pressed her down onto the carpet so that he partly lay across her body. Removing the few pins from her hair, he spread the long tresses like a dark cloud. Her eyes turned inky, as her breasts, pressed high above her bodice, quickly rose and fell; but when his lips lowered to hers, she tensed. "No, I . . . I didn't mean . . . don't!"

The look in his eyes faded and he rolled violently away from her. For a long time he lay still, his face averted.

"I'm sorry," she whispered. "I shouldn't have touched you. I thought you were asleep."

"You could test the passions of the dead, girl," he retorted. "And if you don't wish to try mine further, I suggest you retire. I'll be up directly."

She rose quickly as he got to his feet. His face was its usual hard mask as he towered over her. "Liam is due back in the next few days," he said abruptly. A fleeting look of undisguised relief came over her lovely features and his mask slipped a little. Turning his back and leaning against the mantel, he lifted the brandy snifter to his lips as she closed the door. Moments later, the thin glass burst into sparkling fragments. He stared at the blood trickling down his fingers and idly picked the tiny crystal daggers out of his flesh, welcoming the pain as a distraction from the greater, unexpected pain her unguarded look had caused him. After wrapping his hand in a napkin, he began to drink steadily out of the decanter, finishing it just before becoming too drunk to manage the stairs.

As Catherine's eyes opened in the morning, her nose wrinkled in distaste, sniffing overpowering alcohol fumes. Turning on her side, she saw an unconscious and partly clothed Culhane lying on his back, his discarded shirt twisted under him, his right hand clumsily wrapped in a blood-soaked napkin. He stank of brandy and he looked pale.

Quickly wrapping a sheet about herself, she slipped out

of bed and found a towel by the washbowl. After she soaked and wrung it out, she brought it back to the bed, then carefully pried his fingers loose from the makeshift bandage. The hand, badly gashed, was still seeping, though the fingers were stuck together with dried blood. Careful not to awaken him, she bathed the cuts and found a few tiny glass splinters. Swearing softly, she checked more carefully, but he seemed to have found the rest.

Catherine gave the bell rope a brisk tug, then began to undress him. There was no need to worry that he might awaken. She had just pulled a sheet over him when Peg poked in her head. "What ails him?" she asked curiously, coming over to the bed. "He's white as that sheet."

"Drunk," Catherine said briefly. "He's hurt his hand. Can you find some bandages and wine to wash the wound?"

"Aye." Peg frowned. "That's no trouble, but it an't like Sean to tipple overmuch." She looked at the younger woman suspiciously. "The two of ye still fightin'?"

"No, Peg, we weren't fighting." With a look of anxiety, Catherine sat down on the bed. "I have no idea what made him drink. I doubt if my customary rejection of his advances could have set him off. He was worn out last night; perhaps he simply couldn't hold it."

"Ha!" snorted Peg. "That boyo can outdrink the British fleet when he sets his mind to it! He meant to get drunk."

"Well, he ought to sleep it off, even if he takes all day. He's practically dropping in his tracks." She gave the reeking Irishman a jaundiced look. "If he weren't drunk, it would take a clout with a broadax to keep him in bed."

"Aye, that's true," agreed Peg placidly.

Catherine frowned, considering. "Perhaps Liam could take over some of the work. Last night, Sean said he'd be returning this week. Surely he's not entirely useless."

"Mayhap. And what did you say?"

"About what?" Catherine asked, preoccupied.

"About Liam's homecomin'."

"Oh, I'll be delighted to see him." A soft smile stole across Catherine's lips. "Liam's really rather like an engaging boy. These last months would have been unbearable without his kindness. I'd probably still be up to my

160

elbows in fish and laundry if it weren't for his intervention."

Peg cocked her head to one side. "Ye're right about one thing: Liam's more boy than man. But as for his gettin' ye out of the fish heap, it an't likely. His intercession with Sean nowadays is as unlikely as Saint Peter kickin' my old man's backside. If ye're dolin' out gratitude, place it where it's due. This unconscious lump may not be in any shape to say 'ye're welcome,' but it's to him ye should turn, not that so-called lily-white knight. Liam an't walkin' home on water, ye know. He's comin' on a ship." Peg stalked out to find bandages, leaving the bemused girl to dress.

CHAPTER 8

The Idiot and the Butterfly

Catherine left her jailer freshly sponge-bathed and bandaged, then headed Ellie to the infirmary at a brisk pace. Except for Doctor Flynn, the infirmary was empty and remained so throughout the day. They had only two visitors: a solitary drunkard suffering from delirium tremens, and the half-witted boy, Padraic, who cleaned the place and emptied dry bedpans as if they were full. She spent the morning reading to Flynn. After lunch they walked across the fields to the bluff of Malinmore, which overlooked the bay.

The view was enormous. On the way to the bluff, Flynn pointed out the drumlins, which he jokingly called "fairy hills," whale-shaped mounds that rumbled up from the rocky soil in huge piles of gravel and dirt. Much of the rock sheeting of the area was exposed, leaving coastal soil thin and untillable, the local inhabitants forced to take their living from the sea. The coastal mountain range, which ran into the Derryveaghs, rose in a blue haze around the bay. From atop the bluff, he pointed out the distant River Eske, which twined like a thick silver serpent deep in the opposite curve of the bay. From the great height of Malinmore Head one could view the spectacular coastline for miles. Mammoth limestone escarpments hundreds of feet high jutted outward along the coast like stone ships at anchor. It was wild and rocky and savagely beautiful, the crashing surf at its base forming plumed white ranks.

Monotonously, they attacked the shore, only to be thrown back to march again.

On the way back to Shelan at day's end, Catherine was singing her bawdy song to Ellie when a horseman barreled around a bend in the road, nearly upsetting the light wicker cart. Barking, Ellie pulled at her traces until Catherine could barely manage her. When the dog quieted, she twisted about on the wooden seat and glared angrily up at the horseman, who stared back. Abruptly, her anger was snuffed. "Liam!"

The young lord slid off his horse and walked over to the cart. "I'm sorry I startled you, Catherine. Are you all right?"

Catherine was by now accustomed to apologies from the young Irishman, but this one was different: less fumbling, less . . . apologetic. His fair hair bronzed by the setting sun, Liam was deeply tanned, his eyes a more startling blue than a month past. "Yes, of course, I'm quite all right. Welcome home!" She smiled up at him.

He rested a gloved hand on the woven rim of the cart. "I rode out to meet you. Flannery said you'd be at the infirmary." His approving eyes took in her attire. "You look lovely. Apparently your lot has improved in my absence."

She regarded him intently. "Perhaps *because* of your absence. Did you make a pact with Sean to go away if he eased the terms of my imprisonment?"

He shrugged. "Yes, we had an agreement."

"But why would he want you to go?"

His lips tightened. "We quarreled. I'll not say I'm sorry for it. The rift has been a long time coming. I didn't fight him physically, so in that, at least, I kept my promise."

"Liam—"

"Listen," he interrupted urgently. "I can see you now. Sean's too busy to keep track of me." Noting her silence, he plunged on with determination. "You said once you wanted to go painting with me. I can come after lunch if you can elude Flynn for an hour. I'll signal with a scarf from the bluff. You can see the rise from the south end of the infirmary and signal back."

She still hesitated, without really knowing why. "But the patients . . ."

163

He flattened the objection. "Flynn hasn't had patients since his wife died seven years ago. Say yes. There's no harm in it," he pressed, then laughed lightly. "Surely you know my intentions are honorable?"

She flushed. "It's not that. I . . . you're right, of course. I admit to a raging case of spring fever . . . I suppose because I'm sometimes afraid this spring may be my last."

Seeing her face cloud, he took her hand. "Don't worry, Catherine. You'll soon be free."

Catherine gazed at him thoughtfully. He was no longer the shy, hesitant young man he had been. Now he sounded confident, as if he knew what he wanted and how to attain it.

Still, she was uneasy after he left. She gnawed her lip as the cart rolled along. She ought to be delighted by Liam's new assertiveness, but she was not. His temporarily leaving Shelan to ease her lot had been one thing; to be asked to leave his ancestral home forever was another. Yet she must persuade him to leave in order to disband the rebels at Shelan. Could she lead him into poverty and certain exile, even peril of his life if his brother discovered his intent? She did not dwell on her own fate as his accomplice.

Sean was still asleep as Catherine eased into the bedroom. Slipping off her shawl, she looked down at him for a long moment. Asleep, he seemed vulnerable, alone, no longer a killer bent on revenge. If he hated her once without reason, how much more would he hate her for destroying his life's work, his bitter reason for existence? She had an eerie premonition that disaster for them all had been set into motion.

Even as she watched him, Sean's lashes flickered and his green eyes gazed into hers with an unguarded intensity that was almost painful. He propped up on one elbow, letting the sheet fall carelessly down his lean body. An unexpected wave of desire almost dizzied her and she tightly hugged the shawl to still her tension.

Sean stared at her as if she were some wraith, the light from the windows at her back throwing her into relief. Mercifully, his attention instantly shifted to the light. "Good God, is it twilight? Damnation!" He swung his legs out of bed and threw the covers back, angrily looking for his breeches. She drew back as he brushed by to find his clothing neatly folded on the chest. "I know you meant well, English, but I don't thank you for letting me waste the day." He winced as he quickly drew on his breeches. Noticing his neatly bandaged hand, he glanced at Catherine, who stood with her face in shadow. "My carelessness in my cups was no less foolish than you letting me play indolent country squire." Faintly puzzled by her lack of response, he lightly teased, "You're an oyster tonight, English. Afraid I'll trot you back to your dungeon? All in all, by letting me sleep you've probably saved me from an aching head at best, and cost me tonight's sleep for a bout with the accounts at worst." Favoring the injured hand, he dragged on a shirt, muscles running taut across his belly and back. As he buttoned awkwardly, he peered at her more closely. "Why so grim? Or are you? I can hardly see your face."

"Liam is home," she answered quietly.

His fingers hesitated, then continued more slowly. "You were glad enough to hear of his return last night. What's wrong? Did he bring a rich heiress back from Baltimore?"

She turned away and walked toward the windows. He could just see the strangely beautiful planes of her face in the dusky light. He moved to stand close behind her, his hands coming up to clasp her shoulders lightly, naturally. "What's the matter, Kit? When you don't rise to my barbs, I feel I'm winning. Call me a foul name and you'll feel better."

His lips were close to her hair and her mind foundered. In another moment he would kiss her and her resistance would cave in. "Sean, let me go back to England. Kill me. Do whatever you like, only let it end *now.*"

Sean dropped his hands and padded away. Silently he prowled, looking for his boots, then found them and sat on the chest while he awkwardly pulled them on with one hand.

"Do I merit an answer?" Catherine asked.

"It's no," he said briefly, rising to his feet, and without looking back he strode out of the room.

* * *

Catherine dined alone, and after spending some hours studying a book borrowed from Flynn, she went alone to bed to lie sleepless as the new moon's thin, thready line of molten silver trickled across the black, polished sea. Finally she drifted into troubled sleep and at dawn awoke to find Culhane's side of the bed unused. Rain obscured the horizon; the room was chill and damp. After washing, she pulled on a dark blue velveteen dress with pantalettes and an extra petticoat added for warmth. Downstairs, she persuaded Peg to find one of Culhane's old cloaks, then wrapped herself well before going out in the wet, gray weather.

After a morning of studying and reading with Flynn, she had slipped into the infirmary ward at midday to scan the bluff, but no white scarf waved through the haze. Liam would hardly arrange a meeting in the rain, and a walk in such foul weather would be difficult to explain to Flynn. When nearly two weeks of uninterrupted wet weather followed, she was almost relieved. She saw Liam only on brief occasions, never alone.

Flynn dismissed his charge early in particularly foul weather that she might get home before the light failed entirely; on one of those stormy days, as Catherine entered the foyer she saw the ballroom door ajar. The ivory and gilt ballroom, although the same size as the great hall, was unused because Liam refused to expose its frescos and chandeliers to the careless vandalism of his brother's mercenaries. Curious, she took a peek, and finding the room empty, slipped in, then carefully shut the door. Leaving a trail of puddles across the polished parquetry, she hurried to the gleaming walnut pianoforte silhouetted against rain-washed Venetian windows. Despositing her cloak on the floor, she sat down on the bench and lifted the pianoforte cover, then struck a note that timidly hovered in the long room. Above gilt chairs in lonely ranks along the wall, painted courtiers and ladies seemed to listen critically from the garden fresco. Wincing at her own clumsiness, she ran through limbering exercises. Thanks to early training from a demanding French master, she had been by far the finest pianist at the academy, but now her fingers were stiff from lack of practice. Finally she ventured

Schubert's rhapsodic "Ode to Spring," and gradually her fingers began to respond. Fancifully, she imagined the one-dimensional audience was beginning to smile and tap its toes with the urge to dance.

Suddenly a few crystals on the chandeliers tinkled, and she realized the audience was not all a creation of paint. A round-eyed Moora with a scrub bucket in one hand stood just inside the door. "Come in and close the door," Catherine called softly.

In an agony of shyness, Moora obeyed, coming hesitantly to the pianoforte, her heavy shoes echoing on the bare floor. "I heard the music. It was so soft and pretty, I thought it was fairies." She paused, swallowing. "Nobody here plays but Lord Liam, only he an't touched the pianoforte since he come back from Rome."

Catherine smiled ruefully. "I'm out of practice, too, but playing for myself is a bit lonely. Would you like to hear the rest?" Moora hesitated, then nodded. As Catherine continued to play, the Irish girl's eyes took on a glow of wonder.

" 'Tis lovely," she breathed, still swaying when the last notes died away. "Like magic."

Catherine smiled. "Yes, but a magic you can learn to summon as easily as I. Would you like to try?"

Moora's rapture faded and her eyes dropped. "I don't deserve it. I thought Master Sean'd be hangin' me sure for what I done; I got twice as many chores, is all. I don't even have to clean fish no more." Her eyes lifted, warming with shame and confusion. "Ma says ye kept him from punishin' me like he wanted."

Unaware Sean had heeded her pleas for Moora, Catherine felt a catch in her heart. Would she ever understand the Irishman's mercurial moods? She squeezed the girl's hand. "Desperation can drive one to do perilous, unlikely things."

"That it can, Countess," said a clear, definite voice from the doorway.

Moora involuntarily shrank against Catherine as Liam Culhane strolled toward them. "There's no need to be afraid." Catherine steadied the girl with a firm pressure to her back. "Lord Culhane has simply come to join our recital. Haven't you, my lord?"

"That I have." The fair-haired young man grinned. "Shall we play a duet, Lady Catherine?"

Giving him a winning smile, she dragged the limp Moora onto the seat. "I was just about to show Moora a few simple scales. Naturally, any addition to the lesson is welcome."

Moora had difficulty even with basic scales for she could not read; letters assigned to notes made no sense to her. With simple rhyming phrases, Catherine taught her to play a timid scale and silently vowed to teach her the alphabet. Noticing Moora's nervousness in the presence of her subtly yawning master, Catherine lured Liam into a light, bantering conversation that gradually allowed Moora to relax and even to take part. When the girl doggedly managed her scales several times without error, Catherine showed her a simple song; then, to give her an idea of musical structure, she elevated the piece into an easy minuet, changed the timing to a fugue, then expanded it into a waltz. Liam clapped with tactless enthusiasm, oblivious to Moora's faint flush. "My lady, you make me glad I stayed awake."

"It's just as well you did; it's your turn to play." As Liam eagerly slid onto the bench, Catherine silkily slipped off the other side, propelling Moora gently but purposefully ahead of her. Liam sat alone, baffled once more. "If you'll play a minuet," she coaxed, "I'll show Moora a dance suitable to a ballroom." Giving him no chance to demur, she quickly led Moora, clopping awkwardly, onto the floor.

"We'll have to remove our shoes," Catherine told her. "I'll teach you a lady's part, then play the gentleman and partner you." The Irish girl showed a surprising aptitude for the steps and easily mimicked her partner's casual grace, despite Liam's initially rusty playing. Saucily grinning at one another, the two girls began subtly to compete. Catherine led the way to increasingly complicated steps and the Irish girl followed virtually without error. Liam, completely surprised by Moora's unsuspected ability, was openly admiring. At last Catherine spun to a halt and swept her a deep curtsy. "I declare," she laughed merrily with a teasing brogue as Liam applauded, "you've outdone me entirely!"

Moora playfully imitated the curtsy as aptly as a mirror while Liam applauded. "I do dance nice now, don't I?"

"Beautifully!" Catherine assured her. "In fact, so marvelously well you may have the talent to succeed at ballet."

Moora looked dubious. "Ye mean, where doxies flit about in their unmentionables for rich geezers to gawk at?"

Liam laughed. "Moora, you've got the idea exactly."

Catherine glared him into amused silence. "Ballet is more than a display of anatomy. My grandmother, who studied with Beauchamp at Louis's court, considered it an indispensable part of my education." Seeing the girl's still-doubtful face, she gave Liam a defiant look, then began to unhook her dress.

"Christ," he swore softly. "What are you doing?"

"If you've seen a ballet, my lord, you're sophisticated enough to accept the necessity of light attire for freedom of movement." Moora's jaw dropped as Catherine stripped to camisole, petticoats, and pantalettes, briskly tied her hair up with a dress lacing, then addressed the goggling lord. "Do you happen to know Mozart's Concerto in G Major?" Vaguely, he nodded.

Though quite warm, she went through a brief barre to limber her muscles, then nodded to him and began to move airily to the gentle opening passage. Soon her movements acquired quick, hummingbird precision, then again changed to a fluid, dipping, turning waltz, her bare toes pricking out the intricate designs of the more stylized phrases. With her arms taking on the liquid, soaring grace of a winging lark, her fleeting *bourrées* and *piqués en tournants* skimmed the entire ballroom. Splitting darts seemed to hover breathlessly, impossibly, in space. *Ronds de jambe en l'air* followed quick, scissoring flicks of the feet. As the music slowed, the control necessary to the technically more difficult pace seemed unnoticeable. With flawless balance, she finished a *pirouette en attitude* with an extension into *arabesque*, petticoats falling in a gentle blur of white as she was silhouetted in a deepening *penchée* against the rain-streaked windows. Liam's fingers almost ceased to move as the living poetry of the dancer absorbed him like a cool, intense flame, blue white in the fading light, incandescent. He would have happily gone on forever, but Catherine sagged to the floor. He quickly went to her. "Are you all right?"

Wet with perspiration, she looked up at him and panted, "Quite all right! Though I shall regret this in the morning . . . I feel like a wheezy grandame!" He helped her to her feet, and, despite her gasps, she gave him an impish look. "Are you still convinced, my lord, that ballet is a bloomer parade?"

"You make me feel like a fool; less, an incompetent," he replied penitently. "I've never realized more keenly the limits of my art. When you ceased to move, it seemed my heart ceased to beat. Such elusiveness is sublime agony for me."

Her mischief faded and she murmured softly, "Yet there is freedom in the loss." She turned to Moora, who sat tensely on her gilt chair. "What do you think, Moora? Would you like to try?" The girl's eyes, already unaccountably strained, grew desperate and she looked past them at the door. Silently lounging against it with a faint, sardonic smile was Sean Culhane. Slowly, he straightened, turned, and strolled out of the room.

When Catherine, out of breath and disheveled, entered the Rose Salon, the Irishman regarded her with the same mildly amused, slightly nasty look he had worn in the ballroom.

"I'm sorry to be late. I lost track of the time," she babbled, hastily dropping into her chair like an errant schoolgirl. She gave her hair, stuck damply to her face, a quick wipe with her sleeve. She looked nothing like the exquisite dancer of moments before.

"I'm sorry too. I'm hungry. Moora will be sorry too. She'll be up until all hours finishing her work. And Liam . . ." His smile grew a shade nastier. "Liam will be sorry too."

Instantly, her hackles rose. "It wasn't his fault, or hers! I slipped in to play the pianoforte."

"And here I thought Liam had radically improved. Tonight was the first time his Mozart didn't sound lead-fingered."

"You heard him play, and very well, too. He adores music!"

"And you think it would be nice if he were to adore you. I'm sorry, my pet, but you're already sufficiently appreciated by your current lover. You don't have to prance about in pantalettes to attract another."

"You . . . hypocrite!" she stormed, stuttering in rage. "You pompous, uncultivated oaf!"

"You conniving, derriere-waving little show-off!" he roared, his brows meeting in a black scowl.

"What!" she choked, backing up in her seat.

"Don't give me that innocent look!" he snarled. "What better way to wrap Liam about your finger than to play the ethereal nymph. He's slavering after you like a hound after a hart!"

"My dancing was neither lewd nor unseemly! I was not trying to entice him!" Half sobbing, she began to fear he was right in judging his brother's reaction. "Why must you drag everything into the dirt!" As tears seeped from her eyes, Sean saw she had been genuinely unaware of Liam's infatuation. He sighed as she dissolved in tears and dropped her head on her arms.

Finally he dunked his napkin into his water glass and went to her. Dropping on one knee beside her, he firmly clamped the wet, cold cloth on the back of her neck. She yelped and tried to wrench away. "Stay still. You've made enough of a mess." His voice was gruff, yet oddly gentle. Catherine stilled obediently, shoulders still shaking. Frowning at the hasty snarl of ribbon that missed several loops, Sean began to relace her dress.

She became silent as he did her up, and when he finished, she said in a muffled voice, not looking up, "You think I behaved like a trollop, don't you?"

He smiled crookedly. "Both trollop and angel, little one. I can hardly reproach another man's taste in women when it coincides with my own."

"I don't want him to be in love with me," she sniffled.

"Look at me, you soggy little witch," he ordered softly. She turned her head and warily peered at him. He offered her a dry napkin. "Who could fall in love with a woman with a runny nose? Blow." He pushed her hair gently out of her face, then returned to his own chair as a servant brought in dinner. When the man retired, Sean quizzically regarded his companion. "Do you have any idea of what you did this afternoon, not only to Liam, but to Moora?" She silently shook her head, her eyes two big, wet, shining stars. "For a lark, and out of a misplaced sense of philanthropy, you gave Moora a glimpse of a world entirely closed to her. You taught her scales—"

"How long were you listening?" she demanded.

"The acoustics in this house are peculiar. Sounds from the ballroom are often audible in the study." He continued placidly as if she had not interrupted. "Will you teach her letters as well?"

"Yes, why not?"

"What about words? Like *andante, allegro, pizzicato, fortissimo?* You will, of course, have time to teach her to read?"

"I'd like to try . . ."

"And her court dancing? What will her gentlemanly escort say when she inquires if she danced 'good'? Will he supply her a wardrobe appropriate for her elevated status? What will he ask in return?"

"You're distorting everything!"

"And ballet. Where will she dance? The kitchen garden?"

"She has far more ability than you imagine. And if she has talent for ballet, there's no reason she cannot go to Dublin—"

"No reason? She's already eighteen. Ballerinas debut at sixteen. And she'll have to find a protector, for she hasn't a shilling. In Catholic Ireland, professional dancers and actresses are considered prostitutes, as she will doubtless become when she's too old to perform." He paused suspiciously. "Dammit, don't cry again!"

"I'm not!" She glared at him mutinously, her eyes swimming. "You could send her to London."

He snorted, "With what? Fond wishes and a benevolent smirk?"

"That Botticelli alone over there would educate and

train her ten times over! Theatrical performers have been respected in England for years."

"Unlike backward Ireland?"

"Yes! Why shouldn't something alive and beautiful come out of this slaughterhouse? God help you if you ever win your war, for you'll plant your flag of independence upon a heap of carrion!"

He glowered so ferociously that in spite of her rebellious words, her lips trembled. She wilted, sagging disconsolately. "What's the use? I might as well bay at the moon."

"Welcome to earth, Diana," Culhane murmured. She looked up, startled. "I may be as idiotic as you," he said slowly, "but I'll send the wench to Dublin. She can live with a friend of mine and be tutored. If she wants to go on the stage, that's up to her. I hope she has some modicum of talent. I'd hate to waste a Botticelli."

With a whoop of joy, Catherine hurled upon him, nearly toppling his chair.

"Wait, woman! I have a price."

She disengaged as if she had found herself nose to nose with a wolf. "What is it?"

"That you never again wheedle me with tears."

"I didn't wheedle . . ." she began haughtily.

He ignored her. "I cannot afford them. That last sparkler was prohibitive."

"You really mean to send her, don't you?" she said softly.

Sean felt his gut melt. "Aye, but I consider it a ridiculous notion. She'll probably end up on the streets . . ." His voice trailed away. He knew his need was naked in his eyes, but he was unable to shield it. At that moment Catherine seemed to be as truly fey as Merlin's Nimue, for he felt her kiss, yet she had come no nearer. Her face appeared to be lit by interior candlelight as she leaned toward him.

"Sor!" An insistent knock at the door crashed across their senses.

"What is it?" Sean asked hoarsely.

"There's a message in yer study, sor. The signalman said ye'd be wantin' to know."

Sean looked at his mistress a long moment. "I'm com-

173

ing." He waved a hand to the untouched dinner. "You may as well eat now. There's no point in both of us starving." He gave her a wry smile and left.

The message was brief. John Enderly had entered his daughter's stallion, Numidian, in a private race on the 15th of April. The horse, never publicly raced, had been privately run for a select group of Enderly's most influential friends, who intended to bet heavily on him as did the viscount himself. Apparently Enderly needed immediate cash, Sean mused as he scanned the note. He quickly jotted a return message.

When he entered his room, Catherine was cozily sitting Indian fashion on his bed. Her black hair was loose to her waist, she wore one of his shirts to ward off the drafts. Her nose was buried in a book. She waggled a finger toward the commode. "I saved bread and cheese for you. A decanter of wine is on the desk."

Sean descended on the folded napkin and grinned happily. Not only had she brought bread and cheese, but meat, fruit, pastries, and several chocolates. "Hardly ethereal fare, Diana," he mumbled between mouthfuls. "There's no substitute for a sensible goddess"—he cocked an eyebrow at her—"though domesticated ones are invariably fat."

"If you prefer plump domesticity," she retorted without looking up, "perhaps you should invite Ellie to share your bed."

He popped a chocolate into his mouth. "Even a backward Irishman has the sense to leave pork in the barn."

"Sean?" Catherine looked up, blue eyes serious. "Have you ever heard of 'phlogiston'?"

"Good God, are you reading chemistry?" Wandering over to the bed, he glanced at the book's flyleaf. His eyebrows rose slightly, but he made no comment other than, "This book is out-of-date. Have Flynn review and annotate the sections before you study them. You'll ruin your eyes by squinting in candlelight."

"But that would be a bother to him. I can hardly ask him to take time . . ."

He scoffed. "Flynn has all the time in the world, barring natural calamity."

174

She regarded him thoughtfully. "He seems to be an excellent doctor. Why has he so few patients?"

Sean leaned against the bedpost, enjoying his view of her.

"Flynn is a good doctor. Too good. He had a flourishing practice until his wife died, then withdrew into books and became a fanatic about reforming rural medical practices; most of them still dispense a hash of midwifery and veterinary medicine. Unfortunately, fanatics are apt to lose their sense of humor. He alienated his colleagues and his patients. Other doctors began to decry his methods as heartless, dangerous experimentation. Gradually his patients left him, as did his three daughters." At Catherine's surprise, he grimaced. "I'm not surprised he didn't mention them; they're a vain, fleabrained lot. One is married to a doctor who defamed him, another to a nitpicking clerk. The youngest became a prostitute in Dublin; her sisters claim she has 'entered society.' " He grinned. "Actually, it's the other way around."

"How could they behave so shabbily?" she protested in indignation. "He's the kindest man in the world!"

He shrugged. "There was little love lost. Still, he gets by. I send him patients from Shelan. The Sisters of St. Therese in Donegal Town send him beggars and derelicts who flee as soon as they become either sober or well enough to realize where they are."

Catherine's blue eyes acquired an ominous glint and the Irishman quickly straightened. "Oh, no you don't minx! No more taking forlorn chicks under your wing. Flynn is entirely able to look after himself; he won't thank you for meddling."

She gave him an innocent look. "You overestimate my presumption."

"Ha!"

"And you still haven't answered my original question," she added sweetly. "Phlogiston?"

"Doesn't exist," he replied briefly. "Lavoisier disproved its theory some fifteen years ago." He proceeded to describe the successful experiment that isolated oxygen.

Her lips curved. "For a backward Irishman, you're informed on a surprising range of subjects. May I ask where you went to school?"

Wondering how much to tell her, he did not answer for a long moment. "Eton," he said finally.

Her eyes widened. "Good heavens, whatever for?"

He smiled faintly. "To teach myself restraint." He began to strip off his shirt. "After two years, my restraint gave way; I killed a man."

"In . . . self-defense?"

He folded his shirt with chilling precision. "It was more of an execution."

The book slipped from her fingers. She felt suddenly cold.

"What's wrong?" His green eyes bored into hers.

Forcing herself to meet them, she quietly replied, "I'm wondering when my turn comes."

"You're so certain I mean to kill you?"

"You killed Father's foresters without a second thought. I should imagine you're completely unemotional about executions."

Culhane's hands went to his hips as his handsome face darkened. "Those foresters are as hale and hearty as you and I, if unemployed. The poor beasties you fretted over are happily dining on one another all around Holden."

She stared at him. "But, why didn't you tell me? You let me think . . ."

He scowled. "Did you ask? You prefer to think me a murderer." He dropped into his desk chair and impatiently yanked at his boots. "Treating me as a man would be too complicated."

Moments later the Irishman looked up, wary, as Catherine slipped off the bed and snuffed all but the candles on the bedside table, dimming the room until the two of them were enclosed in a pool of light. Eyes uncertain, she fumbled at her shirt buttons.

Sean's heart began to thud painfully. He rose slowly to his feet as if drugged. "Kit . . ."

As the last button came undone, the shirt fell open and she slipped it from her shoulders. When the Irishman made no movement, she approached him, but so slowly she seemed to fear some terrible precipice would open under her bare feet. Her hair, falling in a dark cloud to her waist, drew his hungering gaze from softly curving breasts to the slow swell of her hips. Then she was within his grasp, but still he remained immobile. Her breasts slid against his bare chest; her breathing quickened to match his own. When she shyly offered her lips, her eyes dark as starlit tropic seas, Sean lost his private war. He pulled her roughly against his hard-muscled length and his mouth came down on hers as if starved for its warmth, lips slanting across their softness. His fingers caught in the silk of her hair, dragging her head back. Unnerved by the brute force of his desire, she moaned like a trapped animal.

Hearing her defenseless whimper, he groaned and thrust her away so desperately she stumbled and barely caught herself against the bedpost. She shrank against the post as he stared tensely at her nakedness. "Don't," he said hoarsely. "Don't come to me like this."

"I thought you wanted me," she whispered, almost sobbing with humiliation and confusion.

"Christ," he cried. "Not like this! Not for a favor! For a price, I can have a slut from a gutter!" She flinched away as if he had struck her, and his voice lowered. "You try me sorely, girl." Then he went on more softly still. "Don't you think I realize you're still afraid? But if you'd suddenly fought me, I'd have raped you! I'm sick to my soul of taking you by force, but I'll be damned before I settle for a placebo! Moora be damned! Your father be damned! And damn you for the most tender cheat it's been my ill fortune to want." His shoulders sagged, then he jerked his head toward his armoire. "Take my robe and go out onto the terrace to cool your injured pride. Don't worry, the rain has let up."

Silently, Catherine obeyed, her mind numbed. Hugging the robe about her shoulders, she stood under the sullen sky watching clouds shift across the moon. Culhane was right; the chill night air was like a ducking in ice water. She had been deluded by misplaced gratitude and sympathy, she warned herself with deliberate harshness. He was, after all, no more than her jailer. If he had persuaded himself to check his lust in hopes of rich response, that was his concern. He was nothing to her.

Her bare toes curled in complaint against the chilly

stone flagging and she turned to go inside, then halted in shock, fascination, and pity. Sean Culhane lay naked on the bed, his lean, powerful body arching as one hand wrenched at his sex. He thrust desperately against his hand, his face twisted in mysterious, age-old agony, his bronzed hide gleaming with sweat in the candlelight. Suddenly he groaned and his hips strained in a final spasm as his seed spurted into emptiness and fell across his thighs and belly. The taut muscles relaxed and he lay spent and still. His black lashes flickered; slowly he looked into the eyes of the silent girl by the door and felt her pity like a blow. His lips twisted. "Where's your disgust, Diana? The act is crudely known as self-abuse." He watched her, green eyes hard. "Well? Have you lost your tongue? Have you no barbs of condemnation to sink into my degenerate flesh?"

"Don't you think your own self-laceration is sufficient?" she said quietly. "Is that why you strike at others? Because you demand of yourself more pain than you can bear?"

Culhane swore at her, sat up, and swung his legs over the side of the bed. Deliberately, he paraded his nakedness as he went to the commode and seized a towel. Slowly wiping his belly and loins, he surveyed her insolently. "You're a fool," he sneered, "and that bucolic state has little to do with your lack of experience."

"My experience of brutality has come from you," she replied evenly, "never beauty, tenderness, or affection, because you don't permit them in yourself. So long as I have a teacher no wiser than Flynn's poor, slackwit boy who repeats his assigned tasks like an unthinking machine, then I'm condemned to remain what you say I am. A fool. How can I give you affection when you seek to wrench it from me and crush it as heedlessly as that dull-minded boy might a butterfly, tearing off its bright wings to keep in his pocket, then startled to soon find them colorless and dead?"

Culhane went pale. Catherine felt his despair as if she were part of his flesh, but, desperate to be free of him, she summoned all her resolve and struck the blow cleanly. "How can one who is nothing but a charred void of hatred, who parades in the mere shell of a man, presume to demand love? You, who can expect no more than bleak fulfillment of vengeance and the pity of those who watch you stumble like blind Oedipus to some solitary end!" Culhane's cheekbones stood out whitely as if they would split the taut skin that covered them. She ached to comfort him, but dared not. If he would not willingly release his hold, she must irrevocably sever it, whether the blow brought freedom, grinding years of imprisonment, even death. This battle between them could not continue. She feared his demand for her love above all.

"You loose no barbs, Diana," Culhane replied quietly with strange, lyrical self-mockery, "but killing lances. If I am a husk and mockery of a man, why do my sides now run red? If blind, why do my empty eyes see a fair illusion that leads me to hope? Like that slackwit, I gape at love and rend it with clumsy fingers, yet still hold its tatters close in idiot hope it may live again. Solitary death is no more welcome than solitary life, so yet I stand and refuse to fall on my sword. It's you, fair Diana, who must lower me and all my bleeding dreams to dust."

"No blow is needed," she answered softly. "You cannot stand forever."

"No, I cannot stand forever."

"I shall always hate you," she whispered, as gently as a kiss.

The next morning he was gone. He had spent the night in the study and she had gone to the infirmary without seeing him. When she returned in late afternoon, a brief note lay on the desk, stating that he would return in three weeks. She sank into the chair, a sleepless night aggravating her tension, her imagination doing its worst. What nefarious errand was the Irishman contemplating? Culhane had made no real defense the night before. Had he been merely waiting to strike back in deadly reality? She flung herself from the chair and paced back and forth. Had he perhaps been hurt so badly he could not bear to see her and had crawled away to lick his wounds? Even to die in some reckless venture? She paled at the thought. According to Flannery, Culhane courted death as ruthlessly as he courted her. Pressing her palms to her temples, she tried to

179

curb her apprehension. The note did say he would return. And his defenseless pain the night before had cost her the battle at the last moment; no doubt he knew it. Why should he seek revenge when he had proved the victor?

She clung to the bedpost and stared about the room, which now seemed bleak and deserted. Aimlessly, she wandered, straightening things that were straight, fiddling with her brushes. His shaving gear was gone, his jacket missing from the brass hook. She checked his drawers and wardrobe. Several suits, his Spanish riding boots and fine riding clothes were missing. He must be going where a proper social appearance was required. Where beautiful, sophisticated women would admire him, flatter him, and no doubt bed him. She sagged disconsolately onto the empty bed. Why should he want to come back at all to a skinny schoolgirl who cut him at every turn, called him foul names, and reacted like a dusty mummy every time he tried to seduce her?

CHAPTER 9

The Mongoose and the Cobra

With one impeccably tailored shoulder against the Palladian mantel, Sean lit a thin cigar as he surveyed the Hunt Room at Ingram House, Norfolk. Late-afternoon sun streamed through arched windows across the shoulders of a small group of men. Above them, on maroon and white striped walls, were paintings of hunting scenes and racehorses. A portrait of Charles II mounted on a thoroughbred hung above the fireplace where Sean lounged. Lackeys scurried about relaying port, claret, and cheroots on silver salvers to gentlemen who represented most of the countries of Europe.

Sean smiled to himself. So far, everything was going exactly as he wanted. Even his short hair was not unusual in international society. After sailing to Dublin, where he had settled Moora with Lady Duneden, he had met with two barristers, John and Henry Sheares, whom he had known in Paris during the early days of the Revolution. Both on the Executive Committee of the United Irishmen, they in turn arranged for him to see the committee's leader, Lord Edward Fitzgerald, in secret. Afterward, he had spent a pleasant though rather sad evening with the ailing Lockland Fitzhugh, marquess of Menton.

Lockland Fitzhugh was the last surviving male of a venerable Scots Protestant family who had been in Ireland since the days of the Plantagenets; they were ardently sympathetic to the plight of their vanquished countrymen.

In the great rebellions against the Tudors, the Fitzhughs had protected Irish rebels at no small cost.

A lifelong friend of Brendan Culhane, Lockland Fitzhugh continued the family tradition in his own quiet way. After Brendan's aborted attack on the Dublin Armory, Lockland narrowly saved him from hanging and finally managed to secure his release from prison. When, because of their Catholic ancestry and their father's dubious allegiance, Sean and Liam could not attend university, even Trinity in Dublin, Fitzhugh had passed Sean off as his nephew, Robert Fitzhugh, and sponsored him at Eton, while Liam had preferred to study in Rome. Although a revered member of Irish Parliament and himself loyal to the crown, Lockland was aware Brendan and his sons were involved with the United Irishmen, whose secret meetings and underground presses organized sedition. After Sean's deadly London brawl with Megan's killer had made continuance at Eton unpolitic, Fitzhugh had sent him to the École Militaire in Paris and had rarely seen him since his graduation.

The marquess was clearly delighted by his protégé's visit, but somewhat embarrassed to receive him in shabby quarters. Partly because he refused to submit to the flagrant bribery and prejudice of the Irish Protestant Parliament and partly because he neglected his own estates in the interest of his country, his wealth had declined. To conserve his finances, Fitzhugh had taken a modest house on Canal Street near Parliament, his failing health no longer permitting the journey to his home in Kildare.

Sean was grieved to see Fitzhugh's condition, but in deference to the old man's sometimes stiff pride he made no mention of it. After a simple but excellent dinner and several glasses of fine port from Fitzhugh's dwindling stock, Sean asked his mentor for an introduction to the forthcoming race in Norfolk. The old man was delighted to be of service. He also added a crisp bit of advice. "The Dublin authorities are hanging suspected subversives from lampposts of late, 'croppies' along with them. You may get away with it in England, but I advise you to keep your collar high over that short hair in Ireland, lad, if you don't want to be thought a French sympathizer." He waved

182

Sean to the divan, then chose a cigar from the box the younger man had brought him. "You had best steer clear of Fitzgerald's crowd, too. He's wanted by the authorities. Not everyone is convinced he's in Paris, you know."

He lit his cigar, then pensively looked at Sean. "I'm not the first Irishman to die certain his nation's sorrows are not ended, but I'm equally certain hope lives as ever in our young men. I've not told you before, but I've been very proud of you, Sean. Keep faith and patience. Don't seek Ireland's freedom in England's blood. Our destiny lies in the law."

"Thank you, sir, but I'm no barrister."

Fitzhugh grunted. "No, you're a fighter, like Owen Roe and the rest of your clan back to the dawn of Niall. Twelve hundred years of blood. I had hoped your stay at Eton might suggest another course, if only to show you not all Englishmen are tyrants."

"I was aware of that, sir, before I left. You've been like a father to me."

Startled, but pleased by the younger man's uncharacteristic remark, Fitzhugh barely managed a gruff tone. "Yet, like all your clan, you regard me as English though my family has been in Ireland for six centuries. We're English to the Irish and Irish to the English: colonists, ever viewed as temporary citizens."

"A most welcome addition to our culture in your case, my lord."

With a shrug, Fitzhugh rose and went to his desk. Shortly, he handed a note to Sean to review; then, after attaching his seal, Fitzhugh gave the letter to a servant for immediate delivery. He looked at Sean for a long moment. "I dislike good-bys. So I'll wish you a good night, and a fair voyage."

Sean grasped the statesman's proffered hand. "Thank you, sir. May you have the same."

As Sean paused on the narrow stair to his room, he saw Fitzhugh with a woolen rug over his legs, still sitting at his desk in a pool of candlelight. His white hair mellowed, he scratched at parliamentary proposals pleading for eased circumstances of Irish Catholics. The proposals would be rejected as they had been for all thirty-five years of his sporadic tenure, but the pen moved as strongly as it ever had. Feeling a tightness in his throat, Sean sensed he would not see the frail old man again. He touched his forehead in an unnoticed salute. Good-by, sir.

Three days after leaving Dublin, Culhane landed in Norfolk, then went overland to Ingram. Upon arrival, Sean supervised Mephisto's installment in a large, airy stall as clean as his own quarters. After leaving Michael Shaunessy, a groom from Shelan, in charge, he drifted through the stables. As he passed Numidian's stall, a glance told him Mephisto had keen competition, if not a virtual brother; the resemblance between the two stallions was amazing. A wizened Arab in a burnoose was rubbing the horse down as he crooned to him in Arabic. Carrying a feed bag, Tim O'Rourke, alias Tim Carson, trotted past his commander without a blink of recognition.

Whistling, Sean strolled back to the house, gave his cloak to the bewigged butler, and wandered into the drawing room.

"Rob! Robert Fitzhugh! Oh, I say, it's good to see you after all these years!" A ruddy-haired young man with an engaging grin bounded up and wrung Sean's hand with high enthusiasm.

"Terry, it's good to see you, too." Sean grinned back with real pleasure.

"I say, old man, you left rather suddenly. I was hoping to have the pleasure of your company at the old schoolyard for another two years at least. You look fit as ever. Married?" Sean lifted an eyebrow. "I thought not!" Southwick slapped his shoulder. "Shrewd fellow. My father's bent on trotting me to the altar before my next birthday. A cheeky lot I grew up with. She's all right and not a bad looker, but I've only nine months until I'm twenty-six; that leaves only two hundred seventy nights for debauchery."

"Your mathematics have improved."

Terence grinned. "Wait until you see the crop of fillies here for the race, and I don't refer to the ones with fetlocks. What a swath we'll cut together."

"I'm presenting my stallion, not myself, as stud at this race. Besides, I always range alone, you know that."

"Damme if I don't. Perhaps if I'd gone with you to London that night, you'd have been back at classes next morning. Rumors were afloat about a British sergeant."

"You always were a good influence," teased the Irishman.

Their conversation was drowned out by rising voices at Terry's elbow. A gesticulating young man was in hot argument with the duke of Norfolk. The blustering, red-faced duke, although a fervent Whig, obviously wanted relief from his antagonist's Tory harangue. The duke's enthusiasm for racing had won him the nickname "Jockey" among his intimates, and this week he wished to talk horses rather than politics.

Terry glanced over his shoulder and murmured to Sean, "The little firebrand's George Canning. You've met the duke, I think," he added dryly, then turned to the men with an engaging laugh. "I say, George, let His Grace off. You cannot alter a man's convictions by sheer lungpower."

"I daresay I should bow to Mr. Pitt; he has the most noted lungs in the House and seems to have excellent luck," was Canning's retort.

"Indeed, perhaps he might persuade you to curb your tongue, sir!" The duke stalked off.

"Why antagonize him, George?" queried Terry mildly. "He could so easily sympathize with your objectives. After all, you want the same things for England."

Canning snorted, looking about for a lackey with claret. "The old stag blunders about in the briar while the dogs of change snap at his heels. King George is no better. God save us from the rule of old men. Why, those Privy Council dotards have even dismissed George Fox."

"But whatever for?" asked Southwick in consternation. "I had not heard of this."

"He affirmed the right of Irish sovereignty to His Majesty," supplied Sean quietly. "Mr. Fox proposed the notion that a small country has as much right to its independence as a large power."

Canning gave him a sharp glance.

Terry flushed. "I am remiss, gentlemen. I plead I was distracted by your debate with the duke, George. May I

185

present my friend, Robert Fitzhugh, nephew of the marquess of Menton. Robert: Mr. George Canning, delegate from Westminster and a member of our prime minister's Tory support."

Canning selected a cigar from a passing salver and Sean leaned forward slightly to offer a light from his own cheroot. "I take it by your surname that you're an Anglo-Irish Protestant, hardly sympathetic with the cause of Catholic emancipation."

"My uncle's parliamentary record of endeavor in behalf of the native majority in Ireland may speak for my inclinations."

Canning nodded. "I share your uncle's sentiments. Ireland's future lies in the law, not continual butchery."

"Unfortunately, sir, those sentiments are paradoxical. The governing law of Ireland is English. By English law, a Catholic Irishman is an enemy of the Crown, unprotected by any law save the rubble of the Gaelic codes."

Lightly, Canning toasted Sean. "*Touché*, sir. Perhaps legal barbarism is no less heinous than chaos, but civilization cannot survive in chaos. Man is obliged to live in order, if he will live at all."

Then his voice abruptly became biting again. "It appears we're all damned, for Chaos Incarnate approaches." The room fell into a hush as His Royal Highness, the Prince of Wales, entered with his closest confidant, George Brummell, in tow. The prince was floridly handsome and elegantly dressed, but his ribald pun of "Hi, ho, whores' men" reduced his audience to guffaws, nervous titters, and gossip. The crowd gave way before him as he greeted various individuals in fluent French, Italian, or German.

Terry turned to Canning. "Perhaps less Chaos than reprieve, sir. You importune Youth for England's guidance and there you see it."

"Better an inane king than insane one, sir?" quipped Canning. "If that were to become our party policy, we should endure in office until the Last Trump. Inanity is ever with us."

"I say," said Terry, eager to interrupt the argument, "there's John Enderly. Let's have him over. A charming fellow. Knows everybody and has the most famous parties." Sean's eyes narrowed, following Southwick as he disengaged from the group and went to speak to Enderly, who was in conversation with two men. After some discourse and a hasty bow from Terry to the pair, the four men joined the group by the crackling fire, which had been lit to dispel the growing afternoon chill. Somewhat nervously, Terry rattled through introductions that included John Enderly, viscount of Windemere; Charles Philippe de Bourbon, the powerful duc d'Artois and brother of Louis XVIII, king of France in exile; and finally the duc's twenty-three-year-old son, Louis Antoine, duc d'Angoulême.

Artois's hooded eyes regarded them unwinkingly as Enderly suavely explained the Bourbons were in London from their residence in exile in Edinburgh for a conference with the Privy Council. As Enderly talked, his gray eyes surveyed the group, only to return coolly to Sean's green ones and linger. Sean looked back at him lazily and sipped at a glass of port.

As Enderly searched his mind for recollections of the old marquess's relations, talk turned to Napoleon's campaign in Egypt and speculations about the possibility of his attacking English colonies in the south. Terry disclaimed the notion. "Napoleon is simply attempting to lure us into war. If left to his own devices, he will roast in the sands of the Nile."

"If I may beg to disagree, sir," smoothly interposed the duc d'Artois, "Napoleon has the appetite of a leviathan. Unless checked early, he will embark on more and more conquests. He is unlikely to mummify in Egypt. After all," he continued silkily, "war policy as administered by Mr. Pitt's pacifist cousin, Lord Grenville, has not proven overly successful."

"But Pitt feels Napoleon will fail because the Directorate is jealous of him," persevered Terry. "The longer he remains in Egypt, the more precarious his position. There's no need to involve English troops with enemies surrounding France. Napoleon cannot last."

"But I believe Mr. Pitt is deceived, sir, as he has been deceived in his support of the decrepit Ottoman Empire and his underestimation of the ambitions of Catherine of

Russia. Poland now lies dismembered. Will he linger while Napoleon gorges on the whole of Europe, and eventually England?"

Dark-eyed Angoulême said nothing. He was accustomed to his father's verbal battles, since Artois's one actual military engagement had ended in disastrous defeat by the Republican Army during the ill-fated Vendée expedition. Still a child when forced into exile, Louis had grown to manhood shadowed by constant conspiracies and political wrangling. His father's leadership of the Bourbon faction in England was the most viable position in the Royalist cause. The fat, conniving Louis XVIII, buried for all purposes in a Russian province by the erratic good graces of Tzar Paul I, endeavored to extend his tentacles throughout European governments to no avail. In Edinburgh, the young duc had learned patience if little else.

Suddenly a voice cried, "Damn me if it's not Fitz!" A silk-clad arm thrust through the circle and its owner pumped vigorously at Sean's hand.

Sean smiled politely. "Your Highness . . . hello, Buck."

Brummell, who wore a captain's uniform of the prince's regiment, nodded as he appraised the Irishman's flawlessly cut dark blue clawhammer coat and fawn buckskin breeches, which molded cleanly to his long legs and fit without a ripple into darkly polished russet boots.

Enderly was startled by the prince's recognition of the man whose manner and intense green eyes so aptly fit his foresters' description of the chief saboteur of Holden Woods, but his bland expression gave no hint of it.

Prince George raffishly threw an arm about Sean's shoulders. "Gentlemen, whatever your various gilded titles and offices, prepare to salute the whoremaster of us all. My own lechery pales beside his black reputation. He got more than one bastard at Eton, one of them by my own mistress, Kitty Fells. A green-eyed brat she dropped, and had the cheek to say it was mine!"

Sean's handsome face was a smiling mask. "Your second equerry had green eyes, as I recall, Your Highness."

George's eyes widened. "By Jove, you're right. The devil! And she married Frank with my good wishes and two hundred pounds a year! Damn the baggage! She's a tub of a trollop today, so the rotter only got a side of pork with my blessing!" The prince threw back his head and laughed uproariously at his own joke.

"If you will excuse me, Your Highness, gentlemen," Sean cut in quickly, weary of the conversation, "I have some unpacking to do."

"You have no valet, Fitz?" sneered Brummell. "However do you dress properly?"

"The same way I relieve myself." As Brummell reddened and the prince roared, Sean bowed to the bemused dukes. "Pick me up for dinner, will you, Terry?" he said affably to his friend, who was preparing to make his own excuses. The hint to stay behind was not lost on the young lord.

Enderly's eyes narrowed slightly as he watched Sean stroll from the room. "I'm delighted to encounter a nephew of the marquess. It had been my understanding that he had no living relatives." He sipped his claret. "Still, I suppose his relationship to Menton is unquestionable."

The prince stared at him. "God's blood, man, I've known Fitz for years. He's a gentleman, whatever his bald remarks to Brummell here."

Growing pink, Southwick sided with the prince. "I had apartments next to Fitz at Eton. He and I visited his uncle one summer at Menton. The marquess called Fitz his nephew, and he ought to know."

Enderly apologized smoothly. "I offer no insult to your friend, my dear fellow. Clearly, my memory is mistaken. You must pardon my vanity for clinging to my first supposition, as my powers of recollection have served me excellently well in the past." He laughed ruefully, as if chagrined. "I must be getting old."

"Not you, milord," said Artois smoothly in his silken, accented English. "You will be a serpent's tooth in the heel of England's enemies for many years yet."

As Sean and Terry emerged from Sean's quarters to go to dinner, they encountered a stunning blonde in the hall. She turned with a whisper of silk and subtle wink of diamonds to watch the Irishman's tall form disappear around a corner.

189

Terry nudged Sean as they trotted down the long staircase. "What did I tell you? The place is rotten with beautiful women. That was Helena Sutton, marchioness of
Landsbury. Isn't she gorgeous?"

"Gorgeous," agreed Sean, "and obviously married."

"Pshaw. Her husband's an old India nabob thirty years
her senior."

"Duels with irate husbands can become monotonous."

Terry laughed. "You ought to know, I suppose. You've
fought enough of them . . ." His head swiveled as they entered a crowded salon adjacent to the dining room.
"There's Lady Anne Trury," he commented. "She's the de-
lectable dark-eyed creature peeping over her father's
shoulder. Worth a fortune but well guarded." He rocked
forward on his toes and craned his neck ever so slightly.
"Ah, I see a challenge for you. Lady Elizabeth Dunaway.
Fabulous horsewoman. Unattached and fond of breaking
engagements. Leveled the prince's regiment. Seems unable to find a man to satisfy her. There! She sees us; or
rather, you. She's a great believer in variety, and you're
exotic fare."

Southwick did not exaggerate. His friend's complexion,
darkly contrasted by a cream silk shirt and stark black
formal clothes, made his hard male beauty arresting, particularly so in a sophisticated gathering. As he roamed
among the guests who circulated under the chandeliers, he
looked like a predator among rich pickings. Women turned
to stare at his lean, long, muscled body and rakehell face,
forgetting to hide their interest in demure glances. Many a
male noted his woman's absentminded lapse in conversation.

His dinner partner, a pretty blonde, giggled through in-
numerable tedious courses; he did not linger at her side
when the overrich menu was exhausted. Terry grinned at
him as they met outside the dining room. "For shame,
Fitz. You're so used to adoring women, you don't even
bother to be polite. That little blonde wasn't half-bad, and
God knows, she was willing."

"Sheep are willing," replied the Irishman dryly, "and
they rarely titter."

As the string ensemble began a stilted minuet, Elizabeth Dunaway strolled up on the arm of a young Italian officer who stared at her miserably with large, liquid eyes while she boldly surveyed his potential successor. "Introduce your friend, Terry darling. I've been curious about that wicked black in the stall next to my Hussar's Red." She swept on, not waiting for Terry to speak. "You *are* his owner, my lord . . . ?"

Sean bowed slightly. "Plain Robert Fitzhugh, Lady Dunaway; however, two such very similar blacks, as I recall, are entered in the race."

"Umm." The leggy redhead tapped her fan lightly against her chin as she considered the breadth of his shoulders and ignored her imploring Italian. "But the one at the far end belongs to the little Enderly girl. She's away for the season, so her father took the opportunity to sneak the stallion into the race."

"I beg your pardon?"

Lady Dunaway's eyes traveled downward, expertly assessing the Irishman's other attributes. An engaging dimple appeared in one cheek as she unhurriedly looked up into his eyes. "He's never been raced because she won't let anyone but herself and her crazy old Arab groom ride him. I hear the nag jumps well though Catherine refuses blind walls. Still, he may provide stiff competition, even for Hussar's Red." She gave him a siren smile. "But after seeing the stallion you present, I feel an even more challenging contest is imminent."

"Indeed, my lady, I'm looking forward to it."

The Italian, reading the lazy appraisal in Sean's eyes, gave a sigh of resignation.

Just after dawn the next morning, Sean, dressed in a stocked shirt, black jacket, fawn breeches, and Spanish leather boots, walked toward the stables. Shortly, he was riding Mephisto along the outside edge of the steeplechase course, a four-mile-long irregular triangle slashed with stone walls and wooden fences occasionally coupled with hedges, brush hazards, and watery ditches. The course would be grueling for both horse and rider. Side bets were made by the more sporting gentry as to just how many riders would be thrown at any particularly nasty jump, but the heavy money was on odds that either Hussar's Red or Numidian would take the purse. After more people got a look at Mephisto, his odds might drop, but Sean was certain a win by his literal "dark horse" would strain John Enderly's ready cash.

That afternoon, Sean set in motion the second prong of his forked attack on John Enderly's finances. With the Englishman's London bank accounts in escrow and his income-producing forestry and smuggling operations broken, Enderly was close to financial ruin. Culhane's next move was designed to discredit the Englishman with his influential friends.

For most of his career, Enderly had played one government against another to advantage, subtly warming to one side or another as it suited him. While he cultivated the Bourbons, he also dallied with Napoleon. Ironically, some munitions he sold the French army found their way through corrupt Directorate officials to Ireland and his enemies via Culhane ships and those of other Irish smugglers.

Although he had lost the syndicated ships, John Enderly maintained a vessel in his own name to import antiques from France and the Low Countries. While it was technically smuggling, the cargo evaded customs, virtually immune from the law because purchasers were usually either English aristocrats or French emigrés recovering family treasures. Many parvenu Directorate officials were prepared to offer cheaply acquired or confiscated property for resale. The cost of smuggling put a stiff fee on the merchandise, but the heavy English import tax was higher still. Special requests were frequently paid for in advance, and were often described in minute detail, sometimes with accompanying sketches, by someone trying to recover a family heirloom. Occasionally, unrequested rarities were offered at private auction.

Now that the viscount was in serious financial difficulty, his French agent welcomed a handsome offer by an Irish concern. As Enderly's requests for private-auction cargo dwindled for lack of ready capital, a smooth-tongued Irishman named Kilpatrick even persuaded the French agent to provide copies of the viscount's orders. Those *objets d'art* now eluded Enderly and were quietly offered to the very clients who had ordered them. In addition, unknown to the viscount, the consignments he did obtain shared space with his Irish competitors in his own Calais warehouse. As the place was nearly empty, the sensible French manager saw no reason not to pick up private rents to line his pockets.

For some months Culhane had been holding a copy of a most important order. The viscount had requests by the duc d'Artois, several prominent Girondists, and the duke of Norfolk, which the French agent had gradually filled. There had been time, however, for Culhane to send descriptions and Liam's sketches of four items on the list to Halloran with orders to have them duplicated. Duplication had been hasty, for they could not delay the agent overlong. The viscount's cargo now awaited shipment in the warehouse, side by side with the reproductions. That afternoon at Ingram Culhane met Halloran at a whist game. When Sean "learned" the other Irishman would be leaving for Calais immediately, he asked him to post a letter. Its contents were cryptic: "Begin the exchange." The originals soon were shipped to England aboard the *Mary D.*, while the reproductions, salted among Enderly's other cargo, set the trap for the viscount's undoing.

Sean skipped dinner and the evening's entertainment, an enactment of Alexander Pope's "Rape of the Lock" by a troup of Drury Lane actors. Wearing his oldest clothes, he went to the stable. While Michael Shaunessy rubbed Mephisto down with liniment, Sean stripped the bandages off the black's legs and reworked salve into his briar scratches. After checking the stallion's shoes for signs of loosening, Sean shrugged into his jacket. "Michael, see that Tim gets the sailing time for the *Mary D.* Tell him not to overdose Numidian when he rides him in tomorrow's race. I don't want the horse broken."

The boy nodded. "Aye, sor."

Culhane drifted down a line of stalls filled with some of the world's finest racers. Large, soft eyes watched him as hooves pawed restlessly along corridors where grooms roamed like flitting owls. He paused at Numidian's stall, the one place in this alien throng that conjured up Catherine Enderly's presence. In front of it, as if he were a guardian of a temple, squatted the old Arab, his black eyes as alert and unwinking as a mongoose when it scents a cobra's presence. "May Allah be with you, old one."

The old man nodded impassively. "And with you, Mr. Fitzhugh." The phrase was polite, but the sounding of Sean's adopted name had a faintly mocking ring.

"Do you know me?"

"You own the brother black," said the old man flatly.

Sean squatted before the Arab like a devotee, ignoring the stares of the passing grooms. "I have heard Numidian's sire, Ethiop, is a magnificent stud. I would like very much to see him."

The old man tilted his head as if to see Sean better. "He is dead with my lady."

"Dead? Her father says she is abroad."

"I refer to the Viscountess Elise. She was killed in a riding accident."

Thinking of Catherine's fearless skill with his own huge stallion, Culhane ventured a probe. "I'm a bit surprised. I was led to believe the viscountess's horsemanship was remarkable."

"When a field hayrake is left behind a high stone wall, skill is of no significance." The old man's voice was toneless, but Sean felt a tinge of nausea. He had seen death in many forms, but the countess's end must have been hideous; no wonder her daughter had nightmares. "I spoke in ignorance. I mean no slight to your mistress," he said quietly.

For a long moment the Arab studied the young man's features, noting their subtle Saracen cast. As if he accepted Sean's concern as real, he nodded, then asked a question of his own with unnerving abruptness. "Ethiop covered many mares. Was yours called Antigone?"

"I purchased the black from an Irish lord," Sean lied smoothly. "His papers record Andromeda as the dam and Belial as sire."

"The Irish lord who owned Antigone would never sell a foal of my lady's stallion," the old man said softly. Their eyes locked.

"Surely it is as you say," Sean murmured. "I bid you good evening. May Allah smile on Numidian's efforts tomorrow."

"Allah smiles on all that is incorrupt." The Arab's thin lips curved like a scimitar's edge.

That night Sean dropped instantly into dreamless sleep, but toward morning he began to stir uneasily. Thinking he heard a forlorn cry, he bolted upright. Only a faint coo of doves on the balustrade outside his windows broke the predawn stillness; the Irishman dropped back, realizing he was listening for Catherine. He lay awake until dawn, forcing himself to think of the race.

By ten that morning, Culhane, mounted in the stable-yard, surveyed the other entries while Shaunessy adjusted his stirrups for jumping. "We've a bit o' trouble, sor," the Irish groom muttered as he shortened the straps. "The old Arab an't taken his beetle eyes off the nag for a minute. Tim may have to wait 'til the start of the race. That means the stuff'll work when Numidian's on the course."

"That's too dangerous. I don't want the nag caving in on a jump."

"It's too late to tell Tim, sor. I can't get near 'im now!"

Frowning, Culhane twisted in the saddle to see Tim, already mounted, lean over Numidian's neck to feed the horse a carrot. Across the stableyard, the Arab saw the same thing; he closed quickly on horse and rider. Spurring Mephisto to reach Tim first, Culhane snatched the carrot from his accomplice's fingers. "You don't want to do that, lad," he advised briefly. "Any little thing gives 'em cramps in a race." As he trotted the course, the dark Irishman leaned down to hand Shaunessy the carrot on the way. "If the Arab looks like he wants an inspection, eat it."

"Gor, sor!"

Shaunessy stared at his master's retreating back, then at the carrot. A plug had been cut out of its center, coated with a powerful narcotic, and replugged, leaving only a faint incision. When he looked up, the Arab was advancing on him at a determined, bowlegged clip. With a sigh, Mike stuffed the carrot into his mouth in two large munches and stood grinding the faintly bitter vegetable as blandly as any rabbit while the Arab frowned up at him. The tobacco-colored little man gave a sardonic grunt, then seesawed off to watch the race.

Southwick was among the riders, as was Elizabeth Dunaway. After greeting Sean cheerily, she began to warm up her mare on a path parallel to Mephisto's working area while the other riders paced up and down in the same manner. He grinned at her. "Would you care to wager a few pounds on whose posterior lands in the mire today, m'lady?"

Dunaway twitched the mare's head away from Mephisto's nuzzling nose. "You *are* a yokel! My mode of wager is well known. I never bet a farthing on Hussar's chances. If I win, I accept only private wagers and the purse. If I lose, I bed the stalwart winner. So, you see, I never really lose."

He chuckled at her imperturbable impudence. "What shall we wager? Say fifty pounds?"

She nodded. "Done. I thought you'd never enter the stakes, you gorgeous dolt!"

Sean touched his hat as he danced Mephisto away. "Not too doltish to collect my winnings. Be in my bed by five sharp." Elizabeth gave an unladylike hoot.

Observers lined both sides of the course. Dotting the rolling green meadow, those not afoot were in carriages or on horseback in order to move quickly from one part of the course to another. Parasols hovered like bright butterflies above the crowd. As the horsemen lined up, Sean took a position just left of center, Elizabeth Dunaway fell in near the end of the line, while Tim entered Numidian a few horses to Sean's right. Terry Southwick, next to Elizabeth, gave Sean a puckish grin and a hearty wave.

Tension crackled through the crisp spring air as horses fretted and chafed at their starting positions. Then a warbling blast of a hunting horn sent twenty riders thundering down the turf; seventeen hit the first wall at the same time; fourteen cleared it. Culhane's right foot was crushed painfully as the horses jammed, but Mephisto, well trained, displayed no skittishness. He ran easily, eating up the greensward in great strides, taking the hurdles cleanly. Here and there, horses went down in melees of churning hooves and scrambling riders. The luckiest riders managed to lurch away with smudged clothing; others went headlong over their horses' necks in bone-jarring crashes to lie in mortal danger of being trampled. While Sean gave Mephisto his head at each hazard, he held him back slightly on the throughway. He had gotten a length behind Tim at the second water hazard and had taken a splashing but had made up the distance by the next wall.

Finally, only a handful of riders continued on the course: Elizabeth Dunaway and Tim among them. Terry had gone down. After passing a jump of felled trees, Sean let the stallion out. Mephisto lunged forward at a frightening pace, great hooves tearing the turf in spraying clots. Sean's thighs felt like liquid fire, but Elizabeth faded from his peripheral vision, then another rider and another, until Mephisto and Numidian drummed down the final stretch neck and neck, sweating like a pair of hell's couriers. A double jump, two singles, then a ditch and wall. Dumbfounded to see Numidian begin to pull away, Sean used his crop and yelled in Mephisto's ear, "Run, you black sonofabitch! The bastard's forgotten he's supposed to lose!" Mephisto roared with fiendish abandon across the last jumps and final brick-and-water hazard, leaving the less impressionable Numidian the loser by half a length.

Sean let Mephisto into a canter, then eased him to a steaming walk, the stallion's ribs expanding and contracting like a bellows. Caps gone, hair clinging wetly to their heads, the two finalists rode slowly to meet each other as the crowds converged on them. Tim's freckles stood out brightly on his pale face. "Congratulations, sor," he said tensely, stretching out his hand.

Culhane took it in a bone-crushing grip. "Be glad it's not your glory-seeking neck, laddy buck."

Both riders slid off their mounts into a sea of pushing, shouting people. First Sean, then Tim were thrust up onto sturdy shoulders and paraded about, then carried in triumph to the winner's circle. To an earsplitting din of cheers, they were toasted with champagne as a garland of flowers was hung about Mephisto's neck. A frigidly polite John Enderly, chief sponsor of the race, presented Sean a massive silver bowl and purse of five thousand pounds; Tim received a smaller cup and colder congratulations. A glassy-eyed Shaunessy led Mephisto away, pulling well-chewed roses out of the horse's mouth with a vague admonition about thorns.

Sean was escorted back to the house in a landau filled with trilling young women, one of whom dipped her silk glove in champagne to wipe his sweat-streaked, dirtstained face. At the house reception he collected private stakes and looked for Elizabeth Dunaway, nowhere to be found.

John Enderly's smooth, handsome mask appeared at his elbow. "Mr. Fitzhugh, I believe my friends and I owe you a good deal of money: some nine thousand pounds, to be exact. In this envelope you'll find the appropriate vouchers. Mine is coupled with that of the duc d'Angoulême on his account with Lloyd's." His gray eyes narrowed. "Your venture has proven most profitable. I hope I shall have the advantage at our next meeting, sir."

The Irishman took the envelope with a polite smile. "I look forward to seeing you again, my lord."

As Enderly faded into the crowd, Culhane felt oddly detached. Since meeting his sworn enemy face-to-face, he had dispassionately observed him as if the man were a viper in a glass case. There had been no rush of gall, no urge to do murder. Though he fully intended to kill Enderly, the prospect now seemed inevitable and montonous.

Hands thrust at him, champagne dribbled on his clothing, women whispered in his ear, and men offered investments. Wary of them all, he pulled away and left the room, firmly closing the doors. The silence of the deserted foyer was deafening, and as he crossed to the stair, voices clearly carried from the partly open door of a salon. The conversation was in French, the speaker the duc d'Artois. His mention of Catherine Enderly's name brought the Irishman to an abrupt halt.

"My son was most distressed your lovely daughter could not attend the race. I had hoped she might be induced to curtail her travels by a few weeks."

John Enderly's voice was placating. "This may be Catherine's last unmarried season abroad, Your Grace. Surely your son will wish her to be settled, with girlish whims behind her. Catherine has spoken with great affection of the duke. Surely a few weeks cannot matter when two young people are admirably matched."

Sean listened with swiftly mounting anger, understanding now why Enderly's note was coupled with Angoulême's: it was prepayment for delivery of Kit to the royal bed. His knuckles whitened on the banister. So Catherine had spoken with "great affection" of the slack-jawed young degenerate, had she? Kit wouldn't look at that uniformed pudding except in pity.

Artois seemed to be shrugging. "I regret Louis cannot offer marriage, my dear viscount. Marriages exclusive to the royal house are sometimes an unfortunate tradition, but I am at heart a traditional man. Louis must wed within the next year or so. He finds the Countess Catherine most appealing and I would satisfy his choice of a companion if at all possible. You will assure her my son's impatience is not only due to the natural eagerness of a lover, but the pressures of his position?"

The conversation seemed to be drawing quickly to a close. Sean headed up the stair, sore muscles protesting at every step and mind roiling with anger. Oily bastards! Condescend to make her a whore, would they? So the royal brat was impatient to mount her, was he? She was better than the lot of them in a pile. She had more breeding in her little finger than that shambling, leftover duke could summon from all his blue-blooded, yellow-faced relatives. Storming down the hallway, he pictured Angoulême in bed with his new toy, putting clammy hands on her, climbing like a toad onto her slim body. He jerked open the door to his room, then slammed it with a crash that dropped the mirror in shattering shards from the wall.

Elizabeth Dunaway's maid, Felice, stared at him from where she was pouring a bucket of steaming water into a huge copper tub. "Do you not wish a bath, Monsieur Fitzoo?"

Sean stared back, eyes glittering in fury, then sobered to some confusion. "Where's your mistress?"

The dark-eyed maid dimpled. "She will come. Is not yet the bewitching hour, is how you say, *non?* Please." She came forward, holding out her hands. "Your clothes? Do not be shy."

A boneweary Culhane boarded the *Mary D.* before dawn and saw Mephisto walked aboard and secured in the hold. A closely matched stallion in the next stall whickered nervously. After soothing both animals, he climbed up to his cabin and stretched his tired body on a narrow bunk. Shaunessy lay senseless in the opposite bunk. Tim, hugging his knees, sat on the floor.

"Good work," Sean said as he pummeled a pillow into submission and crammed it under his head. "Any problems?"

"Some," Tim admitted. He cocked an ear as the mooring hawsers hit the deck and the *Mary D.* was warped from the dock. "Thought I'd have to clip Amin to get the stallion away, but the old sod went lookin' for Shaunessy here, to see if he was walleyed. And he was, laid out like a sack o' feed in Mephisto's stall. I gets to Shaunessy a step ahead of the Arab, shoves him onto a nag, and heads him out to the east meadow. Then I cuts back, grabs Numidian, and lights out after 'im. 'Twas hard keepin' 'im headed for town, but after that, 'twas a cinch, like ye said. I boards Numidian by the eleven-bell watch; the harbor patrol passes the nag off as Mephisto and Shaunessy off as drunk. When you came in at four bells, sure enough there was a different limey patrol, and the real nag trots aboard. Only one thing worries me . . ."

Sean gingerly eased his back into a more comfortable position. "What's that?"

"Rumor was hot round the stables about Mephisto bein' put up to stud. Ye didn't enter him in the stud registry, did ye, sor?"

"Of course not. That ruse kept the odds in his favor."

Tim's face cleared. "I was thinkin' they might trace him through the breed line."

Listening to the sails being hoisted, Sean stared at the base of the bunk overhead. "Mephisto's papers were forged. If Enderly could prove anything, he'd have called our hand before the race. But the old Arab seems damn certain Ethiop sired both Numidian and Mephisto." The dark Irishman frowned. "Brendan kept no papers for Mephisto. I wonder why the Arab's so sure about Ethiop?"

"The old heathen's a weird one. When she married, the viscountess brought him from France; he adored both her and her daughter. Since the girl's disappeared, he's stranger than ever."

"Will he tell Enderly he thinks you tried to drug Numidian?"

"Dunno. He hates the viscount. When he was told Numidian was to race, he was fit to be tied." Tim grimaced. "Still, he's proud as a sultan. He'd not want his mistress's pet to lose or be cheated. He thinks ye saved the nag from bein' drugged by a villainous horse thief and ye beat me fair and square."

"I had little choice," said Culhand dryly. "What the hell got into you, pushing Numidian to win at the end?"

Tim looked at his toes, then up with a trace of defiance. "I know 'twas against me orders, but 'twasn't Enderly I was ridin'. 'Twas a dumb beast that don't know about hatin' and hurtin', just runnin' for a man 'e trusts." Tim sat, stoically waiting for his master's wrath to crack about his ears.

"When did Enderly have your family wiped out, Tim?" Sean asked quietly.

"I was but a babe," Tim replied. "Mr. Flannery said the soldiers missed me in a pile of rubble. I like to have starved."

"Eighteen years. A long time to hate, isn't it?"

"Aye, sor."

Culhane rubbed his head. "Try and work the kinks out of my carcass for the next quarter hour, and we'll call it square."

"Yes, sor!" Sean rolled over on his face with a muffled groan as Tim obeyed with alacrity. The dark Irishman winced more than once when Tim discovered aches not previously realized. "I'm a bit sore meself, sor, but not so bad as this. Ye must have had a fearsome wild ride of it."

Sean thought of Elizabeth and Felice and their tubful of champagne. "More than you know, boy. More than you know."

CHAPTER 10

The Eye of the Painter

Time at Shelan passed serenely for Catherine in Sean Culhane's absence. When not reading to Flynn, she found time to add bright curtains to the infirmary windows and coddle his flowers until they bloomed with renewed vigor. She met Liam nearly every clear afternoon. To prevent Flynn from growing suspicious, she agreed to allow Liam to paint her as a pretext for seeing each other.

The first pose Catherine struck for her portraitist was hardly a marvel of inspiration: her arms sawed akimbo and knees knocked together. When he laughingly protested, she feigned innocence. "Didn't you promise to paint me exactly as I am?"

"And what are you, pray? A perch for boobies?" he teased. When he found charcoals and looked around the easel again, a cross-eyed hunchback awaited with slack-jawed grin. At his exasperated look, she became the perfect model, assuming poses with unstudied ease in her old-fashioned white muslin dress. The wide-brimmed hat she had been previously dangling from its ribbons as if fishing for cod now wrapped itself against her wind-ruffled skirts. His charcoal flew as he halted her at one point, then another. Suddenly the hat went swinging from its ribbons and she lightly danced away, muslin swirling like a frisking cloud as she cut a swath through the heather. Liam became almost frantic to capture her abandon, cursing once when his charcoal snapped. His hand moved in

203

deft, loose strokes until his model sailed the hat toward him. "Time for tea, Master Painter!"

Liam exasperatedly ruffled his hair. "What a bother!" Her teasing laughter sounded oddly muffled over the rocks, as if a ghost from a bygone era had come to beguile unwary mortals.

At tea, Catherine was a polished hostess, serving sugared oatcakes, keeping cups full and steaming. She was uncharacteristically demure, and both doting gentlemen were startled when she announced a wish to go into the harbor village for ribbon. With Liam as escort, of course. Liam and the doctor looked at one another. "I don't think . . ." began the doctor.

"My lord and master isn't here," she said briskly, "and he doesn't have to know. My hat requires a new ribbon." Innocently she dragged up the broken ribbon from her bodice where she had stuffed it. The doctor flinched and Liam fidgeted. "The hat will be barren without a fresh ribbon." She seemed to notice their discomfort for the first time, then protested as if hurt, "Surely you don't think I'd try to escape while I'm your responsibility?" She looked at the old ribbon, then forced a brave smile. "Oh, well, it's only petty feminine vanity that yearns after little furbelows. I've managed decently so far."

Liam nibbled the bait. "For God's sake, Catherine, Ruiralagh is just a fishing town. You'd stand out like a Tudor rose in a shock of shamrocks. To parade you outside Shelan is risky."

"Not if you parade me as Doctor Flynn's niece from Killarney," she said quickly.

"I don't have a niece in Killarney," protested the doctor.

"Kilkenny?" Catherine suggested brightly.

"I don't have any nieces!"

"Besides," said Liam, "you don't sound Irish."

"Bite yer tongue, ye Irish mick, how dare ye be tellin' a good Irishwoman she don't sound like she come from the ould sod. 'Tis insultin' y'are, and fair to be havin' yer ears boxed!"

Flynn blinked. "Grotesque, but amazing."

The male arguments continued to meet with blithe rebuttals until Liam sipped his cold tea and made a face. "Just ribbon, mind you, then straight home."

Little choice of finery was to be found in the general shop where Catherine pondered the articles with maddening leisure. In nervous impatience, Liam paced up and down as she puttered, fingering this and twiddling with that while the middle-aged proprietress regarded her balefully. Two other women in sparrow-drab dresses eyed the stranger's rose-colored gown and softly draped heather shawl with sidelong disapproval. She was dressed no differently than they, save in the vastly becoming shading of her clothing and the appealing dip of her neckline, but in their minds she was far too beautiful to be good, and the fact Lord Liam waited attendance spoke for itself.

By now that lord was well aware his charge had far more on her mind than ribbons. Their carriage had barely rolled into the street lining the harbor, when she had cried out, "Begorra, what a darlin' dog!" slid out of the carriage as if it were buttered, and scampered up the wharf after a moth-eaten mutt that cringed when she petted him.

Despite Liam's protests as he hastily tethered the carriage and hurried after her, Catherine insisted on walking to the village's one dress shop and introducing herself to everybody. Her smile was so infectious people involuntarily smiled back, and generally heard some scrap of conversation concerning "my uncle, Doctor Flynn." The lovely stranger and tense young lord inched along at a snail's pace because the young lady could not resist impulsively complimenting villagers on their flowers or freshly painted shutters. However taken aback at being accosted the individual might be, inevitably he began to thaw.

Rare indeed the malcontent who would frown at a blooming rose, but eventually that being made her appearance: staunchly dignified Mrs. Agatha Flynn Leame, Doctor Flynn's eldest, stuffiest daughter. Her faded blue eyes and strong profile were her only resemblance to her father. She marched into the shop with a cheap sealskin muff mounted on her front and an ugly bonnet trimmed with cock's feathers jammed on her head. "Where's this Kitty Flynn?" she barked.

"Why, Aunt Agatha, how good it is to be meetin' at last. I'd have recognized ye anywhere from Uncle Michael's lovely miniature!"

Agatha's chin jutted out and Liam quailed. "I don't remember me father havin' a niece, from Kilkenny or anywhere else!" Lowering her voice to a furious whisper, she hissed, "If ye think ye can pass yerself off as kith and kin of decent folk so ye can play the whore for my fool of a father and fancy Lord Liam, think again!"

Catherine's eyes rounded as if astonished and she whispered back, "Why, Aunt Agatha, 'tis ungracious ye're bein'. Perhaps 'tis you who should be havin' a thought or two. Ye might not remember me, but I remember Flory Flynn, me social-minded aunt, passin' well. 'Tis a foin time she's havin' herself in Dublin, meetin' all sorts—"

A gloved hand spasmodically caught her wrist. Catherine's voice had grown subtly louder phrase by phrase and Agatha's chin sagged with each increase in volume. "Please! Lower yer voice," the woman whispered hoarsely.

"I'd be delighted, but I'll thank ye to be considerin' yer father's reputation as well as yer own."

Liam began a frantically noisy, mostly one-sided conversation with the shop proprietress while Catherine continued in a lower tone, foiling the craning attention of the customers. "If ye haven't learned by now yer father's an honorable man, ye're a sorry lot indeed! I'm his nurse: nothin' more"—she stuck out her own small chin—"and nothin' less." Her eyes narrowed. "Now, ye've abused his good name fer years and yer husband's practice has fattened because of it. If ye don't start rememberin'—and loudly, mind ye—what a foin gentleman and physician yer father is, ye may see how much of a dent in yer own reputation a flaptongue lass from Kilkenny can make!" Seeing the woman start to bluster, Catherine spiked her guns. "Would ye like yer neighbors to know how much Flory the Floozie charges?"

"Stop! . . . Stop." The gloved fingers twisted at the muff. "I'll do like ye want. But it won't help. The folk hereabouts'll have no part of Da."

Catherine ignored her protest. "Speak to yer sister this afternoon, if ye please. Two mouths run better than one. I expect to be seein' patients come up the hill beginnin' next week. If ye can't send somebody, ye'd both better develop dire disease and pay a call yerselves.''

"But my husband's the village doctor! How would it look?''

"No worse than it looked when ye deserted yer da and left him to bear gagglin' tongues alone. 'Tis only sorry I am it takes a bit of blackmail to make ye see it.'' Catherine's voice resumed its normally blithe volume as she bobbed a curtsy. "Good day to ye, Aunt! Ye're a dear to invite Lord Liam and meself to tea, but I fear we've too many errands this afternoon. Perhaps another time.'' She gave the dazed woman a hearty hug, rescued Liam from the shop mistress, who was swaying ostrichlike to see past his shoulders, then swept out of the shop with the silently fuming lord on her arm.

Determinedly heading away from the carriage, she turned in the direction of the small stone church at the village outskirts. Completely exasperated, Liam dug in his heels. "This is insane. I was an idiot to bring you here. Donegal County hasn't been so stirred up since Cromwell! And that remark you dropped to those fishermen about a mumps epidemic! You've bent the sword of medical ethics to a hairpin! I'm taking you home this minute!''

Wide blue eyes looked up at him beseechingly. "I know I've sorely tried your patience, but won't you allow me to go to confession before we leave?'' She caught his hands. "I promise to be good. I'll not say another word to anyone but the priest.'' He looked dubious. "I won't involve you and your brother,'' she said quickly. "I swear it.''

"But what can you have to confess? You were brought here against your will and . . . abused. God won't hold you responsible.''

Her eyes dropped. She dreaded to admit to a priest lust for a man who had raped her; still more that she must promise in good faith not to repeat the offense. She could not bear for Liam to know how low she had sunk.

Liam caught her chin, his eyes narrowed to hard demand. "You aren't falling in love with Sean, are you?''

She paled. "No! My God, no! How can you ask? Have I no privacy, even in contemplation of my sins!'' She had not meant to speak sharply, but Liam's perceptive question had cut too close to the truth. His hurt, angry expression brought a pang of remorse. "I'm sorry, Liam. Truly, I don't mean to hurt you. My relationship with your brother is one of complete antagonism. We rarely pass an hour in each other's company without quarreling." She paused a moment, watching the shadows clear on his handsome face. "I have need of a priest. Will you take me to the church?"

He sighed. "If you require forgiveness, I can hardly deny you." He tucked her arm in his. "But I'm afraid you'll glean little consolation from Father Ryan."

On the edge of the village they passed a ruined Gothic arch that spread in powerful, spinelike grace from the rocky beach.

"How beautiful! Liam, what place was this?"

"A Franciscan chapel built by the O'Donnells during early Tudor reigns. At the time, the O'Donnells and O'Neills were the ruling families of Ulster and the greatest powers in Ireland. The church was destroyed during Henry VIII's Catholic suppression."

"Your mother was an O'Neill, was she not?"

His face tightened. "Purely descended from Hugh of Ulster. She came to Ireland from Spain when she was fourteen and married my father."

"She was very young."

"Not too young to know what she wanted. She had no desire to thin her royal blood through an alliance with exiled and distant kinsmen. She chose an Ulster man of lesser but equally pure lineage, then waited for a son to restore the O'Neills to the throne. Even as a child I was obviously unlikely to prove a terror to the English. After Father was thrown into prison, she was able to see him for a month out of every six, thanks to a powerful friend in government. After two years she gave birth to Sean. When she had word Father was returning from prison, she took Sean and left. Some say she left because she wanted the future prince to herself; others, because of my parents' long separation, that she had borne a bastard and couldn't bear the gossip."

Catherine squeezed Liam's hand in quick sympathy. "Surely your mother must have loved those she left behind. Your father is respected by all who knew him and you were her firstborn; she cannot have been heartless."

"Who knows? Perhaps she was more heedless than heartless. Sean grew tall and dark like Father. None would have slandered his legitimacy long if she had stayed, but her leaving made his bastardy seem a certainty. That's why Father's retainers cleave to me and not to my brother, for all his skills." Liam's lips twisted and the rankling of bitterness showed in his last words. "It was her one great error and typical of her arrogance."

"But how could she hope for Sean to draw all Ireland to his cause, when his own father's men won't follow him?"

"Megan had little more than contemptuous tolerance for Culhane support. Had she lived, Sean's surname would have been O'Neill. She planned to ally with the great hereditary vassals of the Irish crown, confident the sheer magic of descendancy from Hugh and national desperation would conquer any hesitancy. The Culhanes were only a small link in her aim. But it worked out differently. Sean cannot command the great clans without first establishing himself, and with Megan dead, he cannot do that without the Culhanes. Like that ruin, he would only be a relic of past glory."

The village church resembled a Romanesque fortress; squat and stolid, it offered no welcome. When they stepped into its dim interior, Liam dipped his fingers into the stone bowl by the door, crossed himself, then rang a bell for the priest. Passing crude benches that served as pews, they knelt at an iron rack of lighted candles at the side of the simple altar. Surreptitiously, he studied the young countess's profile as she prayed. Strangely, even here her dark beauty appeared sublimely pagan, her oblique eyes reminding him of hieratic mosaics of Theodora, the courtesan who became empress of Christian Byzantium. Her face gilded by the flickering tapers, she seemed enveloped in a tension that increased as the minutes dragged by, her hands more clenched than clasped. At length she whispered almost frantically, "Where's the priest?"

"The bell can be clearly heard in his house; if he were there, he'd have arrived by now. I'm sorry, Catherine.

We'll come another time." She stared at him, then sagged slightly as if she had lost some inner battle.

Silently they walked along the wharf back to the carriage. Liam handed her up, then tucked a packet into her hand with an ironic smile. "Your ribbon."

Sometime later, as the carriage rolled lumpily along the road, she spoke. "The Culhanes are originally Catholic, aren't they? You seem accustomed to Catholic worship."

Liam nodded. "Catholic as Saint Paddy himself. But native landholders in Ireland cannot afford the luxury of adhering to their private beliefs today." He swept a hand to include the barren land about them. "All this area bounding Shelan is shireland, confiscated property of the Crown since Charles II. If I were Catholic, I could no longer own Shelan. I would be forced to rent land that has been in my family for over a thousand years from an absentee owner at the usurious rate of two-thirds its income each year. I'd have no recourse to law for crimes against my property and person, no representation in government. I couldn't send my children to university, or even keep a decent horse."

Catherine listened to this litany of repression in stunned anger. How monstrously unfair! How could any God-fearing nation squeeze another so selfishly? No wonder rebellions are such a threat to English peace, she thought with sudden guilt. The Irish had no chance. Each time they rebelled, they were crushed; each defeat brought more oppression.

Without looking at her, Liam continued ironically, "It could be worse. Cromwell was for slaughtering us all, funneling us into the barrens of Connaught to starve or extraditing us as slaves to Barbados. He massacred three thousand at Drogheda, five thousand at Stafford. Our numbers were our salvation; in time of famine, it's less of an advantage."

No wonder the retainers hated me, Catherine thought. No wonder Sean Culhane hated me. It wasn't just my father. A huge hand seemed to compress her chest, smothering her.

Suddenly noticing her pallor, he halted the carriage. "Catherine?" Fearing she was about to faint, he seized her in his arms and she swayed against him, hardly aware of her surroundings. With her hair spilled from its covering as the shawl slipped away, she looked so helpless that Liam's concern was replaced by a strong male desire to overpower her. He crushed her to him and his mouth covered hers with desperate urgency.

Startled, Catherine began to struggle. "No, Liam! Please . . . don't! Let me go . . . please!"

Desperately she pushed at his chest, and with a groan, he released her. Her anxiety froze his desire, but not his ever-growing rage with Sean. Misreading her distraught state of mind, he was only too ready to blame her rejection on Sean's bestiality. Still, he was aware he had thrown himself at her in precipitate haste. "I'm sorry. I never meant to do that." He looked away. "I wanted you to like me of your own accord," he murmured. "I . . . I just lost my head."

His dejection reminded Catherine of the old, boyishly uncertain Liam and the lonely, rejected child he once had been. "Part of the fault was mine. I didn't realize how strongly you felt." Liar, she thought, sagging into the corner of the carriage. Sean warned you not to play with fire. How could you not know? "We've been so comfortable," she added lamely, "so at ease together, I didn't think . . ." His face grew progressively more wretched until she caught at his shoulder. "Oh, Liam, you aren't in love with me?"

He looked at her miserably. "I have been for ages. There's no help for it, so we're both out of luck. Obviously, you don't care for me in the same way. I've become just one more difficulty for you."

"That isn't true! You're gentle and kind. How could I not be fond of you?" She stared out over the rocks toward the sea. "Even if I *were* to love you, what good could come of it? I cannot live in your world, surrounded by hatred. Today, for the first time, your people looked at me as a human being, not as an oppressor. Now I find they have every right to despise me. Father assisted the viceroy here, yet he might have been keeping a kennel for all I cared! I'm stifling, Liam!" she cried almost hysterically. "Please

211

don't speak of love. It's a crueler word than you can imagine."

In wretched silence, he drove home and saw her to the door before returning the carriage to the barn. As he unhitched the horses, he saw Catherine's shawl crumpled on the carriage seat. He held it momentarily against his lips, catching her subtle scent. Reassured by a decision he had just reached, Liam folded the shawl over his arm and strolled out of the barn.

In the house, Catherine flung herself upon Culhane's bed, cursing him for forcing her to this dilemma. It was not as if he had sheltered her; indeed, he had dumped her into the mire. But even then she had not known how callously contrived Ireland's agony was, how relentless the cycle of systematic ruin. As a diplomat's daughter, she was no stranger to the venality of government. She knew perfectly well Ireland had no help in George III, whom she regarded as an intermittently insane, narrow-minded monarch of no imagination and less adaptability; his amoral, self-interested son offered no better promise. Whether she turned traitor to England or traitor to Ireland, she was damned. And now two proud, passionate men wanted her; the one she rejected must be dreadfully hurt. "I hate you, Sean Culhane, you swaggering bastard! You would keep me here and call me to hand at whim. I won't answer! Whatever happens, I won't stay in this miserable place!"

The next week was uneventful. Catherine welcomed her medical lessons with Flynn, in fact, welcomed any distraction from her turmoil. But occupants of the house were awakened by screams during her increasingly frequent nightmares. She grew secretly terrified of a recurrence of her childhood mental collapse. This brooding fear was evident in the sketches Liam continued to make of her. She posed as he wished, but her withdrawn sadness held him at bay.

Knowing he must soon begin the oil, Liam prayed for a change in her mood on the last day of sketching. He had been tender and gentle, bringing her flowers, drawing conversation to light topics, yet each day it became harder to hold himself from her. She was so vulnerable, responding with almost pathetic gratitude to his friendship. Hoping to encourage her to move with less constraint, he asked her to loosen her hair and let it fall about her shoulders to let it catch the cliffside breeze. But as she unbound it, he knew wrenchingly he had suggested the wrong thing. If she had undressed for him in a boudoir, she could not have aroused him more. Her hair was a long, caressing shadow. As she raised her arms, her breasts lifted against the thin material of the dress. Glancing up, she flushed when she saw his tense stare. Quickly she assumed a pose, forcing him to begin sketching. But finally he dropped his charcoal in the easel well and went to take her by the shoulders. "This pretense is useless. I'll take you away, go anywhere you like, love you with all my being forever. Be my wife. Marry me."

She touched his cheek. "Have you thought of all you'd be giving up? What your exile would mean to your people, to your brother?"

His lips curved in a bitter but oddly triumphant smile. "I'm not a poor man. I have certain legal rights to Shelan my brother cannot usurp, no matter where I am. He has poisoned this place with his hate and his hopeless cause. If you weren't here, I shouldn't wish to remain. While I cannot keep you in diamonds at court, I can keep you in comfort wherever you choose."

"You do me honor, my lord," she murmured. "I have no wish for luxury; I do have need of love." She smoothed his hair. "But what of you? Could you be satisfied with a woman who might never learn to love you in equal return?"

Liam buried his face against her temple. "I'd risk anything to keep you near me. In time you might learn to love me, and until then, my love would be more than enough to warm us both. Say it, Catherine. Say you accept."

She drew away slightly. "Is marriage the price of my escape?"

"I'll help you whether you marry me or not," he answered levelly, "but I dared not wait to ask your hand in England. Your father would never permit you to ally with an Irish exile."

Catherine had to agree. She and Liam might have to go to the Continent. In Rome, where he had once been happy, they might be content. Content. She loved the idea, yet loathed its flat salvation. Was she to spend the rest of her days in penance for Ireland's wrongs? Yet, as she looked into Liam's pleading face, she thought how like a child he looked, how needful of the simplest affection and reassurance.

Liam read her gaze as acceptance, and with the avid strength of a drowning man, pulled her closer into his arms.

"Liam, wait . . ."

Her protest might have been the thin cry of a sandpiper for all he heard. "Don't be afraid. Never be afraid of me. I only want to kiss you. I need to kiss you." Feverishly his mouth sought hers, and she let him kiss her as long as he liked. Gradually, she was able to relax. If not as compelling as his brother, Liam was not inexpert and his touch was pleasant. But as his lips sought her throat and shoulders and she felt the hardness of his manhood against her thigh, Catherine tried to twist away, realizing he would not be satisfied with kisses. "Please, let me love you," he whispered roughly against her throat. "I need you so. Please."

She ached for him and for herself. Did honor matter so much that compassion had no place? And even more important, she could not linger in indecision. Armed warfare could not be far off; the Irish must seize their advantage while Napoleon threatened England. Though she could not prevent the eruption, she could stem Shelan's contribution of men and arms to a fray which must lead to yet another bloodbath and defeat. All she had to do was yield her body and the rest of her life to this man. She could hardly ask him to give up everything for nothing.

Her mouth dry, she let him push her down to the heather, and lay still while he fumbled at her bodice fastenings. As his ardent mouth explored her breasts, his sharp teeth occasionally hurt, which tempered the automatic response of her senses. She shivered slightly as he undressed her.

"I've wanted to see you naked, like this," Liam muttered as he feverishly stripped. The bronze of his skin

214

stopped at his throat and forearms; elsewhere, his body was marble white. "I've imagined this moment a thousand times. All the long nights my brother used your body." As he knelt, Liam's blue eyes were dark, almost wild from the goad remembrance gave his passion. "Can you imagine how those thoughts tortured me? The thought of his making you respond maddens me! Your body is an altar; I shall purify his desecration of it." He positioned himself. "You're my goddess. I adore you."

As his body lowered, Catherine recoiled despite her resolution. "Liam, don't you see this is wrong? Please, let me go!" She pushed with desperate determination, and with equal determination, he clung to her; but unaccustomed to rape, he was unable to still her thrashing long enough to find entry. Suddenly he cried out hoarsely and she felt a sticky wetness on her thigh. She dragged painfully at his hair until he flung away with angry frustration. As soon as his weight left her, Catherine rose quickly and clambered down the rocks to the sea. Shivering, she slipped into the water and swam until her body felt scoured. Looking up toward the bluff, she saw him pulling on his clothes, sun-streaked hair blowing in the wind. She climbed up the rocks and, as proudly as any goddess he could desire, strode past him to her own garments.

"Catherine, I don't understand. You seemed to want me."

She dragged on her dress. "I thought you offered marriage, Liam, not enshrinement. You offer escape, but to what? A soft prison of adoration?" She turned to him, fastening the bodice. "The worst of it is, you desire me because I'm your brother's whore. You want to snatch away his plaything. How you must hate him!"

"I didn't always hate him." He met her eyes coldly. "Once, in the manner you think so disgusting, I idolized him despite his theft of my father's affection." He went to his packet and dug through the sketchbooks, finally selecting a worn one. "Look for yourself." He flung it at her bare feet and she stooped quickly to keep the loose pages from scattering. For the first time she saw Sean Culhane as a boy, rapier slim with a feral strength of feature and body magnetic even then. The set of mouth and jaw was

215

hard, the eyes already brooding and insolent. Liam had been untrained in those years, but his strokes had been sure. She recognized now-familiar knife-fighting positions in quick studies that recalled his early training with Flannery; sections of his body had been carefully molded, others merely indicated, producing an illusion of slashing movement. The eyes were guarded; the mouth never smiled.

Catherine turned the page. Liam had drawn Sean at sixteen galloping a bay stallion bareback along the cliffs. At the artist's request, he rode nude, his body balanced slightly back, pelvis easily forward as he deftly controlled the powerful animal.

Quickly flipping to the next drawing, a study in colored chalk, she caught her breath. Liam smiled crookedly. "His first mistress. Her name is Fiona. They're still lovers." The pair stood on the rocks, Sean just behind and above Fiona. The flame-haired girl had a woman's lush body though she could not have been more than fourteen. She wore a simple India-cotton dress hiked up about long, strong legs; Sean, only a pair of frayed breeches. They were both barefoot and insolent and touchingly young. "He sent me away after the one sketch, but I hid in the rocks and watched them. He's never seen these next drawings."

Her fingers refused to move and Liam deliberately turned the pages. They were beautiful, as beautiful as two young people could be, free and abandoned as wild things, their bodies intertwined, sometimes impatiently fierce, often restrained as they were content to explore one another's senses. Their profiles were clear-cut, one like a young hawk's poised over his mate. They were beautiful and proud and they cut into her heart like daggers. To hide the unexpected pain, she studied the remaining drawings, but they became a blur of mocking green eyes. Finally, mercifully, there were no more and Liam gently reclaimed his book. "A few months later, I went to Rome. There's no place like it for idolatry." Striding quickly toward the sea, he carried the book far out onto the rocks, then hurled it outward over the waves. Catherine's mind shrieked as the sketches scattered on the breeze and kited down to the

216

water, became logged, and sank. When the last one disappeared, Liam returned to find her still staring at the water.

"My admiration of my brother began to die when I returned from Rome and saw how far his hate had taken him, but I was still awed enough to become his accomplice. You should be the last to underestimate his ruthlessness. Women are things to Sean. You intrigue him momentarily because you loathe him. But if you ever began to love him, he'd discard you like a bit of rubbish. As you discard me because you find idealization repugnant." He reached out and shook her until her teeth rattled. "If you expect to be loved like a woman, start acting like one. If you don't like altars in the bedroom, stop pontificating!" He released her abruptly.

"Who do you think you are, Saint Joan of Ireland?"

Catherine pushed him away and, stumbling over long skirts as her feet slipped on the wet rocks, fled toward the infirmary. Liam scrambled after her, but on reaching even ground, she outdistanced him like a frightened gazelle. Realizing pursuit was pointless, he slowed to a halt. Numbness filled his heart. After all his patience and care, he had snatched like a thief at her first hesitant offer of affection, then smashed his chances in fury at her recoil.

Catherine's subdued demeanor and Liam's failure to call over the next few days led Doctor Flynn to the accurate conclusion the two had quarreled. He was unsurprised by a visit from the young lord. After Liam's departure, Flynn drifted into his dispensary to find Catherine pasting neatly copied labels over worn ones on his apothecary bottles. Peering quizzically over his spectacles, he held out a freshly cut rose. "It's from Liam. Take pity on the lad; he has no dissections of pollywogs and newts to divert him, only a portrait he cannot finish without his model. He asks if you will consider posing tomorrow." Silently, Catherine smoothed a label on a jar of sulphur crystals.

"Don't you think you owe him at least the completion of the project to which he has devoted much time and labor?

217

How can Ireland hope for peace if one person cannot accept another's offered hand?"

She stared at the label. "Will you come with us?"

"Alas, no. Tomorrow I face the dreary prospect of tea with my daughters."

Ah, Catherine, she thought bitterly, you see where meddling has gotten you. "Very well. I'll see the portrait done."

And she did, taking care the sessions were conducted in clear sight of the infirmary. Although dismayed at her distrust, Liam had sense enough not to protest. The portrait steadily progressed without either participant's enthusiasm. Catherine was resigned to having the thing done, while Liam chafed at the remoteness of the figure taking form on canvas; his model's essence, the impudent wit and vivacity, was missing. Her eyes were more hauntingly beautiful than ever, but had a shadowed quality as did her smile. The pose seemed oddly familiar; he painted surely, as if he had repeated it often. Finally he applied finishing touches and stood back, then had an eerie feeling of *déjà vu.* The barefoot girl in white standing on the windswept rocks was a ghost; another lovely, dark-haired girl. And suddenly he remembered who she was.

With a trace of her old roguish smile, his model ventured curiously to the easel. "You look as if it were a disaster. I warned you I'd be difficult to paint." Turning to look at his work, she fell silent for some moments. "She's beautiful, Liam. Too beautiful to be me. But how strangely like Mother. . . . Is it finished?" Glancing up at him, she was surprised at his blanched face.

"Yes . . . yes, it's done. Except for the varnish." His voice was harsh, almost strangled.

"What's wrong?" she asked, involuntarily touching him for the first time since the quarrel.

He shrank from her touch. "Nothing! I've been cheated again, that's all." He turned away abruptly and knelt to frenziedly load his saddlebags, not caring how they were filled.

Catherine stooped beside him. "What is it, Liam? Have I said something to offend you?"

He stared at her, his face twisted, then burst into wild,

hoarse laughter. "No. What could you do? You were only the lure! The gods have had another joke at my expense!" His voice turned to a despairing croak. "You never wanted anything more to do with me once the painting was finished, did you? So now it's done and you can go your way. Liam has his love to keep forever, her duplicate." Wrenching away, he grabbed the painting to hurl it, like the sketches, into the sea.

Catherine scrambled after him. "No! Liam, stop!" Fiercely, she dragged at his arms. "You cannot obliterate Sean and me by wrecking your images of us. You only hurt yourself." He hesitated as she pleaded, "You speak as if I hated you! We've hurt each other, but that's past. There's yet time to learn. We're friends. Nothing can change that."

"Nothing?" He laughed harshly. "I want a wife, not a painted substitute. My idolatry doesn't extend that far."

"Liam, please give me the painting. I'll take it to Doctor Flynn to keep for you. You may feel differently later."

His torment altered to cunning. "No. You're right. The painting's mine. I'd be a fool to discard it."

Wary of his abrupt about-face, she looked at him dubiously. "You won't destroy it?"

"On the contrary," he said tightly, "I'll keep it ever close." He gently disengaged her hand from his arm. "You'd better go back to the infirmary. The wind is growing chill and you have no shawl." Then, ignoring her, he slid the painting back onto its pack frame, folded his easel, and threw the saddlebags onto the gelding. Without a backward glance, he rode away toward Shelan.

CHAPTER 11

Remembrance of a Spring Day

Several daisies narrowly missed being crushed by a worn pair of sea boots as Sean slid off Mephisto and chose the shortest path to the infirmary door. On the way home from Norfolk, he had cursed the *Mary D.* for a lumbering scow, snapped at the crew for minor errors, and generally made every seaman aboard as spiny-tempered as himself. Upon landfall at Shelan, he had paced impatiently until the horses were ashore, then with the English black in tow, pounded off down the beach in the direction of the bay. Watching his commander disappear, Captain Shannon sighed under his breath, "Now I know how the whale felt after he puked up Jonah."

For all his headlong eagerness to see Catherine, Sean hesitated at the infirmary door. He had nearly forgotten the underlying reason for his trip to England in the first place. Probably, the girl wished him halfway to China. Assuming a mask of indifference, he pushed the door open. The mask slipped. The customarily deserted waiting room was filled with men, most of whom uneasily rose, doffing their caps as he entered. He nodded automatically as he worked his way through them to knock on the closed dispensary door. It snapped open. "I have a patient. Would you mind . . . ? Sean, lad!" A beaming Flynn clapped him on the shoulder. "Well, well. You weren't expected for several days yet." He eyed the startled look on Culhane's usually impassive face. "Come in, come in! I'm nearly finished with this gentleman." He pulled Sean into the room and

220

shut the door. "Do you mind, Rory?" The patient, an elderly fisherman, warily squinted at the tall Irishman from a horizontal position on the examination table. "Mr. Culhane is just back from a sea jaunt and I do believe"— Flynn poured whiskey for Sean and his patient—"he looks a bit landlocked." He handed the drinks around, then poured for himself. Ignoring Sean, who was staring at the fisherman as if the man were a walking whale, he raised his glass. "Gentlemen, to my niece, Kitty Flynn."

The bearded salt broke into a gap-toothed grin. "Here, here!" He hoisted his glass, bolted its contents, and belched.

Draining his own whiskey, Sean continued to stare at the fisherman until the doctor blocked his view and finished prodding. He gave the man a medication and dismissed him.

After the door closed, Sean leaned against the wall. "How did you lure him here? And the others?"

Flynn cocked his head owlishly to one side. "They're here for a glimpse of Kitty."

"She must be quite an eyeful. I didn't know you had a niece."

"I don't."

Sean looked at him questioningly, then frowned as suspicion raised its hooded head. He snapped upright. "Blast! Kitty is Catherine. Damnation, Flynn, I sent her here because the place was deserted, not Mecca for craning louts! How did they know she was here?"

Flynn regarded him calmly. "Don't get your hackles up. The men pay her all respect. As you know, she's not likely to tolerate less."

When she can help it, thought the younger man, not a whit reassured.

Flynn began to put his implements in order. "You may as well know, because you'll find out sooner or later, the lass persuaded me to permit Liam to escort her into Ruiralagh." He went on, ignoring the muffled curse behind his back. "The villagers haven't seen so beguiling a smile since Queen Maeve cozened them into fighting her battles. It's no wonder they all come trotting up the hill for another glimpse of the same."

221

"Like a herd of horny goats!" Sean muttered disgustedly.

Flynn grinned at his friend's sour face. "If that's true, how do you explain my daughters' sudden visits? Although every moment they spend under this roof puts fleas in their drawers and they're convinced Catherine's the lively mistress of my frivolous declining years, their courtesy to her is almost painful." His smile turned obliquely shrewd. "I hope your inventive mind can reach a conclusion where mine has woefully failed?"

Knowing exactly how his witch had cast her apparently magic spells, Sean demanded ominously, "Where is the baggage?"

Flynn shrugged pleasantly. "Last seen, she was in my office. I believe you know the way . . . Ah, keep it down, will you?"

As he entered the office, all Sean could see of Catherine was a small bottom protruding from under the desk. Strongly tempted to kick it, he restrained the urge to a mere spine-jarring bellow instead. "Kitty Flynn! Whatever your customary greeting of your village swains, kindly present me with your face instead of your backside!"

His roar was rewarded by a resounding bump under the desk followed by a muffled yelp. The trim derriere disappeared like a ferret down a hole, and a smudged face with enormous dark blue eyes tilted up at him from the far side of the desk. Her mouth forming a small O, Catherine's eyes lit with a sparkling fire he missed altogether. "Get up, you conniving little hellcat, so I can wring your meddling neck!"

Catherine's surge of happiness at first startled sight of the tall Irishman was eclipsed by his scowl and unexpected attack. Her own ire rose. "I've done nothing to you! How dare you charge in here and shout at me!" She scrambled to her feet and, clamping both hands on her hips, glared up at him.

"I'll do more than shout, you scheming witch! I no more than turn my back and you're soliciting in the village!"

Her eyes widened in outrage. "Solicit? Me, solicit! How dare you! You, of all people!" A healthy kick caught Sean painfully in the shin. "Who took *whose* virginity, pray?"

Clamping his arms around her, Sean hoisted her off the floor. "When the village fleet is anchored on Flynn's doorstep, I come to one conclusion, wench! Maeve's beguiling smile, rot! It's not your teeth those fishfarmers come to see!"

"It's not my fault I've turned pretty!" she hissed. "Every time you ogle me, I wish I had a face of mud!"

"Vain, now, too," he gritted. "A few moth-eaten rags and you think you rival Godiva! You did wear clothes into town, I hope?"

Catherine's temper exploded. "I'll carve you up! Put me down, you slandering Irish ape!"

He stuck his nose against hers. "It's no slander to say you're a blackmailer! I've no doubt you coerced Flynn's daughters by threatening to reveal what I told you in private, didn't you? You played at being Irish and simpered at Liam until he put his head and mine into a noose. Irish! You're as Irish as Josephine Bonaparte and about as discreet!"

"And what would you know, ye blitherin' lummox? I can fling drivelin' blarney with the likes of you any day!" His startled look and relaxed grip allowed her to knee his groin. He dropped her like a hot coal. Bouncing away from her doubled-up aggressor, Catherine cooed, "Ohh, I've been waiting for that! But to think I've waited all these weeks to . . . you swaggering bully; you smug, hypocritical sermonizer! You're so careless of rutting, you assume everyone else is indiscriminate!"

The Irishman sagged against the wall while she railed, and slowly Catherine's anger ebbed as she saw beads of sweat on his brow. Uneasily remorseful, she took a hesitant step toward him. "Are you all right?"

He shrank back. "Stay away."

"I didn't realize . . . let me help you to a chair," she urged.

A hand shielding his groin, he sidled along the wall. "Oh, no, you don't. I'm hanging on to the remains of my manhood . . . literally."

Averting her eyes, Catherine fidgeted in embarrassment. Suddenly, a quick, slithering movement riveted her attention. "Now I've got you!" she exulted.

Sean flinched as she pounced toward him. Triumphantly, she snatched up a field mouse. Cupping it in her hands, she stroked the creature to ease its fear. As its bright red eyes peered at him nervously above twitching whiskers, the Irishman let out his breath. "I should have known you'd have a familiar about."

She arched a dark brow. "It's ever a witch's habit. If I had intended to render you impotent"—her head jerked at a broom resting in a corner—"I only needed to wave my wand."

Ruefully, he stared down at himself. "I wonder if mine will ever wave again."

"Of that, I've no doubt. You'll be swaggering about, intimidating everyone again in all too short order."

He grinned crookedly. "You weren't much impressed."

"Oh, but I was," she answered quietly. "Even afraid."

He straightened, his grin fading. "You hid it well enough."

"Haven't you ever smothered fear with hostility?"

He was thoughtful for a moment, then admitted slowly, "Perhaps that's part of the reason I attacked you. Anger removed the uncertainty from our meeting again." He fell silent, for the first time letting himself enjoy the quiet pleasure of her nearness. Her hair fell in a black, silken torrent down her back from a head that seemed too small to carry such luxurious weight. She appeared unchanged, her exquisite, fine-boned face, if anything, more flowerlike. Blue eyes met his with a child's unwavering candor. He yearned to take her in his arms, yet dared not touch her, for he could not trust himself not to whisper impossible words of need. "I've a peace offering," he said quietly.

"Not my freedom?" She searched his eyes. "No, I thought not. Never that." She slipped the mouse into a small cage on the desk. "This mouse and I are much alike." She turned, adding ironically, "Slaves aren't permitted to be ungrateful; therefore, I most humbly accept your gift." The remoteness that held Liam at bay transmitted its chill to his brother.

Though he found her change of manner disquieting, Sean did not retreat. "I bring only what is yours already."

"A slave has no possessions. All is her master's."

"Even so. What is yours is now mine. Come . . ." He took her hand and led her to the window. After pushing it open, he swung across the sill and indicated for her to follow. Intrigued in spite of herself, she adroitly obeyed. "No need to alert the fleet," the Irishman muttered as he led her at a trot to the front of the building.

She caught sight of the stallions and broke into a run. Both blacks whickered a greeting, but it was her own pet she threw her arms about. "Numidian! Oh, darling. I thought I'd never see you again." Her head buried against the animal's neck, she was only dimly aware of Mephisto's nudge at her shoulder.

"My nag thinks it's a fickle wench y'are," came a soft lilt behind her. "He's jealous."

She turned to him, her eyes luminous. "How could you know?" she whispered. Tears blurred her vision and the words drifted away. The tall Irishman and the slim girl looked long at one another as the sea wind whipped silently about them. Then Mephisto broke the quiet by impatiently poking his head at Catherine's shoulder. Her eyes reluctantly slipped from the Irishman's as she stroked the sulky stallion's nose. When her eyes lifted, they were uneasy. "What have you done?" she asked softly, joy shadowed by growing apprehension. "You must have stolen Numidian. Father would never sell him and Amin would die before letting a stranger . . ."

"I picked him up in a horserace," Sean replied quietly. "Your father and the old Arab are well."

She stared at him. "Race? But Numidian isn't raced. Father promised . . ." Not wanting her father's enemy to catch some slur, she bit the words off and turned to play with Numidian's forelock. "How did he place?"

"If I had been his rider, he'd have won," was the flat reply. "You've made him a pet. Mephisto won by a half-length for that reason alone."

"Numidian will run for me!" Her blue eyes flashed. "He's not used to strangers."

Culhane smiled faintly. "Neither is Mephisto. I've trained him to tolerate no other man on his back, and he's trampled two who tested his schooling. It never occurred to

225

me a bit of fluff could sweet-talk the big lummox into heading for the hills.''

Catherine jumped to the stallion's defense. "Mephisto
isn't a lummox! He's a better horse than you're likely to
see again!''

"The best in Britain," agreed Sean inconsistently with a
complacent grin. "Not another horse in the islands can
beat him.''

Her small chin lifted in blunt challenge. "Want to bet?''

His grin widened. "What have you to wager?''

She flushed, remembering she could claim nothing, not
even the clothes on her back. Then her chin lifted a notch
higher and her tone suggested an offer of the crown jewels.
"You've heard me play the pianoforte. If I lose, I'll play for
you whenever you like.''

He nodded graciously. "Done. I'll throw in a new dress.''
Catherine kicked off her slippers; Sean tucked them into
his jacket pockets, then gave her a hand up onto Numidian's bare back. She sat casually astride, long skirts
hiked to her knees. After vaulting onto his own mount, he
led the way down the bluff to the beach.

Ahead of the cantering riders, low tide bared a stretch of
pebbles in a shimmering sweep at the base of white limestone cliffs. Slicing through a silver haze, seabirds screamed
over surf the sheen of pearls. Sensing they were to be let
out, the stallions snorted restively. "We'll line up with
that rock fault," Culhane's voice lifted above the surf's
rumble, "and use that far outcrop as the finish." He
pointed to a prominent wedge of weathered limestone a
few hundred yards down the beach toward Shelan where
the *Mary D.* was already raising sail for departure. Catherine nodded, hair drifting out on the breeze like a ban-
ner. When a side glance assured Sean she was ready, he
shouted, "Go!" and kicked Mephisto sharply in the flanks.
Both horses leaped forward, haunches bunching and
hooves spattering grit, then leveled out. As the riders
leaned low over their necks, they pounded up the beach.
Intent on proving the folly of coddling a racehorse, Sean
gave his challenger no quarter, but when the outcrop was
passed, he was irritably stunned to find himself the loser
by a full length.

Perched like a gull's feather on Numidian's broad back, Catherine grinned as she circled and slowed to an easy trot. "There's no need to scowl like a jilted suitor! After all, I'm much lighter than you, and Numidian knows I adore him; he'll run his heart out for me."

Still frowning, Sean shook his head. "I've left light riders eating dust, and Mephisto's belly-deep in awe of me. It doesn't make sense."

She laughed. "Only if you persist in basing his efficiency on fear."

Culhane kneed the stallion impatiently down the beach. "Mephisto obeys because he knows I won't tolerate less, and punish disobedience."

Catherine was silent for a moment as they cooled the sweaty horses. "What is *my* punishment to be?"

"Which offense do you have in mind?"

"Take your choice. You seemed to have a rather long list when you barged into the infirmary. I don't expect a man with your stringent demands of his possessions to dismiss such transgressions."

Knowing she was forcing his hand to make a point, the Irishman thoughtfully regarded her fine-boned profile and rigid expectancy. "So I have," he said quietly, "and I'll do so now." Leaning over, he caught her bridle, pulling Numidian to a halt. Catherine tensed, her slim body ramrod straight as he turned his mount in a tight circle to face her; their knees brushed. "The price of your crimes is a kiss."

Her sapphire eyes went wide. "A kiss?"

"Only that."

She shifted. "Now?"

"Now."

Resignedly, she leaned toward him, closed her eyes, and waited. After a moment, when there was no response, she peeked at him. "No?"

"No," he intoned with mock gravity. "You're to kiss me."

She blinked. "Oh." Squeezing her eyes shut, she leaned hesitantly toward him again, rising slightly to reach the required target.

Just as her lips started to hastily brush his, Sean whispered, "No pecks, little miscreant. Pay the hangman his due."

Her eyes opened half-wary, half-mesmerized by green eyes that seemed to draw her into their darkly clouded depths. She steadied herself with one hand against his chest. Her lips brushed his shyly, then clung as his mouth warmed to hers.

Sean had resolved to retain control, but instinctively his hand moved to lift her face gently to his and his lips parted, luring her to kiss him more deeply. Irresistibly drawn, Catherine answered the lure and kissed him fully, holding back nothing. A vibrant current flowed through her limbs as if his lips offered the only warmth in the world. She put all her longing for the haven his strong arms had strangely come to promise into the softness of her kiss; and Sean's need for her welcome found release in his gentle acceptance of it. When at last he let her go, they looked at each other silently, without lust, both at peace and content to wait.

That night, Catherine was asleep long before Sean finished reviewing the work piled up in his absence. Though the hour was late, he lay awake, studying her profile in the streaming moonlight, knowing its perfect serenity to be an illusion. Peg had told him of Catherine's worsening nightmares. Something or someone must have triggered her old terrors. The housekeeper thought her distress had increased at the same time Flynn's patients had returned, but that made no sense. His mind prowled restlessly. What had been different? In the village, she had encountered strangers for the first time in months; one of them, a street, a name, might have recalled an obscure memory.

His mind cast farther. Liam had been her escort. Had he made advances? Peg's advice echoed in his brain: "She'd bloom in the arms of a lovin' man." Catherine's spirits had drooped during Liam's absence in America, despite her protests of mere friendship. He had believed her, but had he deluded himself? Once the idea of her warming to his brother's caresses hooked into his mind, he could not wrench free of its barbs. Liam was no longer an insignificant dreamer, but a determined rival with odds grossly in his favor. Her tenderness was no proof she did not yearn for another man's arms, yet more than ever, he wanted to protect her. Once he had coldly sought the key to her dreams in order to break her; now he was determined to break their spell. Still, he wondered whether recalling intolerable memories would end their recurrence or drive her mad.

Sean began to take Catherine riding in the afternoons. To make up this time from his work, he spent long hours at night in the study where he often slept on the sofa to avoid bedding with her, for he trusted his restraint less and less.

As a horsewoman, Catherine fearlessly managed her mount with a reckless though elegant grace. Had her precision been less than faultless, Culhane would have curbed her perilous inclination to speed, but observing her ability to take any jump as easily as himself, he was shortly inclined to believe Elizabeth Dunaway's assessment of her rival was colored with jealousy. Astride Numidian, Catherine reverted to the careless, impudent hellion she had been in England. She delighted in showing her heels to Mephisto and took outrageous chances to do so.

Although the rides were a needed diversion and both he and Catherine reacted like unruly children on holiday, at night her dreams left her shaken and confused. The nightmares, which had briefly abated at his homecoming, returned. He knew the broken French lullaby by heart; its childish monotony made his skin crawl.

One hazy day he led her to a high stone breastwork, which ranged across the barren moor not quite a mile from the house. He was galloping when the barrier appeared, but slowly fell back to allow her to take the lead. Almost casually, she veered away and cantered along the wall looking for a place to negotiate it where visibility was unimpeded, then slowed to a trot when she found none. Her head snapped around when the Irishman drawled, "I knew you'd find an obstacle that mollycoddled he-goat would refuse." He looped a leg over his pommel and gave her a grin as he scratched Mephisto between the ears.

She frowned. "Numidian didn't refuse; I did. I won't risk him foolishly."

"Ha! You've run him ragged over wooden gates higher

229

than this. Come, Miss Enderly, admit it. That nag is a sham of a competitor. He's a big pet, nothing better."

"He's not afraid! I told you I reined him in!"

"Why? Why check him at this particular jump?" He trotted close to her.

"I dislike blind jumps." Imperceptibly, she tried to ease Numidian away from Mephisto, whose big body blocked the way to the open field.

Sean casually kneed the stallion to cut her off. "Dislike? You're afraid. Why not say so?"

She stiffened. "I wouldn't dream of marring your complacency. Think what you please." Numidian sensed his mistress's tension and began to paw the ground.

Sean scoffed, "So plucky Catherine Enderly is a mewling babe after all. Would you like me to go first, Miss Snivel?"

She bridled at the unlooked-for insult. "Why not? Break you arrogant neck, if you cannot bend it! See if I care."

"Such is your concern for my hide, lady," he replied sardonically. "No doubt it would please you best, stretched on yonder wall." Roughly, he jerked the big stallion around, trotted some distance into the field, and wheeled. Catherine's fingers twisted at the reins as the Irishman spurred Mephisto forward. The mighty stallion's muscles rippled under glossy hide as he thundered across the rocky ground. The wall loomed closer with each hoofbeat.

Suddenly Catherine heard herself shriek. "No! No! Stop, please God . . . ." Her terror ended in a whimper. A dark blanket abruptly settled over her head.

Something brushed her face, and involuntarily she twisted away. Light played around the edges of the shadowy blanket, then grew blinding as the darkness lifted. She clearly heard her name. With an effort, her fingers lifted to touch a hard chest under a woolen jacket.

"Aye, lass, my neck is still stiff enough to defy the king's hangman." Culhane's voice was gently teasing, yet its strained note made her wonder.

"Did I faint?"

"Slid overboard like a green cabin boy on a well-greased whaler. Anything hurt?"

She grimaced and sat up woozily. "Only my pride. I've

always considered vaporous females idiotic." She blinked. "Did you jump the wall?"

"With a squalling banshee ruining my concentration? Not likely!" He pulled her to her feet and held her until she steadied. "All right now?"

She eased out of his arms. "Quite."

During the next weeks, blind obstacles bristled all over the countryside. Culhane permitted her no excuse to discontinue the daily rides which quickly became an ordeal. Inevitably he would drop back from the lead, forcing her to take his place, never again attempting a wall she refused. One by one, she rode around barriers or turned away. He never pressed, only waited silently. Despite their recent relaxation of hostility, Catherine was almost convinced he had finally determined to destroy her, yet his gentle patience was bewildering.

She dared not turn to Liam, who avoided both her and his brother and spent many days away from home. Distantly polite at their rare meetings, he too seemed to be waiting for her to break, to be forced to recognize him as her salvation. Even Flynn, busy with his practice, was preoccupied and she struggled alone with increasingly complex studies. While Sean labored in the study, sometimes until dawn, Catherine, fearing sleep, poured over medical books. Occasionally sheer fatigue overcame her at the desk; hours later, Sean would put her to bed. During the day she hid from him at the infirmary, unaware Flynn also observed her carefully. Sean and Flynn were apprehensive. How much her mind could endure if forced to relive her mother's death was impossible to guess. But neither of them could know she was under an additional intolerable strain. Racked between irreconcilable political and moral responsibilities, she would tell them nothing of her current dilemma and could remember nothing of the old.

To Sean fell the dangerous decision. He would have yielded to the obvious solution and sent his hostage home despite the pain of losing her, but according to his spies, even at Windemere Catherine had been haunted by the past. To return her was to condemn her to that condition for life. Would the man who purchased her for a bride care for her hurts? How would he react to her nocturnal screams?

When Culhane led her again to the stone wall on the moor, Catherine followed with mute docility as if through a ritual. She seemed drugged as she automatically veered Numidian away at a monotonous trot. But lethargy escalated into panic as the Irishman crowded Numidian to the wall so closely she feared injury to her beloved stallion. When she flung up a fist to ward off her tormentor, he seized her wrist in a firm grip. "Not today, Kit. Today you don't refuse."

Her pupils shrank to pinpoints. "Let go!" Her voice dropped to a low snarl. "I won't take the wall and you'll not make me!" She goaded Numidian to rear, but Sean's hard downward twist on her wrist forced her to quiet the stallion. "I'm sick of being toyed with! You think I don't know what you're trying to do?" Her voice rose in hysteria as she wrenched against his hand with a strength that surprised him. "You're a monster! Let go of me, damn you!"

"I'll put you up in front of me and take us both over! Take your choice."

Viciously she kicked at his leg and, dropping the reins, clawed at his head. When Sean ducked, she slid out of the saddle, crying out at the strain on her wrist. Still she punched and kneed at Mephisto's flank until he tore the earth with his heavy hooves and reared. As Sean loosed her wrist for fear of trampling her, she scrambled away and ran like a panicked deer. Culhane kept Mephisto close at her shoulder, ready to twitch the black aside if she stumbled, and flushed her toward the wall. Back and forth she darted, but flying feet were no match for the black. Panting and exhausted, she was forced against the stone barrier, where she turned at bay and caught up a jagged rock. Instantly Culhane slid off the stallion and pushed the nervous horse away.

Catherine shrank against the stones but, instead of hurling her missile, began to edge away. "Get back! Get back!" His hand shot out and planted itself beside her left shoulder. She recoiled, only to meet his other hand blocking escape. Twisting to the wall, she pressed against the rough surface as if attempting to dislodge its stones. "Leave me alone! Stop hounding me!"

"What are you afraid of?"

"Nothing! Nothing! Leave me alone!" She was screaming now.

"Catherine, who's behind the wall?" She froze. Abrupt silence fell over the sunlit meadow. "Is someone in trouble?"

Fingers clawing weakly at the rocks, she whimpered. "Please. Please. Stop . . ."

"Kit, do you hear a woman crying?"

"No . . . Maman, don't. Don't cry."

"Is it your mother, Kit?"

"She . . . was hurt . . . she needed help . . . but no one came." Her head sagged against the rock and for a moment Sean thought she had fainted.

"What happened? Why was she hurt?"

"Her birthday," Catherine muttered dully. "It was her birthday." Catherine's voice was strained and faraway and he had difficulty catching all the words, but the picture they recalled was all too vivid. Windemere had been crowded with guests for the week-long birthday celebration and Elise Enderly had been at her best, exhilarated by dancing and a midnight supper. Toward dawn, she had left her bleary-eyed guests gaming at whist and piquet and gone to Catherine's room to rouse out her daughter for an early-morning ride. They had whispered like mischievous schoolgirls while she helped Catherine dress. An usual, they had saddled the horses without awakening the grooms and had left the stable before first light. Dawn had come as still as a silence between heartbeats, the birds just beginning to call as light threaded the sky. The spring fields were blooming and green, the fecund scent of raw earth fresh on the breeze. Elise, riding Ethiop, had teased Catherine into a race to greet the sun. "A wonderful secret's the prize!" she had cried gaily.

"I couldn't keep up with her on Boswick," Catherine murmured. "She began to outdistance me. She was laughing when she took Ethiop over the east meadow wall, then . . . screaming. I would have followed her if she hadn't screamed." Her fingers splayed on the wall. "When I reached them, they were still alive . . . hanging on a hayrack like gory butterflies. Ethiop was nearly gutted."

"Kit, that's enough."

"They wouldn't die and Ethiop kept trying to run . . ."

"Kit . . ."

"Mother always carried a small pistol; it looked like a toy. I took it and shot Ethiop. She pleaded for the other bullet. I wanted to go for help, but she clung to me, begging. Blood came from her mouth and I thought she was dying. She was terrified to die alone. So I stayed and she kept living and moaning through those bloody bubbles. Finally, I put the gun to her head. Then she was quiet." Distractedly, she crooned, "Maman, don't cry. I'll never leave you . . . never."

Turning her to him, Sean held her tightly. "Kit, it's over."

But the soft, terrible voice went on. "When Papa and the men finally came, they stared at me. My habit was covered with blood. Then I began to see she might have lived if I had gone for help. Papa took away the gun and put me in a room. I wasn't permitted to go to the funeral. I stayed in the room and sang. She hated the dark, to be alone . . ." Catherine's head rested on his chest as she pondered idly, wistfully, "I wonder what her secret was?"

"How long were you in the room?"

"I don't know. A few weeks . . . months."

"What was it like?"

Her voice grew stronger, more aware. "There were bars and a cot and two servants who tied me down when I became violent. Finally a doctor had them throw cold water on me and I stopped singing. After a time, I was sent to school . . . Papa was very angry, you see."

A harsh note edged Sean's voice despite his effort to keep his words even. "He blamed you?"

"He never said so. But he never came to see me. I knew."

"Kit, you've begun to learn something of medicine," he said carefully. "Your mother's lungs were pierced. She couldn't have lived. Don't you see your father and the men who found you in the field must have pitied the terrible choice you had to make? The horror you thought you saw in their eyes was a reflection of your own uncertainty and grief."

"If Papa understood, why did he send me away?"

"Grief can be a selfish emotion. Some people best bear their sorrows alone. Perhaps he felt you would recover more quickly if your surroundings no longer suggested bad memories." Privately, Sean thought the viscount could not have done more to ensure his daughter's mental collapse. Denied every normal form of mourning, even painful but necessary relinquishment by witnessing the burial, she had been given neither support nor solace. Enderly's callousness seemed incredible, yet the girl loved him with all the forlorn hope of a rejected child and sought some miserly token of forgiveness. With all his soul, Sean wished he had killed the man at Ingram. "Kit." He tilted her chin up. "Look at me." Even in direct sunlight, her eyes were dark and filled with loss. "You know I'm a coldhearted villain who gives no quarter. Why should I pity you? I could easily tell you you're a murderess, but it would be a lie."

"You lied about Maude . . ."

"But not this. I'm telling you now what someone should have told you then. *Your mother could not have lived.* You had little choice that day. The only evil involved was the delusion she might have survived." His hands locked at her temples. "She cannot feel the dark or hear your singing. She cannot be any nearer to the sun than she is now. She loved you. Weep for her. Then remember her joy." Desperately, he searched his memory of his own brief childhood. "Remember her kissing you at Christmas, smuggling sweetmeats after you were tucked in for the night, her lullabies . . ." Finally Catherine surrendered to the healing grief she had been denied, and he held her while she wept for a long, long time in great, tearing sobs. When at last the sobs slowly eased and she relaxed, he stroked her hair until her tearstained face lifted to his.

"What sort of demon are you, who plucks his victims from the abyss?"

"Like Lucifer, little one, I envy the power of God; one day He may demand an accounting." He smiled faintly. "Will you give a hand to a ruined rebel when he lies smoking in the Pit?"

"If he's the same sooty fellow who once fished me from a pond. Aye. I'd see his wings well laundered."

That night Sean accompanied Catherine to bed, where she slept quietly in his arms for the first time in weeks.

CHAPTER 12

Stormfire

Catherine awoke to see Sean giving the bell rope an impatient tug. With only a glance at her, he began to rifle through his chest. He was pulling out clothing and throwing it on the bed when Peg came puffing in. "Well, what is it, for heaven's sake?" She frowned. "What a mess ye're makin'!"

"Fetch Tim O'Rourke's sea gear, Peg. He won't be needing it for a week or so. I'm taking the lady for a long sail up the coast."

Two jaws dropped simultaneously. The plump one snapped shut when Sean's eyes fixed on her with more than a hint of impatience. "Sure and why not?" she muttered, and backed out the door.

Catherine sat up straight as Sean turned to his shaving. "But what of my infirmary duties? Your work? Surely we can't just leave . . ."

"The devil we can't." His retort was muffled by lather. "We've earned a holiday."

Catherine's eyes brightened. The thought of filling her lungs with sea air made her bounce out of bed.

Amused green eyes met hers from the partly scraped face in the mirror. Sean turned around, scraps of lather clinging to his jaw. "So you relish going alone to sea with a rogue?"

She gave him a feline smile. "For a rogue, you're remarkably reliable."

He dashed his face with cold water. "But not without

purpose, my pigeon. You'd best remember naught but a truce is between us."

She hugged her knees to her chin and retorted softly, "Even now you guard me. You make a sorry villain, Sir Rogue, divided against yourself."

Peg pecked at the door and hurried in with a bundle of clothes under her arm. Dropping it on the bed, she gave Catherine a conspiratorial wink. "I'll be back with breakfast."

"No, you won't," Sean said as she threw up the lid of his chest. "We'll breakfast at sea. Have a couple of weeks' rations taken aboard the *Megan.*"

Catherine felt a faint chill at the name. Suddenly the holiday's bright promise was dimmed. As Peg left the room, Catherine went through the clothing in silence. There was a pair of brown whipcord breeches, a change of shirts and stockings, a warm jacket, and an Aran sweater. She slipped off the bed, and a moment later the nightgown settled in a puddle on the rug.

Sean had concentrated on his own dressing, but in spite of himself, his eyes lifted. Catherine felt his stare. Seeing the look in his eyes, her own darkened and her fingers went involuntarily to her throat. Abruptly he turned away and dragged on his shirt. "Tim's feet are a near size with your own," he muttered, "so don't use both pairs of socks to stuff the boots. You'll want a pair dry."

While Catherine dressed, Sean quickly packed a small bundle of toiletries, a flint box, and needle and thread. When he finished, she was regarding him soberly with grave, dark blue eyes from the foot of the bed. Her fragility was accentuated by male clothing; even without the raven hair falling in a silken stream over her jacketed shoulder, her femininity was apparent in heavy, shadowing lashes and a delicate line of jaw. Sean picked up a scarf from the commode and crossed to her, but as he approached he sensed she was somehow wary. Still, she looked up unwaveringly and he had a momentary sensation of falling into a starlit sea. As quickly as the illusion came, he banished it. If his feelings were so badly shielded that Flynn had been aware of them, he must have the dazzled look of a smitten schoolboy.

"Turn around, English. We'll be taking a private short-cut to the beach."

She hesitated, then turned. After the blindfold was secure, she heard the Irishman shrug into his jacket. The bundle he had packed was pushed into her hands. "Hold this. I'll have my hands full."

Suddenly swept off her feet and easily held in strong arms, she was revolved until she lost all sense of direction. There was a slight click and intrigue stole her earlier uneasiness. A wooden panel in the bedroom must be a door.

The passage was narrow, steep, and circuitous, but Sean never once bumped her against the walls. She itched to brush an exploratory fingertip down one of them. Brick on an upper floor would mean the passage was built into the chimney area; granite, along the exterior wall.

Sean felt a furtive movement. "No, you don't, English. That small nose may be atwitch with curiosity, but it'll not catch the first whiff of salt if you don't play fair."

The air grew progressively more cool and damp, the stairway ended, and they crossed an open space. Catherine caught a faint odor of wine. When on kitchen duty, she had never been permitted in the wine cellar. That she might have been originally smuggled into the house via the cellar had long ago occurred to her, but the door was always kept locked unless opened with one of the keys Peg always kept at her side. Catherine's quick mind was still humming when at last her hair lifted on the sea breeze. Sean set her on the sand and removed the blindfold. He grinned faintly at her alert look. "You shouldn't work so hard at playing compass; it will put a pucker between those pretty brows."

She thoughtfully watched him stride toward the surf's edge where a man waited with a dinghy. The two exchanged a few words, which were lost in the rush of the waves. Culhane had taken a chance bringing her through the passage, she mused. Was it because he was beginning to trust her, or because he thought she'd never have the opportunity to describe it to the authorities?

He came back at a trot. "The supplies are aboard. Come on, English, time's wasting."

He rowed through the pounding surf with long, sure

strokes, keeping the bow well quartered to oncoming breakers. Surrounded by white, crashing walls of foam, Catherine, her hands clutching the gunnels, tried to concentrate only on Culhane's rhythmically moving body, which blocked out the wildness of the water and part of its lashing spray. Thank heaven she'd had no breakfast; her stomach was cringing somewhere in her throat. She mustn't be sick; he'd never let her forget it. Suddenly she heard a chuckle over the water's roar, then an amused drawl. "Never fear, lass. You'll come to know when the Sea Beast is more sound than fury."

Her lips moved stiffly. "I'm not afraid."

"No. Just a bit thoughtful."

Oddly, she was not really afraid, for though the tiny boat tossed like a cork, Culhane had no fear. He obviously enjoyed the challenge to his skill and muscles. His white teeth were bared in effort and concentration, seeming to match the ferocity of the sea. With his wet hair a ragged black satin cap, he might have been the Sorcerer Prince battling the elements. Abruptly the roaring muted behind them and they skimmed across the swells to the yacht riding at anchor. As the dinghy came alongside the clean-lined hull, Catherine saw "Megan" painted in green and gold across the stern. Sean secured the dinghy to a deck cleat, then swung over to straddle the gunnel of *Megan's* teak afterdeck. "Now we'll try your sea legs, English. Give me the blanket." He bent down, and before she realized what was happening, he had caught her about the waist. He slid her over the gunnel and across his thighs until she was safely in his arms. Green eyes teased her wide blue ones. "Next time, you'll be heaving your own ballast aboard."

"I could have managed," she retorted.

"Like to try?" His grip abruptly slackened, and with a gasp, she grabbed for him. Instantly he caught her close, feeling her heart quick against his chest. "Nay, lass," he whispered against her hair. "No games. We're alone with the sea and I'll not have a mutinous crew. While we're aboard, you'll take my orders without thinking. I may tolerate your impertinence, but the sea won't." He caught her face up to his. "Well?"

The long lashes swept up. "You're the captain."

He grinned. "Possibly the only one in the world with a countess for a cabin boy."

Culhane deposited her on cushions in a partly sheltered niche just aft of the cabin. From this vantage point she could view preparations for getting under way. Shortly, the mainsail ran up the mast and he took the helm. With rustling snaps, the mainsail bellied out and the jib filled. Picking up speed, the *Megan* began to dance. Waves slapped against the snowy hull as Sean brought her about and headed southward. "I've an errand below Ballyshannon, across the bay. After that we'll run south to the Arans, then turn back north as far as Malin Head."

Catherine pushed hair out of her eyes. North, she speculated. Less likelihood of British patrols to the north. Culhane could hang for this holiday. How does it feel, my conniving girl, to have a man risk hanging to bring a bloom to your cheeks?

Sean noticed his companion seemed oddly silent after her first eagerness for the voyage. Possibly the motion of the boat was making her regret coming. She seemed well enough; pale, but no more so than before. He had not realized how much he wanted this voyage to please her. He sensed she was somehow afraid, not of the turbulent sea, but of him, ever since she had seen him staring at her body. And why not, when she had been abused because he had hated her? She looked at him suddenly and her clear eyes held his as if searching for some clue to his thoughts; then, as if realizing her confusion was apparent, she turned her head away.

As they rounded Malinmore Head and beat across the chop of the bay, the mouth of the Erne gleamed pewter in the distant haze.

"Malinmore is the largest headland we'll encounter before we reach Malin to the north. That harbor at the mouth of the Erne is Ballyshannon. We're headed just to the right of it."

"Where do we put in for the night?"

"Broadhaven Bay, with any luck."

Three hours later they approached a narrow jetty below the tiny fishing village of Pullendiva, and Sean wasted no

241

movement as he maneuvered the craft downwind of the jetty, brought the schooner about with a hardover rudder, then eased alongside, gently bumping against the oxhide bags he had thrown over as fenders. The sails slapped loosely as he leaped to the wharf to make the *Megan* secure. He came back aboard, dropped the sails, and ducked into the cabin. Reappearing a moment later, he handed her an oilskin bag. "Breakfast," he said briefly. "I'll be back with tea."

Before the sound of his boots on the wharf died away, Catherine dove with keen appetite into the bag. Bread, cheese, and apples. Heavenly! Breaking off generous chunks of bread and cheese, she wolfed them. When she became thirsty, she bit into an apple, then almost as it crunched noticed someone watching her from shore. A tall, red-haired girl stood alone on the beach and an uneasy thought crept into Catherine's mind. At that moment the girl came out onto the jetty and regarded her with amber eyes, hair flaming out in the gray wind. "So ye're the one." Her voice was expressionless, a low, husky contralto that suggested color and vivid speech under ordinary circumstances.

"I'm Kitty Flynn. I don't believe we've met," replied Catherine quietly.

"Kitty Flynn, is it?" the girl said ironically. "I heard it was English Kate. Or was it Cat? Ye're better lookin' than they said. But then, no hag'd keep Sean between her sheets."

Catherine's eyes flashed violet. "If you've heard so much, you must have heard as well it's the other way around."

The amber flickered. " 'Tis your witch eyes. His mother spun tales of the Old Ones about him. Now they've sent a witch woman to destroy him. Sean Culhane was never meant to be *ri eireanne.*" The Irish girl sounded as if she were uttering an incantation to ward evil from her lover.

"You must be Fiona," Catherine replied. "No, I've cast no spells to learn your name. Liam told me." Then more softly, "I no longer hate Sean. In some ways, I even understand his need for revenge." She saw no reaction in the Irish girl's face. "As for bringing ill fortune, how could the

242

Old Ones have sent me? Surely they cannot summon one who has no Irish blood."

Fiona made an impatient gesture. "Ye seek Sean's ruin even as ye veil his eyes. But Megan waits in Kenlo. Among her shadows, she's powerful. She'll destroy ye."

"Megan's dead. I'm not afraid of her."

The flame hair lifted and coiled. "No? Megan's at the heart of the demons in Sean Culhane. He'll never resist her biddin' for she's the only woman he'll ever love. When ye see the devil in his eyes, commend yer schemin' soul to hell."

Abruptly the fisher girl turned and went back the way she had come.

Sean, emerging from one of the whitewashed cottages near the shore, frowned as he saw Fiona walking away from the *Megan*. Quickly he intercepted her on the beach. They exchanged brief words and he caught her arm, then slowly released it. The red-haired girl left him and disappeared into the village. He swiftly returned to the yacht and jumped aboard. Catherine regarded him silently.

"What did she say to you?" he demanded.

"She was concerned for your welfare," Catherine replied quietly.

"The devil she was . . ."

"There's no need to be angry with her. I've known about Fiona for some time. She's lovely." Her voice sounded clear and faraway, as if she were fighting exhaustion.

Sean went down into the cabin, then returned with two mugs and poured tea into them from a narrow tin he had carried aboard from the village. He handed her a mug. "Here, drink this. Careful, it's hot. Peg forgot to pack the tea, so it's the last we'll have for a couple of days . . . that is, if you still want to go." His voice was carefully expressionless.

She wrapped her fingers about the mug, hugging its warmth. "I still want to go."

"I'm taking you below for a while." He carried her, unprotesting, into the cabin and tucked her into a bunk. A brass lantern swung above the bulkhead. "Try to get some sleep, English."

By the time they had left the dock and the waves of the

open bay had begun to slap against the hull, the tea was gone and Catherine burrowed into the woolen blankets. Finally she drifted into sleep.

She awoke some hours later to Sean's touch. "Would you like to face the Beast now, Beauty, or go on sleeping?"

"Is the Beast growling?" she mumbled sleepily.

He brushed a tendril from her forehead. "Not much. He's just a bit lonesome."

She gazed up at him through her lashes. Culhane had never hinted at need for anyone before, only the single time she'd flung it in his face. "Perhaps he just needs his ears scratched. Take me aft, Captain, and show me where he itches."

Culhane tapped her nose. "You'd be shocked." He handed her Tim's jacket. "Button up. The wind has changed and we've a stiff breeze."

He settled her in the downwind curve of his body behind the tiller he had lightly lashed in position. Spray dancing high off her windward quarter, *Megan* was tautly heeled over and making a steady ten knots westward through a hazy, leaden sea. "We're moving so quickly!" Her eyes lit with excitement. "Ships never fly through the water like this."

"Aye. We're running on a beam reach. You'll notice I've added a staysail to the jib and mainsail for greater speed."

"The staysail is the small, triangular sail near the bow?"

"Aye." He went on to describe the rigging, then finished, "The webs running up the mainmast are ratlines. They're not often used on a craft this size, other than for unsnarling tangled rigging or repairs . . ." He noticed her disappointment. "Sorry, monkey. Still, if you've an inclination to go aloft, I've no objection so long as I'm on deck."

She peered up at him. "You really mean it?"

He shrugged. "It's your neck."

With a pleased sigh, she resettled against his warmth. After a few moments of gazing at the rugged beauty of the passing coastline, she ventured another probe. "I don't suppose you'd let me take the helm?"

"Why not? Put your hands here." He tugged a line and

244

the lashings on the helm fell free as the wheel began to move. He slipped his hands over hers.

As the afternoon passed, Sean let her guide the *Megan* under his hand until she could hold the sleek craft steady by herself. When her confidence grew, he showed her how to avoid a jibe. "If you let the wind get too much behind her, she'll jibe, which can break a mast. Be ready to duck. The boom will come around in a hurry . . ." Catherine gasped as suddenly the *Megan* heeled clumsily sideways and the boom sailed past her ear.

"Lesson one," said the unruffled voice in her ear as the boat swung immediately back on course and the boom came whacking back, "keep a cool head. Mistakes at sea are dangerous, but panic can be fatal."

Toward sunset Catherine became drowsy, but was determined to miss none of the primordial beauty around her. The cliffs now burned dark russet against the intensely purple moors.

Sean noticed her stubborn effort to stay awake. "We anchor in Broadhaven in a couple of hours or so. I'll tell you if you're going to miss anything."

Nodding, she nuzzled her nose into his jacket and was instantly asleep. It seemed only moments later that he was gently nudging her. "Wake up, lass. I have to go forward."

He dropped sail, secured the halyards, and anchored in a harbor sheltered from the Atlantic blasts by a large duned island. The backwater was quiet after the foaming rush of water under the *Megan*'s hull all day. Lowland fields rolled away under a huge, ruddy, upturned bowl where tiny cloud scraps drifted in white sheets. Catherine stretched. "The sky looks like pink porridge. What does that portend, Master Mariner?"

"Fair sailing tomorrow." Sean finished lashing the mainsail to the boom and looked skyward. "That ruddy look in the morning indicates foul weather." Wiping his hands on his breeches, he dropped into the cabin through the forward hatch. He emerged on the aft deck with the oilskin sack, dining utensils, the lantern, and a bottle of wine under his arm. He squatted beside her, dug into the bag, and pulled out a stewed chicken. Placing it on one of the tin plates he had brought, he sawed the bird in half with his boot knife, then cut up cheese, divided gooseberries, and poured the wine. "Hungry?"

"Starved. I could eat a well-salted sail."

He grinned as he lit the lantern in the gathering darkness. "Well, you'd better enjoy the feasting while it lasts, because the fresh grub won't keep long. We'll shortly be dining on salt pork and hardtack." He handed her a mug and clicked it lightly with his own. "*Slainte*, Countess."

"*Slainte*, Captain."

The delicious food, the lantern light, the wind, and the gentle rock of the boat combined with lulling treachery. Catherine fell asleep in the middle of the most pleasant meal of her life.

She was awakened by sunlight streaming through a porthole across her pillow. She stretched with a contented purr, eyes slitted against the light. She realized she was wearing nothing under the blanket, that Sean had undressed her. Strange, how she had come to trust him. His manner was almost brotherly, even if his eyes often warned his desire was on short tether. Gradually she had grown accustomed to his touch. Often she awoke to find his body intimately entwined with her own, as if a night of love had left him unwilling to part with her. Grown now unused to sleeping alone, she wished he were lying warm against her in her bunk rather than already moving about the deck.

Donning shirt, sweater, and breeches, Catherine poked her head out of the aft hatch to feel the sun warm on her upturned face. The morning was fair as promised, the breeze light. *Megan*'s topsides and brass mirrored the play of sun off water as she rocked at anchor. "Oh, what a gorgeous day," Catherine breathed, realizing how a bird must feel and wanting to turn inside out with song.

Sean, splicing a rope near the bow, glanced up and noted her steady walk. His teeth flashed their startling white in his dark face. "Sleep well, Beauty?"

"Like the proverbial stone." She grinned back, swinging the hair out of her face. "You're a passable wizard. Weather as ordered, I see." Her grin turned impish. "Your wand seems to be back in working order."

He shot her a wicked look under his lashes. "For all I know, it's rusted away entirely."

She lifted an ironic brow. "Surely it has more than earned its rest."

"True," he observed slyly. "To rest in your willing warmth is a consummation devoutly to be wished."

She flushed. His words had a seductive pull beneath their teasing surface. She should not have begun to fence with him.

She sat on the deck and dangled her feet over the side, toes just clearing the water. Her wavering reflection blended with that of the hull, then was cut by a sheet-white gull that skimmed low, mewling over glittering azure water. Its head snapped down and came up with breakfast. Catherine trilled clearly after him as he flew off, wings occasionally taking a lazy beat toward the gray-blue shore.

"Like it here, English?"

"Very much, Irish." Her heels drummed against the hull. "Where are we going today?"

"We'll explore the islands off Achill. We can reach them by afternoon if we get under way within the hour."

She watched his long brown fingers deftly splice strands of rope together. "Is that complicated?"

"No. Want to try it?"

She crawled over to him on hands and knees and sat cross-legged beside him. He taught her the movements and showed her how to use the splicing awl, and with a bit of practice, she managed the maneuver almost as easily as he. Pleased by her quickness, Sean demonstrated some basic knots. His pupil paid sharp attention; her wits had been her sole defense in the past months. Finally, he let her help run up the sails before he weighed anchor.

By noon they were roaming the out islands, scattered like a school of gray whales across the glitter of the blue, sunlit Atlantic. A few scrub junipers, limbs twisted landward by merciless Atlantic winds, struggled in the worn rocks. To these inhospitable islands and others like them from Inishmurray to the Dingle Peninsula on the world's edge, Christian monks had fled from the barbarian hordes after the fall of Rome. Here, the monks practiced asceticism, copied manuscripts, and wrought art objects in gold. To survive, they fought the Celts from the mainland and later the Norse from the sea. All that remained of those ancient battles against oblivion were crumbling watchtowers and hivelike cairns. Here, was loneliness. Resistance. A scream of faith.

The next day, well south of the Achills, Catherine and Sean stood like pinpoints atop the grand escarpments on the windward side of the largest of the craggy Aran Islands. The island was a monstrous fortress against the sea, and as the weather had turned foul for the day, giant waves assaulted the cliffs in legions. Geysering spray wet their faces three hundred feet above the boiling water as the stormy Atlantic tried to smash the island out of its path into Galway Bay. Billowing clouds of mist swirled about the base of the dripping cliffs and wind howled through the rocks. Standing behind her, Sean held her closely as they faced the sea, their dark heads capped and jacket collars turned up against the penetrating cold. "Frightened?" he questioned against her ear.

"Awed."

When the weather slackened, the *Megan* turned again northward, keeping well out to sea. More sail tops, particularly Britain's, had cropped up in southern waters, and teaching Catherine to identify them had become a dangerous lesson. During the next two days the weather warmed. Catherine spent the hottest hours sunning on the foredeck. She undressed in the cabin and stayed out of Sean's sight as much as possible when unclothed. He reciprocated by not watching her.

They spoke little, other than exchanges during lessons in seamanship. Bit by bit he explained how sea and winds affected a vessel's course and behavior, how certain signs could be read for clear sailing directions, which cloud formations portended storms and how much violence they indicated. She learned to stay well clear of the precipitous shores whose high, rocky formations confused and troubled the sea winds, sometimes becalming a ship until it was helpless to avoid the rocks.

Catherine was a likely shipmate, not as strong as a boy, but willing and quick—and utterly fearless. She learned to

248

clamber up the mast above the briskest seas and once crawled out on the lunging bowsprit while under sail to unsnag a line before Sean could reach it. His rebuke was sharp but he was proud and she knew it. She wanted to match him on his own terms, in his own element; and at sea, he was at home as he was nowhere else on earth. She came to understand the source of his pride in his heritage and slowly realized he was showing her his soul, its wildness and freedom, in the coast he had roamed since boyhood. His spirit, like the lonely, windswept sea, was ever-restless, ever-changing, sometimes howling down to savage the unyielding land, then caressing it with a lulling embrace, inevitably wearing away its resistance. He was asking her to become part of him, without reservations, without ties that would inevitably be wrenched apart, leaving her battered on the rocks and him lonelier and wilder than before.

When Sean was restless, he was inclined to stay at the helm until the moon sheared the water in a quicksilver streak and glittering stars scattered their ancient runes across the black sky. Catherine stayed with him, curled against his shoulder. Usually he was silent, but sometimes he would tell her the Gaelic names of the stars and point out their positions, or recount in his melodic lilt the old legends, repeating the refrains in Gaelic to let her hear their strange, lovely music.

In a few days *Megan*'s white sail skimmed like a tiny paper dart under awesome Malin Head at Ireland's northermost tip. "Nothing's beyond this, lass, but the fogbound Hebrides and Faeroes."

"We cannot go on?" she asked with a note of desperation. "Is there nowhere?"

For a moment he said nothing, then, "There's Lough Swilly just east of Malin." The tiller shifted in his hands and *Megan* winged on toward the mouth of a fjordlike inlet.

Swilly was a wide sheet of water blocked from the reach of Atlantic gusts by sheltering heather-shrouded Fanad Head, and the range of the Devil's Backbone. Foyle, she knew from the maps in the study, was Swilly's sister lake, only a few miles east. And at the heart of Foyle lay the garrison city of Londonderry, hardly a safe spot for a man with a hostage.

After a while Culhane pointed to the eastern bank, where a misty summit rose some eight hundred feet from the water. Its cap was crowned by the ruins of a great concentric stone fortress. "The Grianon of Ailech. It was built by Niall's sons Eogan and Conal over fourteen hundred years ago."

"Niall . . . O'Neill: he was the founder of your line, wasn't he? The first high king of Ireland."

"Aye. He was *ri eireanne,* King of the Irish. O'Neill is among the oldest dynastic names in Europe, and Niall's son, Donell, was first to bear it. *Donegall,* or *Dun na nGall,* means Fort of the Strangers, possibly after the Grianon."

They anchored below the fort; then Sean let Catherine row the dinghy into shore. They spent the hazy afternoon climbing the fortress and exploring the ruins as he recounted the bloody history of the O'Neills. If his ancestors weren't fighting to subdue other Irish chiefs to their standard, they were feuding among themselves, brother slaughtering brother. When she heard how, in the sixteenth century, Shane, younger son of Conn Bahach, first earl of Tyrone, had murdered his illegitimate brother, Matthew, with the cooperation of the man's traitorous troops, a chill ran through her that had nothing to do with the wind sweeping across the Devil's Backbone. Why did a fear creep darkly about the edges of her mind? Why should she want to shield Culhane? He was true to his line. A Prince of Death.

The O'Neills had been stubborn fighters and audacious leaders. Hugh, the last O'Neill and greatest earl of Tyrone, had carried on an incredible war of guile and blood resisting the English, even recruiting the aid of Philip of Spain. An ill-timed rebellion mounted by the Irish and Spanish alliance against his advice, coupled with delay in rallying the rest of Ireland, proved fatal. The ensuing Flight of the Earls to the continent had dispersed the O'Neills, although the Clandeboy branch fought the Cromwellians viciously to reestablish Owen Roe, the O'Neill heir in exile. They gave Cromwell his worst defeat in Ireland, but were eventually crushed, their leader executed outright for his stubborn defense despite his honorable surrender. And then it was over. Until now.

After lunch, as the two wandered the cloud-shadowed heath at the summit, they found an ancient stone cross with four arcs framing a wheel-like base. Catherine knelt and crossed herself. Culhane waited, his own ties with faith long since severed. He could not know she prayed for him.

The *Megan* remained anchored under the fortress for that night. Catherine was already lying in her bunk when Sean came to bed. From her silence during their brief supper, he knew she was thinking Shelan would be the next anchorage if they sailed through the following night.

When he stripped off his clothing, his male nakedness in the close cabin quickened Catherine's pulse. By the wavering glow of the lantern, his deeply tanned skin was a smooth, dark gold; his lithe, lean symmetry like a beautiful satyr's. Knowing his body would be warm to the touch, she wanted to trace the line of his slim flank, of his hard belly and lower, to feel the slow rise of his desire, the tremor of his flesh. Between her thighs. Moving inside her. Desire coiled in her loins and struck with a piercing force. She turned her head swiftly away, lying rigid until he slid beneath his covers.

Furious at the lust that held her, she heard the pages of a book turn and silently cursed him. If he would only extinguish the lantern and let her hide in sheltering darkness, she could exorcise the thought of him lying within a whisper's reach. Could quell this serpent whose fangs pumped sweet poison into the blood.

Still the pages turned, and finally her tension exploded. "Please put out the light! It's shining in my face."

His eyes narrowed at her sharpness. "Is it? Those wide, dark pupils don't suggest an overdose of light. Still, if my inattention annoys you . . . ?"

The mocking, appraising insinuation dampened her desire and allowed her to retrace her wits. "Of course not. Why should it?" she answered coldly. "Only it's been a long day and I'm tired. . . . What are you reading?" Briefly, he held up the binding for her to see. "John Donne. My guess would have been Machiavelli."

"An apt choice. 'I laugh, and my laughter is not within me; I burn, and the burning is not seen outside,'" he quoted lightly. She snorted. "Why the sudden bitchiness, Kit? I'm no more eager than you to end the cruise."

"I know," she answered dully, staring up at the cabin roof, "but you'll take me back. Back to shrivel under your ambition. The Prince and his English Whore in Residence. Is that relic up there on the hill what you've been fighting for?" She rose on an elbow and looked at him. "Ireland held in the grip of the bloody fist of Ulster? The O'Neill resurrected from a line of royal killers? Would you have me bear your sons? Sons to smash and kill and rule?"

Sean whitened in anger. "Would you rather breed a brace of Bourbons! They've not been butchers quite as long as the O'Neills, I'll admit, but they've admirable aptitude!"

"What are you talking about?" she asked in angry puzzlement.

"Angoulême, petite. Go back to Papa and see how long it takes you to find that whelp in your bed!"

"Louis? You cannot be serious! I'm not of royal blood . . ."

"Ah, but le grand Monsieur Artois says you'll do as a concubine. Don't underestimate your gamine charm, chérie. Little Louis wants to fuck you and Artois intends to keep him happy. Of course, they assume you're a virgin. Angoulême has paid your doting papa a stiff price for the right to wave your nonexistent scrap of virtue from his royal standard."

Her eyes flashed fire. "You're obscene. And you're lying."

Sean's temper unleashed. "Am I? Would you like to see the Lloyd's draft your father had cosigned by Angoulême, transferable to me for a gambling debt? It's your bill of sale. I haven't cashed it yet. Perverse of me, isn't it? Holding that draft makes me feel you're mine: bought and paid for."

Sitting up, careless of the covers slipping to her waist, she lashed out at him, "Father's one of the richest men in England. He'd never sell me for a paltry wager!"

"But he would for political gain, wouldn't he?" Seeing her eyes flicker, he pressed. John Enderly was the last real barrier between him and Catherine and he was determined to smash it. He had to have her. The sight of her half-naked, her black hair falling across high, taunting breasts turned his guts to a volcano. "Don't tell me Papa doesn't crave the favor of a man who might someday rule France. You know damned well he does. And he's no longer rich, Kit. He's near ruin. I did it to him. He had to race Numidian because he needed money; otherwise he wouldn't have required a cosigner to cover his losses when Mephisto won. All his accounts connected with his smuggling dealings have been in escrow for months."

"Smuggling?" The Irishman's words came like a hail of arrows. Her eyes faltered in bewilderment and Culhane would have pitied her if he had wanted her less.

"He's a thief, Kit. An urbane one. A good one. I know, because I'm a thief too. But I'm not a traitor, and he is. He's been selling arms to the French—"

"Stop it! You're lying! You'd say anything . . . anything!" She was deathly pale under the tan.

"Yes, I'd say anything. Do anything to beat you down. Down on your back and open to me. With nothing between us. No clothes, no country, no father! But I'm not lying and you know it. Only you've been cheating. You want me now as much as I want you." Culhane jerked away his covering and rose slowly from his bunk. "Do you think I haven't seen desire in a woman's eyes before? Yours are full of it. You know what I am. And you want me. You want me inside you, like the beat of your heart. Kit . . ."

"Stop it!" she sobbed. "Don't touch me! I cannot . . . don't you see? It would be like dying." Her resistance foundered in a gold-flecked green ocean and she wildly seized at anything. "It's useless, Sean. I know! I know about your guns!" He hesitated, still crouched over her. "I've seen them. You care nothing for your own life or anyone else's! You'll push your people into a hopeless rebellion to serve your own ambition and they'll die! And you'll die more horribly than any of them if you're caught!"

"For a woman who finds a killer's touch so distasteful, you sat around long enough hoping for a pat on the head from Papa! Adder-eyed Papa, up to his armpits in blood!"

Catherine clawed at him viciously and he caught her

253

wrist, twisting until she gasped, then pushed her roughly
down on the bunk. Lying atop her, he deliberately slid his
body over hers as she sobbed and twisted. Holding her
wrists, he bit her nipples with soft savagery until they
were hard, begging peaks of desire and she whimpered.
"Get used to it, Kit," he muttered hoarsely. "Tomorrow,
the truce is over. It's time you saw some of your father's
handiwork." Abruptly he released her. Sobbing into her
pillow, she heard him pull on his clothes and go on deck. A
half hour later, the *Megan* was under way.

The next day was overcast, with threatening clouds on
the western horizon. Jacket buttoned high, Catherine huddled near the bowsprit, as far away from the Irishman as
she could get. Her last refuge was crumbling. Had he
planned it all, even to this? The elements themselves had
been his allies. The lazy, sunlit days; the soft, starlit
nights. Like a fool, she had followed him, and now he'd
burned the bridges home.

Dully, she noticed the *Megan* was coming close to shore;
too close unless Culhane planned to land. On the windswept heath above the rocky beach, a village lay scattered,
its few buildings ruined and open to the sky. Their white-
wash had worn away to patches of pale gray against blackened stones. She saw the place had been burned until only
the rock remained. Kenlo. Inevitably the *Megan* had come
home.

Although she was cold, she turned her back to Culhane
and without hesitation pulled off her boots and jacket. Intent on bringing the *Megan* in, he did not notice her movements until he saw her slim body arch outward in a clean
dive toward the rocks. Hearing him call out as her head
cleared the turbulent surface, she struck out strongly for
shore nearly a hundred yards away. The wind whistled
about her ears. The water, Gulf Stream current or not, was
cold, with treacherous rocks that bristled under the offshore surf. She had gone overboard without thinking, only
knowing she had to get away, hide. With nothing left to
lose except the last shreds of respect for her father and herself. And her life.

Sean anchored on the spot, not caring that *Megan* jerked

and heeled about in the water like a broken-winged bird. He hauled the sails down as fast as he could, tensely keeping a shoreward eye on the small black head increasingly obscured by the waves. By the time he pushed the dinghy away from the *Megan's* side, Catherine was fighting rollers among the rocks and his belly was knotted. The waves were breaking over her head and she was weakening, the cold seeping into her limbs, slowing her reactions. Then mercifully, she emerged from the breakers, stumbling and falling as they beat her down, but stubbornly making for shore. She collapsed on the rocky beach; he willed her to stay there, but when he looked again over his heaving shoulder as he rowed, she was gone. The white shirt flashed once among the rocks, then disappeared.

Kenlo's single, irregular street was overgrown with heather, and scabrous lichens crawled up ruined walls that distorted the sea wind into moaning, keening sighs. Doorways and windows stood dark and empty, framing bloated, sullen thunderheads in a gunmetal sky. Catherine sensed rather than smelled a stink of death; a faint, sweet, clinging perfume. Fiona's warning echoed in the rising wind. Megan is powerful among her own shadows. She'll destroy you. Catherine straightened. She had been coming to Kenlo ever since leaving England.

Knowing Culhane must be already searching the beach, she moved quickly from house to house, but no cranny proved safe from discovery, and too late, she realized she should have stayed in the rocks, away from the cold wind that turned wet garments to clinging ice and sent her hair whipping in sodden tangles. Away from Culhane.

A ruined chapel stood apart from the huts, its terraced steps broken and weed-bound. Shivering, she crept in, her fingers pressed along walls rough with seashells imbedded in native rock. The altar was open to the sky and streaked with droppings of seabirds, its relics vandalized or stolen. Long slits in the building's seaward side were blocks of angry surf grumbling against wet rocks. Crudely carved limestone faces of saints in niches about the room had been worn away by the salt wind to noseless, blank-eyed effigies. They resembled less Christian saints than the Old Ones who were even older than the Druids. These were saints returned to pagan primal beginnings. Were they now her allies? Or Megan's?

A small cell adjoined the nave. Roof still partly intact, it was barren except for a rotting chest with hieratic carvings. A small alcove, unnoticed until she advanced several feet into the room, dented the near corner wall.

A stone scratched outside and she whirled. Wind whipping about his frame, Culhane was picking his way along the deserted street, examining the interior of each house. Shivering, Catherine pressed into the alcove, trying not to let her teeth chatter. He might not look too closely if he had not seen her come up from the beach. The ruins had drawn her like a magnet. Megan's lure? No, Fiona's suggestion. Megan's dead. Her thoughts swirled. Stay, Kit. Stay where you are. Not breathing, not moving. Kit. His name for her. His will, still commanding her. Don't. Don't think. He'll go away. Please God, make him go away. Tears streamed in icy rivulets down her face and she shook. I'll never be warm again. Never. She closed her eyes. Never again enfolded in arms that held tightly, fiercely defying her, anyone, to break his grip.

"I thought I might find you here. I used to study in this cell."

Eyes flaring, she tried to bolt past him but a steel grip closed on her arm and spun her around; his other hand locked in her wet hair. He jerked her to him. "So you'd rather freeze than burn. Stubborn Kit. Almost as stubborn as me." His voice was soft, but taut.

"Rape me and be damned to you! You'll never have me any other way!"

"Words, Kit. Just words now. The spitting of a cornered cat. Surrender. You're all out of ammunition. I'm taking you back to the boat. I'm going to make love to you and it won't be rape. Never again." He held her head immobile as his mouth came down on hers, searching softly, then urgently, igniting a slow flame in her belly. Ice and fire. She melted against him, then stiffened and savagely bit his lip. He swore and shook her. "You little bitch! I ought to break your neck, but I've a better way of breaking you."

He dragged her stumbling to the nave with its distorted saints. With a hand locked in her hair, he jerked her to the front of the altar and clamped her in front of him with an arm under her breasts, her head dragged back against his shoulder. "You know where you are, don't you? That's why you ran. What do you see, Kit? Papa's face above the altar? Damned right you don't!" He shoved her to sprawl on the altar steps. "Those stains under your hands are blood. A priest's blood to be exact. He was murdered on this spot by your father's order. But first he was buggered with his own crucifix by your Papist-hating countrymen. You do know what bugger means, don't you, chérie?"

Before she had time to react, he dragged her up and after him out into the street. Every foot of its length, she fought him, kicking and scratching, deliberately falling down to tangle his feet. Anything to silence the hard, relentless voice that made Kenlo alive again with slashing cavalry and bayonets. Hacked bodies and flaming, gutted infernos. Mass murder. Finally he half shoved, half threw her into a building apart from the others.

Instantly she scrambled to her feet, turning at bay, her eyes black and wild, fingers raised like talons to come at him again. He caught her slashing hands easily and pushed her back against a blackened, burned table. "My home, girl—what's left of it!" he snarled. "This is where my mother was raped by one of those bastard's sergeants. I watched while she submitted to give me time to run for my life."

Catherine bucked against him and he bent her further back as he told her the rest, forgetting that her eyes were hardly lucid, forgetting he was hurting her—everything except the agony of reliving that night. "I heard him and a lieutenant name the author of their orders: a certain aide to the viceroy who figured slaughtering some villages might incite a rebellion so he could confiscate the rebels' property. *Your* father, you damned bitch!" Sean's face and chest were beaded with sweat, and at that moment, he hated the girl helpless under him more than on the night he had destroyed her innocence.

With deadly swiftness he drew the boot knife and pressed it against her belly. Catherine's eyes glazed back with terror as the knife dug into her skin. "The sergeant gutted Megan with a bayonet. After the soldiers were gone, I doused the body with oil and set fire to it so nobody would see her mutilated. Then I put what was left into a bag and threw it into the sea.

"When I was seventeen, I found that sergeant in a tavern. He almost killed me, but I left him gutted, like my mother!"

Catherine saw murder flare in the green eyes slanting hellishly down at her.

Later, Sean could not remember what had stopped him in time. He remembered Catherine's screaming; the walls seemed to ricochet the sound of her helpless terror. He put a hand over her mouth, and above it her eyes, utterly lost, tore into his soul. Then they fixed on nothing and she went limp. At first he thought he had driven the knife home. As swift fear flooded away the killing daze, he slowly took his hand away from her mouth. "Kit?" Mind barely functioning, he started to lift her and her head dropped back against his arm. "Kit?" His fingers sought the pulse of her throat; it fluttered weakly. She was unconscious, lashes jagged against a bloodless face. He touched her everywhere and found no blood. With a cry, he flung the knife away. Almost, he had killed her. As he looked around distractedly for something to cover her, his stomach rebelled and he retched, falling on hands and knees in the rubble. His body heaved until nothing more was in his belly, and yet he convulsed.

Naked beneath Sean's blankets and her own, Catherine regained consciousness in her bunk. Despite the covering, she was cold, her mind and spirit sere as an arctic waste. No tears were left now. Nothing except a terrible alienation. Even being alive meant nothing. Culhane had been ready to kill her. Why hadn't he? Was it for the same reason her thoughts had reached his, like a child seeking a reassuring hand, even when she hid from him? Reached for a hand that held a dagger. Papa . . . don't. Don't think. Thinking hurts.

Holding her head, she sat up and huddled against the bulkhead. The cabin was dim, the twilight murky with promise of a storm. Land was nowhere in sight and wind whined nastily in the rigging. Thunderheads mounted in a squall line on the southern horizon and the *Megan*'s bow dipped clumsily into troughs, spray blowing high over her deck. On the horizon was an approaching sail, one of the few they had encountered this far north. Tiredly brushing away clinging cobwebs of thought, she dully watched it through the porthole.

The sail became a mass of sails, tall and commanding. A merchantman? A cruiser. The Irish had no cruisers. Catherine fought to clear her head. She had to gain the vessel's attention. The lantern thumped against the bulkhead. A light. But there would be no chance to use it long enough to be spotted unless . . . A small hatchet was mounted on the wall below Culhane's bunk. Silently she unhooked the lantern, then shook it; a healthy slosh answered. At the helm, visible through the partly open doorway, Culhane was watching the cruiser and beginning to veer subtly away, knowing *Megan* would be unnoticed once the squall line struck.

Barefoot, Catherine moved soundlessly about the cabin. She laid the hatchet on Culhane's bunk, then fished in the food bag for the flintbox. Using a blanket to shield the glow, she waited until the cruiser loomed closer, then lit the lantern and took a firm grip on the hatchet.

Intent on the warship, Culhane did not see his hostage until she was already through the forward hatch; then it was too late. In one stroke of the hatchet she severed the main halyard, burying the blade deep in the mast. With an ominous ruffle, the mainsail dropped in a leaden tangle of canvas and rigging, slamming him to the deck and sending the boom slashing out of control. Catherine swung the lantern in a high, wide arc and tried not to think of the man who might be injured. Tried not to think of what a British tribunal would do to him.

Stunned at first, Sean lay tangled under the sail, then began desperately to fight clear as he heard the muffled lash of raindrops against the cloth. Swearing, he pulled a knife and split the sail. Catherine, still signaling, saw him emerge from his trap much sooner than anticipated. She wrenched at the imbedded hatchet. He warily closed on her. "Douse that light!" She jerked at the hatchet; it stuck solid. No longer trying to wave the light, just trying to keep a footing on the slippery, lurching deck, she backed toward the bow. Sean watched tensely. A wild-eyed, beautiful siren bent on destroying him, she was desperate, trembling with cold and fear. At any moment she might lose her balance, even jump. "Want me dead that badly, little one? Here, catch!" Knowing she would snatch at it and poised to hurl himself forward to pin her down, he sent the knife skittering across the deck.

She grabbed fast enough, almost losing her grip on the lantern, but he was forced to freeze in midlunge just out of reach of the glittering blade poised all too professionally at his belly. She had learned more in captivity than he realized. "Kit, you're going to have to use that knife if you bring in that cruiser. I'll not swing from a British yardarm."

"Take the dinghy but don't come any closer." Her tone was flat, although her teeth were clenched from cold and rain that lashed her dripping body. "I've nothing to lose."

"Nor have I," he said softly. "Only you."

"You were going to kill me," she spat.

"Yes."

"You should have. It would have been over for both of us."

"Is that what you want? Then use the knife." His advice was quiet, almost brotherly, and she watched him with wary uncertainty. "Shall I help you make up your mind? I'll never let you go, girl. Not while I breathe. If you don't kill me, I'm going to take you and go on taking you. I may even give you a child. And if you run away from me, I'll bring you back. If you want to be rid of me, it's now or never."

Her heart raced sickeningly as her desperation grew. The cruiser loomed closer.

"Don't be afraid. I won't stop you. Take your revenge and be free. It's only the matter of a moment." Clutching a shroud line above his head, he leaned toward her, rain-soaked shirt flapping about his bare chest as lightning snapped across the sky. His voice was seductively soft. "We're close as an embrace. Kiss me with the knife."

The weapon slowly backed for the lunge, its point glinting with a razor's wicked edge.

"Now, Catherine. Strike now, or yield."

She thrust the knife forward, but at the last moment looked into eyes that reflected the storm. This strange, brooding man had become part of her. Frighteningly, he needed her now, though she had denied him in rage and pride as he had her. Even if she died by his hand, she could deny him no longer.

As the knife clattered to the deck, a fleck of crimson over the Irishman's heart smeared against her breast as he swept her into his arms and crushed his mouth down upon her cold lips, kissing her as if the tempest raging about them were centered in his soul. He paused to kick the lantern overboard, then picking her up, moved quickly across the careening deck to the cabin's shelter. He laid her down, then swiftly tore free of his sodden clothing. Lightning illuminated the cabin. Their hair dripping in points, they looked long at one another while off the starboard bow a British man-o'-war labored north through the storm. As her stern light disappeared, Sean's mouth plummeted down on Catherine's and she answered his raging desire with equal hunger as she drew him down onto the tumbled blankets. Their wet, slippery bodies met and moved in wanton heat that raged like the storm howling about their battered craft. Passion rose in fiery waves pouring over the edge of the world, a descent into the inferno, bodies locked in a fusion of molten desire. Ice and fire. He possessed her with a tender savagery that not only claimed victory but wreaked annihilation.

For a long time they lay still joined, Sean's dark head resting on Catherine's breast. As the storm slowly abated outside their drifting sanctuary, she touched his damp, curling hair, reveling in its thick softness. Lifting his head, he gazed into her lambent eyes with a wonder his shadowing lashes could not veil. A slow, boyish smile softened the hard lines of his mouth. "Shivering sea witch," he murmured, brushing her lips with his. Gently he explored her face with his fingers as a blind man might, as if he had never seen it before and might never again. "Yea, thou art fair," he breathed. "I fear I'm caught in some siren's spell, for your starry eyes are not of this world, sweet witch, and I shall ever see them, dazzled, dreaming."

She smoothed the damp hair from his temples. "And what of my Sea Beast? When I look into his eyes, I see no wolfish gleam, no fiendish glare, but a man, and such a man as I've never known. I . . ." She fell silent, a shadow crossing her face.

"You wonder when the reprieve ends," he supplied with a trace of his old bitterness.

She stopped his lips with a quick, clinging kiss that scattered his troubled thoughts like dead ashes. "We've gone beyond promises. Everything but this moment."

She drew his head down and his hard body reclaimed hers with a fierce yearning that aroused her own longing to a dizzy pitch, then slowly fulfilled it with piercing, welling intensity until her cry was swept away with the wind.

As Catherine buried her face in his neck and drifted peacefully into dreamless sleep, Sean, staring into the dark, watched fitful lightning play over the still-angry waves.

When dawn rose over the quick-running, sullen seas, he left her sleeping and, naked as an ancient mariner, went up on deck. Wet teak slapped under his bare feet as he surveyed the debris of sail and rigging choking the cockpit. With the severed halyard clamped in his teeth, he climbed up into the swaying rigging. Though he worked quickly at the damage, he grew chilled almost immediately. Perversely, he wanted the discomfort, the astringent of spray and wind on his skin. Least of all did he want to look down and see Catherine staring up at him like a brazen pirate wench with black hair whipping about her naked body. She eyed his nudity with a glance that made his blood run hot. Half angrily he growled, "Put on your clothes, girl. You'll catch a chill."

"You're evidently in no danger," she teased, a dimple appearing in her cheek as she surveyed his long, supple limbs and bronzed, lean frame with the appreciation of a woman proud of her lover.

He flushed and swore under his breath. One night of pleasure and the bold little baggage was as coolly appraising as a Paris madam.

He swung in midair from a ratline to a stay and slid

down to land with a scowl at her feet. She swirled a playful finger in the black, curling fur of his chest. "I'm so glad you didn't persuade me to kill you. If I'd been brought to trial before my feminine peers, I should have been hanged outright as a traitor to my sex."

"God help us all if women ever sit in court!" he snorted derisively to distract her from his all-too-eager response to her touch. Damnation! There was no justice in the world when a man could not disguise his interests while a woman could toy until kingdom come without turning a hair.

Catherine looked up impishly, trailing her fingers along the fine line of fur that traced down his belly. "Sir, do you suggest that justice in capable hands might be too equally dispensed, or that women aren't sensible? Only an insensible woman could deny the upright evidence of your appeal." Her lips curved mischievously.

He firmly plucked her fingers out of his pelt. "If you don't want to be pitched overboard for a water sprite, keep your itchy little fingers to yourself." He moved to the halyards, and a cool, teasing voice came from behind him. "Actually, I had thought of perfecting my backstroke in a more pleasant fashion."

"Damned if your mouth doesn't need another soaping!" Angrily he turned, and somehow she was all soft in his arms, the boat's rocking under his feet only part of the dizzying effect on his runaway senses. Swearing softly, he pulled her upward, hard against his nakedness, and kissed her roughly until she was breathless. Lowering her to the shining mirror of the deck, he took her under the sky, swiftly, urgently, until a shuddering, sweet, swelling agony seized them both and left them clinging tightly, spent and trembling.

Rising slightly, Sean looked down at her exquisite face like a golden, exotic flower against her disheveled hair. Her eyes under their long lashes still smoldered with tiny fires that made him want to take her again although his body could not immediately answer his craving. "It's no good, Kit," he said reluctantly. "We have to go back. Another storm's coming."

The fires guttered in her eyes and the old look of tension returned. "Sean . . ."

"Look, if I thought this rigging would take another beating, I'd head straight out to sea. Do you think I want to take you back there now?"

"It's not the rigging. You're as much a prisoner as I."

"I have responsibilities, Kit. Lives depend on my facing them."

"Is it responsibility? Or revenge and ambition you're loath to forget?"

His jaw tightened and he quickly got to his feet, pulling her with him. "That's part of it." He held her close, his lips against her hair, his voice half-angry, half-pleading. "Kit, trust me a little. Try to understand . . ."

She stood motionless, not resisting, not responding; then her voice came low. "I understand. Nothing's changed. Except now I'm your whore in fact."

He wanted to shake her, cover her face with angry kisses, persuade her with words, his body, anything; but he knew it would be useless. Defeated, he dropped his hands. "Get dressed, Countess. The holiday's over."

CHAPTER 13

A Scent of Orchids

Catherine knelt before the glowing peat fire, her skin tingling with the intense heat. During the last leg of the trip home the weather had been rough, and the *Megan* had limped into Shelan long after dark. Now, her shawl and Elizabeth Flynn's nightgown provided scant protection from the damp, faintly musty chill of the bedroom. Stirring the fire until it flared up, she thought of the holocaust Sean Culhane had ignited. They were both lost to sense or caution, existing only with blind impatience to be one flesh again, to be made mindless in a sensual delirium. She both exulted in and was frightened by a desire that made her capable of such submission. Was it only lust that made her wish to lie forever beneath his body, supine, endlessly yielding as he endlessly took? In every sense a whore? His whore. Far better that than to be the blessed of Heaven, if Heaven had cast him out.

And then Culhane was there, his dark presence like gently demanding hands touching her everywhere. She looked up. "Is everything all right?"

"Yes. No thanks to Liam. He was gone most of the time." He placed an object on the desk with a metallic clink, poured two brandies from the decanter, and came over to her. He handed her a snifter. "Flynn misses you." He was looking at her strangely but his face was unreadable.

He pulled up a chair, dropped into it, and stared into the fire; then as she inhaled the aroma of her brandy, he reached down to finger the lace at her throat. She stiffened involuntarily, feeling a rush of blood to her cheeks. "You've donned lace armor tonight." His fingers slipped to the delicate line of her jaw. "You've no need to wear armor with me, Kit. Take it off."

"May I not finish this brandy first? The room's cold . . ." she faltered.

Culhane frowned, then shrugged with a touch of his old indifference. "As you like." He quickly drained his own glass, then rose and went to his armoire, removing his shirt as he did so. Swiftly, he stripped and put away his clothing, then turned to see Catherine flinch from his nudity. Silently, he went to her, removed the glass from her fingers, and drew her up. He slipped the shawl from her shoulders. In the long, high-necked gown she looked like a bride, untouched, unawakened, glossy hair still coiled up from the bath. As he began to undo the long row of tiny buttons that fastened the garment, he wondered how Flynn had had the patience to work through them on his wedding night. Perhaps he had simply pushed the gown up. His throat went suddenly dry as at last the garment parted to the waist, revealing the shadowed swelling of her breasts. He started to slip the gown from her shoulders and felt her trembling. "Kit, haven't you learned I've no wish to force you?"

"I don't understand the emotions you arouse," she whispered. "When you touch me, you take my will."

"Kit . . . sweet . . ." Sean whispered against her throat, exploring its fragile hollow with his lips, tracing a burning path from the fragrant curve of her neck and lower until she sighed and let him roam where he would. Gently he cupped her velvety breasts inside the gown, stroking them, tempting their peaks to press eagerly against his fingertips. Then he parted the gown to let it fall from her shoulders until she was naked; his warm lips sought the sun-tinted flesh it revealed. "Aye," he breathed, "this is how I would have you."

Drawing a gleaming mass from the desk, he turned her to face the pier glass that reflected her nakedness full length against his, then fastened a necklace about her neck. An intricately worked golden collar with smooth amber and sapphire studs set in mazes of uncut amethysts rested against her skin. Warm from his fingers, it was surprisingly heavy, the irregular stones subtly echoing the shading of her eyes. He loosed her hair and let it fall in a wild, stormy mass to her waist. "For fourteen centuries, only Gaelic queens have worn the Niall Torc. From this night, it's yours. *Ta in gra le tusa,* Catherine."

For a moment she could say nothing, feeling as if the necklace had enclosed her in a spiraling, ancient current of time. As if his quiet Gaelic had sealed her destiny. "Sean," she breathed, "you mustn't . . ."

"Why?" he asked tightly. "Do you find the Torc barbaric in comparison to your grandmama's diamonds?"

She turned to him. "You know it's priceless . . . and never meant for one who is English."

"The Torc was never made to gather dust in a museum, love, but to be worn by a woman against warm, living flesh; to be worn by the chosen of the O'Neill, high chief of the Gaels. I am the O'Neill. And you are the woman I choose."

"But how is this collar different from the other, for all its beauty?" she asked softly. "Once you shackled my body, but my mind and heart were free. Now . . . now I'm less than your thrall." Tears slipped down her cheeks as she lowered her head.

"Nay, I think not. Whatever shackles you bear are fastened in my heart." He carried her to the fire and laid her down in the furs, spreading her hair until it spilled across the blue fox in a shimmering torrent. "Aye, this is how I would have you," he whispered, his mouth coming down on hers in a kiss that seemed to draw her soul from her body.

The surrounding shadows scattered, past and future retreating until only the demand of now remained. His hands moved slowly, seeking love's secret places, reducing her into pliant surrender until her body succumbed and she arched against him with a soft cry. But as he sought entry, she whispered, "You play on my senses with the ease of a practiced seducer. May I not take part in the game?"

With a teasing grin, he rolled onto his back. "Seduce away, wench; I've no objection."

"But, where shall I . . . ? What . . . should I do?"

He shrugged lazily. "Whatever you like. You'll know quickly enough what I think of it." He closed his eyes as if prepared to be bored into sleep.

Catherine considered the supple brown body that reclined in the furs. *Quel beau sauvage, que c'est magnifique.* Startled that her reaction had been in French, she recalled his taunt about her Gallic blood and her expression subtly altered to a mysterious smile. *Au secours, ma chère grand-maman, Nathalie.* You conquered France. Let me humble just one Irishman. She scattered light butterfly kisses on his closed eyelids, then trailed down to his lips. Without moving a muscle, he kissed her back, letting his lips part under hers, arousing her easily to impatient desire with no effort and no apparent counterreaction. Piqued to inspiration, she nuzzled his throat and temple, then lightly darted the tip of her tongue into his ear and was rewarded by the swift intake of his breath. *Merci, Grandmaman!* She wandered down to the hollow of his shoulder and discovered his nipples, nibbling them to the hardness of bullets. But by the time her slim fingers stroked his inner thighs and hesitantly explored his sex, Sean lay like a gathering explosion. Then her tongue delicately flicked him and he gasped, his belly contracting. She caressed him until he was trembling and involuntarily spread-eagled in the furs, surrendering completely to her seeking mouth.

"Sweet Jesus . . . Kit . . ." he groaned. No longer able to bear her gentle torture, he seized her and rolled her beneath him into the fur. He drove deeply between her thighs in sweet revenge even as he sought her mouth. His thrusts quickened until she wrapped her legs about his hips and raked his back in primitive response to the ravenous demand of his driving body. With a harsh, moaning cry, Sean lost his last shred of control and felt his lover violently convulse beneath him at the same moment. As the fire burned low, they lay locked together, shaken and dazed from the terrible force of their passion. So long at odds, they now hardly dared to breathe, afraid to be parted.

"Bitch," Culhane murmured. "Beguiling witch. My innocent wanton. You have the mouth of a child . . . a whore. I no longer care whether you offer salvation or damnation. Like Alexander, I've done reveling at the victory feast, only to seek defeat in a woman's arms. Never leave me, Kit."

"If love were my only prison, I should not know where to go," she whispered. "When you hold me, I'm bound and blind, heeding only your voice, the touch of your lips, your body claiming mine. What have you done to me? I'm lost. Please . . ."

As Sean answered her plea with his lips, he began to move with slow, age-old rhythm in cadence with her breathing until they moved as one and Catherine felt as if her entire body were an incandescent extension of her lover. At last she splintered and floated within his being. As he gathered the furs close about them, she lay against him in warm oblivion, partly covering him, still containing him.

Late the next morning, Liam paused in the shadowed hall outside his door as he saw his brother and Catherine emerge from their room. He knew their relationship had changed. As they descended the stair they were not touching, yet were. Silently he followed, and as they reached the landing saw Sean take Catherine in his arms and kiss her lingeringly. Her body molded to his, and when Sean's head lifted, Liam wanted to be sick. She looked like a sleepwalker, eyes still dark with desire, lips swollen and bruised. Even her body had a new, beckoning ripeness, but invited only one man, whose green eyes were clouded with a look Liam had never seen there before. They parted in the foyer, and when Liam heard the study door close he quickly descended the stairs to catch Catherine on the terrace before she reached the carriage.

"Liam! Where did you come—"

Motioning her to be quiet, he pulled her back toward the house, out of view of the study windows and earshot of the carriage. "I must see you alone. Meet me by the cliffs today."

"Liam, I . . ."

"I *know*, damn it. You look like a bitch in heat. But there are things you don't know and you'd better hear."

She jerked away. "I don't want to hear anything!"

His fingers tightened on her arm. "Don't be a fool. You're not the first to play harlot for my brother. Will you turn traitor as well? I'll be waiting by the cliffs at noon. If you're not there, I'll come to Flynn's." He gave her a push toward the carriage and its curious driver.

She met him. He waited, his hands in his pockets and back to the sea, blond hair silver in the hazy light. He was thinner, harder, more bitter.

"Welcome home. I trust the holiday was refreshing?" He smiled sardonically.

"I've no time for recriminations, Liam. A great deal of work must be waiting at the infirmary."

"Ah. Ever the cool lady. Only, you're hot enough for my brother of late."

Impatient, she turned to leave, but he spun her about. "Is it rape you've learned to prefer?" Jerking her to him and twisting one arm behind her as she struggled, he closed his free hand over her breast. "Is this what you want? And this?" He thrust his hand down into the bodice so abruptly the material ripped. This time, to his surprise, he met no resistance, only implacable contempt.

"I don't care what you do! I'm going to stay with him as long as he wants me!"

Liam's look of desire altered to hopelessness, then to cold fury. He pushed her away. "Then you're a fool, like all the rest of his women! Is the bastard really that good in bed? Are you in love with him?"

"I don't know if I love him, but . . . yes, he *is* that good in bed."

Liam started to slap her, then slowly dropped his hand. She stared at him coldly, brazenly refusing to close her bodice, and he had never seen her look so magnificent. She had become a sensual woman, tawny-skinned and ripe. Her houri eyes filled with a promise that made him want her more than ever. "Did you know Sean has ruined your father? That the bogus antiques shipment he's just arranged will not only destroy your father's hope of financial recovery, but his reputation as well?"

Again, the reaction was not at all what he expected. Catherine only looked at him. "Sean told me about Father. In Kenlo."

He stared. "You believe him?"

"Yes," she said bleakly, "because my father is a murderer . . . and worse."

"Did you also know Sean's mounting an armed rebellion against the Crown?"

"I've known for months. I saw the guns in the blockhouse. At first I meant to use you to get away."

Liam's bitterness welled up. "But you couldn't. You'd spread yourself for my whoreson, rutting brother, but you'd not let me make love to you, even to save England!"

"You exaggerate, Liam. England's in no danger. Rebellion is hopeless. By escaping, I could have saved Irish lives."

He smiled grimly. "Do you think my brother intends to fight alone? I suppose he neglected to mention we expect company tomorrow?" He was rewarded by a blank look. "Ah, at last I see there's something you don't know. Our guests are French."

She went pale. "Sean's bringing in French troops?"

"Not just Sean. The United Irishmen are sponsoring this entertainment. Theobald Wolfe Tone, Lord Edward Fitzgerald, and Arthur O'Connor are only a few of the conspirators who riddle the government and every level of society. Tone has been in Paris arranging a campaign with the Directorate. We've been promised at least three warships under the command of General Humbert, who will shortly embark from France to support the rebellion. Napoleon sends his regards."

"But Napoleon wants Ireland as a door to invasion of England!"

"But of course, my little amateur."

She caught his arm. "Liam, Sean cannot . . . you mustn't let him!"

"What, pray, would you have me do? Thrust my neck into a noose for the sake of a nation I detest?"

"For Ireland! If you bring in the French, you'll be exchanging one yoke for another! Doesn't Sean realize

271

that?" At his indifferent shrug, she flared, "Damn you, you self-pitying ninny! Get up on your hind legs and fight! If a weapon fits ill to your hand, then ply your wits!"

Liam stared at her. This wild-haired, brazen termagant was no longer the woman with whom he had been obsessed, but now he determined to meet the challenge of breaking his brother's hold on her, of breaking her to his own hand. "What do you expect me to do?" he asked sullenly.

"Where's the main gun cache?"

"You've been sleeping over it. The cellar wine racks conceal chambers cut in rock. He has artillery pieces hidden in the silos. Shelan has the largest stockpile of arms outside Dublin"—his lips quirked sardonically—"and apparently the best hidden. Your British General Lake has disarmed practically all the rest of Ulster this past month."

She looked at him intently. "If we could think of a ruse to clear the house, we could blow up the magazine and the silos."

"The hell you say! I'll not scatter my inheritance to dust. It's all I have, after all." He paused. "Besides, how do you think your lover would react to his harlot's treachery?"

Oh, God, Sean! . . . Napoleon in Ireland! She turned away. This decision had been inevitable. To think it could be avoided had been foolish, only now she would be twice a traitor, to Ireland and Sean.

"I see you have the idea. He'd kill you with his bare hands."

"The authorities must be warned. Help me escape, as you promised."

"That was before I knew you'd been using me. Now, there's a price."

She knew, but she had to hear him demand it. Hear her own irrevocable answer. "What is it?"

"Marry me before we leave."

"Liam, I'll never love you in the way you want."

"I don't care."

She silently stared toward Shelan, then answered tonelessly, "I'll marry you."

"In Ruiralagh before the priest? With nuns as our witnesses."

"Apparently, you've made all the arrangements."

"Every step of the way. I've plotted and covered our route from here to Londonderry. Sean will never see you again. Not until the day he hangs. And I'll expect you to watch, Catherine. You'll be mine from then on." He cupped her breast.

She stiffened, then shrugged away from him. She would have to keep him on the run, moving continually. Anything to keep him from consummating their union. Liam's vengeful hatred of Sean canceled her former desire to repay him the loss of his homeland. Once in Londonderry, she would get an annulment.

Liam had not lied about their visitors. At Shelan, servants scuttled about, abristle with cleaning paraphernalia. Peg cheerily greeted her at the bedroom door. "I see the sea air agreed with ye! Yer cheeks have blooms like Spanish roses." She closed the door behind them. "Sean, he always turns black as a pirate." Her smile turned gleeful. "I knew ye'd do him good. He's been grinnin' like a heathen all day."

"If only I *were* good for him," Catherine murmured, then tightly hugged the housekeeper. "Stay with him, Peg. He needs you more than you realize."

The older woman patted her shoulder. "Now, now. 'Tis a young woman the scamp needs." She held Catherine away, studying her face intently. "He's in love with you, did ye know that?"

"I wish for his sake he weren't."

Peg frowned. "Do ye feel nothin' for him?"

"I feel something . . . I cannot think when he touches me, and yet when he lets me go . . ."

"Ye harken back to him like a lark to the wind. 'Tis nothin' to fret about, lass. It's gentleness he needs." She took Catherine's hand and drew her to the bed. "See what came on the *Sylvie* for ye! I've been atwitch since late mornin'!"

Flung across the counterpane were gowns in a profusion of muslins and silks, all in Le Roy's deceptively simple cuts; all fabulously expensive. Dainty gold, silver, and tinted silk sandals were matched to each dress. Peg pointed to a velvet packet. "There's even paints and pomades like Josephine and the society ladies wear." She flipped open a silk-lined box to reveal crystal vials of perfume. Removing a stopper, she wafted it under Catherine's nose. "An't that sinful?"

Catherine almost flinched. A flacon of the identical scent was evaporating on the dressing table at home. Sean had overlooked nothing, even a broadcloth riding habit in the latest style with a short jacket and saucy veiled hat. By the armoire, Spanish riding boots gleamed next to his own. She sagged onto the bed and gazed numbly at the splendid array.

With a mock frown of disapproval, Peg waved a gossamer wisp of lingerie from a finger. "Disgraceful."

Waiting impatiently in the Rose Salon, Sean replaced his wineglass on the mantel and turned as his mistress entered the room. His breath caught. Catherine's beauty had often taken him unaware but never more than now. By the firelight's glow, she was a slender column of white *à la Diane*. Amused by the name of the creation, he had included the dress as a prank. Caught at one shoulder in imitation of a tunic of ancient Greece, it was split at the sides from waist to ankle to reveal a slim underskirt and golden sandals. Tiny bell rings were at her toes and fingers and polished black hair fell to her hips. Gilded eyelids fired her opal eyes with Circean allure and her lips had the ripe warmth of pomegranates. In that moment, Sean knew she was more beautiful than any woman he had ever seen or would ever see again. "I thought that little rig might suit you," he said lightly. "In Paris, *les merveilleuses* dispense with the underskirt and wear nothing but tights, sometimes nothing at all."

Ignoring his teasing suggestion, she replied softly, "You're most generous. Alexander's Roxanne could not have been more richly dressed."

"I've no wish to be an Alexander." He traced the line of her jaw with a fingertip. "I have all the world I need."

"Have you?" She gazed up at him. "Sean, you cannot have Ireland *and* me. Your people would never support a leader with an English mistress. I would continually be

274

suspected of twisting your judgment. They would call you a self-indulgent fool, even a traitor."

"Chérie, I've no illusions about the difficulties of keeping a woman like you, even under ordinary circumstances. I might as easily take a stroll through Soho at midnight with gold coins stitched to my coat. And becoming *ri eireanne* was my mother's ambition, not mine. Ireland's freedom is all I swore to gain. I've no wish to rule."

"You'll have no choice. The abilities and ancestry that rally Irishmen to your standard will also compel you to accept their leadership in peace. To remain free, Ireland must remain united; and for a time, perhaps all your lifetime, your name obliges you to supply focus for loyalty." She turned away. "There's another difficulty."

He came up behind her. His closeness made her feel weak, but she forced herself to go on. "You must have legitimate heirs. My . . . my children would become liabilities. Inevitably, another woman would take my place in your arms, perhaps in your heart."

He lightly caressed her throat. "Would that matter, my taking another woman?"

"Yes," she whispered.

He caught her shoulders and turned her to accept his mouth, obliterating resistance and all thought save the one of melting into his body. Her head slipped back on his arm, her hair in an ebony stream, and he became aware only of how small she was, how desirable.

"Please take me away," she whispered against his mouth. "Anywhere. I need . . . I want only you."

"God, you tempt me." His arms tightened and her response to his kiss took his breath away. He lifted his head at last with an effort. "Kit—"

She was never to know what his answer would have been for it was interrupted by a knock at the door. It was Flannery, eyes widening in frank appreciation of the woman his commander's arm still encircled.

"What's the problem?"

Flannery gave him a sheepish grin. "The *Meridian* has been sighted off Annagh Head. She's makin' fair wind and likely to reach Shelan by mornin'."

Sean nodded, unaware his mistress's smile had become

subtly set. "Very well. Have Fournel and his officers report to my study after they come ashore. Give Rafferty a nudge with dinner on your way out, will you?"

Dinner was quiet, both young people preoccupied with their thoughts. Sean restlessly fiddled with his brandy snifter as Rafferty cleared the table. "I've an itch for a hard ride tonight, Kit. Want to come?"

"Yes. Numidian needs the exercise."

"Run up and change. I'll have the horses brought around."

Sean led the way down the treacherous cliff path to the beach. The night was crystal clear and unusually warm. Soon Catherine regretted throwing on Tim's pea coat over the shirt and cords. She struggled out of it and was awkwardly knotting its sleeves about her waist when Sean ordered abruptly, "Pay attention to your riding. It's a long drop to the beach." Meekly she waited until they reached bottom to secure the jacket. She wanted to ask about Fournel, but seeing Sean's withdrawn expression, thought better of it.

They put the horses into an easy canter down the pale, winding beach. Moonlight painted the pebbles blue-white and transformed the tidal pools into flickering mirrors below cliffs white and mysterious as Oriental palaces, their walls and spires carved ivory. A scent of wild orchids that climbed the rock face hung on the wind. The surf tumbled sleepily on the shore, teasing the horses' hooves into a hard gallop along the luminous sea. The stallions and riders crashed through glassy sheets of water, shattering their surfaces to fragments and thundering on like hurrying ghosts. Only when their mounts began to falter did the man and woman rein to a halt in a swiftly settling spray of sand. The house, a pale silhouette with glowing lights, was barely visible atop the cliffs far to the south. Sean slid off his sweaty horse, then lifted his companion down, his fingers lingering at her waist. Hand in hand, they wandered down the beach leaving the horses to follow, their reins caught around their saddle pommels.

"A French warship is due here tomorrow, English," Sean said quietly. "Can you guess why?"

Her fingers tightened in his. "Yes."

"Ireland will be rising soon, possibly within days. We cannot turn the tide without them."

She stopped and looked up at him. "Sean, it's dangerous to tell me these things."

"Not unless you intend to betray me."

"Would you have me betray my country?"

"You're half French, Kit. Does it matter so much?"

"Napoleon is born to war, Sean. He'll drench the earth with blood. England is his most formidable obstacle." She paused. "Ireland has had foreign allies before and failed."

"Philip II of Spain and your exiled Charles I weren't in a league with Napoleon, Kit. He's the best and only chance we have. We have to gamble now."

"Do you think you'll be more than his puppet? If he lets you rule? He wants no native dynasties in his dominions any more than does England. He'll prove as great a tyrant as Cromwell. England's monarchy is weakening, Sean. Parliament is gaining power . . ."

"If you're asking me to wait until the English bourgeoisie take their turn at wringing us dry, forget it." He put his hands on her shoulders. "You've overlooked one thing about Napoleon, Kit. He's already shown his military genius doesn't extend to government. He left no permanent fortifications to protect his holdings in Italy: just troops and a skeleton government headed by his relatives, and they're impotent without his presence. If he repeats that pattern in each territory he conquers, eventually he must run short of French troops to back them and depend on untrustworthy foreign ones in satellites increasingly distant from home. Even if he retains his power, his hegemony will probably die with him. This all assumes the conspiring Directorate doesn't depose him and return France to the chaos of the Revolution. With England's grip broken, Ireland has a real chance at self-government."

"What if he succeeds and has a son?"

"Josephine had an abortion while she was Paul Barras's mistress; it left her barren. If the Corsican wants an heir, he'll have to divorce her."

"But divorce is easily obtained under Republican law, and he has the grounds of Josephine's open promiscuity.

My father says his brother, Joseph, is using all his influence to have the marriage dissolved; Napoleon may agree. His infatuation with Pauline Foures in Egypt is common knowledge."

"Foures isn't Josephine, Kit. Napoleon will have to return to Paris sooner or later to put down Barras's intrigues in the Directorate. My wager is that when he does, Pauline will stay in Egypt."

"Like a discarded boot."

He caressed her neck. "I daresay Madame Foures isn't without ambition."

She pulled away. "Perhaps she loves him." Her clear eyes momentarily caught the moonlight. "But love has no place in war, does it?"

"Doesn't it?" He caught her gently, then stifled any possible answer with his mouth. Catherine clung to him, knowing that it might be for the last time. That she loved him and that it was too late and that he would never know.

As her breasts thrust maddeningly against his chest, Sean parted the loose shirt to find their soft warmth. Desire pulsed at his groin with a slow, sweet ache and he released her, whispering, "Wait." Retrieving the jacket, he spread it on the sand. They dropped their garments and turned to touch with growing impatience. Pressing his lover down, Sean slowly sheathed himself. Then he was moving inside her, loving her. Velvet sliding through satin. Pale bodies twining under the moon like a night-blooming flower, tenuous, its petals unfurling in transcendent luminous beauty.

In the morning, leaving Sean to meet the French, Catherine went to the infirmary. When her listlessness drew Doctor Flynn's attention, she snatched a cup of tea from the kitchen and retreated into his office to do the billing. All too soon the ink on the paper spotted as her shoulders shook with sobs. A rap on the door made her straighten and swipe at her eyes. Flynn stuck in his head. "You've a caller. Liam wants to take you for a ride. I've only a few patients. You have permission to go if you'd like."

"Thank you. I'll only be a moment." Hastily she dunked a napkin into the cold tea and soaked her swollen eyes.

When she joined Liam in the carriage, she was clear-eyed and controlled; so much so that, when he bluntly told her the priest had agreed to dispense with the banns and marry them within the hour, she did no more than nod.

The ceremony in the village chapel was a mercifully brief ordeal. Like a marionette, she repeated the vows before the rock-faced priest and, after Liam's cold lips brushed her in a decorous kiss, accepted the congratulations offered by the nuns who had acted as witnesses. She sensed Liam was as miserable as she despite his bitter triumph. She had always dreaded a loveless marriage, but this travesty surpassed her worst imaginings. They were to leave at the height of the ball the following night. Liam had arranged a diversion for the eastern patrols. With luck and hard riding, they would reach the Londonderry garrison in three days. From there, word could be sent to General Lake, commander of the British occupation forces. Altogether, Sean would have nearly a week to evacuate Shelan.

Leaving her at the infirmary door, Liam narrowly missed the escort who had come early to return her to the house. Sean was already in need of his hostess.

As Catherine entered the foyer at Shelan, a short burst of male voices and scent of tobacco followed Peg out as she shut the study door behind her. "Put on yer habit, lass. We've a pack of sea-weary horse soldiers on our hands. They've all clamorin' to tear about the countryside on a hunt. Yer things have been moved to the room next to Sean's; it has a connectin' door. Liam's on the other side."

Catherine nodded and climbed the stairs. When she had changed, she critically surveyed her image in the mirror. The habit was beautifully cut in severe black, the white stock of the blouse accentuating her vivid coloring. Gleaming black hair was sleekly twisted up under the high-brimmed hat and her dark blue eyes had an elusive mystery behind the black veil. You look like a gypsy whore in stolen finery, she thought in disgust. Beautiful, yes. Very. Accursed bitch. Catherine Enderly, Catherine de Vigny, Kitty Flynn, Lady Liam Culhane. Kit. You're none of them now. You only exist as a betraying cheat. You've made mockery of a sacrament, every vow a cynical lie, the confession before the ceremony a travesty of omission. Wear black for your love, lass. You've killed him sure. All for a worthy cause.

The young French lieutenant speaking animatedly to Sean of Napoleon's modernization of the Polytechnique changed track in midsentence and stared past his host's shoulder. *"Mon Dieu,* what a ravishing creature!"

Sean turned. Catherine was sauntering down the steps. By now all eyes were on her, the hush dropping like a blanket, the appraising Gallic appreciation evident. Sean's eyes narrowed. The bit of veil had all the effect of a black negligee. The witch was seducing the lot of them without flicking an eyelash. Even as a coltish adolescent she'd had a strange allure; as a woman, that quality was devastating. The Frenchmen surreptitiously jostled one another to have a better look. Grimly he plowed through the crowd to the foot of the stair. "Miss Flynn, you're just in time to meet some of my *other* guests before the hunt."

"I'm looking forward to it, Mr. Culhane." She accepted his offered arm.

Sensing her underlying tension, Sean nodded to Rafferty, who was playing lackey, to offer port. "Thank you." She sipped gratefully and briefly looked up into Sean's eyes as he began introductions. He was incredibly handsome in his riding clothes, a polished stranger, his French flawless. There were so many things she did not know about him . . . and would never know.

General Fournel, Humbert's representative, was introduced first. Wearing civilian riding clothes as did his men, he was a tall, hawk-faced man with graying temples. His distinguished looks and smooth charm reminded her of her father, but his eyes held a less than paternal expression as he bowed with a smart click of his heels. "Your servant, Mademoiselle Flynn," he murmured in suavely accented English. "If General Bonaparte had heard even a whisper of your beauty, he would have come himself rather than allow so fortunate an envoy to extend his compliments. May I present my corps?"

"You are most gallant, General," Catherine replied in clipped French. "I shall be pleased to meet them."

Sean's lips twitched. The regal little devil's company

manners made Napoleon's emissary seem like a lapdog merchant.

"Colonel . . . but where is he?" said Fournel, looking about for his executive officer. "He was here a moment ago."

"He's outside admiring the horses, *mon Général*," eagerly volunteered the Polytechnique lieutenant.

"Ah, yes, I might have known." Fournel went on to introduce the convenient Lieutenant Andre Courbier, whose brown eyes grew melting as he offered his compliments. One by one, the officers tried to outdo one another with flattery as they were presented.

Several Ulster landowners and their wives were scattered among the group along with a newspaper publisher. As Catherine greeted them, the landlords were polite, their wives distant, and the newspaperman shrewd, his addresses no less eloquent than those of the Frenchmen, but lightly barbed. He was just beginning a pointed inquiry about Catherine's family and Sean was preparing to interrupt when the front door opened and the missing officer came gaily into the foyer. "Magnificent! But those blacks are *formidable!* French barbs mixed with Irish strains. Mesdames, messieurs, we shall do brilliantly together in this enterprise. There can be no doubt . . ." His eyes came to rest on the dark beauty surrounded by his fellow officers.

Catherine stared back. It was Raoul d'Amauri, the young Frenchman who had courted her at Windemere.

Fournel waved him over. "Mademoiselle Flynn, my wandering executive officer, Colonel Raoul d'Amauri."

"Mademoiselle Flynn." Amauri's usually expressive brown eyes were polite, no more.

His commander glanced at him. "I fear my young friend is overwhelmed by your beauty, mademoiselle. Ordinarily, he is most eloquent, even for a Frenchman."

Amauri bowed. "Indeed, *mon Général.* I assumed my brother officers had already pressed their fortunate advantage in my absence and numbed the young lady's ears with paeans to her charms. Mademoiselle Flynn may find the welcome silence unforgettable."

Sean smelled a rat. For all her calm response, Catherine

281

looked as if she had seen a ghost, and the handsome Amauri resembled neither a neuter nor a pederast. The Frenchman's facile cover-up and easy smile concealed a control Sean had employed himself when in the presence of a man he had cuckolded. Had he been less than certain he had been Catherine's first lover, he would have been cheerfully inclined to dismember the young Frenchman. As it was, he decided to give Amauri a bit of rein.

At that moment, Liam came downstairs. He tersely nodded to this guest and that, having met the officers earlier that morning. Ignoring both his brother and Catherine, he took a glass of wine from Rafferty, tossed it down, took another, and began to converse with an acquaintance from a neighboring estate. Finally everyone was assembled. Pulling on their gloves, twenty riders filed out onto the terrace.

The hunt master, Tim O'Rourke, waited with a pack of sleek Irish hounds, some frolicking about his mount's heels, the older dogs sitting quietly, tongues lolling.

Accustomed to letting Catherine mount by herself, Sean suddenly noticed three Frenchmen vying for that honor. His own Irish officers, though equally eager, wisely kept their distance. Catherine laughingly bestowed upon Courbier the honor of assisting her up, and Sean eyed the fellow's hand on her tiny waist with the goodwill of an Apache. On his left, Amauri watched with tolerant amusement. "My friends are like pups, all standing on each other's ears."

"I take it your approach will be less awkward?"

Amauri looked pointedly from Numidian to the big black Sean sat and laughed. "I have been known to poach, monsieur, but not under the gamekeeper's nose."

"Don't jump to conclusions, Colonel. Miss Flynn has a mind of her own, and my brother is more inclined to gamekeeping than I."

Amauri glanced at Liam; certainly the young lord wore the look of a jealous man. His efforts to keep his eyes from the English girl were almost pathetic. Still, it would be wise to be careful. Catherine Enderly had the potential of a spark in a powder keg. He cocked his head. "So? Mademoiselle Flynn and your brother have an arrangement?"

Sean shrugged. If the Frenchman knew Catherine, it was best to let him think she was visiting Shelan incognito to have a private dalliance. Amauri would play a close hand if he knew his host was her lover. Only an idiot would make overtures to an ally's woman before going into war beside him—or in front of him.

The Frenchmen surrounded Catherine like a school of fish as the riders rode out across the countryside, but shortly after Tim sounded the horn and the pack set out in full cry, her big black led the pursuit. Amauri maintained the pace until they neared the fringes of a sparse wood. That such a rarity must be Klendenon's Bog, he realized from study of Irish campaign maps, and he remembered a shortcut lay down a rocky ravine. Sean saw him veer off, and guessing why, let Mephisto have his head and drive through the main group of riders until he alone was in sight of Catherine. As he came over the rise, she was turning south to follow the hounds when Amauri cut her off and waved her to follow him. Without hesitation, she disappeared after him into the wooded glen.

In the shelter of the trees, the Frenchman dismounted. He helped Catherine off her horse, then after leading her by the hand to a fallen tree, indicated for her to sit. He stood watching her. "I had to see you alone. *Tu comprends?*"

"Yes."

"What are you doing here, Catherine?" he asked in French. "Your father said you were in Capri, then Montebello. Every time I inquired about you, it was somewhere different."

"Is that so strange? You know I was bored by school. And I adore traveling," she drawled with light defiance, almost daring contradiction.

"Does your father know you're here?"

"I suppose so. But then, he's a busy man. Too busy to bother keeping track of my every movement. And I'm a busy woman. I'm enjoying my freedom." The lovely smile was teasing.

"You've changed."

"Have I? In what way?"

"For one thing, you've become beautiful." He walked

283

around her. "I anticipated it, only not like this. It's quite incredible."

"I was leading the hunt, Raoul. Have you really brought me out here for belated flattery?" The smile still played about her mouth.

He lifted a quizzical eyebrow. "You don't even bother to blush when a man looks you over. Yes, you are very different, I think. No longer just a cocky little schoolgirl. You're more assured, less . . . virginal."

She looked him in the eye. "We'll soon be missed, Raoul. I suggest you return to the house. A loose shoe, perhaps. I shall have taken a tumble, unfortunately joining the others after they've gloriously mangled the fox."

"Très facile. But, *chérie,* you dislike hunting. Why pursue the fox so hotly if you don't wish to claim the trophy?"

She stood up. "I take pleasure in riding an unpredictable course." Her head tilted up at him. "Women delight in perversity. Any good Frenchman knows that."

"Ah, yes. Perversity." He snapped his fingers. "Perhaps that's it. I should have thought Lord Liam Culhane to be a most predictable man. His brother seems to promise more challenge. But possibly you didn't realize that when it began and now continue your affair out of . . . perversity."

Catherine's expression did not change. "I don't know what you're talking about."

"Your affair with Lord Culhane. That's why you're here incognito, isn't it? His brother hinted as much." He sighed. "You've broken my heart, *chérie.* I should so much have liked to be first."

She tapped his chest with the crop. "With a cocky little schoolgirl? *Chéri,* don't speak to me of challenge."

His eyes crinkled teasingly. "Oh, I'll survive the disappointment of missing the appetizer, so long as I may enjoy the banquet at leisure."

"An invitation to dine is not forthcoming, Raoul. I suggest you satisfy your appetite elsewhere."

He struck his forehead in mock chagrin. *"Quelle déesse cruelle!"* He looked at her beseechingly. "Don't you like me anymore?"

For the first time, a trace of her old familiar smile flickered about her lips. "Yes, Raoul, I like you. How could I not? You're irresistible, always able to make me laugh."

He looked at her shrewdly. "Even now, when you don't want to?"

She deliberately misunderstood. "But you're wrong, Raoul. I'm not angry—although you've spoiled the hunt—just a bit disappointed. There will be so little of this sort of amusement for a long while."

"Why do you say that?"

Her lashes flicked up. "What do you take me for? I know why the *Meridian* is here."

Amauri's brown eyes imperceptibly hardened. "Did Liam Culhane tell you?"

She smiled. "That would make him not only a reassuringly boring lover, but a dangerously unreliable ally. Not the sort to be cozy with, especially in war. No, Liam told me nothing, but it's not difficult to put two and two together. Papa, too, has had arrangements with your government for some time. That must have been why you visited Windemere in the first place. What will he gain from this? A dukedom? That's next on his agenda, I'm sure . . . even better"—the thought struck her even as she spoke—"a dukedom and the chair of the governor general of Ireland." She laughed lightly at his frown. "Naturally you've promised leadership of the government to the Culhanes as well. They have a legitimate claim, I believe. What a scramble that will be!" She ran the crop along a log. "I suppose poor Papa will be disappointed. Now that he's disgraced, he cannot be of much use to you. So it's either Culhane or one of Napoleon's numerous relatives on the throne of Tara. Which do you put your money on, *mon cher* Raoul?"

"I reserve gambling to horses. Losses may be expensive, but rarely fatal." He came up behind her. "Would you like to be a queen, *p'tite?*"

She laughed scoffingly. "I want more pleasure out of life." Then, as if toying with the thought, she began to adjust her veil. "Still, being a mere princess might be convenient. I suppose Liam *would* be a prince?"

She turned her head, her eyes luring him as if behind a

harem veil, and he caught her shoulders in spite of himself. "So you are having an affair with him!"

She smiled slowly. "It was you who said he was predictable, not I."

Amauri pulled her close and his senses began to take over as he felt the ripened body beneath her habit. "Catherine, don't meddle in this. It's too dangerous. We're all sitting atop a powder keg. You're behaving as if it were all a game."

"Your concern is endearing, but—"

"Catherine, don't be stupid! You must leave Ireland. Every day you spend with that fair-haired fop—"

"Don't play the jealous suitor. I admit I was infatuated with you once, but then, you said yourself I was a child."

"You still are!" His voice dropped to a murmur. "Only now you have the body of a woman. You're maddening . . ."

She eluded his lips. "You don't have to seduce me to ensure my reliability. It must have been quite a surprise, finding an English bomb in the midst of your conspirators. I have no intention of interfering with your plans, for you see, I *am* in love. The end of this rebellion will see me married to Liam Culhane, my fortunes a barometer of France's success in Ireland."

He released her abruptly. "You're not serious! You don't know your own mind."

"I've never been more sure of anything." Catherine went to Numidian and gathered the reins. "And now, I think we should consider the matter closed."

The Frenchman clicked his heels in an angry bow. "As you say, *Comtesse.*"

She mounted easily without assistance and watched as he vaulted into his own saddle. "Raoul?"

"Yes?" he replied curtly.

"If anything should happen to Liam, I would hold you personally responsible."

His eyes narrowed. "Do you take me for a murderer?"

She regarded him levelly. "Nothing so crude. For instance, if I had proved difficult this afternoon and unfortunately suffered a broken neck in a fall, my demise would have been classified as an assassination under the circumstances, *n'est-ce pas?* A very detached word, assassination. Nothing personal about it at all."

He gave her an appraising look, then rode away at a hard gallop.

Catherine nudged Numidian into a walk in the opposite direction. She felt curiously light-headed and cold, even though the sun streamed warmly though the wasted oaks and rowan trees. She did not even turn her head when Sean's voice drifted over her shoulder. "Well done, Kitten. Though there were moments I thought I might have to shoot him." The Irishman reined in beside her on the path. "Do you play whist?"

She smiled faintly. "Dare I say when I learned?"

"Never mind. Stay away from him, Catherine." She gave him a sidelong look. "It's not that, though his balls make a tempting target. He hasn't swallowed your story yet."

"The story you fed him," she retorted ironically. "Still, I hadn't come up with a better one. If I'd admitted being involved with you, he might have thought you were setting a trap with Father's backing. After all, Papa's allegiances tend to be somewhat shifty."

Sean smiled faintly. "Not anymore. He's becoming a faithful Englishman in spite of himself."

"More of your conniving?"

The Irishman shrugged. "Even I didn't guess Napoleon might have promised him a place in government. That was a deft shot. You're beginning to show a scheming streak, pet."

"Uneasy?"

"Should I be?"

"As Raoul said, things could go wrong. If . . . something did, what would you do?"

"What would you want me to do?"

"Cut and run."

"To end up fighting for Napoleon instead of for Ireland? Not likely. I don't like his ideas of conquest any better than you."

"Then fight against him."

"It's a fine choice you're giving me, girl: to join the English army or march with that Corsican bastard all over

287

Europe. If I'm going to fight and die, I'd as lief do it on my own turf, for my own people."

"Then you won't leave?"

"The others can if they want."

"You'd die, uselessly?" she whispered incredulously.

"Brooding before battle has a way of fouling luck. You'll come to no harm in any case. I'm sending you to Canada to stay with friends until it's over. You sail on the *Sylvie* the morning after the ball. I've set an income aside for you. In case of my death, you'll inherit everything I have. The day the fighting's over, for good or ill, you're free to spit in my eye or on my grave, whichever the case may be."

"You said once . . ."

"That I'd follow you anywhere? I'll never be sure of you unless you're free to turn away and not come back. When those men looked at you this afternoon, I felt as if I'd been making love to a mirage." Abruptly, he twitched Mephisto off the path. "We'd better separate here." He did not look back.

CHAPTER 14

Duels

The provocatively cut gown left Catherine's breasts and shoulders alluringly bare. Her sapphire silk shimmered in the light of massive candelabras that lined the dining table. Sean had chosen to dress her with scandalous, if excellent, taste, and with reason. She felt like another woman, one who had never endured hard work. Exactly what I might have become, she thought behind a smile that expressed nothing but attention to the subtly suggestive repartee of her dinner partner, General Fournel.

"Your eyes are fascinating, mademoiselle; at once inviting a man to the most wicked imaginings, yet distant as the stars."

Amauri lazed in the chair opposite. "Ah, one must beware of cold goddesses, *mon Général.* Wasn't it the huntress Diana who had her lover turned into a stag and torn to bits by her hounds for venturing too close?"

"Actaeon was not her lover, Colonel," drawled Catherine. "He was merely impertinent."

Courbier, the puppyish young lieutenant, leaned forward laughing. "Surely, mademoiselle, a woman so lovely as you could never be cruel."

"If men transform women into goddesses, they must expect less than docile behavior."

Liam, on her left, sardonically raised his glass. "Heed the lady well, gentlemen, lest you become dog food ere morn."

The lieutenant looked at him good-naturedly. "Have you had sad experience with goddesses, milord?"

"There are no goddesses, Lieutenant. They're an artistic fiction. As the lady suggests, all lies."

Liam was more inebriated than Catherine had ever seen him. Her eyes flicked toward Sean at the far end of the table. He seemed to be listening to a guest with polite boredom, but when his eyes met hers, she knew he had missed little of the conversation between Liam and the lieutenant.

"But, milord," another officer was protesting, "men must be permitted a few pleasant illusions."

"Especially if they insist on dying for them; otherwise, who would fight to protect another man's potatoes," inserted Amauri, slyly eying Liam. "And women, too, must have their illusions, love being their particular favorite. What do you expect of love, Mademoiselle Flynn?"

Catherine lifted her glass. *"C'est merveilleux,* when one can afford it." Secretly, she was furious with Amauri for taunting Liam through her.

"Quel cynisme. C'est dommage," Amauri sighed. "Still, surely you believe in the immortality of glory?"

"Immortality is a masculine word. To a woman, only life matters."

"Then you cannot be in favor of war, mademoiselle?"

She gave him a slow smile. "I'm relieved I'm not obliged to be a soldier."

The lieutenant laughed. "Bravo, Mademoiselle Flynn! To waste such beauty as cannon fodder would be idiocy!"

Amauri glanced at Liam, then looked at her. "But surely courage should be coupled with beauty?"

Catherine laughed. "If you doubt my nerve, Colonel, why not call me out?"

"You, mademoiselle? Have you no gallant protector?"

"Will I do?" interrupted Liam nastily.

Catherine lightly tapped his sleeve with her fan. "No, milord. You shall not cheat me. I am the one whose ferocity is questioned."

Amauri gave a Gallic shrug and grinned. "My dear young lady, I cannot fight a woman."

"Why not? Every tradition needs a little airing, *n'est-ce pas?* Come, it will be amusing."

Amauri, in expectation of some parlor game, sighed. "Very well, mademoiselle, if you insist. I challenge."

"I choose knives," said Catherine swiftly, rising to her feet and flicking the fan open.

Amauri blinked and a rustling murmur went round the table. Liam was livid, Sean's eyes almost slitted. "But, mademoiselle, surely you must reconsider!" Amauri protested. "Pistols loaded with paper pellets, perhaps? Then you may have a fair chance."

"Colonel, you questioned my courage. I haven't been in awe of paper wads since a tutor made me eat those I had leveled at him." The fan waved languidly. "You *are* familiar with knives, Colonel? I shouldn't wish to put you at the disadvantage."

Amauri reddened. "But of course."

"Good. The foyer in fifteen minutes? My lord Culhane won't want his ballroom parquetry scuffed." With a snap of her fan, Catherine sailed out the door.

Faced with a barrage of questions, Sean was unable to follow Catherine upstairs until the guests crowded from the dining room into the foyer. He met her just outside her bedroom door. Barefoot in Tim's clothing, hair in a knot atop her head, she slipped a long knife into her belt, then saw him. Waving a warning hand, she backed from his intent look. "Oh, no. You're not stopping me. Raoul's getting his fight."

"Where did you get that knife?"

"Flannery gave it to me. To fend off undesirables."

"Give it to me."

"No," she said quietly. "Amauri tried to bait Liam into making a fool of himself, perhaps a dead fool. If I can make *him* appear the fool tonight, he won't dare cause any more trouble."

Sean caught her arms. "When Amauri sees you're in earnest, he'll stop playing games. I'll not have you sliced up."

Their eyes locked. "You said I was free."

His hands dropped. "I did, but you're taking wild advantage of it."

She smiled impishly. "Don't worry. I mean to prick the colonel's pride, not his hide."

"I'm not concerned about that."

Her smile faded. "I won't be careless."

Sean let her go down alone. He stood in the hallway for a moment, his mind in a knot. Was she trying to force him to split the alliance? If he had to interfere in the duel to save her, she would have created a nice mess. And it was probable her increasingly devious mind had entertained just that notion. He wondered if he was trying to tame a filly that couldn't be broken.

When Sean reached the foyer, his mistress and the colonel were ringed by military men and muttering civilians. The women were scandalized by Catherine's bold manner and masculine attire. She stood boyishly with hands on hips, bare feet spread on the black-and-white marble. Having removed his coat, Amauri stood rolling up his sleeves. He eyed her with some amusement. "So, mademoiselle, we are about to have a demonstration of your formidable needlepoint skills."

She cocked her head and drawled, "It's time you had a lesson in stitchery, Colonel. Our good doctor will explain everything as he sews you up."

Lieutenant Courbier and two of the Irishmen snickered, but immediately stifled as General Fournel shot them a look and stepped forward. "You do intend to use point-guards?"

She smiled. "But of course, General. I was only teasing your handsome colonel. I shall take every precaution, naturally." She turned to Sean. "Mr. Culhane, have you guards?"

Grimly, he nodded and waved a servant toward his study. The man returned with weapon guards and presented them. Catherine selected one and slipped it on her knife. "Thank you. We shall not need the other."

Fournel turned red as Amauri's smile grew a bit tight. "Monsieur Culhane, I protest! This is impossible."

Sean leaned casually against the stair rail and shrugged. "Miss Flynn was challenged. She may dictate rules concerning weapons."

"Don't be concerned, General," Catherine said lightly.

"We're only playing. You must agree a duel is more divert-
ing than the usual pianoforte repertoire after dinner." She
saluted Amauri with the knife in the formal manner of a
swordsman. "Are you ready?"

Amauri smiled and returned the salute. *"Comme vous
voulez, mademoiselle. En garde."* His smile soon vanished.
The Frenchman handled his knife with facility, but Catherine's better training, sharper reflexes, and quicker footing were quickly evident. His first feints teased as they
circled, but if he advanced, she retreated, and her blade always blocked any opening before he could attempt to take
advantage of it. Without warning, her knife blurred toward his chest and there was a clink on the marble.

"You've lost a button, sir," one of the adjutants called.

"The one over your heart, Colonel," his small opponent
murmured helpfully. *"Faites attention."* The knife flicked
out again. "Tsk. There goes another. Colonel, you really
must learn to sew if you lose buttons like a schoolboy."

Amauri's smile became grin. "I think it's the schoolgirl
who needs a lesson." He began to circle intently, and Sean
palmed his dagger from the sheath beneath his silk cuff.
Amauri made a calculated jab, but Catherine faded before
it like a wraith. He tried again, with due respect for a possible counterattack; again she was out of range without
seeming to move.

For once in his life, Amauri was confused. The girl was
making an idiot of him. One part of him wanted to slice her
to ribbons, but the other simply wanted her. The countess
was magnificent, he thought, a beautiful, wily panther.
What must she be like in bed? Before he knew what was
happening, he felt a slice across his midriff and heard a
husky, teasing murmur. "For shame, Colonel, now I know
your mind is wandering." Flushing, he took a furious
swipe and she laughed, easily avoiding him. "Ah, Colonel,
you're wearing a sour face. What a pity when you have
such a charming smile. It has just a suggestion of mischief
. . . la!"

A feather brush across the corner of his mouth left a fine
white scratch across his flushed cheek. Angry now, he attacked her as he would have a man. Suddenly he held a
handful of stinging fingers, but nothing else. His weapon

lay near the foot of the stair; when he would have retrieved it, he found a polished boot firmly planted across its blade.

"The duel is at an end, Colonel." Without looking around at Catherine, Sean continued lazily, "I trust your honor has been satisfied, Miss Flynn."

"Completely, Mr. Culhane."

Sean nodded pleasantly. "Good. Any objections, Colonel?"

Amauri was angry, but not foolish. He smiled sheepishly. "No, monsieur. It is I who have been objectionable." As Catherine was slipping the knife back into her belt, he took her hand and kissed it. "Please accept my most profound apologies, mademoiselle. Believe me, I shall never underrate you again."

Catherine laughed, then curtsied. "I think it's time I resume a skirt, Colonel. It's hardly fair for a woman to amuse herself by wearing breeches. After all, how many men can enjoy the option of petticoats?"

As she responded to a witticism from Fournel, Sean turned to a lanky Irish officer and ordered quietly, "Halloran, circulate and invite all officers into the study. All except my brother." He nodded toward Liam, who was sullenly plying his wineglass as he leaned against the dining room door. "Lord Culhane is in no state to lend our allies confidence. We've a good deal to cover tonight."

Leaving the throng, Catherine retired to her room and locked the door in case her audacity might tempt a visiting male to further test her unconventionality. As she stripped off Tim's shirt, she noticed a small bouquet of flowers by the bedside: tiny, starlike white wildflowers from the startings she had planted on Maude Corrigan's grave. The Irishman was asking her to have faith in him. She fought back tears. It was too late to change course now; the marriage had taken care of that.

Quickly, she donned the satin peignoir and slippers newly brought from Paris, then brushed out her hair. If she was to discover anything from the conference in the library, there was no time to lose. Quietly, she took the service passage to the ballroom.

The great room was thunderously silent, its tall windows shaping ghosts of moonlight. Sean had said the house's peculiar acoustics enabled ballroom sounds to be perfectly distinct in the library; surely the reverse was also true. She crisscrossed the room methodically and heard nothing but a droning mumble, until finally, near the foyer wall, the voices clarified. Not everything was audible, but during the next hour she heard enough. The rebels planned to seize the Dublin mail coaches; the failure of the coaches to arrive at their destinations would signal the uprising throughout Ireland. The initial objectives would be to control Dublin and Wexford. Weather permitting, French support would come ashore at Killala across Donegal Bay and somewhere else she could not make out. Fournel appeared concerned with infantry, while Amauri discussed artillery, talking of roads and horses, fortifications and counterbatteries. Mostly she heard fragmented snatches, but the tone certainly suggested a major French buildup after the initial invasion.

Finally, the conference began to break up and she returned the way she had come, anticipating a hand at her throat at every turn. Not until safely in bed did she draw a complete breath. The candle was barely snuffed when the door of Sean's room clicked open into hers. Heart thudding, she forced her breathing to seem regular. After a moment, the door closed and she was left alone to lie sleepless until dawn.

As the sun came up, Catherine finally drifted wearily into sleep, not to awaken until she felt Sean's presence. Tall against the window light, he stood in his riding clothes at the foot of the bed. The look on his face tugged at her heart and she lifted her arms to him. In a moment, he lay across the bed, his mouth slanting first fiercely across hers, then slowly, savoring the heady wine of her lips, feeling the lushness of the slim body under the clinging satin, the softness of breasts barely contained by filmy lace butterflies. His fingers caught in her hair and he drew her head back, murmuring against her throat, "You'd tempt the devil, witch."

Her fingers stole inside his shirt, touching him, luring him. Desperately, she wanted to hold him inside her, to shield him like a child from the hurt she must give him.

295

With a sigh, he traced a finger down her cheek. "But even the devil cannot always suit himself. Fournel and Amauri are cooling their heels on the terrace even now."

She touched his lips. "Be careful."

He looked at her quizzically. "Of Fournel? He'd sell out his own mother. But, if he turns on me, he'll catch a bullet with his perfect teeth."

"Not just Fournel. Everyone."

"Even you?"

"Even me."

He pushed back the tendrils of her hair. "Nay, lass, it's not in you to bury the knife with a kiss. Not in me. Not now." His lips reclaimed hers with a searing sweetness that left them both shaken. At last, reluctantly, he tore away and headed for the door. "Sleep as long as you like. You've nothing but entertainment of country biddies this afternoon." His piratical grin flashed. "Why not give 'em a rousing chorus of 'The Tart of Whitemarsh'?"

The afternoon dragged unbearably as Catherine amused the visiting ladies on the pianoforte, startling them with her skill and smoothing their ruffled sensibilities. Deftly, she dodged pointed queries about her background until, piqued by the mystery and her polite indifference to local gossip, the ladies concluded she was some French emigré's bastard in pursuit of a life of profligate indulgence.

Peg stole time to help Catherine dress for the ball. As excited as a girl making her own debut, the Irishwoman murmured over the dragonfly iridescence of threads that ran subtly, almost invisibly through the blue-green cobweb silk of her ball gown, making it seem alive with hidden color. As Catherine gilded her nails and eyelids, she forced herself to listen to the housekeeper's chatter. Concentrating on holding the hand mirror steady, she was startled at the stylish coiffure Peg had produced. Catherine, pleading a very real headache, had dined in her room, but Peg had massaged the ache away. Now, when she donned silver sandals and crossed to the pier glass, no sign of strain was visible. About her throat, accentuating its delicacy, was the Niall Torc.

Peg smiled inwardly. Sean was no idiot. By publicly displaying Catherine Enderly as his woman, even were she Cromwell reincarnate, any man, even an Irishman, could see his reason; and once intrigued by her beauty, to be beguiled by the woman was inevitable. Peg handed Catherine a silver fan, then tilted her head as a rap resounded at the door. "That'll be Liam. He's to escort ye." She stood back a moment, surveying the final effect, then hugged Catherine tightly. "Ye're a blazin' beauty, girl. Yer man'll be that proud. Stand by him tonight." She let Liam in from his room and left.

Liam's blond brow lifted slightly as he surveyed his bride's attire and tucked her arm in his. "I'm richly anticipating my marital rights, love. Any woman who could induce my tight-fisted brother to spend so much on a wardrobe must be an extraordinary bedmate." Impassively, Catherine flicked open her fan and scrutinized him. Handsome in dark blue velvet, her husband smiled ironically. "No, dearest, I'm not drunk. You see?" He extended his hands to demonstrate their steadiness. "Tonight, I'm giving my all for love. The white knight is rescuing the lady fair at peril of life and fortune, but I expect you'll be worth it." He inclined his blond head toward the door. "Shall we go down, Countess? Most of the guests are already tooth to tusk with the musicians."

"Where are we to meet?" she asked as they strolled toward the stair.

He squeezed her hand. "You'll reserve the twelfth dance for me. At that point, we'll stroll out onto the terrace to take the air. The north steps have been screened with potted shrubbery and trees to shield our exit. The horses are waiting in the ruins."

"What of the tower watch?"

"I'll deliver drugged wine to them during the orchestra's second relief. At the same time, a messenger will carry news to the eastern patrols that a spy has been spotted trying to breach the southern pickets. They'll be given directions to reinforce the line."

"It all seems so easy."

"Yes," her husband said dryly. "Only it won't give us more than two hours' start."

Catherine's fingers tightened on his arm. "Less with Mephisto in pursuit."

Liam's handsome profile was serene. "The black will be useless tonight and for several to come. I angled a nail into his shoe. He'll pull up lame minutes from Shelan."

She felt sick. It was the beginning. The beginning of hurting all who trusted her.

Liam's sharp voice cut across her thoughts. "You look suspiciously pale." He spun her around and sharply pinched her cheeks. "Pull yourself together. This *was* your idea." For the benefit of the couple immediately behind them in the hallway, he tilted her now falsely radiant face up to his and lightly kissed her, murmuring, "Remember the first time, *chérie*?"

The woman nodded significantly to her husband.

When they walked into the blaze of light under the great ballroom chandeliers, Catherine felt faint. She forced deep breaths until the lights ceased to blur. Over the musicians' heads hung a draped French tricolor flanked by flags of green: one emblazoned with a harp, the other with a scarlet fist. Uniformed Frenchmen stood in clusters, and for the first time, Sean's officers wore Ireland's green and gold with harp insignia at their breasts. The women turned to look, fans fluttering.

Then, out of the crowd strode a tall man in black whose green eyes claimed her before his lean fingers lifted her cold hand to his lips. "Miss Flynn, will you do my brother and me the honor of opening the ball with General Fournel?"

"I should be delighted, sir," she murmured.

With a short, ironic bow, Liam released his partner to Sean. Fournel's eyes roved, expressing barely concealed desire as they exchanged amenities. When the music started, Catherine felt as if she were entering an eel's embrace. Fournel was dismayed not at all by her deft rebuttal of his suggestive flirtation, and the others who eagerly followed him no less so. Courbier in particular gazed at her longingly, and she had the urge to break into hysterical giggles. Liam saw something in her face and quickly cut in. He whirled her so rapidly around the ballroom, that she was forced to concentrate to stay in step. "Don't lose control now, damn it! I have to drug the pickets in half an hour."

Her head snapped up. "I'm quite all right now, thank you. You won't need to intervene again."

"Good. I'd hate to be shot for a tittering female."

She jerked away from him and practically ran into Amauri's chest. Smoothly, he steered her back into the waltz, blandly smiling into her flushed face. "Quarreling with your fair-haired boy, *chérie?* I seem to be always rescuing you from disagreeable men."

Valera's ghost flickered briefly and Catherine glared at Raoul as they danced past the musicians. "Liam is no more disagreeable than you. You're rather a sugar-coated bully, Raoul."

His grin was unabashed. "I'm only concerned for you, *chérie.* Perhaps in my eagerness to save you from a dreary liaison . . ."

She grimaced. "Your General Fournel suggests I wear kneepants and a moustache to vary my lackluster *vie d'amour.* What, pray, is your remedy?"

Amauri's grin widened. "Champagne and intermission in my room for a start."

"A fifteen-minute toss? Your staying power is hardly encouraging."

"La, la, *chérie,* what a sharp little tongue. I can think of better employment for it."

She tried to pull away. "I don't have to listen to this . . ."

His fingers tightened and the teasing smile faded. "Ah, but you do. You don't love that popinjay. I saw your face when you looked at him last night. He's a fool and a tippler. I don't know what game you're playing here, but it's dangerous. Your father's finished. You cannot help him, if that's your wish. Neither Napoleon nor the Bourbons will touch him now. But you need not join him in disfavor. Come to Paris, Catherine."

"With you?"

"With me. You need a man, not a weakling fool."

"You underestimate Liam, Raoul," she said coldly, "and the profits to be made in Ireland in the wake of insurrection. I'll not be leaving until I've used my advantages here."

Raoul studied the cool, lovely face turned arrogantly up to his. "You're your father's daughter after all."

299

"*Mais naturellement, mon Colonel.* Surely you're not disappointed? After all, how long would an ingenue have sustained your interest?"

The dance ended and Amauri raised her hand to his lips. "Forever, if she became the woman I see now."

Then a Captain Rodier was bowing, politely waiting for his superior to make his adieus. Amauri frowned at him. "What is it, Captain?"

"I . . . I have this dance with Mademoiselle Flynn, *mon Colonel.*"

Catherine withdrew her card from her glove and waved it under Amauri's nose. "Ah, yes. Captain Rodier. I've been looking forward to trying a quadrille with you. You danced so beautifully with Madame O'Connell. Will you excuse us, Colonel?" She strolled off with the flattered but uneasy subordinate.

Dance after dance followed until suddenly Sean was holding her in his arms, his dark hair like ragged black satin under the flickering candles, his green eyes shadowed under their lashes, caressing her. The tall man in black and the slim girl in a whisper of green moved perfectly together. She wanted to touch his face, his lips that lost their hardness when he held her to his breast, but her heart was cracking and the agony turned her limbs to lead. *You couldn't drive in the knife with a kiss. Not you. I love you. I love you. My God, help me. Let me die now. Now, this moment.*

She stumbled and he caught her close, his murmur husky against her ear, as it had been so often in the night when he was loving her. "Kit? What's wrong?"

She shook her head, unable to look at him. The music was shrill. "It's very hard, that's all."

He lifted her chin gently. "I know. Only a little longer. The Frenchmen will be gone soon. Amauri has already gone to prepare the *Meridian* for sailing." The misery in her eyes deepened. "You look sad, kitten. Is it possible you'll miss me a bit?"

How could he know? Liam . . .

He misread her distraction and whispered, "You still haven't given up entirely, have you? Part of you still fights. But there's love in your eyes tonight, and before dawn I'm going to hear you say the words. Then all the cannon in Ireland and ice in Canada won't keep me from you when the fighting's done."

Canada. Of course. He was talking about Canada. Not the escape. He didn't know.

Suddenly, Liam was tapping his brother's shoulder. "The gavotte is mine, brother," he said tautly.

Sean carelessly shrugged off his hand, then kissed Catherine's fingers. "I'll see you later this evening, Miss Flynn." Then he was gone.

Liam's grip threatened to snap her fingers. "Stop mooning as if the earth had swallowed him!" He pulled her into the brisk gavotte. "It's too late to turn back. The watch are trussed like Christmas geese." They spun into the pattern of dancers. "Don't fool yourself, love. If you confess to Sean now, he'll throttle you. You're my wife, remember? I'll tell him I've had you from the first, all the time you were at Flynn's . . ."

"Stop it!"

"That something went wrong in the escape plan . . ."

"Liam, for God's sake, I'm not going to tell him. I have to go through with this, in spite of Sean, in spite of *you*. Don't threaten me." Her voice was cold and steady, although she felt light-headed. The whirling . . . "I'm dizzy. Let's leave now."

He nodded and steered her toward the terrace. The cool breeze hit her like smelling salts and, fighting for air, she leaned briefly against the stone balustrade.

Liam's voice came from behind her, gentler now. "Are you all right?"

"Yes." She straightened.

"Very well. We'll stroll toward the ruins. If someone sees us, they'll assume we're having a moonlit tryst."

No one saw them. Nebulous shapes in the shadows, the horses whickered and Liam put his hands over their noses. Quickly, he tossed Catherine a cloak, then threw one over his own shoulders. Without waiting for assistance, she mounted. Bending low over the horses' necks, the riders walked the horses a few hundred yards north of the ruins. At a safe distance from the house, they spurred to a gallop.

* * *

"Pardon, Monsieur Culhane, have you seen Mademoiselle Flynn? I am promised the last dance and I should be most unhappy to miss it. General Bonaparte himself would have difficulty in combatting the contestants for her favors."

Culhane smiled faintly at the anxious young officer. "I've not seen the young lady in some time, Lieutenant Courbier. Perhaps she has retired." Courbier's face fell, then he glumly wandered off toward a servant bearing a tray of port.

Sean surveyed the dance floor. Catherine was indeed nowhere to be seen. He strolled out onto the terrace, idly noting fanciful arrangements of greenery at either end. Perhaps she *had* retired. The light rouge on her cheeks had not completely disguised their pallor. The last strains of music faded away and impatiently he wanted the place cleared. *Sylvie* was to hoist anchor by late morning, and he would not be free to retire until the *Meridian* sailed after midnight. That left only a few precious hours to hold Catherine, perhaps for the last time.

"Mr. Culhane, the French are waitin' to take their leave."

"Thank you, Halloran."

Mercifully, those farewells were brief; unfortunately the other guests, unobliged to catch the tide, were less pressed. Last-moment trivial gossip and reassurances about the forthcoming conflict made it difficult for Sean to maintain his civility. When the last carriage rolled away, he sighed in relief.

Pelting up the stairs, he loosened his stock and tugged off his jacket as he entered his room. Disappointed not to find Catherine waiting in bed, he unbuttoned his waistcoat as he opened the connecting door to her chamber. His fingers missed the last button. Lingerie neatly lay across the bed where the maid had left it. Uneasily, he lifted a bit of lace and rubbed it between thumb and forefinger. He had taken great care to display the desirability of his mistress. What if some randy buck had become dissatisfied with mere observation? Courbier had been eager enough. But the French were gone . . .

Then another thought occurred to him. Trying the door

to Liam's chamber, he found it unlocked on both sides; Liam's room was empty, his things undisturbed. Sean's trust flailed desperately. Liam had brought Catherine downstairs. Peg would have let him in from Catherine's side. That was it. That had to be it. Kit wouldn't . . .

But somehow, he knew they were gone. Dying slowly inside, he knew it even as he ordered a search and sent Halloran to question the tower watch. When the man returned with two woozy, panicky guards in tow, an agony exploded inside his soul, sending sheets of pain arching like sunbursts, blackening finally to a dull, smoldering ache.

When Mephisto pulled up lame and he saw the deliberately angled nail, the first hate began.

CHAPTER 15

The Arena

A few hours from Shelan, the fleeing riders entered the Derryveagh foothills. They picked their way precariously as the incline grew steep, then dismounted. The horses' hooves slipped on wet bracken and twice Catherine fell, reducing the Parisian gown to a muddy, sodden wreck.

Just before dawn, they reached a high, narrow valley and secreted the horses in a moss-blanketed niche in the mountainside. Liam hung feed bags over the animals' heads, then pulled a fishing net from a canvas sack hidden in a rock cranny and strung it across the corral opening. He nodded to the rocks above. "There's a cave up there. We'll rest for a couple of hours, then move on through the high passes. Sean will think I've headed for Omagh. By the time he knows differently, his mounts should be dropping in their tracks, while we'll be halfway to Londonderry. He won't be sure where we'll emerge from the mountains, but once we do, we'll have to run like hell. . . . Go on, climb up. I have to tie the horses' mouths after they're fed, just in case. And be careful; the stones are loose."

As Liam had warned, the rocks were treacherous; negotiating them in a ball gown was no simple matter. She crawled into the cave through a narrow double entrance divided by a boulder whose shadow formed bars of waning moonlight into a blunt triangle across the cavern floor. The ceiling's peak, less than head high, sloped to the back of the cave. She recoiled as her knee hit something that fell over heavily and cracked. In a few moments, an entrance blacked out and Liam whispered hoarsely, "What was that noise?"

"A pot of some kind. I broke it." He swore and dragged himself inside, then squatted to brush pebbles and crockery away to clear a sleeping space. "What is this place, Liam?"

"A prehistoric burial cave. You just dumped the occupant's remains into the dirt."

"What?"

"You'll see when the sky lightens."

Absently, she pushed the collapsing coiffure out of her face. "When did you hide the net here?"

"While you and your stud were at sea. At the time, I was certain you could be persuaded to come with me."

She could almost see his bitter expression, though his face was in shadow. "When do we leave the mountains?"

"At nightfall after we rest again. Once in the open, we rest one more time, thirty miles from Londonderry, then run the final leg."

"You've planned efficiently."

"I had time. And reason." He paused, a dark shape made vaguely inhuman by the cloak's contours. "And now that I've kept my part of the bargain, it's time you kept yours."

Her fingers, tangled in her hair, stilled. "What do you mean?"

"We're man and wife in theory. When we leave this cave, we'll have been joined in fact."

"I'm tired, Liam, as you must be, and we've yet a long way to travel," she answered levelly. "We need rest. Surely your marital privileges can wait until we reach safety."

His lips curled. "My privileges, madame? You mean my rights. As for fatigue, if you had kept to your bed last night . . ."

"You!" Anger bubbled up. "Were you that drunk, or simply fool enough to try to bed me within Sean's grasp? What if the conference had broken up early? A meeting you should have been sober enough to attend. Then we might have more information, not just scraps!" She felt like hurling a pot fragment at him, knowing even in her

305

mounting rage she was releasing the pent-up tension of days.

He laughed dryly. "So that's where you were. Playing spy. And you talk of discretion! Devious little Kitty Flynn." He shrugged off his cloak and spread it on the ground, then began to undo his clothing. When she made no movement to disrobe, he looked at her calmly. "I suggest you undress, my love; otherwise, I'll tear that dress to rags. As we're shortly appearing in public, you may prefer to keep it intact."

Catherine's anger became edged with uneasiness. "I'm not your whore. I'll not be taken like one."

"No. You're my wife," was the unruffled reply. He pulled off his shirt and vest and folded them for a pillow. "In a few hours, we may both be recaptured or dead. Would you deny me a few moments of wedded bliss?"

Realizing his implacability, she tried a new tack. "Liam, we may have years together. Would you begin our marriage so callously? Would you destroy any affection I might have for you?"

His eyes were the shade of steel in the moonlight, like the cool sheen of his hair. "I've waited long enough for your affection. Tried to earn it with gentleness and consideration. I was an idiot. You simply required a stud. Now you have one for life." He pulled off his boots, his lean chest and arms gleaming white above the remaining breeches. "Don't be too forlorn. My brother would never have married you. Ireland will always be first in his heart, and the only woman he ever really craved was Megan. I have no distractions. I want only you."

"Liam, please. Wait until we reach Londonderry. Only two more days. We'll go to the finest hotel . . ."

"Ah, my sweet, you're so lovely and so transparent. Do you really think I'm fool enough to give you grounds for annulment?" His eyes glinted dangerously and his voice lost its coolness. "If you have a stitch on after two minutes, I'll tear it to shreds."

He had her. She had given him the opportunity and the right. Now there was no choice. To find the way out of the mountains without him was impossible. She undid the catch of the cloak and let it fall, then the ball gown and chemise.

Liam's roughened breathing was the only sound in the cave as he unfastened his breeches. "Lie down." She started to spread the cloak. "No. In the dirt. No more altars for you, love." Lying down, she waited, stiff with loathing. The dirt was a powdery dust and she wondered what once-living refuse was mixed with it.

"Open your eyes, wife, and get used to the sight of me." Reluctantly, she obeyed. Naked, he was kneeling over her, his torso ghostly white, his sex jutting above her belly. "Touch me." She did not move. He caught at her wrist, dragged her hand downward, then covered her. He forced entry, and the knowledge that he was forcing her to submit, that he was dominating her, made him buck exultantly until sweat glistened on his flesh. He moaned in private ecstasy as all too quickly his ejaculation burst; then he fell away, panting.

Catherine lay unmoving, sprawled as he had left her, her body a dry husk, capable of feeling only a terrible, irrevocable loss. She had utterly betrayed Sean's trust; lack of choice made no difference. Anguish for his pain as well as her own suddenly rocked her with helpless, silent sobs.

Out of the dark, Liam's fingers brushed her cheeks with unexpected gentleness. "I didn't want it to be like this," he whispered. "I needed you so much and I waited so long. Then to see you begin to love him." His fingers stilled. "I couldn't bear it." There was no response. "I swear I'll be a good husband. You'll be happy, you'll see." He hesitated uneasily. "Don't hate me. I love you so much."

"I don't hate you." Her whisper was a monotone.

"You won't try to leave me? You promised before God . . ."

"Yes. I promised God and now I'm your wife." Catherine sat up and dragged the cloak about her, then stared at him over her shoulder. "But if you ever force me as you did tonight, you'll never see me again. Do you understand?"

He flushed. "I understand."

She curled up in the cloak in the back of the cave, leaving him to seek his own makeshift arrangements.

* * *

The day was damp and overcast, the rumbling thunder-heads lending a blueish cast to lush verdancy of rugged mountain slopes that surrounded the two riders threading through the vales. "Stay alert," Liam called back over his shoulder. "Sometimes rain-swelled rivers flood the valleys."

By daylight, he looked incongruous in his dusty formal clothes, particularly so far from civilization; but, Catherine reflected wryly, she could look no better. Her hair was a mass of tangles, gown filthy. Her face must be dirty as well. Dripping foliage brushed her sandaled foot. Green. Everything in Ireland was green. Like the shadowed green eyes that would haunt the rest of her days. Her chest began to ache as she fought away the memories and eventually lapsed into dull, swaying blankness, not thinking of the future, far less the past.

Liam peered through the gloom cast by the copse of trees that sheltered them. At their backs, mountains almost blocked the moon. Nothing visible moved across the grassy plain. To the northeast, the River Foyle glinted like a silver bangle. He finally nodded. "It's time."

They mounted quickly and urged the horses to an easy canter. Controlling the pace in the open country that stretched to Londonderry was crucial. They were far north of where Sean would expect them to exit the mountains, but rest and irregular terrain had cost precious time.

Dawn paled the sky without sign of pursuit. Toward noon, they reached a stream choked with weeds and yellow water lilies. After watering the animals, they wearily collapsed on the bank for a few minutes' rest. Long meadow grass fanned under a serene blue sky filled with the puffy clouds of a perfect spring day that reflected no hint of the threat that lay over the land. Catherine's mind drowsed wearily, lulled by the sun's warmth and the fragrant fields. Only moments seemed to have passed when Liam nudged her shoulder. "We have to keep moving. Sean will have picked up our trail by now. We've another fifty miles to cover."

* * *

By moonlight, the cashel resembled a low hill; only within a few hundred feet did the stone appear to be regular, like a giant's battered teeth set around an earthen tongue. Its boulders loomed high against the moon as the two riders dismounted. Liam pointed at a black-mouthed doorway formed by a crude, monstrous stone lintel. "We sleep in there."

"What is it?"

"A primitive fort; one of several about the countryside. The interior is a maze of souterrains that open out into a cleared area. Over there"—he nodded to a gap in the southern wall—"the roof has collapsed."

"A hospitable haven," Catherine remarked dryly. "Tons of earth must be atop the remaining passages."

Liam shrugged as he unfastened his saddlebags and slung them over his shoulder. "This is the best cover in miles and offers a chance of escape if we're surprised. Several souterrains open to the interior ring and the plain beyond."

He led Alcazar into the black maw of the doorway. The passage they followed was pitch-black and they stumbled over the debris of centuries, but Liam seemed to know exactly where he was going. "I explored this place as a boy," his voice echoed hollowly in the darkness. "There's a chamber where we can rest for a couple of hours." Shortly, he stopped. "This is it." She felt about to discover a dank cell only slightly wider than the passage. The horses whickered nervously and she could smell them and the mold in the place. She heard Liam drop his saddlebags. "Follow me with your canteen."

They negotiated a short, curving tunnel into a open space brilliant in the moonlight. It resembled an ancient Roman arena pierced with dark passage openings like the one from which they had emerged. Like blunt, stubby columns, huge stones were overturned among the sporadic holes and mounds of rubble that dotted the rocky, mossy floor. A cistern lay at the center. Liam dropped down at its edge and lowered his canteen by a long string. The canteen hit water far below with a faint slap and slowly filled. He hauled it up, then lowered the second canteen.

Catherine stooped by the well and looked down. A faint,

moonlit glimmer of water shattered as the canteen struck it; rings rippled into darkness. She stood up, wincing at sore muscles. She was nearly asleep on her feet, the arena merging into moonlit, rubble-strewn dreams with dim, shapeless figures moving in their shadows. Her spine prickled. "Liam," she whispered unevenly, "don't look up. There are men in the passages."

He froze. "Where?"

"Ahead of me and to my left. Wait. I'll adjust my hair . . ." Fingers trembling, she reached for the tangled mass at her nape and turned slightly. Her knees seemed to melt as she sobbed under her breath, "Oh, God." No longer bothering to keep to the shadows, they emerged from the tunnels and moved silently like nightmares across the clearing. Liam got to his feet, swiftly drawing his pistol from his waistband.

The foremost specter spoke icily. "Try it, brother, and you'll have a bullet through your skull before you level the barrel."

Liam hesitated, then snarled, "These are my liege men. They'll not shoot me on a bastard's orders."

"No?" Sean stepped full into the moonlight. He was a clear target, and from several yards away, Catherine felt the dangerous look in his eyes. "They're accustomed to following my commands automatically and quibbling later. Care to test that theory?"

Sensing Liam's slight movement behind her, Catherine stepped forward to block his aim. Pistols cocked. With tongue turned to parchment, she fought to speak evenly. "I'm the one you want. I appealed to Lord Culhane's honor to help me escape."

Sean walked forward with his deceptively lazy, silent stride. His dark face was expressionless, his comment conversational. "You've a curious choice of timing, Miss Enderly, and an even more curious choice of route. Why Londonderry, when Donegal Town promised safety?"

"You have spies there, haven't you? I was afraid of being retaken so close to Shelan."

"You're lying in your teeth, Miss Enderly," the Irishman said amiably, beginning to circle to her left. Catherine moved stealthily to stay between him and Liam. He stopped and looked at her quizzically. "I'm not going to shoot your tongue-tied Galahad, Countess. He's really quite safe unless he intends to be more of an idiot than he has been."

"If you've no quarrel with me, then we'll leave," Liam snapped.

Culhane hooked his fingers in his belt. "You can go to hell if you like, brother. But the lady stays with me."

Liam jerked Catherine back against him. "That's where you're wrong. The lady is my lawful wife."

For an instant, Culhane tensed and his eyes flickered as if he had been struck. "You're lying."

Liam laughed ironically. "I see for once I've surprised you. If I may be permitted to reach into my waistcoat pocket, I have a marriage document. You may inspect the copy in Father Ryan's records. Naturally, other duplicates are less accessible." Sean held out his hand. As his brother scanned the paper, Liam commented, "As you see, properly witnessed . . ." His voice took on a grim note of pleasure. "And duly comsummated."

Sean's dark head came up slowly. "It seems you were willing to go to any lengths to escape me, Lady Culhane. I badly misjudged your talent for duplicity." The stunned pain and contempt in his eyes as he looked full into hers belied his soft voice. "My apologies for interrupting your honeymoon, brother, but I must insist on detaining your bride."

Liam's arm tightened about his wife's waist. "I'll kill you if any man makes a move to take her."

Sean's lips curved as subtly as a patient wolf's.

A sob rose in Catherine's throat. "Please! He means it."

The Irishman's eyes idly flicked over her. "Aye. You've a way of twisting a man's mind into knots. Lovely, lying Kit."

"You'll stop insulting my wife, bastard," Liam snarled. "You've shamed her for the last time." He turned to the nearest Irishman. "Give me your sword, Halloran."

Sean's eyes narrowed. "Don't be a fool. I've no wish to kill you."

"How noble. Or is your reluctance merely practical? You

311

know my father's men won't follow the bastard murderer of his legal son and heir!"

Sean's eyes glinted. "You've no proof I'm a bastard."

"No? In Father's absence, our mother was no better than a common whore. One of her many lovers was an English naval lieutenant. Perhaps the source of your attraction to the sea?"

Catherine's hand flew to her lips to stifle a scream as Sean pulled his pistol. His eyes were full of death, though he spoke gently. "Still, I'll kill the man who yields you his weapon. Go home, brother. Yon scheming bitch isn't worth your life. She doesn't love you . . ."

"Doesn't she?" Liam's voice rose, almost cracking. "We've been lovers since you took the expedition to England! Catherine swore she'd never forgive you for destroying her father and dishonoring her. Each time you touched her, she was thinking of me to keep sane until we could be together. You pathetic, infatuated—"

"Shut up!"

"You're the fool, brother, to believe a woman you used so contemptibly could ever love you. You disgust her!"

Stunned with horror at Liam's vitriol, Catherine dimly heard Sean's harsh order. "Give him your saber, Halloran."

"No!" she cried, bolting toward Sean. "Please. You cannot murder him! He isn't responsible."

"Get her out of the way," Sean snapped. As she dragged desperately at his sleeve, his arm lashed out. Smashing against the side of her head, it flung her to the ground to lie tangled in the cloak.

When a man pulled her up, she clawed hysterically until she saw it was Flannery. Desperately, she clung to his arm. "It's murder! Stop them! Please!"

Flannery hoisted her up with an arm about the waist and muttered against her ear, "Be still, girl! Too much has been said to let pass. This has been comin' for years. Ye cannot stop it now!"

He dragged her away, still writhing like a madwoman; then she heard sabers rake steel. She went limp and watched in horror.

Surrounded by watchers whose features glowed like

312

banked red coals, the circling adversaries were etched harshly against the smoky flare of torches. Although Liam was a fair swordsman, Flannery had not exaggerated Sean's skill. As supple as a panther, he moved silently, a rippling in the torchlight, part of the night itself. Yet, as he persisted in retreating, seeming to be intent on wearing his brother down, she was terrified Liam might achieve a lucky thrust. At length, the young lord began to strain, face flushed from exertion. He must have known his fiercest attacks were for nothing, for they continually met thin air, never the mortal target he craved. He was becoming exhausted, his saber increasingly heavy and unwieldy; still, he asked no quarter, and she had to admit that whatever else he was, Liam was no coward. He was reeling, guard nonexistent when, without warning, Sean sent the saber spinning from his numb fingers into a rock pile. Liam stumbled after it, only to see his brother lightly ascend the pile, flick the saber up with the tip of his own weapon, and break it across his knee. Swaying, Liam stared at him, then turned to the rebel soldiers. "Give me another weapon," he muttered hoarsely.

"You're done, Liam. Go home."

Liam whirled, arms dangling. "The hell you say! You've stolen my home, you misbegotten thief! But you'll not steal my wife . . ."

Sean nodded to two men. "Tie him to a nag."

They hesitated. One looked at the other, then at several of his fellows and stepped forward. He cleared his throat. "We follow yer orders, sor, always have. But . . ."

"But what?" Sean's voice was coldly clipped.

"We . . . we've no right to lay hands on Lord Culhane."

Rouge shouldered forward from the group and raised a belligerent fist. "Aye, that's the way of it! Ye've swaggered about in Lord Brendan's boots long enough; it's time they went back to the man who ought to be wearin' 'em."

Liam sensed potential allies and turned to look at the uneasy men. "He's right and you all know it! My father was your clan chief and friend. Many of you swore allegiance to him and his lawful issue. I'm Brendan Culhane's elder son and Irish law gives me sole title to his estates. It's *English* law that gives a share to a younger brother. A few weeks hence, *Irish* law will rule the land. Will you decry your oath to my father and raise this bastard upstart to bring you all to the gallows as outlaws? He'll never be the next O'Neill! There is no legal right to the succession through a woman. He plans to steal the high throne of Ireland as he stole my inheritance! You'll have to kill me before I return to my own lands as that thief's prisoner!" He staggered around the circle of torches. "Choose here and now. Follow the bastard or me!"

Encouraged by Rouge, a ragged cheer went up.

A grim smile curved Sean's lips. "Will you follow *this* into battle, lads? Beat back the enemy with paintbrushes? Oh, aye, my brother's picked up a bit of skill with the blade, but we all know where his talents lie. You see the sorry wreck an experienced adversary makes of him. Even Enderly's English brat can reduce his brains to pudding."

"You're not the only competent commander in Ireland!" Liam snarled. "If I've not the present skill to lead men, we'll join with one who does. And as for a pudding, every man here knows of your obsession with my wife! On the very eve of battle, you've dragged them halfway across Ireland to indulge your jealousy!"

Sean stepped down and slowly walked toward his brother, his green eyes glittering in pure fury. "I didn't follow the witch out of affection, brother! Whether you know it or not, she's carrying information for General Lake. If you don't know it, you're a fool; if you do, you're worse. I ought to stand you both against a wall; but you're my brother, and for Brendan's sake, I'm letting you off with your life. Take it and go while my patience holds."

Liam felt his confidence and growing alliance among the men begin to ebb. Even Rouge looked unsure. There was no way in hell he would be able to leave with Catherine now; still, he desperately persisted. "You'd use any lie to retrieve Catherine, wouldn't you? What do you intend to do with her?"

Sean's smile grew nasty. "I've thought of several things. They wouldn't amuse you."

"I won't surrender her to torture or death! Give me your word . . ."

The smile faded. "I've given you all you're going to get. Go."

Liam whitened. "You'll pay for this. I'll have my own back, and your black heart as well!" He whirled. "Who'll join me against this rogue?"

There was a silence, and then Flannery stepped into the firelight. "I, my lord."

Culhane's eyes narrowed. "Aye, why not? My brother's prowess with the blade reeks of your tutelage. The same can be said of the wench. Did you hope she'd murder me to put your pet in the saddle?"

"I've no wish for yer death," replied the redhead quietly. "I'm bound by oath as ye well know."

Two others, then a third stepped forward. "We're oath held, too. Sorry."

"You're *sorry*, right enough," said Sean coldly. "Your lord called you to heel with his gallows talk, didn't he?" Disgusted, he rammed his saber in its sheath. "Go and be damned to you! I've no use for lily livers."

One man stiffened and reached for his pistol, but found Flannery's big paw on his wrist. "There'll be no more fighting among good Irishmen tonight. We go now." He looked at Liam and jerked his head at one of the passages. Liam shot a last promising glower at his brother and led his small band out of the cashel.

Sean's arm tightened about the limp, small form that drooped with exhaustion before him in the saddle. His prisoner was nearly asleep, head nodding with each stride of the horse. Grimy, her hair in tangles, and now barefoot, the fragile sandals ruined by the swift stumbling exodus from the fortress, she was still beautiful, still proud, though the despair in her eyes had mocked the erectness of her stance as he ordered her to horse after the fight. She had looked up at him without flinching, the eerie beauty of her eyes shaking him even then, even while he hated the tear streaks through the dirt on her face that betrayed fear for his brother. He had wanted to hit her, to exhaust his fury hitting her; but she was ready for that and worse, with the stubborn courage he had always unwillingly admired. That so frail a wench could defy him, could bend him like a feather to her wiles made his gorge rise. He should have tied her across one of the fresh remounts they had picked up in Balleybofee. The faint, familiar fragrance of her body that taunted him into restless memory, the silken tendrils at her nape that tempted a man to lift them and kiss delicate flesh . . . Entirely asleep now, she sagged full against him, filling his arms, the swell of her breasts and body between his thighs warming his loins unbearably. "Sit up," he snapped in her ear.

Startled, she stiffened and clutched the pommel. Five minutes later she was asleep again and Sean swore under his breath—but let her be.

Stopping only a few hours to rest, they reached Shelan late the following night. Restored to her old cell, Catherine, utterly worn out, slept again, then awoke to find a plate of kitchen fare near the door. She ate the food, slept. There was nothing else to do until they came for her. But no one came.

The pattern continued for weeks. When awake, she lay on the cot, mind inert, wondering almost idly if there came a point when a living thing could no longer be terrorized because fear became too familiar; probably the same could not be said of pain. She wondered if she could endure what the Irishman might do to her. *God, let him come back alive and help me not to be a coward when he does. I've failed at everything else.*

CHAPTER 16

The Reckoning

Late one night near the end of June, a tired, dusty Halloran came for her. He roughly jerked her hands behind her, then tied them tightly. After shoving her through the darkened house, he thrust her into Sean Culhane's bedroom. Culhane's tall frame leaned against the mantel as he gazed into the fire. He did not acknowledge Halloran's salute or departure. Catherine saw his clothes were stained with dirt, sweat, and blood. A streak of dried blood from a scalp gash was partly hidden by his hair, and a barely averted saber blow had grazed the curve of his shoulder and back, narrowly missing his neck. Involuntarily, she stepped toward him. His head turned and the look in his eyes stopped her. Before he spoke, she knew the rebellion had failed. His body seemed to remain erect through sheer force of will.

"My compliments," he said dully. "You've evened the score; better, you've helped level a country." When she made no reply, he walked to the desk and wearily sat on it, took up the brandy decanter, and slowly untwisted its stopper.

"You need bandaging. Please untie me. I won't try to escape."

Taking a drag on the bottle, he nearly choked. "Madam, if I didn't know how deceitful you are, I'd believe you concerned. The truth is, you're green with disappointment I didn't return strung over my saddle. I'm sorry to have disappointed you."

"You don't believe I acted out of revenge," she said quietly.

"Don't I?" His green eyes narrowed dangerously. "What should I believe when standing knee-deep in the bodies of my countrymen in Wexford. They cut down men like wheat, there and at Tara Hill, and in Antrim. The wounded were bayoneted where they lay and the survivors hanged." He dragged at the bottle and stared at her. "I should have died with them, but at the last moment, I ran. Back to you. The bitch engineer of it all."

"If General Lake knew about the uprising, I didn't tell him. I didn't have the chance."

"Not for lack of effort, madam. But Liam had the chance. The Committee was surprised while it was in session; most of them were taken. And Fitzgerald was shot in his hiding place; he died in prison. It seems Liam got a message through before your escape. He also smashed our musket flints, ruined the powder, and spiked the cannon." He dully nursed the bottle. "You destroyed years of work in a single night . . . if one doesn't count the nights you squirmed in my brother's bed."

"Sean . . ."

"After our duel, my men deserted like rabbits. Barely enough were left to load what muskets we could salvage on the wagons. We met British artillery with clerks and farmers armed with pikes." He went on staring. "It's one thing to hate and ruin me; you had reason. But Liam never hurt anyone in his life. I put him up to kidnapping you. He just wanted to be left alone with his paintpots. We had our differences, but he used to follow me like a pup. You turned him into a killer and a traitor. I'm unable to find an excuse for that, though God knows I tried. Like the weak-witted, pathetic fool he called me, I tried!" His voice dropped to a despairing whisper. "Even if you told me he was lying; even now, I'd want to believe you." Hardly aware of what he was doing, he came to stand bare inches from her and she looked up at him as she had the first time he had seen her, only now her eyes were filled with a terrible sadness that seemed to rise from his own torn soul. "Was he lying, Kit?"

Oh, God, how can I tell him Liam was never the friend

he remembers? Catherine thought in anguish. I've already mutilated his love, his life, his hope. He owes it to his dead to kill me. If he lets me live, he'll despise himself for it. She took a breath. "Liam, didn't betray you. I destroyed your munitions and listened to your conference with Fournel from the ballroom, then sent a message by Padraic. He, of all of you, believed I was Irish. He thought nothing of delivering a note via the Donegal Town mail coach addressed to Lord Camden's sister. I daresay he's forgotten all about it by now." She knew Sean, even in rage, would never hurt the idiot boy, but now his fury threatened to break over her.

"Did you love Liam?" His voice was a ragged whisper.

"Never. I used him."

His long, powerful fingers caressed her throat. "As you used me. Yet you married him."

"The Vigny name still carries enough weight in Rome to assure an annulment."

"You thought of everything." His fingers tightened and his voice became a silken, deadly, crooning whisper. "Papa's girl. Papa's lying, murderous little whore. And all the time you kept prating of honor! Pulling Maude and Moora out of the pond was sheer genius. You fooled us all, but no one more than me." His fingers closed like steel bands, cutting off her breath. "Only you should have planned for this. You've such a fragile neck, my love. Like porcelain. So easy to snap. I've been hearing the sound for days . . ."

She made no effort to resist, and even hating her with a force that choked him, Sean wondered if he could bear to see the strange, lovely fires in her eyes fade to ash. He had loved her so deeply even her death could never exorcise him. His hatred turned on himself, exploding in a low, tigerish snarl. "You want a quick death, don't you? Do you really think it'll be that easy?" He released her and, almost unconscious, she stumbled, falling until his hand caught in her hair and he jerked out his knife. For an instant, utter terror leaped into her eyes. "No, madam, I'm not going to slit your throat. You're going to live, until living is intolerable." He slashed the dress and chemise from bodice to waist, then cut them away. Fingers still knotted in her hair, he pushed her roughly to her knees. Twisting

319

up the thick mass of her hair, he sawed it off next to the scalp, then hacked at the rest until it was scattered refuse on the carpet. "Irish tradition for traitresses, usually followed by tar and feathers; but I've a better notion."

Leaving her huddled on the rug, he stripped off his shirt, then dropped into the desk chair where he applied himself steadily to the decanter. Most of the blood on the shirt was not his own, though his torso was a mass of bruises and cuts. Sitting laxly in the chair, he stared at Catherine with the fixed attention of a man who sees nothing. He had hoped shearing would diminish her beauty, but the rough crop gave her the look of a stricken, lovely child, by accentuating the delicate, breathtaking sculpture of her face and making her eyes, now dark amethyst and glistening with tears, seem larger. She was more an enchantress than ever, and he raged against the spell that held him like a steel chain.

With a low growl of anger, he spun out of the chair and found his knife. Severing the bonds at her ankles with a single jerk, he threw her to the floor and assaulted her. Hating, hurting, until all she could feel was his hatred, permeating her soul. There was nothing he did not do to her. And the moment came at last when she felt nothing; then a time when he finally left her alone and fell into exhausted, drunken sleep, muttering incoherently. Once she felt his hand clumsily ruffling her hair. "Lambsoft . . . soft bitch."

After dawn, she too slept with sheer exhaustion until he roughly shook her shoulder. It was night again and his voice was slurred, the odor of brandy heavy on his breath. "Get up. Time to get dressed." He cut the bonds and jerked her to a sitting position. His jaw dark with rough stubble, he had thrown on his stained clothing, the torn shirt unbuttoned and hanging loose. The look in his eyes pierced her lassitude.

"Sean?"

"Shut up." He dragged the butterfly negligee over her head and arms, snapping a strap in the process, then daubed rouge and pomade on her face. Pulling her after him, he dragged her downstairs and into the barren mess hall. The five men morosely idling there turned to stare at the unsteady apparition of their leader and the garishly painted girl who began to fight frantically with dawning comprehension.

"I've a fresh wench for you, lads. Who'll be first to top the English whore?"

More than one of them had eyed the girl surreptitiously in the past, but none stepped forward.

Almost unbalanced by his mistress's struggles, Sean swayed on his feet. "Well?" he bellowed. "You were hot enough for the bitch once! Doesn't she suit anymore?"

He jerked her in front of him and, placing his forearm under her jaw, dragged her head up. "I warrant she's not much to look at now, but you can always close your eyes, eh?" He ran his free hand down her body as she twisted. "Soft and sweet as cream . . ." His voice dropped to a confidential whisper. "But don't ever look into her eyes. She's a witch."

The men stirred restlessly, riveted by the roving hand. Sean laughed disjointedly. "You don't believe me, do you? Nay, lads. She's yours. I don't want her anymore. I'll prove it." He jerked the negligee down to her waist and she froze as he fondled her breasts. "Beautiful, aren't they?" The lust unleashed in the room was almost tangible as he taunted them, pushing the negligee from her hips; it dropped to the floor. A man in the shadows caught his breath and another licked his lips. With a crooked smile, Sean shoved her toward them, and before he turned to go, three of them were already dragging her to the floor.

After bridling the first horse he found in the stable, he flung himself onto its bare back, then kicked it ruthlessly to a gallop, spurring away from what was happening back in the house, from the look in Kit's eyes as he gave her to them. As if demented, he took walls he could barely see and with no thought for treacherous footing smashed through streams, goading the frothing horse until it stumbled and threw him. He lay where he fell for a time, then stumbled to his feet, reeling as the moon swooped about his head, and took another step into bottomless darkness.

The sun was pleasantly warm on his face when he awoke. He lay quietly, listening to the bees' low drone and the faint rustle of field flowers. Lifting his head, he winced. His temples pounded with a familiar ache and his mouth tasted of stale brandy. He sat up and rubbed his head, remembering Catherine's foul antidote. Then, remembered all of it. The shattered dream. And what he had done to her, even to the last. Two men holding her down while a third tore at his breeches. And the others, waiting. They would all use her over and over. They might even kill her. He clawed to his feet and screamed for the horse, but it was gone. He began to run—run until his chest was a white-hot band, and the bile rose, and his legs refused to obey, then slowed to a hopeless stumble. Whatever they had done was done.

The messroom was empty. Only bottles and dirty glassware remained; those, and a blood-soaked negligee wadded and thrown into a corner. Softly, Sean shut the door and went into the study. He took a dueling pistol from the weapon collection and, out of habit, polished its barrel with a sleeve. Perfectly balanced and without ornamentation, it was Brendan's finest.

"Ye'll not be needin' that. The lass is safe," Peg spoke behind him, having entered without knocking.

"Where?" He did not turn.

"In her cell. I saw ye bring her downstairs and sent Rafferty after a gun before ye left the terrace."

He looked at her then. "Her nightgown was covered with blood . . ."

"Tim O'Rourke tried to talk the others out of rapin' her and some of them were leery of what might happen when ye sobered. That Callahan, though, he was ready to take the risk. He tried to put a bullet in Tim when the lad jerked him off her. Tim was unarmed and Rafferty had to shoot Callahan. Somebody picked up the nightdress and tried to stop the bleedin', but he died in minutes."

"You liked her, didn't you?"

The Irishwoman's mouth tightened. "I didn't do it for her. I knew the state ye'd be in when ye came to yer senses."

Sean sagged into a chair and stared at the carpet. "I cannot kill her and cannot stand the thought of anyone else doing it. She's a barb in my guts that won't be cut out."

"Then stop tryin'. Ye'll not heal yer hurt in whores and

liquor. 'Twill take time." Gently she drew the pistol from his unresisting fingers. "Much of the blame in this is mine. I thought that girl could ease the festerin' hurt inside ye, but instead she's brought ye low. I'd like to take this pistol and put a ball through her schemin' skull, but it wouldn't help." She touched his shoulder. "Have ye thought of what to do with her?"

He rubbed his head, trying to clear it. "The English will come to search the house for rebels and guns. . . . Transfer the wench to the cellar cell. She can rot there," he added bitterly. "Revenge might have been sweet, but I'll be damned if she'll relish the aftertaste." He dragged his long frame out of the chair. "Have the portable art shifted to the wine cellar. The English will steal the wine, but I doubt if they'll break through the racks." He crossed to the painting behind the desk and opened the secret wall compartment it concealed. He withdrew pouches of gold and jewelry, then dropped them on the desk. "Bury these tonight with the Celtic artifacts in the ruins. Have Tim take the best stock into the mountains." He closed the compartment and turned. "How many servants are left to help you?"

"A handful. The rest stole some fishing boats and put out to sea before ye returned from Wexford. Most of the men who came back with ye followed them last night. Tim's gone, too. Said he'd had enough. 'Tis sorry I am, lad, but there it is."

"It was bound to happen." With apparent idleness, he toyed with a brooch from a loosened pouch. "Liam said Mother took lovers in Brendan's absence. He mentioned a particular English lieutenant . . ."

He looked up and Peg's heart went out to him. "I don't know, lad, and that's God's truth. I was Megan's personal maid. If I didn't know, then Liam couldn't. She was wild. I disliked and mistrusted her. But to my knowledge, she was a faithful wife."

He slipped the brooch into the bag and drew the strings. "Then let's get on with it."

Catherine dully surveyed stone walls, now as familiar as her own hands. The boredom of confinement was incredible, the lack of a window to tell the difference between night and day disquieting after . . . how long? She estimated two weeks by counting the barren meals. Her appetite was far from titillated by the inevitable fish, watercress, and potato diet. She sat on a pallet; the cot frame and webbing had been removed along with anything that might permit suicide, which left a stool, a slop bucket, and a candle. Asphyxiation by firing the pallet was possible, but her religion forbade that release even though God seemed to have turned a deaf ear to prayer and no human appeal was possible. She had not seen Sean since the terrible night he had thrown her to the human wolves. She still awoke in cold sweats, remembering their holding her down to endure the man's obscene groping before he suddenly collapsed atop her, blood spurting.

There was another fact even more terrible to contemplate. She was pregnant.

The cell door creaked and a servant with a shawl about her head brought in the ration, set it on the floor, and straightened in the gloom. "Fiona!"

The Irish girl smiled coldly. "I'll be lookin' after yer needs from now on, but mostly Sean's." Her smile grew triumphant. "He's fair sick with hate of ye, but I'm making him forget. Every time he makes love to me he forgets. We spent yesterday in bed. Soon he's goin' to forget ye're alive. He'll not even notice when ye ain't. I'm thinkin' maybe I'll let ye die a bit at a time, maybe for years."

When Catherine finally picked up her food, she found only half the usual ration and the fish, while not actually spoiled, had such an unsavory odor that she left it. The next day was the same, but the rations were halved and the candle not replaced. The dark closed in like a blanket.

Squinting against late-afternoon sunlight that glanced in a blinding glare off the water, Sean finished lashing the *Megan*'s mainsail and reeled in the dinghy. Fiona slipped her arms around his chest and leaned against his bare back. " 'Twas glorious today, just like the old days when we'd sail and make love on the deck for hours." She giggled and ran her hands down his belly. "Rememberin' makes me hot all over again."

He eased away her hand. "We've all the night, girl, and naught else to do."

She bit his ear before releasing him to retrieve their luncheon basket. "Aye. Long, sweet hours. Just us. It's as good for you as it is for me. I knew for certain this afternoon. Ye *can* forget. 'Twas *my* name ye cried." Silently, he held out a hand to help her into the dinghy. She caught his fingers and kissed them, amber eyes aglow. "I want yer child. 'Tis right, Sean; I know it is. My love is more than I can hold within." He drew her close and tenderly kissed her, then handed her into the boat.

As he rowed ashore, the Irishman glanced down into sunlit blue water that deepened to beckoning shadows. Forget? How could he, when each moment recalled her, the ghost at his shoulder? Forcing him to cry out another woman's name to keep from groaning hers with a longing that tore him apart. He had not seen Kit in three months, yet she haunted him, a gentle harpy. Fiona deserved marriage and children. She was ripe for it with a man faithful in body *and* mind. Their frequency of lovemaking made a child inevitable. He had been accused of siring more than one bastard, but as the results were from casual relationships with women who entertained more than one lover, he had felt no obligation. Fiona was different. He had to make a decision; that meant he had to see Catherine.

Sean unlocked the cell, then muttered a startled, muffled curse when he saw the tiny room contained the Stygian darkness and stench of a tomb. "Catherine? . . . Damn you, answer me! Where are you?" His reply was a ratlike scuffling in a far corner. With a chill in his gut, he wasted no more questions, but snatched up the candle he had brought, stepped into the cell, and swung it high. In the corner, crouched against the wall, a small wraith flinched from the light. As he approached, stunned by Catherine's appearance, she shrank away, shaking uncontrollably. "Kit?" He touched her shoulder, and wild-eyed, she tore away as if he had branded the candle to her flesh. Too weak to do more than crawl a few feet in an effort to escape, his prisoner huddled like a trapped rabbit in the seeking pool of light.

After planting the candle in a wall niche, Sean pulled her up. She beat at him weakly. "No! No! Don't! Don't hurt my—" She stopped abruptly as if she had revealed a terrible secret, and he thought her mind had gone. "Let me go," she whimpered against his chest, "please . . ."

"I won't hurt you . . . hush." Without thinking, he stroked her hair and held her close. Stricken with terror, she was skin and bone under the shapeless shift. The small face had lost its beauty. Only the eyes were recognizable, but they were black with fear, their brilliant glory ruined.

"Shh, little one. Be still. It's all right. I haven't come to hurt you."

Slowly, her trembling lessened and he heard her whisper, "Please . . . the candle. I'm not used to it."

He blocked the light with his shoulder. "Why not, Kit? Have you been living in the dark?" She was silent. "Where's *your* candle?" he prodded gently.

"You . . . told her to take it away." She sounded vague and sad, like a dazed child. She sagged in his arms, and he picked her up. Never much more than a hundred pounds, now she could not have weighed more than three quarters of that. She clutched something against her breast. After he laid her on the pallet, he tried to remove it from her fingers. With surprising tenacity, she resisted and for the moment he let her be, continuing to stroke her hair. She was unconscious when he spoke to her again. He pried the object loose and relit the candle to see bits of straw roughly tied with thread pulling from her clothing into the form of a cross. With fury rising in him like a tidal flood, he took her up in his arms. As he carried her out of the cell, he saw on the floor the slop she had been fed.

Fiona sailed into the bedroom with swirling skirts and a teasing laugh. "We've the best of a brace of fresh rabbits for supper and a champagne Boney couldn't afford. When do I have Peg bring it up? Before or after . . . ?" The words died on her lips as she saw the girl on the bed. And green eyes that blistered her with revulsion. "Sean, I . . ."

"Don't bother. Unless you want to take her place, leave now." The words came out like separate chips of ice.

"Sean, I did it for us. She's a witch, sent to destroy ye.

326

She's evil." Fiona came toward him, pleading, eyes golden in the fading light of sunset.

"You starved her like a dog," he snarled. "You made a coffin of that cell, and God knows what else—"

"*You* were the one who put her there!" she flared in defensive anger. "Ye said she could rot! I know. Peg told me!" She came close. "I niver touched the slut because ye forbade it. I did not a whit more than ye wanted. I *let* her rot! Only I'd not the patience to wait years. The witch can't die fast enough!" Her voice rose in hysteria and her hands reached out like claws toward her wasted rival.

With a blow that sent her to the floor, Sean gritted, "Because there's truth in what you say, I'll not kill you. But if I ever see your face again, I'll put a bullet through your murderous heart."

She got to her knees and crawled toward him. "Sean, ye're my life! I'd as lief spend my days in that cellar than be shut away from ye."

He scooped the cell keys from the bedside table and threw them in her face. "Be sure to lock the door."

Holding her cut cheek, Fiona shrieked, "She's bewitched ye! Ye're not a Gael anymore! Bastard traitor!" Stumbling to her feet, she fled.

Mothwing lashes flickered on pale cheeks as Catherine groped weakly through the blankets; then what she sought was tucked into her hand. Her eyes opened. Like a child awakened from a nightmare, she gazed up at the man sitting on the edge of the bed. "Am I dying?" she asked softly. He shook his head. "Then . . . why did you come for me?"

"I nosed you out on the stair," Culhane teased gently. "You were in sore need of a bath, lass."

Unexpectedly, she tensed. "No . . . I don't want . . ."

"Easy. Peg has bathed you already. Haven't you noticed a change in your perfume?" She eyed him furtively and again he wondered if confinement had affected her mind. "You're also in need of fattening up." He lifted a spoonful of custard from a cup on the side table and placed it temptingly near her mouth.

Her nostrils quivered, but she shook her head. "I'd just be sick."

Culhane returned the spoon to the cup. "Have you been sick long?"

"A few weeks."

"You have to eat, girl, or be sicker yet."

Her eyes were bottomless pools. "When I'm well . . . will you send me back to that place?"

"No, lass. Not ever."

Something in his eyes made her put the cross in his hand and close his fingers over it before she slept.

After that, Catherine ate obediently, and was nauseated after each effort until Peg made a concoction that allowed her to hold soft food down. In contrast to the passivity, she insisted on bathing herself, flatly refusing to let anyone either touch or see her body. Attributing her modesty to his sexual abuse, Sean did not force the issue.

After a month, she looked less like a small skeleton and was able to walk for limited periods on the terrace. Sean was gentle with her, but more coolly polite as she regained health. At length, she became restless and asked him if she might walk on the lawn. He studied her silently, then spoke. "You're almost well again. You'll have to be confined."

She paled, then said quietly, "I see. Where is my cell to be this time?" The small, cropped head was high, and her eyes held his unflinchingly, but the mouth was vulnerable.

"A room has been prepared on the top floor. It's plain, but livable. There's a view of the sea."

Her eyes darkened. "Through bars?"

"Yes," he said tightly.

"Shall I never leave that room?"

"You'll be permitted out on special occasions."

She smiled ironically. "Weddings and funerals."

"What did you expect," he snarled suddenly, "a personal jester? You've had that!"

"I never laughed at you," she replied softly, and stood up, gathering the heather shawl close, shivering slightly against the late breeze. "I'm a little cold. Could we go in now?"

As he eased off the balustrade, she looked up at him. "Shall I see you on these special occasions?"

"Yes."

She gave him her arm.

CHAPTER 17

Cry of the Bean Si

As the breeze ruffled her cropped hair, Catherine leaned her cheek against the bars to feel the final warming rays of a brilliant sunset. Shorn hair made her resemble a skinny boy but there was no one to see her as a woman except the taciturn, hard-faced guard who brought her food. The plainly furnished room was bright and airy, with a choice of books. Still, it was a prison, and on sunlit days she wanted to beat her wings against the bars. Her tension increased with advancing pregnancy, although the swollen curve of her stomach was not yet apparent under her high-waisted dresses. Nearly six months pregnant, she worried because the child was undersized. Still, she could not bring herself to tell Sean, aware her condition would seem a mockery to him.

The key turned in the lock, and her heart lurched as Culhane entered the room. To hide the transparent longing in her eyes, she quickly turned to close the window.

Sean watched her fumble awkwardly in an attempt to capture the swinging frame, and easing her aside, he closed the window, then turned to look at her. By sunset, her face seem to glow like a burning rose and desire went through him like a hot wind. He veered away and began to pace the room, reminding her of a jungle cat wary of a trap. "I'm expecting guests for a fortnight. I thought you might like to join the group—in a limited way, of course."

"When will they arrive?"

"Tomorrow. At dinner, you may join us as Flynn's invalid niece. He'll be present, so with your skill at deceit, the masquerade shouldn't be difficult. You'll return to your room at an appropriate time in the evening and keep to your chamber by day."

"Very well, I shall do as you ask."

"You'll do as I *tell* you, madam, or I'll lock you up until Christmas next!" Slamming the door behind him, he left his prisoner to wonder what she had done to antagonize him.

To meet the guests, Catherine donned a cinnamon silk; but she was still too thin to do justice to the long-sleeved dress, and touches of rouge added scant color to cheekbones strained against the skin. I *look* the languishing invalid, she thought as she surveyed her image in the mirror. Now that she anticipated seeing people again, the possibility that Sean might find her appearance embarrassing and banish her upstairs seemed unbearable. Wistfully, she hoped they would like her.

When Catherine entered the dining room and the door closed discreetly behind on her guard, the men all stood up at once. Like multicolored penguins bobbing about a candlelit iceberg, she thought a bit wildly. Nowhere was the masculine admiration to which she had grown accustomed. The seated women in their brilliant plumage clearly dismissed her as a dowdy bird despite her expensive dress. "I . . . I'm sorry to be late." Uncertainly, she sought Sean's eyes, but they were expressionless as he came to take her arm and made introductions before seating her next to Doctor Flynn. The doctor did not look at her after his initial, startled stare. Dear Lord, she thought in growing dismay. I must look dreadful!

General conversation resumed as Rafferty and Peg served dinner. After managing small talk with her neighbor, Milton O'Keane, a thin, elderly member of Irish Parliament, and beginning a second glass of wine, Catherine felt brave enough to peep at the dinner party: three men and two women. George Ennery, a portly, powerful-looking man was saying, "We were all grieved to hear of Lockland Fitzhugh's death, Sean. He'll be irreplaceable. The deaths in the revolt must have broken him."

331

"He was in ill health for several years," Sean said quietly, "and he had borne many defeats."

The guest on his right, a spectacularly beautiful patrician in her thirties with rich auburn hair that reminded Catherine uncomfortably of Fiona, laid a beringed hand on his arm. "You loved Lockland; we all did. Perhaps it's best he's not here to witness Ireland's last humiliations."

"Ellen's right," said Kevin Tralee, the mustachioed blonde next to her. "Viceroy Camden was utterly ineffectual in curbing the brutality. Lake hanged rebels in scores, even butchered our wounded in their hospital beds. There's hardly a family in Wexford and Ulster who hasn't a man dead or in jail. The repression is terrible."

Catherine's dinner partner said quietly, "I heard all the survivors of the French Killala expedition were captured."

Sourly, Ennery looked at his wine. "After one paltry victory at Castlebar, which they threw away in a fortnight of revelry, they were surrounded. The other warships did not even land."

Catherine felt a violent wave of nausea. Amauri, all those charming Frenchmen. She had not even really disliked General Fournel.

"Canning has replaced Camden in the viceroy's chair and appears to be putting together some semblance of order," Ennery put in. "Lake has been recalled; his excesses managed to shock even the English Parliament."

O'Keane shook his head. "Unfortunately, our own Parliament may be dissolved. Pitt is pushing for union."

Doctor Flynn frowned. "You mean we may lose our nationhood?"

"I fear so. There's a great deal of resistance to the idea, of course, particularly in our Parliament, but Pitt is noted for his persuasive bribery. Many have already sold their birthright for porridge."

The sable-haired woman next to Ennery leaned forward. "Even so, perhaps the future is not altogether black. Pitt proposes that union will promote our economic development. Some say he hopes to slip concessions to Catholic factions without annoying the king too greatly."

"Pish," Tralee snorted. "Pitt may mean well but he's a

provincial innocent. England will exploit a union to bleed us dry."

Catherine was pale. I mustn't be ill, she thought. Mustn't . . .

The woman called Ellen touched Sean's sleeve. "You've encountered some personal losses, haven't you, darling? I noticed furniture missing. I hope the troops didn't confiscate your father's Celtic collection?"

Darling? The redhead's magnificent breasts seemed to gleam like the underbelly of a dead fish, and suddenly Catherine retched.

Flynn caught her shoulders and held her head down, so that the guests were spared the sight of her sickness. When she could expel no more, she caught a napkin to her lips, cheeks flaming with humiliation, and pushed back the chair in awkward panic. "Please excuse me. I'm not feeling well." She rose and stumbled against the chair.

Flynn stood and steadied her. "Quite all right, my dear. Ladies, gentlemen, if you will excuse us, I'll see my niece to her room." Gratefully, she leaned against him as he assisted her escape from the stares and Sean's glinting eyes, which softened as he turned to his stunning companion.

"Thank you, doctor," Catherine murmured as Flynn lifted her feet onto the bed and propped a pillow under her head, then got her a drink of water. She sipped it and lay back in some relief.

He studied her. "Does this happen often?"

"Not so much of late. Peg made an herbal remedy for me. It helps." She hesitated. "Tonight was . . . an unusual occasion."

"Still, I'd like to examine you."

"That won't be necessary; I'm quite all right now. But there is something I would like to ask you." She looked up at him. "That woman, Ellen. What is she to Sean?"

Flynn felt uncomfortable, but realized she would know soon enough. "They're old friends. Fitzhugh introduced them. They had an affair, which cooled while Sean was in school in Paris, but they remained close friends after Ellen married Lord Frane Duneden. Widowed, she retired to her villa in Italy. When the rebellion broke out, she returned home. Ellen's a remarkable woman and a great patriot." The reproach in his last remark was gentle.

"I see," Catherine said quietly. "Thank you for telling me." She touched his hand. "I know what you must think. I used you badly and I'm deeply sorry. Believe me, I didn't choose to deceive you."

He cocked his head. "For a young woman who has helped to bring the world down about her enemies' ears, you seem singularly disinclined to gloat; but that would be hardly prudent under the circumstances, would it?" Her hand fell away. "Good night. Try to rest. I suggest you refrain from drinking wine until these bouts of nausea end."

Her eyes closed as he left. "Yes, doctor. Thank you."

After the other guests retired, Sean, Ellen, and Flynn lingered in the Rose Salon. As the young couple began to eye Flynn with polite impatience, he tossed his cigar on the fire. "Sean, I wonder if I might have a word with you in the study. It's urgent, I believe, or I wouldn't interrupt your evening. I'm sorry, Ellen; I assure you we'll not be long."

Gracefully lounging in her topaz silk gown on the divan, she nodded lazily, eyelids languid over hazel eyes. "Oh, yes, you will, Michael, but you have my permission. Sean and I have the entire fortnight to reminisce." She smiled up mischievously at Sean. "Pour me another brandy before you go, will you, darling? It does wonders for my memory."

After leaving Ellen with her brandy, Sean selected a cheroot from a humidor in the study. Twirling it slowly, he lit it and eyed Flynn expressionlessly. "Well, doctor?"

"I want to examine Catherine. I don't like her color. Six months ago she was a radiant young woman; now she's a shadow."

Sean blew out a controlled cloud of smoke. "I confined her under Fiona's keeping. My former mistress became somewhat neglectful."

The doctor's temper exploded. "For God's sake, man, what did you expect? Are you completely uncivilized? Why not shoot the wretched girl cleanly?"

334

Sean ironically lifted a dark brow. "You, too? Everyone wants her executed: Peg, Fiona. Even Catherine herself. Will you do it, doctor?"

Flynn looked exasperated. "Of course not!"

"Then what do you suggest? Sending her back to England with a brass band?" Sean's lips tightened. "She's responsible for slaughter, Flynn. She owes payment to the dead with her life."

"But you cannot kill her, can you? If she should die naturally, it would be a relief, wouldn't it?"

Sean cut him off abruptly. "If you can persuade her to submit to an examination, I've no objection. Catherine *was* ill, but she's recovered. She was extremely nervous tonight; no doubt the conversation disturbed her digestion." He walked to the door and pointedly held it open. As Flynn started to leave, Sean said curtly, "Don't try to play on my sympathy as you did in the past. For all her look of pathos, Lady Culhane is a coldhearted, scheming bitch. She admitted everything."

Flynn regarded him thoughtfully. "I rather thought she had, but then . . . she *is* deceitful, isn't she?"

The prospect of seeing Sean with his former mistress was disheartening, but Catherine managed a calm, if not vivacious, demeanor at dinner the following evening. Carefully avoiding the richer foods and wines, she contented herself with soup and custard. As the group became increasingly animated by champagne, she took little part, sharply aware of Ellen Duneden's sparkling, teasing intimacy with her former lover.

Flynn, seeing Catherine's darkening eyes, tried to distract her with amusing anecdotes about his patients. Soon, everyone was listening, but he could tell his dinner companion barely heard a word. An apricot dress enlivened her complexion and showed off her brilliant eyes; evidently, she had chosen it carefully. She was almost pretty again and the men paid her more attention, but she was easily eclipsed by Lady Duneden in emeralds and cream silk the shade of her flawless skin. She was witty and charming, with a casual warmth that made it clear why she invariably remained friends with her lovers. Ellen

Duneden was a man's woman—intelligent without sharpness; gay without insipidity; utterly feminine. Under other circumstances, Catherine would have been drawn to her; instead, she was wrenched with jealousy.

After dinner they withdrew to the ballroom, where Lady Duneden sat with a flourish at the pianoforte. She began to play, her white arms and shoulders golden under the chandelier, her voice a rich contralto. As the voices resounded in melodic Irish ballads, Catherine felt utterly, irrevocably alone. The music reminded her miserably of her single waltz with Sean on the eve of the rebellion. Her heart had died that night. Why . . . *how* could it yet feel such pain?

Suddenly, she realized they were looking at her and Flynn was speaking. "I said, will you play for us, my dear?" As he coaxed her forward, Ellen encouragingly withdrew from the pianoforte. Uncertainly, Catherine looked at Sean's impassive face, but shyness faded when she touched the keys. She let the pain in her heart flow out with music she had sung in prison darkness, never believing she would hear it again. With the uncanny sensitivity of one blind, she summoned a soft, clear beauty that enchanted, filling the shadows with light. She captivated them with music alone, pure, effortless; and with soaring passion, she expressed her love for Sean, for their unborn child: the joy of love, and the intolerable pain of loss. Finally she was still, stunned with grief, unable to move.

Lady Duneden leaned across the pianoforte and said quietly, "Miss Flynn, you play like an angel. Would you give us a song in memory of those lost in these terrible months?"

Slowly, Catherine looked up. "Forgive me. I'm a little tired now. Perhaps you . . ."

Lovely hazel eyes captured hers. "Not I, Miss Flynn. I could never match the beauty you express."

"Oblige us, Miss Flynn. It's fitting." There was steel underneath Sean's velvety politeness.

Pale, she obeyed. The ballad, "Cucullen," was very old, a Gaelic saga song Sean had taught her on a glassy sea under the stars. Under her touch, it became a mourning lament, a keening cry across the years evoking the lonely, haunting beauty of the misty land and the sorrows of its people. It ended with:

Soft be thy rest, in thy cave,
Chief of Erin's wars.
Bragela will not hope thy return,
Or see thy sails in ocean's foam;
Her steps are not on the shore, nor
Her ear open to the voice of thy rowers.
She sits in the hall of shells, and sees
The arms of him that is no more.

When the last notes died away, Culhane's hate was like a thing alive, winding about the English girl's throat. In his mind, she mocked them. She had twisted the remains of his soul in knots with her witch's lays, taunted them all with eerie mimicry as if Ireland's ruin had broken her heart.

Melancholy dispersed the group quickly; Doctor Flynn and Catherine were among the last to leave. As the doctor turned to close the great double doors, Sean deliberately drew Ellen into his arms and kissed her lingeringly, knowing a small face watched behind Flynn's shoulder.

"Sean!" Ellen pushed against his cheek as the door closed. "Really, you are impatient!" she murmured in mild reproach. "Don't you think you should have waited until we were alone?"

He smiled lazily. "Worried about your reputation?"

She laughed. "You know better. I tossed my reputation in the soup long ago; it had a marvelous tang. But that little niece of Flynn's looked as if she'd never seen a man kiss a woman before. Heaven knows, the girl's no beauty, but surely she cannot be completely innocent." She toyed with his cravat. "Still, if your little neighbor were as lovely as her music, I should be quite jealous." She threw back her head, shining auburn hair catching the light. "You haven't developed a taste for waifs, have you, darling?"

Sean tightened his hold and, kissing the arch of her throat, murmured, "Prefer ditchwater to champagne?

337

What do you think?" His lips burned the curve of her breast as he loosened her bodice. When he took her, Catherine's music still lingered in his mind until a more savage rhythm took its place.

Catherine was roused out of bed by a summons to appear in the study. Her night had been sleepless, and she dressed in a daze while the guard waited outside the door. She gave her short hair a mere pass with the brush. Shunning rouge in the revealing morning light, she pinched spots of color into her pale cheeks, deciding grimly she looked as dismal as she felt and little could improve that fact. Sleepily, she followed the guard downstairs.

Sean glanced up as she entered the study. In the simple white muslin, she looked particularly feminine in the masculine room with its dark greens and mahoganies. Even the gently curling crop made her seem more fragile. She looked at him with the sleepy gravity of a child, eyes dark blue under their heavy lashes.

He sat back in the chair. "I've given Doctor Flynn permission to examine you. He'll see you in your room at eleven."

The sleepiness disappeared. "It isn't necessary. I haven't been sick since the dinner."

"Flynn thinks it's necessary. He may be right. You look like a hant."

She flushed. "I cannot help that." A trace of the old defiance sparked. "Even *you*, Signor Casanova, might lose a bit of your dash if you were kept in a hole for three months."

"Are you by any chance referring obliquely to my attentions to Lady Duneden?"

"What you do is your own affair," she shot back. "All I ask is to be let alone."

"Ah. Sullen this morning, aren't we? Didn't breakfast suit you either?"

"If you're so intent on shoving your mistress down my throat, why not just tie me to the bed again?"

"I should have thought you'd had a bellyful of rutting of late, but if not . . ." He came out of the chair with a swiftness that made her retreat a step. "Yes, madam, you

338

would do well to consider your position before you make snide remarks. Can it be jealousy that whets your tongue?"

Violet fires flared in her eyes. "I don't envy Lady Duneden her place in your bed, if that's what you mean."

"No whore like a reformed whore, eh?" he snarled. "Since you've lost your taste for spreading yourself around, you've decided to hide your bony strumpet's charms in virginal smugness." He caught her chin and dragged it up. "It won't wash, pet. I wouldn't put it past you to invite Rouge to the barn."

She bit his hand like a cornered cat; swearing, he caught her by the hair and twisted until the tears came, but she glared up at him defiantly, refusing to cry out.

"So now the pious act begins to break down, doesn't it, sweet? Underneath, you're still alley cat, pure scheming slut!"

Catherine exploded with all the pent-up pain of the past months. "You *dare* call me slut! When that dyed creature you were pasting yourself against last night is nothing but a celebrated whore?"

He struck her with all his force, sending her spinning to fall against the desk corner. Catherine clung to the rim, almost fainting with pain that lanced through her side. Dimly, his voice came from behind her. "Don't ever insult Ellen again, you little viper, if you value your wretched existence. You're not fit to clean her boots . . ." His voice lowered. "But you will. Put on your riding habit and join us on the terrace after lunch. It's time you learned what a lady is!"

Catherine pushed away from the desk and managed to face him, but was unable to speak.

"By the time Flynn gets to your room, be stripped and ready for that examination. Perhaps you can persuade him to climb on your skinny carcass. Guard!"

Still half-dressed, and pleading the daggerlike pain in her side, Catherine tried to divert the doctor's attention from her stomach; but as he slipped down the straps of the chemise, he noticed her tension. "Catherine, I've seen your body," he reminded her.

"I . . . I'm sorry." Shivering as he lowered the shift to her waist, she quickly caught it and securely tucked it over the telltale rise of her belly. A bruise had formed under the right breast. Carefully, Flynn applied pressure to it and she gasped. "Easy. Just a moment longer." He pressed his hand lightly over her side, his sensitive fingers telling him what he wanted to know. And confirming the pregnancy his practiced eyes had guessed. "You have some cracked ribs: three, I should say." He withdrew a bandage roll from his bag. "Put your hands on your hips." After binding the linen so tightly about her ribs she could hardly breathe, he knotted it and snipped off the excess. "How did this happen?"

"I tripped over a skein of knitting and fell against the bedside table."

"A likely explanation, but then you've not seen your face." He daubed her cut lip and she winced at the sting. "Someone struck you. Sean?"

"We quarreled. I insulted Lady Duneden and he lost his temper."

Flynn sighed. "Will you never learn to play the willow and bend to his storms?"

"I won't grovel." Her jaw set. His face skeptical, Flynn tossed the bandage roll back in his bag and indicated for her to lie down. "Could you defer the examination until this evening?" she said quickly, then added the desperate guile, "I've been ordered downstairs. Sean will be even angrier if I'm late."

He frowned, knowing the reason for her reluctance. "You're simply postponing the inevitable."

"Only by a few hours. I promise not to be difficult." A few hours more to pray Sean's anger would abate.

After Flynn left, she rocked, hugging her swollen belly. What if Sean determined to destroy the child? A blow would be sufficient. Oh, my little one, to come into a world that wants you not. To be taken from my love into the bitter cold.

The new habit had not been included with her prison wardrobe. Dressing in the old one, its dated shabbiness apparent for all its fine cut, took a painful half hour because of the cracked ribs, and she had to leave the bottom button of the straining jacket undone. Without hat and gloves, she would appear to be a country frump, as no doubt Sean intended.

As Catherine followed the guard downstairs, her resolution faltered. Dizzied by mounting malaise and the pain stabbing her side, she tightly gripped the stair rail when she saw Sean impatiently waiting just inside the front door, his crop tapping his boots with angry flicks. "You're late. My guests are mounted."

"I'm not feeling well . . . certainly not well enough to ride this afternoon. May I return to my room?"

"You may not. You may hold down little else, but you'll digest this dish of crow if it kills you." He changed tack abruptly. "What did Flynn have to say? There was some emergency at the clinic and he lit out like a smoked hornet . . . unless," he added sarcastically, "he was tempted to oblige your invitation?"

"Abuse me if you want; I can hardly stop you, but if you have any decency, spare Doctor Flynn your insinuations."

He snapped the door open. "The sorrel gelding is yours."

Under a gray November sky, the riders idled on their mounts, a perfectly turned-out Lady Duneden gracefully perched on Numidian's glossy back. Acknowledging the greetings of the other riders, Catherine walked to her mount. Sean perfunctorily gave her a foot up to the saddle and she swayed, fighting a wave of dizziness. Not looking at her face, he caught up the reins and thrust them into her hands, then turned to his own horse.

"How delightful that you're able to join us, Miss Flynn," Duneden's warm, melodic voice stroked her. "None of us will ever forget your lovely concert last night. I'd give anything to play so well." When Catherine did not answer, she added, "But I suppose you hear this sort of praise often."

Catherine turned with an effort. "I'm sorry. You must think me rude. You're most kind."

"No, not rude," the redhead said thoughtfully. "Are you quite sure you feel like riding today, my dear?"

Sean, giving his cinch a jerk, threw Catherine a warning look. She stared him in the eye, then answered the Irishwoman. "I've been so closely confined of late, my lady, that a breath of freedom is somewhat overwhelming. I wouldn't miss this ride for the world."

They set out across the lawn at an easy trot. The gelding lacked Numidian's satin gait, but with some effort, Catherine was able to adjust a post to absorb the jar. Luckily, the party was in a lazy mood, content to keep an easy pace. Soon, however, the brisk weather made the horses impatient to be let out. She managed fairly well for a while; then, her legs lacking their former strength, the pace became increasingly difficult. The injured side aching badly, she lagged behind. Lady Ellen dropped back. "Forgive me, Miss Flynn. In my absorption with Mr. Culhane's superb gift, I've neglected everyone." At Catherine's puzzled look, Ellen smiled. "You'd not yet joined us when Sean presented me with this stallion. His name is Numidian. Isn't he wonderful?"

"Yes . . . he's wonderful."

Ellen guided the stallion closer. "My dear, I realize it's none of my affair, but you're deathly pale. May I see you home?"

Catherine was silent for a moment, then answered quietly, "Numidian has found a good mistress. You're very kind, my lady, but I cannot go home. Please don't disturb yourself. I'll rejoin you in a moment."

"Are you sure?"

"Quite sure."

Ellen galloped ahead and reined in by Sean. "Darling, I think we should go back. Miss Flynn is ill; I'm sure of it."

"The young lady's no mean actress, Ellen. She's polished her skills on far less trusting people than you."

"But, why?"

"To gain sympathy. She's made a virtual profession of it. She'd gull the devil to get her way."

Ellen frowned. "Are you saying her illness is contrived?"

"Was the Trojan horse full of sweetmeats?"

Duneden quickened her gait to match Sean's. "You seem to know her rather well," she said calmly.

"She lives not two miles away. Why shouldn't I know her?"

Duneden arched a russet brow. "Carnally?"

342

"I'd sooner lie with a cobra."

"I think you're exaggerating. I offered to take her home, but she refused."

"Why not? She's having a field day. You're clucking over her like a mother hen."

"If you're wrong, she might be injured. She can hardly stay in the saddle."

Sean snorted. "Our Miss Flynn has led you a dance! The wench rides like a cossack." He wheeled Mephisto away. "Wait here."

Sagging in the saddle, Catherine had dropped far behind, unable to endure a pace faster than a walk. Then, with a prick of fear, she straightened as a tall horseman left the group ahead and pounded across the stubbled field. Cleanly the rider cleared the stone wall where she had relived Elise Enderly's nightmarish death.

Sean's fury rose. The English bitch sat the slab-nosed gelding like the queen of England. Let her stiff-necked pride be crushed; if she thought the misery of the Irish so amusing, let her squirm on the enemy pike as they did. "Well, Miss Snivel," he sneered as he reined in with a clatter of rocks, "you have Ellen believing you're at death's door. God knows you look the part, but if you think I'll let you play your tricks on her, you're grievously in error. Get that nag moving! Do you believe me idiot enough to let you drift blithely off to Donegal Town?"

"I cannot—"

"I don't want to hear it! I'm sick of your whining. Even the sight of you alive sickens me."

She lost her straightness then and seemed to huddle against the wind. "You want me dead so much?"

His green eyes slanted wickedly. "How could I *not* weary of maintaining your carcass like stinking carrion? For all your rottenness, madam, you once had courage. Now you mewl about everything. You're afraid of your own shadow." He whipped the big stallion around. "Are you coming or do I have to tie you over the nag's back?"

Her lips twisted slightly. "I'm simply offering you a chance to stay upwind." Scowling, he kicked Mephisto into a gallop. In a moment, he cleared the wall.

Catherine patted the gelding's neck. "We can make it,

343

my bucko, if you do your part. Just keep moving after we touch ground, because I'll only be able to hang on. Then you must take me home. Come, sweet."

Sean slowed to a trot. The wench would be forever coming around the barricade if she kept to her current pace. Then, distantly, he heard the gelding scratch into a hard gallop. She could not be fool enough to try to outrun him? Then he had a growing fear that she had no such intention. He twisted in the saddle, a strangled cry tearing from his throat. "Kit! No! That horse won't . . ."

The gelding and rider seemed to float into the air, rising perfectly to hang impossibly suspended. Then the horse's hind hooves blended with the wall, and the illusion crumbled. As if smashed by a massive hand, Catherine hurtled forward and her foot caught in the sidesaddle stirrup. The gelding screamed on impact, rolled on the inert bundle that lay on the ground, then heaved its bulk upward and stumbled away, reins dragging.

Sean cleared the distance to her in moments, sliding out of the saddle and running before his horse skidded to a halt. She lay face down, a hand outflung by her cheek. She might have been asleep, but for the odd angle of her foot. "Kit?" Icy with apprehension, he knelt and turned her over with infinite care. Her lashes flickered against her bloodied face. "Kit? Can you hear me?"

Her eyes opened, confused and filled with pain. Her lips moved, and as he touched them, she whispered against his fingers, "Daggers . . . shining." She choked with an ominous, bubbling sound. "I . . . cannot breathe."

A stain was spreading under her breast and he began to undo the jacket buttons. "Hush, baby, don't try to talk anymore."

With an effort, she turned her head toward the wall and he heard a bewildered whisper. "There's . . . nothing there." Then she coughed blood. The pain crushed her and let her go.

Sean dropped his ear to her heart and heard nothing. Fingers shaking, he tore open her clothing. Yards of tight bandage encased her chest and he paled, remembering flinging her against the desk. Praying she had not suffocated, he fumbled for his knife and slit the bandage. The linen peeled back, revealing a narrow, blue-white sliver of bone protruding through her side, a bubble of blood forming where it emerged. A scream rising in his brain, he groped for her wrist. He felt a dim, erratic throbbing and cradled her. Alive. Still alive. Dimly becoming aware he was not alone, he looked up to see Ellen. Two of the other riders were closing quickly.

"How bad is it?" she asked gently. In the years she had known Sean, she had thought him incapable of fear; now, terror leaped from his eyes.

"Kit's hurt." He touched the girl's face, trying gingerly to wipe away the blood, but his hands trembled so that the dirt smeared. Ellen quickly dismounted and gave him a handkerchief. He dabbed awkwardly at the pale face turned to his chest. "She's alive," he muttered distractedly. "I have to get her home."

"Shall I fetch a wagon?" Ennery asked, sitting his horse a few feet away. His companion, feeling uneasily sick, pressed a gloved hand to her lips.

"There's not time," Sean answered flatly. Carefully, he gathered Catherine in his arms and got to his feet. Her head lolled back over his arm and a blood-streaked hand dangled limply. He looked at them. "Go back to the house. Tell Flynn to be ready for surgery."

"But he's—" Ennery began.

"Find him!"

"He'll be there," Ellen said quietly.

Sean turned toward Shelan and started walking.

"Take one breath at a time, little one, just as I'm taking one step at a time, and I'll get you home," Sean muttered. "Live, even if it's just to spit in my eye. Fight me . . . Mother of God, you've all the brawn of a feather. How is it I could never beat you down? You showed me, though, didn't you, girl? You'd have made it; only you were already broken and the horse was no damned good. Kit . . . oh, Kit. Rest and let me do your fighting for a while."

A small, silent gathering waited on the terrace as Sean, with a fatigue that had not yet reached his mind, stumbled across the lawn. Ennery and Flynn went out with a blanket to meet him. "Let us give you a hand. Wrap her in this."

Like a blind man, he continued past them. I need to hold you a little longer, just a little. Believing you're alive. I don't want to know. Death is forever. Stay warm and asleep in my arms. Don't leave me.

"Sean. Sean!"

He became aware of Flynn gripping his shoulder. "What do you want?"

"We've made a place ready in the messroom."

"Not there."

"I can't use a bed. I have to have a firm surface for surgery, and from her color, I'd say it had better be fast. Don't argue!" Flynn snapped, his anger giving up.

Sean laid his burden down on the appointed table and stood like a zombie while Flynn made a quick examination. When the older man looked up, his eyes were the color of steel. "What possessed you to put a girl with broken ribs on a horse, much less goad her to take a jump? I know you threatened her! She was in pain. She'd never have gone voluntarily."

"Is she dead?" Sean asked hoarsely.

"Not yet," Flynn said curtly, "but that punctured lung alone makes surgery pointless. With any luck, she'll never regain consciousness."

"If anything can be done, you're going to do it, or so help me . . ."

"You'll what? Blow out my brains? I should think you'd have had enough of threats for one day!" Flynn headed for the door.

Sean lunged in front of him. "You took an oath, dammit!"

A faint moan from the still form behind them abruptly altered Sean's insistence to desperate pleading. "Don't make me have to shoot her like a broken horse. Please!"

Flynn looked for a long moment into the young man's tormented face. "Have a servant fetch boiling water; it's already on the fire. And more candles. It'll be dark before I finish. Then get back here; I'll need someone to hold her down. You might fetch Ennery, too." Sean spun on his heel and went to carry out the orders. But instead of Ennery, he asked Ellen.

"Of course, if you think I'm strong enough to hold her."

"Kit's too weak to put up much of a struggle. I wouldn't

ask it, Ellen, but if she sees some man holding her down . . ."

"I gather you courted your little neighbor rather forcefully," Ellen observed dryly.

"I raped her," he said bluntly, "then gave her to my men."

Duneden paled. "Oh, Sean, why? I never believed you could love any woman as you clearly do that girl."

"She's the English spy who warned Camden of the rebellion. I couldn't ask you to help without knowing the truth."

"It's you I'll be helping. She can escape pain in unconsciousness; you cannot."

Sean stood ready to hold down Catherine's shoulders and arms, while Ellen took her ankles. Catherine fought for breath, lips moving in inaudible murmurs, while Flynn cut away her clothes. Sean's eyes had not left her face until Flynn muttered, "Just as I thought, she's well along."

Looking up, Sean saw the distended belly. And fled. Flynn caught him at the door and spun him around. "Damn you! You were swaggering stud enough to put a child in her; you'd better be man enough to stand by her now."

"I didn't know. I didn't," Sean muttered. "But Kit did . . . down in that hole."

Flynn shook him. "If it'll help you get through today, think of the child as Liam's. I've neither time nor inclination to play your confessor!" Summarily, he pushed Sean back to the makeshift operating table.

Ellen had swaddled a blanket around the patient to ward off drafts. "That's a bright girl, Ellen. If she takes a chill, she has no chance at all. Let's begin." He began to tap Catherine's chest with a forefinger. "The left lung seems undamaged but the right one is filling. I'll make an incision here and try to stop the bleeding. Keep her completely still. She'll faint quickly enough; then, Ellen, hold the bowl near her head to receive the drainage. Quickly, we must begin. She's awake."

Catherine's eyelids fluttered as Sean pressed down. "What . . ." Her whisper turned into a scream of agony as

347

the scalpel went into her side. Her eyes went black with pain, widening in terror and shock as she tried frantically to escape Sean's tightening grip. "No . . . no, don't!" The pleading was cut off by another piercing cry and spasmodically she arched against his hands. "Please, merciful God, don't torture me, please!"

"Kit, don't be afraid. It won't last much longer."

She whimpered, then convulsed again. "Don't . . . hurt my baby. Please, don't take my baby! . . . Please . . ." Her pleas faded into silence and she lay still. Slowly, his cheekbones jutting under taut flesh, Sean released her and mutely waited, flinching once as Flynn set to work with needle and thread.

At length, Catherine's struggle for breath seemed to ease. Flynn tapped her chest and listened. "Better. Much better. I want Ellen to stay here, but you leave, Sean. You're as pale as the patient. No, no, go on. You've done your part. I'll be hours yet. Tell someone to relieve Ellen in a bit."

"That isn't necessary," she said.

"It won't get any prettier."

"I've become a veteran nurse of Dublin's hospitals in these past months, doctor. I've seen all there is to see."

"Very well, then. Sean, for God's sake, get out! You'll not do the lass a favor by staying underfoot."

It was nightfall by the time Flynn entered the study, wiping his hands with a stained towel, his shirt sleeves still rolled up. "I could use a whiskey, if you're not too drunk to pour me one."

The young Irishman's tall frame was loosely propped against the mantel. A bottle hung slackly in one hand and a glass listed precariously in the other. He laughed hoarsely. "Drunk? I'm not nearly drunk enough, doctor. I'd have to drink myself to death to get that sodden." He twisted away and dully stared into the fire. "She's dead, isn't she?"

"Not yet." Flynn looked around. "Have you got another glass?" Without looking at him, Sean held out the bottle. Flynn took it, drank, then sagged into a chair and swigged again. "Well, you were bent on breaking her, boyo, and now she's broken. Three ribs, collarbone, and left leg in two places. Those jagged ribs were like knives. One of Marie Antoinette's gowns couldn't have required more stitches." He dragged at the bottle. "She lost the baby on the table."

"Then I've murdered her child as well," Sean whispered, "perhaps my own."

Flynn looked speculative. "Has she had intercourse in the past six months?"

"No."

"Then she must have carried the child at least that long. Amazing. The boy that miscarried was an undersized but perfectly formed fetus of nearly four months. I should say it died of insufficient nourishment."

"Jesus!"

"Catherine carried a dead child for two months or more that should have miscarried but didn't, perhaps because she was confined. Inevitably, her system would have been poisoned. Whether her nausea is due to foul prison fare or gradual poisoning, I don't know, but if she hadn't fallen off that horse this afternoon, she'd have died within the month."

"Because she was afraid I'd take her child."

"She was sure of it. Probably even thought you might destroy it in a fit of temper."

Sean threw his glass into the fire. Hardly moving to evade the violent burst of flame from burning alcohol, in its glare he looked like a creature from hell. "Can she be moved?"

"You mean to a bed? Absolutely not. She's held together by thread and bandages. But she could use a pillow and blankets. That room is freezing without a fire."

Already on his way out of the room, Sean began to shout orders to the few servants.

Fires were built in the former messroom's three massive stone fireplaces, the drapes pulled, and the surgical table moved closer to the central fire. Sean carefully swaddled his unconscious charge in blankets and tucked pillows under her head to assist her breathing. Then he sent the others away and began the long night. Hour after hour, he kept vigil alone, rising occasionally to feed the fires, then returning to his place to watch them beat high, weaving weird, staccato patterns on the walls as they undulated in restless, ominous cycles. Outside, the wind mourned in the crags and the servants whispered that the *Bean Si*, the harbinger of death, was near.

When the sun's first rays needled through a torn drapery, Catherine yet lived. As the sun climbed and sank, Sean watched her face, retracing its features against the time when they would be shut from his gaze forever. For all his defiance, he believed she would die.

Ellen came to say good-by, but seeing his haggard face, she smoothed his hair. "Eat something and sleep. You'll be ill."

He shook his head. "I brought her here, from everything she loved. I cannot leave her alone now."

"Why not let someone else—"

"No."

She went down beside his chair. "Sean, when your Kit awakens she'll need your strength without reserve. I'll call you if there's the slightest change. You can make a place here before the fire." She took his hand. "There'll be time enough later for penance." So, Ellen persuaded him to eat something and lie on a blanket to sleep. She covered him and took his place in the chair to sit gazing at the wasted features of the other woman's face.

Sean awoke on his own. He sat up, rubbing his stubbled beard. In her chair, outlined against the green drapery, auburn hair piled high, Ellen reminded him of Megan, only she had a quiet warmth his mother had lacked. Megan had been tempestuous, even incandescent, but never warm. "You're a rare woman, Ellen. Thank you for staying."

She smiled. "George Ennery will wait. I tucked him into bed with a bottle of your best whiskey."

"How is she?"

"Becoming feverish. Doctor Flynn was here. If she hasn't regained consciousness by nightfall, you're to send for him."

"Would you continue to be an angel and keep watch a bit longer? There's a thing I must do."

"Yes, of course. I expected you to sleep for hours."

Sean found Peg dusting aimlessly in the Rose Salon. "Peg, where's the child?" he asked quietly.

She tucked the duster under her arm. "I bathed and wrapped the little fellow in a linen pillowcase. He's in my room."

"Take me to him."

A tiny bundle lay on the bed. The odor was horrible.

"You didn't take him outside?"

"To feed the dogs? Whether he's yours or Liam's, he's a Culhane . . ."

"You knew two months ago, didn't you?"

She could not read his voice or his mood, but she looked at him straight. "Aye. Ye had enough trouble without a babe into the bargain. I figured ye'd be findin' out in good time. Only I didn't know the babe was dead. I had no wish to see the lass and her child die in so mean a fashion, and ye haunted the rest of yer days."

Sean touched the linen and she caught his head. "Nay, don't be lookin'. Naught of life's there. Bury him deep and remember him decently."

High on the hill near Maude Corrigan's marker, Sean dug a hole with his hands and knife, then carefully laid the bundle in it, but could find no prayer to say nor the heart to push the dirt back into the grave. Rubbish. Burying his own son and Catherine's like rubbish. A spasm took him then and a keening cry welled in his throat like the howl of an animal across the gray, windswept heath.

"You don't have to go."

Ellen kissed Sean gently. "You want to be alone. She may come around soon."

"Ellen, I . . ."

"Don't say it." She pressed a finger against his lips. "We've had wonderful times together; but I've always thought you were incapable of loving any woman deeply." She smiled with soft regret, her lovely eyes drawing him as they always had, but now with an irrevocable difference. "If I ever find a man to love me as you do your Kit, I'll snap him up like a starved trout." She took his hands.

351

"Good-by, darling. Good luck. For your sake, I hope the girl lives, but whatever happens, don't let it destroy you. My house is yours. Don't stay here alone."

He held her close for a long moment, but she knew it was for the last time.

There was no need to call Flynn. Near sunset, Catherine, murmuring incoherently, stirred weakly in the blankets. Sean bathed her face and tried to trickle gruel down her throat, but aware only of mounting pain, she dazedly avoided the spoon. Her breath came in shallow pants; then a sharp spasm raked her eyes open, and with a cry, she strained against the pain as if it were a fearful, consuming lover. He held her shoulders. "Easy, little one." But she did not know him, could not distinguish his voice over tidal sweeps of agony. The dull pulsations rose into a livid, incoherent shriek, then plunged her into soundless depths where she drifted.

For the next few days, Catherine, unable to endure for long the pain that lay in wait, wavered in and out of consciousness. Sean dreaded feedings; as careful as he was, the gruel induced coughing that left her torn and trembling.

On the third evening, he carried her, wrapped in a blanket, up to his room, the splinted leg stiff from the knee down, the small head lax like a tired child's against his shoulder. Her cropped hair tickled his chin and he looked down at the long, ragged lashes that swept her cheeks. Aye. Rest, little one. Rest to fight again . . . and again. You've the heart of Conal, and a good English backbone, and my arm to lean on. Just don't let go.

Peg followed him into the room and pulled the draperies, then came to stand with him by the bed. " 'Tis hard to hate her now. Just the day the Frenchies came, she asked me to look after ye. I'd have taken oath she wished ye no harm." She fell silent for a moment. "There's somethin' about the whole matter that's awry. . . . Will ye sleep now? I'll watch a bit."

He left, but wandered instead to the empty ballroom. As he lifted the cover of the pianoforte and pressed a key, a single tenor note lingered in the room, evoking the image of a dark-haired girl poised *en penchée* before the long hazy windows; fleeting, ephemeral glimpses of a slender body in flight, vibrant as a firefly in the gloom. That spirit had been the real Catherine, the Catherine he had never known, had tried to touch. To seize. The idiot and the butterfly.

When the doctor came that night, Sean asked the question that plagued him. "Where was Padraic those last days before the ball?"

"With me," Flynn said, deftly changing dressings. "And he slept over, as he often does. Why?"

"Kit said she had used Padraic to send a letter to Lord Lieutenant Camden, probably on the mail coach out of Donegal. But she couldn't have known exact details of the rebellion until after Fournel arrived. Wasn't there any time the boy could have gotten away for several hours, even as late as the day of the ball?"

Flynn shook his head. "I kept him hopping."

"Would he have passed the message to someone else?"

"Not likely. Padraic worships Catherine and he's literal about commands. If she told him to take the message personally, he'd not have thought of relinquishing it." Flynn frowned. "He might have hidden it out of shame . . . you know, conflicting orders and all. He wanted to obey me, too."

"No, Camden got a message, all right; only it wasn't sent from Catherine."

"So, she *was* lying?"

"Aye." Sean felt oddly relieved and wretched at the same time. Had Catherine loved Liam so much she would protect him to the last, knowing she might die for it?

"Do you think Liam betrayed us?"

"Not us. Me." Sean rubbed his head as if it ached and dropped it against the back of the chair. "At the last, he hated my guts. Maybe always; I don't know."

Flynn finished bandaging, and took the patient's pulse. "Well, there's something you'd better know and face. Catherine's side is beginning to knit, but her strength is failing."

"She'll live," Sean said flatly. "She was able to say a few words this morning."

"Gibberish. Calling for her mother, the baby. I've heard her. Most of the time she has no idea who or where she is."

"She'll remember."

Flynn pulled on his jacket. "Then what? Her body has been fighting of itself, but given conscious, rational choice, do you think she'd choose life?" He opened the door. "If she awakens, you'll have a real fight on your hands."

If only the pain would end. Late that night, nerves taut, Sean held Catherine down as she twisted with shrieks that slowly subsided as the pain exhausted her. He eased his grip and bathed her hot forehead and parched lips. "Maman," she mumbled, eyes slowly opening and following the movement of the cloth as he withdrew it. She tried to speak, but was unable to get past the pain. Then, almost inaudibly, she whispered, "Help me."

Sean stroked her hair. "Easy, little one, I'm here. Don't try to talk . . ."

"Please. I hurt . . ."

"I know, kitten. The pain will pass. Try. You have to keep trying."

Her fingers caught in his sleeve. "I . . . cannot . . . bear any more! You've . . . made me suffer as your promised." Her fingers tightened. "End it. I beg you!"

Realizing what she was asking, he clamped his hands on both sides of her face, her heat seeming to sear him. "Damn it, no! You're going to live. I'll make you."

"You . . . cannot hold me now." The dim flare of rebellion guttered in her eyes as her head slipped to one side.

He left the room at a run and yelled down the stair, "Peg, get Flynn!"

Flynn looked up from the bed. "She must have a priest."

Sean stiffened. "No. I've seen it before. She'll give up."

"That has already happened. Catherine's a practicing Catholic. Would you have her die believing she's damned?"

Distraught, the young Irishman twisted away. "Do you want me to hand her over to Ryan? Where's the solace in that toad?"

"The man matters not. It's God he represents, and only God can give her peace."

Sean stared furiously at the small, still form in the bed. "Where was God when I brought her here?"

Father Ryan's toadlike eyes slid up, his plump hands folded neatly under his cassock as he leaned back in his chair. "So, ye expect me to absolve yer whore?" The priest keenly savored the moment; it was almost the equivalent of a miracle. Never had he expected the stiff-necked Culhane to beg the aid of the Church, much less his.

The dark man leaned across the table. "You will not call her whore, priest."

Ryan felt a prick of apprehension. He withdrew his pale hands and fanned them. "But how should the Church regard her, Mr. Culhane? I've heard talk—"

"Fishmongering gossip! Whatever Catherine is, I made her. She had no say in the matter."

"I've heard differently," the priest purred.

"*How* differently?"

"She incestuously seduced her uncle, Michael Flynn."

"You married her to Liam! You know she's not Flynn's niece!" spat the Irishman.

"She willingly serviced ye and yer brother . . . she took part in orgies with yer men . . ."

"Who fed you this incredible filth? Flynn's harpy daughters?"

"I'm the father confessor of this parish," the priest answered blandly. "How should I not be hearing its sins?"

Sean reached over the desk and jerked the man up by the front of his tunic. "Off your fat backside, you miserable turd! I've no time to play devil's advocate!"

Sheer pig rage stifled Ryan's natural cowardice. "Yer bitch can die and be damned!" His last phrase ballooned out from a ruthless punch in the belly. He moaned.

"Is that your last word, *Father?*"

The priest gathered his bile and spat. The next blow was to his genitals; he screamed and fainted.

Hearing a knock, Flynn left Catherine's side and went to the door. "Father? How good— Perdition! What the devil!" He was summarily dragged outside the room by a tall, hooded figure who closed the door behind him. "Sean! Where's the priest?"

"Ryan is unavailable," was the brief response. "Is she conscious?"

"Barely, but you cannot impersonate a priest! It's sacrilege! Besides, she'll *know.*"

"Kit's half out of her head. She'll not see my face. As an altar boy in Kenlo, I assisted at the Last Rites." He removed Flynn's hand from his arm and opened the door. "It will be on my head."

Catherine's face was translucent, her breathing labored. "Father?" she whispered as Sean tucked her cold hand into his warm one.

He stroked her eyelids closed, his voice a low, rasping brogue. "Peace, lass. Rest quietly."

Her fingers tightened imperceptibly. "I would make . . . confession."

Sean hesitated, the awful travesty of what he was doing seeping into his marrow. " 'Tis not necessary, child, if ye repent in yer heart."

She did not seem to hear him. "Forgive me, Father, for I have sinned." The confession poured out in a faltering, widening stream from a bursting heart. "I willingly became mistress of a man who raped me, then . . . came to love him . . . beyond honor, beyond life; but he would have opened the way to . . . endless bloodshed. I . . . betrayed those who trusted me. I defiled God's Holy Sacrament of Marriage . . . by pledging faith . . . to one whose wife I did not intend to remain. I . . ." She faltered, fighting for breath. "I brought misery and death to this land. And to a man . . . oh, God, help him! He's so alone." The murmur became almost inaudible. "Father . . . forgive . . ."

Brokenly mumbling the Latin, the Irishman drew a jagged cross of oil and ash on his lady's forehead and took her hand. With ebbing strength, she pressed his hand to her lips, opening her eyes as she did so. And saw his heavy Celtic ring. She stiffened in horror and looked full into the shadowed face under the cowl. "You . . . mock me!"

Desperately, Sean threw back the hood and planted his hands on either side of her head. "I mock you as you mock God! Would you die so easily and give your child to darkness? To stifle unanointed in your womb? To be damned to wander Limbo for eternity while its mother basks in God's limitless forgiveness?"

"No." Her eyes went wild. "The baby's . . . dead. It must be!"

"It lives."

"No!" she gasped. "I don't . . . believe you! You're lying, lying . . ." The words died away.

He could not find her pulse. Jerking out his dagger, he held it to her parted lips. A faint film of mist formed and faded, then another. He clamped her hands in his. "Stay. Hold on, little one. If God won't help you, cling to your demon!"

And so, drawing her bit by bit from the seductive shadows that promised release, he clung to her, hour by weary hour, day after day, feeding her, coaxing, bullying until he scarcely knew what he was croaking. When she lay senseless, he bathed her and changed dressings as Flynn had taught him. And when the pain mauled her, he held her until finally his own helplessness and exhaustion strangled his hope.

Is there no mercy in Heaven? She's suffered enough. I'm the one to blame. Give me her pain. I don't know how to pray. I only know she hurts.

Early one morning, the girl's breathing eased and sweat beaded her brow. As the sun came up, she slept, worn out with the battle. Light-headed with fatigue and relief, Sean opened the curtains to let pale, golden light stream into the darkened room. In the mirror, he glimpsed a beard-stubbled face with burning eyes in hollow sockets.

An hour and a hefty breakfast later, Sean fell asleep again in the big chair beside the bed and did not awaken until late afternoon. His eyes opened to meet Catherine's, still so dark their blue was difficult to distinguish, but without the blackness that spoke of intolerable suffering. "You look exhausted," she murmured softly as he rose and came to the bed.

He wrapped an arm around a bedpost. "There's not much I can say about what I've done. As soon as you're whole again, I'll send you home. You and your father will never see or hear from me again. I'll have a private account set up for you in London. You can begin a new life to lead as you see fit, without interference from your father or anyone else. If I may make a suggestion, America would be a good choice of residence." He turned away to gaze out to sea. "A new wind is blowing there, sifting away the old rotten seeds of this plague hole." Catherine said nothing. He had not expected paeans of joy. She had little left of home and family, even reputation, but still he had hoped she would feel some relief. "Don't you believe me?"

"I believe you," she replied quietly. "May I sleep now? I'd like to recover as quickly as possible."

He retreated behind a polite mask. "Of course. If you need anything, I'll be in the adjoining room. Just ring that bell on the table."

"Thank you." She closed her eyes.

He left the room, feeling like discarded rubbish. But then, what had he expected?

He was even less surprised when the remaining servants transferred their loyalty to their former master's elder son and left. Only Peg, Rafferty, and a young scullery maid remained.

Because too few servants remained to care for the livestock, Sean auctioned the breed stock to neighboring landowners and gave the rest to local villagers. Only Mephisto, two coach horses, and a draft mule remained. The estate became as silently deserted as the original ruin brooding above the cliffs.

Unaware of Shelan's alteration, Catherine slept most of the time, her body beginning to mend. Though Sean read aloud to distract her from pain-nagged waking hours and patiently fed her, their conversations were brief, polite, and impersonal. They might have been strangers. When she slept, he worked like a peasant in the stables and kitchen garden, deliberately losing himself in toil, breaking up hard clods of rock and dirt with pitchfork, boots, and hands; hacking peat from the bogs with a slane until his mind dulled.

Nora, the scullery maid, sidled up to Peg's elbow as she rolled out a piecrust. "Ma'am?"

The housekeeper jumped. "Will ye scare the wits out of me, girl? Ye're supposed to be sittin' with Lady Culhane 'til she wakes." The girl looked at her nervously and Peg softened. "Lunch, is it? I'm runnin' a bit late, but 'twill be ready in an hour. I'll not forget ye."

The girl made no move to go. " 'Tisn't that I came for, ma'am. It's . . ." she faltered. "It's milady. She's awake, but . . ."

Peg caught her arm with a floury hand. "What about her? Out with it!"

"She don't know me."

Peg sighed and relaxed her grip. "Oh, that's all, is it? Well, goose, I doubt if she's laid eyes on ye before."

The girl's eyes widened. "But I don't think she knows *anybody.* I spoke to her plain and she didn't answer a word. 'Twas . . . scary, like she wasn't really there."

Peg pulled off her apron. "I'll have a look. We'll not disturb the master just yet."

Sean stroked the curls back from the still face. "Can you hear me, little one?" There was no sign his voice or touch registered. Dark blue eyes looked through, beyond him with a sadness that tore into his soul. He caught her head between his hands. "Kit, don't hide from me."

Flynn gently caught his shoulder and nudged him out of the way. He pricked her instep with a needle, then again, harder. He looked up grimly. "I've seen this condition in asylums."

"Ye mean, the lass is daft?" queried Peg.

"It appears so."

"I told her the baby survived," Sean said dully. "It was the only reason she tried to live. Finally, she must have realized the truth."

Silent for a moment, Flynn rolled down his sleeves. "You'd do well to send her to England now to be among loved ones in happier surroundings. In time, she may recover."

"Enderly has no love for her, no money or inclination to look after her!" the younger man argued. "She'd be carted off to a madhouse to be starved and beaten and live in filth! They'd tie her up and worse."

359

Flynn sighed in exasperation. "I find it difficult to believe he'd send his daughter to such a place, if only to protect his reputation."

"Kit's nothing but merchandise to him. Like this, he cannot even make a paying prostitute of her, though I wouldn't put even *that* past him." Sean turned away. "Kit has to go back whole and able to deal with him on her own terms."

Flynn spread his hands in resignation. "Suit yourself, as always. I can certainly do nothing for her." He tugged his jacket from a chair back and shrugged into it. "As she no longer requires my services, I'll be moving to Edinburgh for further studies. I've bemoaned the lack of medical skills in rural areas too long, ignoring my own inadequacy. I've arranged for a younger man, Doctor Edwin O'Donnell, to take over the clinic in my absence. His brothers were killed in the uprising, leaving him with a mother and family to support. He's glad for the opportunity."

"You'll be missed here."

"I doubt it."

CHAPTER 18

Into Eden

Winter faded, spring bloomed into summer, then blazed into fall. Viceroy Canning's government brought moderation and peace to the land, although the proposed union with England was ominous, as was Napoleon's return from Egypt. The world outside the windows of Shelan was gray and mistbound, like the shadowed barriers of Catherine's mind that the Irishman circled like a prowling wolf in the fog. The pianoforte he ordered from Londonderry arrived in early September. Like a doll, she allowed him to press her fingers down on its keys, but he could only summon an echo of his lack of skill in a world of gentle learning he had long ago abandoned.

Still hoping to reach her with music, he asked a distant cousin, Arthur O'Neill, a famous harpist and music collector, to visit Shelan. O'Neill was blind; his sympathy for the afflicted girl was of a depth few capacitated people could imagine. Hour after hour, he played for her. As Sean went about his work, he would come into the room from time to time to listen, and finally he lingered with a sense of peace lost to him for over a year. Her profile hazed by silvery light from the long windows as she reclined on a divan, Catherine was as tranquil as a dream and as far removed from reality. When O'Neill departed, the house was more silent than before. The winter of 1799 closed in.

The following summer, Culhane carried Catherine down to the beach. In desperation, he waded into water nearly up to his chest, thrust her under, and held her there. There was no sign of struggle, only fragile bubbles rising with increasing slowness. Almost sobbing, he lifted her and caught her to him. "Don't. Don't be afraid. I won't hurt you. Please, I only want to talk." She lay against his chest, a sodden dripping bundle.

Buffeted by the surf, the Irishman stumbled back to shore. Laying her down just above the tideline, he crouched over her. "Can you hear the sea rushing up the sand, trying to touch us like the night we loved on the beach? We loved, Kit." He lowered his lips to hers, hair forming dripping black points about his dark face. Her lips were cold, but inside her mouth was warm. "I'll never stop loving you," he whispered.

From the beginning, Sean had doggedly persisted in treating Catherine as if she were not incapacitated. He read to her for hours and spoke as if she were listening until Peg wondered if he himself were becoming unbalanced. She could not deny that the daily outings either in the carriage or on the sloop did wonders for the girl's color. Sean spent most days grubbing in the stable or wrestling with rocks in the thin soil, not because Shelan suffered want, but to occupy his mind and allow him to sleep. Even after giving a fortune away to war-ravaged families, he was rich, his reserves left intact due to the rebellion's brevity.

After taking a spartan supper, he would wearily mount the stair to sit beside Catherine and read. Before retiring to his roughly furnished quarters in the adjoining room, he would brush out her hair, now shoulder-length, lifting it and plaiting it to watch its shimmer in the candlelight. Each night she seemed more beautiful, his sad-eyed, lovely doll.

The spring of 1800 arrived, and with it, budding life. A litter of mewling kittens in the stable caught Sean's attention as he fed the stock. Hunkering down, he waggled a finger in their midst. A taffy-colored mite, braver than his fellows, reached up and caught the invader with all four feet. "Ouch, you little demon!" The Irishman tried to withdraw his finger and the kitten clung tenaciously. Sean's lips twitched. "You're bloated with milk; now it's meat on the table you're wanting." He picked the kitten up and rubbed it against his cheek. "You're a bit soft for a man-eater." The kitten scowled as he held it up; Sean scowled back and the kitten kicked at his hand. "Ha! You remind me of someone, cat." He tucked it against his chest and stroked it. "You two should be introduced, if you can stay awake that long." Already beginning to drowse under the petting, the kitten butted its head into the curve of his elbow.

Catherine lay on the chaise on the terrace where crocuses peeped from flowerbeds near the steps. Sean slipped the sleeping kitten into her lap and curved her hands over its warm fur, moving them to stroke the mite's softness. "Best make friends with the tyke quickly, lass. He'll be howling for his mother soon." Catherine gazed past his shoulder as if at some distant sail on the horizon. Leaving the kitten in her lap, where it seemed content to sleep, he headed for the garden.

The kitten dozed for a bit, then began to groggily explore his perch. Nosing about, he planted his paws on Catherine's chest and sniffed her chin, then grew bored and crawled over the intriguing mounds and valleys of the blanket, falling over heavily and worrying with tiny teeth those which hampered his progress. The blanket monsters subdued, he peered about for further adventure.

Culhane nearly sank the hoe into his foot when he heard a dog's furious barking and, mingled with it, an urgent cry for help. Dropping the hoe, he pounded toward the sound, then rounded the house corner at a sharp angle. The chaise was empty. An Irish staghound, one of two kept as watchdogs, crouched snarling not five feet away from Catherine, who lay on the terrace trying to reach the kitten spitting practically in the dog's face. Sean snatched up a handful of pebbles and flung them in the staghound's face. With a startled yipe, it fled, leaving a heap of shattered crocuses in its wake through the flowerbeds. Swiftly, he picked Catherine up and carried her to the divan. "The kitten," she protested weakly.

He snatched at the tabby, which promptly sank its claws into his hand. Sean yelped, not unlike the dog, and dragged the offended hand out of reach. There was a sound suspiciously like a giggle. He carefully picked the little brute up by the scruff, then took it to Catherine, who murmured to it and stroked away its fright. Then her eyes met his like sunlight on clear water, and his legs slowly ceased to support him. He sagged to his knees and buried his head in her lap. As the kitten wandered down the chaise and curled up, the girl gazed down at the dark head. Slowly, her fingers touched his hair.

An unspoken alliance developed between them. Catherine did her utmost to recover full health as quickly as possible, and Sean gave all his time and concentration to help her achieve that end, although he knew his effort inevitably hastened their separation.

On fair days, they went to the beach, where he held her hands as she kicked in the surf. Sometimes they were even able to laugh as waves pelted over her head and she sputtered; but more often, as the cut-off shift clung wetly to her slim, sinuous body, her nearness taunted Sean, who had not had a woman in over two years. At these times he let her swim without assistance, but one day, when an unexpected wave choked her, he caught her in his arms without thinking. She felt iron hardness at his groin and froze, eyes dilating, then, completely unnerved, began to struggle. He released her, and instantly she waded warily out of reach, breasts heaving under the wet material. "Sweet Jesus, Kit, I'm not made of wood," he said hoarsely. "That shift is transparent." Her lashes swept down and a crimson flush rose under them. She dropped into the water up to her neck. Sean dived under an incoming breaker, then drove in a hard crawl out to where he could scarcely see her head. When his breathing evened, he struck out slowly for shore, giving Catherine time to leave the water and wrap up in a blanket they had left on the beach.

Uncertainly, she looked up at him as with harsh strokes he dried glittering beads of water from his body, hard muscles playing under darkly tanned skin. He jackknifed to his heels. "I'm sorry, but I cannot help it," he said flatly.

"I know," she replied softly. "Why didn't you say something before? I've been wearing this shift for weeks."

"I didn't want you to begin remembering." He brushed water from his hair. "Besides, what you wear makes no difference. You're covered to the neck now and all I can think of is jerking that blanket off and driving into you until you forget your name, the past, everything except the way I feel inside you. Until *I* forget, though God knows *that* would take more endurance than I've got." He rose quickly and picked her up before she had time to react. "Unless you're up to walking home, love, you'd better relax. It's a long climb."

In the early days of Catherine's recovery, a goal had been set. When she was able to walk up the main staircase on her own, Sean was to take her up the hill to the baby's grave. Three days after the swimming incident, she climbed the stair, and he knew it was because she had grown wary of him and increasingly anxious to leave.

On the way to the grave, he made her stop to rest. Her gaze followed the well-worn path. "You come here often, don't you?"

"Humility's a bitter draft to swallow," he replied tersely, "but more effective in regular doses." He offered his arm again. Finally, they reached the place. Bobbing in the wind, white Stars of Bethlehem covered the green hill. Catherine knelt to read the inscription scratched on the crude stone marker. "Beloved son of Sean and Catherine Culhane." She looked up questioningly at the tall man towering above her. He shrugged. "The other claimant wasn't here to argue the point." His eyes were unreadable. "The name is uncut. I figured you might have something in mind. A proper stone will be ordered when you've decided."

"Michael," she said softly, "after Doctor Flynn."

Sean knelt and scratched in the name. When he had done, he stayed hunkered, brushing stone dust out of the new scrapes with a finger. "Sean," Catherine said quietly, "I believe Michael was your child. Liam took me only once, forcibly, the night we ran away."

"Why did you marry him, Kit?"

She looked out toward the bay. "I was fond of Liam; but I couldn't love him, not the way he wanted. He became embittered. He told me about the French and we struck a bargain. He sensed I never meant to keep it, but he knew if the marriage were consummated I'd stay with him; I had committed enough offenses against God." She stared at the white stars dancing over the mound. "Our child died for those offenses."

"You didn't kill Michael!" Sean returned vehemently. "He died of starvation, as you might have, months before the accident. You'd never have lived to carry him full term. Even if he'd survived . . ." His eyes went tawny. "You might have gone into labor in that cellar."

"Animals deliver their young alone. I was less afraid of giving birth than what would happen after." She looked at him. "Fiona said you gave instructions—"

"Damn Fiona! I don't blame you for believing her. God knows I gave you reason." Sean stood abruptly. "I didn't know what was happening, though that in no way relieves me of responsibility. You were right to be afraid. I would have sent Michael away." His voice grew strained and husky. "But I swear I'd never have hurt him. Not this. I never meant this, Kit. Just as I never wanted to hurt you." His mouth twisted. "Why don't you *hate* me? All I see in your face is pity! You lied to keep me from finding out Liam was a traitor. At first I thought you lied because you loved him, but it was out of pity for me, wasn't it?" Fury rose in him and his fist clenched. "Don't, damn it! Don't ever pity me! Why should you?" Stooping down, he caught her shoulders. "I degraded you because I was jealous. Because there was a part of you I couldn't touch. Because I thought Liam had. That you could give yourself willingly to any man but me." His voice hardened. "Don't look at me like that!" Roughly, he jerked her against him and kissed her brutally, holding her head immobile until, with a bitter relief, he felt her stiffen. Abruptly, he let her go with deliberate harshness. "Are you finished here?"

Swiftly, she rose. "Yes, I'm finished." On the way down the hill, she tired, but when he offered his arm, she drew away. He let her continue alone to the house.

Sean could not have said why he chose a particular day to say good-by, but in the mellow sunlight one morning as she stood on the terrace brushing her hair, Catherine was so lovely he found it painful to look at her. Each day could only hurt more. Going up behind her, he drew her close, his lips against her hair. "This is our last day together, little one. What would you like to do with it?" He had not wanted to see her gladness, but her sudden tension clearly communicated it.

"You mean it, don't you?"

"Rafferty will take you to Donegal Town. From there you'll take a coach to Dublin." There was a long silence. Now that the moment was here, they both felt a plummeting sense of unreality.

"Why don't we have a picnic?" she said finally. "We've had little time for quiet pleasures."

He nuzzled her ear. "I never courted you properly, did I, lass?"

"Nay, sir, you did not," she replied with a trace of sadness, and turned to look up at him. "You took me by storm; I'll never see another so wild and unpredictable. How dull the world will be without your filling the sky."

He sensed she was only half teasing. Something of his agony must have come into his eyes, for she drew away. "I'll tell Peg to prepare a lunch," he said quietly.

The day was clear, the sun unusually hot as the carriage rolled northward along green-carpeted parapets patched with red thyme and plum tones of heather. The Atlantic was a hard, brilliant blue, the sunlight sequined with gulls kiting off the ramparts. They reminded Catherine of the day Sean had distracted her from despair by teaching her how to swear; even then, he had tried to protect her. She watched his hands, long-fingered, strong on the reins. Hands that could be brutal. Tender. She and her Irishman had fought love from the beginning, perhaps sensing it could only come to this ashen end. She regretted suggesting the picnic. Her mouth had a bitter taste.

She set out the food as Sean lay on his back, eyes closed, arms under his head. They had said little after starting out, each lost in his own thoughts. Perspiration stuck the white Dacca muslin to her back, and she pushed hair out of her eyes for the third time as she leaned over to slice bread. Bees droned about the hamper with irritating stubbornness. As she flicked a poaching insect off the butter, Sean turned on his side and propped his head on a hand. His steady regard made her nervous. She began to slice faster with short, hard strokes, sweat beginning to trickle down her spine and between her breasts.

"Careful, kitten; you'll cut a finger."

Her head shot up, but sharp words died on her lips. "What shall I put on your bread?" she asked lamely.

He shrugged. "Whatever you like."

She selected roast beef, added fruit to the plate, and held it out to him.

Sean reached past the plate and touched her nose. "You're getting freckles." Then he sat up and took the food, thanking her politely.

She threw odds and ends on her own plate, then sat staring down at it. She put something in her mouth and chewed it slowly; it tasted like sawdust. Almost eagerly, she accepted the glass of wine Sean poured, and drained half before he restored the bottle to the hamper.

"More?" he asked, as if she had done nothing strange.

"Yes, thank you. It's quite good. I . . . was thirsty."

He poured impassively. "It's a Haut-Brion; it ought to be good."

Liquid gold and she had gulped it like water. She sipped more slowly. It would be easy to become drunk, just when a clear head was mandatory.

Sean eyed her over his glass as she toyed with a pear slice. With the demure white gown and her piled-up hair windblown, she looked like a polite, beautiful child restlessly putting up with an elder's company. "Would you like Flynn's address in Edinburgh?" he asked suddenly.

The long lashes flicked up. "Very much. I've never thanked him for all he did." Her eyes lowered again and she prodded the pear. "I've never thanked you either."

"You've nothing to be grateful for."

"I disagree."

"I told you once I didn't want your gratitude," he said curtly, "especially when it's misplaced. I murdered our child. I nearly murdered you."

"We were both responsible for Michael's death, Sean. We're both selfish, each wanting to punish himself by taking sole blame. You hurt me horribly, but I did no less to you." She cut off his attempted interruption. "I *was* a spy. I would have betrayed you if I had reached Londonderry. I knew you might hang, that everyone involved in the rebellion might be killed. I did what I had to do—as you did." Her eyes held his. "In that cellar, I prayed Michael might be spared the unhappiness of a world that had no love for him"—her voice hardened—"and he was spared, but I lived because you refused to let me take the easy way out. As Mother might have lived, had I refused her. I'll never know now whether I made the right choice. I must live with that doubt, *despite* that doubt. But you?" She leaned forward. "Will you stay here at Shelan and stew in your own martyrdom? Hack at rock to keep sane? Walk that empty house until your ghosts are more alive than you?" A sob of anguish and fury rose in her. "How long before you blow your brains out? How long—"

Culhane jerked her hands forward, then twisted her under him and stopped her mouth brutally with his own, ravaging it until she lay limp and unresisting under him, all the fury done except for the heaving of her breasts against his chest, maddening him with lust, anger, and loss. "Kit. Kit. Damn you," he muttered hoarsely against her lips. "I love you." His mouth slanted across hers and Catherine felt torn asunder with the sudden force of a terrible desire. Fatal. Fatal wanting. Needing. God. No. Not now. His hands burned through the thin bodice and his hardness pressed fiercely against her. Desperately, she clawed at his back, his face, feeling sickeningly the tearing of his flesh, hearing his muffled gasp of pain. Rearing up, he raised his hand to slap her into submission, then realizing what he was about to do, flung off her. "Get away from me, then, damn it, if you don't want to be raped!"

Still dazed with desire and wretchedness, Catherine retreated. A fat raindrop struck her forearm, then more spattered the blanket. Eyes averted, she began to dump things into the hamper. Intent on their quarrel, neither had noticed storm clouds moving in from the sea. With a muffled curse, Sean caught her arm. "Leave it! We're in for a drenching." Dragging her to her feet as the downpour let loose in earnest, he headed for the carriage. Lightning cracked the heavens. The horses bolted in fear, tore up the tether posts, then raced homeward with the carriage rattling behind.

Catherine pushed streaming hair out of her eyes. "What are we going to do? It's miles to Shelan."

"There's Flannery's old place. Come on, run!" Racing under the storm, he led her across the gray, rainswept heath.

At last Catherine huddled against the cottage wall while Sean battered the lock off the door. The door crashed inward and he caught her wrist, pulling her in with him. Dripping, they surveyed a dusty room containing a crude bed and table with stools. Except for cobwebs and field-mouse droppings in the corners, everything was as Flannery had left it. The windows whitened in the storm's glare and Catherine shivered. Sean thought to wrap the bed counterpane about her, then saw the roses of her chill-stiffened nipples clearly through their wet, transparent skin of muslin. His hair was a sleek black helmet, and his green eyes slanted like a cat's in the gloom as he stared at her, wet clothing defining his rising desire. With her hands crossed over her breasts, Catherine shrank away. "No," she whispered. A roof post abruptly stopped her. "Please!" She was still pleading when he caught and gently drew her wrists behind the post.

Holding them loosely with one hand, he unfastened the laces of her bodice; as it parted, his eyes veiled under his lashes, then lifted. "You're the most beautiful creature I've ever seen. All the rest of your days, men are going to tell you that and they're going to want you in the same way—except for one thing." His lips hovered above hers. "This is the time you're going to remember when you hear the words 'I love you.' " With infinite tenderness he kissed her lips, then her throat as it strained away beneath his mouth, then her shoulders and the swell of her breasts, arousing the sleeping, burning serpent in her belly. Ignoring her struggles, he returned to invade her mouth with slow, ravaging hunger until her head fell back. With his free hand, he eased the sodden dress from her shoulders, then peeled the filmy stuff away from her breasts. Tugging her wrists back so the twin mounds thrust forward, he took each nipple into his mouth and teased them into jutting peaks of desire.

Catherine groaned and thrashed as her body turned to liquid fire. "Stop it!"

Almost angrily, Sean picked her up and threw her on the bed, then shoved the sodden skirts up about her waist and tore away the soaking silk undergarments. She thrashed, long legs gleaming in the cool light, as he tore open his own clothing. "No more lies between us, Kit. You're swollen with wanting. Just like me. Tell me you want me."

"No!"

"Love me, Kit," he whispered hoarsely. "One last time." She bucked, and with a despairing curse, he wrenched her thighs apart and plunged into her. Felt the clinging velvet drag of tight sheathing. Wild with long-pent desire and frustration, he drove more deeply and more demandingly with each stroke. Suddenly, with a low, keening cry of surrender, she caught him about the neck and arched to take him even deeper, deeper, until he was battering at the entrance of her womb and still she convulsed under him, still crying out with need, holding him as if she would never let go. "Sweet God, Kit!" A spasm twisted his face. Desperately, he fought to withdraw, but she wrapped her legs about him. Past control, he flooded her in convulsive spurts that seemed to drain his guts. He collapsed, sagging. In the stark silence, their hearts thudded like tiny savage drums.

His eyes sought hers in confusion. "Why, Kit? You cannot want my child. Tomorrow you're free of me for good."

Her eyes smoky in the darkness, Catherine's lips curved slightly as she traced the line of his jaw. "You arrogant bastard. Always telling me what I want. Then making me want it. Telling me what *you* want. Then making me want that, too." Her voice was soft and husky. "I'll never be free of you, you devil-eyed mick. I love you. I've always loved you."

"Kit?"

"Yes."

"Marry me."

Her silence brought a tension. Then she spoke of the thing that remained unsaid between them. "What of Liam? What if he comes? Why hasn't he?"

"I don't know, kitten. Possibly he doesn't dare press the issue. He'd hardly invite English magistrates in here to ultimately confiscate the place. Nobody likes a turncoat, especially one whose usefulness is done."

"Where is he now?"

He nuzzled her neck. "Holed up somewhere in Ulster, no doubt. I've been too preoccupied with you to run him down. Are you afraid of him?"

"He hates you, Sean."

"If he could take you away from me, he'd have tried by now. You don't have to stay married to him. The banns were never posted and you agreed to the terms under duress."

"Liam didn't twist my arm; he simply gave me a choice. And the marriage was consummated. Neither the Vatican nor any law in Christendom recognizes rape by a husband."

"Don't you want to marry me, little barrister?"

In answer, Catherine slid atop him and lowered her lips to his with a kiss that could have rekindled the London Fire. When her head lifted, Sean Culhane lay a smoking ruin. As he let out his breath in a beatific sigh, she gave a low purr of delight and rubbed her nose in his fur. He stroked her nape. "You're not afraid anymore?"

She burrowed closer, whispering, "I died inside when you hated me. Even after the hate was gone, I felt like glass only glued together each time you touched me. Then, suddenly, there was no more time and nothing mattered anymore but never losing you."

"I never stopped loving you, little one. I nearly went crazy. Christ, what a battleground we made of what should have been."

They made love again, lingeringly, rediscovering each other in the darkness. Then it was still, the easing rain lightly drumming in somnolent rhythm as they lay entwined under the faded counterpane. They slept, still locked together, then loved again as the sun sank, turning their bed to pale gold, their bodies to burnished bronze.

Throughout the golden days of summer and fall, they gorged on one another, not trusting the future. There was only now, and they took it as hungrily as they took each other. Reexploring the coast and islands, the two sunned

for endless days on the *Megan*'s deck and made love until
their skins turned Indian dark and they looked like a pair
of jewel-eyed primitives. As the weather cooled, they went
back into the Donegal mountains, into Eden. Part of the
debris of war, blasted and scarred, they slowly healed their
wounds and found peace. The stubborn seed of their love
gave flower as Sean found a happiness with Catherine he
had never known. Increasingly, he became aware of the
difference between Megan, who promised all but only took,
and Catherine, who gave warmth and love without measure. He learned to laugh easily and often as Catherine's
playfulness surfaced after years of repression. In many
ways, he had never really known her, and the emerging
woman beguiled him. All contrasts, all mesmer, she
wrapped him in love and he adored her.

As Sean opened his study door one crisp October afternoon, the only warning of an alien presence was a faint
cloud of blueish smoke rising above the back of his
wingback chair. He silently eased back into the foyer. A familiar voice with an unfamiliar note of bored mockery
floated across the room with the smoke. "Don't bother
going for a gun. You've grown careless in the ruins of your
dreams. I daresay ambition has lost its gloss?"

Sean crossed the room, dropped into the desk chair with
a carelessness he did not feel. "What do you want, Liam?"

The dissipated face that regarded him from the chair
was shocking, even more so than its sudden appearance.
The fine, fair hair was the same, if untrimmed; but the
handsome aesthete was now a bloated Parsival disappointed to find the Grail a beggar's cup. Wine and misan-
thropy had taken a hard toll of Liam Culhane. His skin
was blotched, his mouth indulgent; eyes secretive, bright
with malice. "Why, what a question, brother. I saw you on
the beach from the cliff. My wife looks fit. She was ill, I
gather?" He might have been discussing the weather.
When Sean said nothing, Liam continued with a derisive
smile. "A charming couple you made, playing children's
games and stealing kisses. I was a bit surprised you didn't
heave her skirts up and have at her." Sean's jaw tightened, but he held his tongue.

Liam sipped his whiskey, then toyed with the glass and smiled into space. "All kissed and made up, even to the point of my wife being your cheery whore until the divorce papers are served and husband Liam is out on his noble duff." Sean's head lifted slightly. "Oh, yes, I received due notice. Actually, you could say I've been waiting for it. Two years." He waved the glass. "Holed up like a troglodyte in a cave of all my worldly wealth. My minions were afraid to come and cut your throat. You made a nasty impression on them—"

"You've become a sot and a bore as well as a traitor, Liam," Sean interrupted bluntly. "Why not take the bottle and crawl back to your lair?"

"I've been off liquor for a week so I might pay you and my wife a polite visit," his brother snarled. "Don't patronize me. And as for boring"—thin lips curled around the word—"here is titillation for you: you rut upon your own sister."

Sean stared at him. "You're deranged."

Liam chuckled. "You'd like that, wouldn't you? I believe my wife has that honor. Is that how you persuaded her to spread herself in your incestuous sty?"

Sean vaulted over the desk and wrenched Liam out of the chair by his shirtfront as whiskey spiraled onto the rug. "Why would I lie?" Liam challenged. "She's my sister, too."

"You'd contrive any rot to get her away from me, you slime!"

"I'm not lying. And if you close my mouth now, Catherine will hear the truth from the Pope and nothing will keep her with you!"

Slowly, Sean released him. "Let's see your concocted proof. I've an itch to cram it down your throat!"

Liam shrugged his jacket back into position, reached down beside his chair for a leather portfolio, and laid it on the desk. He drew out a canvas. "Recognize it?"

"Of course," Sean said impatiently. "It's the portrait that used to hang in Brendan's bedroom."

"Does the woman look familiar?"

"Should she?"

"You know her intimately, or rather, her daughter."

Liam drew out a second painting. It was a portrait of Catherine in an almost identical pose to the one in the older canvas. Catherine was by far the more beautiful, her eyes and cheekbones more dramatic, the mouth more provocative, but the two women were undeniably related.

"It won't wash, Liam. This is no proof of anything."

"That's what I thought at first. It left too many loose ends." He restored the paintings to the folio, then pulled out a vellum envelope. "Then I found this. Brendan gave a codicil to Father Ryan's predecessor along with a copy of the will to safeguard in case either of us ever contested dispensation of the estate." He casually handed it to Sean. "You'll find it most interesting."

Sean suspected forgery, but he knew Brendan's writing as well as his own and the document was authentic, even to the subtle weighting of the ink in certain letters. The pages held answers to questions he had wondered about all his life, including some answers he would have given that life not to have known.

My dear sons,

I have added this codicil to my last will and testament to be opened only upon question of the dictates of my will. The major actors it discusses are all dead now, and it may explain my actions.

At the age of eighteen, I sailed on one of Grandfather Ruadric's barques, which foundered off the French coast. I washed ashore near the Convent of Saint Anne, where a young girl, Elise de Vigny, aided the sisters in attending me. She was innocent as the dawn and as lovely. When I regained health, she invited me to stay at her father's estate until a ship might take me home. In that brief time, we loved with all the joy of children who cannot believe their love is impossible. Inevitably, desire overcame restraint. I asked the comte de Vigny for her hand; one of the richest men in France, he refused, enraged. I was forcibly put on the next packet boat and kept under guard until passage to Ireland was effected.

Word soon arrived of my lady's marriage. Wild with

grief and anger, I returned to sea, sailing to the Americas, around the Horn to the Pacific. On my homecoming, marriage to Megan was proposed. I wanted a mate to ease my loneliness, to bear my children; Megan wanted a sire for future kings and a man to match her desires.

In the beginning, we were well matched; then Liam was born, I was often away in Dublin, and we grew apart. In Dublin, I saw Elise again, as wife of an aide to the viceroy. She had been sold into marriage to conceal her pregnancy with my child, a child that was stillborn. Enderly was a discreet homosexual, interested in her only as a possession. Although we were faithful to our separate marriage vows, tongues began to wag.

When I was imprisoned, Elise, with the aid of Lockland Fitzhugh, used her influence and private income to gain my release. She concealed money bribes to officials in expense lists for the restoration of Windemere. On one of her prison visits, Megan encountered Elise in my cell and was convinced by Dublin gossip that we were lovers. She left for Shelan, where some months later she gave birth to Sean. Upon my release, she took him to Kenlo.

After Megan's tragic death, I went to Dublin and pleaded with Elise to leave Enderly. She refused to believe the extent of his crimes, and as a devout Catholic, felt bound to him. In a desperate effort to lure her away, I made love to her, virtually by rape. Like the release of a raging river, our love could no longer be checked. Yet, when her husband returned to England, Elise, unaware she was pregnant, accompanied him. Because he had not slept with her in years, there was no doubt of the sire. He accepted the child, my daughter, Catherine, but his relations with Elise became even more cold. After twelve years of misery, she became convinced of his vicious nature and resolved to end the marriage. A week before she was to leave England, she died horribly in a riding accident. My heart died with her. Your sister, Catherine, was shut away in school. I have never seen her, the living love of my Elise. The above is explanation for this further provision: in the event either of you refuses to abide in any manner with the dispensation of your inheritance or dies without issue, that portion of the estate allotted to said heir shall revert to my daughter, Catherine de Vigny Enderly, through anonymous investments to her mother's American estate.

I ask your forgiveness for my failures as a man and as a father. With the hope for happiness for all my children, I am your loving father,

Brendan Culhane.

Sean felt as if a sword had emerged from the grave and slashed out his entrails. Liam took the document from his unresisting fingers. "I take it you're no longer bored?" He tucked the codicil back into its envelope and gave his ashen brother a bitter smile. "Perhaps you'd like a drink; you'll need a great many to catch up to me." He put the bottle down on the desk. "Do you tell her or shall I?"

Sean slashed the bottle away to shatter against the wall, leaving a spreading stain. "Leave Kit out of this! She's endured enough."

"How do you propose she be left out? We've both had her. It would seem Rouge Flannery is the most virtuous suitor of us all."

"I'll take her home." The words came out slowly, grating in Sean's throat like bloody cinders. "I'll never see her again, but you have to give her an uncontested divorce."

"Your gallantry is uncharacteristic, brother," Liam sneered. "How can I be sure you'll keep your part of the bargain?"

"For Christ's sake, Liam, do you think I could take Kit into my bed again, *knowing*? No, of course you don't! That's the revenge you've been waiting for all these years." The agony in his eyes hardened to a deadly glitter. "But I'll tell you something. If you ever go near Kit, or speak a word about this to her or another living soul, I'll blow your sick, sodden brains out!"

Liam shrugged. "Somehow, I think you may perform

that exercise on yourself first, brother, but I agree to a divorce as soon as Catherine is safe at Windemere."

"I want that codicil burned."

"We'll burn it together, after she's in England. Then we'll drink a toast to the sister we both adore." He eyed a brandy decanter. "In fact, why don't we have a drink now?"

"Damn you, get out!" Sean shook with shock and helpless rage. "Get out!"

"Very well, brother. Have a pleasant journey to England."

Of late, everyone at Shelan took meals together in the kitchen. The cozy gatherings, which often dissolved into gay bouts of laughter and songs the house had rarely known, provided Sean with the family intimacy for which his loneliness hungered. Occasionally, Catherine glimpsed a subtle shyness about him, a wistfulness in the midst of the hubbub that made her heart go out to him. The alienation she had felt in Ireland had been the lot of her man all his life. A private dinner in the salon indicated a special occasion, hopefully one which promised news from Rome; but as soon as she opened the salon door and saw Sean restlessly stirring the peat in the grate, Catherine knew better. She went to him and took his arm. "What is it, darling? Bad news?"

Sean's heart lurched as he looked at her. The Diane gown made her beauty luminous, but again it presaged disaster. "You're particularly lovely tonight," he said bleakly.

So terrible a void was in his eyes that they seemed blind and she felt a surging fear. "Are you trying to tell me the divorce has been denied?"

"Your husband was here today." Catherine paled, waiting. "He's agreed to an uncontested divorce on the condition we separate permanently."

"What! But he must know . . ." She spun away. "We'll obtain a divorce without his consent! He knows I'll never live with him now!"

Furious, eyes slanting like a catamount's, Catherine was more beautiful than ever and Sean never wanted her

378

more than at that moment, as he lied to her. "I've had word from Cardinal Manzetti. Without Liam's cooperation, divorce is impossible. The Pope considers that too many witnesses disclaim our position."

Her shoulders sagged and the fight went out of her. "Oh, Sean, I'm so sorry." She came into his arms and tensely he held her. "Let Liam have his hollow victory. All that matters is staying together." She lifted her lips to his and, gently but firmly, Sean put her away from him.

"Divorce matters to me." He poured her a favorite pale Rhine wine. "To your happiness, Catherine."

Automatically, she drank, then put the glass down deliberately. "You're terrifying me. Please say what you must."

"You've made these last few months the happiest of my life," he said dully, "but they were an illusion. Reality is living a lie. Cohabitation. Fornication. Breeding bastards. Everyone assumes I'm a bastard; even I don't know the truth. I won't bring that down on my children."

Numbly, Catherine put the glass to her lips again. He was not saying this. Not now.

"You'd never be sure of me, Kit, if we simply lived together. Now, you're young and beautiful; no man in his right mind would leave you for another. Later, you'll have doubts. I've never been faithful to any woman long. And what of me? I've mistreated you more than once out of jealousy." He paused. "It's marriage or nothing."

There was a silence. "You're full of malarkey, my love," she said definitely and melodically. "What our children never know won't hurt them. But you love me so much it does hurt, the same way I love you. You were faithful when I was deranged, when there was little hope I'd be any more than that. There will never be any woman for you but me, and you know damned well I'll never want another man! What did Liam really say to make you lie?" The last word was slightly slurred.

"Believe what you want, Kit, but we're done," he said flatly. "I'm sending you home."

She stood up, feeling an unsteadiness that increased dramatically, sending the room into a blur. "I won't go. You don't want me to go." She caught at the table. "Don't lie to me anymore! Don't . . ." The world dimmed into a warm, enveloping mist. Then arms closed about her, cradling her. "You deceitful . . . bastard. I'll come . . . back."

Just before the mist turned black and silent, she heard his reply. "I won't be here."

CHAPTER 19

Trapped

The mist moved over Catherine as if creeping in from the sea, then receded until nearly penetrable. She felt something beneath her heavy head as hot fluid trickled down her throat. The mist drifted in again, thicker than before. Finally, it parted to reveal cherubs gamboling about a naked, reclining Venus painted on a ceiling. Cupid leaned over Venus's shoulder with a coy, familiar wink. Nostrils flaring at the room's stale odor, Catherine clutched a satin counterpane. Her bed. Home. After nearly three years. Her eyes closed. Sean, come back. You're my breath, my life. She lurched from the bed to the armoire, then scrabbled through her musty clothes: several Le Roys, but nothing from Sean. She threw a habit on the bed, then dug for her boots.

"Welcome home, my lady. Will you be needing me?" Catherine jumped and looked over her shoulder. The maid, Mignon, regarded her unblinkingly.

Catherine turned deliberately. "Yes, you can help me. Where is he?"

"Who, my lady?" The woman's French was clipped, like Sean's.

"Don't play games with me. You're his spy."

"My lady?"

"Damn it, Mignon, I have to find him before . . ." She stopped. This was no Moora. In this hard little face were eyes the color and warmth of Toledo steel. "Mignon, I'm not his enemy. I won't betray him. And I'll give you anything."

"I need nothing, my lady." Mignon went to the bed and began to unbutton the jacket that lay there. "Will you be riding before breakfast? My lord Enderly is anxious to see you."

Catherine caught the maid's wrist. "I have proof. I have . . ." Then she remembered. Sean had never given her Flynn's address. There was nothing to indicate her captivity had been anything but unwilling.

The girl regarded her with contempt. "If the gentleman in question has no wish to be followed, you have little choice but to accept his decision."

Catherine sagged down on the bed. Mignon was right. Sean had made it clear, whatever his reasons, he never wanted to see her again. What twisted weapon had Liam used? Growing anger drove back raw pain. If it took the rest of her life, she would find out the truth and she would find Sean. Yet nilly, willy, first she had to deal with her father. "Mignon, I shall want the emerald silk."

For one of the rare times in his life, John Enderly was startled. The breathtaking creature who embraced him was not the moon-eyed child of three years before, but an assured woman, a dramatic beauty with fire and promise.

"Papa," Catherine said warmly, "how good it is to see you. I cannot tell you how happy I am to be home."

He took her hands. "Are you well, my dear? I had lost all hope of your safe return."

"Quite well, Papa. Older. Wiser. With a reputation that I assume is in tatters." He looked somewhat taken aback at her frankness. She squeezed his hands. "Poor Papa. My resurrection must embarrass you greatly."

He lead her to the breakfast table, bare of candelabra and usual flowers. "That you must never believe, my dear. You are all I have, and most precious." He seated her. "So lovely a creature is rarely at a disadvantage in society, I assure you." He resumed his place at the end of the table and flicked out a napkin. Catherine, opening her own, found it frayed and less than clean. Pale spots on the walls demarcated absent paintings. The sideboard and its silver were missing. Enderly noticed her glance. "As you may have no-

382

ticed, the rest of the house is even more barren. The vendetta was rather complete. I depend on you to assist me in locating the author of our misfortunes."

John, the butler, came in with a tray. He bowed as he presented Catherine with a segmented Madeira orange surrounded by dried figs. "Good morning, John."

"My lady." Stiffly correct, he served Enderly and left the room.

Catherine dipped into the fruit. "In some ways, it seems as if I've never been away. Nothing ruffles John."

"He's one of the few servants I retain."

"Surely Alice is here?"

"Your former maid succumbed to heart failure two years ago."

"Poor Alice," Catherine whispered softly. "I had so missed her."

"She did nothing but talk of your childhood. One would have thought the woman had been your mother."

"In a sense she was. I was fortunate to have had two such mothers."

Noticing he frowned slightly, as he always had when she spoke familiarly of the servants, she thought dispassionately, How could I have adored him so blindly? What a narrow creature he is. Outwardly, he was unchanged so far as Catherine could tell: his clothing no less well cut for all its simplicity, his face as handsome as ever, the few shavings of silver at his temples merely adding to his distinction.

Kidney omelets arrived with hot, black tea. The meal was blandly pleasant, the conversation no less so. How civilized we English are, she thought, faintly amused.

After breakfast, Enderly led her to the study. As he spread out a map, she noticed the terrace beyond the window was leaf strewn, the gardens weed choked. "You must tell me all you can remember. Where were you kidnapped?"

Careful, my girl. Not too much or too little. Dear Father has not been sitting on his hands. Tell him only what you think he knows. Her tale was an adroit mixture of scant truth about the actual abduction and blatant fiction about Caribbean Island smugglers and their vengeful leader, who had first maltreated her, then made her his mistress.

"He was a Spaniard of education who called himself Perez, and he never left the island, to my knowledge. I managed to make him infatuated with me. The past two years have been fairly comfortable . . . if somewhat exhausting."

Enderly lifted an eyebrow, but made no comment. "Why did this Perez let you go?"

"He married the daughter of a rich French planter. Louise was plump and given to ruffles. She and her equally plump papa heatedly objected to my remaining on the island. Apparently, the Spaniard had completed his plans for you, so with considerable regret, he sent me home as abruptly as I was kidnapped. Except this time, I was drugged. Perhaps he thought I might go into hysterics at the prospect of leaving him," she added dryly.

"The green-eyed man, what of him?"

Although she did not twitch a hair, her heart sank. "A paid mercenary. I rarely saw him."

"Did Perez ever say why he initiated this vendetta?"

"An old grievance. He held you responsible for the death of his mother, but where or how, he never said, and he was a dangerous man to prod."

"Do you believe his story?"

"Of course not," she lied blandly. "The man was obsessed. You know how Latins are about their mothers."

Enderly eased into his desk chair. "You've endured a great deal, Catherine, but I never expected you to turn into a cynic."

"As I said, Papa, I made adjustments. I don't think of myself as cynical, merely practical." She looked at him cooly. "For instance, my absence must have been awkward to explain. How did you?"

"At first, you were abroad; later, you visited relatives in America."

She laughed lightly. "How embarrassing to claim colonial relations; no one could doubt such an admission to be true."

"No one believes it now, of course, but no one can disprove it."

She played with a curl at her cheek. "Still, no virtue, no dowry, no marriage. Even a rich bourgeois couldn't begin to restore our fortune." She appeared to mull the problem

384

over. "I may have to become a discreet courtesan, an expensive one only the richest can afford." She cut Enderly a look. "Would you mind very much?"

"What makes you assume you're suited to be a courtesan?"

Dear Papa. You'd feed me to the wolves if they had gold teeth. "Perez was a man of jaded tastes," she stated matter-of-factly. "I never bored him. I'm new, mysteriously scandalous, well-bred and available . . . for a price. But I want more than money." She leaned forward deliberately, breasts swelling against the low-cut décolletage. "You could see that I'm introduced to the proper men. Artois and Angoulême are still in Edinburgh, aren't they?"

"Angoulême is to be married next year to the princess of Savoie. Not a wise choice, my dear."

"I wasn't thinking of Louis. *Monsieur* is the one who controls the purse strings."

"He's no fool, Catherine. He has a mistress of some years with whom he's well satisfied. He indulges no one but himself. He would have you for an hors d'oeuvre."

"Such a nibble may intrigue a gourmet." She smiled wickedly. "I believe *Monsieur le duc* might be tempted to sample the whole feast."

"Perhaps."

She leaned over the desk. "Papa, there's no time. How much longer before we lose Windemere? Months? Weeks? I don't question your judgment; I only urge you to make use of me while I can be a valuable tool. Public poverty is no whetstone."

"I'm aware of your point, Catherine. I'll consider it." He rose from his chair. "Now, regretfully, I have pressing business in Liverpool. I beg you to excuse me until this evening, my dear. I'm sorry about the distraction, but your arrival was precipitate." He took her hands. "We'll spend a great deal of time together, I promise. I'm sure you're tired after the journey and would like to rest quietly in your room. John will be near if you should want anything."

John the Jailer. "Thank you, Papa. I am tired. I should

like something to read. Is the account of Artois's Vendée Expedition still in the library?"

"Yes, of course. Perhaps I can correct its Jacobin slant for you after dinner."

Ushering her out of the study, he locked the door and strolled with her to the foyer where John handed him his hat, gloves, and crop. He kissed her cheek. "Until this evening, my dear."

Catherine watched him mount a bay stallion and trot down the drive. Dear Papa doesn't trust me as far as he can throw me, she mused, and that's exactly why I'll get to Edinburgh to see Flynn!

John Enderly reviewed his daughter's brief story. Although she had made no slips, the tale had yawning gaps; its comparison to the prisoner's version might be interesting. Her return was awkward, but her unusual beauty presented possibilities. She was not yet twenty-one; that left nearly two months to decide whether she would prove more useful dead than alive.

To receive his first real information virtually on the eve of her return was a peculiar coincidence. The anonymous note had simply stated his daughter would be reentering England via Liverpool within the week. If he were to have men about the docks and the Cockcrow Inn, he might intercept the man who had ruined him. It had cost them, but the marines had taken him alive. When the prisoner awoke in his cell and catlike green eyes glared through the bars, the watch officer knew he had his man.

Without delay, Sean was taken to Sergeant Worthy to have his tongue unlocked. Despite his rigid control, his nerves crawled as Worthy slit off his clothing. His boots were neatly placed, as if by a valet, near the door of the two-storied stone room. Worthy was fastidious despite his huge-muscled bulk. His amiable pug face did nothing to dispel the icy knot in Sean's gut. A cat-o'-nine-tails hung on the frame that held him suspended by the wrists, ankles tied apart to the support columns, his toes just touching the floor. He blinked, a sweat of anticipation pricking his skin.

Worthy tested the ropes at his wrists, which were

wrapped in coarse cotton to absorb perspiration and keep the prisoner from slipping free in an effusion of his own fear. "Well, lad. That about does it." The man held out a handful of wicked iron points hooked to the rawhide strips of the cat. "Any time ye've had enough, sing out. I an't the sort who likes to hurt a man more than necessary, but I do my job, see, and I'm good at it." He backed off, then seemed to remember something and tapped Sean's shoulder. The young Irishman flinched. "Don't tense up. The cat can tear tight muscles permanent."

Sean tried to concentrate on the rope cutting into his wrists, the pounding ache in his head from the pistol butt, anything but what he knew was coming. But he could not know, could not imagine, the searing claw of pain that made him gasp and snap against the bonds. The second raked across the first and he bit blood. Relaxing made him feel exposed, and with all his will, he fought the urge to knot his muscles against the pain. Tried to go inside himself. Hide. With the methodical timing of a clock, Worthy cut his back to shreds. Darkness was a long time in coming; when it did, Worthy had to pour three buckets of stinging salt water over him to bring him around. He pulled his dripping head up by the hair. "Anything to say, lad?"

Sean blinked, trying to focus, then shook his head like a tired dog.

The pug sighed. "Well, it's up to you." He dropped his victim's head, then placed a heated brazier on a nearby tripod. "After I was pressed into the marines, I spent fifteen years in the Orient. Might say I learned the finer points of my trade there." He propped long needles into the brazier. Thick fingers slid along Sean's nape. "Them yellow devils can make a man howl just by a touch." He applied a subtle pressure to the medulla and the Irishman's head jerked back, lips drawn across his teeth in a rictus; the boring pain was a nail driving into his brain, making the pain of the lash a comparative caress. Then Worthy's hand shifted to his spine and he tore at the bonds; when it moved to his groin, he made animal sounds of fear, then began screaming and went on screaming as the fingers finally became white hot needles that explored the nerves in his body until no sound emerged from cracked, bloody lips though he still screamed. Until he didn't know Worthy. Didn't know his own name. Anything.

The viscount on the balcony above went home to dinner.

"Papa, I'm going to the stables this morning to see Numidian. Why not join me?"

"Unfortunately, my dear," the viscount murmured, "the horse was stolen by a stableboy, the one who was your driver the night of the kidnapping. I suspect he was in league with . . . Señor Perez."

Catherine's brisk spirits plummeted convincingly. "Numidian, gone? Oh, Papa! Amin isn't gone too, is he?"

"Your mother left him a legacy. I daresay he'll be with us until doomsday." The last was sardonic. No love was lost between the Englishman and the Arab.

"I suppose I'll have to make do," Catherine sighed. "We haven't ridden together in years, Papa. Do come."

"You know I detest horses," he replied lazily. "Having to do without a coach is tedious enough without riding as sport." Then he relented gracefully. "I've another errand in Liverpool, but tomorrow we'll do something together, I promise."

"Dear Papa, you are good to me." Catherine ran upstairs and hastily donned a habit, then hurried to the stables.

After a gravely dignified but happy reunion with Amin, she led him to the riding ring out of earshot of John, who had followed to lurk behind a nearby boxwood hedge. Once Amin realized she had come to despise her father and knew of his vicious career, he was a mine of information. Finally, she dug to its core.

"I remember Mother's death now. I'm free of it except for one thing. She promised to tell me a secret the day she was killed; she never had the chance."

"Your mother had resolved to separate from my lord Enderly."

She felt a cold dread. "The accident was rather oddly timed." Amin said nothing. "Amin, Father didn't really love her and he had all her money. Why would he care so much what she did?"

"My lord Enderly is an exceedingly proud man." He

388

stressed the last words with an inflection of hatred she had never heard him use.

"He murdered her? Out of pride?" she whispered, aghast.

"Pride and greed. Had she persuaded you to go with her, he would have lost all possibility of her fortune."

"What fortune?"

"On your twenty-first birthday, you will inherit the Vigny estates."

"But there are none. The Revolution took everything."

He shrugged. "If the Bourbons return to power, you will be rich. The château and its lands, the Parisian and European properties are impressive when united under a single heir. You even own an island near Jamaica."

"Then by encouraging my mental collapse, Papa would have been executor," she mused. "How inconvenient for me to return just now."

"Particularly so because you are not his daughter. I would have preferred to keep these secrets for a time, but you are in immediate danger, my lady."

Shortly, the tale was out. "Brendan Culhane is my father?" The color drained from her face so suddenly he thought she must fall. "Oh, dear God!" Stunned with horror and grief, she clung to the fence.

"My lady, please!" She slowly straightened, standing as if propped. "My lady? What is the matter?"

"The man you suspected at Ingram is Brendan Culhane's son, Sean." Her grip on the rail tightened. "I was his mistress. I married his brother Liam two years ago." She twisted at the rail in growing fury. "That was the weapon Liam used! He must have discovered the truth in the legal contest for the estate. No wonder he was so willing to allow an uncontested divorce! I had grounds to divorce him whether he agreed or not!" Tears welled from her eyes as her head bowed. "Oh, my Sean, we are surely the forsaken of God!"

"Is Sean Culhane the one who returned you?" She nodded. "My lady, they knew of his coming. There was an informant."

"Only Liam knew Sean was coming here!" She gritted

her teeth. That malevolent . . . there was no word sufficient! "Did they intercept him?"

"I have inquired discreetly, yet I do not know."

Her dazed wits sharpened. "If they've caught him, a yacht called the *Megan* may still be in the harbor." She picked at fence splinters. "Enderly may let me go to Scotland if he hopes I'll lead him to the people he's after." She waved at the breeze ruffling the grass. "By sail, I can reach Edinburgh in three days, God willing a steady wind. It's the only chance," she added bleakly, "for if Sean's in prison, I can do little alone."

A bottle waved under Sean's nose; his head jerked weakly, trying to avoid the biting smell of ammonia.

"That's enough. He's coming around," came from a nebulous shape wavering on a gray horizon. Another shape was attached to the bottle and he peered at it with dull curiosity. His entire being felt like an open wound.

"Wait. A little more. He's blacking out again." The Irishman's head twisted away.

"Good morning, Mr. Fitzhugh. Can you hear me?"

Sean moved his lips, but all that came forth was a groan.

"The prisoner seems rather inarticulate, Mr. Worthy."

Worthy shrugged. "I worked on him just shy of the point where he'd die or go barmy. It's my opinion, milord, ye'll get nothing out of him."

Enderly's crop tapped against his hand, his only sign of irritation. "You're a stubborn man, Mr. Fitzhugh, but that won't save you. Your refusal to break confirms your guilt. You're too headstrong to follow orders and you're not stupid enough to die for another man." He pushed the crop under his prisoner's chin, abruptly forcing his head up. "I may not be able to retrieve my fortune and my sullied reputation, but like Shakespeare's Shylock, I *will* have my pound of flesh and more, beginning with your vaunted manhood."

Sean rasped each word. "You . . . envious . . . faggot!"

Enderly's mouth whitened and his knuckles strained on the crop. "You'd like to taunt me into killing you with a blow, wouldn't you?" He turned to Worthy and dictated

calmly as if giving an order to a tradesman, "Geld him."
He lifted a finger and let it fall.

Listening in numb, incredulous silence, Sean went berserk, shrieking a lifetime of hate at his enemy. Finally, he hung, twitching, semiconscious, eyes as sulphurous as a demon's from hell. Enderly gracefully withdrew a packet from his pocket. "In this package, Mr. Worthy, you'll find a woman's undergarment. Bring me his equipment in it. I intend to present the package to my daughter."

"Leave her alone! She has no part in this. Leave her alone!"

"Thank you, Mr. Fitzhugh. The last few minutes have been most rewarding. Now, if you will excuse me, I'll leave you to the expertise of Mr. Worthy."

After witnessing the Irishman's violent outburst, Worthy took no chances. He summoned four guards to take the prisoner from the flogging brace and spread-eagle him, still fighting, to an X-shaped stone slab in the center of the room. Adjustable iron manacles imbedded in the stone stretched limbs to the straining point and securely locked wrists and ankles. The condemned man was trussed for butchering in less than five minutes.

Worthy dismissed the soldiers and began to strop a knife that resembled a medical scalpel. "Watchin' only makes it worse, lad. The sharper the blade, the less ye feel. I'll be as quick as I can."

The knife flittered blue-white, and sweat streamed from the Irishman's bleeding body as he strained against the bonds.

Worthy tested the blade against his thumb, then took a position between the prisoner's thighs.

"Jesus, Mary, Mother of God," Sean whispered, unable to take his eyes from the descending blade.

Suddenly, the spread-eagled man arched like a drawn bow, tendons standing out like crawling snakes as the knife sliced cleanly. His body convulsed, his hopeless howl of outrage tearing through the roof of his brain, up, up, echoing against the stone walls. Blackness filled his mouth and eyes and he plummeted backwards, headfirst into a twisting pit.

CHAPTER 20

The Nadir

Persuading Enderly to permit her to go to Edinburgh proved as simple as Catherine had supposed, and less than two weeks after setting foot in England, she dressed in an inn in Scotland to catch the eye of a royal duke. The claret velvet dress and pelisse were trimmed in ermine, the muff of the same luxurious fur, with pendant tips. A flicker of admiration in Mignon's eye, although quickly suppressed, was a greater boost to her confidence than a host of male compliments.

"Mignon, I wish you to go to the university and copy a posting of this week's surgical lectures. You may be followed. I assume you can elude an interested party?"

Although the narrow streets were snow-drifted below their creaking ornamental shop signs, Catherine ordered an open carriage and directed the driver to the park. As the man cracked his whip and urged the horses toward the broader avenues of the city, a second carriage followed discreetly after them. Beautiful in a strange, brooding way, the stone buildings of Edinburgh spilled over a series of gorges. The massive bulk of Edinburgh Castle on its bluff loomed over misty rooftops. Although the park was bleak in winter, its formal flowerbeds barren, ornamental shrubbery formed fanciful sculptures under blankets of white, and children in bright caps shrieked as they frolicked through the formations.

Watching them, the young countess felt a quiet happiness. Now certain Sean's life was within her, she shared her mother's joy and pain when she had carried a child of the man she loved, but could never have. Catherine could not hate her parents; she understood their anguish too well.

Shortly, she saw the innkeeper was an accurate gossip; a group of riders trotted along a path at the far end of the park. She signaled the driver to take her closer. Slim and dark among the riders was Angoulême; with him were three young men and an older one. As they walked the horses, snatches of male laughter drifted across the snow. With a quick order to the driver to stop, she dismounted the carriage. Running lightly toward the children, she scooped up a handful of snow, packed it expertly, and let the nearest boy have it in the back of the head. He grabbed up ammunition of his own, spun around, then gaped at the elegant culprit. Her teasing laughter tinkled invitingly in the crisp air. "Are you going to let me get away with that?"

"I canna pelt a lady, ma'am," the boy faltered.

"Why not? I duck like a trooper. Retaliate!"

Two other children goggled as their companion nervously tossed a timid snowball in the lady's general direction. Catherine batted it with her muff, sending it exploding into powder. "Come on, you can do better than that! *I* can do better than that!" So saying, she scooped up another wad of snow and knocked his cap off. The boy reddened as another caught him in the shoulder. Indignation conquered gallantry, and he responded with energy. Soon Catherine's missiles began to connect with the other children. Merrily, everybody pelted away.

The men on horseback, noticing the furious battle and the lovely girl defending a hedge fort, drew near with predictable masculine curiosity. Suddenly, the young woman whirled. With marksman's accuracy, she dispatched a wet lump of snow into Angoulême's left ear. He gasped and grabbed at his head. The older man behind him quickly kneed his mount forward to block the duke's body with his own, intending to jostle the assailant aside. Catherine sidestepped and dug the horse sharply in the ribs. He shied, neatly unseating his rider in the snow. The children

393

cheered and in defense of their new friend hurled a flurry of snowballs at the mounted riders. Angoulême ducked, trying to get a glimpse of his initial assailant. She giggled and called merrily, "Are you prepared to surrender, gentlemen?"

Louis's eyes widened. "Catherine! I mean . . ."

"Good day, Your Grace."

Brushing snow from their shoulders and hats, the others stared aghast at the reckless young woman. The children paused, hands full, watching the men.

A mischievous smile lit Catherine's lovely face. *"Quelle assassine,* to dispatch a duke in so ignoble a fashion! *La Gloire de France* and all his forces leveled by a snowball bombardment!"

Lips twitched, but no one quite dared to laugh. Louis was thoroughly embarrassed, even more so because of his engagement and the Enderlys' disgrace, but *Dieu,* she was a gorgeous creature! The countess's eyes sparkled like a rajah's jewels and the snow on her lashes was entrancing. "There is no danger, Rochand. I know the young lady," he said edgily to the man scrambling to his feet.

Sapphire eyes slanted up at him under fantastic lashes. "Are you so certain I'm not dangerous, Your Grace?"

He flushed. "My lady, may I present my equerries . . ." He rattled off their names unhappily, finishing with the dismounted rider, Rochand, his father's aide. "Gentlemen, Lady Catherine Enderly, la comtesse de Vigny."

Catherine swept a curtsy a shade deeper than necessary. The children, recognizing the spew of titles even in French, faded away, thinking better of a new attack. The young duke's companions were openly intrigued. The beauty's scandalous reputation was an open challenge. And how well she knew it.

Even Louis, against his better judgment, felt a sharp twinge of regret. What a desirable wench! And she had deliberately sought him out. Obviously, she wished to curry favor for her father. How far would she be willing to go? He curbed his fancies with an effort. Seeming to know what he was thinking, she smiled up at him with a roguishly assessing glance. He stirred uncomfortably. Best to end this charade quickly and meet her privately later. "I apologize,

Countess, but I have pressing duties this afternoon. Will you forgive us?"

A succulent lower lip protruded softly. "Don't you mean to invite me to court, Your Grace? I may be forced to leave the city tomorrow. Papa asked me specifically to present his compliments to *Monsieur le duc.*"

Louis whitened. Damn the girl!

His equerries looked at each other. The lady did not lack for nerve, but she clearly stirred the young duke's imagination. If he snubbed her now, he could say good-by forever to enjoying her favor. If he claimed her, they would have to wait their turns, and no one wanted to wait.

Catherine's eyes widened, their mysterious depths lovely beyond imagining, her soft mouth vulnerable, somehow pleading now. The fur drifted slightly in the softly falling snow. Louis imagined that mouth parting under his in gratitude, those eyes darkening as her body answered his desire. His father might rebuke him, but what difference could one brief audience make? It was so little to yield for so rich a reward. The others regarded her like so many epauletted vultures. "If his appointments permit, I'm sure my father will be happy to receive you this afternoon, Countess. May we escort you?" Her smile, suddenly radiant just for him, warmed his vitals like hot wine.

"Thank you, Your Grace," she said softly.

Ah, how vulnerable, how feminine she is underneath the impudence, he thought as she signaled her driver. How I shall enjoy her.

Artois's hawkish brows lowered as his son hesitantly asked permission to present the countess. "You're aware, Louis, I've no wish to receive her?"

"Yes, Father, but I thought it could do no harm to be civil. After all, she's not responsible for her father's misdeeds."

"As parents are not always to be held accountable for the idiotic indiscretions of their children," said Artois ironically, staring coldly at his reddening son. "This is unlike you, Louis."

"I apologize, Father," Louis said, shamefaced. "Shall I send her away?"

The duke sighed in exasperation. Louis's strategy was childishly clear, but if he was bent on an affair, the woman would be better dealt with now in order to avoid trouble later. "Admit her. But Louis"—his head lifted slightly—"don't presume on my patience again."

"Yes, Father," the young man murmured meekly.

When the countess de Vigny swept into the room and curtsied gracefully before him, Artois knew why Louis's usual, clerklike timidity had disintegrated. The young woman's incredible beauty was like that of a subtly perfumed winter rose. The ermine-lined hood, lowered in respect for his prestige, revealed an exquisite face with skin so translucent the pulse of her throat was a faint blue beneath the skin. Ebony satin hair swept up in a sleek chignon emphasized her hypnotic eyes. No trace of the impudent girl in the park was apparent now. An aristocrat of the *ancien régime* stood before him, vintage of lineage apparent in refinement and regal pride of carriage. What a queen she would have made, he thought regretfully as he murmured his greetings. Although he assumed she would shortly begin a plea for her father, happily, the young countess seemed disinclined to discuss the viscount, and conversed with quiet intelligence about the new regime in France.

The ten-minute audience stretched. As there would be no second interview, Artois found himself reluctant to dismiss her. Her claret velvet gown was strikingly effective against the gray stone walls with their heavy, dour tapestries. He detested Edinburgh, and the dank castle in particular. Presbyterians were a grim lot. Catherine de Vigny was like a breath of Parisian summer, warm and lulling to the senses. Even her skin seemed subtly sun warmed. As a man, he was interested; as a prince, he was wary. Undoubtedly, the girl was her father's tool, and Artois knew enough of Enderly's guile to suspect a cobra under the velvet; but her directness and absence of flirtation gave him pause.

He heard himself offering to take her cloak. Her head inclined gracefully as he removed the fur-lined pelisse from her shoulders. A tempting nape and shoulder urged a man to brush them with his lips. A slender, swanlike throat and delicate collarbones curved above lovely breasts, creamy and silken in their low décolletage. It had been a long time since Artois had desired a woman at first sight, yet this one had something indefinable. The mouth and the way she moved suggested a deep and conscious sensuality. She appeared to be a woman for whom men held no secrets, yet who would draw them like a flame, promising realization of secret longings, not all of them of the body. A madonna. A woman. How could the frigid loins of an Enderly produce such a creature? She sensed his keen scrutiny and turned to gaze up at him. Eyes a man could kill for, if only to see himself alone reflected in their depths. She seemed to know what he was thinking, yet while there was reserve, there was compassion, too. "I see now, Catherine, I was foolish to propose you as a mistress to my son," he remarked quietly in French. "A tsar, perhaps; an autocrat; but never Louis."

"Louis is a nice boy," she replied gently.

"Yes, the princess will suit him well." He studied her. "You must resent the offer being withdrawn."

"I never knew of it, Your Grace, so there was no disappointment."

Artois's eyebrows lifted slightly. "I assumed your father would encourage the match. I would have married you to a duke: Guise, probably."

"The viscount was honored by your consideration, as was I upon learning of it recently, after acceptance was impossible. I have been absent from England for the past three years, you see."

"Without communication with your father?" he asked, startled.

"I preferred then, as I do now, to keep those years private from everyone."

He became blunt. "Even at the cost of your reputation, Comtesse?"

"Even so."

No cub of Enderly's could so completely lack ambition. His wariness mounted.

Deliberately, he changed the subject as he guided her through the royal apartments, pointing out masterpieces of art among the appointments. He paused casually by a

Louis XIV clock. "Your father obtained this piece for me. Is it not magnificent?"

She touched the fine inlay of the case. "Forgive me, monsieur, but Mother was a gifted collector; she taught me a great deal. The dark wood in this inlay comes from the South American interior; it was unknown in Europe until about fifty years ago." She turned. "An obvious discrepancy to a dealer, monsieur. The viscount would never present such a piece to you. There must be some mistake."

"There is no mistake. Lesser pieces, presented at auction in London, were so obviously fraudulent the dealers nearly caned the auctioneer senseless." He watched her, waiting to see which way she would jump.

"The viscount may be desperate for money, but he's not idiot enough to try to gain it this way. Fortunes may be recovered; reputations, rarely." She looked at him levelly. "Possibly you know him well enough to realize that power far more than money lures him. He has little real interest in possessions, only in the position they support."

Artois answered with equal frankness, "You defend your father's reputation well, Countess. How do you defend your own?"

"I offer no defense, monsieur. I have nothing to regret."

"Even though you may shortly be unable to retain any semblance of position?"

She smiled slightly. "I prefer obscurity."

"What do you want of me?" he asked softly, his hooded eyes unreadable.

"My life, monsieur."

He frowned. "Are you in danger?"

"This December twenty-third I become sole heiress to the Vigny fortune. I have reason to believe John Enderly murdered my mother to retain that inheritance. He might even murder me. He's not my real father; exposure of that fact will remove him from all claim to my estate."

"I see." His tone was skeptical, but he was intrigued. Though the tale was wild, his experience of Enderly's ruthless cunning led him to believe it held more than a thread of possibility.

"Without his knowledge, I married two years ago. Although I separated from my husband without scandal, I am now with child. That child must be protected."

"What do you want me to do?"

"Extend Enderly some reassurance of friendship and proof of regard for me. Under your protection, I would be invulnerable. No amount of money would lead him to risk your wrath if he thought his future depended on your favor. If he also believes my child is yours, the baby and I would be safe forever."

He marveled at her cool audacity. "And if I refuse?"

"Then, if I should die before the age of twenty-one, I ask you to make public my parentage; also to become executor of my estate."

He let out a faint whistle. "You ask a great deal. How do I know this tale isn't some incredible concoction to reestablish your father's position? My own honor would be forfeit."

"My death will provide proof, monsieur."

"You wager for high stakes, Countess," he said slowly. "What have you to put on the table?"

She offered her lips. Without hesitation, he crushed his mouth down on hers.

He kept her the night. He was an expert lover, but with none of his many mistresses had he felt this need to infuse his soul into a woman's body as he drew both pleasure and tenderness from her. This woman was sad; he knew it and that he could do nothing to dispel it. So, he had loved her with his man's body and heart. For the time, the prince had been gone; only warmth and need had remained. When she had cried out softly, he knew she had not been pretending. She had loved and been loved. Now she gave without reserve, without cheating.

By the morning light, their faces showed the effects of passion and lack of sleep, flesh drawn against the bone. Artois watched Catherine use his brush to untangle her hair, sending it into a cloud about her naked shoulders. Her spine was straight, the slender back curving to small buttocks. She was pale, mouth still swollen from his kisses. Her breasts lifted as she shook out her hair and began to twist it up into a chignon. As she pinned, he kissed her nape. "I took you many times and I still want you, yet you haven't asked whether I shall give you your desire."

"You fulfill my desire, Charles," she answered quietly. "As for the other, you will or will not help me. You owe me nothing."

"Would you have given yourself to me if your life and fortune weren't at stake?"

Catherine was silent for a moment. Sooner or later, she must ask for her beloved's life. To try to conceal Sean's importance to her was pointless; Artois was no fool. More important, she had already come to respect him too much to treat him like one. "I love another man; I always will. We can never join in flesh as you and I have. He is forever denied to me, while you may fill my nights, my days with life, perhaps love." She carried his hand to her cheek. "I want you to want me. I need you as a man."

"The child is his, isn't it?"

"Yes."

He turned away. "As a man, I wish you were more capable of lying. It seems I must be content with scraps from another man's feast." She said nothing. He touched her mouth. "Isn't your life worth a small deceit?"

"His safety as well as mine depends on your help. He may be imperiled even now, perhaps dead. Before coming here, I was prepared to both lie and whore to save him. Now, knowing you, I can only beg for him and my child, for I love them more than my life."

"Scruples are ill-suited to whores, Countess," was the bitter reply. His hawkish faced resumed its usual polite mask. "However, my compliments to the fellow. He's a most fortunate man."

"No," she whispered. "He's not lucky at all."

A white glare of light needled under Sean's lashes. He stirred, unwilling to leave the quiet, protecting dark, then more restlessly, feeling restraints on his limbs. His back began to sting annoyingly and he jerked weakly, twisting his head to see what held him. Leather straps bound his wrists, loosely chained to an iron bed; his ankles were strapped as well. He strained at the fetters, rattling the bed. Then, feeling the heavy, ominous bandage at his groin, the Irishman moaned in his throat like an animal. He went limp, silent, helpless sobs welling up.

A shadow moved against his closed eyes and a hand touched his shoulder. Sean's streaming eyes flew open, his teeth bared in a snarl. "Damn you, butchers! Kill me and be done with it!"

"Easy, lad." A brown-haired, middle-aged man with spectacles pushed him down, not ungently, although Sean could not have fought him. The fight was gone. He lay inert, face averted to hide tears he was helpless to either stop or wipe away. Like a woman, he thought hopelessly; not even that.

"It's not so bad as you think," the man said. "My name is Thatcher Marcus and I've been medical officer in several prisons. Sergeant Worthy knows his business; he's nearly as deft a surgeon as I am, for all those meaty fists of his. You're lucky to be alive. Many men die of shock or hemorrhage; some simply resolve to die. I had a fight, pulling you through."

"Do you expect gratitude? Do you think I *want* to live like this?"

The hand was at his shoulder again. "Do you think I like seeing men treat other men like beasts? I cannot unshackle a man's body, I can only heal it. His degraded spirit must be left to God."

"God!" The man on the bed laughed hoarsely. "God is a fiend! There *is* no difference between God and the devil. He's the arch neuter, uncaring, unfeeling . . ." His laughter dissolved into a strangled groan.

"You're not a neuter. Haven't you realized why you're still alive?"

The dark head turned slowly. "Worthy cut into me. I felt it."

"He removed one testicle, not both. You're entirely capable of begetting children."

The green eyes were vulnerable. "I'm . . . still a man?"

The doctor smiled. "More than most. It's a rare one indeed that Worthy's unable to break."

Sean closed his eyes. "Enderly thinks I'll bargain for what's left, doesn't he?"

"Yes."

Sweeping fatigue weighted Sean down. He expelled the air in his lungs. "How long have I got?"

"Three weeks. I can stall him a bit, but he's not an idiot."

Sean felt his strength sapping. "You must explain to Enderly's daughter . . . about the package . . ."

"I cannot help you there," Marcus said quickly. "I'd join you on the block. Rest now, lad. We'll talk again."

"You've got to listen . . . she'll be sick again." He fought to press away the fog, but it curled about him and his leaden limbs pulled him down.

Sean awoke to Marcus changing his bandages. "The incision is healing cleanly. You'll be fit soon." When the patient said nothing, Marcus rebandaged him and began to apply ointment to the burns on his body.

"What happens if I don't cooperate with Enderly?" Sean asked abruptly.

"Sergeant Worthy finishes what he started. I advise you to be agreeable. There's always some hope if you're alive."

"Is that how you began to give in? And Worthy? He's a goddamned zombie."

Expressionless, Marcus stood up. "I'm going to unshackle you long enough to do your back. Do I have to call the guards?"

"No."

Marcus unlocked the shackles and helped him turn over. His touch on the lacerated flesh, though gentle, was enough to make his patient grip the bars. He kept talking. "In the past, Enderly has given prisoners who've refused him to his soldiers before returning them to sentence or the cells. Some of those men have been worked over with musket butts until nearly every bone was broken. Some had their genitals hacked off; some were mutilated, rendered mindless. He doesn't recognize a refusal. If you're lucky, you might make them mad enough to kill you before turning you over to Worthy." He wiped his hands on a linen towel. "I'm done."

Sean turned over on his own, lips tightening. "What makes you think I want to stay alive?"

"In your delirium, you repeated a woman's name. You seemed to want to keep her from believing you dead."

"She already does," Culhane answered dully. "Enderly's shown her his rotten proof by now."

"Perhaps not. He's unpredictable. You can be sure of nothing but Worthy's knife."

Sean said nothing. The man was right. But to grovel for a life that had become less than dirt to him! He stared up at the whitewashed ceiling long after Marcus had gone.

That same afternoon, Mignon entered Catherine's room at the Royal Crown Inn, took off her bonnet and pelisse. She looked at Catherine, who stood tensely waiting. "Well, I saw your Doctor Flynn. I don't know the man. He can rattle your praises in Gaelic until the sun blackens. You've wasted your time."

Catherine wanted to burst into tears. She gestured aimlessly, then wandered to a chair and dropped into it. "Mignon, I'm carrying Sean Culhane's child, a child he may never see. He's been robbed, robbed of everything. He's got to have *something!*" Tears began to slip down her cheeks. "Please. Not for me. Hate me. But help me. There's no one else. He's alone." The words ground out from her soul. "I cannot bear to think of him alone."

Mignon looked at the huddled figure for a moment. "Culhane's a fool. But you're no less a fool." Her face twisted. "You may as well hear it now. Culhane was taken into the prison at Liverpool the night he brought you back. Likely he's dead. Lucky if he is, for there's none to help him; save me, he let his agents go their ways after the rebellion."

But Catherine did not hear her. She was already slipping to the floor.

"There's a gentleman to see you, my lady," Mignon said from the bedroom door. "A Monsieur Artois."

Catherine slowly sat up and absently brushed at her hair. "I'll see him. Please get my bedjacket, Mignon." The maid helped her into it, plumped the pillows, then admitted Artois and withdrew.

He quickly crossed the room, concern all over his dark

403

features. "Catherine, you're ill!" He sat on the bed and took her hand. "Why didn't you tell me?"

"I'm not ill, Charles. I saw no need to alarm you."

His dark eyes searched hers. "Did you think I wouldn't come? That I didn't care?"

"No, Charles, I didn't think that."

"Is it the child?"

She touched his face. "The child is well. You're good to be concerned." She smiled. "I hoped you'd come to say good-by."

His grip on her hand tightened imperceptibly. "You're leaving Edinburgh?"

"I leave on the tide."

"That's absurd! I won't let you!"

"Charles, you cannot tie me here like a lapdog. Please don't try."

Angered, he stood up. "What is this? A ruse to force my hand so I'll back your scurrilous father? Become an after-the-fact cuckold for your probably illegitimate child? You take me for a fool, madame! You languish most attractively of a nonexistent ailment, yet you would have me believe you well enough to make your frail way home to a martyr's end. . . .What the devil, woman?" He glowered. "Why do you smile? Do you think me amusing?"

"No, Charles," Catherine replied, her smile fading, "you just reminded me of someone."

"Him?" he snarled. "Your lucky fellow?"

Her face crumpled suddenly. "They say he's dead. I must go home. I have to know. I must find him." Her last words were sobbed against his chest. Artois held her until she stilled. "I'm sorry; this is all so unfair to you," she whispered.

"Shh, I'm an iron man, *p'tite*. I'm only in danger of rusting from your tears."

She smiled wanly against his damp silk stock and curled her fingers into his lapel. "I'll miss your clanking about. You have a terrible temper."

"Yes. I'm even thought to be dangerous. Didn't your papa tell you?"

"He said you would eat me for an hors d'oeuvre."

He lightly chucked her under the chin. "Only because

404

that's all I can get." He tilted her head up. "Tell Enderly whatever you like. That I'm madly in love with you. That there is a baby Bourbon in that small belly of yours. Perdition, I'll tell him myself. Have him come to Edinburgh. Find out what you need to know about the baby's father, then leave Windemere immediately. I want you to come to me."

"Is that an order, Charles?"

"The prince orders you; the man can only hope."

She kissed him then, lips clinging as his arms tightened about her. Artois felt his pulse begin to race, and gently put her away from him. "You tempt me to lock you into this room and throw the key out into the snow." He went to the writing desk and scratched out a note, then sealed it and stamped his signet into the wax. "This tells Enderly about everything but my paternity of your child. As an heir to the throne of France, I cannot put such an admission in writing. Naturally, you'll want to wait a few weeks before telling him anyway. I'll affirm the child's parentage when he comes to Edinburgh."

"Thank you, Charles."

He looked at her obliquely. "Wouldn't it be much simpler, *chérie,* for me to have him killed?"

Her eyes widened as she started to protest, but he waved her to silence. "Princes are inclined to practicality. Direct measures avoid excessive paperwork, if nothing else. I shall abide by your wishes in this, but if Enderly crosses me, he dies. Is your man in prison?"

"Yes, but more than prison walls separate us," she replied bleakly.

He scribbled another paper and sealed his signature. "This may help. You can fill in the name." He rose, crossed to the bed, and stood looking down at her. "You've been honest with me; I will be the same with you. I *am* a dangerous man. I never settle for scraps. I hope your lover is dead, for if he is not, I may be tempted to kill him. Never tell me his name, Catherine, as you value his life." He held out his hand, palm down. "Acknowledge me as your rightful sovereign, Countess, for I will be king." She kissed his ring. Slowly, he turned his hand palm up. "And what acknowledgment for the man?" She laid her cheek against his

405

hand. He touched her hair. "Good. We understand one another. I'll summon a coach with my crest to take you home. Will you be ready to leave within the hour?"

"Yes, of course."

He kissed her lightly. *"Au revoir, petite mère des rois."*

Feeling like a Christmas goose being fattened for the kill, Sean idly picked at his tray. Knowing he had to regain strength if he hoped to escape, he tried to eat everything he was given, starting with the thickly cut meats, but he had no heart for it. The door opened and his appetite was little improved when Enderly strode in with Marcus behind him.

"Mr. Fitzhugh, you're looking well. The menu seems to agree with you."

"I've gotten by on less."

"I daresay. We must have a pleasant chat about your past. Doctor . . ." He waved a negligent hand. "Remove the bandages."

Sean felt a wave of malevolence for the men who appraised his body with the same insolence a rake might look over a whore. He masked his expression by watching Marcus snip through the linen dressing and peel it away. The scar was surprisingly small, a livid line along one side of the reduced sac; Worthy had even taken up the slack. The wound was sore but not particularly noticeable unless someone was looking directly at it. Enderly was. Sean forced his hands to relax; he was starting to grip the sheet.

"Good. Pity you insisted on being maimed, but you're more sensible now, aren't you? I'll send for you tomorrow night." Enderly turned to Marcus. "Refasten those shackles. I wouldn't want him to accidently damage his wound in his sleep."

The guards came for him promptly at eight: four of them, all big, one a hulking bruiser bigger than Rouge. He dumped clothing onto the bench against the wall, then jerked his head to a corporal with hands the size of shovels. When the corporal unlocked the shackles, Sean stood up, two bayonets pointed at his belly. "Try anything funny and ye'll be holdin' yer guts in with yer hands," growled the bruiser. His tiny eyes reminded the Irishman of a mongoose.

After he dressed in a smaller man's clothes, they manacled his hands behind his back. An expressionless corporal attached chain-linked irons to his ankles. The mongoose nudged him in the ribs. "Move out, bucko."

John Enderly spread his hands apologetically. "You must forgive the chains. After a time, I hope we can dispense with them." Sean's guards stayed at either elbow. Mongoose and Shovel Hands took up positions against either wall.

Enderly gestured toward a Louis XV chair opposite him at a lavishly laid table. "I've just finished, but would you care for a glass of wine?"

"Not particularly." Let's get this over with, damn you, Sean thought tautly. The place reminded him of a bordello. The bed was covered with leopard skins and jewel-colored pillows, while on the stone walls incongruous draperies hung in swags. Candles in brass sconces created mosaics of light on the mirrors and oriental carpet.

"You look a bit tense, Robert," Enderly murmured. "Dare I hope you're impatient to confess and have done with any more unpleasantness?" His light mockery was evident as he stood up, the light picking up the curve of his lips as he came nearer.

"No?"

The Englishman began to unbutton Sean's shirt, smiling as his prisoner tensed. He caressed him, watching his eyes.

Disgust wrenched Sean's gut. He focused through the man's eyes to the back of his skull, anywhere but the eyes of the other men.

"Have you *really* nothing to say?"

With a snarl, Sean drove his knee upward with all the force he could muster. And connected with nothing.

Enderly must have expected just such a reaction. He twisted away with practiced swiftness and a rifle butt cracked across Sean's skull, stunning him. The two guards on either side jerked his arms up high behind his back, forcing him to his knees, and dimly he felt the newly healed back open. They shoved him, still dazed, onto the floor, then clamped a rifle stock behind his neck. With lightning efficiency, they had him stripped and spread-eagled face down, one man on each arm and leg, holding him taut. His head clearing, he twisted and bucked like a pinioned stallion.

They took turns with gun butts until he no longer needed to be held down. At some point his will dissolved, ground away until he was broken in body and spirit. He wanted to beg, but only a croak would emerge from his throat. Finally, they rolled him over and stood back. Enderly leaned down and thumbed back the Irishman's eyelid, then, hearing a groan, touched his mouth almost tenderly. "Tell me what I want to know. Say it, Robert, and no one will hurt you any more. Otherwise . . ." There was a silence, then the dark head nodded. "Say it."

"Yes. Please . . ." The words were broken, like a sob of need. The green eyes looked up at him as if he were a savior, then slanted into those of a fiend. Before the guards could react, Sean wrenched at the man's hair with one hand and smashed his nose with the other. The guards went at him all at once, pounding at him with fists and boots. Then a musket butt smashed down on his skull and his grip went lax. They dragged Enderly, still screaming, out from under him, then went on kicking him in the head and sides.

One of them helped Enderly to a chair. "Take him," he croaked. "Tell Worthy. I want him . . . hacked to bits!"

The guard nodded and the four of them carried the slack body out, face down, head dangling.

Faraway, Sean heard the four marines complaining about his weight. Like a gnat's nagging stings in the midst of livid pain, Blankface's thumbnail dug into his left Achilles tendon, keeping him conscious and aware of what awaited him in a room just beyond the opening guardroom door.

"Hah. Looks like the viscount was in a bit of a miff," observed the chief guard, stepping back to let them in.

"That an't half," said Blankface, dropping Sean's left foot. "Ye ought to see old Johnny's face. Nose all over it."

He strolled over to the wall to light a cheroot from a candle. Shovel Hands dropped his leg; he saw no point holding up dead weight if everyone was bent on gossip.

"Pick him up and let's get on with it," Raker growled. "I an't plannin' to spend the night with him. Besides, he's tricky—" The warning came too late. The battered, silent man exploded, jabbing and kicking. With a maniac's strength, he wrenched away as a guard went down screaming with a smashed knee. Shovel Hands sailed headfirst into the wall and Sean jerked the pistol from the unconscious man's crossband. Raker fired point-blank into his back. His body lurched against the wall, seeming to embrace it, then he turned, eyes blazing with hate and pain. Even as the rattled chief guard's bullet pocked stone splinters by his head, he squeezed the trigger. Raker clutched his exploding face and dropped.

Then, with his first animation of the evening, Blankface smiled from across the room and leveled his gun.

Lifting his drooping head with an effort, Sean waited with weary patience for the final bullet; when it came, he seemed almost grateful to his executioner. His body jerked once, then sagged. Leaving a streak of scarlet, he slipped down the stone.

"Appears ye got him square through the heart, Corporal," observed the guard. Sheepshanks huddled, clutching his knee, his eyes squeezed shut with pain. The fourth guard lay inert by Raker.

Blankface nudged the body in the ribs. "We'll pitch him out for the diggers."

He was cold. So cold. Like the night his childhood had been brutally wrenched from him. Tears seeped in icy rivulets down his cheeks as he shivered naked in a surfswept crevice and watched the glare of a blazing village, its sullen glow reflected from low-lying clouds heaped like dirty piles of sheared fleece. Beyond moonlit stones as luminous as skulls, the sea sighed in mourning, lulling whispers like a beguiling lure. The blanket he tried to draw over himself dissolved into icy powder between stiff fingers as he weakly plucked at the snow of the prison courtyard. Mother . . . please, I'm cold.

Go back to bed, Sean. If you are going to be king, you must be brave.

I'm lying naked in the snow. I can feel my life seeping out on the ground.

Men don't whimper. Be a man.

Don't go. Help me . . . please. Somebody. I hurt. Kit, hold me. Warm me. He tried to blink away snowflakes that froze on his lashes. High stars shone faintly through the falling snow and silently he cried out to them. Kit, I fought them. I didn't die the way you think. I'm still a man. I am . . . His head twisted in restless struggle and struck a dark shape beside him. He managed to move a hand far enough to tug at it with numb fingers. The coarse blanket came away; underneath it was a corpse, features already drawn in rigor, open eyes glassy, impervious to the gathering snow. Another corpse lay on the other side of him; and Raker's bulk, stripped of its uniform, beyond that. Hardly knowing what he did, Sean rolled over heavily, seeking warmth against the dead body. The pain of the effort shook him and he moaned against the rough blanket. Oh, God. I hurt. End it. Jehovah, God of Vengeance. You're good at killing. You've killed me over and over. When you made me Kit's brother. Up in that room. Finish it.

Yet somehow, he could not stop huddling for warmth against that corpse, could not roll away and let the cold take him quickly. You hate me too much to let me die, don't you? Inch by inch, bitterness welled up. I lost *both* balls up in that room and you know it. I haven't enough courage left to die; I used the last going for that gun. Damn you! His teeth bared in a snarl. This is how the damned die. With a grimace of outrage. Like this poor bastard I'm hugging like a friend. Well, you won't get me. I'll spit in your Stone Eye.

He pawed with new energy at the body, struggling with it until he had its filthy rags and dragged them onto himself. It took a long time but he did it with grim triumph. He rifled the other corpse for rags to tie around his feet, then clawed the ragged blanket around his shoulders like a shawl.

Finally, he began the agonizing ordeal of getting to his feet. Leaving the snow bloody with his efforts and staggering like a drunken derelict, he wandered out of the deserted courtyard to the street. The guard normally posted at the back entrance was standing on the corner with another watch, rubbing his hands and hugging himself, bored, lonely, and chilled. Shivering in the unblocked wind of the street, Sean kept to the shadows along the wall, avoiding the light from the windows across the street. As he safely turned the corner, he clutched at the bricks, digging his nails into the mortar grooves to keep from sliding to the ground.

With terrible slowness he stumbled toward the harbor, keeping to the darker streets and alleys, until he collapsed. Curled up against the cold in his rags, he lost consciousness. He came to, teeth chattering, shaking violently. From then on, he crawled.

The few people he encountered averted their eyes from his battered, filthy face and went out of their way to avoid him. A marine and his mate were more curious. As they approached, a frown of suspicion creased the corporal's forehead. "See here, what are you up to?"

Sean stretched up a hand that shook. "Thruppence, sir?" he croaked. "Thruppence for a gin?"

"Filthy sod," the mate remarked. The marine shook his head in disgust, and the two walked on.

Near the harbor, a sailor actually gave him a penny to impress his sentimental doxy. They watched him drag himself into a side street. "Lumme, poor bloke. He's leavin' blood in the snow," the girl said. "Mayhap we ought to . . ." The sailor firmly pulled her away.

At last, Culhane came to the haven he sought, an unpainted, narrow house near the harbor. Shivering uncontrollably, he leaned his head and shoulder on the back door and weakly pounded with the heel of his hand. No one came. The place was dark, neglected, the curtains drawn. If the house was empty, he would die here. He could drag himself no farther. It had taken three hours to cover the quarter-mile. He could not feel his hands and feet, only pain that exploded in his chest with each heartbeat. His face was numb, his hair filling with drifting flakes. Too weak to cover himself again, he scratched at the door, almost absently watching the slowly spreading blackness over his heart.

Then the door drifted away and he tumbled into the house with the gently blowing snow.

CHAPTER 21

Lazarus

Catherine twisted her hands about the small pistol in her muff as she waited in the office of the commandant of Liverpool Military Prison. Since her return from Scotland the previous evening, the effort of behaving normally with the battered Enderly had nearly exhausted her control; now her nerves were strung taut. This place is a mountain of stone, she thought bleakly. A man could be buried alive here and no one would know. Scream his life away and no one would hear. Or care. Her fingers twisted, twisted.

The door opened and a green uniform came at her. She put out her hand automatically, warding the officer off; he kissed her fingertips.

"Countess. This is an honor. I am Colonel Deal." A short, blunt man with a ruddy face made ruddier by his powdered white periwig, his small eyes appreciatively took in the rakishly sophisticated figure in chocolate velvet with satin cloche and sable muff. "The general didn't mention your coming. I would have made some preparation . . ."

"That is kind of you, Colonel, but totally unnecessary. I understand military quarters aren't designed to administer tea and scones. You have a prisoner who has been accused of my abduction. May I see him?"

"I . . . am afraid not."

"Why not, Colonel? I'm the sole witness. If you've made an error, an innocent man may pay for it with his life. If he's guilty, I can identify him."

413

The commandant squirmed. "This is a prison, Countess; its prisoners are villainous scum. Hardly a fit place and company for a lady."

Catherine ignored his slight inflection on the last word. "Surely I may trust to your able protection, sir."

"I regret, my lady—"

"Colonel, prisoners not in the military are subject to civil law. Must I display a warrant to see the prisoner? You have no right to hold a civilian incommunicado indefinitely without trial."

The commandant's jowls began to swell against his tunic collar. "I'm sure Mr. Sexton, the magistrate, will tell you—"

She frostily cut him off. "I've been to the chief magistrate of the Western Counties, Mr. Andrew Carton. In fact, Mr. Carton has provided just such a warrant. I wish to see the prisoner now."

His eyes turned piggy. "I'm afraid that's impossible. The prisoner died under questioning."

Stay with me, Kit. I keep thinking this is a dream, that in the morning . . .

"I assume he was given medical treatment?"

"Certainly."

"I should like to see the doctor in charge."

"Most irregular, my lady."

"No more irregular than an immediate investigation of your administration here, Colonel. Well?" Inside, she was shaking, unsure how far Deal could be pushed. Flaunting her title and waving Artois's seal under the chief magistrate's impressed nose had been one thing; it would be quite different if she actually had to use ducal influence to secure a prisoner's release from a military prison. She felt like a juggler, trying to keep her lover out of reach of a rescuer as dangerous as the hunters. Yet she had to see Sean dead; she had to be sure.

"As you wish," Deal said tightly. "Follow me."

"Countess, this is Thatcher Marcus, our resident doctor. Doctor, Lady Catherine Enderly. My lady wishes to know—"

414

"I'm capable of asking my own questions, Colonel," Catherine interrupted. "Please leave us."

The colonel shot Marcus a warning glance, then withdrew from the small office.

"Doctor, some weeks ago a prisoner was brought here. A black-haired, green-eyed man. The colonel tells me he was sent to you for medical attention after being questioned and that he died. Is that true?"

"I attend a great many prisoners, my lady. I don't remember them all."

"You would have remembered this one. He . . . rather made one think of Lucifer." Inside her muff, fingernails dug into her palms as the doctor studied her. "Doctor, I mean you no harm. They may have had the wrong man; if so, I feel responsible. I only want to know if he was given medical treatment." There must have been a note in her voice, a dry sound of crumbling.

"May I ask your given name, my lady?"

Oh, God, please. What a stupid question. If Sean is dead, living is stupid. Stupid. "Catherine," she muttered.

"Are you sometimes called Kit?"

Her heart leaped over. "Yes. Yes! He was here?"

"Yes." His tone was so grave she wanted to scrabble at him, beg for any hope.

"Tell me." The two words were all she could manage.

"The prisoner was brought to me in critical condition after severe questioning. He survived." Marcus looked away from the welling hope in her eyes. "Two days ago, he was shot while trying to escape."

With an incoherent cry, she sagged. He caught her and carried her to his battered sofa. Mute, she curled away from him, into her grief. After checking the ward outside to be sure the colonel was not lurking nearby, he let her be for a time, then touched her shoulder. "Your father will come here, my lady. Colonel Deal has probably gone to send word to him."

"I don't care. I don't care what he does! He's a murderer. Murderer!"

She began to scream uncontrollably and he gave her a sharp slap. "Stop it! Would you endanger us both?"

Eyes glittering, she pushed him away. "Where is he? What have they done with him?"

"He was buried in a potter's field."

She began to rock, keening in sorrow: primitive, ageless, terrible. Marcus shook her. "Listen to me! He didn't want this kind of grief from you!" She groaned, hardly conscious of him. Knowing the colonel would be back at any moment, he had to shock her into reason, even if it were born of rage. "Your father intended to serve you his manhood on a platter to test your reaction! But he was cheated because the prisoner fought to die like a man. If you're weak, that struggle was for nothing."

White-faced, the young countess fell silent. After a moment, she murmured, "I must see his grave. I cannot accept his death. It's as if he were calling me. As if he were a child begging for warmth."

Marcus helped her clean up her disheveled appearance and, leading her away from the commandant's office, took her to the rear gate. "You can walk from here. It's not far to the field." He gave her directions.

The potter's field was a barren, windswept heath lumped with carelessly scattered dirt mounds; there were no markers, no signs of remembrance. Three scraggling trees clustered in stubborn resistance to an icy wind that lifted snow into flurries, scoured the frozen dirt clods bare, then covered them again. She walked toward two men digging at the far end of the field.

Golgotha. The Place of Skulls. I cannot leave him here. I must take him home to Ireland. To the sea.

The men were lowering a dirty gray bundle into a grave hardly deep enough to discourage scavenging dogs. They looked up, peering askance at her expensive clothes and still, white face.

"Is a special section reserved for prison dead?"

One man leaned on his shovel. "No, mum, they're all piled in together."

"Do you . . . remember where you put the prisoners who died two nights ago?"

"The ones pitched out in the court? Well, let's see. There was three. Stiff as boards, they was." He squinted and

416

rubbed his hands. "Cold work, burying in this kind of weather. Ground's like iron."

She gave them each a sovereign. They hastily pocketed the money. "Was a young, black-haired man among them?"

The thinner man shook his head. "Nah. Two was dun-thatched, not all that young, either. And one was Sergeant Raker. Big ox. Took near three hours to get 'im under."

"She must want the other one, Lean," the small digger said. "The one that took off. Must have hated Raker's guts so bad 'e couldn't stand to be in the same boneyard with 'im. Got up and walked away, just like Lazarus."

Catherine dropped to her knees and grabbed his sleeve. "What did you say?"

"I say 'e walked. Filched rags off the others and hauled 'is carcass away. Left blood all over the snow. Guess the drifts covered it up before the mornin' watch come around. We figured no sense in lookin'. Too cold for 'im to do anythin' but freeze. 'E an't showed up yet, though."

Great roses began to bloom in Catherine's cheeks. "You didn't report him missing?"

They looked at her with some hostility.

"No, of course you didn't!" She hugged the first dirty digger around the neck. "Oh, you lovely, lazy old crocks! You wonderful, beautiful angels! Here! Take a holiday! Take ten!" She flung a handful of sovereigns at them and ran across the mounds of snow.

Finding the house was not difficult. According to Mignon, it was Sean's only possible refuge. The place was forbidding even by daylight, its paint weathered in the salt air until only fragments clung to the wood. Sagging shutters once a trim green framed dirty windows; the ground-floor shutters were closed. Heart pounding, Catherine knocked on the front door. Receiving no answer, she tried again more loudly, then stepped back and scanned the upper-story windows. Finally, she went to the rear; it, too, seemed deserted, but while new-fallen snow had obliterated any clues in the yard, it had not completely covered the sheltered back stoop and lower door, which were blood smeared. Thinking it locked, Catherine wrenched at the

417

door, then nearly pitched into an unfurnished room festooned with cobwebs. The other gloomy rooms were empty except for a few pieces of heavy furniture and piles of debris, but a trail of dark blotches led to the kitchen's cellar door. Finding a discarded flint among the litter, she lit a rusty lantern which hung on a nearby nail, and opened the door. A stairway descended into darkness. Slowly, she crept down narrow, rickety steps, then held the lantern high.

Face to the wall, a body partly covered by a ragged blanket lay on the dirt floor. Her heart leaped wildly. "Sean?" The head moved almost imperceptibly and her knees went weak. "Sean, it's Catherine."

As if the effort was terrible, a man slowly turned his head. It's not him! she thought frantically. It cannot be! The bloody face was battered out of recognition. In growing terror, she stumbled forward and knelt, staring at the swollen, twisted nose, the closed, blackened left eye. A wicked gash split the brow and another raked across his bruised cheek. But the good eye, pain-clouded and barely aware, was the green of the sea. She placed the lantern on a rickety stool.

"Kit?" he asked in a ragged whisper.

She touched his broken lips. "Yes, my darling."

"You're . . . real." The relief in his eyes was so intense she fought back tears.

"It's all right now," she whispered. "I'm going to take care of you."

He seemed to relax, then tensed and strained to lift his head. "No! You mustn't stay here!" Gently, she pressed him back, but he resisted with growing desperation. His face twisted in pain and her hands trembled as she started to draw back the blanket. "No." He caught her hand tightly, trying to stay conscious. "Kit, get out of here . . . I'm dying."

"I'll bring a doctor."

"No! No doctor. I'd be turned in." A lost look came into his eyes. "I'll not go back there."

"Don't think of it. You're safe now. Try to rest." She kissed his hand, lulling him. "No one's going to hurt you anymore."

418

"Kitten, go away, please . . ." His whisper died away to quick, shallow breathing. She pulled the covers away. The prison rags were blood soaked from neck to groin.

Waiting not an instant longer, Catherine went out to buy candles, bedding, and food. Shortly, surrounded by supplies and a pan of hot water, she rolled up her sleeves. Then she began to cut away the rags, tears streaking her face. Sean's right arm was broken near the wrist and several ribs were caved in. The bullet wound in his chest was ugly and mounded. She eased him onto his side, and in his back, now a mass of livid scars and reopened cuts, found a bullet hole just missing the spine. His skin was so encrusted with blood and dirt that despite the lantern and candles, she gave up trying to see any more. After slipping clean towels under him, she spent the better part of an hour bathing him. Clean, his body showed the full extent of its brutal abuse. Then she saw how they had mutilated him.

Her head dropped beside his cheek. Unimaginable hatred filled her until at last she knew fully why Sean had devoted his life to vengeance. Their lives were not payment enough. Nothing would be enough.

After she had bandaged him, changed the linen, and finally pulled warm blankets over him, she rested her head in her hands, trying to fight off black despair. Sean very possibly *was* dying. Without surgery, he *would* die.

Clad in shabby clothing found in an old bureau, Catherine huddled in the deep doorway of a house near the prison on the way to the potter's field. As dusk fell, the two gravediggers came along, their empty cart rattling on the cobbles. She slipped out of the shadows and fell in beside them. "Would you like to make another ten sovereigns, angels?"

They squinted. "Lumme, it's the rich lydy. Come down a bit, an't ye, mum?"

"Not a whit. I can pay you well. I need a favor. Are you interested?"

Lean cackled to Short, "We'll have gold-plyted wings afore long. What's up?"

419

When she told them, they became markedly less enthusiastic.

"Fifty upon completion. You'll never dig another grave in winter."

Ten minutes later, in full sight of the marine guard, Lean took a whopping fall on the ice just outside the rear of the prison and set up a groaning like a sea cow in labor. "Gor, 'is crown's cracked!" wailed Short. "Get a doctor!"

The guard frowned dubiously. "Doctor an't goin' to come down for no lousy digger."

"Ye coldhearted rotter, 'e could die out 'ere!"

"Naw, I an't goin' for the doctor. I'm on watch, see?"

"Well, help me get 'im to the back door. I'll tote 'im up to the Bones if the bloke's too fancy to come down. I know the back way. Nobody'll see us. 'Ere, lad, have a 'eart."

The marine sighed. He was well acquainted with Short; the fellow was fully capable of badgering him all night. Sometimes the two did him favors, like picking up that draft of rum for him last night while he stood post. "Alright, alright. Heave 'im up."

Less than an hour later, the two emerged, Lean hobbling along under his own steam, a fat bandage on his head. "What's Doc say?" The marine's breath formed a cloud.

"No work for a while," said Short gleefully. Lean rolled his eyes and gave the guard a smirk as he limped past.

The man stared after them. "Lumme, never met a stiffie yet that an't got a queer sense of wit."

Shortly after, Marcus left the prison's main entrance. "Evening, lads. I may miss curfew tonight. Keep an eye out for me, will you?"

"Night on the town, 'ay, Doc. Ye don't get many of those."

"You fellows keep me too well occupied." He touched his hat in a small salute. "Night."

Minutes later, he ducked into a doorway. "I got your message. 'Lazarus operandus, Kit' puzzled Short a bit; his pronunciation was more imaginative. I realize you couldn't say much, so I brought the basics."

"God bless you for coming." Quickly, Catherine described Sean's injuries. "We should go to the house sepa-

420

rately. I'll leave the back door unlocked. He's in the cellar."

Marcus nodded, then paused. "Your father knows his prisoner wasn't executed. He's talked to Worthy."

"Does he know Sean's alive?"

"Not yet, but he'll dig up all the fresh graves in that field until he's sure; that won't take more than a day."

"Then I must get Sean out of England by tomorrow night. They're sure to begin a house search." Distraught, she looked up. "Can you get word to the diggers? I don't want them hurt. I don't want *you* hurt. You're taking a terrible chance."

"I've always thought I had the only sane attitude possible for a prison practitioner. I've also been a coward. Give me your address, Countess."

Quickly descending the cellar stair, Catherine shook snow from her cloak. Sean stirred restlessly, muttering unintelligible snatches in three languages. She felt his head; he was feverish.

"Kit? Please . . . don't go. Don't leave me in the dark. Where are you? . . . No. Get out of here. Stay away. God . . . I'm cold."

Catherine added another blanket and heated gruel, then, lifting his head, spooned the liquid between his lips. A little went down; most he could not control and she dabbed at the corner of his mouth. His good eye opened. "Thought . . . you were gone."

"I'm not going to leave you."

His face contorted. "I don't want you! Part . . . of revenge . . . to make you think I cared."

"Nothing you can say will make me go."

He turned his face away sharply. "I'm your half brother. I took you knowingly . . . in incest. Now, will you go?"

"Liam told you, didn't he?" She brushed back his hair as he turned back to stare at her. "I know why you brought me home. Amin explained everything."

His eyes clouded. "How can you look at me like that, after . . ."

"I love you. Nothing can alter that. But how did Liam find out?"

"A codicil to Brendan's will. And Brendan's painting . . . of Elise."

As the truth dawned, Catherine's eyes hardened. "Then he knew! Liam knew when he married me! That's why he went into a frenzy when he finished that painting on the cliff." Rage bubbled over. "Oh, God, how could he! Then send his own brother to certain death. It wasn't as if he hadn't done enough!"

A creak at the stair top brought her to instant, breathless silence, Sean to the edge of terror. As polished boots descended the staircase, he fought to reach the pistol. When Catherine restrained him, he lunged against her like a madman. "Give me . . . that gun!"

"Sean, it's Doctor Marcus. Don't you see?"

Exhausted, he leaned against her, staring like a cornered wolf at the surgeon.

"I've come to do what I can, Sean," Marcus said quietly. "No one knows I'm here. You dragged yourself this far. You cannot wish to die now like a dog in this cellar."

"I'll never leave here alive. Why give her false hope?" His voice faded to a dull whisper. "She'll be better off."

Catherine's arms tightened about him and she murmured against his hair. "I'm carrying your child, love. Nothing can make me sorry for your life in me. This child was conceived in innocence; he'll be loved without reservation, but you know more than anyone what being thought a bastard is like. For his sake and mine, you must live."

His arms stole around her, one hand hanging limply, his face against the curve of her neck. "All right, little one. I . . . owe you one."

Finally it was over. "I don't like having to leave this piece of lead in his chest," Marcus muttered as he bandaged, "but if I take it out, he'll not be going anywhere for weeks."

He straightened the nose and packed it. "I see you've been applying compresses; the swelling's reduced." He pulled on his jacket. "You're an excellent assistant, Countess. I've rarely had better."

She walked him up the stair to the back door. "I had a good teacher. And please call me Kit. I owe you Sean's life; I'll pray for your well-being every night of mine."

He took her hand at the door. "I'm the one who should thank you for giving me back my self-respect." He fished in his pocket and brought up a pair of vials. "I almost forgot. If he's in imminent danger of being retaken, pour one of these down him; it kills within seconds." He dropped them in her hand. "I advise you to swallow the other."

Sean, propped against a wall, gazed critically at the slim sailor lad who pommeled a stocking into the toe of an outsized boot. She pulled it onto a foot already encased in three pairs of wool stockings. "Two pairs of mittens, too." The pseudo-sailor waggled woolly fingers. "They'll not look as closely at a boy."

Sean rested his head back against the wall. The thought of merely standing up filled him with dread.

Catherine stripped off the gloves, then stooped and began to dab at his face with a melted paste of coffee grounds and lard, carefully avoiding cuts. "In the dark, this will blend with the rest of your skin. It's a shame the doctor had to shave you; a bit of beard would have helped." She touched up his nose as he tried not to wince.

When she had finished with Sean, Catherine dragged on thick sweaters and a pea jacket and struck a boyish stance. "Well, how do I look?"

The Irishman's broken lips moved in a semblance of a wry smile. "Lovely. Very."

Catherine gave a snort of exasperation. "We'll soon see about that!" Quickly, she brushed the coffee mixture against the grain of her brows to roughen them, then altered the contours of her face. Minutes later, she was unrecognizable. She put her hands on her hips. "Well, as they say, it's now or never. The nine o'clock watch comes by in an hour. Not too many people on the streets and not too few. Ready, bucko?"

"Aye." He took a deep breath, then lifted an arm. She got a shoulder under his armpit, and as gently as possible, helped him to his feet. His lips went white, and he swayed unsteadily for a moment, then lifted his head and nodded.

The Irishman's face was beaded with sweat when they reached the top of the cellar stair, and she let him briefly rest. By the time they reached the back door, Catherine already felt the strain of his weight.

The night was chill with little wind. Snow sifted lazily across streets silvered by a half-moon. His bad arm slung over Catherine's shoulders, Sean tried to take as much weight off her as possible, concentrating on one step at a time, each dull explosion of pain. When they entered an alley across the street, he used a wall to help support himself. They rested at the alley's end, just off a street of lighted taverns where a few sailors, doxies, and stray soldiers wandered. Most townspeople were in bed. When the street emptied somewhat, Catherine took Sean's arm and helped him into the street. Partway across, a hurrying soldier, bending his head against the cold, accidentally bumped into the Irishman's shoulder. Catherine heard Sean's gasp of pain and the soldier did, too. "Sorry, bub." He peered into Culhane's face, then at Catherine. "Say, what's wrong with 'im? I didn't tyke his bloody arm off, y'know. Sod looks ready to pass out."

"He's . . . my brother," Catherine said desperately. " 'E's just a bit soused. A bloke in an inn down the street took a poke at 'im."

"More than one poke, looks like."

"Bloody bashtard," Sean mumbled. He swore incoherently, then began to sing in a slurred voice, "Four and twenty virgins came down from Inverness . . ."

"Best get 'im home, lad." The soldier chuckled.

"I mean to, sir."

When they reached the dark shelter of another alley, Sean almost dropped in his tracks. She eased him against the wall as he fought back waves of pain. "How much farther?" he muttered.

"Just a few more steps."

With painful slowness, they finally reached the end of the alley and the harbor spread before them. Catherine braced him against the wall and his head fell forward, his breathing sick and shallow. "Look . . . for a small boat. Just big enough . . . to be seaworthy."

Scanning the vessels tied at the quai, she almost sobbed, "These are too big and it's time for the watch."

"We'll wait. Further down . . . boats . . ."

He sagged, and she gasped, "Sean, I cannot hold you!"

He pressed upward, thinking how tired he was, how much he wanted to go to sleep in the snow with her holding him.

"They're coming," she whispered.

The watch tramped by, bayonets fixed. They split formation just beyond the alley. The first one peeled off to check the wharf across from the lovers' hiding place. Far down the quai, in the direction of the prison, moving torches flared; already search parties were out posting sentries with torches at intervals along the waterfront.

The guard strolled out to the end of the pier, slowly turned and scanned the building fronts. Catherine's fingers closed around one of the vials in her pocket and eased its stopper out. Sean's eyes were closed. In complete trust, he would swallow anything she put to his lips. Please, God. He's come so far.

The marine turned back to face the harbor, spread his legs slightly, and urinated into the water. She went weak with relief. The man hastened to rejoin his comrades, now dwindling down the quai.

"Sean, they've gone, but the marines are picketing the harbor. We have to go now or we'll be trapped here. Please, love."

"Leave . . . me. . . . Bleeding . . . bad."

With desperate fury, she dragged his arm over her shoulder. "I won't leave! If you give up, you won't go back to prison alone."

His battered face twisted. "Damn it, get out of here!"

"No!" she hissed. "Why should I? You didn't let me off so easily. Walk, damn you! I'll drag you if you don't!"

His eyes opened, their green depths burning with fever and anger. "You little bitch, don't . . . give me . . . orders!"

"Then look after yourself! Any man who won't stand on his own two feet deserves to die!"

He stared at her in disbelief, then his face hardened. He twisted away and felt his way along the wall, nearly falling as he reached the corner. She followed anxiously and put out a hand. "Don't . . . touch me, dammit!" he snarled.

"You'll never make it alone."

His low, derisive laugh ended sharply, bitten off by pain.

"I'm a bloody O'Neill, remember?" Unbelievably, he began to stumble down the quai, pushing along the wall, his bad arm pressed against his side and chest. The few sailors paid little attention, thinking he was drunk, the white-faced boy tagging behind a shipmate. Fifty yards down the quai, he sagged against a tavern wall and slipped to his knees.

With a low cry, she stooped beside him. "Sean, don't do this! You're killing yourself!"

"Pick . . . a boat," he muttered. "Pick . . ."

Terrified now, she obeyed him, running out on a pier. The vessels were still too big to handle alone. Finally, between a couple of fishing boats rocked a catboat, its sails neatly furled. Almost stumbling, she raced back, noticing the picket lights had crept halfway around the harbor.

She stooped beside Culhane, who clung to the wall, his body sagging, his eyes glassy. "I've found one." She slipped a hand under his arm. Unresisting now, he let her pull him upward. She pressed between him and the wall, trying to get him upright, his good arm around her neck.

A sailor came out of the tavern and glanced at their gyrations with amused curiosity. Sean's head dropped forward against her cheek and he groaned. She lifted wide, terrified eyes to the sailor. A slow grin crossed his plain, amiable face. "Blast me, ye're a girl, an't ye?"

Sean's head dropped lower, his lips moving against her neck, "My . . . girl."

The sailor laughed and shrugged. "No offense, mate. I an't tryin' to steal yer lass away." He winked at her. "Though I'll promise ye, missy, he'll not be much use tonight."

"Would . . . would ye give me a hand with him, please? Our boat's just down the wharf, but . . . he's awful heavy."

The sailor cocked his head. Odd-looking little thing. "Sure, lass, why not?"

He started to throw a brawny arm about Sean's other side, and hastily she said, "He's been in a fearsome brawl. Could ye go easy, please?"

"Oh, sure, sure. Handle 'im like a babe."

"You fisherfolk?" the sailor asked as they half walked, half carried the Irishman down the wharf.

"Aye. We've not enough family men to crew the boat, so

426

I help out. Not many spot me as a woman though. How did ye know?"

The sailor flashed her a grin across Sean's dangling head. "Yer eyes. Big as saucers starin' up at me like I was goin' to gobble ye up. No boy I ever knowed had eyes like that."

She managed a faint grimace. "Blokes in the streets scare me a bit at night."

"Yer fella git in fights often?" he asked as they sat Culhane on the dock alongside the boat, his legs hanging over the side.

"Only when he's pushed."

Dropping into the boat, the sailor eased his burden forward, then lowered him carefully. The Irishman slipped into unconsciousness the moment his head touched the deck. "Well, 'e's out like a light. Want a hand with the mainsail?"

"Please."

She unlashed the tiller as the sailor ran up the sail and handed her the boom sheet. He hesitated, then asked shyly, "This fella spoken for ye yet? I mean, I don't live here. I'm out of Marblehead. That's in Massachusetts. My ship's the *Ina Clair*"—he pointed—"the bark yonder. We'll be takin' on stores and cargo." He shoved his hands into his jacket pockets. "I don't know any girls hereabouts."

Catherine smiled up at him. "What's yer name?"

"Tom Carr."

"Well, Tom Carr, ye're a kind man. If I were free, I'd be pleased to have ye call. Ye've got nice brown eyes and I like yer smile, but . . . yonder lad in the scuppers is my true love, that's sure."

"Oh, well." He shrugged and grinned wryly. "One man's famine, another man's fortune." He hopped up onto the dock, put a foot on the stern, and shoved the boat off.

"God bless you, Tom Carr," she called softly as the boat eased out from the dock, the sail beginning to belly out.

"Ah, go along with ye, girl. I didn't do nothin'."

"More than you know," she whispered.

The wind was fitful and the sail often hung maddeningly slack as the catboat glided though the inky water. Catherine imagined every hull that loomed up in the fog-swirled darkness to be the harbor patrol.

She sucked in a deep breath as the sail blossomed in the offshore wind of the harbor mouth, and the boat moved quickly into the open sea. Beyond the sail, a triangular shadow against the hazy stars, cloud cover obscured much of the sky; at this time of year, storms were unpredictable. She managed to sight the North Star and fixed a slightly northwest course. Knowing little of navigation, she wanted to be sure of direction before leaving sight of land. Too far north and they would sail blindly out into the North Atlantic.

She lashed the tiller to its course and moving forward, pawed for the extra sail under the bow. Wrapped in its folds were a lantern and tallow candle. She crawled back to the stern with her finds, then pulled the mended sail closely about Sean. The candle went into her pocket with the vials; feeling them, she looked down at her lover's still, drawn face. Dear God. Help me see him safely home.

CHAPTER 22

Scarlet Beads

Dawn of the second day saw the catboat approach Malin Head, russet and gold, clawed with streaks of snow. In Ireland's interior, the Grianon thrust its ancient stones above the mountains.

"Hail, Conal and Niall," Catherine whispered. "Your son has come home to his fathers. He has given you honor. Grant him peace."

As the sun mounted, she relashed the tiller and knelt beside her lover. His skin hot and dry, he stirred fitfully. She pillowed his head in her lap and scooped snow off a seat where the wind had not yet blown it away. As she let crystals melt on his lips to trickle down his throat, his eyelids flickered and he gazed dazedly up at her. "Where . . . are we?"

"Malin Head's off our port bow. You're halfway home."

"I didn't make it . . . on my own," he muttered. "Couldn't."

She smiled, gently teasing. "You'd be unbearably smug if you had." Then her smile faded and she faltered, "I wanted to die when you refused help." She felt the vials in her pocket. "I nearly poisoned you when that soldier . . . oh, Sean, I was terrified." She burst into tears of latent reaction, sobbing against his hair.

With an effort, his good hand lifted and groped weakly. "Take . . . that damn cap off. I want . . . to see my girl again." She pawed at the knitted cap and her hair tumbled down across his shoulder. His fingers found its silk. "Lovely . . . very." His head dropped tiredly against her.

429

Carefully, she re-covered him and removed the scarf over his eyes. By daylight, the damage was garish and she wondered how they had fooled anyone. She got him to eat a bit of cheese and bread she had slipped in their pockets and took a nip herself from the flask to ward off the chill wind. With a burning throat, she resumed the tiller and focused tired eyes on the horizon.

Sean stirred very little during the long day and night. The cold tempered his fever but the bandages grew sodden, warning that the bullet in his chest had been dislodged. His breathing was faint and shallow, and with increasing apprehension, Catherine watched the sun sink.

Near dawn, Shelan's lightless silhouette loomed high against the moon. What if Peg and Rafferty had heard of Sean's capture and given him up for dead? she wondered. What if everyone had gone? What if Liam . . . ? Severely curbing her imagination, she maneuvered the catboat in as close as she dared, then weighed anchor and scrambled for the lantern.

Holy Mother, no flint. Don't panic. Use the pistol. You've got powder, haven't you? She pulled the pistol out of her waistband. The flash almost gave her powder burns but the candle glowed. Hastily, she dropped lower against the wind as she slipped the taper into the lantern.

Hanging on to the mast, she waved the lantern, fanning it with her cap to make a signal, then moving it to form Culhane's initials, anything. The candle burned low, but still no light answered from the house. In desperation, she was considering running the boat aground when she saw a shadow push a boat through the surf. Minutes later, a flaming head appeared in the lantern's glow. Her heart sank to her toes. Flannery! That meant Liam! She grabbed for the gun, trying to load it with stiff fingers, but when his hand caught the gunnel, she was still fumbling. She lifted the gun butt with a hopeless cry. "No! I won't let you have him!"

"Easy, lass. I mean Sean no harm," the giant reassured her.

"Your murderous master wants him dead!"

"No man is my master, girl," he retorted tersely, "especially not Liam Culhane; I left him long ago. He wasn't exactly closemouthed in his liquor." He nodded toward the long figure outlined under the sail. "What shape is he in?"

"He may be dying," she said dully.

"Then we'd best be quick. Help me with him."

Peg helped undress the wounded Irishman, keening in Gaelic when she saw his body. She crooned to him, touched his face as Catherine bathed him. The indestructible housekeeper was useless. Flannery finally led her to a chair by the fire, where she sat, rocking and weeping. He came back to the bed. "Rafferty shouldn't be long with the doctor." His mouth was a granite line above his beard as he looked down. "The bastards. Nothin' alive should be treated like this."

Catherine covered Sean and sagged into a chair, closing her eyes.

"Had anything to eat?" She shook her head. "Any preferences?"

"Hot." He patted her arm and left.

The next thing Catherine knew, Rafferty was frantically shaking her awake. "Doctor O'Donnell's delivering a babe in Ruiralagh. He'll likely not be back 'til mornin'." Peg began to wail and wring her hands.

"Please take Peg downstairs to bed, Mr. Rafferty," Catherine quietly ordered. "Then ride for the doctor and wait until the baby's safely delivered. Bring him back here. Quickly. Please be as quick as you can . . ."

Flannery stepped aside with the tray as Rafferty coaxed his wife out of the room. "What is it?"

Catherine told him. "I'll need boiling water, plenty of it. The sharpest, smallest knife you can find. A razor. Something for forceps. Candles, bandages, linen, whiskey. Nora can help."

He frowned. "Do you know what ye're doin', lass?"

"I only know he won't live more than a few hours if that bullet doesn't come out. Help me get him to the floor by the fire."

When everything was in readiness, she rubbed her gritty eyes and looked up. "Have you any experience with bullet wounds, Mr. Flannery?"

"I've had a few dug out of me, and I worked one out of a fella's arm once."

"Nora?" The girl shook her head, freckles stark. "Then go back to bed, Nora," Catherine said gently. "You've been a great help with finding things." After Nora gratefully closed the door, Catherine looked over the equipment and took a breath. "I suppose that's it." With the razor, she reopened Marcus's incision, then blotted to see the entrance angle of the bullet. Using a crochet hook, she probed, trying to keep her hand steady. Culhane groaned, pain seeping into his unconsciousness as the shaft buried deep in his chest but encountered no bullet. The firelight blurred. Flannery dragged her head up and put whiskey to her lips. "Drink. More. That's good."

Another quarter inch and she found it. "Ready with the heated one?"

"Go ahead."

When she worked the bullet loose, blood welled up. White-faced she worked quickly to bring the bullet to the surface, then flung it into the fire where it landed with a hiss. Flannery instantly handed her a second hook heated red hot, the handle thickly wrapped in wool, then held Sean down. She inserted it into the wound. He convulsed and screamed, then went limp as she withdrew it. The blood flow ebbed.

Flannery held a cold rag to the back of her neck, then bathed her sweat-beaded face as she gulped air. "He's still losing blood," she muttered. "We'll have to close the others with the flat of a hot blade."

At last it was done and the cauterized wounds bandaged. Flannery carried the unconscious man to bed and covered him. When he looked back at Catherine, she lay curled up in a heap among the bloodstained blankets. He transported her to his own cot in the adjoining room.

Bright light blazing through uncurtained windows struck Catherine's eyes when she awoke, and for a moment, she lay bewildered, almost blinded. Then remembering, she flung out of bed and jerked open the bedroom door.

Flannery sat with stocking feet propped up on the desk. He looked up from his book. "Doctor's come and gone. He'll be back in a bit."

She let out her breath. Sean was still alive.

The Irishman lay on his back, his head turned away

from the windows. Frightened by his terrible pallor, she hesitantly touched his bruised cheek.

A few hours later the doctor arrived and checked the patient. "How is he, Doctor O'Donnell?" Catherine asked worriedly.

"Mr. Culhane has a rugged constitution, but from now on he'll need someone else to do his fighting for him." Keene blue eyes studied her from a typically Irish face. Dark-haired with strong features, he had a dent in his chin and capable-looking hands. "How are *you*, Lady Catherine?"

"Enraged, doctor. I'm in a fighting mood."

"Good. Stay angry for the next two weeks."

"What are his chances?"

He shrugged. "He shouldn't live, but he might. He shouldn't have survived days of neglect, three days at sea, or amateur surgery with a Christ Almighty crochet hook, but he did." He worked into his jacket and picked up his bag. "Personally, I don't like a man who breaks all the rules. He brings out my great green gambling streak and I'm supposed to be a steady man." He tipped his hat. "See you in the morning."

Just before dawn, Sean's fever mounted. Muttering unintelligibly, he fought the blankets. Without warning, his eyes flickered open and he cried out, arching in shock at the pain. Futilely, Catherine tried to hold him down. "Flannery! Come quickly!"

Nightshirt flapping, Flannery tore into the room. He shoved her aside, took her place, and jerked his head toward the pile of rolled linen on the chest. "Tie him down with the strips, girl. Hurry!"

When he felt himself being bound, Sean redoubled his efforts, cursing. Quickly exhausted, he lay pleading, "Don't. Don't cut me. Please . . ."

Cathering measured laudanum into a cup, hands shaking. He twisted away. "No! I won't take that filthy stuff! Get . . . your . . . filthy . . . hands off!" He screamed, and Flannery held his head rigid while Catherine forced opiate into his mouth and held his jaws closed. He bucked against the restraints, choking. When he stopped, she tried a little more. Too weak to resist, he simply lay there, stubbornly refusing to swallow until the medicine ran from the corner

433

of his mouth. She held his nostrils and jaw closed; finally he had to let the stuff go down his throat, his green eyes glittering with fever and hate. "Butcher! Leave her alone, damn you! I'll kill you!" His voice grew weaker, pleading, "Tell her . . . somebody, tell her it isn't me . . . burn it. No, don't . . . don't kill me like this." His raving faded into an incoherent mumble as he lapsed into drugged delirium.

Slowly, the injuries began to knit. The restraints were removed as he was less troubled by pain. He even slept occasionally without heavy drugging, although he was never wholly conscious. They fed him in tiny amounts, building his strength, but although he was lucid near the end of a fortnight, he was dangerously weak, unable to lift his head. Catherine was saddened to see him so helpless, when he had been so fiercely self-reliant. When he was conscious for longer periods, she moved her cot into the room. There, she sang and read to him in the long hours of the night, always keeping a candle burning even while he slept, always being where he could see her. Though he rarely asked for anything, his eyes often followed her about the room.

The day O'Donnell came to take the stitches out of Culhane's head and face, Catherine and the doctor, now easy with one another, bantered with casual good humor. "Well, boyo," O'Donnell teased Sean cheerily, "you may not rival the gods again, but you'll break many a heart before your dotage. When the swelling's gone, your hair will hide most of the scars." He peered at the injured eye. "How's the vision in the left one?"

"Cloudy."

"Um. That may pass. I'm going to take your packing out." A minute later, the doctor applied firm pressure to both sides of the nose and stroked upward. Sean winced. O'Donnell shrugged and dropped his instruments in his bag, then rested his hand carelessly on Catherine's shoulder. "Well, your nose is a bit awry, that's sure."

Catherine smiled down at her patient. "I prefer it this way."

Sean tried to smile back, but he did not feel it.

After the doctor left, Catherine laid her head down beside his and he awkwardly caressed her face. "Is Orfeo still about?"

434

She chuckled. "Haven't you heard him in the hall? He knows you're home. He's most offended to be shut out."

"I'd like to see the little beggar."

When she opened the door, Orfeo got up, stretched, and strolled in, tail tip wisping back and forth. He inspected the room, then hopped up on the bed and nosed Sean's face, sniffing the medicinal odors. When Sean stroked him, he lay down, rumbling rustily, his diabolic amber eyes half-closed. "He's getting fat. Peg's spoiling him."

Catherine laughed. "I'm the guilty one. He's full of cold soup from your tray."

Sean gently thumped the cat's belly and got a disdainful look. "Tight as a drum." He looked at her. "So will you be soon. What are you going to do then, little mother?"

Petite mère. Charles d'Artois's farewell phrase slid across her mind as she answered, "What every mother does: bring new life into the world. Our child's name will be Culhane, as it should be." She knelt by the bed and stroked the cat, now folded up like a mandarin. "I feel complete and at peace. Very aptly, too; next week is Christmas."

In a playful Christmas spirit, Catherine set herself to amusing her patient by relating the tale of Perez and his fat wife. With a waddle and roll of her eyes she imitated the jealous lady, and she swished Orfeo's tail as an imaginary moustache under her nose to depict the swashbuckling desperado. Sweeping Orfeo into her arms in a dripping parody of lecherous ravishment, she murmured saccharine idiocies at the disgusted cat. Sean's laughing face contorted. "Mercy, woman, I'm in pain!" As she curtsied, Orfeo scrambled out of her arms and made an adroit exit.

"Enderly *believed* that swill?" Sean managed at last.

"I doubt it. If I'd known he already had you, I wouldn't have been so brazen. Naturally, Liam would never endanger himself by revealing any more than required to ensure your capture. He was certain you'd never confess anything." With feigned carelessness, she flopped down in a chair. "Let's not talk about Liam. The only time I care to hear his name again is in a divorce decree."

Sean's amusement disappeared. "You may have to, Kit.

435

If he wants to cause trouble, he can ruin you. He'd destroy himself, but he'd take you . . . and our child with him."

"I have to divorce Liam. He must be removed from any possible claim to me and the baby. I'll go to America if necessary." Seeing his eyes, she got up and took his hand. "Please, let's not talk of this now. Don't let's spoil Christmas."

"No, little one," he said softly, "we'll not spoil Christmas."

Christmas Eve morning dawned clear and cold with the Donegal coast blanketed in a rare snow, the ramparts of its massive cliffs banded with white above icy froth of incoming breakers. At Catherine's description of the German Tree tradition, Flannery went to the mountains and brought back an ignoble specimen whose windswept rump had to be tucked into a corner of Sean's room. Fortified by Peg's potent Yule punch, the Shelan inhabitants joined merry forces with Doctor O'Donnell and his family and drenched the tree with cranberries and currants, paper decorations, sugared pastries and candles. The adults became gaily intoxicated, the children wildly excited when they saw the mysterious parcels. Sean was able to sit up for a few hours, propped against pillows, a blue woolen robe pulled about his shoulders. When the candles were lit, Catherine sat on the bed beside him. Lovely in a white velvet gown, she wore his birthday gift, a gold fifth-century madonna, about her neck.

The children squealed as the door opened, then sighed because it was only Peg bringing more punch and a slender gentleman with a harp. Sean's eyes lit up. "Arthur!"

The children looked at one another, unsure whether to be disappointed or not.

Arthur O'Neill bowed. "A Merry Christmas to you all, my friends. I suggest we delay the immediate introductions, for I'm sure the children are dancing with impatience. Peg, pour me a cup of your famous brew, if you will." She obliged, and seated him by the fire.

Flannery proceeded to hand out the presents and the young O'Donnells tore into theirs with shouts of glee, then waved their prizes triumphantly as Orfeo pounced in the empty boxes, pursuing string snakes through the crackling paper.

While the adult presents were passed around, O'Neill took up his harp. After a few soft notes, the group fell raptly silent and Catherine felt as if she were alone with the blind harpist, witched away by the haunting music, pure and warm as the life, love's living dream, within her. Then Sean's hand covered hers and he was inside her too. Their eyes met. Sean slipped a magnificent diamond-mounted baguette emerald on her finger. "It was my mother's, for my bride and mother of my children."

"You are my soul's husband. Your ring will never leave me," she whispered.

She slipped a chain about his neck. "I had Flannery make this from my last gold sovereign." Sean lifted a simple crucifix that bore irregular hammer marks. She touched his face. "We owe your life to God. There were so many times these past weeks when our combined strength was not enough."

"Then He helped for your sake, not mine."

"I'll never believe that. Tonight we not only celebrate the birth of God, but of a man who suffered out of compassion for His brothers. Cannot you, of all men, accept Him as an equal who endured in spite of completely human fear and despair? If I, with all my mortal frailties and limitations, can find so much to love in you, how much more must God?"

He kissed the crucifix. "For your sake then, madonna mia . . . and respect for the better man."

On New Year's Day, Catherine bundled up in a cloak and, carrying Orfeo, intercepted Peg as she was mopping in the foyer. She gave her a letter. "Will you see Rafferty gets this to the packet?"

"Never fear. He'll be off within an hour."

"Thank you. Orfeo and I are just going out for a breath of fresh air."

As Catherine and the cat left the house, Peg absently glanced at the letter before dropping it in her apron pocket. Noticing Doctor Flynn's address, she decided to send him a note herself. Seeing no need to pay extra as it was all bound to the same place, she went to her bedroom and carefully slit off the seal, then wrote a holiday greeting. As she tucked it into the envelope, she noticed a second letter to Monsieur Charles d'Artois. She frowned, then went up to Sean's bedroom. "An't Charles Artoys somebody famous?"

Sean looked up in some surprise. "Aye. After Fat Louis, he's next in line for the French throne. He's also a crony of Kit's father. Why?"

Peg's face stiffened. "Nice friends yer lady's got," she snapped, holding out the unopened letter to Sean.

His eyes narrowed angrily. "What right have you to pry into Kit's affairs? Put that back where you found it!"

"Ye're my right. Ye'd better see the name."

She dropped the letter in his lap. Glaring at her, he picked it up. His face went taut. "Where is she?"

"Out for a walk."

"Have her see me when she comes in."

Cheeks rosy with cold, Catherine sailed into the bedroom and spun snow off her cloak. "Oh, it's glorious out! Orfeo went berserk! Most of the time all I could see was his tail waving above the drifts . . ." Seeing his expression, she dwindled off. "Is something wrong?"

He lifted the letter. "Peg wanted to include a note to Flynn. She found this."

The color drained from her cheeks. "You haven't opened it?"

"It's not addressed to me. I thought you might prefer to tell me about it." His tone had more than an echo of its old hardness.

"I wouldn't."

"Does it concern me?"

Her eyes darkened. "Do you still believe I'd betray you?"

He held out the letter. "Send it. I withdraw the question."

She made no move to take it. "Damn Peg and her thrift! Now this will always be between us. You'll always wonder."

She slowly pulled off the cloak and let it fall over the chair, then went to a window. Omitting nothing, she told him of Enderly's murderous schemes and her subsequent audience with the exiled duke. "To protect our child," she finished, "I asked Charles to claim him in a private interview with Enderly."

"*Charles* stood to lose a lot by helping you, even if he was thunderstruck by your gall. He wouldn't do it for nothing." His eyes darkened. "What did you give him, Kit?"

She said nothing. "Oh, Christ!" The cry tore from him. "You found a stud soon enough! Less than a month, wasn't it?"

"It wasn't like that!"

"No? What was it like?"

She whirled. "I'd have done anything to protect you and our baby! Anything! I'd have bedded Charles, Louis, the majordomo! But it wasn't sordid. Charles is a remarkable man. He's not unlike you . . ."

"Oh? I beg to disagree, madam! He has a nose that centers on his face, and both balls, by God. I'll warrant he was superb, your Charles!"

"Stop it! You're only tormenting yourself and me!"

"You're going to him, aren't you? My convalescence must be driving you mad with impatience. And Angoulême, too, has a 'fondness' for you. Good God, you can gull men! I'm a past veteran of your witchery, but like a dull fool, I believed I sired your child. I tried to crawl for him, believing it! Do you know *whose* bastard you're carrying!"

Catherine whitened as if he had stabbed her. With shaking fingers, she slipped his ring off and put it on the desk, then quietly left the room, closing the door. Alone, she threw herself on the bed and let the tears come, bitter and without release.

In growing misery, Sean stared at the ring. You bloody idiot, he berated himself, what would you prefer? Murdered by Enderly, she would have been exclusive. Is that what you want? You can never have her again. Accept it. Make it part of your blood and bone as she can never be again. Oh, Kit. I can only relinquish you.

"Kit?" There was no response and he tried again. Finally, he tried to go to her, but the carpet sucked him down like Ulysses in an endless, undulating poppy field.

Catherine heard his fall. In quick terror, she flung from the cot and threw open the door. Sean lay senseless, tangled

439

in bed linen on the floor. The bandages showed ominous stains of blood. "Flannery!" she shrieked. "Peg! Help!"

O'Donnell, in the foyer flirting with Peg in hope of snagging a tasty lunch after visiting his patient, pelted up the stair ahead of the housekeeper. Quickly he helped the women get the Irishman back to bed, then sheared away the bandage over the chest wound. "He's hemorrhaging. I'll have to go in."

"I'll help you," Catherine whispered.

"No. Everybody out."

Hours later, O'Donnell emerged from the room to find Catherine huddled against the wall, Peg and Flannery sitting on the steps beyond. "Give that man peace, or he'll be seeing it in eternity. He's got little more blood left in him than that damned cat!" O'Donnell stalked down the stairs and the cat mewed after him.

The three in the hall got up, and Peg, wiping at her puffy eyes, headed for the bedroom. Catherine blocked her path. "No. He'll see no more tears. And he'll hear no more tales. If you have any questions about my conduct, address them to me. I won't permit anyone to hurt or upset him again."

Peg pushed at her shoulder. " 'Twas *you* who hurt him!"

Catherine shoved her back with a low, flat warning. "Keep your voice down. He may have been yours once and he will be too soon again, but until then, *I am his lady,* and you'll answer to me. I didn't claw and fight to keep him alive only to betray him or let him die of meddling. Thanks to you, he carries a pain he need never have known. He's mine now. Either accept that fact and be silent, or leave."

Peg sucked in her breath. "Throw her off the place, Flannery!"

"Leavin' the lad to pine away? Peggie, is yer love for him that selfish?"

Peg began to sob. "She's brought him naught but hurt."

"Nay, she's brought him joy, too. His heart's alive again. Ye hoped he'd love her, only not too much. Ye can't be expectin' people to behave like recipes, old girl." He hugged her. "Poor Peggie. That notion's the same that kept us apart. These two are mixed together; ye'll just have to let the cake rise."

* * *

440

Catherine awoke near dawn to find Sean's eyes looking dazedly into hers as she lay dressed beside him. "I . . . didn't mean to . . . keep you here," he whispered. "I only wanted . . ."

She touched his lips. "I know, love. Don't try to talk. I gave nothing to Charles that belongs to you. He knows that."

He shook his head. "I've no right . . . to you. I know that."

Her eyes burned into his. "We're beyond right. I love and desire you more at this moment than I ever have. I hate the women who'll come after, yet they will come; then one, and I'll want to kill her. You're a man, the kind of man a woman yearns to feel not only inside her body but inside her soul. So much of mine is you."

"I want to touch . . . my son."

She guided his hand. "He's there, waiting." Sean felt the ring on her finger and closed his eyes.

Two weeks passed before Culhane was able to sit up again. In four, he was restless. Although O'Donnell squelched any notions about getting out of bed, he permitted him to be shifted to the divan near the windows. Catherine and Flannery made an occasion of the transfer and Peg brought up brandy-laced cocoa. She did not linger. Noticing Sean's gaze follow the Irishwoman out of the room, Catherine squeezed his hand. "I'll be right back. I think Peg's forgotten some pastries."

She found the housekeeper in the kitchen preparing a roast lamb for dinner. "Peg, are there any pastries?" Silently, Peg pointed to a napkin-covered pan. Catherine peeked. "Oh, wonderful. Eclairs are Sean's favorites." She looked up. "Won't *you* bring them to tea, and join us? This is a special day for Sean, particularly because he spent his birthday in prison." When Peg ignored her, she added, "I imagine you always brought in his cakes."

"Since he was ten. Looked like Satan's imp. Didn't need me then and doesn't now."

"You know better," said Catherine softly. "That's why you've loved him all these years." She left the pastries and went upstairs.

In moments, Peg followed.

Four days later, Catherine scowled as she dropped a

stitch while awkwardly knitting a tiny sock. Sean looked up from a book when she swore aloud at dropping another. "The babe will be more impressed with your lullabies, nimble fingers."

"He ought to have something made by his mother."

"He'll be thrilled. With so many holes, he'll be denied no access to his toes."

"Well, that wooden doll you've been carving is no Donatello," she shot back. "It has ears like a monkey."

"Then it'll *be* a monkey," he replied placidly.

She giggled and his deeper laughter joined in. "What if we have a girl, Sean? We keep saying 'he.' Will you mind very much?"

"Only the mooning swains cluttering our doorstep." His smile faded and he was silent for a moment. "Artois is in love with you, isn't he?"

She put down the knitting. "I won't be living with him for some time, if at all. If Liam creates an uproar, any such arrangement will be impossible." She took his hand. "By now he knows I'm safe and you're alive, but he doesn't know your name. You must never go near him, Sean. We'll devise some way for you to see the baby."

He smiled grimly. "You were right. Charles and I are much alike. I'd like to put a bullet through his skull, too. Shall I see you on these family occasions?"

"Wouldn't that be unfair to all of us?"

"There's nothing fair about this whole mess!" he flared bitterly, then subsided. "I'm sorry. I'm getting edgier these days."

"You're getting well. Another month and you'll be charging around and losing your temper without a twinge of remorse."

He shrugged. "Why not? Even Rafferty's no longer impressed." He looked at her, then said bluntly, "I want you to leave next week, Kit; before I'm on my feet."

Her fingers crushed the knitting. "But . . . must it be so soon?"

"Charles may be interested to know that half a man may lust as much as a whole one. Will Friday next suit you?"

* * *

A few days later, Catherine was reading to Sean when O'Donnell burst into the room. "You've got to evacuate! One of the villagers on his way to Donegal Town spotted troops headed toward Shelan. They're less than four miles away."

"Find Flannery and tell him to set the fuses," Sean said swiftly. "Tell Rafferty to hitch up the wagon and tie Mephisto to the rear gate. Have them waiting out front for Peg and Nora. They're to head north to Kenlo and camp there until things die down. Kit, Flannery, and I will take the boat." O'Donnell nodded and ran out the door, snatching up Orfeo as he went.

"Kit, fetch my clothes."

She stood up. "Not unless you promise to stay in bed until Flannery can come get you."

"Don't argue, woman!" he roared. She did not budge. "Alright, dammit, you stubborn wench!"

She ran to the armoire. Although she was as careful as possible, he was pale by the time she finished dressing him. Knowing she was giving him pain, Catherine fretted as she slipped his bad arm into his shirt. She started to do the buttons, but he waved her away. "Get your things."

She started toward the other room, but as she paused briefly to scoop up his little carving from the rug, a drawl from the doorway chilled her blood. "Pretty tits when ye bend over, girl. Always did have."

"Rouge!" she gasped.

The giant lounged against the doorframe, his pistol pointed at Sean's chest. "Good to see ye remember me." He nodded lazily to Sean. "Hello, Culhane. Ye can live a few more minutes if ye behave. Yer brother's not a bad lot to work for; if he wants the pleasure of killin' ye personal, I got no objections. Me, I get the pleasure of yer doxy before the troops take turns. They'll be along directly. Me and Lord Culhane was more impatient." He smiled at Sean's flinting eyes. "She filled out real nice."

"Touch her, and I'll tear you apart!"

Rouge smiled mirthlessly, his gray eyes flat. "Ye an't in shape to tear paper. Ye're bleedin', boyo."

With a muffled sound, Catherine took a step toward Sean.

"Stay where y'are, girl," Rouge rumbled, then his voice

443

altered. "Better yet, go in that bedroom. Unless ye want him to watch."

White-faced, she retreated as Rouge eased into the room. Sean hurled a candlestick at him. As the big man whirled with a pistol leveling, Catherine screamed, "No! Sean, don't! Rouge, leave him alone! I'll do anything you want . . . only leave him alone."

Slowly, Rouge lowered the gun. "Why not? Start strippin', girl, and be quick."

Hands shaking, she tore at her buttons.

"Kit, don't! They're going to kill me anyway!"

"We're going to fuck her anyway." Rouge's eyes followed the dress dropping to the floor, then roamed the silken flesh above the chemise. "Might even fuck her to death, pretty little thing like that."

Hearing Sean's savage curse and fearing Rouge would lose patience, Catherine pulled desperately at the chemise.

Rouge grinned. "See, Culhane, yer doxy wants it. She'd like to know what a real man's cock feels like." He moistened his lips as the chemise parted to the waist. "God, ye're a beauty." He moved toward her, unfastening his breeches. "Get into that bedroom," he said thickly. He took another step and his head blew apart. Stumbling backward against the desk, Catherine bit her hand in terror as he fell almost on top of her.

In the doorway, Liam's bloated face appeared above a cloud of smoke which issued from a musket bore. A pistol was in his belt. "Good God, darling, I am sorry! Thank heaven I was in time to stop him." A false note belied his tender concern, and sheer rage revived her wits.

"Liar! I think you were in the hall all the time! You deliberately waited until the last possible moment out of sheer spite!"

His eyes narrowed and his attention slid toward Sean. "What *is* my wife doing here, brother? I thought we had a gentleman's agreement."

"Gentleman!" Catherine shot in. "You wouldn't know the meaning of the word, *brother!*"

He paled, then jerked out the pistol. "You told her, you bastard!"

Catherine darted forward, blocking his arm. "Sean

444

didn't tell me! You counted on his being silent, just as you did when you betrayed him! You planned to reclaim me, didn't you? All you had to do was kill him, the only one in your way, the only one who knew!"

Liam's face turned florid and Sean tried to shove her. "Kit, get out of the way!"

She stumbled, but held her ground. "No! He'll have to shoot us both!"

Advancing into the room, Liam tried to placate her. "I've no intention of killing you, Catherine. I love you."

"No, Liam."

"I did it for you!"

"You did it for yourself."

"I'll prove it to you," he said icily. "I'll let him go. The others have left, but Flannery must still be around somewhere. Flannery can get him out of here before the soldiers come."

Her voice shook. "I don't believe you!"

"Oh, I won't do it for nothing. Come with me. Live as my wife. I can kill him and take you anyway. If you come willingly, I'll let him live."

"Always bargaining. Always a price, Judas!"

Liam's mouth tightened. "If you think you can anger me enough to use this bullet on you instead of him, you're mistaken, my dear. I can hold you both here until the soldiers come."

"Flannery will get you first."

"Not before I blow my dear brother's guts out." His voice dropped. "I advise you to decide quickly, my love. If the soldiers meet you in such charming deshabille, I may not be able to restrain them."

Abruptly, Sean thrust his foot against the small of Catherine's back and sent her sprawling sideways across the room. She fell to the floor, one outstretched hand sliding through Rouge's blood.

Liam chuckled. "Bravo, brother."

Frantically, she twisted around. "I'll go with you! Liam, don't hurt him!" He gave her a thin smile. *"Please!"*

"From sparrow hawk to nightingale, how quickly you can change your song, my love; but it alters too late. If I let him live, I'll never be sure of you."

"I'll *hate* you!" she screamed. "I'll hate you the rest of my life!"

"You don't know how to hate," he said gently, "not really hate." He looked at Sean. "You and I do, though, don't we, brother? You, the English; and I, you."

"Stop waving that bloody thing like a handkerchief and get it over with," Sean said in a tone of bored contempt.

"Oh, I'm in no hurry. I've waited a lifetime for this moment . . ."

As Liam talked, Catherine crept toward Rouge's body. Her eyes never left her husband. Intent on Sean, he was unable to see her directly without turning his head.

"Let her go, Liam. To the British, you're nothing but a turncoat. Do you think they'll let you keep this place, keep *her*? You're only trying to frighten her now with threats of rape, but you won't be able to stop them. To them, she's a collaborator. Take her out of here . . ." Sean clung to the bedpost, the stain at his breast slowly blossoming.

"You've gone soft, brother," Liam sneered, face taut. "Delilah has shorn the scourge of her people and he is given unto the Philistines. Will you bring the temple down about our ears, brother?" Suddenly, he stiffened. "That's what Flannery's up to, isn't it? You thieving urchin bastard! You'll not wreck my house!" The gun aimed at Sean's heart, and Catherine scrambled over Rouge's body as Liam cocked the pistol.

A sharp sound spat from the corner. Hunching as if jabbed in the ribs by a playful elbow, Liam twisted, feet awkwardly placed. He stared at his wife. With tears streaming down her face, she knelt on the bloody rug, Rouge's smoking pistol in her upraised hand. "Catherine, not . . . you! You couldn't."

"You'll not hurt him anymore, Liam," she whispered brokenly. "You've taken too much."

Wearily, Liam tried to focus on his brother's chest, but the gun was too heavy now. Its muzzle dropped, even as he dropped, his knees striking first. Catherine crawled toward him and Sean warned him sharply, "Kit, don't. He's still armed."

"Liam won't hurt me," she said softly as she slipped Liam's head into her lap. "It would be like killing himself."

Liam's blue eyes, the last familiar feature in a face dissolved by dissipation, began to fade as Catherine brushed his hair from his brow, where it always persisted in falling. "You . . . almost loved me," he whispered, "didn't you?"

"Yes."

"If I'd only had time. If Sean hadn't . . ." His voice became urgent. "Don . . . leave me here. They . . . hate me . . . British bastards. Don't let them have . . . my house."

"We won't, brother," Sean promised quietly.

"Liam," Catherine whispered, "I'm carrying a child. If you know anything of Sean's parentage, you must tell us now."

He stared up at her. "You're . . . mine. Not his. Only . . . mine." The color went from his eyes and his head sagged.

Half-grieving, half-wild with frustration, she wanted to shake the inert body. "Oh, Liam, clutching and greedy for love to the last." She stroked his eyes and mouth closed and eased his head to the floor.

"We have to leave now, Kit," Sean muttered. "We've no time to wait for Flannery to come up."

Swiftly, she got Sean into his jacket, then threw on her cloak. With his good arm around her neck, she supported him through the hall and started down the stair, but near the bottom, his slender reserve of strength failed. He collapsed, twisting as he fell, to sprawl on his back, head down, his body partly inclined up the last steps. She screamed, clutching the rail, then skittered to him. When she cradled his head, his face was as still as Liam's. She screamed again in terror that grew when pounding feet sounded in the service passage. "Get yerself together!" Flannery gave her shoulder a jerk as he knelt to feel for Sean's pulse. "He's still alive. Come on, girl, get movin' and lock that front door. The British are on the hillside!"

Even as Catherine slammed the open door, red coats beaded the frosted slope. She tore down the corridor after Flannery, who carried Sean in his arms. Once in the wine cellar, the giant nodded toward a fuse running in the concealed armory. "Don't kick that. There's enough loose powder from those cracked kegs in there to blast us to smithereens. Lock the cellar door and get over here." She obeyed, struggling for a moment with the heavy bar. "The

447

door's iron-faced; they'll not come through in a hurry. Hit the fuse with that wall torch, then give this bottle a twist."

A section of wine rack swung back, and seconds later they were descending through a long rock passage cut into the bowels of the cliff beneath Shelan. Partway down, Flannery began to wheeze, and for the first time Catherine realized how old he was, the strain he was sustaining. Head flung back over Flannery's brawny arm, shirt hanging loosely from his bandaged chest, Sean gave no sign of returning consciousness.

"They're at the door by now. Hurry, lass, but for God's sake don't stumble!" They reached the bottom. Flannery sagged against the rock, his lips white. "The . . . lever . . . there."

Catherine threw her weight on it, and a huge rock moved back. They staggered into the sunlight. Quickly, Catherine ran to the curragh overturned on the beach. Slipping on the sand, getting silt mixed with the blood on her petticoat, she wrestled the unwieldy hide boat to the water. Flannery lowered Sean into it and motioned her into the stern. Rowing swiftly, his face now flushed nearly the red of his great beard, he got them to the catboat and helped her maneuver Sean over the side. As Catherine unlashed the tiller, he ran up the sail, then went back over the side. "Weigh anchor, girl; head dead out. When ye're beyond sight of land, bear north to Kenlo. Hurry! The winds against ye. I can give ye only a few minutes."

She grabbed at his hand. "Come with us! Let them have the place, Flannery! Liam's dead. Shelan isn't worth your life!"

Gently, he put her hand away. "Every Culhane since Conal has had a Flannery at his back, girl." His voice turned to a whisper. "Ye do yer real da proud. Thank God it's you and that boyo who'll carry on his line." He pushed off before she could kiss him.

Flannery beached the curragh, flipped it and slashed its bottom, then ran heavily toward high ground. Fanning from the house and pounding down the cliff trail across the beach, soldiers fired at him and the catboat, which danced away on the waves as it tacked out to sea. He clambered to a protected crevice, where he emptied his pistols, picking off two marksmen firing at the boat.

"Save yer shots, men," a puffing lieutenant cried as he waved his saber and charged the Irishman's crevice. "He has only a knife left!" Those were the last words the officer uttered as a slash ripped through his gilt-braided tunic. His sword shimmied with a clatter down the rocks.

A sergeant was less inclined to ration lead. Efficiently, he shot Flannery through the heart, then waved his men to join their fellows reloading at the edge of the surf. As the catboat tacked further away despite their efforts, he paced, scowling. "Hurry up, ye bleedin' blind! They're nearly out of range! Jesu, if I had even a toy of a cannon, I'd blow her out of the water." As if a mischievous demon had answered his wish, the cliff erupted behind them. In a thunderous billow of smoke and debris, Shelan hurled its bowels into the sky to fall in a hurtling, deadly rain of glass, burning timber, and stone. Soldiers on the beach scattered pell-mell like scarlet beads, screaming as their uniforms ignited or they were crushed by falling wreckage. Beyond the rolling breakers, the catboat headed for the horizon.

As the boat turned north, the sky filled with ominous, dark-rimmed clouds. To break the rising wind, Catherine handled the tiller with only her head above the funnels. Tears for Flannery were hard, icy patches on her cheeks. She wrapped Sean closely in the extra sail, pulling it high to protect his face from stinging spray; then with the tiller braced under her arm, she tried to protect her face against frostbite with the cloak.

Even with its sail reefed, the boat heeled under the onslaught of the first gale winds. Catherine gripped the tiller with white knuckles. The boat reeled, fought itself erect, only to bend to the wind's force again. She let the mainsheet slide through numb fingers until the boat righted, then hauled in enough tension to maneuver. The waves grew into black, towering walls of water that slid under the boat just when they seemed about to engulf it. One particular brute hit their stern, slewing it around and filling the small craft with enough spray to set the bailing bucket afloat in the scuppers. Quickly, she lashed the tiller and scrambled forward for the small leather bucket as more water came over the stern. She applied it with frantic determination. The pelting rain became freezing sleet. With the cloak up to shield her head, she kept bailing with numb hands. Suddenly the boat rolled viciously and the tip of the boom caught a wave. As the boat slewed sideways again, the boom whistled over Catherine's head. The backstay parted with a pop, and with a sickening crack, the mast snapped and toppled. Sick with despair, she stared at the spilling canvas. It was over. They were done except for the dying.

Catherine finished bailing as darkness fell, then numbly listening to the silence and subtle hiss of blowing snow, hung against the gunnel. The waves ran by them now, leaving the catboat bobbing helplessly on a sea of black glass. As a last, desperate hope for rescue, she pulled off the bloody petticoat and secured it to the bare mast stump before she crept under the old sail to lie against Sean's comparative warmth. She rubbed her hands and feet harshly until they stung, then did the same to Sean. Luckily, Flannery had padded sail thickly about him to keep him dry. With her cloak pulled over them both, she whispered a prayer and crept against him.

Dawn rose gray-white, hazy with fat, lazily drifting flakes of snow hissing as they met the slow roll of the waves. Catherine stirred to find Sean's arm about her, his breath warm to her face. His legs were wrapped with hers in an effort to keep her warm. She opened her eyes to look into his, dark murky green under lowered lashes. "Soggy little cat," he murmured. "Come closer . . . I'm not strong enough to hold you close."

Shivering, she burrowed against him. "Flannery?" he whispered.

"Dead. Shelan went with him."

He was silent for a long time. When he spoke again, his voice was slurred, as if coherency was an effort. "I hear flapping. Couldn't you reef the sail?"

"There was a sudden storm . . ." Her voice gave way. "The mast snapped. We've blown out to sea. I lost your monkey, too," she finished dismally.

"I know you tried." He caressed her until she lay quiet against him, limbs entangled with his. His lips moved against her hair. "Tiger kitten. I could die so easily making love to you . . . *la petite mort*, then sleep . . ." His hand slipped into the open chemise and found soft flesh.

Catherine lay still, her heart thudding under his hand. Even if she were damned for it, she had not the will to stop him. But there was no urgency in his touch or in his cold lips. "I love you," he whispered against her mouth. "If this is the last time . . . I say it in life, it will be my litany in hell."

Her lips parted and answered his with feverish passion. As his heart quickened against her, she breathed, "Take me now and not even Hell can separate us."

"No, little one. Only your prayers in Heaven can beguile the ear of God. Seeing you . . . He may remember he was once a man and pity me."

"You tease me."

He touched her lips. "I love you, madonna. How much more must God?"

"I love you." Her whisper was a lullaby as they drifted into the mist. *"Mon cher diable. Mon ange de feu. Je t'aime toujours. Il n'y a pas de mort. C'est un mirage. L'amour seulement n'est pas un mirage . . ."*

In the swaying crow's nest of the French warship *La République* as she made her lonely way through the icy seas of western Ireland, the lookout retreated deeper into his jacket until he resembled a turtle even unto that creature's melancholy eyes. He was chilled to the marrow and bone-pricked at the rump, but his gaze kept up its restless lizard's flick over the waves for threatening British sail. The sailor's glum demeanor abruptly enlivened. "Ship ahoy!" he howled.

"Where away?" the deck officer demanded.

"Two points a'larboard."

The deck officer's telescope snapped to his eye and he wrung the tube to focus. Then wrung it again to frame a white petticoat. Slowly, he lowered the instrument, his brows puckered.

"What is she?" called the captain. "British?"

"Well . . . it might be, sir," his officer responded with a quirk to his lips. "I'd have to ask my wife."

451

CHAPTER 23

Tricolor

Death seemed to come easily, a creeping coldness in the extremities, then sleep. Catherine did not know if Sean's heart had ceased to beat, only that she had grown bitterly cold and his body no longer warmed her. The mist surrounding their drifting, shattered boat crept under the sail and filled her heart. Night fell without stars, without moonlight through the winding mist, without Sean, and she was sick with disappointment and fear. The sun rose like a lantern on the horizon and she eagerly reached for it, straining for the light. A hand caught hers.

"Don't disturb yourself, *Comtesse*. You're quite safe."

"What?" Her vision cleared and she peered incredulously at a silhouetted face. "Who are you?"

There was a chuckle. "Not God, *ma chère Comtesse*, I assure you."

"Then if you're the devil, why are you speaking French, and where is Sean?" she demanded faintly.

"Monsieur is safe in sickbay," the stranger laughed, "and I speak French because I'm Doctor Emile Fourquet, not the devil, and this is a French warship, *La République*, possibly hell, I've never been sure. How do you feel?"

She tentatively wriggled her fingers and toes, then stared at him in some amazement. "Alive."

"Quite. Though for a time, I feared I might not have the pleasure of meeting the petticoat sailor."

Fourquet was young, handsome, and sure of himself. As he grinned at her, Catherine recalled suddenly how she

452

must have looked in the battered catboat. She had been wearing next to nothing then, and definitely nothing now. No wonder the man was grinning. Probably the whole crew was nothing but teeth. If Fourquet expected a blush, he did not get it. She regarded him without batting an eye. "As I seem to lack even a petticoat at the moment, may I borrow some clothes?"

His smile became a fraction more professional. "Ah, but you must stay in bed two more days at least."

"I'll cooperate gladly, doctor, after I see Monsieur Culhane."

"I assure you the gentleman is doing as well as can be expected after his considerable injuries, mademoiselle; unfortunately, his chances are poor. You should be prepared for the worst."

Then why aren't you with him? Catherine thought furiously. Instead, you hold the hand of a naked woman with a runny nose, you . . . Frenchman! Aloud, she said simply, "Doctor Fourquet, I intend to visit Monsieur Culhane whether I wear your clothes or this blanket or nothing at all. And I am not Mademoiselle, but *Madame*. Madame Culhane."

Ten minutes later, Fourquet pulled back the curtain of the tiny sickbay to admit a small, unsteady figure in oversized shirt and breeches, then he headed up to the quarterdeck. Catherine knelt by the bunk where Sean lay. She kissed his fingers and the pulse of life in his throat, her tears wetting his haggard face. Alive. He was alive. Like a mother cat going over her cub, she touched him, touched his hair, his face, reveled in his rough, prickly beard. He had been bathed and efficiently rebandaged. Perhaps Fourquet wasn't completely remiss. Food and warmth: that was what Sean needed. A place to heal, to be left alone.

Her scattered thoughts fused together when Fourquet flipped open the sickbay curtain and Raoul d'Amauri ducked his head under the bulkhead. "Fourquet says our petticoat sailor is obstinate," he chided her with a comical scowl that broke into his familiar, endearing grin. "I told him he must get used to it."

He opened his arms, and with a cry of relief, Catherine

flung herself into them. "Oh, Raoul, thank heaven you're safe! I had heard the Killala expedition was a disaster, that you were all captured."

Hugging her, he laughed ruefully. "A disaster definitely, but many of us survived. We were exchanged after a year." He held her back to study her pale face. "It's you who are endangered now. You must behave and go back to bed." His fingers brushed her cracked lips. "You're suffering from exposure and have a touch of fever." Then he added slowly, "Culhane will be well taken care of; I'll see to it myself." He cocked his head. "You had me fooled, *chérie*. When did you marry him?"

With a fading smile, Catherine uneasily slipped her hands from his. "I'm Liam Culhane's wife—his widow. He was killed . . . what day is this?" she asked distractedly, feeling overwarm. Perhaps Raoul was right about the fever.

"Your January twenty-first."

"Two days ago he was killed . . . with the others." She fought off a wave of dizziness.

"Ma pauvre petite. You've had a bad time." He cuddled her again, eyeing the flaring emerald on her finger. "Go back to bed like a good girl. Culhane will be all right, I promise."

Somehow afraid now, Catherine shook her head. "No, I . . . must stay with him." She swayed and clutched the Frenchman's arm to fight the ship's roll. "Please . . ."

"Of course, *chérie*. Sleep now."

As if hearing a hypnotic command, she collapsed in his arms.

After he had reinstated the countess in his own cabin bunk, Fourquet felt her forehead. "She'll be fine in a day or so. Just overdid a bit. What about Culhane?"

Amauri shrugged. "Keep trying. We can use good mercenaries."

"And Madame Culhane?"

"She has carte blanche."

By the next night, Catherine, much improved, was able to sit up with Sean, who had been transferred to Amauri's vacated cabin. Dozing over one of Fourquet's medical

454

books, she was instantly alerted by a slight pressure of the Irishman's hand in her palm. Her fingers tightened and she looked down. Green eyes flecked with golden lights from the candle reflection held hers. He said nothing, only reached up to touch her face, then slept, long and deeply.

She was giving her patient a light breakfast the next morning when Amauri slipped into the cabin. *"Alors,* Monsieur Culhane, Doctor Fourquet tells me you're back among the living!" He grinned. "You must have the constitution of Attila."

"No, just Kit. Thanks for the use of your cabin, Colonel."

Amauri shrugged. *"Pas de quoi.* The officer who was next door left us in Brest, which leaves a cabin free for madame. I don't mind bunking with Fourquet. It's fortunate your boat drifted so far south. We might easily have missed you. As it was, the *République* nearly ran you down. Must have been quite a storm."

Catherine's well-timed spoon saved Sean an immediate reply. The storm had come up from the south. The *République* must have been surreptitiously cruising off the Irish coast. He swallowed the spoonful. "Bring me a cigar tonight, Colonel, and I'll tell you the whole story."

The spoon hit the cup. "You'll do no such thing. You know what Doctor O'Donnell said."

"Nag." He grinned weakly at her and she fiercely wanted to kiss him.

The look between Catherine and the Irishman was like a small crack of lightning, instantly shielded, but sulphur still hung in the air. Amauri was unable to see the countess's eyes but he derived the distinct impression Culhane was as intent as himself on consoling the bereaved widow. It might be well to loosen the Irishman's tongue. "Is the patient permitted wine with his dinner, madame?" he murmured solicitously.

She laughed. "Of course. I'm not so rash as to stand between an Irishman and his poteen, Colonel."

Dinner was extravagant considering the conditions. Although the wounded man ate little and was quickly done, the Frenchman toyed endlessly with his dessert. Finally, Culhane decided to let him off the hook. "Kit is aware of my former negotiations with your government, Colonel. We don't have to play games. What do you want to know?"

"Everything my superiors will want to know when we reach Paris," Amauri answered simply.

"What makes you think we want to go to Paris? Kit's an aristo."

"She'll be safe; better than safe, she'll be welcomed. Napoleon is reconciling—quietly, of course—with the *ancien régime*. He's been duly elected First Consul. France is an established republic. That status must be fully recognized by other legal governments which are, naturally, headed by aristocrats."

"So, the general intends to solidify his position before he makes his next jump."

"Jump?" warily countered the Frenchman. "Napoleon has proven he wants peace; it's the English who persist in war."

Culhane swirled his cognac. "What if he suddenly decides resident ex-Royalists are a threat again? The guillotine isn't all that rusty."

"Madame Culhane's father was of great assistance to France in the Italian campaign. The First Counsel never forgets such favors, though the viscount's services, forgive me, madame, are no longer needed. If Madame Culhane conducts herself as a loyal citizeness of France, she has nothing to fear. Should dissident Royalists approach her, she need only report them to Fouché, the minister of police. Many ex-aristocrats now serve in the highest ranks of the Grand Armée; I'm one myself." Amauri sipped his cognac. "The truth is, *mes amis,* you have no choice for the moment. The security precautions concerning the movements of military vessels are strict. You've drifted into a war. I'm afraid you must be resigned to spending at least a few weeks in Paris until things settle down. We expect a peace settlement with England soon. You'll be my personal guests. Paris is very gay in the winter season, especially now the army is not away on campaign." He looked quickly at Catherine. "But of course, you're in mourning . . . forgive me."

"There's nothing to forgive, Raoul," Catherine replied

quietly. "You may wish to ask your questions now. Sean must rest in a few minutes."

Amauri looked inquiringly at the Irishman and Culhane shrugged. "I was caught by the English and interned in the marine prison at Liverpool. They wanted to know things I was disinclined to tell them."

"Yet you're alive."

Sean explained briefly, substituting an Irish agent for Catherine's part in his escape and leaving out Liam's treachery, saying only that his brother had died defending Shelan.

Amauri nodded. "The English have much to answer for. Perhaps France can become your foster state, Culhane. Napoleon needs men with your skills. After all, we have a common enemy. . . ."

Catherine laid a hand on Amauri's arm. "Could this discussion continue another time? Sean must rest."

"But of course. My apologies, Monsieur Culhane." Amauri stood up. "Catherine." He kissed her hand. "My thanks for a most pleasant evening. I hope we'll have many more together, all three of us. You'll see Paris is more charming than ever . . ." He paused. "But even its allure will be dimmed by your loveliness, Countess."

Suddenly, the cabin became confining as the two men subtly squared off. Then the Frenchman was gone and Catherine silently drew Sean's covers higher.

His engaging charm and conversation undiminished by the bone-jarring rattle of the coach, Amauri smoothly solved the problem of accommodations on the outskirts of Paris. "You two are going to be the talk of the salons. Who could ask for a more intriguing entry into the romantic heart of Paris than to be found entwined in deshabille, adrift in a boat? My brother officers are gentlemen, but such a tidbit is too rich to escape discussion. I think it will be best if Catherine stays with my mother in the Faubourg St. Germaine. You, Sean, will join me in my bachelor quarters off the Rue des Italiennes; it's an ideal location to salve one's memories."

Catherine's hand found Culhane's under the cloak and lap robe that covered him. His pallor after the long overland journey from Calais worried her. "Sean mustn't overdo, Raoul. You'll see to that, won't you?"

"I promise that for a while his only danger will be dying from boredom, but then, *mon ami*"—Amauri tapped Sean's knee—"you and I will make up for lost time."

"Not all of it, Raoul." Culhane's fingers tightened on Catherine's. "Never all of it."

The baronne herself came out of her Louis XIV mansion on the Faubourg to greet them. A tall, distinguished woman in her fifties with a military carriage and a wealth of silver hair, her only warmth was for her son, her graciousness to her uninvited guests impeccable but reserved. She ordered the Irishman taken upstairs to rest, insisting the following morning was soon enough to drive to the Rue des Italiennes. Dinner would be served at seven.

As a maid led her upstairs, Catherine noticed the furnishings of the rooms were reminiscent of the deposed Bourbon monarchy, which suggested the baronne did not completely share her son's enthusiasm for the Republic. Catherine's bedroom at the rear of the house overlooked a stone stable and rose garden on the wooded edge of the Luxembourg grounds. After a long, luxurious bath, she rose from the tub, toweled, and ignoring the maid's shocked look, dropped naked into the bed.

Late the next morning Catherine awoke, mildly embarrassed at missing dinner but glad to have been left alone. Luncheon was served in the sunroom. Although he did not feel up to it, Sean joined the luncheon party because he wanted to be near Catherine. In the slanting, leaf-broken light, his pallor was apparent, and Catherine distractedly answered questions and held up her end of the conversation politely but automatically. Sean said little, merely watched Amauri with deceptive laziness and commented on the excellence of the wines to his hostess. Amauri, however, seemed never to be at a loss for amusing anecdotes and gossip, his cinnamon eyes mischievous as he teased his mother about her dying palmettoes, which speared brown, shriveled fronds through the rich green foliage of the sunroom's exotic plants. "Napoleon won't appreciate such blighted reminders of his Egyptian campaign, Maman. It's a good thing he never calls. This place looks as if it were decorated by Louis Capet's ghost. *Mon Dieu,* you've reupholstered the library divans in lilies!"

"I see no point in bowing to every change in fashion, certainly not in Paris, of all places," his mother replied.

Catherine laughed, discovering the baronne's sangfroid had its own appeal. "Fortunately, I shall not need to be concerned with fashion. This dress your son bought me in Calais is the only one I own."

"Pas du tout, my dear. You're invited to the Tuileries night after tomorrow. Le Roy is coming to fit your ball dress this afternoon. He'll also take your measurements for a suitable wardrobe. Your social calendar will be quite full."

Catherine tried not to show her dismay, aware Napoleon's invitation was a summons. Sean said nothing. He stuck out the rest of the meal, then pleaded fatigue when Amauri suggested the two of them smoke in the library.

The baronne eyed the younger woman's face as her son assisted the Irishman from the room.

Later, from a window, Catherine watched Raoul's carriage drive away among the trees of the Faubourg. She and Sean had had no real chance to say good-by under the watchful eyes of the Amauris. They had dared not even touch. She felt stifled by loss, by a civility that denied any expression of loss, yet knew Sean must feel this piercing loneliness even more. What would become of him once irrevocable separation became daily reality? This beautiful whore of cities would hold few secrets for a man like Sean. And for Amauri, his all-too-willing guide.

CHAPTER 24

Claw Couched in Velvet

The Tuileries palace was ablaze with light, its windows glowing like diamond solitaires through gardens which, denuded by winter and revolution, were discreetly cloaked by darkness. At every door, inside and out, guards stared implacably at the streaming, glittering crowds. Parisian *haut monde* thronged the rooms, the men in their blue tunics slashed with scarlet no less striking than their women, long and justly celebrated as the most elegant in the world. Above the murmuring crowds, chandeliers hung like mighty suns rising to a zenith of French glory yet unrealized.

The baronne d'Amauri listened idly to the orchestra tuning, its sound faint through the racket and the closed door of one of the small salons off the grand ballroom. "Well, it won't be long now," she commented. She was dressed in beige chiffon encrusted with crystals; a magnificent five-strand pearl collar with an emerald and diamond clip was clasped about her throat. "The second violinist invariably manages that horrid F screech just before Napoleon and Josephine make their entrance," she continued. "You'll be presented immediately after they're seated. Napoleon will open the ball with Josephine, of course, and you will partner the war minister, General Berthier. The First Consul himself has the second waltz. It's a significant honor. Don't be surprised if Josephine doesn't like you. She's on edge since the Foures affair. It would do well to be charming to Napoleon publicly and think what you like privately. He's not without charm when it suits him. He can be a great help . . . or hindrance to your future and that of Monsieur Culhane."

"But I still don't understand why he should bother with me. I'm just one more penniless expatriate."

Raoul d'Amauri squeezed her hand. "You recall the best of the old days, *chérie.* Napoleon wants to diminish the difference between the *ancien* and *nouveau* regimes. Peace abroad is his fondest hope, but peace at home is vital." He tapped her nose. "You, my delicious gamine, represent stability—of all things."

The barronne touched her son's shoulder. "Raoul, I believe the First Consul is seated."

The crowd parted as they were announced. The Amauris were referred to as Colonel and Madame, but Catherine's titles were droned out and she felt like an insect on a pin. The First Counsul stood at the end of the opening path across the gleaming floor. A slight man with sharp features, his short-cropped, ruddy-brown hair was Caesarean. Even at a distance, his force was compelling, but she was drawn more strongly by curiosity to see the man whose ambition had cost the lives of so many, the life of her child among them.

Sheathed in white peau de soie, the severity of its cut softened by a low ermine bodice and a starry nebula of diamonds scattered through her midnight hair, Catherine, with the Amauris just behind her, approached the low dais.

She gave Napoleon stare for stare, all the while pitying the woman at his side. Though Josephine was still beautiful, years of private dissolution had subtly tarnished her glow. Without looking, Catherine knew she would have tiny lines about the eyes and her public smile would be a trifle forced. Napoleon must have scrutinized many women under his wife's nose with just this same lack of subtlety. Her curtsy held a hint of abruptness Napoleon did not miss. He put out his hand and protocol bade her take it as she rose.

"It would appear the fabled Helen is returned home, Comtesse. Welcome to France."

"Thank you, General, but I do not flatter myself that Italy and Egypt were conquered on my account."

His gray eyes flickered momentarily, then hooded like an eagle's. "I think perhaps Troy was lowered to dust for less. Will you do me the honor of opening the ball with me, Comtesse?"

Her lashes flicked up in the surprise he had intended. Refusal was impossible. "You honor me too much, sir." Her smile did not reach her eyes.

Turning his cloak collar high against the cold river damp from the Seine, Sean looked up from the quai of the Île de la Fraternité at the brightly lit Hotel Suilly he had just left. Despite the night's winter chill, the windows of Eugène de Valmy's rooms on the second story were open and male laughter and the clink of glasses could be heard. On their way to dinner at Valmy's, Raoul had laughingly warned him the officers present would be some of the best and wildest of the highly competitive, cliquish artillery and hussar cadres. Besides Doctor Fourquet from the *République* and Captain Eugène de Valmy and Captain Emile Javet from Raoul's artillery cadre, Sean had met Brigadier General Emmanuel de Grouchy and Major General Joachim Murat. All were heroes of the Italian and Egyptian campaigns; Murat and Grouchy were military legends. Murat was married to Napoleon's sister, Caroline.

Only two women were present: one, a succulent blonde named Charlotte, who wore nothing but pantalettes and camisole and a cerise velvet ribbon around her neck; the other, Irenée, a stunning Ethiopian Javet had brought back from the Egyptian campaign. Disdaining rich food, she stood with a hand resting on Javet's shoulder as he dined, as if he were a pet. She was strangely suited to the room, its precise, formal patterns of walls and drapery accentuating the barbarity of her hip cloth and beads.

Amauri, seeing the direction of Culhane's attention, gave a nod to Javet. After dinner, as the men lounged about with Charlotte draped across Murat's lap, Javet snapped his fingers and pointed to Sean. With the smoothness of oil, Irenée began to dance with a sinuous, raw eroti-

462

cism. The hip cloth hid little of the smooth muscled body quickening its rhythm into a shivering, insistent demand. As she moved closer to him, Sean heard soft clattering of ivory and gold necklaces against dark-nippled breasts, smelled musky, peppery perfume. With a swift movement, she flicked off the hip cloth, as Raoul whispered, "Take her! You're the guest of honor!"

Green eyes looked into the black's tawny ones. "You are as beautiful as dusk on the Nile, mademoiselle, and as unforgettable. Another time, perhaps." Noting Amauri and his friends were incredulous, and Javet and Murat contemptuous, the Irishman shortly took his leave.

For a while, Sean wandered along the Seine watching mist curl around the bridges. Only a few lights streaked the black, lacquered surface of the winding river. Out of old habit from his École days, he ended up at Madeleine Rochet's door on the Île's shore side and stood watching the glow from the windows above the street, wondering if they were still her lights. Finally, he let the knocker fall. The Indo-Chinese girl who answered the door seemed part of the mist, all subtle modeling and liquid silence as she bowed in jonquil silk, black hair dropping straight like a waterfall. Black almond eyes looked up expressionlessly at him. "Honored Sir?"

"My name is Sean Culhane. I wish to see Madame Rochet."

The satin head inclined. "My mistress will be delighted to see you, monsieur. Please enter." She closed the door behind him. "Please follow me."

The girl led him upstairs. He watched the soft movements of small buttocks under silk. Slightly smaller than Kit and about the same height, she had the same fluid grace and, under the mandarin collar and soft, fine hair, he knew she would have a delicate nape.

"Madame, Monsieur est arrivé."

Madeleine Rochet rose from the divan and threw down her book. "Sean! I hoped you'd come!"

She came into his arms, warm and familiar, and Sean kissed her. "You *knew* I'd come."

"How could any woman be sure of you? I heard you were

in Paris, of course. The castaway story is still circulating. Everyone's dying to meet you."

"You mean, have a look at me."

Her black bangs cut severely across her ivory face, Madeleine's carmine lips curved across white teeth. "Why not? Romance in Paris is not so common as one might think."

"Anyone who thinks freezing in an open boat in the North Atlantic is romantic should try it."

She touched his face. "I'm sorry, *chéri*. It was terrible for you; I can see that." She kissed him quickly again, and pulled him to the couch as the Indo-Chinese took his cloak. "Come. Sit. Put up your feet and let me take your boots. Mei Lih, bring cognac and absinthe."

"When did you take up absinthe?"

Kohled eyes coolly met his. "On my thirtieth birthday. On my fortieth, I shall try opium. To grow old is boring unless one is either very selfish or very unselfish. I'm selfish." Madeleine used her long, curving lashes, like her fingers, forcefully, without coyness, as punctuations to her husky French. In her black silk Chinese wrapper, she was still beautiful, like good architecture, with a long throat and a hard, pure profile, thin-lipped and high-boned.

Mei Lih brought the liquors and they drank together, Sean the dark amber, and Madeleine the cloudy topaz. In some ways, Madeleine had never changed from the thirteen-year-old peasant girl who had been seduced by a young infantryman in the Royal Army. Madeleine had been the mistress of many aristocrats since, but no one was more fiercely Republican than she.

After the first cognac, Sean made no protest when Mei Lih pulled off his boots, only settled his long body more comfortably into the cushions and felt the liquor simmer in his belly. "I wasn't sure you still lived here; old Saint Louis hasn't yet become the exclusive area you predicted. Mei Lih could easily open the door to an unwelcome visitor."

"Mei Lih," Madeleine murmured.

The girl dexterously slid a small gun from one yellow sleeve and discreetly returned it.

Sean grinned. "I'm properly chastised. I should have

known you wouldn't grow careless." His eyes met hers. "Or talkative, when a man doesn't want to talk."

She smiled. "I don't need to ask questions. I lived through the Terror." She touched the scar at the corner of his lower lip. "Will you let me make love to you tonight?"

"There are deeper scars, Leine," he answered quietly. "The English had me in prison for a time."

"*Ça va.* I have some, too. They don't show so much as those of the poor devils who come back from these wars. My own son, Leandre, was killed at Rivoli."

"I'm sorry, Leine. I didn't know . . ."

"I had a son? No. No one did. It seemed important to keep him a secret once. He was sixteen; Hercule's boy. He ran away from his Zurich school to join the army in Italy." She put her absinthe down, then placed her hands on either side of Sean's face. "I've not yet learned to need absinthe. I need to make love to you. Can you understand that?"

He kissed her, then opened her robe to find the breasts still high, still perfect. "You're beautiful, Leine," he said simply. "Time will never be your enemy."

Madeleine laughed lightly. "You made me sound indestructible." She gave a nod to Meh Lih, then took Sean by the hand and led him into her bedroom to sit on the bed. A candle burned on the side table. "Mei Lih will prepare a bath. She'll massage you and then you'll sleep." She blew out the candle and undressed him, her hands gentle, expert, not lingering on scarred flesh.

"All is prepared, madame," Mei Lih's silhouette murmured from the doorway, the yellow sheath rimmed with firelight.

Madeleine slipped Sean into a robe, then led him to the bath. The fireplace gave the only light, but he tensed slightly as Madeleine removed the robe. Their eyes impersonal, the women eased him into the bath, then bathed him. He grew drowsy in the copper tub and accustomed to their hands, until Mei Lih started to soap his genitals. He caught her hand swiftly. "I'll do that."

She began to lather his hair. They let him soak until the water turned tepid, then Mei Lih held out a large towel and, half-asleep, he stepped out of the tub.

Mei Lih indicated for him to lie face down on a thick cotton pad before the fire. She left the towel over his hips and began to massage him with almond oil, beginning with the toes and working upward to the fingertips and neck until he felt liquid. Almost asleep, he idly watched Madeleine, who sat on the divan, her robe parted to the waist, her beautiful breasts glimmering in the firelight. Mei Lih turned him over and began again to slowly work up his body.

As if the heat of the fire were too intense, Madeline unfastened her robe and let it fall away until her body was a luminous white shape against the black silk. Seeming to believe him asleep, she began to slowly make love to herself, carressing her own breasts, thighs and belly, then dipped her long fingers into herself. At the same moment, Mei Lih slipped the towel from his hips and massaged his chest and belly, his inner thighs. Dimly, he felt a vague desire, but his eyelids and mind were leaden and he slept; his last conscious memory was Madeleine's soft moans and disappearing fingers.

His next awareness was of darkness and a warm, slow mouth at his partly swollen sex. He stiffened and a second mouth gently kissed him, then licked his lips, exploring, probing unhurriedly like the soft tongue that caressed his groin. He was too full of cognac and too relaxed to feel panic. Easier to surrender. To feel. Hands stroking every inch of his body, tongues at his nipples and encircling his glans until he felt a full, sweet pressure. At long last, he felt almost unbearable relief.

"Sleep again, my love," Madeleine murmured.

Later, in the darkness, he pulled Madeleine to him, putting his mouth where her fingers had been.

He awoke to find a stream of sunlight across a sprawled body, only now he was alone with the Indonesian. As she felt him stir, she lifted her head and smiled. Then without giving him time to protest or cover himself, she slid down to his groin and stroked her cheek against him, nuzzling him, her almond eyes half-closed and sleepy. As the girl made love to him, he closed his eyes, remembering Catherine and that stormy night in the deserted cottage. Then just before the moment, he eased Mie Lih up and under him and made love to her, slowing his thrusts to a power-ful, undulating rhythm that made her eyes widen. When her need matched his, he took her with him until her slim body shuddered as if in a storm wind.

"Mon Dieu, mon ami, I've been concerned!" Raoul ex-claimed as Sean walked through the front door of their apartment. "When you didn't return last night, I feared you had either run into trouble or collapsed in the street! After all, you're not long out of a sickbed."

Sean shrugged off his cloak for Guillaume, the waiting manservant. "Sorry to have worried you. I was visiting an old friend."

"Ah, well." Amauri stirred his coffee and leaned back in his chair at the breakfast table. "I suppose you don't feel like going to the artillery drills today."

"I feel fine. Where are they?"

"In a field on the city outskirts. We can wager on the fir-ing times. Want an omelette before we go?"

"I've eaten, thanks, but a second cup of coffee sounds good. *Café noir,* Guillaume." The valet headed for his tiny kitchen.

"La Noire last night was *très bonne, aussi,"* Amauri ob-served. "Didn't you like her?"

"Very much."

The Frenchman grinned wryly. "Too much of a good thing, eh? You may be right. One needs to be celibate occa-sionally, just to purge the system." His smile faded. "Cath-erine's the one woman I cannot get out of my mind. I was wild when I heard she was married. The trouble is, I seem to be in love with her. But half of Paris saw her at the ball. Even Napoleon wants her! How do I fight them all? Christ!" He kicked back his chair and stood up. "I don't want to be married. Catherine's no Caroline a Murat can stroll away from."

"Caroline makes no pretense of being faithful to Murat."

"Well, Catherine's no whore," Amauri replied tightly. "I don't care what they say of her in England. The rumors are already drifting into Paris. Soon, no matter where she goes, lies will follow. She must be protected. Not only that . . ." He hesitated. "I don't want to worry you, but Fouché, the minister of police, has Mother's house under surveillance. I think Napoleon himself ordered it." Sean stiffened and Amauri shook his head. "No, *mon ami*, there's nothing we can do. If we try to smuggle Catherine out of the country, Fouché would pick her up before she got a mile outside the city. She entered France without papers. Fouché can come up with a hundred legal technicalities to detain a possible Royalist."

The Irishman snorted. "So much for détente!"

"Oh, Napoleon's intentions are honorable in that respect, but Catherine's too damned beautiful, that's all. He's made his interest clear to everyone. He wants her as his mistress."

"I suppose it's naive to suggest he might accept a refusal?" Sean asked tightly.

"Of course. He's no boor. He'll simply wait until she changes her mind." Amauri sympathetically touched Sean's shoulder. "I'm sorry, my friend; I feel entirely responsible. After all, I gave you my assurance of her safety. Short of betraying France, I'll do anything I can to help, even to the cost of my life."

"Thanks, Amauri, but as you say, it's too late now."

A week later, after attending a reception celebrating the Peace of Amiens between England and France, Sean reached Amauri's quarters and the laconic Guillaume handed him a sealed note. Recognizing the handwriting, Culhane ripped it open. "I must see you immediately. Catherine."

Although Culhane asked the butler if he might see Lady Culhane, it was the baronne who greeted him in the drawing room. "My dear monsieur, what a pleasant surprise. Catherine will be down in a moment. She's putting on her habit." Her voice altered subtly. "May I suggest, under the circumstances, that you refrain from riding in public areas?"

"Circumstances, madame?"

Her silk dress nearly the color of her hair, she walked to the window. "Did you notice the kite vendor across the park? He's a representative of Monsieur Fouché." She turned. "Those white roses on the mantel came today; the card contains a single 'N.' Similar arrangements are scattered throughout the house. Catherine refuses to have them in her bedroom. Thank heaven, roses are short-lived; the scent is beginning to cloy . . . ah, there you are, and so quickly, too."

With cheeks flushed from a race down the stairs, and blue eyes brilliant under a tilted, feathered hat, Catherine came into the room. Her new habit was moss green velvet with cream silk ruching about a high Medici collar, and Sean thought she had rarely looked more adorable. She said nothing, her eyes widening slightly, drinking him in as he was her. Then she turned to the baronne. "We won't be long, madame."

"Dinner won't be served until eight, my dear. You have plenty of time. Perhaps you will dine with us, monsieur?"

Catherine's face lost a little of its luster as Sean replied, "Thank you, no, madame. I have another engagement this evening. . . . Why don't Kit and I go out the back? The hostler can bring my horse around as if to the stables."

Chestnuts rose tall and straight-shafted against the rusty gold of the setting sun as the riders reached the outskirts of the Luxembourg. With no birds twittering a summons to winter twilight, the wood was strangely silent. Creeping away from clusters of skeletal underbrush, tree roots twisted bare across parchment-dry leaves and lavender, pebble-strewn earth. When the horses reached a clearing, Sean dismounted and Catherine slid off her mount into his arms. Her face was luminous in the golden light and he held her so closely she found breathing difficult, but she clung to him even more tightly. "Take me away from here. I'm beginning to be afraid."

He tipped her face up. "What are you afraid of?"

"Everything. Everyone. Since the ball, this house has been like a prison. Every time I suggest going to see Mother's old friends or into the city, the baronne says it's unwise. This is the first time I've been out. Now even you won't stay to dinner."

"Poor Kit." He removed her little hat and tucked her head under his chin. "Unfortunately, the baronne is right.

It seems Napoleon intends to use your Royalist connections to detain you here until you become more approachable."

Her eyes blazed. "I won't! I'll die first!"

He gripped her head tightly. "Don't say that! Don't even think it!"

Her eyes filled with tears and slowly she wilted. "What can I do?"

"I wish I knew. Fouché's good, Kit. We don't stand a chance of making a run in a coach for the border. Horseback is out of the question in your condition."

"Are you saying I should give in?" she whispered. "The baronne thinks I'm a fool . . ."

"God, no! I'd assassinate the bastard first!"

Catherine's fingers fiercely dug into his arm. "No! He's surrounded by bodyguards. If anything happens to you . . ."

"Don't worry, little one," he hastened to soothe her. "So long as the general behaves, he's safe from me. I'll think of something."

She sighed. "No, there's nothing you can do. I'll just have to keep refusing. Sooner or later, he'll find a diversion." She looked up. "But I need a house of my own; a small place I can keep myself. The baronne will be relieved to have me gone. She cannot relish Fouché's henchmen lurking about."

"I'll find a place." He hesitated. "What do you think of Raoul?"

"He's a godsend, I suppose. If it weren't for him, we'd be dead." She smiled ruefully and toyed with his silver cloak clasp. "We hadn't tuppence between us when the *République* fished us out of the water. Until you wrote the bankers, it could have been a great deal worse."

"He's in love with you."

Her head snapped up. "I don't believe it! He must have a different mistress for every night of the week!"

"Oh, he's energetic, I'll grant you"—he smiled faintly—"and he's not exactly delighted to be in love; that's why I think he means it."

She eased away and wandered across the clearing. "Perhaps that's why his mother watches me like a hawk. She occasionally darts in questions about Ireland and you. I don't think she believes I was ever married to Liam."

"Others may agree with her. Raoul says slander from England is beginning to tint local gossip. We may as well be prepared, Kit. When the baby begins to show, I'm sure to be named its sire."

Catherine stared at the chestnut-framed sky and clenched her fists. "I cannot even present marriage documents without overturning a scorpion's nest." She looked at him suddenly. "Is that why you refused the baronne's invitation?"

"Each moment we're together can only confirm her suspicions." In frustration, he kicked at a lichen-encrusted log. "My feelings must be daubed on my face like clown's paint every time I look at you." He was silent for a moment. "I won't be going with you and the Amauris to Saint Denis this Sunday. It's time I found living arrangements separate from Raoul's. Until the baby comes, it will be better if we see each other as little as possible, better if Raoul and his mother think I'm losing myself in the city."

"That's partly true, isn't it?" she murmured. "You're different. You're becoming hard and withdrawn again."

"Is that the way you see me?"

"I see only the man I love, will always love, no matter what guise he assumes."

"What would you have me do, Kit?" he asked hoarsely.

"Stop loving me," she whispered raggedly. "Save yourself."

"But there's no need to go!" Raoul argued as Sean packed his few belongings. "I thought you and I had become friends."

"Raoul, I've been camped here nearly a month. Your mother has agents on her doorstep. Kit and I cannot infringe on Amauri hospitality forever."

"Look, if you want privacy, that's one thing, but you don't bother me. And if you think Mother's going to let Fouché bully one of her guests out of her house, you don't know her." Amauri distractedly ran a hand through his hair. "Look, with any luck, I may be moving soon and you can have this place to yourself. And Catherine won't need a house . . . because she'll be living with me."

Sean's eyes narrowed. "What did you say?"

"I'm going to ask her to marry me tomorrow when we lunch in the Bois."

The Irishman's eyes slitted. "Isn't that a little precipitate? She's been widowed less than two months."

Amauri sat on a desk edge. "Catherine is pregnant, no? You needn't look surprised; Mother noticed almost immediately. Widow or not, there'll be a great deal of talk. Do you want your brother's child to be called a bastard?"

Culhane's lips tightened. "Since you're aware of my dubious parentage, you already know the answer to that question. But you cannot expect Catherine to go along with the idea; she hardly knows you."

"She knows me better than any man in Paris, except you. Will you marry her?"

"No," Sean said flatly, and turned away to pull another handful of clothes out of his armoire.

"My family name is old and respected," Raoul continued with determination. "Mother's reputation is impeccable. I've already spoken to her and she's fully prepared to give her blessing to the match and back Catherine to the hilt, no matter what the gossip. After all, no woman who deserves a scandalous reputation would refuse Napoleon. Once Catherine's married to me, the general will have to drop his siege."

"He wouldn't thank you, Raoul. You could be a colonel for life."

"Look, I'll admit I'm easygoing, but I'm not spineless."

"If you've made up your mind, why talk to me?"

"Because I have the feeling Catherine won't accept any man unless he has your approval."

Sean eyed him narrowly. "Then you overestimate my influence. Kit has a mind of her own. I'm the last man you should approach for a benediction."

"Are you against me?"

"As I said, Kit can decide for herself. If she asks my opinion, I won't turn thumbs down on you."

Raoul held out his hand. "That's all I ask."

Slowly, Sean took it.

The Irishman laid aside his book and watched Raoul fling his cloak over a chair on his return from the Bois. "How was the *porc rôti?*"

"Catherine refused me," Raoul said quietly. "You knew she would, didn't you?"

"I thought she might. Respectability is a poor trade for freedom."

"I cannot just throw her to the wolves," Amauri said quietly. "I'm not giving up."

The baronne d'Amauri strode into the foyer even as her son shook rain off his cloak and handed it to the butler. Her blue eyes cool, she watched the servant mince around the muddy puddle on the floor as he took the garment away. When the man was out of earshot, she addressed her son, whose rain-streaked face was pale with cold and nervous anticipation. "I see you received my summons quickly enough. Catherine's most upset. You'd better go to her. She's in the library."

As Raoul opened the library door, Catherine started and spun to face him. Fear blanched her face. Raoul swiftly went to her and, eyes grave with concern, drew his arms around her. "Catherine, what is it? You're shaking like a leaf!"

"Fouché just left . . . Fouché himself. My God, that man signed the death warrants for my family."

"Easy, *chérie.* What did he want?"

"He implied that I've been conspiring with Royalists, that Sean might be involved. He considered my father's connection with the duc d'Artois incriminating."

"But you haven't had conference with Artois. Fouché can have no evidence, only suspicions."

She turned away, her face utterly white.

"Catherine? Is there something I don't know?"

"I *have* seen Artois recently. The business was personal; it had nothing to do with politics or Napoleon, but several of Artois's aides and servants must know of it. If Fouché has agents among them, he'll have no difficulty trumping up evidence." She whirled. "Sean had nothing to do with the Bourbons and he knew nothing of my visit to Edinburgh. He was in prison!"

The defiance underlying her last words struck Raoul as incongruous. "It was *you* who tried to arrange his release, wasn't it?" he guessed suddenly, his eyes narrowing. *"Mon Dieu,* Catherine, did you ask Artois to get Culhane out of prison?"

"Indirectly."

He threw up his hands. "Then you're both in up to your necks! Fouché's investigation must be discouraged or you'll end up in the Conciergerie at the very least. Sean could be shot or turned over to the English." He strode toward her and demanded in angry exasperation, "He did escape, didn't he? That much is true, isn't it?"

"Yes." Completely terrified now, she caught his arm. "Raoul, please! You must stop Fouché! He cannot send Sean back!"

"How do you expect me to stop him? Yesterday, I talked myself blue trying to convince you the situation was dangerous!"

"I didn't realize," she whispered.

He clasped her shoulders. "Listen. At the moment, Fouché is only conducting a routine investigation because of your background. Napoleon's interest in you requires that he be much more painstaking than usual. If you're innocent, there's nothing to worry about. The whole problem is easily solved." He tipped her face up to his. "Marry me. Napoleon will be forced to look elsewhere for a mistress, and Fouché, who is a very busy man, will turn his attention to another unlucky soul . . . shh, let me finish." He touched her lips. "I've already explained the advantages—no, necessity—of a father for your child. I've even talked to Sean. He understands and accepts the situation."

"He said that?"

"He promised his blessing." His warm hands slipped down to her cold ones. "Catherine, I learned a hard lesson in Ireland. I love your independence as I love you. I'll be a good husband and your child will be as my own. I'm only sorry my proposal must come on the heels of your bereavement." His cinnamon eyes burned with warm, inviting fires. "You wanted me once with all the innocent passion of a young girl. Now that you've grown up, is it so impossible to love me?"

She touched his face sadly. "If I were capable of loving again, Raoul, it could easily be you."

He grimaced ruefully. "Then you've nothing to lose. If you cannot love anyone, you might as well have me." He tapped her nose and laughed softly. "You underestimate the confidence of a Frenchman. If I should concentrate all my irresistible charm on you, how can you help but surrender in time?" Without asking permission, he kissed her, fully and deeply.

Catherine felt her pulse quicken, and wondered dimly whether it stemmed from sexual excitement or her highly strung nerves. Amauri's kiss hinted at considerable skill as a lover. His lips sought her throat, and breathlessly she pushed at his chest. "Raoul, you must let me think. You're making me dizzy."

His eyes took on a sleepy look. "Good. I want you to feel dizzy. I want you to fall into my arms, to let me feel like a conquering hero. I want you, Catherine. When I make love to other women, it's you I see." His lips caressed her cheek. "You, I feel."

"Raoul, you haven't thought this out."

"I've thought about it for three years, but you'd disappeared."

Gently, she disengaged herself. "Raoul, please try to understand. Everything's happening too quickly. I have to think. I must see Sean. Liam was his brother; he'll be affected more than anyone."

"Of course," he said easily. "Do you want me to contact your father?"

"No, I'll write him," she responded quickly.

"I'll invite Sean to dinner; he'll come once he knows what's at stake."

The private discussion between the Culhanes was charged with bitter grief and hard silences. Knowing Sean would not let her sacrifice herself to preserve his safety, Catherine was evasive about his danger. Sean, not wishing to frighten her even more, was equally evasive. More

475

than Catherine, he realized a visit from the minister of police at this point had to be a scare tactic. Now, Napoleon only meant to bring his quarry to ground, but if he found out about Artois, he might have her guillotined.

Sean's own inquiries to Madeleine had turned up only good reports of Amarui. A hell-raiser, but no worse than most, Amauri was a good commander, respected by his men and fellow officers. He drank and gambled, but not foolishly. He could easily afford a family and seemed ready to settle down. Culhane had nothing against the man except his allegiance to Napoleon, but Amauri could hardly be rebuked for patriotism.

Finally, Culhane could only stand by silently, trying to hide his wretchedness and sense of loss, but knowing he was failing completely because Catherine's eyes were luminous with tears. Not daring to touch, they moved about the library like carefully precisioned planets, knowing divergence from the prescribed orbits promised disaster. All the while, some devil kept whispering to them, "Run. Take your forbidden love and flee. No one will know." Until Catherine suddenly clamped her hands over her ears. "I'll marry him! Only let's have it done quickly!"

Amauri and his mother were waiting in the drawing room. Sean extended his hand and said simply, "Congratulations, Raoul."

The baronne kissed Catherine's pale cheeks, then Amauri drew her to his side. The happiness of the betrothed pair was toasted in champagne, but Sean's throat recoiled as if the wine were gall.

CHAPTER 25

Lilies and Pearls

The champagne at Amauri's bachelor dinner three weeks later was no better, and Culhane bluntly ordered whiskey from a passing waiter. He drank it raw, letting its fierceness eat at his innards as he watched a line of skimpily clad nymphs prance through a burlesque ballet. Their shrill squeals and lascivious wriggles, encouraged by raucous shouts from the disheveled males who crowded Madame Hortense's Maison Rouge, did little to relieve his depression. As a satyr-boy chased the nymphs through silver-painted paper laurel trees, they threw flower garlands to the noisiest of their admirers. The reigning champion was a chasseur with the lungs—and apparent ardor—of a Zeus transformed into a white bull. Festooned with garlands like a maypole, the chasseur let loose with another languishing bellow. Seeing a lackey with a tray, Culhane abruptly exchanged his empty glass for a full one and tossed it down, no longer caring what the contents were.

"Surly bastard, isn't he?" Javet, barely sober himself, murmured none too softly to a brother officer.

Apart from the others, the Irishman, a grim half smile curving his lips, silently eyed Javet. The man had been egging him on all evening, his subtlety decreasing as his liquor consumption increased.

Javet made another deliberate aside. "Perhaps Culhane's disposition can be traced to his missing equipment."

His companion laughed. "He might be better pleased by a private performance with that satyr-boy."

Javet laughed mockingly. "He'd much rather seek his pleasures between his sister-in-law's thighs, if he can find room between Amauri and Bonaparte."

The Irishman reached Javet in two strides. "Keep your mind on me, Javet. If you want a fight, you've got it."

Javet grinned mirthlessly, his eyes glazed with liquor. "Sabers. I want the satisfaction of carving up what's left of you! La Place des Vosges at sundown tomorrow evening. Name your second.

Sean shrugged. "I don't—"

"May I offer my services, Monsieur Culhane?" Emmanuel de Grouchy, his long face impassive, appeared at Sean's elbow.

"Thank you, General."

"I am Lieutenant Antoine Le Clerc. I'll second Captain Javet, sir," offered Javet's friend, chagrinned to have become involved in a questionable quarrel over a woman favored by Napoleon.

"Very well, gentlemen," the general replied. "I suggest we adjourn until tomorrow."

After Javet and Le Clerc had gone, Grouchy lingered with Culhane. "Javet will have second thoughts, you know. Once he sobers, he'll regret everything he said."

"Until the next time he gets drunk. See you tomorrow, General."

As he left Hortense's, Sean flexed his right wrist and fingers. The fingers were still stiff and the wrist without its former strength. He could not sustain a drawn-out fight with a cavalry saber.

Catherine turned as Culhane was admitted to an anteroom beneath Notre Dame where she waited with the baronne d'Amauri and twelve bridesmaids, all strangers, all hand-picked by the baronne from families of the *ancien régime* and the Republic. The bride's incredible beauty struck the Irishman like a blow, though she was as white as the lily-embroidered satin dress, its train a gleaming river across the burgundy carpet. Long-sleeved and high-necked with appliquéd lilies edging the fragile curve of her

478

jaw and wrist, the dress drifted into satin loosely studded with tiny pearls as it swept to the ground. Atop her sleekly chignoned hair was a coronet of lilies, pearls, and diamonds. A vivid memory of her chipping at the *Megan*'s varnish and grinning at him with paint on her sunburned nose put a hard knot in Sean's throat. He bowed slightly to the girls in aqua satin, then kissed the baronne's hand. As he took Catherine's icy hands, he felt their trembling. "You're lovely, little one."

She looked at him as if she longed for the earth to crack up and swallow her.

Sean noticed his medallion through the appliquéd lace at her throat and remembered. Gently he slipped his ring off her finger and put it onto her right hand as her fingers dug into his, her eyes going the color of ink.

The baronne noted the slight convulsive movement and her smile became determinedly set. "Archbishop Lepec will be ready by now, I believe. I hear the opening chords."

"Are you ready, Kit?" Sean asked quietly.

"Yes." The reply was little more than a whisper, but her head came up and her hand moved to rest gracefully on his arm. Two bridesmaids settled the cloudlike veil over her face.

The organ was thunderous in the stone cavern of Notre Dame, but the shattering color of the soaring stained-glass windows diminished even the music as they arched toward the April sky, the fabulous rose window like an overturned goblet spilling claret light across the tiny humans below. Catherine felt lost, surrounded by implacable, impersonal centuries as she watched her husband-to-be and his honor guard, a vague mass defined only by the scarlet slashes on their uniforms, slowly approach through the gray gloom. On either side of them, the cream of Paris, ostrich plumes waving and jewels gleaming in craning masses of color, lined the strip of scarlet carpet that arrowed to the altar where she waited with Sean. Then Amauri and Fourquet, his best man, in gold-emblazoned blue tunics, came into focus.

As the two officers assumed their places, the archbishop, resplendent in white and gold, began to drone the opening passages of an interminable High Mass. Yet too soon,

Catherine felt a rigid tension in Sean's body just before he gave her hand to Amauri; then he was gone. She would have bolted after him like a panicked animal, but the archbishop was clasping her hand into Amauri's. She mumbled the last phrases and Amauri's deeper voice firmly undertoned them. He slipped a heavy diamond onto her finger and lifted her veil. She stared up at him like a vacant doll as his lips brushed hers, then they turned and walked quickly up the long aisle as the dress swords of the honor guard flashed up to form an arch. On the front left row of wedding guests, Napoleon's thin face smiled easily. Suddenly, Catherine wondered if the cascading lilies on her dress, like the aristocrats among her bridesmaids, had been Napoleon's idea. Then from somewhere, green eyes tore through the crowd to hers and her own paper smile began to crumple.

The smile, however, outlasted the wedding reception and the hundreds of guests who dropped crumbs and admired the elaborate wedding gifts as they flowed through the baronne's house. Even Josephine was envious when she saw the fabulous Celtic jewelry the bride had been presented by her brother-in-law. As Josephine ran her finger across a massive gold and ruby brooch, Fouché quirked an eyebrow. "Undoubtedly, the fellow has access to the Irish National Treasury."

Napoleon laughed. "To some extent, he's entitled to it." He turned to Murat. "Find Monsieur Culhane, Joachim. It's time I met him."

"Madame." Sean Culhane kissed Josephine's hand, then Caroline Murat's, and his face impassive, nodded slightly to Napoleon and Fouché.

"We are delighted to welcome you to Paris, Monsieur Culhane," Napoleon said amiably. "I regret recent occurrences in state affairs have prevented me from inviting you to the Tuileries." Though his head barely reached Culhane's shoulder, Napoleon showed no sign of feeling overshadowed. Confidently, his eyes seemed to bring all men to his level.

As Napoleon and Culhane exchanged guarded pleasantries, Josephine, having heard the gossip about the Irishman, eyed the newcomer to Paris. His Spanish-style beard and moustache gave him the look of a ruffian, but an elegant ruffian. With a connoisseur's eye, she studied the savagely cut cheekbones and irregular nose. A raw scar was barely visible under the short-cropped, curling black hair at his temple; a second wickedly slashed across his cheekbone and the left corner of his mouth. She found him dangerously attractive, but because of the cool assessment in his eyes, as he had lazily kissed her hand, her long, silent perusal was deliberate and a little cruel. In contrast to Napoleon's energetic movements, the Irishman had an almost languid grace, and she remembered the other stories. Seeing his eyes, she wondered. When talk turned to ballistics, Josephine, as if disenchanted, drifted away with Caroline. "I don't agree with Murat, Caro. I think the man may be dangerous."

The sun was setting over the narrow, red-brick houses lining the Place des Vosges when two black carriages pulled into its deserted expanse of cobblestones. On the surrounding rooftops, narrow chimney silhouettes sliced the sun and streaked the courtyard below with dimming bars of copper light. Grouchy, accompanying Sean Culhane, stepped from one of the vehicles and waited as three men dismounted from the other: Javet, Le Clerc, and Doctor Emile Fourquet were still in dress uniform from the Amauri wedding. Grouchy preceded Culhane as the two groups approached one another and halted a few feet apart. "Gentlemen. Captain Javet, do you wish to apologize to Monsieur Culhane?"

Javet bit his lip. He looked pale, as if still under effects from the party the previous night. He knew he was in the wrong, and sensed the others knew it, too. He could only brazen out his rash insult. "I do not apologize, sir."

"Monsieur Culhane, do you withdraw your challenge?"

"I do not."

"Very well, gentlemen, choose your weapons."

The combatants discarded their cloaks, headgear, and jackets. Le Clerc presented a long black bundle, and from it unfurled a pair of sabers. The two men selected their weapons. Culhane slashed his saber in an experimental *enveloppement*, then waited, one hand on his outthrust hip, the saber point resting on the toe of his boot while Javet tested his own weapon.

"Gentlemen, are you ready?"

"Ready." Javet took his position. Sean nodded and the opponents crossed sabers. For a few moments, nothing seemed to happen, only a tentative brushing of saber tips. Then, at the same instant, Culhane and Javet slid backwards and the sabers flashed dimly in the gathering gloom. As Le Clerc was to relate later, the duel was not a fight, but an execution. In less than a minute, Javet lay sprawled on his back on the cobbles, his jugular pulsing away his last moments of life from an angled slash to the left side of his neck and shoulder. His shirtfront rapidly turned black in the dusk until the whites of his eyes gleamed like gray pearls.

That night on the Île de la Fraternité, the door of Number 15 opened and Mei Lih stepped back into the shadows, the white silk of her dress forming a nimbus behind the candle she held. Sean took the candle and placed it in a wall sconce. Silently, he reached for her, pulling her to him even as he kicked the door closed, crushing his mouth down on hers and tangling his hands in the silk of her hair until her heart battered against his chest.

He carried her quickly to the sofa in Madeleine's drawing room and tore the thin shift from her slender body. Half closing his eyes, he buried his face against her breasts then entered her swiftly, urgently until he did not even hear himself harshly gasping Catherine's name as he drove deeper into oblivion.

"The house looks remarkably as it did before the Revolution, Raoul; even Grandmère would have been amazed at what your workmen have accomplished, and so quickly, too."

Raoul d'Amauri laughed as he showed his bride the last of the ground-floor rooms of the old Comtesse de Vigny's handsome seventeenth-century mansion on the former Rue Royale. "I'm glad you didn't see it before. The last oc-

482

cupant was a former stableboy, now a treasury official. The furniture sprouted antimacassars like mushrooms."

Catherine had to smile. Raoul's irrepressible good temper and effort to ease the strain of the long day had earned her gratitude, but images of Sean, hoarded in brief, miserly glimpses at the reception, still haunted her. Where was he now, the one who should have taken holy vows by her side and claimed her tonight forever? She tucked an arm about her husband's. "It's difficult to thank you properly, Raoul. You've done so much."

He smiled confidently and brushed a tendril loose from her chignon. "Oh, I'll think of many ways to make you appreciate me, but you must thank Napoleon for the house."

She stiffened. "Napoleon?"

"It was his wedding gift." He paused. "He has also arranged for the Vigny holdings to be returned to you. You've a stack of papers to sign, even before beginning to answer all the social invitations piled up with the wedding gift replies." He tapped her nose. "Being the wife of an ascending general is going to keep you busy."

"You're to be a general?" she said incredulously. "And Napoleon is giving my property back? I don't understand. I thought he'd be furious. . . ."

"The First Consul is a generous and gracious man," Raoul said impressively, his faint note of pedantry at odds with his usual lightheartedness. "Undoubtedly, his chagrin has been outweighed by his desire for domestic alliances. What more delightful way than a fairy-tale wedding?" He looked teasingly crestfallen. "Aren't you even going to congratulate me? After all, I'm the most fortunate fellow in the world today."

"Of course, I'm . . . very happy for you, Raoul. I'm sure you've more than earned your promotion."

Amauri chose to ignore the uneasy note in her voice. "Come, let's celebrate," he said coaxingly, and drew her into the dining room. The long table was set for two. On the table and sideboard gleamed some of the baronne's massive silver pieces, loaned until the wedding silver and porcelain could be transferred. Perhaps, she reflected as Raoul seated her, the place would seem less sterile after her own things arrived. Then silently, she sighed. Her own things, for all their lavishness, included nothing she had chosen herself, not even the furniture: all Directoire. How much more appealing had been her grandmother's pieces, which had ranged back to Frances I. Grandmother's bed had belonged to Diane de Poitiers, mistress of Henry II; it had been a tiny bed, perfect for the petite comtesse.

Bed. She tried not to think of it.

But too soon, dinner was done. Although she had eaten slowly to conceal her lack of appetite, Catherine knew Raoul was not fooled; he even looked faintly amused and she wondered how their dinner conversation might have slanted had the butler not been present. She had already met five servants: butler, cook, gardener, and two maids. She would have little to do but smile once the obligatory correspondence was completed, and Raoul had even suggested a secretary for that!

Now he was suggesting they retire, and feeling the butler's eyes boring into her brain, she fixed a smile on her face and laid her napkin by her plate. After all, my girl, you're not a virgin. There's nothing your husband can do to you that hasn't been done already.

Balustrades topped with flambeaux set off the staircase where, as throughout the rest of the house, cream walls blended with peach marble floors. Raoul led her along the upper landing. "This is your room."

Grandmère's old room. As he opened the door, she held her breath, expecting a travesty of the senior comtesse's femininity. A moment later, she impulsively flung her arms around Raoul's neck. "You found nearly everything, even Grandmère's bed! It's just as it was. . . . How did you ever do it?"

He grinned and his arms tightened. "Maman remembered how the room was from the old days."

"She's recalled everything wonderfully. Oh, Raoul, thank you!"

When he kissed her, taking his time, she made herself relax and, trying to block a swift, bitter pang of memory, answered his ardor. After his head lifted, his eyes were dark with desire. "Don't be too long, *chérie*. I'm impatient for you."

When he came to her, wearing a dark green velvet robe,

Catherine stood tensely waiting in a white Grecian negligee that had been laid out on the bed. She knew what her bridegroom saw when he caught his breath. Caught simply at the shoulder, the filmy fabric draped across the breasts leaving the arms bare. Slashed to the hips on both sides, it hung straight, revealing her body: the long legs, the soft darkness between her thighs; the high, haughty breasts. Her handspan waist was thickened but not yet misshapen.

Raoul came close and lifted the cloud of her hair in his fingers to feel its softness. His lips lightly brushed hers, and as his fingertips brushed her nipples through their diaphanous covering, she shivered. "I'll warm you, *p'tite;* never fear." He unhooked the shoulder catch and let the negligee fall, then caught it just under her breasts. "Beautiful." But as he dropped the negligee, he noticed the scar under her right breast. "Where did you get that?" he asked abruptly.

Startled by his change of mood, she murmured, "I was injured in a riding accident. Does it disturb you?"

He frowned. "No, of course not. It's just that otherwise, your body is perfect." He felt her stiffen slightly and his teasing manner returned. "I want a woman tonight, not a goddess." Suddenly, he caught her face up to his with one hand and kissed her almost brutally; his other hand undid his robe and pulled her close to feel his hard nakedness. "Touch me," he whispered against her lips. "Hold me." He smiled as her eyes widened at his size. "I'll keep you very happy, *chérie.*" He lifted her and laid her on the satin sheets, then cast off his robe.

Involuntarily, she thought of Sean's lean, hard beauty, the fierce arrogance of his virility, and a knot of desire grew in her belly. Ruthlessly, she tried to concentrate on Raoul. Raoul was real, inevitable. But for all her resolve, a ghost entered her that night, green eyes burning into hers even as his lips seared her body. She moaned and arched, wanting him so badly that his rhythm broke cadence and, startled, elated and greedy, he plunged into her. It was over quickly for them both, for Catherine's impassioned response had excited her lover to shuddering, precipitate release.

"*Dieu, chérie.* What a woman you are!"

His voice brought her back to reality, to guilt, and a kind of fury that led to hard resolution. "I want to be everything you need, Raoul."

Because she meant it, he believed her. "If only you knew what you're saying," he whispered, flushed with pleasure. "Nothing will be denied us. I have dreams beyond anything you can imagine. We'll share them all. The past will fade, you'll see."

Thoughtfully stirring her café noir, Madeleine Rochet listened to the downstairs door close and the whisper of silk as Mei Lih ascended the stair. The Indo-Chinese entered the bedroom and bowed. The girl's youth and beauty were useful, but this morning, the Frenchwoman felt a twinge of jealousy.

The night before, Culhane had carried the Oriental directly into the front bedroom; then there had been only sounds of lovemaking and the clink of a decanter behind the closed door. Perversely, Madeleine had felt like demanding money before he left, but then he would never have returned. Gentlemen knew what was expected of them, and Culhane was generous.

She sipped the coffee. "Did Monsieur Culhane say anything of interest?"

"He intends to leave France within the fortnight, madame."

"Anything else?"

"No, madame."

Madeleine's mind began to click, the momentary distraction enough to make her miss the oblique opacity of the Oriental's eyes. "Bring pen and paper, Meh Lih."

A few hours later, Raoul d'Amauri kissed her wrists and smiled. "How beautiful you always look, Madi. I received your message, but you're wicked to use perfumed paper; after all, I'm a married man now. Is there some problem?"

"Perhaps." She drew him to the sofa, then glanced up at the girl. "You may leave us, Meh Lih."

The girl's dark lashes fanned downward as she bowed.

With her light, graceful walk, she left the room, carefully closing the door behind her.

"Her resemblance to my wife is remarkable." Amauri smiled lazily. "You're a devious womam, Madi. I'm beginning to see why my brother-in-law is letting the women of Paris languish."

She inclined her head, demurely accepting the compliment. "Still, I'm not so clever as you. May I congratulate you on your promotion, *mon Général?*" She rose and went to the sideboard, where she drew a chilled bottle of champagne from an ice bucket for his approval.

"Merci bien! Here, let me open it." She rejoined him on the sofa and handed him the bottle. Moments later, blond liquid bubbled into waiting glasses. They sipped. "Excellent year." The new general leaned back into the cushions and stretched comfortably. "Now, what's this possible problem?"

"Culhane plans to leave Paris within a week or two."

"Damn, I was afraid of that." He looked at her over the glass rim. "This is where you really begin to earn your money, Madi. Culhane has to stay. Persuading you to discourage your current patron in order to be available to Culhane has been expensive, but I'm prepared to be far more generous if my plans go well. My wife signed the papers reclaiming the Vigny estate this morning."

Madeleine smiled. "Everything seems to have gone as you wished. You're now possessed of a promotion, a great fortune, and a very beautiful wife. I've heard the comtesse is even more beautiful than Josephine."

"You've only to look at Mei Lih for proof of that." He paused. "But how did you ehoose the girl without seeing my wife?"

"La comtesse was described to me and Madame Hortense suggested this girl." She watched his eyes. "Monsieur Culhane won't return until this evening. Would you like to see her privately?"

He thought a moment. "Culhane was here last night?"

"He was with her from early evening until dawn."

"I suppose I can spare an hour before I drop by Maman's." He smiled slowly.

CHAPTER 26

Rotted Roses

Catherine soon learned her husband's playful manner hid more than a shrewd mind. Far from being disappointed by her lack of virginity, he reveled in her skilled ability to arouse him and appeared bent on teaching her every technique of a courtesan. While patient and considerate, he was also insatiable.

The newlyweds first rift came almost immediately and another facet of Raoul's character was clarified. The quarrel was over the house. Its original facade had been clumsily renovated to the neoclassic style in the early days of the Directorate. "Raoul, do you suppose we could restore the exterior of the house?" Catherine suggested one evening as they returned from a dinner party. "The old facade was much more graceful."

"You've inherited your mother's penchant for remodeling," he said lightly as he held the gate open for her. "Do you have any idea what such changes would cost?"

"Surely we can afford it. This house was one of the architectural jewels of the city. You said yourself the former occupants had deplorable taste."

"But the good sense to adjust to the times." Raoul clicked the gate shut. "To alter my house to reflect the pomp and greed of France's worst despot immediately after marrying an aristocrat would create a most unfavorable climate for my career."

She stared at him. *"Your* house, Raoul?"

Scenting battle, the coachman headed for the stable.

"No, of course not," Raoul soothed, mentally cursing his careless slip. "But you must realize you have reason to assist my advancement. After all, your future is linked to mine." He offered his arm.

Catherine hesitated, then accepted it. But as they moved up the walk, she observed quietly, "Somehow, that role in your life suggests a shadow. You said Napoleon wanted to ally with the old regime. I should think he would be delighted to see this house restored. If one can believe his admirers, he's no poor judge of architecture." Her soft voice grew more determined. "It won't cost you a franc. I'll use my own income."

"Our income, *chérie*," Raoul corrected firmly. "Certainly you'll have a generous allowance for house management, couturier . . ."

Catherine stopped dead. "I'm not an idiot, Raoul. I intend to learn to manage the estate."

He looked grim. "Do you think I would cheat you?"

"No, of course not, but why should I behave like a doll with sawdust brains? I won't be managed!"

Raoul lightly gripped her shoulders. "Catherine, be reasonable. By law, your property became mine when you married me; you knew that."

"I didn't know I possessed an immediate fortune at the time; certainly, I never assumed you'd appropriate it. You said you loved me!" She pulled away from him. "Perhaps I was naive. Perhaps it's the money you wanted."

"That isn't true," he flung back. "I had no idea Napoleon intended to return the property. I do love you." He hesitated, then said slowly, "I'm only behaving as I've been trained. I'm used to taking command. Perhaps I've gone too far. Forgive me, *chérie*. I'll teach you whatever you wish to learn. And I'll have an architect look at the house."

"You mean it?"

"Yes." He shrugged ruefully. "Even if we're crossed off the guest lists of every Republican in town."

She laid her hand on his arm. "I don't mean to be a spoiled brat, Raoul. If you're so certain renovation at this time is unwise, I don't mind waiting. But I would like to

489

see the accounts tomorrow. I don't even know what I . . . we own."

That night, they made up the quarrel as lovers do, but in the morning, after Catherine had gone over the accounts with Monsieur Armand Lessier, her husband's solicitor, she saw only one extranational property listed under the Vigny holdings. No mention was made of either the Caribbean property, or of holdings in southern Switzerland and the Ruhr, which Amin had described. "Is that all, Monsieur Lessier?"

"*Oui, madame.* You are a very rich young woman."

"Certainly richer than one might think," she replied coolly.

That evening, she held out an aperitif to Raoul and lightly kissed his lips. "Thank you for sending Monsieur Lessier today. The accounts were most interesting."

He nuzzled her ear. "I'm relieved to hear you weren't bored. That sort of thing quickly becomes dreary."

"Oh, I wasn't bored; far from it. Unfortunately, Monsieur Lessier could only stay for an hour." She sipped her drink. "Perhaps we can finish tomorrow or the day after."

Raoul looked startled. "Didn't you finish today?"

"Heavens, no. Not half. We've still . . ." And she listed her international holdings.

He rotated his glass. "You're too modest, *chérie;* you seem to know the exact extent of your estate. I'm more surprised your father discussed financial matters with you so frankly. Unfortunately, he recently sold those properties."

She smiled. "Papa is extremely private . . . and shrewd, like you. You once said you'd never underestimate me again; certainly, Papa isn't like to make that mistake. A successful arrangement between us is dependent on complete trust and frankness, don't you agree?"

But even as Amauri began to spill oil over the waters, they both knew she would never completely trust him again.

Sean frowned critically at the rough drawing of a single-limber gun carriage he had just sketched. At first glance, it was much simpler, lighter, and more maneuverable than the double limber commonly used, yet far more complex to build to the required strength. His concentration kept wandering and he hardly knew why he bothered, except to occupy his mind. The single limber had been tried before with poor results; so far, his ideas showed no more promise.

Yesterday, Grouchy had informed him Napoleon wished an interview. Sean knew he should have held his tongue about artillery at the Amauri wedding reception, but the chance to tap the mind of a genius had been irresistible. His tour of armaments factories and barges had been another mistake. Grouchy had made sure he had seen things no foreigner should have.

To avoid incidents with Javet's cronies, Sean rarely left his rooms. He had not been back to Madeleine's since the night of Catherine's marriage. Meh Lih had been strangely subdued, and he remembered his drinking and demands on her body. Even more callously, he had made Meh Lih Catherine's surrogate. Catherine. Slamming her out of his mind, he grabbed for the wooden triangle.

Sean had drawn no more than a few lines when he heard a knock at the door. He swore and went to answer it.

"Gil, you skinny bastard! I was beginning to think the British had rammed you down a cannon bore!"

The slim young naval lieutenant grinned. "Not a chance! Maman is preventing that with her cooking. I've only been home a week and she's already letting out my breeches." Beneath his sandy hair, Gil Lachaise's fine-boned face had the innocent charm of a young Parcival; his gray eyes, the lucid clarity of dew. His grin softened and he held out his hand. "It's good to see you again, my friend. I heard you were dead."

Sean clasped his hand, then they embraced tightly. He drew Lachaise into the room. "You haven't changed much, Gil."

"More than you think." Gil winked. "I'm to be a captain within the month.

Sean grinned and slapped the young naval officer on the shoulder. "We'll have a drink to celebrate."

An hour later, the two men sat, legs stretched out, a fire crackling in the fireplace, their reminiscences well warmed with Irish whiskey.

An old classmate from the École, Gil was the illegitimate son of an aristocrat. Generously, he had left Gil a legacy and, though married with other sons, had seen him regularly. When he and his family died in the Revolution, Gil and his mother had genuinely mourned them.

Although Gil had not suffered from the question of illegitimacy as had Sean, the young cadets had reached an understanding that ran far deeper than did their relationships with others. Besides Catherine, Gil was the truest friend Culhane had ever known.

"You will come to dinner, Sean? Maman's upset that you haven't called. All she heard was that a wounded Irish rebel had floated practically to Paris in a wrecked boat." He grinned wickedly. "When we learned the fellow was wrapped in the arms of a meagerly clad beauty, we knew he had to be you."

The Irishman's easy manner ebbed. "The woman in the boat was my sister-in-law. She'd been widowed only a few days before when Shelan was overrun by the English."

Gil sobered instantly. "I'm sorry, I didn't know."

"Don't be too sorry. You're not entirely off." Hesitantly, the story came out of him like the draining of a long-cankered sore, in a way that once would have been impossible for him before Catherine had made him face his need for other human beings. The only thing Sean could not admit, even to Gil, was the extent of his degradation in prison.

When he was at last silent, dusk had fallen along with one of the last light snows of the season, which left the dome of Sacre Coeur a ghostly mound of white hovering above the indistinct rooftops of the city. The room had grown cold and Sean threw wood on the fire.

Gil watched the fire's red reflection play about his friend's dark face. Agony of spirit seemed to burn under the flesh, pitilessly searing away its prison.

The Frenchman hated to say what he had come to say, but now it was doubly necessary. "Sean, you must leave Paris. The officers are debating about who should have the honor of calling you out. They're after your blood. Not just Javet's friends. The city is full of idiots who haven't spent their recklessness on the battlefield."

Sean leaned against the mantel. "I'm leaving day after tomorrow. My staying on can only compromise Catherine. Amauri will protect her now; God knows the poor devil will probably have his career ruined for his trouble."

Gil frowned. "Why do you say that?"

Sean shrugged. "Napoleon can hardly be delighted to be eluded at the altar."

Gil sighed. "Sean, I think you've been duped. Amauri made brigadier general on the eve of his wedding; his friends congratulate him, not only on his bride's beauty, but on her magnificent dowry."

"Kit has no dowry," Sean said tightly, "not a sou she can claim."

"Napoleon ceded the Vigny estates back to her as a wedding present. Does that sound like the act of a thwarted lover? Now that he's First Consul, he prefers his mistresses to be married; it prevents embarrassing accidents from being laid at his door."

Despite the heat of the fire, Sean felt suddenly, clammily cold, and utterly stupid. He was not accustomed to feeling stupid, but now the sensation gripped him like a mailed fist and he smashed his hand against the mantel. "The whole damned thing was an arrangement. I'll wager Amauri even suggested Bonapart have Fouché present his calling card!" God, what his stupidity had done to Catherine, whom he had sworn he would never hurt again. He had been too preoccupied with his own misery to see the trap. "I'll kill the slimy bastard."

The deadly whisper galvanized Gil. "Look, Amauri may be innocent. I'll grant you he's ambitious, but I've never heard he was unscrupulous. Besides, even if he is, you'd only make things worse. God knows what information Amauri might have already fed Fouché. You say your lady's five months pregnant; surely she's safe until the child is born."

Culhane's muscles contracted as he gripped the mantel in self-disgust.

The Irishman thought for a moment. "I'll have to make myself valuable to Napoleon, in case France's latest boy general should fatally choke on his recent good fortune."

* * *

Catherine wandered the ruins of her grandmother's rose garden. Revolutionary mobs had trampled the gardens. Swaddled in shallow, drifted snow, the remaining rose bushes were diseased. Restoration would take years, but she had years; to think of how many made her shiver.

Careless of her fur-lined kid gloves, Catherine dug at the roots of a damaged lilac bush. The shrub showed promise. Letting dirt and snow sift off her fingers, she watched sunlight wink off the snow's minute facets. Her heart felt as if it were cracked into tiny, frozen crystals like the ones that blanketed the garden. Her spirit had pointlessly endured only to die of creeping frost.

The marriage was a disaster. She was beginning to recognize Amauri's lies; like Enderly's they came fluently, as if they were part of his charm. He wanted something from her, beyond money, beyond her body, beyond even love, and fear of that something made her shake from head to foot.

That night, as Catherine brushed her hair before bed, Amauri nuzzled her ear and purred, "I've a wonderful surprise, *chérie*. Josephine has chosen you to be one of her ladies-in-waiting."

Even prepared for an outburst, he flinched as she whirled. "That's absurd! She wouldn't choose me if I were the last woman on earth!"

Hastily, he tried to calm her. "Josephine desperately needs a suitable lady, Catherine. One of the three she has is leaving with her husband for an Italian post. To be asked is a spectacular honor. After all, I'm only a general and the army has scores of generals—"

"So soon dissatisfied, *mon cher?*" she cut in ironically.

He flushed. "Not at all. I'm just trying to make you understand. It's a political appointment, not a matter of favorites."

"I daresay it depends on *whose* favorite one is," she muttered as she turned back to the mirror and resumed brushing her hair with studied carelessness.

Amauri pretended astonished anger. "Are you insinuating Napoleon still has designs on you? How can you abuse his honor after accepting his generosity?"

"He merely returned what is rightfully mine." Coolly,

494

her eyes met his in the mirror. "Besides, what has his so-called generosity done for me but transfer my property into the hands of one of his faithful servants? Every time I request a conference with our solicitor, he's either conveniently in court or out of the city, or contracting measles from one of his children; from the time he spends in bed, he must have dozens of them."

"Catherine, you aren't being fair," Amauri said sternly. "We aren't his only clients." He scowled and began to pace the room. "Do you think I'd let you accept this position if I thought Napoleon would abuse you?"

"I'm beginning to think you'd do anything to get what you want, Raoul," she said flatly. She tossed her hairbrush on the dresser. "What *do* you want? What is worth being not just another general, but the foremost cuckold of Paris?"

He slapped her. "I ought to kill that Corsican and you, too!"

"So, at last you're honest." She did not touch her face; she had not even shielded it.

With a kind of dull pain, he stared at the livid marks of his hand and wondered what they had cost him.

She looked at him levelly. "I won't agree to become Napoleon's mistress to further your career, Raoul. You'll just have to take your chances like all the other generals."

Raoul saw now he had tried to maneuver her stupidly. Catherine had proven she was as intelligent as she was beautiful. He could not lose her. Ever. Not to Napoleon and certainly not to a ghost.

"I suppose I could force you into anything I wanted," he said quietly. "I checked Culhane's story about the prison; also your marriage. Father Ryan in Ruiralagh was most informative."

She stiffened.

Good. Let her worry. "So, you see, I do have ways, but I have no intention of using them."

She said nothing, watched him.

"You're right about one thing; our marriage was arranged, but not because Napoleon desired you. At the time, he couldn't have cared less. You were only seventeen."

She stared at him. "You?"

With a wry smile, Raoul nodded. "Remember you were afraid your father had selected Valera, the Spaniard, as your future husband? Valera was only a ruse to turn you to me. I was to save the lady fair from his lecherous grasp." His smile grew even more rueful. "Only everyone stepped out of character. The schoolgirl turned out to be the most intriguing nymph I'd ever seen, and the villain was in earnest when he tried to rape her; to this day, I cannot blame him. I had all I could do to keep from taking you myself, but if I had taken your virginity, I would have been killed. Valera was, you know, less than a day's ride from Windemere."

Her unblinking expression made him feel awkward, but he plowed on, "On the other hand, I . . . wanted you as a woman, not an innocent."

"You were willing to marry me in that condition."

Now he felt his way. "I cannot deny that. I . . . didn't love you, although I was delighted with the prospect of having you. I was to return to England in the spring. Then the Egyptian campaign threw everything awry. By spring, your father was reluctant to negotiate, I thought because he thought Napoleon would be trapped in Egypt." He hesitated. "I was disappointed, more than I believed possible. Then when I saw you in Ireland, I became determined to have you whether anyone approved or not, although I'll admit I was keener on a mistress than a wife. As it was, Napoleon still desired the marriage for exactly the reason you hit on: a legal transfer of your property to the Republic and an alliance with the old regime."

"Why does he want to convert the property according to pre-Revolutionary laws, Raoul?" she asked.

"That, you will have to ask Napoleon. I only know it takes a lot of money to outfit an army."

Her eyes narrowed. "Then, to finance his campaigns, he's draining the Vigny estate?"

"Among others."

"But he could use the estate without my cooperation."

"Easily."

She stared at him. "You were telling the truth when you said certain properties had been sold."

He grimaced sheepishly. "I didn't really think you'd accept the ruse of patronizing husband."

"What a wretch you are, Raoul," she sighed, and sagged into a chair.

"But I do have a certain boyish charm, you must admit," he coaxed, "and I do love you. I was even glad to marry you." His cinnamon eyes grew warm and yearning.

"Will you still love me when I cut off Napoleon's supply of money?"

He appeared genuinely astonished. "But why would you do that? He'd simply rescind the conversion of property and imprison you. Culhane and I would have adjoining cells."

"Not you, Raoul," she said amiably. "You'd be sole heir and director of my fortune. But I don't believe there's any immediate danger of my confinement. It would be too embarrassing for the First Consul to pack his fairy-tale princess off to a dungeon; it might even look as if he was piqued because she'd refused his advances. So that just leaves Sean Culhane's neck on the block, doesn't it?"

He held his breath.

"I have no intention of thwarting Napoleon. I just wanted to hear what you'd say if I proposed it."

He did not quite know how to take her ambivalent reaction. "Does . . . that mean you'll become Josephine's companion?"

"Why not? It seems a silly charade. It would be so much simpler to escort me to the First Consul's bedroom and hold out your hand for your reward; perhaps his valet will expect a small percentage, but after all, these transactions are a pimp's function, are they not?"

His fingers trembled with the urge to hit her again. "Jesu," he breathed, then his face contorted in real pain. "I don't want you to go to Napoleon! On my life, I don't! You're my wife. The idea of sharing you sickens me."

"Prove it. Tell me to refuse this appointment."

"It would destroy my career," he whispered in genuine misery.

"You're a general, aren't you? How much more do you want?"

"For God's sake, I'm twenty-seven years old! I cannot just stand still!"

"I'm pregnant. Plead my condition. After all, I can hardly be expected to appear at court functions after this month."

"Josephine is prepared to make allowances. Besides, Napoleon would just send over his personal physician to examine you."

"Let him. I'll give the doctor a show! He'll believe I'm about to produce a dancing bear!"

"Catherine, be serious!"

"I am serious," she said calmly, though inside, she felt paralyzed with dread. Still, the axe might as well fall all at once than an inch at a time, for she had no doubt of her husband's reaction. "Either you refuse the appointment or I do. Which is it?"

"You must accept, Catherine," Raoul said tightly. "I cannot permit you to do otherwise."

"Then why continue to play games?" She rose abruptly. "This marriage was a farce from the beginning, and it will be until the end. If you want me again, you'll have to take me by force."

"You don't mean that," he whispered. "Ryan said Culhane kidnapped you, raped you; yet you endured it. You even gave yourself to Artois in trade for Culhane's prison release." His face twisted as his voice rose. "You *whored* for a man who raped you! Why not have a little understanding for me? I saved both your lives!"

Her eyes held his. "What would you have done if Sean had been my husband, Raoul?"

His eyes flickered. "Why, the same . . ."

"The devil take your lying tongue," she flared impatiently. "You'd have murdered him! He would have simply succumbed to his wounds aboard the *République* and been conveniently buried at sea."

Desperate resolve took the place of Raoul's pleading despair. "If you whored for that bastard once, you'll do it again. Don't think what the British did to him cannot be finished in France. Or perhaps I should notify your father? Why cheat the man of his revenge? After all, he was cheated of attending his only 'daughter's' wedding!"

Although she had known they were inevitable, Catherine went paler with his every word. She had fought with the only weak weapons she had.

But Amauri realized from her silence that while she might submit, the victory was not his. No matter what happened, Culhane had won. He suddenly hated the Irishman. He caught Catherine's chin. "Warn him and he'll die imagining you in Napoleon's bed."

Her blue eyes, hard as minerals, glared back at him.

"And you'll satisfy my wants, too. A whore's first duty is to her pimp." He jerked her to him, dragged her head back, and kissed her brutally. It was like kissing a dead woman. He twisted his hands in her hair. "Show me, Catherine. Show me how much you want him to live . . ."

She kissed him back, startling him with a passion that drove him against her in desire, then pulled back. "How long, Raoul? What guarantee do I have you won't betray him?"

"As long as Napoleon wants you, Culhane is safe from me. Then it's a matter of how long I want you . . . and Culhane's luck, of course. You cannot very well expect me to save him from natural calamity, can you?"

"Can I not? The day he dies is the day you lose all hold on me."

"Haven't you forgotten the child, *chérie?*" he murmured as he pushed her down onto the bed. "I think you'll be with me for a long, long time."

Sean tugged on leather gloves as he strode out of Napoleon's receiving room. He was glad to be free of the artillery sketches Napoleon had kept. Most of the expensive changes involved alterations in current casting procedures, which might take months, even years to perfect; but Napoleon had been keenly interested, particularly in the gun carriage modifications.

As he rounded a corner, he glimpsed a woman he could have sworn was Catherine at the end of an adjoining corridor. He took an involuntary step in that direction, then caught himself. Paris was glutted with slender brunettes.

"So you see, Madame Amauri, your official duties are not demanding. I daresay your informal ones will consume even less time."

"I am at your service, Madame," Catherine murmured politely, noting the only subtle barb the First Consul's wife had permitted herself while she and her ladies-in-waiting toured their new companion about the palace.

Josephine was the consummate official's wife: charming, diplomatic. The tiny lines about the eyes Catherine had expected were there, but Josephine had long been celebrated as the most beautiful woman in Europe and she still deserved the accolade.

But since the Pauline Foures affair and a near-divorce, she had become wary. Obviously, the young countess knew why she had been appointed to the First Consul's family circle, and was wretched. Josephine felt a bit sorry for her, but that twinge of sympathy was dispelled when she saw quickly hidden hunger for the girl in Napoleon's eyes as, flanked by two aides, he entered the room.

Napoleon lightly kissed his wife's fingertips, then nodded to his sisters, Caroline and Pauline, as they curtsied. He turned to Catherine, who curtsied with a rustle of apricot moire.

"We're introducing Madame Amauri to the Tuileries and her duties, my love," Josephine murmured.

Napoleon extended his hand, and slowly, Catherine laid her fingers across his. He carried her hand to his lips. "I hope you will find your connection with my household pleasant, madame."

"To serve France is pleasure enough, *mon Général,*" she said obliquely.

"True," he replied with an impish quirt to his lips. "The attitudes of patriotic fervor are infinitely variable."

Josephine shut her tiny fan with a click. "Will you join us for luncheon, Bonaparte?"

He eyed her. "Unfortunately, I cannot." He bowed slightly. "I bid you good afternoon, ladies. Why not show Madame Amauri the view of the gardens from the ballroom? The first narcissus are in bloom."

Tucking his foil under his arm, Guy Lavalier slipped off his mask. "Technically, Monsieur Culhane, I can teach you little." He flipped the mask onto a rack and turned to watch the tall, black-haired man remove his equipment and flex his wrist.

"One never knows enough, Monsieur Lavalier."

Lavalier rubbed his nose. "How long do you plan to stay in Paris, monsieur?"

"Indefinitely."

"I see. May I suggest we work together privately to strengthen your wrist?"

Culhane looked at him with an ironic smile. "No profits in dead pupils?"

"Your fight with the late Captain Javet wasn't exactly a credit to me, Monsieur Culhane; he was one of my pupils too." The fencing master's smile echoed the Irishman's irony. "The place is usually empty before noon; you can come up the back way. What do you say?"

Culhane slipped his foil into the rack and hung up his mask. "Same time tomorrow?"

"Of course . . . are you going to your lodging now?"

The Irishman's eyes narrowed, and Lavalier quickly added, "I only mean to suggest you stay elsewhere until your wrist is recovered."

Culhane nodded. "Thanks for the warning." Then went on slowly, "Why not just let matters take their course?"

"Grouchy says you're a good man. That's enough for me."

Culhane went to Madeleine's; he had no other choice. To seek refuge with the Lachaises would endanger Gil. Madeleine welcomed him with open arms and transparent relief. "Merciful God, I was afraid some idiot had killed you! Why didn't you come back? Did Mei Lih say something?"

"No. How did you hear about the fight?"

"Madame Hortense. Half her military clientele are bragging to their girls about taking you on! I've been out of my mind . . ."

He kissed her to quiet her questions. "Leine, may I stay here for a few days?"

"But of course. As long as you like." Knowing he never would have avoided trouble in the old days, she looked at

501

him intently, but held her tongue. "Come, you're tired. I'll have my cook prepare something for you."

As Sean dug into a bowl of soup, Madeleine twirled a glass of Chablis. "I'm glad you came, *chéri;* I was afraid you wouldn't be so sensible. I've been wanting to talk to you."

He glanced at her and buttered his bread. "You sound serious."

Madeleine listened until the cook's footfalls faded. "Mei Lih overheard my cook gossiping. Apparently your sister-in-law and her husband aren't getting along too well."

Culhane kept his voice expressionless. "How would your cook know that?"

"Her sister is Catherine d'Amauri's maid."

"Every couple bickers. It takes time to adjust."

"Last night they had a violent quarrel. Raoul d'Amauri isn't given to quarrels."

"I'd be surprised if Catherine picked a fight without provocation. She's determined to make the best of this marriage."

Madeleine laid a hand on his arm. "Heavens, I'm not accusing her! I just thought you'd like to know. After all, you'll be leaving shortly, and she'll have no one to turn to if something is seriously wrong." She squeezed. "Of course, servants do exaggerate. It's probably nothing. After all, they did make up the fight in the usual way."

Sean abruptly displaced her hand. "I'm not interested in the Amauris' intimacies."

"No, naturally not," Madeleine murmured. "I daresay in that area the bride is deliciously happy."

Ignoring the glint in his eyes, she rose and wandered over to the decanter of absinthe, fabric whispering against her thighs. "As I recall"—she smiled as if to herself— "Raoul is extremely well-endowed." She turned. "But I've been talking too much. You've hardly touched your food."

"I'm more interested in bed now."

"But of course. How thoughtless of me."

Culhane crossed quickly to her. Catching her chin up in his hand, he said roughly, "No, Leine. You're thinking all the time." Pushing her against the sideboard, he kissed her so brutally she thought her neck would snap.

For a week, Napoleon had been no more than polite,
Catherine mused as her coach moved away from the Tuileries. Perhaps obviously pregnant women did not appeal
to him and she would have a few months' reprieve before
he demanded her surrender. Maybe he would even discover another mistress. But as she glanced idly at the
surrounding debris of the Carrousel, which was being de-
molished to make way for Napoleon's new design for
central Paris, she knew she was building false hope. He
was merely giving her time to get used to him, taking special care to be charming. He must know she found the
situation revolting. Yet, perhaps he enjoyed anticipation.

Well, she was not anticipating. In the past week, she had
become the consummate whore, capable of feeling nothing
but contempt for the husband who took her over and over,
finding increasingly perverse ways to excite her because
he sensed her abandoned response was exactly that: a body
abandoned of soul and passion. Only Raoul could change
the course of their lives together, but even if he made the
decent choice, she could never love him. His threat to Sean
was too stark. She would cooperate until she could retaliate. God, what black thoughts to mingle with the first
lovely hints of spring.

She ordered the driver to turn toward the Seine. At
the Pont de la Concorde, she signaled him to stop. As
she walked along the sunlight-dappled river, the vehicle
trailed her. Paris skies were blue, trees dotted with tender
nubs of green. Clots of wildflowers stubbornly poked up in
the excavation for the Place de la Concorde. As barges and
water coaches ferried cargo and passengers under the
bridge, vendors paraded the quais with Marseilles lan-
goustines. It was a long time before she had breathed
enough clean air to face the house on Rue Royale again.

"I lunched with your brother-in-law today," Raoul said
casually as the butler placed a bowl of soup on his plate.

"Oh?" Catherine returned with equal calm. "I trust he's
well?"

"Quite. In fact, when I asked him to join our cadre
tchembourti match this Sunday, he agreed."

"But he has no ponies," she objected.

"He's ordered that magnificent black of his brought from Ireland. Of course, the animal is too big to be used in tchembourti, but I offered the use of a string from my stable."

"That was civil of you," she said dryly. "I didn't know we kept a stable of sufficient size to accommodate two players. You *are* playing in the match?"

"I wouldn't miss it." Raoul took a sip of his wine. "I keep most of my racers and ponies near Longchamps. They've won a tidy sum this month."

He smiled to himself as he envisioned his teammates' reaction when Culhane joined them. They would not challenge the Irishman at the match in deference to a brother officer, particularly because they believed Amauri ignorant of Javet's insult to his bride. Too, some of them probably thought Javet had been out of line. No, he was not worried about a scene, but he had not expected Culhane would have the audacity to strut in front of a pack fairly panting for his blood. A good thing the Irishman could take care of himself; he would not have enjoyed calling off the pack.

Mounted on Mephisto, Sean spotted Catherine in the crowd assembled for the match. Even among many beautiful women who strolled with their gentlemen about the fringes of the playing field, she was extraordinary. The day was chilly, and despite the change of season, Amauri had insisted she wear a dramatic, high-necked black dress with a cashmere shawl fringed in sable tips draped over one shoulder. A large opal-and-diamond pin secured a peacock aigrette to a turban cloche which covered her hair. One gloved hand held a heavy sable muff; in the other was looped the leash of a cheetah, which sat tensely on his haunches as horses uneasily minced around him. She was a vision out of Omar Khayyam, her incredible bone structure and oblique eyes drawing attention from all over the field.

As she turned away from a small group of officers and ladies, Catherine saw Sean almost at the same instant, and for a moment, the world dropped away to leave a harsh silence. Need unmasked. Later, neither knew who moved first: Catherine, who left the crowd; or Sean, who urged the black to follow her across the tawny field speckled with shoots of new grass. It was unwise and they knew it. They were too conspicuous, the First Consul's newest mistress and the notorious killer reputed to be the father of her unborn child. Yet, as irresistibly as lunar tides, they were drawn, one to the other.

Away from the crowd, Catherine looked up at Sean in his Cossack-style tunic with team colors banded on his arm. She lifted her hand, letting the sable slip down her arm in a black glossy fall. Leaning down from the saddle, Sean touched her fingers with his lips, then reluctantly released them.

"You look tired, love," she said softly as she let her hand drop to stroke Mephisto's neck.

"You look beautiful." Sean's lips twisted in a slight smile. "There's little resemblance to the greasy urchin of Liverpool."

She laughed huskily. " 'Tis fickle, y'are. You said I was beautiful then, too."

"You were," he murmured, then harshly, "I miss you like hell."

Her eyes glimmered too brightly for a moment, then Mephisto, exasperated because she had stopped stroking him, stepped forward and nudged her. The nervous cheetah backed, fangs bared. Its leash dragged on Catherine's hand and Sean's hand slipped toward his knife. Catherine turned. "Sit, Salomé." The cat obeyed edgily.

"That's quite a house pet," Culhane commented with a frown.

"Raoul likes me to make a display. He gave Salomé to me a few days ago. She's quite tame." Her voice lowered. "Too tame. She's afraid to be dangerous."

Sean caught the faint inflection. "And how are you, Kit?"

She soothed the cheetah, her heavy lashes hiding her eyes. "As happy as can be expected. The life of a general's wife is a busy one, thank God." She looked up and smiled suddenly. "With my social schedule, our child should be a natural dancer. He was tapping his toes in time to a polonaise at the Russian ambassador's the other night."

Sean laughed, his release what she had hoped, but somehow the boyish note in his mirth stabbed her to the heart. "Your team is moving onto the field, Sean. Hadn't you better join them?"

He reluctantly nodded. "I have to switch horses." His voice lowered. "Wish me luck?"

She slipped a crumpled four-leafed shamrock from the heel of her glove and tucked it into his. "I found it in the garden this morning."

"More cognac, *chérie*? Your hands are like ice," Amauri asked his bride solicitously as they rode back into the city.

"Yes, please." He poured and she sipped gratefully, then thrust her free hand deeper into her muff. Reclining like a skinny dog on the opposite seat, the cheetah watched them.

"How did you like the match?" Raoul inquired.

"It was wonderful. Your cadre played beautifully, and with such vigor. They deserved to win."

"That Georgian cossack officer who showed us the game last year rode with even more vigor, just as brutally as Culhane. He said that in Tibet and Afghanistan, tribesmen use enemies' heads for balls. From watching him on the field, one would think Culhane is a savage! Doesn't he play at anything?"

"If he weren't a fighter, he'd be dead."

"Well, he broke Rodier's shoulder with that damned playing stick."

"Rodier was blocking his shot," she replied placidly.

"That's no excuse."

"Rodier deliberately interfered with his shots all through the match; so did some of the others. Sean might have scored at least three more goals if they'd let him alone."

Amauri scoffed, "The man isn't God. He's never played the game before. How can you blame his misses on others?"

"If Sean were God, Ireland would be free and I wouldn't be married to you," she said bluntly. "I know what I saw.

506

The others in your cadre ostracized him after the match. You and Grouchy were the only ones who spoke to him."

"Aren't you forgetting Madeleine Rochet and Hortense Castel's barouche of well-rouged young ladies?"

Catherine's fist clenched in her muff, but her voice was even. "Why did your fellow officers treat him so rudely, Raoul?"

"Your brother-in-law makes enemies far more readily than friends."

Her lashes flicked up. "Have you been helping him make enemies?"

"No, for God's sake! He does well enough at that by himself!" he exploded. "I'm not his keeper, though I ought to keep closer watch on you. You made a spectacle of us both by going off with him. Don't you realize for your child's sake, you mustn't be seen with the man?"

"Sean Culhane is my brother-in-law, Raoul," she said calmly. "To ignore that relationship will cause gossip too. It's best to treat him normally, as a relative. Surely you know there is no man on earth with whom I would be less likely to compromise your honor."

As the carriage entered Paris, Raoul stared at her serene, beautiful mask in the twilight. He itched to tell her of Culhane's mistresses, but dared not. Ironically, he had to fan the heat of her longing to ensure her obedience.

CHAPTER 27

The Outcast

"En garde . . . engage!" Shining foils flicked in delicate, explorative movements. Lavalier and his opponent were well matched, their opening movements a deft formality. Wearing old-fashioned steel fencing masks penetrated by a single horizontal slit, they resembled medieval knights, formal and mysterious. The matched pairs in the loft drifted from their exercises to watch the two swordsmen. The light foils skimmed in undulating bands of reflected light with flawless precision rarely seen in a century increasingly dominated by sabers.

Shortly, behind his mask, sweat ran into Lavalier's eyes. It was one thing to meet his equal, another to meet his superior. His opponent was too accustomed to the deadly reality of infighting to shield his expertise. When the match ended, the little Gascon held out his hand. "You're the better man, Monsieur Culhane. It gives me no shame to admit it."

Murmurs went up as Culhane slipped off his mask and grasped the offered hand. "The more fortunate fighter, perhaps, Monsieur Lavalier, but not the better man."

Lavalier grinned, his white teeth surprisingly large in his small jaw. "Will you join me for dinner, monsieur? There's a certain little maneuver I'd like you to show me tomorrow. You can understand how awkward it would be for the teacher to pay his pupil?"

As the two men laughed, several spectators, including one of Javet's cadre officers, approached a trifle hesitantly to be introduced. Others held back; some, awed, hurried off to spread the news that the Irishman had surfaced and to enthusiastically embellish his skill.

For all his appearance of carelessness, Culhane prowled the Lautier drawing room as edgily as a panther among alien scents. Relief that he was at last able to take action was neutralized by the certainty serious trouble would come of it. On the surface, things were beginning to go his way. Napoleon had given him authority to supervise construction of the artillery modifications; better yet, he wanted more designs. Grouchy had openly befriended him. General hostility was tempered by their association and the match with Lavalier. Now, all he had to do was look tame. He took up a post against the wall where he met furtive stares with sardonic amusement.

Gil deftly negotiated the general retreat of the Lautiers' dinner guests from that particular area and angled in with two glasses of champagne. "Here. Drink up. Our hostess is fretting about which woman she's going to seat with you at dinner. Your partner lost her nerve." He grinned. "It looks like you're going to draw either one of Madame Lautier's arch enemies or Yours Truly." As Sean laughed, Gill grimaced. "How can you look half-asleep? Haven't you seen Arcôt and his friends glaring daggers?"

Sean grinned. "I haven't got my back to the wall for nothing, *ami.*" His eyes flicked toward the uniformed malcontents, who glared like sullen organ-grinders' monkeys on the opposite side of the room. "They'll wait until the party's over to start the fur flying."

Gil shook his head. "Don't be too sure. Fourquet and Murat have spread a pretty black picture of you."

"Why should Murat discredit me?"

"He's a crony of Javet's, for one thing; for another, he's an idle gossip." Gil hesitated, then plunged on, "He's labeled you as a homosexual."

The Irishman's abruptly tightening fingers threatened to snap the stem of his glass.

"Easy, *ami.* It's not just his way of revenging Javet. He isn't a bad lot. He's brilliant at manipulating the enemy in field maneuvers, but when he carries his intrigues into civilian life, he's an idiot; even Napoleon says so."

His eyes glinting like dark bits of glass, Culhane said nothing, half wondering if Gil may have chosen this moment to tell him and force him to conquer the shock and rage quickly, but he still craved to do the murder everyone expected.

Sean watched almost absently as Arcôt selected a pistol from the case Gil offered him. With Levet, his second, standing behind him, the Frenchman looked determined but pale, even in the chill gray mist of early dawn. The aged trees of the Luxembourg loomed like druidical wraiths in the seeping mist that spread outward from the river. Squirrels scampered across the ground and skittered with tiny, scratching claws up the bark to branches, where they flicked nervous peeks at the five men who silently took positions below on the damp, silvery grass. The teams of the two coaches dozed in their traces, heads drooped. High in a chestnut tree, a single bird trilled a warning to his hushed tribe. Then a voice began to count and the bird fell silent. On command, the two armed men turned, aimed, and fired. The horses' heads jerked up with low whinnies and the animals danced restlessly, then settled down, reassured by familiar hands at their reins. Long before they quieted, one duelist lay on his back, his white shirt unstained by blood. Confused, his second knelt at his side as the other men closed in. Then Levet saw the black, welling emptiness where Arcôt's left eye had been and looked up with a hoarse rasp. "You cold-blooded bastard!"

Culhane said nothing, simply replaced his gun in its case as Gil gently tugged the other one from the dead man's fingers.

As the coach rolled lumpily over the uneven ground of the park, Gil abruptly pulled Sean's cloak free of his left arm. A sleeve was steeped in blood. The young Frenchman swore. "I thought he got you. Thank God Marius and Levet were too upset to notice."

"It's just a scratch."

Gil frowned. "If Arcôt hadn't been so tense, he might

have done a better job; but then, he wanted to live." He cocked his head. "You don't much care, do you? The girl is all that matters."

"These fights will get uglier, Gil," Sean said impassively. "Sure you want to tag along?"

Gil eyed his friend's careful mask. "I know you've been brutal to discourage challengers. It's you I'm concerned for, don't you know that?"

The Irishman did not reply, but the mask faded, and for Gil, it was enough.

By the time Culhane reached Madeleine's, his arm throbbed painfully, and he was relieved to find Mei Lih there. Without protest, he let her clean his wound. Her fingers were cool on his bare skin; he tried not to think about the way they felt. Though he had often wanted her, he had not taken her since he had been living at Madeleine's. He tried to relax but the twinges that shot through his arm each time she tweezed a thread out of the seeping groove kept him tense. Finally, she swabbed the fissure with whiskey. After bandaging him, she started to move away with the bottle. He caught her arm. "Wait." He took a long pull at the bottle, then handed it back. "Thanks for the doctoring."

The Oriental looked up at the man who towered over her. "I am honored to serve you, my lord."

Sean suddenly wanted to lift her against him like a child and kiss her. Feel the long course of her hair stream through his fingers. Make love to her, then sleep with her small body curved against his like a kitten. Like Kit.

Without a word, he went to collect his artillery diagrams and set to work at the desk in his bedroom. In late afternoon, he threw himself across the bed, a familiar ache pounding behind the scar near his left eye. The headaches were less frequent now, only returning when he strained his eyes.

He was nearly asleep when he felt Mei Lih tug at his boots. When she went on to undress him, he cooperated dully, oblivious when she threw a blanket over him.

It was night when he came partly awake to find her sitting by the bed. Serene as a silver lily in the moonlight, she looked so much like Catherine in the shadows that he felt a pang of longing. "There's no need to keep watch, Mei Lih," he murmured. "The wound is slight."

"No, my lord. The wound is deep," she replied softly. "You may die of it, I think."

He realized she was not speaking of the bandaged cut. "Perhaps," he agreed quietly. Obviously, out of his head with self-pity and drink, he had babbled more than he ought on Catherine's wedding night.

"Let me give you peace, my lord."

He touched her cheek. "How lovely you are. I don't want to hurt you. How can I make you understand?"

She held his fingers against her lips, then smiled for the first time, allowing him past her impenetrable reserve. "As a girl baby of poor family, I was given to the Sisters of Saint Marguerite in Saigon and educated. I hoped very much to become a nun. When I was twelve, my father demanded my return. He sold me to a pavilion of love where I remained until a French naval officer brought me to Paris. In a fit of drunkenness, he sold me to a place called Antime's to pay his debts."

Sean had heard of Antime's, a rat hole of disease down by the river. Sickened, he wondered what kind of man would condemn another human being to that living hell.

"Fortunately, I was there only a few days. The officer had first tried to sell me to Madame Hortense; she told Madame Rochet, who, after making certain I had not contracted a disease, took me in." She stroked his open palm. "Since the convent, no one has been concerned with my feelings. Only you."

He shook his head, his voice low and dull. "You're wrong, *p'tite*. I've used you."

Unexpectedly, she smiled again and tilted her head. "Because you see in me the illusion of one denied to you? Perhaps I am a gift of God."

His lips twisted in the darkness. "An interesting theory, *ma petite philosophe*. Will it ease the hurt when I blurt out the wrong name, as apparently I've done before?"

"Long ago I gave my heart to God. He does not mind sharing."

"Are you certain this is an acceptable way to save a sinner's soul? I'll never see you as a nun."

"A nun is not what you need," she said firmly, with a gleam in her eye that startled him. "God knows what He is doing."

The Irishman's final protest was stopped by the softness of her mouth on his.

Despite Catherine's steely resignation, Amauri saw a growing wildness in her that threatened their fragile arrangement. Abrupt to the servants, taciturn to the point of hostility, she roamed the house like a caged animal. Hardly a promising courtesan, he decided. At this rate, Napoleon would be put off. Steps must be taken to end the problem.

A visit to Madeleine's was out of the question, so, as if for an exercise bout, Amauri went to Lavalier's fencing school. After watching the Irishman in a brilliant exchange with the Gascon master, Amauri invited him out for a drink.

Stone drunk, the young Frenchman arrived home well after dinner. Silent and morose, Culhane returned to Madeleine's. Each, determined to wrangle information out of the other, had merely succeeded in acquiring the requisites for a brain-splitting hangover. As he was put to bed by his wife, Amauri did remember one thing: the object of his visit to Lavalier's. "Culhane'sh goin' opera th'us tomorra night. Just a cozy m'nage à trois to oblige my blushing bride." He tugged her head clumsily down to kiss her before he passed out with a lopsided smile.

Sober, with the traces of a pounding headache still lurking at his temples, Amauri found his rival's presence far less easy to shrug off when he and the Irishman flanked Catherine's chair in a box at the Opera. Before they left for the theater, he had served Culhane cognac in the drawing room while Catherine finished her toilette. He had insisted she wear her prettiest, most seductive dress, and when she entered the room, he felt triumphant. Catherine had chosen the perilously low-cut black Alençon lace. Besides her rings, she wore only a pair of magnificent diamond studs in her ears. But when Raoul saw the starved longing in the Irishman's briefly unguarded eyes, he realized his wife could have worn rags. And Catherine's eyes, which Raoul only saw of late as cold, brilliant sapphires, warmed with deep-fired radiance as she gazed at the Irishman; then their yearning melted to stark unhappiness within a heartbeat. Raoul had meant to remind her of her love for Culhane so forcefully that she would never dare to resist Napoleon. Now, all he knew was that Culhane had her love and no other man could beg, borrow, or steal it.

He glanced up automatically as the orchestra finished the *Alceste* overture and the corps de ballet swirled into their opening steps. Fetching wenches. Why the hell did he have to be married to a raving beauty who made other women seem insipid?

For Catherine and Sean, the performance was torture, their frustration almost tangible under the indifferent masks they had worn as they had passed through the lobby crowds and climbed the stair to their box. Catherine's black moiré evening cloak formed a dramatic foil to the tall man in black at her side, and Amauri realized he had erred in ordering the black lace. In his blue and scarlet he, himself, appeared to be the stray escort.

Because the gilt chairs of the two men were placed slightly behind hers, Catherine was unable to see Sean without turning her head. But she felt him in the darkness. Warm reality. Sensed his nearness as if his hands caressed her skin. Sensed his heartbeat as if it lay beneath her ear. How tired he looked. How tense and wary, as if he held the world at bay. She could have wept as she remembered the shy efforts he had once made to meet people halfway. His loneliness now was so transparent she ached to touch him, even if only to take his hand as a friend. And how transparent was Amauri's reason for this miserable farce.

Grim thoughts that had plagued her for weeks whirled through her brain. If she warned Sean, he would realize her danger and refuse to leave France. Whether he went or stayed, he would eventually know if she became Napoleon's mistress. He would do something desperate and be killed. And if he stayed in Paris, sooner or later Amauri would destroy him anyway. There seemed to be only one thing to do; she must hurt him to keep him alive.

Tantalized by the subtle scent of Catherine's perfume, Sean remembered glimpsing the roses of her nipples beneath her lace bodice as he had kissed her hand in her drawing room. He had not dared to dwell on the thought before, but now it went straight to his groin. As he tried to divert his mind, Catherine reached out and took her husband's hand. Missing Amauri's look of surprise before the Frenchman smiled back at her, Culhane felt jealousy rattle through him like an angry snake. He tried to fight the fury down. After all, she had married the man. They had done far more than hold hands; then, as he imagined *that*, he nearly went berserk.

As he watched Catherine's small, affectionate attentions to Amauri through the remainder of the performance, Sean sensed she loved her husband. He was utterly unprepared for her rejection piled on top of the stark hostility he met everywhere. He felt as if he were some nameless dead planet blindly hurtling away from its sun.

Then his jaw set. He had nothing left to lose, but Catherine had a chance. Unless Amauri turned out to be Napoleon's puppet. Catherine would want to know the truth, no matter how much it hurt. But could he hurt her?

As the performers took their final bows under a rain of flowers, Amauri turned with his easy smile and lightly caressed Catherine's bare arm. "We've been invited backstage to meet the prima donna. You'll enjoy Madame Wetzl, Sean. She's more of a roué than most men."

Sean managed a noncommittal smile and opened the door of their box, not looking at Catherine as she passed through it.

Madame Wetzl held court backstage, her fleshy face dampened with perspiration under heavy makeup. Catherine felt drained. She fixedly stared at the web of ropes and pulleys overhead, the stacked flats, anywhere but at Sean's set face. The diva had unabashedly looked him up and down, then claimed his arm, her body powder smearing his sleeve.

The couples who had come backstage eyed Culhane with wary curiosity, then, disarmed by his polite manner, engaged him in conversation when La Wetzl allowed anyone else a word. Catherine had known she would have to contend with other women in Sean's life, but that knowledge did not make it easier as she felt the electric interest of the attractive Parisiennes who vied for his notice. Even the dancers peeked at him as they mopped uninhibitedly at their pretty, perspiring faces and shoulders, hitching up their muslin costumes like so many tired butterflies. One blonde stared outright, and made no effort to respond to the quips tossed at her by the attentive rakes.

Suddenly, Catherine stared back, eyes wide with astonishment. "Moora!" she breathed. She slipped out of Amauri's clasp. "Pardon me, Raoul; I see someone I know." He watched curiously as she flew across the stage to a golden-haired dancer who met her partway with open arms.

"My lady!" Moora sobbed with confusion and joy. "Oh, my lady!"

"It's plain Kit to you and don't you ever forget it! Oh, you look wonderful!" Catherine hugged her tightly, then looked her up and down. "You're so sophisticated!" She did not exaggerate. The Irish girl's blond hair was sleekly caught back from a porcelain face dominated by impudent blue eyes that made her resemble a lively, lovely doll.

"I'm Marya Alexandrovna now, dahlink," Moora replied grandly with a heavy Russian accent. "I lif on vodka and caviar, slip on satin sheets cofered with roses, and svat men away like mosquitoes." She grinned impishly. "The only trouble is; raw fish still heaves me stomach, I've scratches from thorns, and I slide out of bed the livelong night." She shrugged. "And what use has a woman in love for swarms of men?"

"You're in love? How wonderful! Who's the lucky fellow?"

"There are three actually; I just haven't the heart to discard any of them."

Catherine laughed. "Sean warned you'd take to a life of sin like a duck to water!"

Moora's eyes slid over Catherine's shoulder. "That's *him*, isn't it?"

"In the flesh. He'll be so glad to see you . . . but for heaven's sake, behave, or he'll never let me hear the end of it."

"I knew ye'd win him over!" Moora said triumphantly, lapsing into brogue. "Will ye be lookin' at that boulder on yer finger! I knew he was a goner when he pulled ye out of that pond. Scared silly, he was—"

"Moora, hasn't your mother written you?" cut in Catherine, her smile slipping.

"We've been on tour. The troupe just opened in Paris a week ago. With the war and all, I imagine I've letters waitin' in six cities."

Moora stole another look at the Wetzl crowd. "For a minute I was worried when I saw you with General Amauri. There's a skirt chaser! He's been after every girl in the corps!"

"He's my husband, Moora," Catherine said quietly, "not Sean."

Moora went white. "Oh, Lord, what can I say?"

Catherine smiled faintly. "Nothing. Raoul's infidelity is no surprise."

Tears came to the girl's eyes. "But why? What's Culhane doin' here if he's not with you?" Suddenly, her eyes fell to Catherine's gently protruding belly and she fell awkwardly silent.

"We cannot talk here," Catherine said. "Can we meet tomorrow?"

"We can go to my lodgings after the matinee."

"I'll be there. Now, come and see Sean." Catherine's fingers suddenly dug into her hand. "He ought to know something in his life has been a success!"

CHAPTER 28

A Distant Music

Sean finished his last drawing. Inspecting each diagram of French armaments, he scribbled notes on them. He rolled the drawings, then inserted them into the barrels of dueling pistols.

He replaced the pistols in their case, swept his cloak over his shoulder, and pulled a hat low across his face. After dousing the lamp, he checked the windows overlooking the street. The man was there; no doubt, his confederate was in the rear courtyard as usual. They were Fouché's people, who had scared off the hotheads who skulked around.

Quickly, Culhane tied his boots around his neck. Like a ghost, he crept out of an alley window with the dueling case in a saddlebag over his shoulder. He hauled himself up to the roof via the knotted rope looped around the chimney; it had proved useful in evading Javet's friends. Now over the rooftops to a side street, then to Gil's where he stabled Mephisto. It would be a long ride to the *Sylvie* in Calais. She would deliver the drawings—ironically, to England.

A week later, after Sean's return to Paris, Napoleon reviewed his latest artillery designs. His gray eyes did not reflect his praise of them, however; and he was indifferent when Sean again declined his offer of a colonel's rank in the army. "Undoubtedly a wise decision," Napoleon observed coolly. "Good duelists make poor soldiers."

Sean waited, tension pricking his muscles.

Napoleon smiled faintly. "If I blamed you for these duels, *whatever* the cause, Monsieur Culhane, you'd be in prison; however, the loss of your skills would inconvenience me. Lieutenant Tourney, the current challenger, will publicly apologize to you at Maison Thäis this evening; I hope you'll oblige him by being there to accept it graciously." He idly brushed his jaw with his pen. "In future, the instigating party will be arrested. I hope you understand my position?"

Sean left the office with a feeling of unease, not because of the admonition about dueling; but because Napoleon had scrutinized him as carefully as a gambler who suspected a cheat. Apparently Bonaparte had nothing incriminating or he would not have sent him to watch yet another secret test. But why the sudden scrutiny?

Only moments later, with a sickening sense of dread, he thought he knew the answer. From a salon down the hall, he heard music, the Mozart piece he had heard Catherine play at Shelan. She was playing it now; no one else had her special touch. He followed the sound, only to be stopped at the salon door by a guard. "Sorry, sir. These are private rooms."

"Is that Madame Amauri playing?"

"Yes, sir, I believe so." The guard's stern demeanor broke. "Pretty, isn't it?"

"Yes, very."

As Sean turned to leave, the door opened. Josephine stood there in champagne muslin. "Ah, I thought I recognized your voice, Monsieur Culhane," she murmured. "I wasn't certain, over the music. Won't you come in? Your sister-in-law is entertaining us with her wonderful virtuosity. I'm certain she will be upset if you don't stop to speak to her," she added as she perceived Sean's hesitancy.

"You're most gracious, madame." As he followed her into the room, he noticed the guard had resumed his usual stiff expression.

The lovely flow of music ended in a jarring note as Catherine looked up. Dismay crossed her features, then blended quickly with the bright, gilding sunlight that

519

streamed from the windows behind the piano as she rose to greet the Irishman.

For a moment, her gown of butter-tinted lace with a tiny ruffle edging its low neck and cap sleeves seemed part of the sunlight. A cream silk ruff with a single matching rosebud encircled her slender throat. "You startled me," she said lightly, as she silently cursed Josephine's malicious caprice. "But what a delightful surprise. Will you join us for cocoa? If you don't stay, we'll begin to gossip again. We know everyone's sins as well as our own." She extended her hand coolly, but as Sean brushed his lips against it, his mask as carefully placed as her own, she nearly lost her hard-won composure. The desire to touch his hair was so intense, she felt weak. How handsome he looked in his gray suit, how tall and fine. She drank him in with her eyes as they exchanged trivial remarks and Josephine introduced him to the other ladies, who quivered like roosting pigeons with a wolf in their midst until he lazily charmed them into a flurry of fascinated excitement.

How easy he finds it to make women bend to him, Catherine thought with a twinge of jealousy. As she watched him lounge on a flimsy chair and sip cocoa, which he detested, she felt a wave of tenderness for him and a less friendly wave of sheer green possessiveness.

Josephine shot her a sly glance. Catherine played idly with a wisp of her hair and gave the woman look for look. But when Sean took his leave half an hour later, she wilted as if the brightness of the morning had gone with him, and Josephine could not resist a dig. "Perhaps we should invite Monsieur Culhane more often. He seems to make you come alive."

"He has that effect on every woman he meets," retorted Catherine sweetly. "You may wish to remove your rouge; you have quite a glow without it today."

In a black mood, Sean left the rocketry tests at the Polytechnique. The uneasiness he had felt during his interview with Napoleon had been radically intensified by the sight of Catherine so intimately connected with Josephine. Napoleon must see her regularly. How could any man help but want her when she seemed to grow lovelier with each passing day? Pregnancy made her skin bloom and her eyes glow with a hushed waiting that filled him with awe. The stark dismay on her face at his visit troubled him, but her accompanying flicker of guilt disturbed him even more: that and the tiny white rosebud at her neck. Visions of white roses with overpowering scents filled his mind, and the memory of Madame Amauri's remark that Catherine would not permit white roses in her bedroom.

Lieutenant Tourney's apology was brief and Culhane accepted it briefly, prolonging the young man's humiliation no longer than necessary. Napoleon had sent several officers to accompany the lieutenant, which increased his embarrassment. From now on, few military men would be eager to challenge the Irishman at the cost of their commissions—and their pride—at the very least. Unfortunately, Napoleon's tactic also agitated resentment.

After that, Culhane was seen with several dancers and an actress or two, and Josephine shook her head. "Really, it's become chic to appear with your brother-in-law. At least for women of a certain reputation," she added archly as she picked up her teacup.

"Most celebrated women have a certain reputation, if one believes gossip," Catherine returned calmly, determined not to let Josephine detect her hurt, although she herself had asked Moora to take Sean under her wing.

"Yes, I daresay even you've attracted a few rumors."

"I wouldn't know. So far, no one's been rude enough to repeat them to my face." Catherine tasted her own tea. They were alone in the sunny little salon that adjoined Josephine's bedroom, where they had been taking turns reading Villon to each other.

"Your brother-in-law hasn't been so lucky," the Creole said as she poured more tea. "All sorts of people have been rude to him. After all, he's fought two duels in less than two months and been challenged to a third. Bonaparte is quite irritated."

Catherine went white. "He's been dueling?"

"You must be the only person in Paris who hasn't heard!

521

The first one was over the black mistress of one of your husband's cadre officers. The two fought only hours after your wedding."

Raoul stared coldly at his wife as she glared at him, taut with fury. She had accosted him the moment he had returned from Longchamps. Now they were closeted alone and her immediate accusation annoyed him. "I'm not responsible for your pet ruffian's peccadilloes."

"Javet was one of your cadre officers," she said tightly. "Why didn't you intervene?"

"Culhane challenged. What did you expect me to do?" His eyes narrowed slyly. "If you heard about that fight, you must have heard about Irenée, too."

"Irenée?"

"Javet's African mistress and don't pretend you don't know. That's what eats at you, isn't it? Well, now he's taken up with an Indo-Chinese whore and her procuress. I've had the Indo-Chinese myself. Next to her, you're as exciting as a wet rag!"

"Don't decry my sodden appeal too much," she gritted. "It's all that links you to your next promotion."

Warily, he eyed her. "You wouldn't do anything stupid?"

"Of course not," she retorted coolly. "Whatever Sean does, I have my child to consider."

Raoul felt a sweep of hope. Perhaps the Irishman could be dislodged from her heart after all. He poured two glasses of sherry, then held one out to her.

"No, thank you."

"Take it." He pressed the glass into her fingers. "It's good for you. Doctor's orders, remember?" He leaned against the mantel. "It's foolish for us to fight over Culhane. There are things you don't know about him."

"Really?" She ignored the wine.

"Do you know what happened to him in that prison?"

"He was tortured."

"Did you ever wonder why he wasn't tortured to death?"

"If you had seen him after they'd thrown him naked into the snow to die, you'd know how stupid that question is to me."

522

"Your precious lover became the sodomite of the prison guards to save his neck, only for once he underestimated his appeal. The colonel tired of him."

"Indeed?"

Raoul should have been warned by her lack of surprise, but he attributed it to her control. "Apparently, Culhane cannot forget his prison experience. He still has women, of course, but one of his lovers is a young man, Gil Lachaise."

"Would this . . . quirk in his nature be responsible for some of the other duels? I mean, people must be talking . . ."

Amauri jumped at the suggestion. "I've even heard Murat speak of it. I'm sure everyone's heard by now . . ."

"Thanks to you, my pet," she drawled ominously.

"Me?" Amauri looked genuinely startled. "How can you blame me? Culhane and Lachaise are seen everywhere together. Doesn't it strike even you as strange that Culhane is seen with so many women, but only one man?"

"Not strange at all, after what you've done to him, you sneaking wretch!" she hissed, her whole demeanor changing to that of a tigress circling its prey. "There's only one place such a filthy lie could have started." Eyes like frozen fire, Catherine advanced on her husband. "Sean was nearly beaten to death in that prison because he wouldn't submit. He was shot trying to escape being gutted on a block."

Deliberately, she threw the sherry in Amauri's face and smashed the glass. The broken bowl jaggedly pointed at him.

His eyes narrowed. "Are you insane?"

"No," she said bluntly, "but I have been. And I've killed before, too. My own husband, as a matter of fact. He didn't die heroically at all. He was just as vicious, just as devious, just as selfish as you. And if I were to kill you," she went on softly, "say, some night when you crept into my bed, everyone would just think I'd gone crazy again. After what you've done, I'd gladly spend my days in a madhouse reviewing the pleasure of cutting your throat."

Amauri's face had gone gray. "Don't forget I can have you arrested," he muttered hoarsely, "and that whoreson, too."

Unexpectedly, she smiled. "Go ahead. What have you given us to live for, anyway?"

"You *are* mad!"

She laughed almost gaily and tossed the goblet into the fire, where it shattered; then she turned and hissed, "Just keep your doors locked, husband."

CHAPTER 29

The Rat From Venice

Culhane paid little attention to the slim, dark stranger who watched him fence, but he did notice his opponent's lack of concentration. He pressed Lavalier harder to force his attention, but the Frenchman fell back and finally gave an irritated wave of his hand. *"Suffit, suffit.* That's all for today."

Sean lowered his foil. "What's the matter?"

The stranger smiled slightly and strolled away to join three officers lounging in the corner. He said something, using one hand expressively. With a low burst of laughter, the men slid glances in Culhane's direction.

Lavalier looked at them with acute dislike. "What's wrong?" the Irishman repeated quietly. "Who is he?"

The Gascon thrust his foil into the rack and tugged off his mask. "That's Antonio Neri. Ever hear of him?"

"Should I have?" Sean put up his equipment.

"Get your coat and come with me," Lavalier said abruptly.

"Mind if I ask where we're going?"

"I need a drink. I suggest you have one, too."

Lavalier fiddled with his glass and stared into its depths. Cradling his own drink, Sean waited patiently, scanning the other occupants of Pascal's dingy café. Pascal's was Lavalier's favorite haunt.

"Merde." Lavalier downed most of his glass. He waved for the proprietor to bring another. "You're in trouble,

ami," he bleakly announced. Sean smiled faintly. "No, not like before. Neri's a Venetian. A professional. He's been called in to kill someone and I think it's you."

"So?"

"So, he's good; some say the best. He's also very expensive. They must have taken up a collection to bring him in."

"The military?"

"They aren't permitted to fight you; that humiliates them."

"Too bad. Besides, if he challenges me, Fouché will be on him like a shot."

"Neri never challenges. He's no fool. You'll be the one to call him out."

The two men fell momentarily silent as Pascal, the proprietor, brought Lavalier's drink. He gave Sean's full glass a disapproving glance and lumbered off.

"I'm not about to call him out," Sean said softly to Lavalier. "I'm not going to land in prison."

"Oh, you'll fight him all right. He'll find a way to make you."

"I'll wear my most fetching smile when he insults me." The bitter reference to the perverted rumors about him embarrassed Lavalier, and the Irishman regretted his remark. "Look, he can call me anything he likes. I have a tough hide."

"What about your sister-in-law? Has she a tough hide, too?"

Culhane stiffened.

"You see?" Lavalier murmured, then shrugged. "Perhaps he won't dare involve her. Napoleon would hear of it."

Culhane's eyes narrowed. "Why should Napoleon care about Kit when Josephine is called harlot by the whole world?"

Lavalier looked at him impassively. "Josephine is protected by her position. No abuse of her reputation can topple her unless Napoleon lets it." The Gascon went on as if Sean were not still staring at him. "Neri is a superb stylist, but he can revert to gutter tactics. Beware of his feet. He's also been thought to poison his blade."

526

"Why should Napoleon care about Kit?" repeated the Irishman softly.

"Josephine's current lover sometimes gossips. He says the lady is afraid of la comtesse. That one does not fear shadows."

Sean stared at some point fixed between Lavalier's ear and infinity. "So the bastard sold her . . . ."

"Sean, if you go for Amauri, Napoleon will throw you in prison until you rot. You'll be of no use either to her or the child."

"I'll get him. If not today, then another. Even if I have to cut his throat in an alley."

The next day, on return from fencing, Sean had barely unlocked his door when it jerked open from inside. He crouched toward his boot knife as the door moved inward; Mei Lih's frightened face in its opening did nothing to dispel his readiness to attack. "My lord, you must go quickly! Your friend has been hurt!"

Moora impatiently pushed Mei Lih aside. "Gil Lachaise was taunted into a fight as he was leaving the École Militaire. It was Neri." Then she added awkwardly, "He accused Gil of being your lover."

His face contorted, he spun away.

Mei Lih shrieked after him, "Don't go unarmed! Come back!"

Antonio Neri was dining at Justine's with three officers in a private room. Handsome as an El Greco don, he courteously stood, his companions also rising in his wake as Culhane and Lavalier were ushered into the room by a waiter. Neri was slightly younger than Sean, a head less tall, and less well shouldered, but he was as alert as a ferret. *"Buona sera, signori,"* he said easily, crooking a finger at the waiter to linger. "Will you join us? The veal is particularly good tonight."

"Thank you, no," drawled the Irishman, "but you must enjoy it before it gets cold. No point in ruining your last meal."

Neri waved the waiter away. "Are you calling me out, signore?" he murmured after the door closed.

527

"You don't leave me much choice. Monsieur Lavalier will act as my second."

"I am at your convenience."

"Will the courtyard behind the Ursuline Convent at midnight suit you?"

"Admirably." He gestured to the man on his right. "Colonel La Rousse will be my second. Captains Marquand and Rossiers will observe, if you don't mind. You may, of course, invite your own friends if you wish. I suggest rapiers." His eyes flicked to the weapon partly concealed by Lavalier's cloak. "Ah, yes. I see you have anticipated my choice." He bowed slightly. "Until midnight, signori."

The Ursuline courtyard, normally deserted at midnight, had the appearance of a fair. Word of the duel had passed like wildfire and officers ringed the court. Among them were women in masks and hooded cloaks. Torches in brackets along the arched stone colonnades and lanterns among the spectators gave sporadic light. More lanterns bobbed like fireflies through parklike gardens which bordered the court entrances as the last arrivals picked their way through ancient flowering trees and flowerbeds.

Lavalier's lips curled in disgust as he eyed the crowd. One of the women had brought her opera glasses. "Voyeurs. They find a killing better entertainment than the Opera Buffa."

Leaning against a column, arms crossed over his chest, his tall companion stared into space as if unaware of the shadowy crowd, its murmurs and low laughter lifting on the damp night air. The scent of lemon and lilac drifted in from the garden, their heady perfumes incongruous with grim tile-topped walls. The arcade lined three sides of the bricked court; the fourth side, along the garden, was fenced with ornamental ironwork with a gate. Secluded from the busy Carrousel by the construction of the new Rue de Rivoli and Rue de Castiglione, the court, used for centuries to settle affairs of honor, offered little danger of official interruption.

A murmur of anticipation ran through the crowd as four cloaked silhouettes filed through the creaking gate of the iron fence; the figure in front gestured gracefully to the crowd, then strode to the center of the courtyard and turned slightly to face the tall, still man in the shadows. Culhane eased off the wall, removed his jacket and waistcoat. Lavalier handed him his rapier, then followed him out to meet Neri, who was by now similarly prepared, his second at his elbow.

Colonel La Rousse rattled off the obligatory offer to the dissidents to reconsider honorably their intention to enter into combat. The offer was politely declined by both men. The duelists took their positions, arms as elegantly arched as fencing masters on exhibition. The illusion was swiftly shattered. With the swiftness of rattlers preparing to strike, they separated, disengaging with an ominous slither of steel as each sought unsuccessfully to hook the other's guard. White shirts sculpted by torchlight, they warily circled, barely engaging, playing with the ends of each other's blades, tiny counters and feather-touch parries. Neri uncoiled in a blurring attack, was parried and riposted with equal swiftness and skill.

Very quickly, Neri saw the Irishman was as deadly as himself. Neither his wrist nor his wariness would give out. He would have to be taken by guile. One successful thrust and his rapier would leave its light burden of oily poison in his opponent's body; in minutes the Irishman would falter. Death was inevitable, but long before the poison killed, the dizzied victim would fall prey to his opponent's sword and appear to die of his wounds.

The Irishman lunged. Neri countered and fell back slightly, answering the next thrust with a riposte, was counterriposted. He answered in remise; the Irishman parried, then disengaging unexpectedly, attacked in headlong advance, steel ringing. Falling back, Neri parried the attack, lunged, but at the instant he attempted a beat, Culhane disengaged and in a split second jabbed him in the bicep.

A disappointed mutter went up among the watchers. They had not expected the Irishman to draw first blood; neither had Neri, and his confident smile turned grim.

Ignoring the sting in his arm, Neri attacked with the calculated concentration of a serpent slithering after a mongoose. Steel spat fire as he pressed Culhane back toward the dark end of the courtyard, forcing his opponent to rely on his backlit silhouette to distinguish his movements, while Culhane was still illuminated. Sean did not clearly see the *poussée cachée* Neri made from *prime,* and the Italian gave a triumphant laugh as his point passed into Sean's side. The crowd cried out with muted cheers, but as Neri withdrew his sword too easily, he sensed his error. Culhane slipped under his guard to jab at his thigh. Neri swore as he slashed downward to beat the point away. He had missed the Irishman's body and ripped through the loose shirt.

Neri, knowing each moment was precious, tried every trick he had learned as an alley cutthroat. He began to work close, pressing, luring his opponent to try for him, using his body like an acrobat, trying to trip or kick when *corps à corps,* using the rapier guard to attempt steel-accented, vicious blows. But Culhane was equally fast and ruthless. Eluding a knee to his groin with the deftness of a cat, he jammed his guard into the Venetian's diaphragm and drove his heel toward Neri's instep, narrowly missing it as the Italian leaped backward. He lunged forward as quickly, catching Sean barely off guard; but the Irishman failed to fall back, parrying strongly instead, and suddenly they were locked, muscles corded, jaw to jaw. His teeth flashing in the torchlight, Neri laughed, and sprang back as his opponent did. As they separated, Sean sliced Neri's face. The crowd fell silent.

Suddenly, a prearranged signal ran through some of the officers. Their lanterns doused with a distracting clatter of shields, and Neri, with the advantage of the torches, drove home. The culprits cheered as Sean, unable to ward off the entire force of the attack, stumbled back, a dark splotch at his shoulder. Then, as Neri's attention concentrated on the kill, his blade accidentally grazed the bell of Sean's rapier. Momentarily startled, he was off guard just long enough for Sean to counter, then knock his blade from the center of the action. Sean disengaged into *sixte* and lunged. His blade went through the Italian's chest.

The assassin looked surprised, then sagged at the knees as Culhane freed his rapier. Neri's lips tightened, then

530

smiled twistedly through the gore. "Death has wearied at last of her complacent lover, but I do not think she will be more faithful to you." He choked and blood trickled from the corner of his mouth.

Sean looked past his shoulder and eyed the men moving forward in the gloom. He lifted his rapier to Neri's throat. "Tell them, Neri." His tongue felt swollen. "Tell them you lied about Gil Lachaise."

Neri's smile became mocking. "I have nothing to recant, signore. 'He who breathes in pain, breathes truth.' " With a snarl, Culhane cut his throat. Neri jerked forward to the pavement.

With a glitter of steal, the nearest advancing silhouette drew his saber, then another flashed from the shadows, and another. Sean braced, trying to detach his mind from the searing throb in his shoulder, trying to keep the ground from undulating like a heaving sea of brick. Cries of "Murder!" echoed off the walls.

The officers were thrown into confusion. "We've got to get out of here!" "No, kill him!"

A more strident voice snarled, "He fought well despite you damned cheats! Leave him be. Where's your precious honor now? Get out of here and take what's left of it with you!" It was Lavalier, his sword drawn.

The crowd milled, the women shrinking toward the exits, pleading for their escorts to come with them. Some of the military, appalled by the breach of the code, joined Lavalier; others stood uncertainly as the ringleaders blustered.

Lavalier glared. "With all this noise, the police will come. Do you want that? Go! Only your consciences will know what you've done here tonight!"

Marquand grabbed La Rousse's sleeve. "Come on. Look at the bastard. Neri's poisoned him. He's done for, anyway. Come on, let's go!"

Lavalier whirled to see Culhane going slowly down on one knee, head dangling as the rapier slid from slack fingers.

The crowd broke.

"He's coming out of it now," Lavalier murmured as his own physician, Doctor Mariot, cleaned the Irishman's wound. Sean's lips and eyelids were slightly swollen and blueish, his breathing labored as he stirred.

The Irishman tried to focus. "Where . . . what's going on?"

Mariot peered into his eyes. "Dilated like a cat's in a cave."

Lavalier dipped a cloth in cold water and wiped his friend's pale face. "You're at my brother's house. That's him, Louis." A slight man, older than Lavalier but with the same shrewd eyes, nodded. Culhane tried to lift his head, but dull pain shot through it and he let it fall back on the pillow. His body, too long for the bed, slanted across it with his left foot projecting between its brass bars. His shoulder throbbed sickeningly and he swore under his breath as the doctor briskly secured the bandage knot at his shoulder.

Lavalier laid a hand on his arm. "Take it easy. You've been poisoned, but you'll be fine. Rest now."

CHAPTER 30

Veil of Deceit

Angry voices penetrated the drugged, fitful sleep to which Catherine had succumbed after Raoul had sedated her during the night. She restlessly flung a hand over her eyes to shut out the light, wishing whoever was shouting would go away, then caught a trace of brogue in the louder voice. Her eyes flew open. "Moora?" She fought to an upright position, then distractedly brushed a hand across her forehead as the terrifying memories of the previous night returned. Pawing off the covers, she heaved her thickened body off the bed and stumbled toward the door to drag it open. "Moora?"

At the foot of the staircase, Moora paused in mid-tirade, her parasol brandished under Antoinette's outraged nose. Antoinette turned to her mistress for vindication. "I told this . . . lady . . . you were not receiving, madame. The general gave strict orders—"

"But I am receiving, Antoinette," Catherine said with an effort. "Please take Mademoiselle Alexandrovna's parasol. I shall call you if we want anything."

Antoinette hesitated. "Madame, are you certain you feel able to have callers? You're not well."

Looking at the haggard young woman who leaned against her bedroom doorjamb as if it were the only thing keeping her on her feet, Moora felt inclined to agree with the maid.

"Thank you for your concern, Antoinette," Catherine

said quietly, collected now that her head was beginning to clear, "but I wish to speak to my friend."

The parasol held stiffly like a marshal's baton as she stalked to the kitchen, Antoinette wondered how an imitation Russian tart could possibly be an intimate of her mistress.

Moora mounted the steps. In her lilac muslin dress, she might have been a Botticelli naiad, except for her pert straw bonnet trimmed with violets.

"How lovely you are today," Catherine said softly, her voice somewhere outside herself. How ironic for a girl wearing a spring bonnet and violets to be a messenger of death.

"I wanted to be first to reach you," Moora said slowly, "but I see you already know." She stopped just outside the door.

"Raoul told me," Catherine said dully, her eyes dilated by laudanum. "It must have been an entertainment, like a bear baiting. People came to watch him die." Her eyes grew darker, frighteningly disoriented. "Only it was less of a show than they expected. He'd been poisoned, you see." She stared dazedly at the Irish girl. "But you know all this. How stupid of me. You've come to tell me he's dead." She caught Moora's arm, whispering brokenly, "Where is he? Where have they taken him?"

"Oh, God," Moora breathed. She slipped her arm around her friend, firmly drew her back into the bedroom and closed the door. Like a sleepwalker, Catherine made no protest as the Irish girl helped her to the bed and vigorously chafed her cold hands. "Listen to me. Sean's safe, do you hear? Alive and safe."

Catherine's eyes grew enormous and her lips trembled. "Don't. Don't lie." She began to sob helplessly. "I cannot stand any more. I heard . . ."

"I can imagine what you heard, no thanks to that husband of yours," Moora said angrily, "and it's true enough, mind you, but he'll not die. The wound's little more than a nasty scratch." She smiled at the expression in Catherine's eyes. "Cross me green Irish heart."

Catherine sagged against her shoulder. "Oh, merciful God."

534

Moora patted her back. "He's been taken to a safe place to hide until the fuss dies down."

"I must see him."

Moora shook her head. "You might be followed. Neri's body won't be found any time soon," she said in a voice that held a note of grim relish, "but news of the duel is out. Napoleon may already know. Fouché is bound to put a man on you to locate Sean."

A sad resolve filled Catherine's eyes. "There can be no waiting, Moora. Sean must leave Paris *now*. Will you arrange a meeting?"

The next morning, Catherine, telling her driver to return in an hour, dismissed her coach opposite Notre Dame. Slowly, she walked to Sainte Chapelle and climbed to the upper floor and the chapel proper. As she stepped into its interior, she paused, dazzled by a spectrum of light. Surrounded by gemlike windows, arches flared from slender gilded stalks that supported a deep blue ceiling spangled with gold stars. To Catherine, the small chapel had the intimacy of a jewel box. That this sublime artistry had risen from apolcalyptic horrors of the Middle Ages awed her. Its survival seemed to be a promise of hope, for it represented the best of man's faith and the grandeur of his heart. Catherine crossed herself. What an eye for theater Moora had developed, she thought with sad irony as she looked for Sean. Moora was kneeling on the stones near an old woman, the only other person in the chapel. Then Catherine saw Sean walk slowly toward her from the shadows on the far side of the nave, the light distorting his tall silhouette. Although she had prepared for what was to come, she could not prepare for the treacherous leap of her heart. Then he was too close, invading her fragile wall of control, and the words she had carefully planned caught in her throat. He was pale, and his eyes, God, she could hardly bear to look at them, could hardly bear to speak the terrible words that would sever their bond forever.

Indeed, she had dressed with infinite care, as if she were preparing for execution. The coral silk dress and gauzy shawl draped about her face made her eyes and skin come alive, simulating a blush of health and well-being.

Sean lost his powers of speech as well. He was afraid for the first time since prison. Not in any duel, even the one with Neri, had he really felt fear, but now he was helpless against the mortal blow he sensed was coming; when it did, it was so quick and clean he went numb.

"Sean, I want you to leave Paris within the hour. You must never come back." Catherine wanted to shriek with the reflected pain that arced from his eyes. She wanted to bury his face against her, hold him and cry out her undying love, but she could not. He must go thinking her a jealous, peevish woman, for certainly he would attribute his banishment to rumors of his affairs.

"And if I choose not to go?" The phrase came like a dying murmur.

"You have no choice." Her voice was cold with despair. "When Napoleon finds out about your last duel, even I may not be able to help you."

"What particular act did you perform to obtain this little favor," he whispered hoarsely. "Does he prefer it Greek style?" She gave a little cry and stepped back. He caught her wrist. "What about my child? Do you deny me him, too?"

"Please," she whispered, "you're hurting me."

He dropped her wrist as if it were a hot iron. "Hurt *you?* Do you think me a block of stone you can hack at whim?" He twisted away in an unthinking blaze of bitterness. "Forgive me, madame. My inconsiderate survival must have inconvenienced your standing with your lover. I'll go. I'll go and be damned to you!"

Dear God, not like this; I cannot let him leave feeling betrayed. She caught his sleeve, then murmured like a fervent prayer, "I love you with my whole heart, my whole soul, and my whole mind. Believe I know something of what you've suffered to stay near me; but you're killing me. Each time I hear you've dueled, I die a little more. Even if Napoleon doesn't imprison you, he'll look the other way when the ringleaders hire more killers. They won't bother fighting you now; they'll shoot you in the back or cut your throat." She put her hands to her ears remembering Raoul's gloating triumph. "Poison. Dear God."

He had slowly turned as she was speaking and caught

her to him, burying his head against her neck. "Don't. Don't remember. Just remember the time we had in Ireland before Liam came. Don't let's tear each other apart now."

The old woman stared until Moora glared at her so pointedly she laboriously rose and huffily left the chapel.

Sean's arms tightened. "If only I knew you'd be safe . . ."

"I'm in no danger. Raoul and I have come to terms; each knows where the other stands. Napoleon's planning to transfer him to Spain indefinitely."

"And Napoleon, once he has you to himself?"

"Once Raoul is gone, I'll have no reason to oblige Napoleon. I shall retire to the Convent of Saint Therese near Saint Jean de Luz where Mother received her education. When our son is old enough, I'll send him to you."

"You'd give him up?"

"A convent is no place for a boy."

"A convent is no place for you."

"Darling, I have a need for peace only God can give me now." She anxiously scanned him. "Are you well enough to ride?"

"With luck, I'll be across the border in two or three days." There was so much and yet no more to say.

She placed her hands on both sides of his face. "God protect you and give you peace, my love."

"Oh, God, Kit," he cried softly as his head swooped down. His lips crushed hers as if he sought to draw her soul from her body to take with him. Her fingers caught in his hair and she sobbed against his mouth as she clung to him; then he tore out of her arms and away toward the stair, his stride quickening. Abruptly, without looking back, he was gone. She stood there, mute and immobile under the weight of a terrible premonition of disaster. She put out a hand and took a faltering step after him, then another, whispering his name; then the black weight pressed down and she heard Moora's faraway cry of alarm fade into nothing.

When Catherine heard the front door slam downstairs, her hand slid into the pocket of her white satin dressing gown and her fingers curled around the grip of the tiny pistol she had taken from Raoul's gun collection. She had refused Moora's offer to stay with her and finally, reluctantly, the young Irishwoman had taken the Celtic jewels for safekeeping and left. Now Catherine wished with all her heart Moora had stayed, as Raoul walked into her bedroom, his face taut.

"Guillaume followed you to Sainte Chapelle," he said tightly. "Your divine Irishman has risen from the dead once too often. Where is he?"

"I'll tell you nothing, Raoul." She drew the gun. "Now, get out."

He took a wary step toward her. "If you pull that trigger, you'll die for it."

"The prospect of living with you is less palatable."

"You'd condemn your child as well?" he countered suspiciously.

"Sentence cannot be carried out until after the birth. The baby will go to a safe place." She smiled. "Take another step and make it easy for me."

He turned on his heel. "I'll find Culhane soon enough. I know his hideouts." He kept going and she heard the front door slam. Still holding the gun, she went to the bedroom door to call her maid. She must find a hiding place in the city. When Raoul discovered Sean was gone, he would be more dangerous than ever. As she stepped into the hall, the thought spun from her mind as her wrist was seized and the gun wrenched from her hand. A blow cracked across her face. "Raoul!" She twisted away with a shriek. "Antoinette! Help me!"

He grabbed her hair and cut off her breath with a forearm locked across her throat. "Tell me, you bitch, or I'll beat it out of you!"

Her slippered foot slammed down on his instep; the heel was not heavy enough to make him lose his grip completely but the pain startled him. She wrenched away and ran toward the steps. "Antoinette!"

He caught her arm, spun her around, then slapped her again and again, hissing, "Tell me where he is, damn you!"

"No." She clawed out at him, trying to shield her head,

until she lost her balance and fell to the floor. She curled up desperately as she saw his foot go back to kick her.

"Mon Dieu, Général!"

Raoul jerked around to see Antoinette's horrified eyes staring up at him. With a witness, the game was up. He bent over his moaning wife and rasped, "I'll kill Culhane just like his brat! You'll have nothing!" He hurtled down the steps and pushed past Antoinette into the library for pistols before racing out the door. Catherine barely heard him go. The first contraction tore through her even as Antoinette knelt by her head.

The three policemen searching Culhane's quarters snapped to attention as Police Minister Fouché entered the room, a lieutenant of police behind him. "As you were, gentlemen. Moulin, have you anything to report?"

"No, sir. We've found nothing personal in his belongings: no letters, no addresses, not even money."

"A man of remarkably pristine habits." Fouché walked slowly about the room. "There has to be something. Even if Culhane's alive, he wouldn't have risked returning here after his fight with the Venetian." Fouché fanned through papers on the desk. "This is no longer a matter of apprehending a duelist, gentlemen, but a spy. I want this place taken apart, even the floorboards. If you find anything immediately, I'll be at 15 Île de la Fraternité."

Mei Lih seized Culhane's hand and dragged him into Madeleine's house with surprising strength. She peered out at the darkened street, then swiftly shut the door. "Minister Fouché just left. He had only one man with him; otherwise, I'm sure he would have left a watch on the house."

"Napoleon heard of the duel quickly enough."

"It's not the duel he cares about now. Fouché has a warrant for your arrest as a spy!"

The Irishman swore under his breath. That meant his drawings had fallen into the wrong hands and his courier was probably dead.

Madeleine's angry voice floated down from upstairs as she leveled a pistol at his chest. "I don't thank you for this,

Culhane. How dare you sell out my country while you enjoy my hospitality!"

"I haven't betrayed France, Leine; just Napoleon," he shot back coolly. "The Terror was nothing compared to the blood France will spill for that vainglorious runt. You know he doesn't give a damn for the Republic. You're more pissed than patriotic."

Tears of rage streaked the kohl around her eyes. "Oh, you *canaille!* You *cochon!* You . . ." She hurled the gun at him and stalked off in a swish of black silk.

Culhane eyed the scar the gun had made in the wallpaper, then headed up the stairs. He silently went up behind Madeleine as she poured absinthe with a shaking hand. His familiar hands closed on her shoulders and she swore, starting to swing the bottle. Instantly, his grip slid down her arm to her wrist. "Put it down, Leine. I'm not going to hurt you."

"Go to hell!"

"Directly, ma'am, if that's what you want." He kissed her neck. "I'll do anything you want if you help me, even surrender to the police."

"What!" She spun. "What are you talking about? Get out of here!"

"Not until Kit's safe," he said flatly. "Fouché can work up a nasty case against her now. He has bits and scraps he can twist to look like a Bourbon conspiracy; piled on top of her association with a known spy, the evidence is more than enough." His hands tightened on Madeleine's shoulders. "I swear on my life she's innocent, Leine. She has no love for Napoleon, but she doesn't want the Bourbons back in France any more than you, and she knows nothing about my work here."

"What in hell do you expect me to do about her?"

"Hide her until the baby's born and she can travel."

"Hide her?" Madeleine threw up her hands. "Where? Under the bed?"

"You survived the Terror, Leine. I know you have a place," he cajoled softly. "I'll keep you covered in diamonds for the rest of your life."

She looked at him with hostility and began to pace nervously, finally stopped and bit a nail. "Would you marry me?"

"If you want," he said slowly.

"You love her that much?"

"She's my sister." He knew better than to tell her the whole truth.

She blinked, surprise incongruous on her jaded face. "The hell you say!" She swept a quick look from him to Mei Lih and back and her lips tightened. "You never mentioned a sister."

"You never mentioned a son." His eyes held hers levelly. "Think, Leine. If we were lovers, would I have let her marry Amauri?"

The tension was abruptly broken by a violent pounding on the door downstairs and they all froze. Carmine lips a blotch in her chalky face, Madeleine pushed the Irishman toward her bedroom. "In there. Hurry!"

Quickly scanning the dark garden below for police, Sean threw the bedroom window open. As he flung a leg astride the sill, he heard a strange woman's voice cry hysterically, "Madame, you must help! He may come back! I don't know what to do!"

Then Madeleine's voice, sharply pitched. "Control yourself, Antoinette! You're making no sense at all. What are you talking about?"

"The general beat Madame Amauri. The baby's coming now! No one's with her and he may come back!" She choked in mid-sob as Sean slammed into the room, his face terrible. "Monseiur Culhane!"

Sean wheeled on Madeleine. "Leine?" he pleaded hoarsely, desperately. She hesitated, then nodded and he was gone.

The front door of the Amauri mansion was unlocked, and Sean, pistol drawn, eased into the foyer. Flickering candles in wall sconces cast uneasy shadows that made the rooms seem more eerily deserted. Silently, he mounted the stair, wondering which door to try; then a faint cry told him.

Catherine lay on her bed, sweat-damp hair fanned over the pillows, face contorted, her belly a swollen bulge under

541

her hands as she pressed at it, gasping between pains. Suddenly, her teeth clenched and she tried to draw into herself, then went limp, panting. As Sean moved toward her, her far hand came up with a pistol even as her head turned, eyes determined, only to flare wide in horror. "Oh, God . . . why are you still here?" She struggled to push him away as his arms closed around her. "No! Run! Run, or it will all have been for nothing!" Beginning to sob with frustration, she ineffectively pommeled his chest as his arms tightened.

He held her until she quieted, his lips brushing her temples and cheeks. "Hush little one. I'll go, but first I'll take you to a safe place."

"There's nowhere to hide. No time." A spasm stole the words and she turned her face away, gasping, "Too quickly . . . it's coming . . . too quickly."

Swiftly, he wrapped blankets around her and scooped her up in his arms. He had left Madeleine's carriage by the stable at the rear of the house. Depositing Catherine in the carriage depths, he drew the blankets high. As she leaned her head against his shoulder, he whipped up the horses, praying Fouché had not yet sent a guard to Madeleine's. He kept to dark, labyrinthine streets, taking them at a perilous pace that caused the wheel hubs to spark against stone as the carriage careened around building corners that jutted like misplaced teeth. Tensely, he counted the minutes between Catherine's pains. She made no sound; only the stiffening of her body indicated the spasms. At this rate, the baby would come within an hour or two. Seeing no suspicious loiterers about Number 15, he drove the carriage into Madeleine's stable, then swept Catherine from the carriage and headed for Madeleine's back door.

Mei Lih showed no curiosity about the woman whose hair fell as black and long as her own over Culhane's arm as he carried her into the hallway; but upstairs, Madeleine scrutinized the Englishwoman like a hawk.

Catherine, through waves of pain, was only vaguely aware of the starkly beautiful woman who led the way into a storeroom adjoining the upstairs sitting room. A dress mannequin amid a jumble of clutter brushed Sean's elbow as he ducked the low, sloping ceiling. Madeleine twisted

542

the knob of a large armoire; it swung back with a creak. Inside was a tiny alcove with a cot prepared with heavy layers of linen. Catherine suddenly cried out and pressed her face against Sean's shoulder.

"Quickly, put her down." Madeleine pushed blankets aside as Sean laid the writhing woman on the bed. "Mei Lih, see if the water's boiling."

Catherine gripped Sean's hands as the contraction became more violent. When it passed, she gasped, "Go. For God's sake, go. Raoul's looking for you. He has a gun. Please . . ."

Madeleine touched his arm. "She's right. You can do no more here. Go, drag that great black goat of a horse out of my garden and ride."

"Coming," he replied absently, but did not move, just brushed the damp hair from Catherine's face and gently blotted the seeping blood from the corner of her mouth where Amauri had struck her. Her glistening eyes in the candlelight were dark pools of torment as they locked to his in farewell, her lips compressed as she fought to hold back another scream. He kissed her hand, then pressed a small figure into her palm. "Hold on to this, little one. It's a gift for the child. Kiss him for me."

"Go with God," she whispered. Her azure eyes told him the rest as Madeleine dragged firmly at his shoulder. As he followed the Frenchwoman back to the sitting room, Sean looked back once to see Catherine staring blindly at him, clutching, as if it were a crucifix, the crude little monkey he had carved.

Instead of leaving, Sean caught up a brandy decanter in Madeleine's sitting room and took a long draught to dull the ache in his shoulder. Mei Lih, having noted the slight stain of blood on his shirt as he had carried Catherine up the stair, slipped a linen pad under his shirt and secured it under the bandage as he leaned against the sideboard. Madeleine eyed him bleakly. "You're not leaving Paris, are you?"

He looked at her while Mei Lih worked. "Not until I relieve Kit of a bad bargain."

"You made me a bargain too, remember?" she returned

harshly. "You're no good to me dead. You go after Amauri and it's all off."

He smiled faintly. "You know your trouble, Leine? You have no faith in men." His eyes went dark as a muted cry came from the other room. "Go to her, Madeleine," he said softly. "I must keep a promise to myself first; then I'll keep the one to you."

Amauri and Fourquet stealthily crept through Madeleine's garden toward the house. The moon cast an uneasy light through breeze-stirred pear leaves, which mottled the stableyard and garden. From the shadows came a potpourri of scents—hawthorn, violas and primroses, parsley and shallots. And an incongruous sound of munching. A massive black shape nuzzled the herbage where the shade of the garden's wall obscured his presence. A prickling across Raoul's neck warned him to turn, pistol drawn, to face a crouching figure, a quicksilver streak of moonlight along the gun barrel near its center. "Stalking alley cats, General?"

Raoul was momentarily speechless. Finally, he said carefully, "I've come to offer a way to settle our differences."

"Is there more than one way?"

"I see we're in agreement. Will pistols suit you?"

"Anything you like."

"Emile and I will meet you in Mother's garden directly. You'll agree it might be awkward for Madeleine if one of us was to be shot here." As warily as retreating wolves, they parted.

Raoul reached the mansion just ahead of Sean. His mother was unsympathetic. *"Bonne chance, mon fils.* I hear he's an excellent shot."

"I can handle myself, madame. All I ask is for you to be present. Napoleon must be satisfied we took no part in Culhane's intrigue."

Her beringed fingers drummed lightly on her cigarillo box. "Very well. Wait in the garden. I'll join you directly."

The grounds behind the Amauri mansion were patched with moonlight under massive chestnuts. Between them and the Faubourg Sainte Germaine with its light, late-evening traffic of lantern-dotted carriages, the house windows gleamed silver. "The moonlight seems bright enough to do without lanterns, gentlemen," the baronne observed, her white hair sculptured, her dress catching cold light in its folds. "I see no need to draw the servants' attention to this affair." She looked at the tall, dark man who silently waited as Fourquet loaded the pistols. "Have you no second, sir?"

"No, madame."

"Will I suffice?" She continued implacably as Raoul and Fourquet stared. "I am ill-suited to support your defense, but seconds serve essentially as witnesses, do they not?"

"I'd be honored, Baronne."

"May I ask your grievance against my son, monsieur?"

"There is more than one, Baronne; most of them, I believe you know. Most recently, he brutally beat my sister-in-law and tried to abort her child."

The baronne's face went gray. "I see. How is she, monsieur?"

"She is in a safe place, madame, but the child is coming even now. It may be stillborn."

Her lips trembled slightly. "I am deeply sorry." Then, refusing to look at her son, she stepped back and ordered coldly, "Proceed, gentlemen."

Fourquet offered the pistols, first to Raoul, then Culhane. The Irishman shook his head. "I'll use my own gun."

The doctor started to protest, but Amauri waved him aside. "It doesn't matter. Let's get on with it."

As Fourquet turned away with the pistol case, the baronne held out a hand. "You may give me the remaining weapon, doctor. I've been called here to ensure the fairness of this fight, have I not?"

The two men took their places, back to back, guns lifted, then paced in opposite directions as Fourquet counted. At twelve, he ordered them to turn, then take aim. At the order "Fire," Amauri squeezed his trigger a shade faster than Culhane, but instead of standing his ground, the Irishman twitched aside and shot his opponent between his incredulous, horrified eyes. Even as Fourquet leveled his gun with a cry of, "You filthy swine!" Culhane whipped the knife from his sleeve and sent it into the man's throat. He straightened and turned, unsurprised to find the white-faced baronne aiming the gun he had rejected at his heart.

"You're no gentleman, Monsieur Culhane!"

"No, madame, but neither was your son. You can fire, but I'll wager you'll not hit me, whatever your skill."

"Are you saying this weapon has been tampered with?"

"My guess is that Raoul was no more willing to chance losing than I was."

"You wager your life on that guess, monsieur." She fired and the gun jerked slightly to the side, its charge missing him by a good yard.

"Fourquet pared the ball," he said quietly.

She tossed the gun in its case and drew a small pistol out of the shawl looped over her arm. "It appears I should have been forced to kill Raoul if you had not." Her chin lifted and he glimpsed a glisten of tears on her face. "Thank you for relieving me of that obligation."

"You enjoy the honor your son and I lack, madame. I'm sorry that virtue has been so ill-rewarded."

"Honor often covers weakness . . ." She turned to look at her son. "And there lies mine."

Madeleine brushed a straggling lock of hair out of her face with a perspiring forearm and muttered, "Christ, this is hard work. Push, girl, push!"

Her teeth sunk into the monkey doll, Catherine strained against Mei Lih's hands. Fouché's guard had arrived. Bored with wandering the street, he smoked a cigar in the garden.

Suddenly, Mei Lih said urgently, "Here it comes! There's the head!"

Catherine dazedly saw the women bending over her somewhere beyond the barriers of pain, but she had known worse pain after her accident in Ireland, and fiercely, she bore down, knowing she was stronger than this pain. The powerful final seizures gripped her and she felt the last gush of agony as her body expelled its burden.

Madeleine held it up, her hands bloody, her black silk rolled up past her elbows. The baby was silent, a tiny pink form glistening with blood and protective coating from the womb. Too exhausted to lift her head, Catherine stared at it in growing panic. Mei Lih, who had assisted many a birth in the pavilion in Saigon, abruptly smacked the child on the buttocks. A gurgling cough, then an angry bellow of surprising volume answered the indignity and Catherine's eyes lit. Madeleine handed the roaring baby to Mei Lih to bathe. "He's a Culhane, that one!"

A month passed before Sean knew he had a son. Under an assumed name, he had written Madeleine from Belgium, then a carefully worded note to Catherine via his agent in Hamburg. Catherine's reply sent his heart soaring. He spent the day on a rented yawl off the coast near Brussels, getting roaring drunk with the captain and singing about sea sirens with wild, black hair.

Shortly, Catherine and her hostesses felt a comradeship against the world. She knew the part they had played in Sean's life, but uneasiness and jealousy had been subdued. Mei Lih informed her privately that to disabuse Madeleine of the impression Sean was her brother would be unwise. On the other hand, knowing Catherine might show telltale aversion to the Frenchwoman, Mei Lih told her nothing about Madeleine's association with Amauri and her marriage bargain with Culhane.

Madeleine found Sean's attraction to his sister only another of his unpredictable aspects. She was certain he would not go so far as incest—until three months later when she caught the first hints of emerald in the baby's eyes. Knowing Sean's brother to be a blue-eyed blonde, she felt fury begin to rise. She had sheltered the bastard's incestuous whore! Even encouraged her to stay because Fouché's intensifying investigations made it dangerous to leave, even though the police had come to the house twice and taken Mei Lih once for questioning. Madeleine had corroborated Mei Lih's story that they had both been working with Amauri and that Mei Lih would have been returned to Antime's if she had betrayed her employer. Mention of Antime's had turned the tide; the women had not been bothered since.

Damn the bastard! She cried hoarsely, sloppily. Dis-

547

gusted rage was still in her eyes when the other women, hearing her weeping, came into the room. "That's his bastard," she grated, almost choking, then more stridently, "That's your brother's brat, you lying bitch!"

The baby, startled by the noise, began to cry. Catherine protectively scooped him up. "Don't ever call my son a bastard again! Ever! Sean and I didn't know of our relationship when Brendan was conceived, but we're not sorry."

"You're lying! Just like he did, that sneaking spy! He promised to *marry* me if I saved your skin! Isn't that a laugh? After thirty-seven years and the worst life could do, I trusted him like a green peasant wench!"

As Brendan shrieked, Catherine stared at her. "What spying?"

"Don't tell me you didn't know he was giving French military secrets hand over fist to the enemy!" The profound relief on the other woman's face sent Madeleine into a frenzy. "Get out! Take his brat and go! I ought to turn you in." Her voice quieted ominously. "I *will* turn you in. I'll pay him back—"

"No, madame," interrupted the Oriental, "for then Monsieur Fouché will know you've hidden Madame d'Amauri. You are an accomplice."

Madeleine's face drained. "Go . . . get out."

Catherine left the room to gather her few belongings. Mei Lih followed her. "Where will you go?"

"I have a friend with the Russian Ballet troupe."

CHAPTER 31

Wings

Through a downsweeping meadow wearily walked a dust-covered man leading a limping black horse. Sean ached in every bone and Mephisto's left front fetlock was swollen. From Austria to Saint Jean de Luz near the Gascon-Spanish border was a long way; every mile felt impressed into his rump. Beyond the meadow sparkled the Bay of Biscay. Ahead sprawled buildings topped with terra-cotta tile. Wisteria and lilac crept up white walls that muted to mauve under the leafy shade.

He tethered Mephisto outside an ornamental iron gate; beyond it was a mimosa-lined patio with a fountain. He tugged at the bell rope.

A white-robed nun appeared, her white-winged cap reminding him of a gull in flight. "God be with you, monsieur. How may we help you?" She stared in spite of herself at the haggard, dirty man who looked like the devil's messenger.

"I'm Sean Culhane. I'm here to see the comtesse de Vigny," he told her. "Monseigneur Messier wrote me."

The nun recovered her composure. "One moment, please." She disappeared, and Sean wondered how old she was; seclusion had left her face free of lines of worldly hardship. Would Kit stay eerily beautiful long after youth had gone? For four years, she had buried herself in this place.

The sister returned. "You may enter, Monsieur Culhane. Reverend Mother will join you directly."

After she left again, he splashed water on his face from the fountain, then wiped it on his jacket sleeve. As he ran his fingers through his tangled hair, he sensed he was no longer alone. A tall woman watched him impassively.

"I am Mother Jeanne Vincente. We are pleased to see you have had a safe journey, Monsieur Culhane. May we offer you refreshment?"

"I would be grateful, Reverend Mother, but later, perhaps?"

"Yes, of course. You are naturally anxious to see the countess and your son. Please." Her hand appeared from under her surplice and, with unexpected grace from so gangling a frame, indicated he was to follow. She had not smiled, and as he followed her, Sean wondered if those colorless eyes had missed anything in their appraisal of his shabby appearance.

In fact, Jeanne Vincente had assessed him thoroughly, from his muddy cavalry boots to the gaunt, guarded face with cheekbones savagely cut above the unshaved jaw and the faded scar that raked into the ragged hair. Most of all, she had noticed the bitter set of the mouth and the cold demonic eyes, their strange, thick-lashed beauty unexpected in such a harsh, forbidding face. Yet her voice betrayed nothing of her dismay at sensing his deep hostility and despair in contrast to the happy, untroubled child he had sired. "By fortunate chance, Monseigneur Messier is dining with me today, monsieur. He's most anxious to see you. Perhaps in an hour you could bring Catherine to my study?"

"Of course, Reverend Mother." As they passed through a maze of arcades, Sean noted they encountered no nuns; he deduced she had taken him a special route. Reverend Mother opened a second grill gate to an arcade which surrounded irregular green plots, shelled walkways, and twisted fruit trees. Massed under the trees were white and vivid pink begonias sparked with scarlet against paint-spatter caladium. "This is our central courtyard. The countess spends much of her time here when not working in the hospital." She scanned the garden, then pointed, but Sean had already spied Catherine despite her novitiate's cap. She had paused to wipe her forehead as she knelt among yellow violas.

As Jeanne Vincente saw the look in the Irishman's eyes, she was no longer disturbed by his harsh appearance. When Catherine looked up as if she had been touched by his hand, Reverend Mother had no doubts at all. Catherine's eyes widened to burn a blue, molten path to the dark man who walked toward her as if drawn by their consuming flame; then she was up and running to close the last distance between them. Slowly, he opened his arms to receive her, then buried his head against her neck and held her as if she were part of his flesh. Reverend Mother turned away, painfully reminded of the depths of human love and passion she had renounced. She did not think she could bear to see them kiss.

When Sean's lips lifted at last from hers, Catherine felt he had taken her breath, her very being away with the starved plunder of that one long kiss. Nearly blinded by tears of joy, she whispered, "Oh, Sweet God, to answer all my prayers . . ."

He kissed her again, knowing he should not, but helpless to stop himself. The sweet insanity swept them both, making them aware only of each other in a delirium of need and response. Then, dimly, Sean felt insistent pounding on the back of his leg and reluctantly gave up his ravenous attention to Catherine to look down at a soot-haired imp. A small stubborn jaw jutted and green eyes glared. "It's a sin to kiss nuns!"

Catherine leaned down to touch her son's chin. "You kiss me, don't you, Brendan? Your kisses aren't sinful."

"I'm allowed!"

"All the kisses you want. Why do you suppose that is?"

"You love me." The small brows met. "You don't love him!" Then suspiciously, "Do you?"

Catherine stooped. "You exist because he and I love each other. He's your father, Brendan."

The four-year-old looked at Sean warily. "Where's your black dress?"

Culhane's lips twitched. "I'm no priest, lad."

"Then how did you get in here?" pursued the boy craftily.

"Because he's your special father, darling," Catherine

told him. "Remember Sean, the O'Neill I told you stories about?"

Brendan had envisioned a paragon seven feet tall in a cassock with epaulettes and a flaming sword like Saint Michael's. His father rode a huge black stallion through the sky and sailed ships single-handed and walked on water if they sank. "You don't look like a hero," he said slowly. "Generals have gold buttons."

"I've brought something for you." Sean dug into a pocket to produce a handful of gold and brass, all that remained of his military career.

Brendan tentatively touched an epaulette, then a button. "They're real, aren't they? Did you fight in real battles, too?"

The rapt fascination on Sean's face altered subtly and Catherine took his hand tightly. For a moment he glimpsed Austerlitz's acrid smoke-drifted fields covered with slaughtered carcasses, some not recognizable as human in their scraps of brave color and gilt. "Aye, lad. A few."

The boy's eyes had grown dazzled and dazzling. Christ, his son had lashes like a girl's. Lucky he had a jaw like a little mule or he would be too pretty to piss.

"Will you tell me a battle story . . . sir?" Priests, the only men in Brendan's life, were never addressed as "sir," and the boy struggled to adjust.

"Someday, when they'll be more to you than stories." Sean longed to embrace the boy, but knew no son of his would tolerate such presumption from a stranger.

The boy examined the buttons, then looked up, awed. "May I show one to Sister Marie Angelique?"

Catherine squeezed Sean's hand. "Of course."

He hugged her, selected the shiniest, and scampered off, then skidded to a halt and turned, attempting a show of dignity. "Thank you, sir." He took off again.

"Who's Marie Angelique?"

"A friend." Catherine gave him a mysterious smile. "There's no need to worry. The sisters won't betray you."

She stood up, drawing him with her. "What do you think of your son?"

He told her and she threw back her head and laughed,

not at all nunlike. "Your spittin' image, me darlin'. Likely, his grandfather thought the same of you." Sean turned scarlet and she giggled.

"Well, at least he's an O'Neill. He knows what's his and intends to keep it." Sean grinned suddenly. "You don't need a convent, Kit; the lad's watchdog enough."

She leaned over to pick up her workbasket. "I've been content here, Sean."

"Without a man? How could you be?"

She straightened. "Don't be cruel. I wanted you. I'll always want you. It's both my curse and my blessing, but I cannot have you and that's that."

"I only want you to be happy, Kit," he said slowly. "Are you?"

"My work at the hospital has given me deep satisfaction. It isn't the paradise on earth I knew with you, but yes"—she looked directly at him—"I'm happy. At least I will be now that you're safe. You're not going back to the army, are you?"

"I couldn't if I wanted to," he replied with a crooked grin. "I deserted."

"Oh, Sean! They'll be after you too."

"It doesn't matter. Austria is going to be defeated. You just saved me from another lost cause, that's all."

"I?"

"Didn't you know Monseigneur Messier had written me?"

"No," she said, suddenly tense. "I didn't know you were coming until I saw you. What did he say?"

"Not much. I expect he'll enlighten us both in a few minutes. We're to report like dutiful children to the study . . ." He grimaced. "After we've had our chaste reunion."

His bitterness stabbed her and she touched his sleeve. "You mustn't think of it anymore, Sean. Our lives run in very different paths now. Take Brendan to America and begin again."

Sean began to pace aimlessly. "He hardly knows me. How can he be expected to accept the loss of his home and mother?"

"He must go, Sean. You've seen his distorted view of the world."

"Hell, he thinks I'm a bloody hero," he protested. "I'm a professional butcher."

"You're more man and hero than he'll ever find in dreaming! Can you ever know my pride that *you're* his sire?"

He wanted to believe, yet found himself only grateful for her stubborn faith. "Be proud for both of us then, Kit, for I've not a scrap of pride left, save in the boy."

Brendan appeared leading a slim nun by the hand. Sean swore softly as the girl grew close enough to recognize. "Mei Lih."

"My lord, I am very happy to see you well." She smiled and bowed.

Brendan bounced impatiently. "He's not Jesus, Sister, just my father!"

Marie Angelique's eyes danced as Sean laughed ruefully. "Out of the mouths of babes . . . Perhaps we can talk later, but Monseigneur Messier is waiting now to see Kit and me. We shouldn't be longer than an hour."

"Of course. We'll have a picnic, won't we, Brendan?" Marie Angelique looked down at the boy who was gazing upward, fascinated by his father's beard.

"What's a picnic?"

"Something especially nice, darling." Catherine kissed him. "Run and help Sister get everything ready."

The boy regarded her uncertainly. "Will you be here when we come back?"

"Yes, darling," Catherine answered unevenly, wondering if he had sensed something. "Your father and I are just going to talk with Monseigneur for a little."

Marie Angelique led the boy away. Sean started to speak and Catherine put her hand on his breast. "Don't say it, my love. I've been at war with myself for four years and my heart is sore."

Messier stood up as he greeted Sean from behind a desk in the small, book-lined room. Arched windows opened on the courtyard, their panes brushed with branches of lilac. An occasional bird twitter carried in.

"I've wanted to meet you for a long time, Monsieur Culhane," Messier said. "Catherine has told me much about you."

I'll bet, Sean thought ironically. Catherine's confession must have been the liveliest tale he's heard in years. "I'm grateful to you, Monseigneur, for befriending her."

"Catherine is a most charming young woman, but I have a greater interest than friendship; rather, say, an obligation."

The silver-haired prelate indicated they should sit, then resumed Mother Superior's high-backed chair and wedged himself into an elegant slump. "Many years ago, against my better judgment, I married Elise de Vigny to John Enderly. Now, I realize the disasters that union begot. When you arrived here, Catherine, I made inquiries about your background but had little luck. After you expressed your desire to enter the Church and cede it your inheritance, I had an idea. Most of my investigation was blocked by Father Patrick Ryan in Ireland and his refusal to contribute information that might shed light on your case."

He smiled. "I must confess to a certain duplicity. I wrote Father Ryan again and implied that Catherine Culhane planned to leave her property to the Church and certain Vatican officials would take it kindly if he could help untangle difficulties concerning claims to the Shelan estate. As far as Father Ryan knows, you, Catherine, are the last surviving heir of those properties, and you, Monsieur Culhane, are dead." His fine hands spread. "As to the last, I did not enlighten him. I requested a copy of the will and codicil, which unfortunately he no longer possessed. Apparently, Liam Culhane took the only copy; but, being now eager to serve his Church, Father Ryan suggested Brendan Culhane might have entrusted a copy to another priest as a safety measure, Ireland often being in turmoil, Catholics persecuted and their records destroyed. He mentioned several possible clerics, and eventually I traced a copy of the will to the archbishop of Londonderry; I have it here." He indicated a sheaf of papers. "It is as you described to me, Catherine, except for one vital part, which I will read to you now."

He found the page. "Your mother, Monsieur Culhane,

had become convinced her husband and Elise Enderly were lovers."

He began to read. " 'Megan vowed revenge that would hurt me most. My dearest friend, Lockland Fitzhugh, had been in love with her for years, yet certain his honor would never permit a sordid venture against mine, Megan and I continued our close association with him. She seduced him. I cannot blame him; I, once bewitched by her, freely forgive him, who will not forgive himself. There was no doubt Sean was not my son. Now, I forgive her; but then, I wanted a son like that proud, fiery boy too much.

" 'When you returned to Shelan, Sean, I had your presence, but I never had your heart. In my mind, you are my son. I hope one day you will accept this indulgence.'

"It goes on from there in the same vein as the other will."

The dumbstruck young people stared at the priest as if he were some hobgoblin sent to torment them further.

"Something's wrong." Sean muttered hoarsely. "The other will was in Brendan's writing; I know his hand. I was looking for a forgery."

"The other will was probably authentic, for the most part. I never saw it, so I can only surmise, but I would guess the division of pages lent itself to partial forgery. Your brother was an artist. He probably gambled on your being too shocked by the revelation to think clearly. He didn't allow you to handle the codicil for long, did he?"

"No," the Irishman said numbly.

"And after all, he *appeared* to have as much to lose as you by such a document. But as you see, *you* are not related to Catherine at all." The Jesuit handed the will across the desk. "Here, see what you think."

Sean went through each page, then finally looked up at Catherine, who sat transfixed with a kind of horror in her eyes. "Kit," he whispered, "it was all for nothing."

Her eyes closed. "When Liam was dying, he said, 'Not his . . . never his . . . only mine.' We thought he was possessive to the bitter end, but perhaps he was trying to tell the truth."

"One thing you should know," Messier interposed. "My investigation was greatly assisted by the duc d'Artois."

Both dark heads snapped up and he smiled. "I presumed he had assigned agents to Catherine after the Irish prison incident. He was most relieved to hear you were spying *against* Napoleon, Monsieur Culhane; it corrected the impression that Catherine had betrayed his trust.

"He offered a guilty conscience as his reason for assisting me. You see, he had ordered Enderly's extermination after Catherine's apparent defection, but someone else intercepted Enderly on the way to Edinburgh at the invitation of the duc—an invitation to assassination. The men hired to perform the killing found Enderly decapitated on the road."

"Amin," whispered Catherine. "He must have ridden him down in the dark. I've seen him cap strawberries at a gallop."

Sean shook his head, still dazed. "I cannot believe Artois would help us. He wants Catherine for himself."

"The duc knows well the privations of exile and disappointment. Is it so strange he might wish to spare one he loves from the same fate?"

An hour later, they stood before Monseigneur Messier at the chapel altar. Neatly buttoned and brushed, Sean had taken a quick bath and shave and given his boots a buff. Over the braided coronet of her hair, Catherine wore a delicate garland of mignonettes and marguerite daisies Marie Angelique had woven to cap her white novice's veil. In her hands was a small matching bouquet. Marie Angelique, Mother Superior, and Brendan were the only visible observers; others were shadowed behind a screen in the choir loft, their singing pure as a nightingale's call at sunset. Catherine's eyes glistened as Sean repeated his vows. His eyes met hers and he almost drifted into silence. Behind her cloudy veil, her exquisite face was luminous.

Later, as they walked alone through the convent gardens, Sean felt peace, yet subtle suspense, as if not yet assured of awakening from a nightmare. Above the convent roof the cloudy scales of a mackerel sky curved against the setting sun like massive, fiery fish. The convent's simple cross rose against the sun. A smile flickered unwillingly across the Irishman's mouth. If You're a Fisher of Men,

You're as stubborn as I am. You wait until the fight's gone out of me, then ease the line. If You've reclaimed my soul through this woman, I'll buy each day with her with my life, my soul, only don't ever let her stop loving me . . . .

"What is it, darling?" Catherine looked up at him with concern. His grip had tightened almost painfully on her hand.

"I was praying, I suppose." His lips sought hers as if they were children tasting the innocence of a first kiss.

A long moment later, Sean chuckled softly. "Our son isn't going to relinquish his place under your blankets so easily every night. A night with Mei Lih is an irresistible temptation to any man, but in the morning he'll know he's been had."

"He isn't the only one who'll know he's been had." Catherine impishly tugged him in the direction of her room.

"Are you sure this haste is seemly, ma'am?"

His bride slowed to a maddening amble, eyes demurely downcast. He snatched her up in his arms. "No more nonsense, woman. You're about to become a respectable wife and mend your wicked ways."

"*My* wicked ways?" She lifted a derisive eyebrow.

He grinned. "Suitably matched, aren't we?"

They came to the end of the building, but nothing was beyond but more garden. "Where is this room of yours anyway?" Catherine gave him a feline smile. "Out with it, madame! I'm hot!" he demanded in his best general's bellow. Flushing scarlet, she pointed hastily to the door nearest her groom's broad shoulder.

As he kicked open the door, she gave his hair a sharp tug. "For shame, to shock the sisters so!"

"I'd have given 'em a far ruder shock if you'd persisted in the game—" He broke off.

Catherine followed his gaze to a small table decorated with white damask, lighted tapers, and a bowl of marguerites. Steaming pilaf and Messier's best champagne stood ready. "How thoughtful of them," Catherine said softly.

"These nuns of yours are like leprechauns," Sean muttered as he reluctantly set his bride down. "One never sees them. Things just appear."

"Aren't you hungry?"

"Starved." He stared wistfully at the bed.

She laughed and tugged at his hand. "Come. You'll need your strength. I'm not likely to let you sleep the night away!"

"Oh, it's sure you are I can satisfy your demands?" With a wicked grin, he seated her and bit her neck.

She gave a little yelp. He slid languidly into his chair and with a drowsy look poured wine. Her eyes widened with chagrin. "You aren't that tired, are you?"

He lifted his glass, his eyes sleepy slits. "I shall do my utmost not to doze off at an inopportune moment, madame."

Biting her lip, she frowned at him, then caught the tawny glint to his eyes and broke into soft laughter. "You liar! Desire turns your eyes exactly the shade they are now . . ."

"I see I'll have to be wary of you, lady. If I hide my passions so poorly, I'll be helpless against your wiles." His voice turned husky and his eyes clouded as he touched his glass to hers. "Yet I would be lost, for I do desire you, even unto madness."

Twilight faded into darkness, candlelight playing on their still, waiting faces and the last drops of liquor in the wineglasses. Sean carried a candle to a wall niche by the bed, then tugged off his boots. When he turned, Catherine was waiting. She unfastened his shirt to kiss warm skin until he went taut with desire. She slipped off the shirt, then unfastened his breeches and eased them down over the slim hips and flat belly to bare the hard beauty of his body.

When he was naked, Sean removed Catherine's veil and garland, then tugged loose the dark, heavy mass of her hair until it fell in a stream through his fingers to her waist. Tugging a marguerite from the garland, he tucked it in her hair. The perfume of her skin filled his nostrils as he slipped her gown from her shoulders, then sought her throat with his lips, and the proud rise of her breasts. Catherine's head fell back and she sighed, filled with longing. The robe slid to the floor and the sweetness of her flesh sent Sean's senses reeling in joy and craving. "Jesu, I've dreamed of you until I thought no woman could be as beautiful as the dream. What poor things dreams are!"

Then, over her shoulder, he saw the lights and led her to the window. The night garden was abloom with candles, haloes radiating from luminous clouds of flowers. Seeing tears glisten in Catherine's eyes, Sean enfolded her in his arms as he said huskily, "I think I understand now what your life here meant to you. Are you sorry?"

She looked up at him. "I weep for happiness, beloved, and because I have more love than I can bear."

With lips and hands, she made love to him, moving down his lean body, rediscovering each smooth, dark hollow and plane until she knelt before him and paid tender tribute to the proud maleness of him. Sean's chest rose and fell more quickly as the burning, sweet ache in his core became pure, raging flame. With a muted groan, he swayed and lifted her hair to bathe his loins in silk. "Kit . . . Sweet God." He felt as if he were lost in an impossible dream that drained him of all his nights of frustrated longing. Catherine pressed her cheek against the graceful curve of his long body and entwined her arms about his hips, the softness of her hair a warm cloud. Silently, he stroked her hair and lifted it, letting the pounding pulse of blood in his body slow, letting the rise and fall of his breathing ease.

How still it was, his own heartbeat the only sound in the darkness. He felt blood surge through his veins and the powerful promise of his own life force. He was alive and a man. Sean slipped downward in Catherine's embrace and enfolded her like a flower, tasted his own potency on her mouth.

As if her limbs were weighted, Catherine was hardly aware when Sean carried her to the bed and lay beside her, but when his lips and hands began their sweet, slow exploration of her body, she opened to him like lush, ripening fruit. Desire focused in a solar glow between her thighs, and when his mouth sought her there, her hips undulated in mute, primitive need until she cried out, burning, begging.

At last, Sean covered her body with his own. With a soft moan, she buried her face against his neck. He poised for a heartbeat; then, without urgency, he consummated their union, slowly giving himself to her. He receded and surged into her like the sea in a rising storm, endlessly arching and curling over her to pound her downward to inky depths, only to lift her up on rising crests of passion until she became irrevocably part of him, part of the spume and savagery of him. Then she felt herself hurtled into the sun in sheets of glistening spray, to fall back in a million droplets of shattered fire through cushioning ether to the enclosing sea. Deep, dark, and silent, its tawny green softened to gold-flecked sunlight like Sean's eyes, so close their heavy lashes nearly brushed hers. Dazed, she felt as if her heart would burst of love for him.

"Wife," he murmured wonderingly. "Mother of my son." His lips brushed hers. "Little love."

She touched his lips. "My husband. My heart's life."

They lay, his head on her breast as she stroked his hair. In moments, he fell asleep, worn out from his long journey. After the last candle in the garden had burned away, Catherine lay awake, listening to the beat of Sean's heart and echoing it with a prayer in her own.

The sun was high overhead when Sean opened one eye, threw a long leg over his wife, and without a word, proceeded to make love to her languidly and thoroughly. She was flushed with both satisfaction and embarrassment when he finally grinned down at her, his green eyes slits of sleepy amusement, but she was too happy to make her scowl convincing. "Pleased with yourself, aren't you, bucko? Couldn't you wait until we were away from here to make me sound like a cat caught in a briar?"

His grin widened wickedly. "Afraid the good sisters will realize what they're missing and defect?" He nipped her stomach and she squealed and tugged his hair.

"Your conceit boggles the imagination! Why, I suppose you even fancy they'd form a line at the door for your favors!"

"Why not, when you're so obviously and loudly uncomplaining?"

"Oh!" Her eyes sparked and she fought to clamber free of him. Laughing, he twisted her easily back under him and with amusement, then a distinct leer, watched her frustrated wriggling. Her lips parted in a soft O as he parted her thighs. "You . . . cheated."

He slid into her like a sword sheathing in silk, his lips hovering in a whisper just above hers. "Anytime you've had enough, I'm yours to command."

His strokes possessively deepened, sweeping her will away, and she groaned in pleasure and vexation. Then, with a sweet, vengeful smile, she retaliated with a special skill of her own until his control disintegrated.

Wide awake now, he stared at her. "Where did you learn that?"

She twirled a curl of his chest fur. "From your little Flower of the East. Did you think we talked of nothing but diapers in Paris, your mistresses and I?" Her voice lowered to a silky purr. "Rare is the man who can leave three women cooped up in a house for months with nothing in common but his lovemaking and have them refrain from carving each other into mincemeat. Not that you deserve any credit for it, bucko." She tapped his nose and rolled away from him, swinging her legs over the side of the bed. "The women in your life are just marvelously tolerant, that's all." She was nearly up when he dragged her back down again, laughing as she fought him half playfully, half in earnest, then dissolved in helpless giggles. "Sean, I have to bathe. I smell like a she-goat!"

"The perfume suits a haughty nanny that keeps her nose"—he nipped a buttock—"and her tail in the air."

She shrieked and pummeled, but inevitably found herself back where it had all begun, flat on her back with him coaxing her thighs apart with a devilish gleam of white teeth and an ease that both infuriated and beguiled her.

Sean's intent was diverted by a sudden, insistent pounding on the door. His pantherlike move from bed to knife was interrupted when the knock repeated itself knee-high, and the Irishman straightened with relief and exasperation.

Catherine laughed softly. "Will you answer the door, Papa, or shall I?"

"Might as well settle it now," her husband muttered. Pulling a towel off a rack near the washbasin, he tucked

562

its skimpy length around his lean middle and opened the door.

Familiar green eyes widened, then glared up into his, and a small foot leveled at his shin. Sweeping downward, Sean caught his son up in mid-kick, heaved the boy onto his hip, and let him yell as he closed the door. "You're not my father! You're not supposed to be in here! Go away or I'll kill you!" The boy struggled violently until he saw his mother, covered to her armpits, in the bed they had shared, then froze into stunned realization that this stranger had been in bed, naked, with his mother and she had not minded.

Before he had time to start yelling at her, the stranger dumped him onto the bed and bellowed, "Pipe down! Whether you like it or not, I am your father and you'd better start getting used to it because I'm going to be around from now on!"

Emerald eyes blazed mutinously into emerald. "I won't! I hate you!"

"Go ahead, hate me, and I'll go on loving you. Where do you think you got your blasted stubbornness?" Sean's jaw nearly touched his son's outthrust chin as they glared at one another.

The Irishman, first to break the standoff, hunkered down. "I'll tell you something. The task of a father and husband is to love, protect, and provide for his family, and up to now, you've had to take my place. You've done it well and I'm proud of you. But just as I can never be a boy again—however I might like it—you're not yet a man, however you might like it.

"You love your mother, but I loved her first. She belongs to you, but first she belonged to me. And you've been sleeping in her bed, but I slept there long before you were born."

Brendan longed to look at his mother for reassurance, but was too proud and too afraid. Maybe she would not want him now that this man had come. Why didn't she say something?

Sean knew the fear running through his son's mind, but knew too they must come to a clear-cut understanding. "Just because you and I take our proper places in her life doesn't change the way your mother loves us."

563

Catherine touched her son's shoulder. "Your father's telling you the truth, darling, and believe me, he loves you every bit as much as I do."

Brendan twisted suspiciously to look at her. "Is he going to sleep in our bed with us?"

"Parents sleep together, darling," she said softly. "Sons have beds of their own." His eyes filled with tears, though he tried to fight them back in the presence of another male.

"That doesn't mean you cannot join us when you're invited," Sean said.

Brendan watched his mother's hand in Sean's. "You want Maman. You don't want me."

"Your father was once so badly hurt he wanted to die, Brendan," Catherine murmured, "but he fought to live, in a more terrible battle than any you've dreamed of, because he wanted so much to see you."

The boy sat there stiffly, uncomfortable.

"Would you care to come into bed with us for a while?" Catherine suggested. "I realize all this is sudden and you may want to talk a bit."

"No," said Brendan, wrinkling his nose and starting to slide off the bed. "You're all smelly."

A gentle but firm hand on his shoulder stopped his slide. "You haven't been properly dismissed yet."

The boy flushed. "May I go, sir?"

"Yes."

After the door closed, Sean looked at Catherine. "He resents me as much as I resented his namesake. I never changed."

She took his face in her hands and kissed him. "Thanks to you, your son's only a frightened little boy. He's never known the horrors you faced. You were forced into manhood by the time you met Brendan Senior." She grinned. "Besides, you didn't resent Brendan for kicking you out of your mother's bed, but her out of *his.*" Her eyes widened with mock ferocity. "And no one's going to pry me out of yours, even our son."

"I'm surprised you didn't take his side when I was yelling at him."

"You're on his side. How could I?"

"I love you," he said huskily.

564

"That's good," she murmured. "Now stop fretting and remind me how much."

As the moon rose high over the fields, Brendan was tense with excitement over his first real venture outside the convent walls and a little frightened, especially after he saw the pistol and saber at his father's belt and his mother in an oriental tunic and trousers. She carried a pistol like his father's. Was he to have one, too? But no, after his father embraced Sister Marie Angelique right under Reverend Mother's nose, his parents led him to waiting horses: the huge one must be the famous Mephisto. His heart thudded. Then, unbelievably, his father swung him up onto the great horse's back. He clutched the pommel as the black's head snaked around.

The Irishman kept an arm around his son and stroked the horse's nose. "Easy, boy." The black nuzzled his master's hand. Sean gave Brendan a lump of sugar. "Feed him this and he'll be your friend. Hold your hand out flat."

Brendan eyed Mephisto and shakily held out his palm. When the great teeth showed briefly in a neat nip at the sweet, he squeezed his eyes shut.

"Well done. You can pet him now."

The boy stroked awkwardly, then peered at his father. "Are you going to ride him with me?"

"No, he has a sore fetlock. He won't be ably to carry a man for a few more days. I'll walk alongside while you grow accustomed to each other."

As Sean eased Mephisto into a walk, Brendan stared back at his receding home. "Where are we going?" he asked tremulously.

"To sea in a ship. She's waiting in a hidden channel."

"A pirate ship?" breathed the boy.

"Some would call her that."

Brendan forgot his nervousness and prodded insistently, "Will you let me sail?"

"Aye, but at first, you'll learn in a boat about twice as long as Mephisto."

Shortly, Brendan nodded with each stride of the horse across moonlit fields and vineyards banded by woodland. He began to slide athwart the saddle into Sean's arms.

Catherine took Mephisto's reins as Sean placed the boy in front of him on the sorrel.

In sleep, the small body was warm and relaxed against his, and tentatively, he touched the boy's hair. The mouth seemed unfamiliar: William Fitzhugh's, perhaps. Had his own lips ever had that fine sensitivity? What a cold-blooded, wary little bastard he had been. He knew now how Brendan Culhane and Lockland Fitzhugh must have felt, hoping for a response that had never come. Fitzhugh was the finest man he had ever known besides Brendan. He smiled, remembering Fitzhugh's indomitability; perhaps his own stubbornness did not stem from the O'Neill strain after all. If he could only hope for his son's respect, he would try to earn it and never let the boy see his pain.

Then Catherine ruffled his hair, her face luminous with more than moonlight. "I love you with all my being," she said quietly, "yet I'm glad my love is no longer enough for you." She leaned over and touched his lips, so like her son's, then kissed them so sweetly his sadness passed.

Abruptly, the moment was broken by a faint sound from a grove of trees ahead. Both reined their horses. "There it is again. A slapping," Catherine whispered.

"Likely the wash against *Sylvie*'s hull. I'll see. Take Brendan." Sean gave her the boy. "If you hear a shot, let Mephisto and the sorrel go, then run like hell. We have a son now. Promise."

"I promise."

Like a ghost of the moonlight, he was at her bridle one moment and gone the next. She waited, cold to the bone despite the mild evening air. Her grip tightened on Brendan and the reins as she breathed a silent prayer, "Not now, God. Not when he has a chance to be happy."

Brendan stirred. "Where's Papa?"

"He's making sure the ship is waiting."

"Are you scared he won't come back?"

"Are you?"

Sleepily, he considered. "Not if I tell God I like him. He's not as mean as he looks."

And your heart is not the stubborn citadel it seems, my sweet, his mother silently noted as he calmly went back to sleep. Then, Sean was lifting Brendan down. "The *Sylvie*'s

566

waiting and ready to weigh anchor. Hand me Mephisto's bridle. We'll tether the others."

Moments later, with Mephisto clattering up the gang-plank behind them, they boarded the schooner. Her decks and paint gleamed below gaff-rigged masts that stabbed upward through black shadows from trees overhanging the creek. Men moved quickly on the decks. After introducing Catherine to the awed Captain Shannon, Sean led her and Brendan to their cabin.

"Brendan's great-grandfather couldn't step in a curragh without turning green," he drawled. "Let's hope he hasn't inherited that habit." He bit her ear and she yelped. "Likely he's a teasing imp, though. How am I to deal with a first officer so smitten with my wife he's liable to order his own head overboard as an anchor?"

"Oh? Mr. Shannon struck me as quite sensible." Catherine ignored her husband's skeptical look.

The cabin's white woodwork was set off by varnished mahogany bunk stanchions and brass fittings. Portholes opened to night air alive with cheeps and croaks from the creek. Catherine heard water slap the hull and a rhythmic rub of oarlocks. "We're already moving."

"Aye, a longboat is towing us out of the creek." Sean strung a gear hammock, then added blankets and tucked his son into it. "Has he a toy?"

Catherine drew Brendan's battered monkey out of the makeshift sling on her shoulder. "Some of the teeth marks are mine from his delivery; the others are from his teething. It's still his favorite plaything, although he sleeps with this because it's softer." She produced a grubby stuffed rabbit.

Sean fitted the rabbit into Brendan's arm, then ran his thumb over the monkey's dents. He pulled Catherine into his arms and held her tightly. "I have to go topside. Get some sleep. I'll be back as soon as I can."

She hesitated. "I suppose women aren't allowed on the quarterdeck."

"It's my quarterdeck." He kissed her lightly, then thoroughly until she was all soft in his arms. "That's to keep your powder dry."

Her fingers brushed his groin and he caught his breath. *"That's* to keep you primed for firing," she murmured.

As they mounted the quarterdeck, *Sylvie* cleared the creek mouth. The rocky coast of France spilled away on both sides of the stern, the sea molten silver below a lunar haze that faded the stars. The night was hardly prime for eluding coastal patrols. The longboat slacked alongside, unloaded, and was hauled aboard.

Shannon saluted. "She's all yours, sir."

"Thank you, Mr. Shannon." With an eye to the sails, Sean gave the wheel a twirl and dictated orders to the first mate. The man took off to quietly relay the number and order of sails to set. In virtual silence, the sails ran up on heavily greased capstans, bellied out with a dull rumble, then snapped taut. The *Sylvie* heeled to the wind, spray fanning over her bows.

"Under full sail, she must be even faster than the *Megan!*" Catherine breathed in awe at his shoulder.

"She has to be fast. We don't carry the guns to fight a pitched battle."

Two men, each with a telescope strapped to his shoulder, scurried up the masts. While the lookouts scanned the horizon for ships, Sean and Shannon conferred over tidal changes in the local shoals, adjusting reckonings by the softly called depth soundings of a sailor perched at the bowsprit. Finally they were clear, and Shannon relaxed slightly as Sean signaled all sail to be set. Once the treacherous shoals were passed, the crew settled into routine while, above them, the masts with their tiny human silhouettes spiked the dwindling moon. At last, the coast of France merged into the glittering wake behind them. At the wheel, Sean curled Catherine into the curve of his arms.

"Now that you have your lady love," Catherine teased, "I wonder how you'll manage me. The convent was no cure; I'm still unruly."

"I mean to be forthright, ma'am. The only way for a sensible man to have any peace with an independent female is to love her and be ready to catch her borrowed breeches when they drop."

"Oh, you!" She tried to squirm out of his arms; then her lips began to curve in a slow, appreciative grin. "Kiss me, you cocky mick, while I filch your belt as well."